YOUNG BLOOD

Book One of The Young Blood Trilogy

T. Marshall Bunn

Belief Creating Reality Publications

ROCKVILLE, MARYLAND

Belief Creating Reality Publications
Rockville, Maryland
www.youngbloodtrilogy.com

Publisher's Note: This is a work of fiction. Names, characters, places, and incidents are a product of the author's imagination. Locales and public names are sometimes used for atmospheric purposes. Any resemblance to actual people, living or dead, or to businesses, companies, events, institutions, or locales is completely coincidental.

"YMCA" written by H. Belolo, J. Morali and V. Willis © 1978 Can't Stop Music
Used by permission

Excerpts from *Dracula* by Bram Stoker, 1897, in the public domain

Cover photo by Nicci Trent

Book Layout © 2014 BookDesignTemplates.com

Young Blood: Book One of The Young Blood Trilogy/ T. Marshall Bunn. -- 1st ed.
ISBN 979-8-9861016-1-3

Library of Congress Control Number: 2022910190

Acknowledgments

This book is the culmination of decades of work, ideas refined over time until they finally became what they needed to be. Many thanks to all of the people in my life over the years who encouraged me to keep going, to stop procrastinating and truly put pen to paper (or pixel to screen).

And thank you to my dear friends Nicci Trent, Rachel Brune, Gypsye Legge, and Stephanie Stewart for their help with proofreading and offering guidance on my early drafts. I couldn't have done it without you.

INTRODUCTION

I made my first kill at the age of eight.

A claim like that might not seem too unusual given where and when I grew up, which was in Augusta, Georgia in the 1980s. I had plenty of friends at my school who around that age had started going off on hunting trips with their fathers, coming back with proud tales of spending hours out in the woods in the cold weather some weekend morning, bringing down their first deer with their first rifle, and so on. That kind of thing never interested me, nor was my father into it either.

My first kill was not a deer, nor were the family and friends who were involved in it hunters. Well, I suppose in a way we were, but not in the traditional sense. We were vampires. For a while, anyway.

The story I am about to tell, while it is about vampires, is not a typical vampire story. There won't be some elegant centuries-old gentleman with a foreign accent and a guilty conscience. And while this is also a story about children, it won't be typical of that, either. What's difficult about relaying this tale is that it happened so long ago, so I see things in a very different light than I did back then, particularly because I'm aware of a much bigger picture. But at the time, I was just a kid experiencing life day to day and not really understanding just how amazing, impossible, and tragic everything was. I suppose the shortest possible way I could summarize everything would be to say that we did some very horrible things when we were young, and it would take several years for us to truly realize what we'd done.

As far as blame goes, there was plenty of that to go around. One could try to make the argument that because we were children, we weren't to blame because we were too young to know what we were doing. But we did know. We just weren't mature enough to know that it was wrong. Actually, that's not true, either. We knew that it was wrong. In fact, that was part of the thrill. Most of us grew up watching a lot of television shows and movies, and the "bad guys" were almost always more fun and interesting to watch, then later to pretend to be on the playground. This was our chance to actually be the bad guys, to get away with things in real life. And we did. We just didn't realize how serious it was, what the consequences of our actions would be. And truth be told, for a long time, we didn't care.

There could be many explanations for our behavior, such as bad parenting or a lacking education, or something to do with the influence of violent entertainment, but I won't bother with any of those dead-end, circular arguments. I'll leave the psychoanalysis of us up to someone more qualified. But there is one more thing I will address: the notion that children are innocent. This is something I cannot believe or accept, partly because of what I went through, because of what we did. In my opinion, the idea that children start out as perfect little angels and only become bad later in life is a fallacy, perhaps a very dangerous one. If anything, I would say that the opposite is true: We start off as selfish, conscience-lacking creatures, and it is only through upbringing and socialization that we are taught to be civilized. Somehow, my friends and I seemed to slip through the cracks, maybe due to the above-mentioned explanations (or excuses). Whether it was negligence, inborn cruelty, or just a bizarre set of circumstances and coincidences outside our control, I can't really say. Maybe I shouldn't try to. After all, I could go on for pages and pages like this and never come to a conclusion, and I really should just tell what happened.

The whole thing started off harmlessly enough, well, as harmless as childish revenge could ever be anyway. We didn't set out to become evil, murderous monsters; that was more an unintended side effect of the original plan, which was mostly meant to be just a prank at the time. But things got out of hand. Way, way out of hand.

PART ONE

"Carolyn, will you please stop singing that song." It was more of a statement than a question or polite plea, the exasperated tone of an adult who is just a few moments away from losing all patience with a child.

"Okay," she said to Susanna, our older sister. She sat still for a moment with a smirk while Susanna stared straight ahead through the windshield, her face set in a hard, humorless expression. Then, Carolyn's face lit up dramatically as she once again threw her arms up and started singing tunelessly, *"WYYYYY EM SEE AY! Da da da da dun dun WYYYY EM SEE AY-AY!"*

Susanna groaned angrily and partially collapsed onto the steering wheel while my two friends and I in the backseat cracked up. Growing up, Carolyn had always seemed like one of the funniest people in the world to me, and I looked up to her, trying my best to imitate her silly sense of humor. There were many nights where she would get me into trouble at the dinner table for making me giggle uncontrollably at ridiculous stuff (funny faces, sound effects, and such), and the more I tried to fight the urge to laugh, the harder Carolyn tried to make me, all the while usually not getting caught herself. Susanna seemed to straddle a line between Carolyn and our parents, sometimes finding the situation funny and occasionally joining in, but usually falling on the side of being too mature for such things, leading her to roll her eyes at us and call us stupid or something similar.

That was how she felt now, Carolyn having broken out in probably her fourth or fifth rendition of the song since we'd left the house. Aside from the fact that it annoyed Susanna and made the rest of us laugh, there was a reason she kept singing the song, which for her consisted of simply shouting out the beginning of the chorus and sometimes the only parts of the verses she could remember: *"Young man, something something something... Young man! Something something something!"* That was because we were in fact on our way to the local YMCA, where a race that my friend Carl was participating in was being held. Actually, this was just the qualifying race; those who performed well enough this evening would take part in the official event the following night.

Carl had come over to our house that morning and had practiced running around our backyard. Some of that was unintentional at first because our dog, King, was a huge, intimidating St. Bernard who really didn't like strangers. Whenever we had company over and anything took place in the backyard, King had to be locked up in a large pen adjacent to his doghouse, at which point he would bark viciously the entire time. He wasn't so much mean as he was protective of the family, and most people were too afraid of him to let us try to get King to get to know them as opposed to just biting their faces off.

This morning in particular, I had forgotten about putting King up when Carl came by. He was going to stay with us for a few days, as was another friend of mine from school, Tim. Carl planned to practice for the race, and Tim had brought along his Atari 5200 video game system to share with us. My family had the older, less expensive Atari 2600, but Tim's family was very well off, and Tim usually had the latest, trendiest things. He was also one of the smartest kids in our class, something he was a bit smug about, but we got along okay. At that age, who your friends were often depended on who your parents' friends were. Carl and Tim were close because Carl's mother worked for Tim's father as a legal secretary, and the three of us got along at school mainly because we liked a lot of the same TV shows and video games.

When I took Tim and Carl out back to show them the yard, King, who had been asleep in a far corner, suddenly sprang to life and began barking, pausing a few seconds before barreling toward the three of us. Carl and Tim ran in opposite directions, and King paused again to decide which of my two friends to have for breakfast. I called out to try to get him to calm down, but he ignored me and began heading in Carl's direction.

He was distracted by the clanging sound made by Tim running into the side of our above-ground pool, which he then tried to climb into for safety. The pool, which had always had a problem with leaks, was empty apart from lots of dead leaves, pine straw, and the occasional dead bird. But Tim didn't seem to care, and he ducked down below the edge, looking back to see if he was being pursued. In the meantime, Carl had made it to a large magnolia tree in the center of the yard, but I wasn't sure if he would be able to climb up its branches before King caught up to him.

"King!!" Carolyn's voice rang out from the patio. He stopped and looked back at her. She repeated his name just as sternly, and he stared at her, then looked back again at Carl as he noisily made his way up the branches of the tree. Carolyn continued to call out to King as she approached, telling him to sit and to stay, and he did as he was told. I wasn't sure why he always listened to her more than to me, but at this point, I was just grateful that neither of my friends had ended up getting killed.

Carolyn reached King and led him by the collar to his doghouse, and he barely protested, looking somewhat guilty. Once he was safely locked away, Carl and Tim emerged from their hiding places, out of breath. Soon enough, though, we were all laughing about it.

"Well that certainly was... um... interesting!" Tim said, straightening his glasses.

"No kidding!" Carl said. "Scared the ass out of me!"

Carolyn, who had been laughing along with us, suddenly went cold. "What?" she asked Carl pointedly.

He looked down, embarrassed. "Nothing." Despite the fact that we were as young as we were, Carl had recently developed quite a repertoire of swear words, but — and I didn't know this at the time

— he tended to get them mixed up or wrong, coming out with things like "you suck-hole!" or "kiss my shit!" Sometimes he just did it to be funny, and those of us who didn't know any better laughed along. But more often as time went on, these words would come out when Carl lost his temper, which was often.

"Good," Carolyn said sternly. Though she could be quite the cut-up, she was still my big sister, and it wasn't uncommon for her to switch between being my best friend in the world and then suddenly becoming an authoritarian figure, bossing me around and telling me what was right or wrong. Because of her age, she felt justified in extending this to my friends, and they seemed intimidated enough by her.

"And Ray," she continued, turning to me, "how could you forget to put King up before your friends came over? You want to be the one to explain to Mom and Dad when they get back why we had to bury two kids in the backyard?"

Tim snickered, then stopped when Carolyn glared at him.

"Yeah, well, shut up!" I said back to Carolyn, suddenly defiant. It wasn't the greatest comeback in the world, but I did the best I could. While I tried to emulate Carolyn's sense of humor and sarcasm, I was still pretty young by this point and not as articulate or clever as I would have liked. "You would have got in trouble, too!"

"Lay off, Carolyn," Susanna said, having come out into the yard from the back door. "Everyone's okay."

Carolyn sighed and said, "I guess." King continued to bark, a repetitive *"woop woop woop, woop woop woop"* sound as he bounced around in his pen, occasionally jumping up against the fence.

"Let's all go back inside," Susanna offered. "Give King a chance to calm down." Tim and I nodded, glancing back at the doghouse. Carolyn seemed to agree.

"But I wanted to practice for the race!" Carl whined.

"You can do that in a little while," Susanna said somewhat condescendingly. "Tim... You're Tim, right?"

"Yeah," Tim said. Although Tim and Carl had both been over to my house separately earlier in the year, Susanna had never met them.

"Didn't you bring your video game thing with you so Ray and the rest of you could play it?"

"Yeah, but it'll take a little bit of time to hook it up. It's kinda complicated."

Susanna smiled. "Well why don't you go in and do that, and we'll come back out later so Carl can run around the yard and all."

Carl frowned, probably annoyed by Susanna's tone. But she was in charge, and there didn't seem to be any point in arguing with her.

This was the second summer in a row where Susanna had been left in charge of taking care of me and Carolyn while our parents were out of town. Every year, my father, who was the director of a local public library branch, brought my mother along with him to the American Library Association conference. My mother, who worked in a different library as an administrative secretary, enjoyed the conferences mainly for the chance to meet famous authors, while my father was more interested in the various seminars and panels on library administration. It was also an excuse to travel and see new cities, and our parents had made the mistake of bringing my two sisters and me along to one of the conferences a few years before. But at the time, we were all too young and too bored, and mostly we were just in the way.

From that point on, they opted to leave us in the care of our aunt and uncle, who lived out in the country in a small town called Appling. Their house, which was the one my mother had grown up in, was situated on a couple dozen acres of land with lots of fields and woods. Susanna and Carolyn seemed to enjoy the change of scenery, but I hated it. It was too quiet and too boring for me. For one thing, they only had three TV channels, not the twenty or so that we had back home. And my aunt and uncle also seemed sort of creepy and too quiet for my liking. Really, they were just unfamiliar and therefore made me uncomfortable, as I only saw them once or twice a year, so they were more or less strangers to me. One year, Carolyn tried to get me interested in exploring the woods and the creeks, and that somewhat intrigued me, but by then, it was our last summer there.

By the summer of the following year, Susanna was almost seventeen years old, so our parents decided that she could look after me and Carolyn at our house in Augusta while they went away to the conference, which that year was in Philadelphia. Most of the week was uneventful, but a couple of days before our mother and father got back, Carolyn tried to play a trick on me.

A week or two earlier, Carolyn and I had been watching a cartoon one Saturday morning in which one of the characters rigged up a bucket of water over someone's door. When the other character opened the door, the bucket turned over and drenched him, then landed on his head. It was pretty funny, so Carolyn thought it would also be funny to do the same thing to me. While I was away from my bedroom, she propped up a plastic trash can full of water on top of my door, which she left partly open. She then hid at the far corner of the room and waited for me to return.

When I came back and pushed open the door, the trash can, rather than tipping over and onto my head, just plummeted to the floor, barely missing me as I jumped backward, startled by the strange object suddenly falling into my field of vision and the scraping noise it made as it fell from the top of the door. As the trash can hit the floor, it turned over, the water pouring over everything in sight. Carolyn, who at first had been laughing with a mean expression — anyone who has older sisters knows this "sister sneer" — gasped and covered her mouth, eyes wide.

"Carolyn!" I shrieked angrily. The noise brought Susanna downstairs, and she found us both standing there, dumbfounded.

"What in the hell happened?" was all she could say.

Carolyn, not immediately removing her hand from her mouth and still short of breath, tried to explain what she'd done, or rather what she'd tried to do. Water was everywhere, though a lot of it was soaking the red rug next to my bed.

"How could you be so *stupid!?*" Susanna yelled. Turning to me, she went on, "Go get the mop and start cleaning this up!"

"Me? She did it!"

"Both of you!" she said angrily. "I can't believe this. Quit standing there like an idiot and go get the mop!"

I hurried to the kitchen and brought a mop and bucket back, angry at both of them. I hadn't heard all of Susanna's recriminations from the other room, but I caught the tail end of them as I got back, her lecturing Carolyn on how lucky we both were that the trash can hadn't actually fallen on me, or else I probably would have ended up in the hospital. Moreover, if we didn't get this cleaned up immediately, the hardwood floors would be ruined.

Still, we got everything tidied up just fine, and we even managed to get the rug dried out and put back in place before our parents got back. They never suspected that anything had happened, but then, they never really asked about what we'd done all week other than a general "was everything okay" line of questioning. My mother seemed more interested in telling us about Philadelphia and the writers she'd met, and my father had several things to take care of before going back to work on Monday.

I think what angered Susanna the most about the incident was that if there had actually been any damage and had we been caught, our parents might have deemed her untrustworthy of being in charge while they were gone, and we probably would have been back in the care of our aunt and uncle the following summer in 1983. Honestly, had it happened that way instead, a lot of people would have been much better off, as we wouldn't have had the chance to do the things we did that year. People died as a result, though we didn't plan for things to turn out that way.

But things happened as they did, with Carl and Tim coming over to the house to stay with us for a few days near the end of June, which was my idea. We played some games on Tim's Atari, and later, we raced around the yard with Carl so he could practice for that evening. Susanna wasn't very involved in things, just sort of the designated semi-adult in charge, plus she was busy upstairs in her room going through her things and preparing for her move to Charleston, South Carolina in a few weeks to go off to college.

Carolyn, though, spent time with me and the others, including taking part in the practice races around the yard. She was somewhat athletic herself, much more than Tim or I were, so she was the only real competition Carl had. He didn't take it well the few times that she beat him, either. The first time she did, he swore at her, calling her a bitch. I didn't hear just what she said to him in response, but she grabbed the front of his shirt, got right up in his face, and whispered through clenched teeth while staring him straight in the eye. I think I managed to make out the words "balls" and "off," but I had no idea what she was talking about, just that she told him off, and he apologized several times in a row and promised not to do it again. Tim and I found this hilarious.

As much as Carl liked to portray himself as a tough guy and a major athlete — as much as a nine-year-old can be, anyway — sometimes his behavior was a bit laughable. He was rather thin and tall, the tallest boy in our class, in fact. At school, some of us were more competitive than others when it came to sports, and Carl definitely seemed determined to prove himself.

Aside from doing his best to win, Carl also had this weird habit of overexerting himself, or rather, making a show of overexerting himself. I first noticed it in a game of kickball when I was on first base and Carl (on the opposite team) raced past me on his way to second. He looked like some Olympic runner, arms pumping by his sides as if he were a locomotive, teeth clenched, and breathing in exaggerated, quick gasps. At first it seemed kind of impressive, but the more I noticed him doing it, the more fake it seemed, more like he was doing an impression of an athletic person than actually being one. It just seemed a little too over the top for a lanky third grader.

Sometimes Tim and I teased him for this, at which point he would get defensive and whip out his latest arsenal of poorly chosen swear words, which, when overheard by a teacher, got him sent to the principal's office more than once. He soon learned to curb his profanity, at least at school. Now he had learned a new lesson, which was not to direct it at my sister.

In these practice races around our backyard, he was again doing his athlete impression, but I didn't want to antagonize him too much, certainly not this early on in his visit. When he went inside to use the bathroom at one point, I mentioned to Carolyn how funny Tim and I found his mannerisms while running.

"Well, maybe it helps him," Carolyn said.

"To look like he's about to explode?" asked Tim with a grin.

She frowned back, looking a little impatient. "I mean that by doing that, acting all *'chug-a-chug-a,'*" — which she said while imitating Carl's arms pumping and making a pained face like he did — "it kind of psyches him out so he believes he can run faster. And then maybe he can." She paused, then smirked and rolled her eyes. "But you're right; it does look pretty stupid." We laughed. "Really though, if it helps him to believe it, leave him alone." I was a little confused over her defending him after their recent confrontation, but Carolyn was just like that, sometimes one of the gang and other times more of a wise older figure. Maybe she just liked telling us what to do, playing the "I'm older and know better" card.

She was still quite the joker, though, which turned on full blast after dinner when we began heading to the YMCA for the qualifying race. Upon hearing that the race was being held there, Carolyn immediately began her repetitive and tuneless attempts at singing the famous song of the same name, bouncing up and down and doing the popular dance with her arms, spelling out the letters from the chorus. We all laughed, even Susanna, but the more Carolyn repeated the joke, the more tired of it Susanna became. This just egged Carolyn on more, especially once she realized that the rest of us were also getting a laugh out of Susanna's aggravation.

But by the time we were halfway to our destination, the song (or bits of the song) had been sung for the sixth or seventh time, and Susanna had had enough. She'd already warned Carolyn to stop once, then been defied, which my friends and I still found hilarious. Sternly, she said to Carolyn, "I swear if you do that one more time, I'm stopping this car and kicking you out, and you can walk the rest of the way."

Carolyn stopped bouncing around, but she was still smiling. She squinted as she said, "You wouldn't dare."

"Try me," Susanna said in a low voice, staring ahead, jaw clenched.

"Fine." Carolyn deflated and sat with her arms folded. I wondered if she would in fact "try" Susanna.

Seeing that she wasn't going to, I took it upon myself to burst into song: *"Young man...!"* which prompted huge laughs from Carl, Tim, and Carolyn.

Susanna braked and began slowing down, and I immediately clammed up, catching her eyes in the rearview mirror.

"Okay, okay, okay!" I said, throwing my hands up. "I'll stop."

"You bet you will." I could tell she meant business, so I sat quietly while the others tried to keep from laughing. The car resumed normal speed, and we rode in silence for a while.

Things began to feel uncomfortable and not fun anymore, which Tim tried to defuse by making small talk with Carl, asking him about the race and how he had gotten involved with it. He had heard about it from his father and been encouraged to compete, and although his family wasn't going to be able to make it to this qualifying race, they would be there for the actual race the following night. Carl had no doubts about qualifying, and his excitement grew as we got closer to the venue.

We arrived at the YMCA around 8:00. It was still light outside, and in the eastern sky, a huge full moon was rising just above the trees. I didn't even notice it until Tim pointed it out to us as we got out of Susanna's car, and we all thought it looked very cool. It looked bigger than normal, and yellowish-orange instead of white like I was used to seeing.

A large white plastic banner illuminated by spotlights bore the words *Run for Life — 1983* in red and blue and hung on the side of the main building, which was on a hill situated above an oval-shaped running track.

"So what's this for again?" Susanna asked Carl, pointing towards the banner.

"I don't know," he shrugged. "Some charity."

Susanna laughed slightly, then smiled. "You don't care as long as you get to race, right?" Carl laughed and nodded. "So where to now?"

Carl's face fell, his eyes going wide. It soon became apparent that he had no idea what he actually needed to do.

Fortunately, Susanna again took on the role of the responsible adult and led us around until we found the people in charge, and we got Carl signed in. We were told where he needed to go in order to join the other racers and get ready.

There were lots of kids there, some with their families and some not, and there was a general excitement in the air. Many of the people, parents and children alike, were joking around and having a good time. A few of the competitors seemed to be taking things more seriously, particularly the older ones, who were doing things like stretches, running in place, or jumping jacks. I wasn't sure exactly what the age range of the participants was, but most of the boys and girls there seemed to be around my and Carl's age.

Two boys, who didn't seem to be accompanied by any parents, ended up walking near us as we headed down toward the track and to the place where Carl had been directed, a smaller building next to a chain link fence. They had been having their own conversation, then suddenly took notice of the five of us.

"Hey look!" the taller of the two said. "More losers!" His friend, a squinty-eyed pale boy with red hair, gave out a sort of hiccup-sounding chuckle and agreed.

"Excuse me?" Carolyn said to them.

"We're going to beat you," the taller one said with a wide, goofy grin. He looked kind of like Carl, skinny with short brown hair, but taller and possibly a year or two older. I wasn't sure if the other boy was his younger brother or just a friend, but they had already made one thing apparent: They were jerks.

"That will be pretty hard to do since we're not going to be in the race," Carolyn said, sneering. Tim and I laughed.

The boy faltered. "Well… Then what in the world are you people doing here?" The second boy managed to add a "yeah," clearly used to following the other's lead.

"*I'm* in the race," Carl said, pointing to his chest. By then, we had all stopped walking. "And *I'm* going to beat *you.*"

"Oh, get real," the boy said. "You aren't beating shit." He and his friend laughed.

"Oh yeah?" Carl said. "I bet I will!" He was getting worked up, growing more defiant and anxious.

"Nah, you won't," said the red-haired one, "fag." I had never heard that word before and had no idea what it meant, but it set Carl off.

"You're the fag!" He started to lunge for the boy, arms raised and fists clenched.

Susanna, who had been silent up until now, stepped in and blocked Carl, who quickly backed down as she held a hand to his chest, her other hand pointed towards the two boys. "That's enough," she said firmly. "Why don't you two all-stars run along and leave the rest of us alone?"

"Ooh, tough boy," the brown-haired boy said icily to Carl. "Gotta have a girl stick up for you, faggot?" His thick southern accent made the word sound like "figgit."

Susanna then turned to him and glared, and she walked a few steps toward him. I couldn't see her face once her back was to me, but the boy looked suddenly intimidated. "I said get inside," she said, her voice lowered and stern, and she pointed to the building, where a stereotypical coach-looking fat man in a baseball cap was standing by the door and holding a clipboard, a whistle on a cord around his neck.

"Whatever…" the boy said, regaining his defiant composure. As the two of them slowly started heading away, the red-haired one shot us a dirty-looking smirk and flipped us the bird. I barely knew what that meant, either, aside from it being another attempt to tell us off.

Turning back to the rest of us, Susanna said, "Okay, enough of them. Carl, do you have everything you need?"

Carl, still angry, began to focus more on why we were there and calmed down. "Yeah, I think so." He was carrying a small tote bag with some supplies in it, and he looked inside to make sure it was fully stocked. I actually had no idea what he had in there, but I assumed it was something to do with the whole track running thing. I'd never been all that interested in sports, aside from whatever happened to bleed over from the other people in my life. Carl was into running track, and Carolyn had played basketball on the school's team for a year when I was younger. Susanna was a cheerleader in high school and a ballerina a few years before that, but I didn't really understand what those things were about. As far as I was concerned, cheerleading was something involving jumping around at football games, and I was barely old enough to just vaguely recall Susanna's ballet recitals.

As Carl headed over to the coach by the building, the rest of us went to the metal bleachers that lined one side of the track. The seats were still somewhat hot, having been baking in the sun all day, and I realized that it was a good thing that the race had been held in the evening instead of during the day. That week had been the hottest one of the year so far with temperatures in the mid-90s. It was probably also a lot easier on the runners, too, not having to sweat to death in the blazing sun. Large banks of spotlights on poles illuminated the area and were becoming more necessary the darker it got.

Eventually, a group of ten contestants lined up by the starting line, though Carl wasn't one of them. His group must have still been waiting for their turn. I wasn't that interested in these people since I didn't know them, but seeing them run their portion of the race gave me an idea of what to expect once Carl got his chance to go. It was pretty straightforward, the coach counting down with the standard "on your mark, get set," and then a shrill blow from his whistle. The runners began making their way around the track, some of them ahead, some behind, until they made their way back around to the finish line (which was the same as the starting line). The first, second, and third place winners were the ones chosen to compete further — either later that night or the following night; I wasn't sure — and the others were immediately out. Susanna, Carolyn, Tim, and I joined the crowd in cheering the racers on, soon caught up in the excitement and eager to see Carl take part.

His group was the second to go, and as he and the others lined up, I saw that the two boys we had encountered earlier were among them. They still had the same confident and snide air to them, and Carl looked angry and defiant. I pointed this out to Tim, who said that they had probably gotten into more arguments since we had last seen them.

The coach again counted down and blew his whistle, and the race began. The two boys stayed up near the front of the crowd as everyone made their way around, while Carl seemed to be lagging behind most of the other runners. But I knew what he was doing, as this was a technique he had used during our practice sessions earlier in the day. He was saving himself up for the last half of the race, letting the others tire themselves out early on.

Sure enough, about halfway through, when the runners were on the opposite side of the track from us, I could see Carl switch into super-athlete mode and begin his dramatic exertion. Suddenly, he was cutting through to the front of the group, gaining on the two boys, who had started to look behind themselves at the other racers.

But as the group began heading around the final turn about three quarters of the way through, Carl suddenly veered off to one side and tripped, almost falling over completely but managing to keep running. The four of us gasped and called out, and Carolyn stood up. Carl managed to keep going, but his stumble had cost him the advantage he'd gained, and he was never able to make it up. The race ended with the two boys and one girl with a ponytail crossing the finish line first, Carl and the others following close behind but visibly disappointed.

As the runners slowed down, the winners looking quite pleased with themselves, I saw that Carl did not in fact slow down with the rest of them. Instead, he headed straight for the brown-haired boy, tackling him to the ground as he reached him. In the bleachers, the rest of us were on our feet, Carolyn leading us down towards the track to intervene.

"You son of a bitch!" Carl said as he thrashed at the boy, attempting to beat him to pieces. "You lying cheating sack of ass!"

The boy pushed Carl off of him, aided by the coach, who had reached Carl and was violently pulling him backwards while he continued to kick and scream. "You cut that out right now!" he said to Carl, who eventually became still. "Now what's the problem here?"

The boy stood up and brushed the dirt off of himself, eyeing Carl angrily. "I don't know. Stupid kid just jumped all over me." The other boy, the red-head, joined him at his side and began pointing at Carl.

"Yeah, you're just mad that we beat you!" he said. He emphasized and drew out the word *"beeeeat"* as snidely as he could, which just angered Carl further.

The coach continued to hold Carl by the arms as we reached him. "Let go of me!" he shrieked, struggling impossibly against the large man's grip.

"All right, everybody calm down," Susanna said.

"Are you okay?" Tim asked Carl, who was dirty and scratched up.

"No I'm not okay!" Carl shouted. "That piss-head cheated! He threw a rock at me during the race!"

The coach finally loosened his grip, and Carl tried to regain his composure. "Is that true?" he asked the boy.

"No, it's not true," the boy said matter-of-factly. "He's lying!"

"Yeah!" the other boy chimed in, pointing at Carl again. "He's just being a sore loser!"

"I am not!" Carl squealed, his voice quaking. He seemed on the verge of tears and was holding his arms, visibly smarting from where the coach had been holding him so hard.

"I don't know what you're talking about," the boy said. Then he added, smiling, "Crybaby." I noticed again that he really did look a lot like Carl, sort of like an older version of him with all of his obnoxious traits but none of his redeeming qualities.

"Did anyone else see this boy throw a rock during the race?" the coach said to the other racers, who had gathered around to see what was happening. No one spoke up; they just shrugged their shoulders and looked around at each other, seeming genuinely confused.

"But I saw it!" Carl insisted. "And that other suck-ass had one too!" He pointed at the red-haired boy, who had been smiling up until that point.

"Did not!" he said defiantly, an angry look spreading across his face. "Loser!"

Carl started to lunge for him, but the coach grabbed him again, this time by the shoulders, stopping him.

"All right, that's enough! I think we've seen enough unsportsmanlike conduct for one night! You and your friends clear on out of here."

"No way!" I said. "He said those boys cheated! That's not fair!"

"I don't need to hear any lip out of you either," he said, pointing at me, and I flinched. Carl started to protest further, but the man cut him off. "Or you! Now get on out of here!"

We tried to convince the man to listen to us and that Carl wasn't lying, but by then, two security guards in dark blue uniforms had shown up, suddenly making things seem a lot more serious. By the expressions on their faces, it was clear that they felt that we were the troublemakers, and any further debate would be useless.

So Susanna led us away from the crowd, Carl still fuming and trying to hold back tears, occasionally muttering a swear word here and there. I was angry, too. We all were. I didn't know exactly what had happened, but I certainly didn't believe that Carl had been lying.

"Well that really stunk," Carolyn said. "Sorry it went like that, Carl."

Carl stared out the car window, not looking at anyone and still trying not to cry. "I know what I saw," he said softly.

"Well, what did happen?" I asked.

Carl paused and breathed deeply, maybe relieved that someone was finally going to listen to him. "It was the other boy who did it first," he said, "that red-headed rat-faced piece of crap. He was pretty slick about it, just kinda letting a rock he'd been carrying in his hand drop out and fall behind him."

"A rock?" Tim asked. "I mean, they were just running the whole time with rocks in their hands? Seems like that would slow them down."

"Apparently not…" Susanna said pointedly.

"No, they weren't big rocks. Just maybe about that big." He held up his hand and made a circle with his thumb and finger. "The boy threw it behind him, well, dropped it, and I just happened to look over and see it. The girl behind him didn't even notice, and it didn't hit her. She just ran right past it. But it freaked me out because I wondered if he might do it again or the other guy might do it, too."

"And he did, which was when you tripped up," I said, figuring out the rest.

"Yeah," Carl said angrily. "It didn't even hit me, but I saw it coming and tried to get out of the way." There was silence for a moment, and then Carl beat his fist hard on the inside of the car door.

"Carl, stop that," Susanna said somewhat coldly.

I could tell that Carl was about to explode at her, so I put a hand on his arm in what I hoped was a comforting gesture. "Carl, it's okay. Just stop."

"Yeah, come on," Tim chimed in. "We'll go back to the house, maybe play some more video games…"

"I don't want to play any more damn video games!" Carl yelled. "I just…" He sighed heavily. "My dad's gonna kill me."

I assured him that he would not, but Carl still wanted to wallow, insisting that his family was counting on him winning the qualifying race so they could see him compete the following night. Now that was out, and he was sure that his father would be very disappointed in him. He was, after all, a P.E. teacher, though at a different school than the one the three of us attended.

Finally he said, "I don't want to talk about it anymore." The rest of the ride home was in silence.

Not long after we got back to the house, Carl insisted on going straight to bed, or at least, to my room where his and Tim's sleeping bags were. He clearly needed to be left alone to fume some more, so we let him.

"Poor kid," Carolyn said once he was out of earshot.

"Yeah," Tim said. "He was really looking forward to the whole thing. And now it ended up like this."

"Well, maybe he'll feel better in the morning," I said. We still had a few more days before our parents got back from Los Angeles and my friends went home, and despite what had happened so far, I was counting on us having a good time. I had been looking forward to that for weeks.

"That's just really crappy what those boys did," Carolyn said, "and even worse that there was no way to prove it."

"Couldn't we, though?" I asked. "I mean, if Carl had explained it better like he did to us, we could have… I don't know… maybe found the rock on the track and shown it to them?" I realized as I spoke that it would have been pretty impossible to find one or two little rocks on that big track and prove that they were the ones the boys had dropped. Carolyn then said pretty much what I had been thinking, adding that it would have been pointless.

"Not like that coach would have listened to us anyway," Tim added.

"Yeah, well," Susanna said. "I've got some stuff to do up in my room. Don't stay up too late." She walked off and headed for the stairs.

Carolyn looked dumbfounded, then shook her head. "I suppose she could be a little more uncaring and cold," she said, "but then we'd probably have to turn the air conditioner down."

"Well, maybe she's just worn out," Tim said. "I guess we all are."

I wasn't. I was wired from all the excitement, and I wanted to stay up and play some more video games like Tim had suggested earlier in the car. Although it was nothing compared to how complex video games would become years later, I was still very intrigued by how detailed and exciting Tim's Atari system was compared to the older one we had. Carl also had a different video game system called an Intellivision, which I'd played once over at his house earlier in the year, but I didn't like it very much.

Tim and I stayed up for about an hour playing Pac-Man, an old favorite of mine. I loved how it looked so much more like the arcade version — which I'd only played a couple of times — than the more primitive one I was used to. Carolyn soon got bored sitting and watching us play, so she got up from the couch and said she'd see us in the morning. And by the end of that first hour, Tim was also ready for bed, so we went to my room, where he crawled into his sleeping bag. Carl was gently snoring in the far corner.

When I had been planning this whole thing weeks prior — my friends coming over, having fun, and spending the night with me in my room — I had pictured the three of us staying awake for a while with the lights out, talking quietly and cracking jokes. Things weren't going according to plan, though, with Carl being upset over his loss at the race, then with Tim wanting to turn in for the night before I was ready to.

Rather than going to bed, I decided to stay up a little bit later playing single-player games on the Atari with the volume turned down, but it wasn't as much fun without someone to compete against. Finally I gave up and headed for my room, but I paused at the foot of the stairs that led up to Susanna's bedroom.

There are certain moments that you look back on and ask yourself what the rest of your life would have been like if you had done something differently at that point, if you had gone one way as opposed to another. You think about what happened as a result of the choice you made, which seemed insignificant at the time, but which led to a very important and pivotal moment, changing everything from that point on. Sometimes, I wonder how many people would still be alive today had I not gone up those stairs.

I knocked on Susanna's door and waited for her to say I could come in, which she did. I found her sitting on her bed, which was surrounded by cardboard boxes, some with writing on them indicating whatever products they had originally been used to sell. Some were taped shut, others halfway full and still open. She was still packing for her upcoming move.

I knew this, but I still asked, "What are you doing?"

"What does it look like?" she said, mimicking my tone. She wasn't being mean; I could tell she was just joking. For some reason, she tended to do that more often when we were alone as opposed to when other people were around.

I wanted to come back with a clever response, but nothing came to mind, so I just moved closer to the bed and looked around at all of her stuff. Her room was pretty much a wreck, clothes and books and all sorts of old things scattered around as she sorted through them and decided what she needed to take with her and what she could live without. At the time, I didn't really understand the impact of it all, how big of a deal this first move away from home must have been for her, nor did I truly grasp the fact that she would be gone for so long. I was just used to her being around, even if we weren't terribly close, being nine years apart in age. She sometimes seemed like a third parent to me, though like Carolyn, there were times when she could shift gears and just be the big sister.

"You know, you could actually help instead of just gawping at everything," she said.

"Okay," I said, sitting down on the bed eagerly. As I did, a stack of notebooks and folders shifted, falling over onto my hip.

"Way to help, baby brother," she said, rolling her eyes.

"I've told you not to call me that," I said fiercely, this being a particular pet peeve of mine. She always used that nickname in a condescending manner, and I hoped that she wouldn't blurt it out in front of my friends. I began straightening up the fallen pile of books as best as I could, but I wasn't doing a very good job, more like scattering them further.

"Just… just… Could you just hand those to me one at a time?" She sighed. "I need to go to bed soon," she added. "But I can't until I get all this stuff cleared away."

While she said that, I picked up a spiral notebook with a red cover on it. In the upper right corner was written *Susanna Young, Latin, 4th period, Dr. Washburn.* I had no idea what Latin even was, so I asked her, mispronouncing the word as "laytin."

"Latin," she corrected. "It's a foreign language." Then she smiled. "Hey, there's a joke about that that one of my friends told me."

"What?"

"A boy asks his father why they have to learn French in school," she began. Having already taken French at my own school, I had wondered this myself, finding the subject rather boring and arbitrary. "And the father says, 'So if you meet a French person, you can talk to him.' So then he asks, 'So why do we have to learn Spanish in school?' The father says, 'So if you meet a Spanish person, you can talk to him.' Then the boy says, 'Well, then why do we have to learn Latin?' 'So if you meet an Ancient Roman, you can talk to him!'"

I could tell that she had reached the punch line, but I didn't get it. "Um…" I managed to say. "That's stupid."

Susanna sighed again. "No, it's… Never mind. Just hand that one here."

I handed her the notebook, and she began looking through it, deciding if it needed to be packed up for the move or left behind. While she did, I picked up the next one, a purple notebook that, according to its label, was for her Chemistry class. I opened it up and looked at a couple of pages, but as far as I was concerned, the big words and complex formulas in there might as well have been, well, Latin.

"What about this one?" I asked.

"Hang on," she said, not looking up from her Latin notebook and still thumbing through the pages. She stopped on one and laughed, rotating the book to read a note from one of the margins.

"What?"

"Oh, nothing," she said, still smiling. "Just where my friend Peg wrote, 'Dr. Washburn looks like a lumberjack.'"

I laughed, too. "Did he?"

"Well, he had this black and red plaid shirt he used to wear, and he was kinda fat… plus there was the beard…" I pictured some kind of Paul Bunyan figure, then a guy I'd seen on a roll of paper towels at the grocery store one time when I was there with my mother. "Anyway, no, I don't think I'll need this one. If I decide to take Latin in college, which I don't think I will, I can always come back later and get this one if I need any notes. Next!" She held out her hand. I handed her the Chemistry notebook, and she began going through that one.

I reached for the next item in the pile, which was a loose-leaf folder, also purple. I was confused because this one was also labeled "Chemistry," so I opened it. Most of the papers in it were typed, pre-printed sheets, official handouts for the class, I figured. Many of them were in faded, purple typescript, which I recognized from some of the handouts I had gotten in my classes as well over the years. I had discovered several months earlier that if I licked my finger, I could press it onto this kind of print and have it come off in a mirror image on my skin, which always amused me. I had come home from school one day and baffled my mother, who wondered why my hands and forearms seemed to be tattooed with multiplication tables.

I was about to repeat the experiment on one of the pages in this folder when I noticed that it also had pockets in the front and back. The front pocket was empty, but the back pocket had some handwritten notes on some pages that appeared to have been torn out from a spiral notebook. The handwriting was different from what I had seen in Susanna's notebooks so far, and at the top of the first page in all capitals was written the title: *VAMPIRE POTION*. Below that were more symbols and words that I didn't understand, but still, I was intrigued.

"Susanna?" I asked. "What's this? A vampire potion?" She looked up sharply from the other notebook as I continued, "I didn't know there was a such thing."

"Give me that," she said, holding out her hand. I did, but I wasn't giving up. This sounded interesting.

"Really? A vampire potion?" I repeated.

"Yes," she said, sounding irritated, or maybe sad, and she began looking at the papers, the folder spread open on top of the notebook she'd been reading. "It was... an experiment."

"But did it work?" I asked. "Like, turning people into vampires?" I was no stranger to the idea of potions turning people into weird things, having seen it plenty of times in TV shows and cartoons. The first one that sprang to mind was a *Tom and Jerry* cartoon where the characters took a potion that made them bigger, stronger, and more menacing, but then they would find themselves in a tight spot when the potion wore off and they suddenly returned to normal.

"Oh yeah it did," Susanna said, looking off to the side, seeming distracted.

"So tell me about it!" I said eagerly. "Was it cool?"

She turned back to me, perturbed. "No it wasn't.... well... It was just... I don't know. It was strange." She appeared reluctant to continue, but I wanted more.

It wasn't like vampires were a huge interest of mine at the time. In my mind, they were lumped in with other monsters and strange creatures I'd been aware of most of my life, sort of silly, cartoony villains like Dracula, Frankenstein, or the Boogieman, the last of which I'd never actually seen any visual depiction of. It being the early 1980s, I for some reason always pictured that one as some sort of weirdly dressed disco-dancing guy that bounded into your bedroom late at night while some funky music played. Not all that far back, Carolyn and Susanna had both watched reruns on TV of some old black-and-white show called *Dark Shadows* that also had vampires in it, and I'd seen some parts of it, too, but it didn't really interest me. What's more, around Halloween the previous year, our teacher had read to our class a funny book about a vampire rabbit, which I thought was pretty neat.

So really, I had been aware of supernatural creatures, monsters, aliens, and even superheroes for quite some time, but it had not yet crystallized in my worldview whether or not these things were real. I was taught the difference between fiction and non-fiction, reality and "make-believe," and I knew that most of what I saw on TV wasn't actually real. But I also knew that some of what I saw on there or read in stories was at least partly true, or at least representations of things that could be true. There may not have been an actual guy named Ebenezer Scrooge who was visited by some ghosts on Christmas Eve many years ago, but no one had ever clearly stated to me — at least not convincingly — that there weren't still real ghosts out there that I might encounter someday.

And so this night, when Susanna told me all about this potion that she and a friend from school developed that could turn people into vampires, the lines became a lot more blurred.

She explained that this boy in her class that she was "involved with," whatever that meant, had sort of accidentally developed this potion, and he had been able to use it to turn little white mice into vicious killers that would drain the blood from other mice who had not been given the potion. He demonstrated it to her one afternoon when they were staying late after class to catch up on lab assignments. It was something they did in secret, not anything their teacher knew about. They were working on school-related things as far as anyone else knew.

"One of us… I can't remember who… thought of trying to develop the potion further to make the mice more vampire-like, so we did," she continued. "After a few weeks, we'd gotten it to where the mice couldn't handle things like sunlight, garlic, crosses, stuff like that. They were also stronger than regular mice, and one of them even turned into a little bat and tried to fly out of its cage. We stopped it, though." She smiled as she said that, though I wasn't sure why.

I listened intently, not feeling any reason to doubt her. She was, after all, older and more experienced than I was, and if she was telling me that there was such a thing as a vampire potion, and there was the formula for it right there on the paper in front of me, then that was reason enough to believe. It also meant that, as I had sort of unconsciously suspected my entire life, there really were strange and magical things out there in the world, extraordinary phenomena like the ones I'd heard about through TV, movies, and fairy tales. Those things really did happen to other people, even if most of the depictions I'd seen of them so far were fictional.

Susanna went on, "So it was at this point that Robert decided…"

"Who?"

"Robert. The guy I've been talking about for the past five minutes."

"Oh. I don't think you ever said his name."

She huffed. "Well, his name was Robert, okay? Anyway, he decided that we'd gotten as far as we could with the mice, and the potion should be tested on an actual person. I certainly didn't want to try it, but he was pretty gung-ho about it."

"So he became a vampire?" By this point, I had pulled my knees up to my chest with my chin resting on them. I wasn't scared, just fascinated.

"Oh yeah he did," Susanna said with an exasperated tone.

"Like with a big cape and all?" I spread my arms out, my legs dropping back along the side of the bed. "Running around going, 'Bluh! Bluh!'" I was doing the best impression of a vampire I could manage given what I'd seen of them.

She scowled. "No, nothing like that. He was just… I don't know… Him, but more powerful and… meaner."

"Oh." I was a little disappointed. "Did he at least have fangs?" I put both of my index fingers up to my mouth to mimic the appearance.

She paused. "Yes."

"So then what happened?"

After looking off into space for a moment, she continued, "Well, long story short, he tried to kill me. But we managed to change him back to normal, and then things were fine."

Oddly enough, that part of the story didn't really bother me or seem any more extraordinary than the rest of it. Vampires killed people, I knew. They were bad guys. Bad guys did stuff like that. And in the end, bad guys were defeated or killed by the good guys, and everything was okay again. That was how the world worked.

"So the potion could be reversed?" I asked.

"Yes, thank God," she said, shaken. "He was very sorry for what he did, trying to hurt me and all, but I wasn't too quick to forgive him until I was able to make him promise to get rid of the potion."

"And did he?"

"Yes, plus he gave me his only copy of all the notes we'd made for it so he wouldn't be tempted to try it again later. That's what these are," she said, pointing to the papers in front of her. "And as far as I know, he never did do it again."

There was a pause. All I could say to break the silence was, "Wow."

Susanna shook her head. "I shouldn't even be telling you about this. It's a secret, okay? Don't tell anyone."

I nodded.

We worked a little more on going through her notebooks, but by then it was definitely getting too late for us to still be up. So she had me help her clear the remaining piles of notebooks off of her bed, keeping them separated so she would know where to pick up the following morning when she continued sorting through them.

"Thanks for the bedtime story," I joked as I told her goodnight and left, then headed down the stairs and to my bedroom.

Carl and Tim were both asleep, and I got into bed as quietly as I could to keep from waking them. It had been a tiring day, so falling asleep wasn't all that difficult, though at first, my mind was veering off in different directions, thinking about all of the exciting and interesting things that had happened.

I thought of the video games we had played, hearing the bleeping and blooping sound effects in my head along with the synthesized music. The computerized images seemed almost burned into my eyes, and I kept picturing Pac-Man running around the maze trying to get away from the evil ghosts. I also thought of Carl, angry on his behalf that he had lost the race to those two mean boys. And I thought of Susanna and her friend's amazing vampire potion, how cool of a story that was, a secret she had shared with me.

The dream I had that night was a further mish-mash of the day's events mixed in with other random elements. My friends and I were at school, playing some game where we had to run back and forth across a parking lot or similar paved surface. At one end of the blacktop was a green painted wall with a white horizontal stripe on it, and the object of the game was to run up to the wall and somehow up onto it, spinning around in the air and then racing back in the opposite direction. Carl was there, exerting himself melodramatically as usual, his arms pumping at his sides, enunciating the phrase "chugga chugga, chugga chugga" rhythmically as he went along. I could see his face close-up, and it was contorted in a dramatic grimace, his veins popping out of his neck as if he were some professional bodybuilder lifting a huge weight. He reached the wall, bounced up against it, and spun around to head the other way. I was racing in this same way, too, as were Tim, Carolyn, Susanna, and some other people I knew from school, but it was as if my mind were a camera that was mainly focusing on Carl.

As we headed away from the wall, we were racing toward an enormous chain link fence in the distance. I could hear people cheering, or screaming, somewhere nearby, along with a computerized sounding police siren. My mind's "camera" shifted focus to farther ahead of us, where there were the two mean boys we had met earlier. The red-head seemed to be drenched in sweat which flew away from his hair as he ran. The taller, dark-haired one looked back towards us with an exaggerated evil grin. He reminded me of a typical cartoon villain who probably should have had a long moustache and a menacing laugh, though he didn't in this dream. He threw his arm behind him dramatically, and as his fingers spread out, several dozen large marbles flew out from them and clattered along the pavement towards us. Unable to stop, we slipped up on the marbles as they reached us, flying off our feet and into the air. I expected to land on my back, which I knew I would hurt, but that didn't happen. Instead, time jumped ahead as it sometimes does in dreams, or maybe I just skipped into another dream.

The next thing I remember, I was standing by a small white plastic table on some grass. On it, there were several small clear plastic cups containing what looked like Coca-Cola. But I knew that instead, it was the vampire potion. I was going to drink it, but then I worried that if I did, the sun might get me.

I looked up, but there wasn't a sky there; instead it was a white ceiling. At the center of it was a round stained glass window, a white sort of tic-tac-toe pattern overlaying it. The glass was a deep red, and no light shone through it. I looked back down at the table, and there was a marble floor beneath it now, which made sense since I was apparently indoors after all. I reached for a cup, picked it up, and drank the potion, which tasted sweet. I felt excited.

After I set my cup down, someone nearby said, "Did it work?" I reached up to feel my teeth, searching to see if I had fangs. My finger touched a sharp fang on the right side of my mouth.

"Ow!" I said, suddenly realizing that I was awake and in bed, having said that word aloud.

Although it was a skill I would master one day, by this point in my life, I was not very good at keeping secrets. By the following morning, I had already told Tim about the vampire potion, but not exactly on purpose. At first I was just telling him about the weird dreams I'd had, and when I came to the part about the vampire potion, he stopped me and asked me what I'd meant. So I told him what Susanna had told me about the potion she'd made, and he thought it sounded pretty cool. Like me, he was interested in science fiction and fantasy, though he read more books than I tended to.

Carl, meanwhile, was on the phone in the kitchen, having called his family to tell them the bad news about not qualifying for the race. He had seemed less upset by it when we'd gotten up that morning, or at least not as afraid to talk to his father about it. By this point, his increasingly raised voice distracted me and Tim from our conversation, and we went into the kitchen to join him.

"I'm… I'm sorry…" he said softly into the phone, and he hung up. He had tears running down his face, and he turned away from us when he saw that we were there, not wanting us to see, wiping his face quickly.

"Carl?" Tim asked. "You okay?"

He sniffled. "No…"

"What happened?" I asked.

Carl, his voice quavering, told us how his father had yelled at him and about how disappointed he was in him. He became more angry as he spoke, slowly shifting from wounded to hostile. When he had asked his father if he could still stay with my family for a few days, he had been told that he could do what he wanted and that his father didn't care. He paused, punctuating his story with a single expletive to describe his father: "Ass-head."

"Yeah," was all I could add.

"Well, maybe he'll forget about it and calm down by the time you go back home," Tim offered, sitting down at the kitchen table beside him.

"Yeah, maybe," Carl said. He had stopped crying; now he was just fuming. After a moment or two, he said, "I want to kill those two jerks."

"I know," I said. "Me too." How serious we were about that is hard to say. People often use the word "kill" in a colloquial way, not a literal one, but at the same time, we didn't really understand the difference. I'd seen bad guys and monsters get killed in cartoons before. After all, they deserved it.

"Hey, tell him about the vampire potion!" Tim said, suddenly brightening up. So much for the secret.

I glared at him, but to be fair, I hadn't actually gotten around to telling him it was a secret earlier. Carl just asked, "The what?"

Tim said, "Susanna's got some potion that can turn people into vampires!"

"Bull crap," Carl said, but at least he was starting to smile again.

"No, really, it's true!" I said. "She showed it to me last night!" I went on to tell the two of them more details of what Susanna had told me, probably embellishing bits along the way, my memory already becoming distorted to make the story more interesting. Carl's eyes widened as I talked, and I could tell he was starting to believe me. "But don't tell anyone," I added.

"Hey," Tim said, a grin broadening across his face. I'd seen this look before. It was the one he got when he was feeling clever, or more specifically, when he was coming up with something sneaky. Despite being one of the top students in our class, he could occasionally misbehave just as much as the rest of us. "Why don't we take the vampire potion, and then kill those two boys?"

"What?" I asked.

"Are you serious?" Carl asked. After a pause, he added, "That would be awesome!"

I had to agree. Getting back at those boys seemed perfectly reasonable, in fact, it felt like the right thing to do. They had no right to cheat in that race the way they did, and they had gotten away with it at our expense. Someone needed to teach them a lesson. I didn't come up with all of these justifications at once, but they quickly built up the more we talked. Besides, the idea of being turned into vampires sounded pretty interesting, to say the least.

We discussed the possibilities some more, and Carl wondered if Susanna would be willing to make the potion. If she did, the three of us would go back to the YMCA that night and get our revenge. Carl was very excited about the idea. We all were.

Although I was disappointed, I was not all that surprised when Susanna immediately rejected our proposal. We had gone up to her room to tell her our idea, and after her initial refusal, the next thing she did was chastise me for telling them about the potion.

"I told you that was supposed to be a secret, Ray." She turned away from us and went back to sorting through her belongings.

"I know, but come on!" I said. "It would be the perfect way to get back at them!"

She had been avoiding eye contact, focusing on going through her things, but then she stopped and turned back to me. "The perfect way," she said sarcastically. "Do you have any idea what you're saying?"

"Sure I do!" I said, not actually understanding her question.

"You really want me to turn you guys into vampires and have you go kill those boys." She was again using that tone of voice where she was technically asking a question, but it came out sounding like a statement.

I honestly did not understand the depth of what she was saying; I just thought she was being mean and refusing to help because she was mad at me for telling her secret. The gravity of actually killing anybody was more or less lost on me, plus I had very limited experience with death.

The only family member who had died during my lifetime was my grandmother, and that happened when I was almost too young to recall it, plus I barely remembered her or what she was like. I vaguely remembered her funeral, a bunch of people in fancy clothes standing around looking sad while I squirmed in my mother's arms and was probably the typical loud obnoxious toddler whose crying spoiled an otherwise somber event. A couple of years later, I'd had a pet lizard that died, and that made me sad, but I got over it eventually. And Susanna had once had a cat that either ran away or got hit by a car — I was told two different stories, or maybe they were two parts of the same story — and while I had been aware of how sad both she and Carolyn were about that, part of me was glad that the cat was gone because it had scratched my face when I leaned down to pet it one time. That had left a small scar on my left cheek that never completely went away.

So that was my limited exposure to death. I was aware that it was something that happened to other people, to animals, or to fictional characters, but I did not really understand it yet. In time, I would.

Carl and Tim tried to convince Susanna to help us, but the discussion ended with her definitively saying, "I said no." We headed back downstairs, defeated.

We still couldn't let the idea go, though. We gathered in the den where the TV was, but we hadn't turned it on. Normally, I would have been eager to play more video games, but this vampire thing sounded much more exciting. We tried to think of a way to make it happen somehow.

"What if we stole the formula from her," Tim suggested, "then made it ourselves?"

"Yeah!" Carl said. "Who needs her?"

At first I liked this plan. If I could sneak into Susanna's room when she wasn't in there and find that notebook again, I could take the formula. But then I realized that someone would still have to make the actual potion, and I certainly had no idea how to do that. It was way too complicated. I told them this, adding, "Not unless one of you can read Latin." They didn't know what I meant, but then I also barely knew what I was talking about.

We continued to toss around ideas. Tim offered that maybe we wouldn't have to actually kill the boys, just scare them. We'd do this as vampires, just not go so far as we had originally thought. That sounded more reasonable, but I was afraid to approach Susanna again for fear of what she might say. Carl suggested that we wait until after lunch to ask her about it.

We hadn't seen Carolyn all morning, by the way. She had gotten up while the rest of us were upstairs talking to Susanna, and by the time we had gotten back downstairs, she was in the other den watching TV.

Our house had two rooms with TVs in them, each called "the yellow den" and "the red den" based on the color of the carpet in each room. The yellow den was adjacent to the kitchen and part of the main house, while the red den, with its shag carpet and wood panel walls, was an addition that was built shortly after I was born. That was usually where our parents spent time reading or watching TV when they wanted to be separate from me and my siblings. While we sometimes watched shows together as a family when I was younger, the older I got, the more things became separated. So in the red den, my parents would watch more adult shows like the news or documentaries on public television, and in the yellow den, my sisters and I would watch sitcoms or more kid-oriented stuff.

When our parents were out of town, Susanna and Carolyn often spent time in the red den, I guess just because they could. They got to feel like they were the adults of the household. That didn't really interest me. In fact, I liked having the yellow den to myself, or in the case of this summer, a place for me and my friends of the same age to hang out.

Lunchtime arrived, and Carolyn made us grilled cheese sandwiches, one of the only things she knew how to cook. She seemed proud of this, but she also had a tendency to burn them. Nevertheless, they were edible this time, and by the time I had finished mine, Carolyn had made one for Susanna, which I then brought upstairs to her room.

I noticed how much progress she had made on sorting through her things from the previous night, particularly the notebooks, which she appeared to be almost done with. I noticed that the Chemistry folder was on top of one of the piles, and I again thought about Tim's suggestion of stealing it. But there wouldn't have been any point. Instead, I took the more honest route.

"So, about the vampire potion," I began.

She paused in the middle of taking a bite from her sandwich and looked up at me impatiently.

"No, wait, really! What if we just scared those boys? Just to teach them a lesson, you know? No one has to get hurt."

She finished her bite and swallowed. She didn't say anything for a moment, and there was something in her expression that I couldn't quite read. "No one has to get hurt," she repeated, but it didn't sound as sarcastic as it might have. Her eyes weren't even on mine as she spoke; she was looking off to the side, like she was thinking about something else. Then she seemed to come back to herself, and she looked at me. "You can't be sure about that. Not unsupervised, anyway."

"What?"

"I mean that if… *if* we were to do this at all, it would have to be *we*. Me, you, and the others. And Carolyn. And I don't think she'd go along with it."

"Why?" While I was glad that she at least seemed to be considering the possibility, I didn't understand why they needed to be involved in actually going there and scaring the boys, too.

"Because if only some of us become vampires, the vampires will probably turn on those who don't take the potion. That's how it works." She took another bite, this time keeping her eyes on me.

I understood. In the story she had told me the night before, the mice who were given the potion attacked the regular ones, and the guy she had made the potion with had tried to get her, too. "Even if we didn't want to?" I asked.

"Exactly." She wiped her mouth with her napkin. "So it's all or nothing. All of us, or none of us. And like I said, I don't think Carolyn will go for it. Besides, in case you haven't noticed, I've got stuff to do. Making that potion would take a lot of time and effort. It's not like making a glass of chocolate milk."

"I know," I said, even though I hadn't. But I at least had some understanding of potions being complex and needing a lot of preparation.

"Ask Carolyn," she said, waving her hand toward the door. "If she says no, then that's it. And don't ask me again."

I wasn't sure why Susanna seemed so convinced that Carolyn would say no, but I felt a certain smugness as I walked back up the stairs a little later to tell her that she had agreed to the plan.

Like Carl, Carolyn had not believed that the potion was real at first, but once I told her a short version of Susanna's story and that she had in fact sent me downstairs to ask for her vote, so to speak, she realized that we were telling the truth. She only started to be convinced to go along with things when I assured her that the potion was reversible, that is, that we could go back to being normal human beings once it was all over. According to Susanna's story, that was how it worked. She was also opposed to the idea of killing people, but once we clarified that we were only going to scare them, she agreed. It probably helped that Tim and I played the sympathy card on her, saying that it was something we should all do to help Carl out given how bad he felt about what had happened.

Once I relayed the news to Susanna, she and I came back downstairs, joining everyone else in the kitchen.

"Okay," she said, sounding tired. "I'm partly only doing this because I've gotten sick of packing. We're just going to take the potion, go there as vampires, and scare those guys."

"And that stupid fat-shit coach, too!" Carl piped up. "He hurt my arm."

Susanna looked at him disdainfully, then just shrugged. "Yeah, whatever. Probably."

"We can't take it now, though, can we?" Carolyn asked. "I mean, it's daylight outside."

"I don't have the potion itself right now," Susanna said. "I have to make it, and it's going to take a few hours. And I don't have all of the ingredients with me. I'll have to go get some of them." I had no idea where she would get such things from or what they might be, but I was so elated that she was finally going along with the plan that I didn't want to ask too many questions. She might change her mind if it turned out to be too much trouble. "You will all just have to find something to do in the meantime."

After she left in her car, the rest of us tried to decide how to pass the time. This sounded like such a cool idea, and we were excited about it, though Carolyn needed a little bit more time to warm up to it. After a while, she admitted that she was curious as to what it might be like, but she insisted that her main motivation for going along with everything was to keep an eye on us and make sure we didn't get into trouble.

For a while, we played some more video games. The games relied a lot on imagination, that is, the primitive, blocky graphics could be interpreted in different ways. This was usually accomplished by reading the instructions that accompanied each game, which pointed out that this pixelated whatever-it-was represented your spaceship, and those other patterns were aliens that you had to fight. For some games, it was clear what everything was supposed to be. For others, the graphics were more abstract, and you could easily imagine the game elements as something else entirely if you wanted to. I found myself doing this with the games we played this afternoon, working in a vampires vs. humans theme whenever I could, at least in my head. I mentioned this to the others after a while, but Tim and Carl weren't too into it. Carolyn said that she thought it was pretty clever of me, and I took what praise I could get from her.

After a while, Carolyn got tired of video games and went back to the red den to watch TV. Not long after that, she called me into the room and pointed at the TV, excitedly pointing out to me that the man on the screen was the same actor who had been in *The Incredible Hulk,* a show I had liked when I was younger. It was one of the ones our entire family watched together, but the show had since been cancelled.

I was not impressed by Carolyn's revelation; I had seen this program before and had found it boring. To me, it was nothing more than a dull show about history, though it was a documentary series intended for children.

"What, so if he's not turning into a big green monster and throwing things around, you don't care?" she asked, sneering.

"Guess not." I started to turn and leave, but I caught myself. Simple disagreements between us like this could sometimes quickly devolve into childish arguments, and that was not something that I wanted to happen this time. If Carolyn got too ticked off at me, she might change her mind and back out of the vampire plan just to spite me. I tried to salvage the situation. "It's just, I don't know, boring."

I stood there and watched a little more, and I realized that just a few days earlier, I had been thinking not only of this show, but of this particular episode, one that told the story of Albert Einstein. I could not remember why I had thought of it earlier in the week, but when the screen showed a black and white photo of a weird man with frizzy hair, it clicked in my head that I had been thinking about that same strange old guy recently and how I had seen him on this show several months ago. I mentioned this to Carolyn, who then accused me of lying.

I insisted that I wasn't, and we bickered some more as the show went to a commercial break. The commercials were mostly not ones that advertised products but the kind that talked about other shows that would be airing throughout the day or later in the week, some of which I was actually interested in.

Carolyn pointed at the TV again, snidely saying, "Yeah, but you still like that crap, don't you?" There was a promo on for a British science fiction show about children with psychic powers.

I shot back that yes, I did like it. "And so did you up until about a year ago!"

Carolyn frowned, taken aback. All she could do in response was to mock what I had just said: *And so did yoooou up until about a yeeear agooo!"* She stuck her tongue out as she said it, bobbing her head from side to side.

This was a recurring theme with us, one of our major sources of conflict. For reasons I couldn't understand, her tastes and interests fluctuated a lot. She would like something, but then after a few months, she would decide that she hated it. This was disconcerting for me, because often, we shared interests and liked the same things, partly because I looked up to her and wanted to be as cool as she was. Sometimes, I would go along with her sudden change of heart, as I did when she inexplicably went from thinking that the singer Boy George was fun and interesting to regarding him with extreme contempt. But other times, I would continue to like the things I did — singers, TV shows, certain video games, and such — and I would do my best to ignore her ridiculing of me for continuing to like something she now considered stupid. I didn't agree with her, and at this age, that meant that she was the one being stupid.

Whenever we argued, I felt pleased with myself when the argument got to the stage it had now, where she clearly could not think of anything to say back to me other than what I had just said, but in an exaggerated way. It felt like I had beaten her. If I pointed this out, she'd just do it again, and we would get more angry at each other.

But this time, I needed to be more careful. An angry Carolyn was not a good thing at this point, or else she might exercise that same fickleness and decide that turning ourselves into vampires was a dumb thing to do, and the deal might be off.

So I backed down, saying I was sorry even though I wasn't. She sighed and said she was too, probably meaning it just as much. We were silent for a few moments, then laughed together at the TV as a girl on the screen reacted hysterically to being suddenly doused by a bucket of water. We were once again on our way back to reconciliation.

Perhaps to further this, Carolyn suggested that we stop staying cooped up inside and go out to the backyard to do something more fun. Carl and Tim agreed, apparently having had enough of electronic battles on the TV in the yellow den. Just as we were about to go outside, Susanna arrived from her shopping trip and came in through the back door.

Tim was in the process of putting the controllers for his Atari away and turning the TV off, and Susanna asked, "Is that all you've been doing the whole time I've been running all over town, playing video games?" She seemed annoyed. I glanced at the clock in the kitchen, only then realizing that she had been gone for hours.

"Well, no…" Carl began.

"We watched some TV, too," I said. She just glared at me. "What?"

She shook her head. "Nothing."

As she headed for the stairs, her arms full of brown paper bags filled with various unknown items, Carolyn waved her hand and said with fake enthusiasm, "Okay, we'll be out in the backyard if you need us!"

Susanna didn't respond and kept walking out of the room.

"Good luck, Dr. Jekyll," Tim said, though only loud enough for the rest of us to hear. Carl and I laughed, but Carolyn just gave him a withering look.

We started to go out the back door, but Carolyn stopped us, saying that she needed to put King up first. We didn't want a repeat of yesterday, so we waited. Once we were outside, he still barked at Carl and Tim for a while, but we did our best to ignore him. In time, he gave up and went to sleep, occasionally waking up and barking again when one of us made a lot of noise.

It was decided that we would play a game called Ghost in the Graveyard, which I had played with Carolyn and Susanna when I was a little younger. Tim was apparently familiar with it, too, but Carl needed to have the rules explained to him. It was sort of a reverse hide-and-seek, where one person, the "ghost," would hide somewhere in the yard as the others, called "detectives," would close their eyes at a tree called the "base" and count from one o'clock to midnight.

After that, the detectives would search for the ghost. Upon finding him, a detective would call out, "Ghost in the graveyard!" Then the ghost would chase after the detectives as they ran for the base. Any detectives who were tagged by the ghost would then be ghosts in the next round. Eventually, when the last detective was caught by a ghost, the game would start over, and that person would be the lone ghost in the next round.

We played for about half an hour with Tim starting off as the first ghost. I wondered if Carl might lose his temper again and start being difficult once he was caught and also turned into a ghost, but it didn't seem to bother him. While there was a competitive spirit among us, there was never really any genuine antagonism. We were just having fun.

After a couple of rounds, I wanted to take a break and see how Susanna was coming along with the vampire potion. I went inside and up to her room, then knocked on the door.

"What," she said flatly.

"It's me," I said, opening the door and peering in. She was sitting at her desk, her back to the door. All sorts of weird chemicals and powders were spread out all over the place, and she was hard at work. I recognized the piece of paper with the formula on it from the night before, now held on a propped up clipboard. As I approached, Susanna picked up a pencil and made a check mark about a third of the way down the page.

"How's it going?" I asked.

"Slowly," she said, not turning around. I moved closer to the desk, but she still did not look over at me. I had gotten this attitude from her before; she got this way when she was studying and didn't want to be bothered.

"Oh," was all I could say. While her dismissiveness bugged me, I knew that, as with Carolyn earlier in the den, I shouldn't antagonize her for fear of her getting mad at me and changing her mind about everything. I hoped that since she was this far along, she was already committed.

A large plastic bowl was off to the left side of the desk, and several small bottles and piles of ingredients were organized around the rest of the surface. Susanna stared intently at the paper and pointed at it with her pencil, biting her lower lip.

"Well, um…" I began, "how much longer?"

"Hmm?" she said, still not looking over.

"When will it be ready?"

"Not for a while. The potion is very complicated, and some steps have to wait a little while for the ingredients to properly interact and settle or whatever." That sounded reasonable.

"So…?"

She huffed, then finally looked at me. She was frowning, but her look softened. "Sorry. Just concentrating. I get like this when I'm really deep into something."

"I know," I said, and gave a weak laugh.

"About three hours," she said.

"Okay, I'll tell the others." I turned to leave.

"And if you could, please tell them to quit making so much noise."

"Oh. Sorry." I involuntarily looked over at her bedroom window, which faced the backyard. Her bedroom was the only actual room on the second floor of our house; the rest was an attic. Like the red den, her room had been added onto the original house some time after I was born. In fact, I could vaguely recall it being built, the house full of strange men and the smell of sawdust and paint. Most likely, it had been built using money my parents had inherited after our grandmother had died. Prior to that, Susanna and Carolyn had shared what was now just Carolyn's bedroom.

By the time I got back outside, I had already forgotten Susanna's plea for us to play more quietly. I found Carolyn, Tim, and Carl waiting for me, and they were eager to get back to the game. It was my turn to be the ghost this time, which I was fine with. In fact, I relished it. It was more fun being the one who was hiding and then chasing after everyone.

We had started to get bored with the original constraints of the game's rules by then, too, with some of us suggesting changes. Carolyn felt that counting from one o'clock to midnight did not provide enough time for the ghost or ghosts to find proper hiding places, so she decided that we should count more slowly and add the word "rock" to every fourth hour in the countdown, as was done in the lyrics to the old song "Rock Around the Clock." I suggested changing the name of the game to "Vampire in the Graveyard" instead, but this didn't catch on. Carolyn either forgot or deliberately chose to ignore my suggestion by calling out "Ghost in the graveyard!" upon spotting me in the next round. I tried to protest that it should be "vampire" instead, but by then, she was running for the base, and I failed to catch her in time.

Later on, when Carl and I were the detectives and were trying to find Carolyn and Tim as the ghosts, he and I had decided to stick close to each other instead of spreading out. Neither of us had spotted them yet when Carl turned to me and said in a low voice, "Hey, watch this." He then bellowed out, "Ghost in the graveyard!" Carolyn and Tim burst from their hiding places and chased after us, and we made it back to the base safely. We were pretty sure that they didn't know why we were laughing.

We changed the rules a little more as time went on, one variant being that instead of staying in one place, the ghosts would creep about and try to sneak up on the detectives. That worked okay, and we were just about to try a new variant in which the ghost was the one who called out the phrase spontaneously and began the chase, but then Susanna shouted from the back door that dinner was ready.

We went inside and washed up, and while I had thought that Susanna was making a joke and actually meant the potion when she said "dinner," she was in fact referring to a real meal. It was just as well; I hadn't realized until I smelled the food just how hungry I had gotten with all of the running around we had done in the backyard. Time had flown by that day, and sunset wasn't too far off.

My family always ate meals at the kitchen table. We had a dining room, but it was reserved for special occasions that never seemed to occur. I could remember only one time that the family had eaten in there, and that was far enough back that I was too young to really know what was going on, still sitting in a high chair at the time.

Susanna apologized for the fact that dinner was just leftovers, which included reheated pizza, pot roast, and corn, but no one really cared. Not only had we built up an appetite from our games earlier, we were still pretty excited about the prospect of becoming vampires and carrying out our revenge scheme.

"So," I said, "are we going to have the potion for dessert?"

"It's not chocolate pudding, Ray," Carolyn said.

"I know! I just meant, you know, after."

"Yes," Susanna said. "The sun should have set by then."

"Good," I said, glancing out the kitchen window. It looked like it was getting darker already.

The five of us continued talking throughout dinner, my two friends and I being the most excited. Susanna seemed a lot more calm, or at least she was more reserved. She was in her humorless, serious mode again. Carolyn joked around more, but I got the sense that she was also holding back, maybe afraid to get too enthusiastic. I didn't really understand their attitudes; I could not understand why anyone would be anything but excited about this. Maybe it was because they were older, or maybe it was because they were girls. Either condition made them difficult for me to understand, and I was used to that.

Finally, we were done with dinner, and Susanna left the kitchen to go upstairs and get the potion. As she did, she told me to check to see that the sun had gone down. I jumped up and ran to the yellow den to look out the window to the backyard. The sun was gone, though the sky was still a dull blue.

Susanna returned with a tray that held five short plastic cups, each filled with a dark brown liquid. As she set the tray down onto the table, Tim asked, "So this is it?"

"This is it," Susanna said.

Carl picked up a cup, but Susanna told him to wait. The rest of us chose our cups and pulled them closer, and Carolyn sniffed hers. I did the same, noticing the way the potion bubbled slightly. For a moment, I wondered if it was in fact Coca-Cola and that Susanna had just played a joke on us, but then I noticed that it smelled different than I had been expecting. The odor, while not entirely unpleasant, was kind of salty, like ocean water.

"Are you sure this stuff is safe to drink?" Carolyn asked, not taking her eyes off her cup. "Maybe one of us should try it out first."

"No," Susanna said. "It has to be all of us at once."

"Okay then," Carl said, smiling and holding up his cup. He appeared to be making a toast, and I involuntarily repeated the move. The others did the same.

"Down the hatch," Susanna said, smiling for the first time in quite a while.

I drank my cup down. The briny smell gave way to an unexpected sweet aftertaste, and some of us gasped after finishing our drinks. We set the cups back onto the table, then looked at each other.

"So," Carl asked, "did it work?"

I turned to Susanna, who was staring straight ahead. She had a faraway look in her eyes as she said, "Give it a second." I saw that she was beginning to breathe heavily, and then I noticed that I was doing the same.

Suddenly, I felt dizzy, and I looked down towards the table, which I had grabbed onto without thinking. We were all standing up, and the sensible thing might have been to sit down, but for some reason, I didn't. I wasn't sure what the others were doing then because I was way too focused on myself. I had never felt anything like this before, and while I was excited about what this meant, part of me was scared nonetheless. I continued to breathe heavily, my eyes pinched shut. Even when I opened them, it was like I was looking down a narrow tunnel, and still down toward myself, not looking out at the others. My arms and legs began to feel numb, and my heart was pounding. I had never really thought about it before, but if I had to imagine what a heart attack would feel like, this was it. I was vaguely aware of heavy breathing around me, presumably the others going through the same thing, but I barely cared. I almost wanted to call out to Susanna or Carolyn for reassurance, but then I was distracted by a strange noise filling my ears. It reminded me of galloping horses, but faint and far away. It grew louder, sounding more and more like a heartbeat. Finally, after what felt like forever but was probably only a minute or two, the sound culminated in a single, dull *boom*. There was also something else, like a low laugh descending in pitch, just a few seconds' worth. My vision, which had turned almost completely greenish-white by then, began to clear, and the other strange sensations quickly faded.

I relaxed my grip on the table and looked up. Susanna was directly across from me, she and the others having recovered as well. We were still breathing heavily, but that was subsiding.

"Wow," Carl managed to say. "That was…"

"…scary," Tim finished, then added, "but cool." He wasn't wrong. As he spoke, he smiled, and I saw the first evidence of the potion's intended effect.

I reached up to my mouth, first with one finger and then also with my thumb, and sure enough, there were two sharp fangs on either side of my upper teeth, the four in the middle remaining unchanged. The others around the table all had them, too. We had done it. We were vampires.

I laughed. "It worked!"

Carl and Tim also laughed, followed by Carolyn, who looked a little nervous.

"Hell yeah, it did!" Carl said, his usual big, goofy grin punctuated with new fangs. "Awesome!"

Susanna was more calm, but she also seemed pleased, a sly smirk on her face. "Of course it did," she said.

"This is so cool," Tim said, also grinning. He felt his fangs again. "We're really vampires!"

"Yeah," Carl said. "And now it's time we paid those ass-heads at the race a visit!"

"Calm down, Carl," Carolyn said. She turned to Susanna. "So what do we do now?"

"Well, first of all, we establish some ground rules. There are certain things we can and can't do."

"Hey, I want to turn into a bat!" Carl said, interrupting. "How do I do that?"

"Carl, wait…" Susanna began.

"Yeah, me too!" I said. Whatever new powers we had, I wanted to try them all.

"Maybe just think about it really hard?" Tim suggested. "Or flap your arms a lot or something…"

Suddenly, there was a flash of light and a small cloud of smoke where Carl had been standing. The smoke quickly faded away, and in its place, a small black bat hovered in the air, flapping away. It was Carl, now a vampire bat.

Had I been older and more experienced, it might have occurred to me that what I had just witnessed was impossible, even silly. But I knew nothing about physics or biology, only that those things existed and were beyond my current grasp. I had, though, seen magic tricks and amazing, fantastic things on TV, like David Copperfield waving his hands and making things disappear or change in a puff of smoke. I had also seen Carl Sagan talk about someday travelling to far away planets and meeting aliens. To me, these fantastic things were out there, possible but just out of my reach until some later point in my life when they would become reality. And on this night, something else I had imagined possible had indeed come true. It would not be the last time.

"Ha ha! Holy crap!" said the bat. It bobbed up and down in place, its wings flapping quickly. "I did it!" The voice was Carl's, but it sounded smaller, sort of tinny, almost like it was coming through a small radio speaker. Little chirps or squeaks also seemed to overlay his voice.

"That's totally awesome!" Tim said, and he repeated the process, a big flash of white light appearing, followed by a quick puff of smoke and then a hovering bat in its place.

"Guys..." Susanna began, exasperated.

I couldn't resist. I had to try it, too. All I had to do was simply think about becoming a bat like Carl and Tim had, and... *POOF!* It happened. I laughed, hearing the same weird effect in my own voice, that tinny AM radio sound punctuated by occasional small squeaks. I felt small and light, and to hover in place was not that difficult. It was like I was treading water, but with very little effort. My perspective was slightly changed, I saw when I glanced over to Susanna and Carolyn. They looked bigger, but not tremendously. It was kind of like looking through a fish-eye lens, or more accurately, having a dream of myself but younger, when I was shorter and things were in a different proportion.

"Guys!" Susanna said more firmly. "Change back *now.*"

Her voice did not leave room for argument, and I couldn't help but notice that she looked more menacing with fangs. Almost simultaneously, the three of us changed back to our previous forms. Doing so was no more difficult than the initial transformation into bats: All we had to do was will ourselves to do it. Once again, we were in person form, standing where we had previously been hovering as bats.

"That's better," Susanna said, frowning at us. Despite her reprimand, we were still giddy, looking around at each other and smiling proudly. This was incredible. Carolyn seemed to be in awe, simultaneously amazed but also bewildered, trying to take it all in.

"Okay, I need to sit down," she said. She did, and the rest of us did the same.

The next several minutes consisted of Susanna lecturing us about the need for self control and restraint, but it wasn't just some boring adult litany about what we had done wrong. What she told us made sense and was necessary for us to understand if we were to successfully carry out our plan.

We were now equipped to do what we intended, to scare the pants off of the people at the YMCA, but being vampires also meant that we were vulnerable to certain things. It had already been emphasized that sunlight had to be avoided, but that was no longer an issue now that it was after dark. But Susanna still listed sunlight along with garlic, crosses, wooden stakes, and running water as things to avoid.

"Wait, huh?" I said. "Water? I've never heard of that before."

"Wet stuff," Carolyn said, sneering. "Kinda clear."

I stuck my tongue out at her. "I know. But water kills vampires?"

"Yeah, I have to admit that's a new one on me, too," Carolyn said.

"No, it's true," Tim said. "I remember reading that somewhere." If both Susanna and Tim said it was true, I had no reason not to believe it.

"Right. So just be sure to avoid those things," Susanna continued. "I don't think there's much chance of us running into them, but I needed to let you all know before we went charging out there. Oh, and fire, too. Stay away from fire."

I had never heard of that being used against vampires either, but by then, I realized that it was better to just listen to Susanna and take her word for things.

"So, do vampires have venom?" Tim asked.

"What?" Susanna asked.

"Like snakes. I've seen in movies where Dracula or whoever bites someone, and they just go all limp while he drinks from them. I thought maybe that was something like snakes have, something that paralyzes the victim."

"Yeah, I remember seeing that, too!" Carl said. "There was this lady getting bitten, and she was all like, 'Ohhhh...'" He leaned his head back dramatically, making a strange face. "Was that because she was being poisoned?"

Susanna seemed thrown. "I don't... I'm not sure. I mean, the mice in the lab... I don't remember if the ones being bitten struggled less than they should have. I don't know..." She had begun looking off into space, then recovered herself, shaking her head and frowning slightly. "But we are *not* going there to bite anybody. Just to scare them."

Carl let out a small *"aww"* sound, and Carolyn kicked his chair, glaring at him.

"And that's another thing. While we're there, we attack as bats, not as people. We can't risk anyone seeing us and recognizing us from yesterday." I could see the logic in that, but it was also a little disappointing. I had already pictured myself running around chasing after screaming people, menacing them with arms raised and fangs bared. But I had also pictured myself doing this while wearing a long black cape, and that wasn't going to happen, either. We didn't have costumes; we were essentially just ourselves plus fangs. At least, that's how it seemed at first.

The lecture was over, and we followed Susanna out the back door. Her car was underneath the carport, and for a moment, I expected us to pile inside, but then I realized that it wasn't necessary. We could become bats now, so we would be flying to the YMCA.

"Sure is dark out here," Carolyn said once we were all outside.

"Do we have some kind of special night vision?" Carl asked. That hadn't even occurred to me, how flying around at night might be difficult because of the lack of light. But then, as I looked at Carl, a strange, yellowish glow began to appear in his eyes. "Whoa…" he said.

Apparently, we did indeed have another special power, the ability to see in the dark. The others' eyes all lit up as well, a somewhat dull, yellow effect like a small flashlight being shone into and around their eyes. And while I couldn't see my own, I could tell that they were glowing, too, as everything around me started to look more or less like it usually did during the day. Sort of. Something seemed wrong, and after a few seconds, I realized what it was: There were no shadows because there was no real light.

"Okay, that's really freaky," Carolyn said.

"Yeah, but kinda cool," Tim said. "You have to admit that."

"Fair enough."

Susanna let out a small laugh and led us to the driveway and out from under the carport. My eyes stopped glowing, as did everyone else's. I looked up and noticed the full moon, which did a decent job of lighting things on its own.

"Aw, I liked the glowy thing," Carl said. His eyes then flared yellow again, and he said, "Oh." Then they faded again. The glowing and the special vision could be controlled, happening when we wanted it to. I noticed that I felt a slight tingling in my forehead whenever I made my eyes light up. We each tested this a few more times, the glows winking on and off.

"Okay, enough," Susanna said. "Time to go." She looked up toward the sky, and with the same flash of light — which seemed brighter outside in the dark — and a puff of smoke, she transformed into a bat. The rest of us did the same, and then we were a circle of small black bats hovering in mid-air. The night vision had returned, each of us having small, yellow-glowing eyes.

"Wow," I heard the tinny, squeaking version of Carolyn's voice say. "This is pretty damn cool."

"Come on," Susanna squeaked, shooting up into the air above us. I followed, losing track of her for a few seconds, but then I spotted her and caught up. I glanced behind me, and the others were catching up to us as well.

They did, and we stopped again, hovering in place. I looked down once more, seeing our house, our backyard, the whole property. I had never seen it from this angle before, and everything looked so small. I spotted King's pen and realized that we had forgotten to let him out earlier when we had gone inside for dinner. One of us would have to remember to do that once we got back.

The height didn't bother me, either, nor did anyone else ever complain about it. I had sometimes had an issue with being high up in the air, but only when I felt like I might fall. That didn't seem to be a problem now. I could fly, plain and simple. I remembered a couple of dreams I'd had before in which I was able to fly, and this was similar. It wasn't like the scary process of learning to ride a bike or learning to swim; I could just do it.

"This is great!" Tim said, squeaking. I only knew it was him because of his voice; we were pretty much identical as bats.

"Come on," Susanna said, flying off to one side.

As we flew, our group was led by Susanna's bat form, which occasionally ascended and descended for no apparent reason. It occurred to me eventually that she was just testing everything out, learning how to fly and maneuver. Although I was mostly fine with the heights as I mentioned before, I felt a light tingle in my stomach during some of the descents, kind of like being on a swing.

And as far as my stomach went, it didn't really occur to me at the time that I was a fraction of my normal size and that I had a bat's stomach, though I would eventually ponder this kind of thing later on as I studied bat physiology and tried to better understand what we had become. But for now, I was just enjoying the moment. I didn't feel like another species or an animal; my mental picture of myself was pretty much the regular me, flapping my arms like a bird to propel myself along through the night sky. It was only through seeing the others in their bat forms that I began to think of myself as one, too, but this was a gradual process.

But really, while I say all of this at this point in the narrative, my thoughts were not nearly this complex yet. Everything was just fun. I didn't indulge in much philosophical introspection about what we were doing or just how fantastic it all was, nor did I truly understand the implications of what happened next.

We arrived at the YMCA just in time. As we flew over the trees and caught our first aerial glimpse of the place, I saw that the racers were lining up, almost ready to start. Everything looked different now, the brown track with its white lines tracing it, the metal bleachers off to the side filled with spectators. There were less of them than on the previous night, presumably because there were fewer racers, the ones who had won the qualifying race. I began feeling resentment towards the participants, the audience, and the people in charge of the race, recalling my anger from the night before.

Off to one side of the track, there was a large, grassy field. On it were some soccer goalposts with large nets strewn about them, and Susanna led us to the top of the one closest to the track, where we landed. We perched upright on it like birds, not upside-down like normal bats did. As there were along the track, there were plenty of floodlights in this area, and they lit the place enough to where we no longer needed for our eyes to glow in order to see. Instead, we each had tiny, black eyes.

"So what do we do now?" Carl asked, perched next to me. I suddenly realized that we did not have an actual plan, just that we wanted to scare as many people as possible, particularly the two cheating boys.

"Wait until after the race starts," Susanna said. "Then we move in."

From that far away, I could just barely make out the two boys in the line-up at the starting line, and off to the side was the coach with his whistle. He counted down and started the race, and the runners were off. So was Carl.

"Wait!" I heard Susanna say from behind me, but by then, I had also taken off and followed Carl. Glancing behind me, I saw that the others were flying close behind. I still wasn't exactly sure what we were going to do. Anticipation overwhelmed me, and it felt like we were just going to make this up as we went along.

I saw Carl head for the taller, dark-haired boy, who was running along looking confident, unaware that we were approaching. Carl zoomed right past his head, and while the boy looked confused and said something, he kept running. I repeated this maneuver, catching him saying something that sounded like "the fuh?" as I flew past his head.

Carl then did a U-turn in mid-air and headed back towards him, and I decided to go for the other boy, the red-haired one. I ended up smacking into the side of his head, but it didn't hurt. It certainly distracted the boy, though, who faltered in his running and batted at his ear, looking around in confusion. I flew back up, only temporarily disoriented by the impact.

The remaining bats had begun menacing some of the other runners, who were similarly bewildered. Some of them tripped up while others flailed their arms in an attempt to ward off whatever was after them. Gasps and sounds of confusion began to erupt from the stands.

By this point, I wasn't sure who was who in terms of the bats since we all looked alike and were spread out, circling and dive-bombing the runners. I wasn't even sure who it was who made the first kill, but sure enough, the red-haired boy was suddenly skidding to the ground in a cloud of dust, clutching his neck as a vampire bat clung to him. Then he just lay there motionless as the bat drank from him.

Part of me wanted to protest, to fly down and tell whichever of us it was to stop, but something strange happened. I just hovered in place and watched as the bat flew away from the boy's body, which lay there lifeless. A steady stream of blood poured from his neck, which I continued to stare at for a few moments.

I looked up and saw that most of the runners had continued on, unaware of what had happened. Nearby, a whistle sounded repeatedly, and at the same time, the other boy went down, also attacked by one of us. I knew that within moments, he too would be dead. And rather than feeling any kind of remorse upon seeing this or the previous killing, instead I felt empowered. Those stupid boys deserved it. This was what we had really come here to do, not just buzz around people's heads like bees.

I saw the coach running onto the track towards the fallen boys, but suddenly, another bat flew at him and attached to his neck. The man screamed and tried to fight back for a few seconds, but it was no use. He too crashed to the ground and did not get up again.

Screams began coming from the people in the bleachers, which I at first thought was just a reaction to what was happening down on the track. But then I saw that some of the people there were also being attacked. Most of the racers had stopped running by then, trying to figure out what was going on. A couple of them continued running, still oblivious.

Finally, I'd had enough of watching; it was time for me to take part. I flew to the edge of the confused crowd, where panic was beginning to take hold. I found my victim, a teenage girl with short, dark, curly hair. I didn't take much time to examine her as I zoomed in for the kill; I just launched myself at her neck, mouth open and fangs ready. As I reached her flesh, I bit down. It was no more difficult than biting into an apple, and my mouth was immediately filled with a rush of rich, warm blood. The girl screamed for a short time, then collapsed as I continued to drink. It felt wonderful. It wasn't so much the taste that I relished but the power I felt, the absolute control and command of the situation, a feeling of accomplishment and conquering. There was no intense philosophizing about the moment or examination of what was happening. It just *was,* and I loved it.

Finishing my first kill, I flew up from the girl's body and looked around, hovering for a bit. People were terrified, pushing and clamoring over each other to try to get away. Some were successful, but others continued to be menaced and brought down by the bats as they randomly picked out new targets, diving onto them and draining them of life. I felt a smug satisfaction seeing all of this, and I flew on to find another victim, then another.

This went on for several minutes, maybe ten or so. I ended up over by the side of a building with a dark green wall, on which was painted a white, horizontal stripe. As I hovered near it trying to decide what to do next, a bat flew down to me, its small mouth red with blood.

"We need to go," Susanna's small voice said to me. I half expected her to tear into me for having attacked those people, but there was none of that. "Head up there to the others." Her tone was flat and unreadable, still sounding strange to me because of the metallic squeakiness of it. I had no idea what she was thinking. I felt like I might be in trouble, but I was also still experiencing the rush of what had just happened, and it was hard to feel guilty.

I flew up and found two other bats hovering in place, which turned out to be Carolyn and Carl. We looked down and saw Susanna heading back toward the crowd, which by then had mostly dispersed, though the few people who remained were still in a panic. There were also plenty of bodies lying around.

"Do you think she's mad?" Carl asked. Like the rest of us, his mouth was dripping with blood. I wondered how many people he had killed.

"I can't tell," Carolyn said. "Maybe."

Soon after, Susanna and Tim flew up to us, and the five of us hovered there for a moment.

"Back to the house," Susanna said, and we flew away.

The flight back took several minutes, and as we went along, I thought about what had happened. It had been amazing. Those people didn't stand a chance against us, and I felt so strong. We had certainly gotten our revenge, and it felt justified. We had been a terrifying, powerful force. I loved it. And while I feared that Susanna might reprimand us upon our return home for being irresponsible and reckless, there was also the fact that she had taken part in the killings just the same, a fact that I would point out to her if needed.

Arriving at the house, we flew back down to the driveway in the same spot from which we had departed, then changed back into our person forms.

"Whew," Carl said. "That was… I don't know… just…"

"I know," Susanna said.

King woke up and ran to the fence upon hearing our voices, and he began barking.

"I should let him out," Carolyn said simply. "I forgot to when we went in for dinner earlier." No one protested as she walked off through the carport and out to the backyard.

The rest of us went inside, and we gathered in the kitchen, where we had been turned into vampires just an hour before. We all looked at each other, unsure what to say.

"Okay, so," Susanna began, then looked down. She looked up again, more confident. "I didn't expect things to go that way." Surprisingly, she smiled, but she also looked a little unnerved. I wasn't used to seeing her like this.

"No, it was better!" Carl said excitedly. "Did you see how those people ran? We scared the holy living ass out of them!"

"You know, Carl," Carolyn said, having come in from outside, "you really shouldn't cuss so much."

"Especially if you can't even do it right," Susanna added, mostly under her breath.

"Oh yeah right," he said. "I'm sure that's the worst thing in the world."

Tim laughed. "Yeah, I'm pretty sure that killing a bunch of people at the YMCA counts as a bigger sin than that!"

We were all quiet for a few seconds, but then we all burst out laughing.

"Oh my God," Carolyn said, covering her face with her hand briefly. "This whole thing is so ridiculous." She didn't seem upset; she seemed amused.

"I know!" Tim said. "Can you believe what we just did back there?"

"Yes, actually," Susanna said, smiling slyly.

The mood had lightened, and I felt relieved, unsure what to say since we had left the YMCA. In terms of what we had accomplished, it felt more or less like whenever my team had won during a game at recess or in P.E. class. We had beaten our opponents.

"Guess we showed them!" I said.

"Yeah!" Tim said, clenching his fist.

"Now I understand what you were so nervous about," Carolyn said to Susanna.

"You noticed that, did you," she asked with her characteristic flatness, narrowing her eyes and smirking.

I was confused. "You were nervous? I didn't know that."

Carolyn smiled enigmatically. "Well, sisters just know things," she said to me, raising her eyebrows.

"Can you tell when I'm nervous?" I asked.

"Sure, that's easy. You just wet yourself." She immediately laughed at her own joke, her wide mouth punctuated with her new fangs, which made "the sister sneer" that much more irritating. What she had said wasn't true, but it was funny enough to make Tim and Carl laugh, which made me mad.

"Shut up!" was all I could manage to say in response.

"You have to admit it, that was a great comeback," she said, still laughing.

"Yes, very funny." I wasn't terribly mad, but I always felt bad when she got one over on me.

Carolyn sighed, still grinning. "So, what happens now? I guess we take the cure for the potion and go back to normal?"

The room got quiet.

Carl was the first to speak up: "No way! I want to stay like this! It's so *bad!"*

Tim agreed. "Yeah, come on! Can't we stay like this just a little bit longer?" He turned to Susanna, a pleading look on his face. I did the same.

Things are different when you're a child. What's important to you then is so different than when you're an adult, when responsibilities, duties, and morals define who you are and what your place is in society. As a child, all of that has yet to form, and most of what matters centers around what you want at the time. This can be something as trivial to adults as getting your next video game or whether or not the family gets to go out for pizza after your sister's basketball game, but to a kid, it's deadly serious and terribly important. Sometimes, adults will even laugh at how seriously children take these things, these desires, even going so far as to ridicule a child if he cries when he doesn't get his way. They may also have a similar attitude towards a child's early experiences with falling in love, or as they see it, thinking that they're in love. But it was still a few years before I would have my first experience with that sort of thing.

Susanna, meanwhile, was not quite an adult; she would turn eighteen in just over a month. But she was the oldest and therefore in charge, though she didn't often employ the "because I said so" defense that most adults did, a concept which makes absolutely no sense to a child. If the child wants something, that's paramount to them, and it's frustrating to throw out arguments that sound perfectly reasonable and then have them shot down by an authority figure. From time to time, Susanna — and, to some extent, Carolyn — and I had conflicts like that, but she was usually more reasonable (that is, more accommodating) than the actual adults in my life. Maybe she just wasn't mature enough to understand the consequences of our actions, to see the bigger picture. Or maybe she was just as eager to continue being vampires for the same reason that the rest of us were: It was fun.

Either way, she did not need much convincing at all, which was a relief. Whatever the reason for her change in attitude, I wasn't about to question it. And Carolyn backed down quickly, too, admitting that Carl was right and that the whole thing was, as she put it, "bad as all." Eventually, the consequences of this mutual decision, to continue being vampires and to keep going around the city killing people, would catch up with us. We honestly had no idea just how bad things would get.

Carl was the first to suggest that we go out and find more victims that night, but to attack in our person forms, not just as bats. He just wanted to experience things that way, he said. We all agreed, but Susanna insisted that we go somewhere far away from the YMCA, again not wanting to run the risk of any of us being seen and recognized.

"And what are all the 'vampire killers' we need to watch out for again?" Carl asked her.

"Sunlight, garlic, crosses, wooden stakes, fire, and running water," she said.

"And dandelions," Tim added.

"What?" I asked.

"Just kidding." He smiled.

I rolled my eyes but still laughed, as did the others.

"We also don't have any reflections, do we?" Tim asked.

"No, we don't," Susanna said. That was something I had heard of before regarding vampires, but it hadn't come up yet.

"Wait, really?" Carl said. "No way." He then ran to the bathroom nearest to the kitchen. After a couple of seconds, a surprised exclamation of "Holy shit!" came from there.

Tim and I ran to join him, but there wasn't really room for all of us in there; it was just a half bath. From the doorway, we saw Carl moving back and forth in front of the mirror, grinning and making little rising and falling *"shoop… shoop…"* sound effects as he did. Then he laughed.

"Oh man, you've got to try it," he said to us.

"Don't turn on the water!" Susanna called from the other room.

"Why…?" Carl began, and he reached for the sink.

"No!" I screamed. "Remember what she said! The running water!"

Carl froze, then slowly backed away from the sink. "Oh," was all he could say, and he walked out of the bathroom and into the laundry room where we were. Susanna and Carolyn had come from the kitchen as well.

"You didn't, did you?" Susanna asked sternly.

"No, he's fine," Tim said. He thought for a moment. "Maybe we should turn the water off underneath the sink. You know, just to be safe in case anyone else forgets."

"Actually, I've got a better idea," Susanna said. "Carolyn, Dad showed you how to turn the water off for the whole house, right?"

"Yeah, there's a cut-off out by the street. I'll need a wrench, though. That thing is hard to turn." Carolyn and I had both assisted our father with home repairs in the past, so this must have been something she learned on one of those occasions. I, meanwhile, knew where the fuse box was for the house, and I had been tempted once or twice to shut the power off to Carolyn's room as a joke, but I was afraid of getting into trouble if I did.

"Okay, well you do that while the rest of us figure out where to go," Susanna told her. Carolyn gave a mock salute and then turned sharply as she headed for the storage shed to get the tools she needed.

Soon after, we were once again flying as bats out toward a lake a few miles from our house. It wasn't too far away and was still in town, and Susanna was pretty sure that there would be people there. She said that it was a popular place for people to hang out and go parking, but I didn't know what she meant by that. I got an image in my head of people driving and lining up their cars next to one another in the grass, but that didn't really make much sense. But another thing I had realized growing up was that there were other people, particularly ones older than me, who did things I didn't yet understand, but maybe I would someday. I knew that the world was bigger than I was, that there were new things to learn and experience. This night had certainly been quite an education so far.

As we arrived at the lake, Tim said in his squeaking bat voice, "Looks like we're in luck."

I saw what he meant, a campfire below with five people nearby.

"Yeah, but maybe not," Carl said. "Remember about the fire."

"We'll be okay as long as we don't touch it," Susanna assured him. "What we need to do is lure them away. Let's land nearby, but don't let them see us."

We did, stopping near some trees. This time, instead of staying bats, we changed back into our person forms. We could see the campers by the fire, but we were too far away for them to notice us.

"What now?" I asked quietly.

"Shh!" Susanna hissed, louder than I had been. "Let me think." After a few moments, she whispered, "Okay, Carolyn and I will try to lead them back this way. Wait here."

Carl, Tim, and I stayed where we were as Susanna led Carolyn toward the campers. The two of them talked in hushed tones as they walked.

When they got closer to the campsite, Susanna called out to them, "Hello?"

They each looked over, surprised.

"Hi, sorry to bother you," Susanna continued as they approached. "Could you, like, help us out? Our car is totally broken down." That wasn't how she usually talked; she suddenly sounded like a valley girl.

"Yeah," Carolyn said, adopting the same attitude. "I think it, like, needs a jump or something."

One of the campers, a boy around Susanna's age, said something as he stood up, but I couldn't quite make it out. It sounded positive, though.

"Let's get closer," I whispered to the others.

"No," Tim said. "Wait for them to lure them back over this way."

By then, Susanna and the campers were too far away for me to hear what they were saying, but the gist of things seemed to be friendly. There were four boys and one girl, and Carolyn and Susanna laughed as they spoke, prompting the others to also laugh with things they said. It wasn't often that I saw Susanna or Carolyn interact with other teenagers, but the few times that I did, it had been kind of like this. They seemed like different people. Sometimes that bothered me, but this time, I was glad to see that our plan seemed to be working.

But then, Susanna and Carolyn were led in the opposite direction by three of the boys, while the other boy and the girl stayed behind at the campfire. I wasn't sure what was happening exactly, but Tim figured it out.

"Oh, crap," he whispered. "They're trying to trick them into taking them to their car, but the car is somewhere over there, not back this way."

"Okay, hang on," I said. "I'll fly over there real quick and bite one of the boys. You two get the other ones by the fire."

Without waiting for a response, I changed into a bat and flew past the two remaining campers, who seemed to be having a disagreement over something, but I didn't know what it was or really care. I needed to reach my target.

I had planned to take down one of the boys as a bat and hoped that Susanna and Carolyn would get the other two, but then I remembered Carl's suggestion that we attack in our person forms since we hadn't gotten to do that at the racetrack. So instead, I flew above the group and ahead of them, then landed and changed into my person form. I had meant to do it far enough ahead where they wouldn't see me, but apparently I misjudged the distance.

"What the hell?" one of the guys said, startled by my sudden appearance. The rest of the group stopped walking, Susanna and Carolyn included.

Instinct took over, and I ran straight at the guy, jumping up onto him and biting his neck. It wasn't all that different from attacking as a bat, though the proportions of everything were changed. This actually felt more natural. My victim screamed as I dug in with my fangs, and he fell backwards from the momentum of our collision.

As I drank the blood from him and felt him quickly go limp underneath me, I heard the other two boys scream as Carolyn and Susanna attacked as well. Not long after, I heard the faraway cries of the two remaining campers as Tim and Carl got them. I would have smiled with satisfaction over the success of our plan, but I was too busy drinking from my prey. I was getting used to the taste of blood by now, its salty and somewhat metallic flavor. More than anything, I loved the power that drinking it made me feel, the sense of accomplishment over conquering yet another helpless victim.

"Hey, turn on the TV!" Carl said, not long after our return to the house. "There might be something on the news about us!"

It was just past 11:00, and Carolyn tuned in to a local news broadcast. One of the first stories was about the tragedy at the YMCA earlier that night. The reporter looked serious and concerned as she relayed the story, in sharp contrast to her smiling and upbeat tone just a few moments before. There were not many details since no one was sure just what had occurred, only that something had attacked and killed several people, including women and children. There was some vague speculation about birds infected by rabies, and both police and wildlife officials were continuing their investigation.

When the story ended and the reporter moved on to another topic, Carl huffed. "Well, that stunk. They didn't even mention vampires at all!"

"Well, yeah," Tim said, "but we know what really happened." He grinned.

"Yeah, and that's pretty cool, too!" I said. I was beginning to realize that part of what was so fun about this entire thing wasn't just the supernatural aspect of it, the new powers and abilities. It was the fact that we were doing something bad and getting away with it. The fact that we had actually murdered people that night didn't even enter into my head, at least not in any real or moral sense. Everything felt like a game come to life.

"Well, we'd better keep it that way," Carolyn said. "The less news coverage, the better."

"But do we all agree to stay like this for a little while?" Susanna asked. We did.

"Hey, you know what I just realized?" Carl said. "I don't feel the slightest bit tired."

"Me neither," I said. "And we've been up all day, plus we sure did do a lot!"

"It's the potion," Tim said simply. "It's made us nocturnal."

"Made us not what?" Carl asked.

"Nocturnal," Susanna said. "It means only awake at night. Like certain animals, ones that stay up all night and sleep all day. Owls, bats…"

"Vampires," Tim said, grinning and pointing to his fangs.

Susanna smiled. "Yes. So that makes sense. You're right."

Tim nodded and beamed. "I am," he said smugly.

Susanna sighed. "I'm guessing we'll be up until sunrise," she continued, "but we'll definitely need to go to bed then…" Her voice trailed off, and she seemed to be bothered by something.

"What?" I asked.

"Well, we can't just crawl into bed and go to sleep when that happens."

"Why not?" That's how I'd done it my entire life, and I didn't see how being a vampire changed that.

"Because the sunlight will still get in, even through the drapes."

"Oh," Tim said. "Right."

"Couldn't we just duck down into our sleeping bags?" Carl asked, crouching down and curling his arms in as he spoke. "And you others could just pull the sheets up over your heads?"

"Too risky," Susanna said. She thought for a few moments, looking pensive. "Well, I guess there's always the basement."

"The basement?" Carolyn asked, sounding annoyed. "We're going to have to sleep down there?"

"Well, it's the only way to be sure to avoid the sunlight," Susanna said.

"That sounds kinda neat!" I said. "It will be like camping out. And we've got enough sleeping bags for it." There were some in a small storage area underneath the stairs that led up to Susanna's room.

"I guess," Carolyn said.

"Okay," Susanna said, sounding more confident. She headed into the kitchen, talking as she walked. "We definitely need to keep an eye on the clock, though, to make sure we make it down there before sunrise." She stopped and looked at the calendar on the wall next to the phone. I knew what she was doing; the calendar was a *Farmers' Almanac* one, which listed on each day the exact times for sunrise and sunset. It also detailed the phases of the moon and the signs of the zodiac, but I had no idea why.

"Hey, I could set my alarm!" Tim said, holding up his digital watch. "My watch has an alarm, calculator, stopwatch, date…"

"And it also tells what time it is on the moon, right?" Carolyn asked sarcastically. Tim gave her a dirty look.

"That's perfect," Susanna said. "Set it for 6:05 a.m. That's fifteen minutes before sunrise. When your alarm goes off, your job will be to let all of us know."

"Got it," Tim said, pressing the buttons on his watch.

After that, we weren't really sure how to spend the rest of the night. We each threw out ideas on what to do to pass the time, Carl first suggesting that we race around the backyard again, this time as bats. That idea was quickly vetoed by King, who barked at my friends as soon as they were out the back door. Carl tried to insist that he was no longer afraid of King now that he was a vampire, though he and Tim had both run back inside and slammed the door. Carolyn said that it would still be a bad idea to spend time out there this late at night as the constant barking, plus whatever noise we might make while playing around, would disturb our neighbors.

We tried watching TV for a while, but by then, it was after midnight on a Sunday (technically Monday, as Tim insisted on pointing out), so there wasn't much on worth watching. Some stations were off the air, and the cable channels that aired around the clock mostly showed boring news programs or old movies that none of us cared about. Susanna went upstairs to her room, presumably to resume packing. Tim, Carl, and I played some more video games, but Carolyn wasn't interested in that anymore, and she also went to her bedroom.

The lack of running water eventually turned out to be a problem, however, when Carl went to the bathroom and flushed the toilet. He came back to me and Tim and told us that the toilet had flushed but didn't fill back up, and we realized the difficulty that this presented. We may have become vampires, but we still had digestive systems. In fact, we also still ate regular food; the three of us had snacked on cheese puffs earlier while playing the Atari. Our drinking blood wasn't really a necessity; it was just a part of what we had become.

We went up to Susanna's room and told her about the problem with the toilet. She had been sorting through her stuff and seemed annoyed by the interruption, but she recognized that this was something that needed to be dealt with, and she admitted that she hadn't even thought about it before. After talking with Carolyn and getting her to turn the water back on outside, we worked out a somewhat complicated solution.

Apparently, water itself wasn't what we had to worry about, only running water, as Susanna explained. She demonstrated this by filling a large plastic bowl with water in the kitchen sink, standing well back from the faucet as it flowed, then reaching around it to turn it off. Whether it was an effect of the potion or just the power of suggestion, I found myself cringing as I watched the water pour. I didn't want to go anywhere near it. I even gasped a little as Susanna reached for the bowl of water, but she put her hand in, then pulled it out and wiped it off with a dishcloth.

"See?" she said. "No problem. But touching that flowing stream of water would be another story."

"So we should turn the taps off underneath the sinks and make the faucets unusable, but leave the toilets running." Carolyn said. Tim pointed out that this was what he had suggested earlier, but she just ignored him, her eyes still on Susanna.

Susanna nodded in agreement, but added that first, we should gather up some bowls of water to use for washing up and such. "Oh, and brushing our teeth, too, I guess. Hadn't thought of that, either."

The next hour or so was taken up with gathering up water in pots and bowls, setting them aside, and being careful not to spill them. Then the water flow to each sink in the house was cut off. The bathtubs and showers were off-limits, Susanna decreed. While this didn't bother me or the other boys very much, Carolyn was disturbed by the idea of having to go for a few days without showering.

"I'll go to the store tomorrow and get some baby wipes," Susanna assured her.

"Baby wipes?" I asked. "Is someone having a baby?"

Tim and Carl giggled, but I was genuinely confused.

"No, doofus," Carolyn said to me. "They're these things that… well… kind of like Wet Naps." I still had no idea what she was talking about, which my expression clearly showed, prompting an exasperated sigh from her. "Never mind. Just don't worry about it."

Although I didn't understand the details, the overall feeling seemed to be that we had settled the problem of the running water, and everyone seemed satisfied.

Not much else happened that night, and we eventually moved our sleeping bags and pillows down to the basement. It felt like a combination of camping out and a slumber party. The previous winter, our parents had taken me, Susanna, and Carolyn on a brief camping trip to a beach in South Carolina. That had been fun, plus it was interesting to see what the beach was like during what my father called "the off-season," a term I hadn't heard before. Our family had been to that place on weekend trips during the summer, and there were a lot more people there then. The beach also filled up with fog one afternoon, which made everything seem very strange and mysterious, all whitish and blank. It might have even been a little scary, but I felt safe with Carolyn that afternoon, who insisted on holding my hand. I was getting to the age where I balked at such mothering behavior, but deep down, I was grateful.

When Tim's watch alarm beeped to signal the approaching sunrise, Susanna got up and turned the basement light off, a single light bulb hanging from a white cord. Carolyn and I laughed when she stumbled as she made her way to her sleeping bag in the dark.

For a while, we stayed awake talking, occasionally cracking jokes and making each other laugh. As time went on, I found myself whispering, a habit developed from previous situations like this when we didn't want our parents (or my aunt and uncle during those earlier summers) to hear that we were still awake. I was also reminded of a time recently when Carolyn had made me spend the night in her bedroom in a sleeping bag after coming home one night from seeing a scary movie with her friends. The movie had scared her so much that she didn't want to sleep alone that night, so I had to keep her company. I wasn't sure why she needed the presence of an eight-year-old to ward off a potential boogieman, but I still had a good time.

While what we were doing felt somewhat normal, there was still the extraordinary fact that we were vampires. It had been an incredible adventure so far, and I wondered what the following night would entail. Carolyn grumbled again about having to sleep in the basement, claiming that it was "stinky," but I hadn't noticed. Tim then brought up the idea that vampires usually sleep in coffins, which led the rest of us to wonder whether or not we could build some for ourselves. Carolyn said that she knew of some spare wood in the storage shed that she could probably use, but that would have to wait until the following night.

We were woken by the beeping from Tim's watch, which Susanna had instructed him to set for 8:45 p.m., just after sunset. It was pitch dark, and as we stirred, I heard Susanna say, "Damn, should have brought a flashlight."

"Here," Tim's voice said, and a faint glow came from his direction. "My watch has a light."

"Of course it does," Carolyn said quietly, shuffling in her sleeping bag.

I saw some vaguely illuminated movement as Tim used the light on his watch to guide Susanna to the basement's light bulb. With a click as she pulled the chain, the light came on, searing into my eyes, which I involuntarily covered up with my arm. I groaned, as did the others.

"You know," Carl said, recovering and rubbing his eyes, "you probably could have just used your glowing eyes to find that." He was right. For a few moments upon waking, we had forgotten our new situation.

"Okay, smarty," Carolyn said, rising from her sleeping bag and standing. "Ow." She said that as she stretched her arms and legs, looking uncomfortable. "Okay, sleeping on the basement floor was not the greatest thing in the world."

It had been a little uncomfortable, but I hadn't thought that it was all that bad. After all, the whole reason we had been down in the basement in the first place was to avoid the sun because we were vampires, and as I woke up and recalled everything that was going on, I began to feel more excited and to forget whatever inconveniences might be bothering my sister.

"So let's go!" I said. "Upstairs and back inside."

"Sure, fine, whatever," Carolyn said, sounding a little more upbeat, or at least less annoyed.

We walked up the wooden stairs and out the basement door, and as we made our way out, I heard Susanna breathe deeply, then sigh.

Carolyn did the same. "That's better."

I wasn't sure what they were talking about, but I followed their lead, taking a deep breath. Nothing felt that extraordinary. We were outside, but that was it. Still, there was some kind of weird feeling in the back of my mind, some nagging feeling I couldn't place.

We made our way around the side of the house and in through the front door, which Susanna had to unlock. Once inside, things looked a little weird and different. I had no idea why. Something was distracting me.

While most of us filed past the stairs and into the yellow-carpeted den, Carolyn broke off and went down the hall to the bathroom, a larger one in the center of the house, not the one Carl and the rest of us had used the previous night. This one was a full bath with a large mirror that spanned the length of its counter and sink. Arriving in the den, I felt uneasy, unsure what to do. Everyone else seemed similarly disoriented.

Suddenly, Carolyn let out a scream, a combination of what sounded like a frustrated *"Oh!"* and *"Ugh!"* at the same time, accompanied by a simultaneous stomp that I could feel through the floor. There were more vibrations as she clomped her way into the den.

"Can't even see my reflection in the mirror!" she said to no one in particular. She huffed, then turned to Susanna. "Does my hair look okay?"

"It's fine," Susanna said to her, then approached her and fussed with her hair. "Really, it's…" She frowned, broke off, and left the room for a few seconds. Returning from the bathroom with a hairbrush, she said, "Here," and began working on Carolyn's short blonde hair. Carolyn continued to look angry, gazing off in one direction away from everyone else.

"Oh!" I said, pitching my voice higher than usual and flailing my hands up. "Carl! Does my hair look okay?" I bounced up and down in a silly manner, knowing an opportunity to make fun when I saw one.

Carl giggled, and Tim did the same, getting in on the joke and reaching for my head, miming tossing my hair about with his fingers and saying in an exaggerated high-pitched voice, "Oh! Here you go!"

"Oh, your haaaaair!" Carl said in a similarly girly voice. "What are we going to doooo?" He flapped his hands around.

We laughed as we continued to make fun of my sisters, which prompted both of them to give us disdainful looks.

"Girls…" Carl said, rolling his eyes.

"You know," Carolyn said, now brushing Susanna's hair in return and not looking over at us, "someday you guys might actually care about how you look, once you're old enough."

I hated when Carolyn or Susanna did that, telling me that I didn't understand something just because I wasn't as old as they were. A phrase often used was "you're too young," but I'd learned to counter this at an early age with: "I'm not too young, I'm *Ray* Young!" That just got on their nerves, which was pretty much what I was going for.

"Okay, calm down everyone," Susanna said, standing up from where she had been kneeling. She tossed her long brown hair back with her hand, apparently satisfied with Carolyn's styling job. As long as none of us had reflections, she and Carolyn would have to rely on each other in order to look glamorous. It all seemed pretty stupid to me. What's more, Susanna had always been the prissier of my two sisters, so it seemed strange to me that Carolyn had all of a sudden been so upset about her appearance. It also occurred to me that I was feeling tense, meaner than usual, and what Susanna said next clarified why.

"We're all on edge because we need blood," she said. The rest of us nodded, realizing she was right.

"Oh…" Carolyn said, reaching up to her mouth. She bit at her finger gently, her fangs exposed. I did the same, almost involuntarily.

"So we need to go out," Susanna continued.

"Yes," Tim said, somewhat absently. Then he smiled and said, "Please."

We hurried outside and changed into our bat forms, then followed Susanna as she led us into the sky. I asked where we were going, and she told us that we would be going to Daniel Village, a shopping center not very far from our house. I had been there many times throughout my life, though certainly never for the purpose we had in mind. I was looking forward to killing again.

"Maybe we should just wound the people this time," Carolyn said in her squeaky bat voice as we flew. "You know, get enough blood to drink but don't actually kill them."

"That's probably a good idea," Susanna said. "And we should stay as bats." She went on to say that there would probably be enough people there to drink from, but the crowds would be thinning out since most of the stores closed at 9:00.

I wasn't too keen on Carolyn's suggestion, but I didn't protest. Tim and Carl also remained quiet, but I wondered what they were thinking.

We arrived at Daniel Village, and it did not take long to spot our prey. A group of four people, three men and one woman, were exiting a pharmacy and heading out into the parking lot. It was a large shopping center lined by about two dozen stores and a movie theater. Across the street was an airport, and I thought of how we no longer needed planes to fly, unlike the helpless people we were about to go after.

When Tim pointed out that there were only four of them, Susanna said that she and Carolyn would take the woman, and the rest of us could have the other three. I wondered if we were loud enough for the people below to hear us talking, and sure enough, the woman in the group looked up, vaguely in our direction.

It was too late, though, and we zoomed down toward our targets, Carolyn and Susanna latching onto each side of the woman's neck as she screamed. As Carl and Tim claimed their victims, I took mine, biting into his neck and drinking from it immediately.

He crumpled to the pavement as I continued to drink, and I loved how the entire experience felt. The taste of the blood seemed so much more distinct than it had the night before, and it was wonderful. I hadn't even realized just how thirsty I was until I'd begun drinking. I also forgot that we were only supposed to take a little bit of blood from these people and move on, but then I remembered. And I didn't care. All I wanted to do was to keep filling myself up from this delicious source until it was all gone. I kept waiting for either Susanna or Carolyn to float up beside me and tell me that we had to leave, but that didn't happen, and I was glad.

But then something else intervened, a piercing scream from someone nearby, and I broke off quickly, hovering a few inches from the drained body beneath me.

"Oh my God! Look, Jason, *look!*" a teenage girl shouted, pointing at us from just a few feet away. A boy in a baseball cap winced as she grabbed his arm tightly, seeming more irritated than concerned. But then he saw what she was indicating: four dead people lying in the parking lot with a small group of bats fluttering above.

"It's vampires!" the girl cried. "Like on the news!"

The boy grabbed the girl's arm and shouted for her to get to the car, and I flew toward them as they ran. The boy was struggling to get his car keys from his pocket as he went along, which was not working very well for him. Still, he and the girl managed to make it to their car, and he fumbled at the driver's side door frantically while the five of us raced to catch them in time.

One of our bat-selves just missed being slammed in the door as the boy slipped into the car, and the girl was beating on the window of the passenger side, screaming at him to open up and let her in. I was on her side of the car by then, and another bat landed on the girl's neck and bit down, causing her to collapse onto the car as she screamed one last time.

I saw the boy inside the car, illuminated by the purplish-blue lights in the parking lot, reaching across to unlock the passenger side door and screaming out the girl's name, which I couldn't quite make out. He froze as he saw me and a couple of the other bats hovering at the window, eager to get in. He then drew back and started up the car, which quickly backed up out of its parking space, leaving the girl to fall onto the pavement while the bat who had killed her detached itself and flew up. The car's tires squealed as the boy sped away, swerving but managing to avoid the other cars in the parking lot. In just a few seconds, the car was gone.

"Come on," the bat said, hovering in place over the girl's body. It was Susanna. "Back to the house."

As we flew back, I thought about how that encounter had been a little more scary. We had been spotted, and one of our intended victims got away, but then, so what? It wasn't like he really could have done anything. In fact, rather than feeling threatened, I began to feel disappointed that the boy had escaped. If this was a game, then one point had just been scored for the other team. But we were still winning.

Some of these concerns were raised in discussion back at the house, but not immediately. The first thing that happened involved Susanna retrieving the newspaper from the front porch. We had ignored it on our way inside earlier, but she was eager to see what it might have to say about our attacks the previous night.

There was a story — but not on the front page, Carl noted — that further detailed our attack on the YMCA, how many people had died, and what the possible explanations were. Susanna read the story aloud to us, which said that it appeared that some strain of rabid birds or bats may have been responsible. Medical examiners had noted the extreme loss of blood in the victims, but a wildlife expert who had been consulted insisted that vampire bats were not native to the area, nor did they normally attack humans or drain that much blood from the cattle and other animals they usually bit. Witnesses, however, were insistent that they had seen bats, but police were reluctant to give any credence to these accounts, claiming that they were the result of hysteria and traumatic responses to the event.

"Well, that's a little better, I guess," Carl said once Susanna was finished reading. "At least they mentioned vampires."

"So?" Carolyn said. "Do we really want them to know that?"

"Sure we do!" Tim said. "They'll be more scared that way!"

Carolyn huffed, rolling her eyes. "And what about that boy who got away in his car tonight?"

"What about him?" I said.

"Calm down, Carolyn," Susanna said. "It's not like he actually saw us. Not really." I knew what she meant: We were in our bat forms at the time.

"Yeah, but..." Carolyn began. "Fine."

She left the room and headed down the hall. When I asked everyone what we should do next, Tim reminded us of how we had talked the previous night about building coffins to sleep in. He followed Carolyn to her bedroom, and I heard them talking as they came back up the hall. She no longer seemed angry like she had a few moments earlier and instead was eager to get me to help her retrieve the wood from the storage shed in the backyard.

"We can help, too!" Tim said.

"No," Carolyn said, holding up a finger. "We don't need King chasing after you guys again."

"Right," Carl said. "I guess we'll just wait here, then."

"And I need to go out and try to get those wipes we talked about," Susanna said. "Too bad the pharmacy is closed, though. Maybe the gas station will still be open."

King bothered us some as Carolyn and I made a few trips to and from the shed to get the wood and tools for the coffins, jumping around and getting excited. I was annoyed, but Carolyn insisted that he was just trying to help. From time to time, both Carolyn and I had helped our father with projects like this, though those were usually conducted on the patio or the carport. This time, Carolyn decided that we would have to do the work inside in the den, again concerned about making too much noise outside in the middle of the night.

We went at it for a couple of hours, but after a while, we realized how impractical of an idea it was. At first, we had thought that we could just hammer together some boards into a coffin-like shape, maybe adding a lid that swung open on hinges. But once we tried to actually make the idea work, we realized that it was more or less impossible. None of the wood we had was the right size, and trying to saw it indoors would be extremely messy. Using either the electric saw or even a regular one outside was out of the question because of the noise factor. I kept insisting that there must be some way we could make it work and offered some suggestions for different ways to hammer the wood together. The guys backed me up for a while, but eventually they too conceded that there was just no way. Disappointed, we were left with several useless bits of wood nailed together and subsequently torn apart, some with crooked nails seemingly permanently embedded within them. These were tossed out onto the patio to be dealt with later.

During all of that, Susanna came home in her car from her trip to find the wipes. I had wondered why she had gone in her car as opposed to just flying to the store as a bat, which I asked her about upon her return, and she said something about "passing as a human," a phrase I did not understand. She explained that she meant that she wanted to fool other people into thinking she was just a normal person, not a vampire. I could see the usefulness of that.

What I couldn't see the point of was this insistence on these new wipe things. Taking a break from attempting to build the coffin, Carolyn joined Susanna in demonstrating to the rest of us how they were used. Basically, they were little tissues with some substance on them that you could use to clean off your hands, face, or whatever without using water, but I didn't see much need for them. In fact, I thought that they smelled rather pungent, and after using one on my hands, I found myself trying not to breathe through my nose and wiping my hands on my shorts over and over to try to get the weird slimy feeling off of them. Carl and Tim didn't complain as much, though, and Carolyn seemed the most grateful for them.

Another thing that interrupted us during the coffin-building experiment was the 11:00 news. We wondered if anything more might be said about our killings, particularly since we had done some more this evening. It wasn't the top story, but there was still some more coverage of the mysterious deaths in the city. While the reporters did mention further speculation about vampires, they also discouraged panic and reiterated the idea that the killings were most likely being done by some sort of animals. "It is far too early to determine the precise cause at this time," urged the well-dressed reporter, "but police advise caution."

"Fat lot of good that will do," Tim said, smiling. I shared his smugness and felt pretty powerful at that moment, proud of getting away with the bad things we were doing.

After the news moved on to another topic, Carl said, "So, those people we killed…" — he said it so matter-of-factly that it didn't even occur to me how odd of a sentence it was, particularly coming from the mouth of a high-pitched gangly nine-year-old — "will they come back to life as vampires?"

This had not yet crossed my mind, even though I knew that it was a common thing with vampires, that their victims also became vampires. Even with my limited experience with them, I knew that part of the legend. But for some reason, I hadn't even thought about it until then.

"No," Susanna said simply.

"Really?" Tim asked. "Why not?"

"Yeah," Carolyn said, looking confused. "I thought that's how it was supposed to work, that a vampire bites someone and then they become a vampire, too."

"Not in our case," Susanna said. "Remember, we became vampires by taking a potion, not by being bitten."

"Oh," Carolyn said. She looked disappointed, maybe even sad.

"So they're just dead then," Carl said.

"Afraid so," Susanna said, though she sounded indifferent, not remorseful. "When we did the experiments with the mice and the potion, the mice that were bitten didn't also turn into vampire mice; they just died. The effects aren't transmittable."

"Hmm," Tim said simply.

Carolyn huffed. "Well, that kind of sucks."

Carl began to laugh, then stopped when Carolyn glared at him.

At that point, we continued our attempts to construct a coffin, but that was soon abandoned. Carolyn became increasingly frustrated as time went on, plus she snapped at me a couple of times when I kept trying to come up with suggestions on how to do things. A little later, once the idea had been dropped and the scraps were tossed out onto the patio, Susanna insisted that we try watching something funny on TV to cheer ourselves up.

Unfortunately, *The Tonight Show* — which we watched in the other den, the one usually occupied by our parents — offered very little in the way of entertainment for me and my young friends. Some old guy in a suit telling corny jokes in front of an audience of other old people did nothing to make us laugh. It wasn't like we understood most of what he was saying, either; we knew next to nothing about politics or topical news of the day. Carolyn and Susanna seemed to get more out of it than the rest of us did, but Carl, Tim, and I were just plain bored.

We left the room after the first commercial break and decided to try to find something else to do instead. Carl came up with the idea of flying around inside the house as bats and playing a sort of hide-and-seek game that way. That was fun, and we quickly learned how to better maneuver as bats, zipping around corners, hiding in small spaces, and just generally being sneaky. We also took the opportunity to annoy Susanna and Carolyn in the red den, sometimes zooming close to them as they sat and watched their late-night talk shows. I also hovered in front of the TV screen once to mess up their view, which prompted Carolyn to throw an empty cup at me. She missed.

Later on, Susanna came up with another alternative to sleeping in the basement, which she said was based on Carl's earlier suggestion of ducking down into our sleeping bags. She was pretty sure that as long as the windows to the house were blocked off with black garbage bags, that would be enough to keep out the sunlight, and we could sleep in our beds and sleeping bags with no trouble.

So we spent about two hours using masking tape and garbage bags to block out all of the windows, a task that took longer than we thought it would. We also had to do it with the lights off, fearing that someone might drive by and wonder what we were up to. But our glowing night-vision eyes made that easy enough. The end result was pretty impressive, and we felt that we finally had a house that was safe for vampires and with no sunlight allowed, as Tim put it.

Sounding bitter but also relieved, Carolyn said, "Well at least we can actually sleep in comfortable beds tonight."

"Don't you mean today?" I asked.

"You know what I mean," she said, rolling her eyes.

"Well, technically…" Tim began.

"I *know,*" Carolyn said, cutting him off. "What time is it, by the way?" She wasn't specifically asking Tim, but he was more than eager to show off his fancy digital watch again.

He shot out his arm dramatically and pulled his wrist toward him, announcing, "3:27 a.m." He paused, then continued, "and 24 seconds, Tuesday, June 28th, 1983…"

"And what's the temperature in Alaska right now?" Carolyn asked, sneering.

"51 degrees Fahrenheit," he said, not missing a beat or glancing up from his watch.

"Oh, shut up," Carolyn said.

The next night, I was again woken by the sound of Tim's watch alarm, this time in my own bed. The blacked out windows had worked, but just to be safe, Susanna had also instructed us to sleep with the covers over our heads, or in Tim's and Carl's cases, ducked down into their sleeping bags. At some point during the day, I had made my way out from under the covers, and I was still okay, so I knew that meant that the garbage bags were enough to keep out the sunlight.

After I had woken Susanna and Carolyn up, everyone gathered in the den, again eager to go out and kill. Susanna decided that we should go to a place not too far from Daniel Village where she knew there would be people, but it would be less open and well lit. It was a bar she had been to with some friends from high school.

"But what if any of your friends are there?" Carolyn asked.

"They won't be," Susanna said. "They're already out of town. Just me now…" She said that last bit softly and without looking at anyone.

"And just how did you get into a bar underage?" Carolyn asked, suddenly stern.

Susanna huffed condescendingly and smiled. "Oh, Carolyn, someday…" She trailed off, shaking her head.

"Look, can we cut the chatty crap and just get out there already?" Carl snapped. Again, we were all feeling irritable from not having fed.

"Fine!" Susanna said, but she sounded more amused than angry or threatened.

Soon, we were in the air and on our way to the bar. We landed nearby and changed into our person forms, hiding under some trees not far from the bar's entrance. I noticed the smell of pizza coming from the place and felt even more hungry than I had been, which only increased my anticipation and eagerness to kill.

The opportunity presented itself quickly enough, though it was unexpected. A voice from behind us called out, "You kids need some help?"

Startled, we turned around to see an adult couple who were walking with a young girl. The girl stood between her parents, holding their hands and gazing up at us with an open, eager look. Her long dark hair was tied in braids on either side of her head and hung down past her shoulders onto her chest. While both she and her parents seemed friendly enough, I didn't like her; she immediately reminded me of a particularly spoiled and snotty girl I had known at school, though this girl was two or three years younger than I was. These people weren't bar patrons; they probably lived in one of the houses just down the street.

"Yes, you can," Carl said, and he launched himself at the father's neck, taking him down instantly. He didn't scream, but the mother and daughter did, the girl letting out a typical, whistle-like screech. This was soon stifled as Tim and Susanna went for the girl and her mother, latching onto their necks and forcing them to the ground as they drank.

That left me and Carolyn standing there and looking around, wondering if anyone might have heard the screams. Almost immediately, two older boys ran up from the direction of the bar, stopping short when they saw us.

"Are you okay?" one of them asked, apparently thinking that we had been the source of the noise.

"Fine," Carolyn said with a smile, and I knew that she was about to pounce.

The other boy, looking behind us, saw Susanna and the others enjoying their dinner, then said, "Oh, God…" He began to back away as his friend asked him what was wrong, but it was too late. Carolyn and I were upon them within seconds.

Once again, I bit down into a delicious human being's neck and felt him crumble beneath me, barely noticing the impact as we hit the pavement together. I was far too preoccupied with the warm rush of blood and its perfect, salty taste. It flowed down my throat as I gulped, filling me with wave after wave of refreshing warmth and satisfaction. This had been the best kill so far, but then, each consecutive one felt like that.

Just as I was finishing, I felt someone tug at my shoulder and say, "Come on!" It was Carl, and I looked up to see Susanna pulling Carolyn away from her prey as well.

I then saw that two more people were approaching from the direction of the bar, but I wasn't sure if they had actually seen us yet. One of them stopped and squatted down for a moment, shielding his eyes from the overhead streetlights to get a better look.

We ran in the opposite direction, almost tripping over the bodies of the first victims we had encountered, then changed into bats mid-run and flew up into the air. I looked back down and saw the two men as they reached the bodies we had left behind, wondering what they might be saying.

We had established a routine of leaving and entering the house via the front door to avoid alerting King and setting off his barking. It was just easier that way, though most of the time in our regular lives, we entered and exited through the back door, which led to the carport. We also weren't very concerned with being seen by our neighbors. The house across the street was empty, owned by a very wealthy family that had since moved into a larger house elsewhere in town, though they occasionally rented their old house to people. The house next to ours was occupied by an elderly couple who went to bed early, and the same was true of the house across from them, the one catty-cornered from ours. Overall, it was a quiet neighborhood, and while I often found this boring as a child, it worked out pretty well for our current situation.

Susanna brought the newspaper in as she had done the night before, and the rest of us talked excitedly about our latest adventure out on the town. At least, my friends and I did; Carolyn just seemed quiet.

The newspaper did mention more about possible vampire attacks but was pretty vague, and nothing much new was said, according to Susanna. Carolyn remained silent and seemed uninterested, and after a little while, she got up from the couch and walked down the hall to her room without saying a word.

While Susanna stayed upstairs in her room as well, the three of us watched TV for a while, settling on a kung fu movie. Carolyn and I had watched this kind of thing before, finding it particularly funny the way that everything seemed so over the top and exaggerated. Sometimes, she and I would pretend to be characters in these films, striking silly fighting poses and speaking to each other in stilted voices, pretending to attack each other while making *swish! swish! chak! chak!* sound effects. I told Tim and Carl about this, then got them to play along.

I wanted Carolyn to take part since she had enjoyed it in the past, so I went to her room and knocked on the door.

"Hmm?" she said, and I walked in. She was lying on her bed and had been reading from a small, red book, which she put away as I walked in, looking up at me impatiently.

"That stupid kung fu stuff is on," I said. "Want to come see?"

"Not really," she said.

"Why not? It's funny. Tim and Carl are all fighting and going 'yeeowww!' 'yah!' and all." I made karate hand gestures as I spoke.

"I don't feel like it," she said.

"Oh." I started to give up and close the door, then asked, "What's wrong?"

"Nothing," she said, looking away and reaching for her book.

"Okay," was all I could manage, but something made me linger there.

She was quiet for a few moments. "Don't you think we've had enough?"

"Enough what?" I asked, releasing the doorknob and taking a step into her room.

"Of... this." She looked up at the ceiling and then back at me. "This vampire stuff. I think we've done enough damage. Let's get Susanna to make the cure and go back to the way we were before."

"No!" I shouted, almost surprised by my gut reaction. "What damage? The windows are okay! We'll just have to take the tape off and get the garbage bags down..."

"That's not what I mean," she said. "Just... I don't know." She looked down at the bed. "Never mind. Forget about it. Don't say anything to the others."

"Okay." I closed the door and headed back up the hall. It sunk in what she was suggesting, and the idea of giving up this incredibly fun thing that we'd been experiencing seemed appalling to me. I didn't want to say anything to Carl or Tim as I reached the den, not so much because she asked me not to, but because I was afraid either of them might agree for some reason.

Later on, Tim realized that 11:00 was approaching and the news was about to come on, so we called to Susanna and Carolyn to come watch it with us. I wondered if Carolyn might not come out of her room, but she and Susanna arrived at the same time and settled down in their chairs. Tim and Carl sat on the couch, and I sat cross-legged on the floor in front of the TV, waiting to turn the volume up once they started talking about the vampires, about us. It turned out that we were the top story.

"More tragedy has occurred in the Summerville area of Augusta tonight in what appears to be the latest in a series of unexplained killings," the news anchor reported, her brow furrowed.

The screen then changed to footage of the same bar where we had attacked earlier that night, showing police cars parked nearby with their blue lights flashing while various people stood around. The anchor went on to say that five bodies were found and that there were witnesses who saw people running from the scene.

A policeman was then interviewed, a squinty, round-faced man in uniform. He spoke with a thick southern accent, saying, "We believe that there may have been people here who saw what happened and fled the scene in a panic, so we're urging anyone who may have witnessed this attack to contact the Augusta Police Department as soon as possible with any eyewitness accounts they may be able to provide."

The camera cut back to the reporter in the studio, who concluded the story saying, "The identities of tonight's victims have been withheld pending notification of next of kin."

After the news story ended, I stood up and turned the volume down a little. "What does that mean?" I asked.

"It means that they can't say the names of the people on TV until they've told their relatives that they've died," Susanna said.

Carolyn let out a loud sigh and looked down at her chest. "See, that's what I'm talking about," she said gravely.

"What?" I asked.

Carolyn suddenly slammed her hands down on the sides of the wicker chair she was sitting in, straightening up. "Am I the only one here who is feeling the slightest bit guilty about all of this?" she said, raising her voice and looking around the room at the rest of us.

"Probably," Tim said.

"Carolyn…" Susanna began.

"What are you talking about?" Carl asked, sounding genuinely confused.

"Like that little girl tonight," Carolyn said, but then she trailed off, looking to one side.

"That little brat?" I said. "What about her?"

"She had a *family,*" Carolyn said, looking at me sharply and emphasizing her words.

"And they were *delicious,*" Tim said, mocking her tone. "Right, Carl?"

Carl giggled. "Yeah." He continued grinning and looked at Carolyn, his fangs showing.

Carolyn seemed even more flustered, so I couldn't resist saying, "And what about that guy you killed tonight, Carolyn?"

"He… I…" she began, then shook her head and looked down. "That's not the point." She continued to avoid eye contact for a while, and the room remained quiet. "I just…" She looked up, then turned to Susanna.

"What," Susanna said flatly.

"I think we should change back now." Even though I hadn't told Tim or Carl that she had already mentioned this to me, everyone knew what she meant: She was ready for all of us to stop being vampires.

"Change back?" Carl said incredulously. "You're nuts!"

"No, I'm not nuts," she said with extreme condescension. "I'm a human being."

"No you're not!" Tim said, raising his hand and pointing. "You're a vampire!"

"Shut up," Carolyn said, rolling her eyes once more. She sunk back in her chair, then turned to Susanna. "Really, though, can we stop this?"

"I don't know," Susanna said. She then looked at me and said, "Maybe we should take a vote."

"What?" Carolyn said, sitting up again.

"I'm serious." She straightened up and took on an official air. "All those in favor of staying vampires, raise your hand." As she said this, her hand was raised as well.

Tim, Carl, and I immediately shot up our hands in agreement. Carolyn didn't bother to change her posture; the vote was decided before it had begun. I felt triumphant, and I was sure that Tim and Carl did, too.

"So it's decided," Susanna said, nodding her head. "We stay this way."

"But…" Carolyn started.

"It's *decided,*" Susanna said, looking sternly at Carolyn. This was a rare victory. My sisters and I had disagreements over the years, and more often than not, Susanna and Carolyn either outvoted me or just won by default due to the fact that they were older. But every now and then, there were times when Susanna and I were in agreement and Carolyn was forced to bend to our will, and this was certainly one of those times, further reinforced by my friends' presence and opinions.

Carolyn relented. "Fine," was all she could say. She stood up from her chair and stomped towards the door to the hall. Then she stopped.

"But we still have to change back eventually," she said, turning back. "Our parents will be back on Sunday." The idea of that filled me with disappointment, but I tried to shove it out of my mind and not think about it.

"I know," Susanna said. "But we'll change back when *I* decide it's time."

Carolyn paused for a moment to glare at her, then stomped down the hall.

"God, she's so dramatic," Carl said.

"Yes, she's always been that way," Susanna said.

After that, things felt uneasy. We may have won the vote and bullied Carolyn into continuing to go along with us, but the fact that she was so opposed to that began to spoil things. Tim, Carl, and I talked about this in hushed tones, not wanting Carolyn to overhear us.

We felt that she was just being stupid, feeling guilty about things and trying to ruin it for the rest of us. Her attempts to appeal to our consciences earlier had not worked at all. That may have been because we were under the influence of the vampire potion, or maybe we simply had not developed proper morals by that age. We were certainly aware that we had been killing people, but truthfully, those people didn't matter to us. We didn't know them, nor did we care about them. They were the enemy, players on the other team. It was fun playing a game that was so easy to win.

Not long after I had been thinking along those lines, Carl also brought up the game analogy, then accused Carolyn of wanting to "switch sides."

"Yeah," Tim said. He paused, looked thoughtful, and then looked pleased. "So why not let her?"

"What?" I asked, catching myself before my voice got too loud.

"She wants to be human again, so let's let her!" Tim said, smiling.

"Because I don't want to!" Carl said, and I had to gesture to him to keep quiet.

"I didn't say you had to, or even that we had to."

I began to catch on. "You mean, just give the cure to Carolyn, and let her change back?"

"More than that. If we can somehow slip the cure to her, make her drink it without knowing it, then we can trick her."

"And then scare the ass out of her!" Carl said, smiling.

"Oh," I said, liking where this was going. I began picturing the scenario in my head: Carolyn would suddenly find herself no longer a vampire, and the rest of us would chase after her, taunting her over how she wanted so badly to be changed back.

We continued to discuss this and tried to come up with a plan, but it soon became apparent that we would need Susanna's help. After all, she was the only one who knew how to make the antidote. I wasn't sure if she would go along with this, but I hoped she would. The idea sounded so perfect.

Upstairs, I asked her what she thought. After pondering for a few moments, she said, "How would you suggest we trick her into taking it? I mean, we can't just point and say, 'Hey, look! It's Superman!' and then slip something down her throat without her noticing." She acted out the exaggerated pointing.

I couldn't help but laugh at the mental image that provoked, but I also felt disappointed, because I knew she was right. "I don't know. Maybe we could have a blood feast? Like blood in cups or something, and you slip the cure into her cup."

"A blood feast," she said, giving me a deadpan look. "And where would we get the blood?"

I deflated again. "Um, rob a blood bank?" I actually had no idea what a blood bank even was; I had only heard the term used in jokes about vampires (and a similar joke about how Dracula drove a bloodmobile).

"Sure, that'll work," she said sarcastically. She thought for another moment. "But we could probably figure out a way."

I was surprised that she was going along with this so easily, but I didn't dare say so for fear that she might shoot down the idea altogether.

"The thing is, though, that I don't have the antidote yet. I was going to make it at the same time as the actual potion, but there wasn't enough time. And it's not entirely… Well…"

"What?"

"Well, it's kind of like there are two cures. One works immediately, but it's, well, more complicated. The other one takes longer to take effect."

I didn't entirely understand this, but after thinking about it, I said, "Well I guess if the other one is less complicated, make that one. The sooner we can do this, the better!"

She looked confused for a moment, then nodded. "You're probably right. I'll have to think about it some more. Give me some time to work a few things out."

Back downstairs, I told Tim and Carl the latest news. They were excited that Susanna had agreed to do it, but I warned them that she still seemed a little uncertain. I wasn't sure if she was doubting the entire plan or just the specifics of making the antidote, but I was not yet convinced that she was committed.

After a little while, she came downstairs and led us into the red den, which was at the opposite end of the house from Carolyn's bedroom. Even so, we still spoke quietly. She told us that she would go ahead and make the antidote tonight, and tomorrow night, she'd arrange a way to get Carolyn to drink it. It wouldn't change her back immediately, but sooner or later, Carolyn would be back to being a human, and we could scare her off. She urged us to keep quiet and not let on, or else the plan might be ruined. Before leaving, she let out a sinister laugh, then added, "This is going to be fun."

When she left, Carl said, "Boy, she's really vicious when she wants to be, huh?"

"Oh yeah," I said, recalling plenty of incidents growing up when she and I had been at odds. More often, my conflicts had been with Carolyn since she and I were closer in age. Still, I'd had my fair share of scrapes with Susanna as well.

"You know," Tim said, "we should probably try to act more casual. All this sitting around and whispering might make her suspicious if she happens to come out of her room." He turned on the TV, saying it would cover up our voices, and we continued to talk about the plan.

Not much later, we saw Carolyn heading into the kitchen. After about a minute, she left with a glass of milk, drinking from it as she walked.

"Hey, Carolyn!" Carl called out. "How's it going?"

Not looking over and continuing to walk back toward her room, Carolyn flipped him the bird. Carl just laughed.

"Yeah, way to not be obvious, Carl," Tim said.

"What? I didn't say anything about…"

I lunged at him, reaching to cover up his mouth. He leaned back to dodge me, then laughed some more.

"Calm down. I wasn't really going to say anything."

"Okay, fine," I said, recovering. "Just don't do anything to mess this up." It suddenly became apparent to me how much I wanted this plan to succeed. It felt good to be scheming against my sister, and I wasn't just thinking of the current situation, the way she had started trying to spoil our fun as vampires. That was foremost in my mind, but more than that, this felt like an opportunity to get one over on her, to get her back for the times she had bested me in the past.

Maybe what happened next was because of that frame of mind, the increased viciousness the potion seemed to have brought out in me, or the aforementioned lack of a conscience. Regardless of what was to blame, by the end of the night, Carl, Tim, and I had developed the plan to the point where we were not simply going to scare Carolyn. We were going to kill her.

When we woke up Wednesday night, things felt different. While much of the previous night had been spent resenting Carolyn, I found myself feeling a new emotion: anticipation. I was still enjoying the sneakiness of everything, and that made it fun again. Carolyn had no idea what we were planning, and to make things more complicated, neither did Susanna. That is, she was in on the plan to change Carolyn back, but only Tim, Carl, and I knew about the plan to kill her.

I had bristled at the idea when it first came up; initially I just wanted to chase after her and verbally abuse her. But really, I hadn't been thinking very far ahead. It was Tim who came to the inevitable conclusion: If she became human, then she was fair game. As the night went on and I thought more about the plan and wanted it to succeed, I thought of the many times throughout my life when Carolyn had made me mad, all of the petty little conflicts we'd had.

So by the following night, I was ready and willing to carry the plan through, and I was looking forward to it. In fact, part of me was more intrigued by carrying out such a fiendish little plot than actually getting revenge on my sister. There was a goal, something to achieve. The nightly routine of waking up eager for blood further fueled this, too.

But Susanna had something else in mind this evening, an experiment she wanted to try, she said. Tim and I exchanged knowing glances at this, but Carl stomped his foot and complained that he wanted to go out and eat.

"That's what this is about," Susanna told him. "I want to see if our usual edginess when we wake up will be curbed by eating a regular meal instead."

"Oh, who cares!" Carl said.

"I care," Susanna said firmly. "So quit your whining and help me."

Carl frowned, but he did as he was told, helping Susanna get out plates and glasses. There was a pot of water being heated on the stove, and next to it, the steamer we used for warming hot dog buns. Susanna's definition of a regular meal may have been a bit of a stretch, but I was pretty sure I knew what this was really about.

My suspicions were confirmed when Susanna suggested that Carolyn, who had mostly been quiet so far but not antagonistic, go outside to feed King. She had been doing that on previous nights after our returning from killing, but we needed time to get the food ready anyway, and it seemed only fair that he should get to eat early, too. Really, this was just a tactic to get Carolyn out of the kitchen while Susanna slipped the antidote into Carolyn's glass of iced tea. It was a clear liquid, and once it was mixed in with the rest of the drink, there was no way to tell that hers was any different from the rest of ours.

Once all four of us knew what was going on, Susanna warned us again not to let on and give anything away. The antidote would not work instantaneously like the potion had, she reminded us. In fact, it might take as long as a full day.

"What?" Carl said incredulously. "An entire day?"

"Quiet," Susanna said through clenched teeth as the back door opened and Carolyn returned. By then, the table was set, as was the trap.

As far as the experiment went, to see if eating did anything to curb our desire for blood, it didn't work. We each wolfed down our hot dogs as quickly as we could, eager to get this fake dinner over with so we could go out and do the real thing. I didn't even want to finish, but Susanna insisted that we all did. This was of course especially important for Carolyn, though we couldn't tell her that. When we finished, we looked around at each other. Whether it was because we had inhaled our food so quickly or just the general anxiety over still wanting to go out, we were all breathing heavily.

"Well, that sucked," Carolyn said. "Stuff didn't even taste right."

My food hadn't tasted bad; it just wasn't what I wanted.

"Yeah," Tim said. "Can we please go out and get some real food now?"

We went out as usual, or at least, we pretended that it was another typical night. But aside from Carolyn, everyone knew that things were different. Carolyn was now the enemy, but we couldn't let her know that until the antidote took effect. This new wrinkle in the plan— the fact that it might take an entire day for her to change back — bothered me, but there was nothing any of us could do. We would just have to pretend for longer than previously planned.

Finding and preying upon a group of human victims went the same as it had the previous few nights, and Carolyn took part just as eagerly as the rest of us, or at least she didn't object like I thought she might. Truth be told, she craved the blood just as much as the rest of us did, even if she was also feeling guilty about it. But she didn't throw a fit when we got back to the house, either, even though I expected her to.

In fact, rather than stomping off to her room again upon our return, she instead enlisted my help in clearing up the scrap wood from the patio, which we had left there a couple of nights earlier after our aborted attempt at making a coffin. I made some small talk with her, asking her if she was still mad at us.

As she arranged the planks of wood in a garbage bag, she said without looking up, "I'm not going to say I'm okay with it. Just the sooner we get this over with, the better."

I didn't know what to say in response to that, and I was afraid that if I kept talking, I might let something slip. So I found myself with very little to say, making the whole encounter feel awkward.

Once we were done, we took two garbage bags' worth of wasted lumber to the trash cans in the driveway, then started to head inside. Carolyn then decided to stay outside and spend some time with King, who had been whining at us the whole time we had been working on the patio. I noticed that it was cloudy, and the moon was trying to peek through the clouds, mostly just a whitish haze lighting up the lumpy grey sky overhead.

The rest of the night was mostly uneventful, but it was nerve-wracking in terms of waiting for Carolyn's return to being human. Based on what Susanna had said, it was pretty likely that it wouldn't happen this night, so basically everything was just a waiting game. Susanna again spent most of her time up in her room, and my friends and I spent most of our time in front of the TV.

Around midnight, I heard thunder, and Susanna came downstairs. When I mentioned that Carolyn was outside, Susanna opened the back door and called out to her. She told her to come inside because it was probably about to rain, so she did.

"Good thing Ray told me you were out there," she said.

"Hmm?"

"You wouldn't want to be out there if it started raining."

"Well, duh." Carolyn was mostly avoiding eye contact with her, or really, with any of us.

"No, not just that. Remember the thing about running water?"

"Oh!" Carl said, his eyes widening. "So the rain would...?"

"It would," Susanna said, turning to him.

I hadn't even thought of rain being an issue, probably because it hadn't rained the entire time we had been vampires. Susanna warned that we should probably keep an eye on the weather forecast for the next few days just in case. We wouldn't want to be out hunting and get caught in a surprise thunderstorm, which she said were common that time of year.

"Lovely," Carolyn said, then clomped off to her room.

"So's your hair," Tim said quietly, and we laughed. It had looked a little rough, I'd noticed.

Susanna just gave him an annoyed look, then left the room.

The following night, I woke up with even more excitement than before. Surely this would be the night that Carolyn changed back to being human, and we could go after her. In fact, I realized as I was urging Tim and Carl to get up that she might have changed back already.

We hurried to the den, but Tim had warned us not to seem too eager. If she was still a vampire, it would be bad to let on that we might be expecting anything else.

Unfortunately, Carolyn didn't seem any different than usual when she came into the den. Susanna walked in with the newspaper and was checking the weather forecast, which she said called for thunderstorms during the day — which we had already slept through — but none for that night.

"Great," Carolyn said. "So can we go already?"

"What's wrong, Carolyn?" I said with a taunting tone. "Don't you want to check your hair first?"

Tim and Carl started to laugh, but Carolyn snapped back at me, "Knock it off, Ray! I'm not in the mood."

I couldn't think of a more witty retort than "whatever," and the others just stifled their laughs and looked away. It seemed like they were laughing at me instead of her, though.

As we flew downtown to look for our victims, I thought about what Carolyn had said to me, how she made me look bad. It wasn't so much that she had said anything particularly biting, just that her tone had been so condescending, and it made me feel smaller, inadequate. This furthered my resentment toward her, but the anger I felt was quickly replaced with an evil glee. Soon enough, she would be human again, and then I would show her. We all would.

We reached downtown Augusta after several minutes. This was the farthest away from home that we had looked for victims before, and it was not an area I was familiar with. Our family just never seemed to have much reason to go there, so I found it to be a rather strange place with its tall buildings and long, straight streets dotted with parked cars. The roads were dark but shiny; I could tell that it had rained not very long ago.

There were plenty of people around, a little too many, in fact, for us to make a discreet attack. It was also preferable to find a group of five people, if possible, so all of us could feed at the same time. Eventually, Susanna spotted just such a crowd walking along a poorly lit side street. No one else seemed to be around.

We landed in a circle surrounding them, changing into our person forms, which caused the five of them to stop suddenly, surprised and confused. They were all adults this time, three men and two women, and they seemed to quickly take in the situation as we bared our fangs and closed in on them.

Carolyn and I had landed behind the group, and as soon as they had turned back and seen us, Carolyn leapt at one of the men and wrapped her arms and legs around him, biting into his neck. I did the same, though somewhat less adeptly, and took down the woman next to him.

When I had finished drinking from her, I looked up and saw Tim finishing off the other woman. Carl had already had his fill of one of the men in the group, and Susanna and Carolyn were still enjoying their victims.

Susanna got up and looked around, and I did the same, making sure no one had seen us. Carolyn, meanwhile, was still on top of the man, gnawing away. This went on for a while, and eventually, Susanna knelt down and began to tug at her shoulder, urging her to hurry up.

Carolyn's arm shot back and struck Susanna in the chest, and she cried out and stumbled backward. She seemed more surprised than hurt. The entire time, Carolyn had not even looked up or stopped feeding.

"Ow," Susanna said under her breath, rubbing the point of impact. "Carolyn, come on. That's enough." Carolyn ignored her.

"Damn!" Carl said. "He can't be that good!"

By now, Susanna had stood back up and recovered. I looked at her, unsure what to say.

Finally, Carolyn stopped drinking from the body and let out a gasp. It sounded like she was coming up for air after a long swim. She stood up and brushed herself off, wiping at her mouth with her hand. The rest of us just looked at her.

"What?" she asked defiantly. "I was hungry."

During our return flight, I found it odd how Carolyn suddenly seemed so vicious and eager for blood. In fact, when we had left the house earlier, she had been the first of us to change into bats and head for the sky, though I hadn't really noticed or thought anything of it at the time. I might not have even thought of this until the second time she killed that night, which occurred not too long after we left our victims' bodies downtown.

It was Carl who pointed out the lone policeman sitting on his motorcycle. He was parked on the side of the road, and while he was clearly visible to us, Susanna explained that he was hidden from view of cars in case they sped by. A "speed trap," she called it. Since she was the only one of us who was old enough to drive, it made sense that she would know about such things.

Suddenly, Carolyn broke off from the group and flew down towards the man, prompting Susanna to call out, "Wait!" The rest of us stopped and hovered in mid-air, wondering what was going on.

Carolyn soon reached the ground and changed form, landing behind the policeman. She called out to him and began walking toward him, and he turned around. As he pulled off his helmet and said something to her, the rest of us flew down to get a closer look.

By that point, she was already upon the man and draining the life from him with the same vigor and viciousness as before. The officer had let his guard down for this seemingly helpless-looking young girl, and it was already too late for him. She didn't drink from him for quite as long as her first victim, but still, the fact that she was doing it at all was strange.

As if the night needed to get any weirder, Carolyn repeated her actions yet again just a few minutes later, this time descending upon a young couple who were walking along a sidewalk. When Carolyn reached the young man and latched onto him, this time staying a bat, Susanna directed Tim and Carl to take out the other person. I doubted that they minded the opportunity to kill again, but I was also pretty sure that they were thinking the same thing I was.

"Susanna," I said in a squeaky bat whisper, "what's going on? I thought she was supposed to be turning back to human, but she seems like more of a vampire than ever!"

Susanna sighed. "I don't know," she said. Because of the lack of human body language when we were in our bat forms, it was sometimes difficult to determine moods and subtle meanings of the things we said. We mostly had to rely on tone. But it was clear that Susanna was bewildered as well, possibly concerned. I certainly was, but I was also frustrated. Things weren't going according to plan.

"Maybe…" Susanna began, but she didn't finish her sentence.

"What?"

"The antidote was always kind of unstable," she said. "I really did think she would have changed back by now. Now I'm wondering if mixing it with that food last night was a bad idea."

"Now you tell us," I said.

"Come on," she said to me, then led me down to the others.

The people were dead, and we hovered over them.

"You sure are drinking a lot tonight!" Carl said to Carolyn.

"What's it to you?" she squeaked back.

"Carolyn, I said that's enough before and I mean it," Susanna said, flapping in place and facing Carolyn's nearly identical form. It kind of looked like Carolyn was turning her nose up at us in defiance, some bat-like variation of "the sister sneer."

"You have to stop," Susanna continued. "Otherwise you're going to leave a trail of bodies leading straight back to the house." That was a good point. I began to think about the policeman we had seen on the news a couple of nights earlier, plus the one Carolyn had killed tonight.

"Fine," Carolyn said, and she seemed to be laughing. She shot back up into the sky.

Once we were back home, Tim asked, "So, really, Carolyn, what was the deal with all that?" He said it with a smirk, which probably didn't help things.

"With what?" she said, but her own snide look betrayed her.

"All that killing and stuff!" Carl said. "I thought you didn't want to be a vampire anymore." I almost glared at him, but I caught myself. That was dangerously close to tipping our hand, but an overreaction from me would have been even worse.

"Well, maybe I changed my mind," she said. "God! You people are impossible." And then, not surprisingly, she stomped out of the room and down the hall.

"Again with the dramatic exits," Tim said, then laughed.

"Quiet, Tim," Susanna said.

"Really, though," I said to her, almost whispering, "what is going on? Do you think the cure isn't going to work?" I filled Tim and Carl in on what she had said earlier about it being unstable.

"I think it's… I still…" She put a hand to her forehead. "I'm not sure. Some of the mice in the original experiments took longer to change back than others. But I think she still will. I'm just a little worried about what will happen in the meantime."

"Me too," I said.

"Or what if she doesn't?" Tim asked. "Change back, I mean. Maybe we should try giving her the cure again."

"I don't know how we could pull that off," Susanna said.

We tried to come up with some possibilities, still keeping our voices down. During a lull in the conversation, we suddenly heard a strange sound, a faint scraping that seemed to be coming from the hall. Then I realized that it was actually coming from Carolyn's room.

I tip-toed as quickly as I could down the hall, then listened by the door, trying to figure out what was going on. The others crept up alongside me. I didn't recognize the next sound I heard, but Susanna did.

"The screen!" she said. "She's trying to go out the window!"

She pushed past me and tried to open the door, but it was locked.

"Quick! Out the front!" We raced back up the hall and fumbled at the door, trying to make our way to Carolyn's window as soon as possible. Both her and my bedroom windows faced the front of the house, so if we were quick enough, we might be able to catch her. I wasn't even sure why she was trying to escape through her window, but I was beginning to get an idea.

We managed to make it into the front yard just in time to see her flying away as a bat, which immediately dashed my hopes as to why she was trying to sneak away. I had thought it was because the antidote had finally kicked in, but apparently I had been wrong about that. Very quickly, the pieces fell into place, both for me and for the rest of the group.

"Holy crap!" Carl said. "She's going out to kill *again?*"

Although she had only gotten a few seconds' head start on us, by the time we made it up into the air, Carolyn was nowhere to be seen. We had no way of knowing which way she had gone, and by the time Carl suggested using our glowing eyes to try to spot her, it was still too late. She was out of range, whichever direction she had flown.

I suggested splitting up to find her, but Susanna said no. She knew her way around the city, but the younger three of us didn't, and we would just get lost. Tim thought that Carolyn may have gone back downtown, and since none of us could come up with a better idea, that was where we went to look for her.

We searched for about an hour, but she never turned up, nor did we see any signs of any other people she might have killed. We did see police cars and officers gathered around the two spots where Carolyn had stopped to kill earlier, and I remembered Susanna's warning that there could have ended up being a trail of bodies leading back to the house.

Eventually, Susanna insisted that we give up and head back home. There was nothing else we could do.

Susanna led us as bats through Carolyn's open window, and as we changed into our person forms, she chided herself for leaving the window wide open like that, saying that anybody might have come by and made their way inside, helping themselves to all of our belongings.

"Well, we would have just helped ourselves to him then," Carl said. Tim laughed in agreement.

Ignoring them, Susanna shut the window and locked it, then unlocked the bedroom door and led us up the hall to the den.

"So now what do we do?" I asked.

"Nothing," she said.

"But we can't just leave her out there, killing all over the place and doing who knows what!"

"And what would you suggest?" she said, fixing me with a pointed look.

Unfortunately, I had nothing to offer. We had already looked for her.

"What's the big deal, anyway?" Carl said. "We wanted her gone, so now she is! Works for me!"

"But she's... I don't know... out of control?" I wasn't sure where I was headed with that sentence, nor all that sure what I was feeling other than frustration and confusion.

"Surely she can take care of herself," Tim said. "She's old enough, right?"

"Probably," Susanna said, looking down. "And I think she'll end up coming back here sooner or later. She's got to have somewhere to sleep to avoid the sunlight, after all."

"So that's just it?" I asked, my voice getting louder.

"Yes, Ray, that's just it," Susanna said, suddenly angry and even louder. She screwed her eyes shut, threw her head back, and sighed dramatically, almost growling. "I can't handle all this," she said to no one in particular.

She started to leave the room, and I asked her where she was going.

"I've got things to do."

"What things?"

"Just… things!" She stomped out of the room and up the stairs, her attitude briefly reminding me of Carolyn.

"More endless packing, I guess," Tim said.

This wasn't good enough for me, and before long, I had gone out to search on my own, telling Tim and Carl not to tell Susanna. I had tried to convince them to come with me, but they had become indifferent. The way they saw it, Carolyn was our enemy anyway, and they no longer cared what happened to her. I realized part of the way through our conversation that they might turn on me if I seemed too eager to help her, thinking I might have gone soft and no longer wanted to follow through with the plan.

As far as that went, I was torn. I still liked the idea of getting back at her and pulling off our scheme, but it seemed that things had gone terribly wrong. I wasn't even sure just what I was feeling. There seemed to be this sense of pervading helplessness, that nothing was going the way I wanted it to. I wanted to fix things, to put them back the way we had originally planned them out, but it was like the picture kept changing. And I certainly wasn't thinking of any long term consequences, what might happen if we succeeded in killing her ourselves.

Or what if she ended up dying some other way? A vision popped into my head of her flying through the air, and then the antidote suddenly kicked in and she became human, plunging several dozen feet to the ground and her death. I didn't want that to happen, either. Was I finally developing a conscience, becoming genuinely concerned for her well being? I didn't know. But there was something urging me on, almost like a voice in my head saying, *You have to go find her.*

I decided to try going to Daniel Village again, where we had killed a few nights earlier. Whether there was any logic to that or if it was just because it was one of the few places in town whose location I knew, I wasn't sure, but it seemed as good an idea as any.

Within a few minutes, I was already lost. Susanna had been right: I did not know my way around the city. On all of our previous outings, she had led our group, and I had taken that for granted, not knowing the extent of my ignorance. Because of a homework assignment the previous school year, I had some sense of which directions were north, south, east, and west in relation to our house, and I knew that Daniel Village was to the southeast. So I thought it would be simple enough to head in that direction, and I would soon find the shopping center.

Not being able to recognize the various landmarks along the way, I ended up heading farther east than intended. I began to panic after a while once I realized that I had no idea where I was, but finally, I lucked out. I recognized my school, though it seemed to sneak up on me since I had not realized I was in that part of town. It also looked quite different at night and from the air. Still, I had been driven along the road from it to our neighborhood enough times to reorient myself and figure out just where I was and how to get back to the house. I had almost forgotten about Carolyn by then and just wanted to get home, but as I followed the road, I also looked around, wondering if I might spot her.

I relaxed and felt more comfortable once I reached my neighborhood, recognizing the familiar houses. Suddenly, I heard a scream from not very far away, and I headed in its direction. As I got closer, I heard more screams, brief and stifled. I recognized the type from our previous attacks, and I knew I had found Carolyn.

I arrived at a house about two blocks from our own. I recognized it, but I did not know who lived there. On the front lawn, I spotted four people, three of them sprawled out in the grass. The fourth was, not surprisingly, Carolyn, who was sitting with her legs crossed beneath her, a boy's upper half draped across her lap. She was bent over, drinking from his neck.

I flew to her and landed, changing form, and I called out to her in a loud whisper, looking around to see if anyone else was nearby. No one was. It was very late at night by then, so it was unlikely that anyone would be out. My main concern was whether or not anyone besides me had heard the screams.

As I approached, Carolyn looked up from the boy's neck at me, then smiled. Like any stereotypical vampire in a movie, her mouth was smeared with blood.

"Hi," she said in a whisper, still smiling. She bent back down and continued to drink from the boy, her head bobbing up and down slightly as she did. The boy was still alive, and he was looking at me. There was something strange about his expression, a sort of pleading look, almost sad. He seemed be somewhere between Carolyn's and Susanna's age. Although it was hard to tell exactly what color his hair was in the purplish streetlight, I noticed that it was longish on the sides and parted in the middle, styled in what I called "the football cut," as the overall shape of that haircut seemed strange and pointed on top, reminding me of a football. It was a popular style for teenage boys then.

"Carolyn, where have you been? We've been looking all over for you!" I whispered. That was not entirely true; by then only I seemed to care enough to look for her. But that sounded more heartfelt and sincere.

She stopped drinking again and glanced up, licking some of the excess blood from her lips before she spoke. "Aw, really?" She smirked, seeming unconcerned, and bent down again to drink some more. The boy winced as she did, apparently unable to struggle against her. I watched as she continued to drink, noticing the occasional little *"mmm"* sounds she made. It occurred to me that I had almost never really watched any of the rest of us feed when we attacked as a group; I was usually too preoccupied with my own kill.

"Carolyn, come on!" I said. "We really should get back to the house. It's not that far."

She looked up from drinking again, this time with a stern expression on her face. "Not until I'm done," she said, her eyes boring into mine. I immediately clammed up, knowing better than to argue. The boy's eyes, meanwhile, were beginning to lose their focus as Carolyn continued to drain him. He no longer seemed to be looking at me, nor at anything. I only noticed his shallow breathing when it stopped a few seconds later. He was dead, but Carolyn kept drinking from him, bending down a little farther then, burying her head deeper into his neck.

Something made me close my eyes and turn away. Had it always been like this? Was this how it was each time we had killed people? Or was this something new, something to do with her newfound viciousness? Did I make that same gulping sound when I drank from my victims?

At last, she was done, and she leaned back, letting the boy's upper half drop from her lap onto the grass. He was just lying there, lifeless, nothing more than a finished meal. Carolyn, meanwhile, was wiping her mouth with her wrist, grinning and looking off into the distance. She leaned back on her arms, beaming at me. "That was good," she said.

I wasn't sure what to say. Finally, I managed to ask her where she had gone.

"Oh, all over," she said. Apparently something about my expression concerned her, leading her to say, "Don't worry. I didn't kill that many people. Mostly I just wounded them as a bat. Maybe they survived, maybe not."

"But… I don't know… where…?"

"All the places we'd been so far," she said. "In order. Kind of like ceremoniously retracing our steps."

"Huh?"

"The YMCA, Lake Olmstead, Daniel Village, Tip-Top, all those." She was naming the places we had made our kills over the past few days, and I began to understand, sort of.

"It was kind of hard to find some of them, but I felt like exploring," she said. Immediately I was reminded of the very first time I'd heard that word: It was at our aunt and uncle's house out in the country, as Carolyn and I were walking around the woods and fields on the property, going places we — or at least I — had never been. She told me then that there was a word for what we were doing: exploring.

"But why?"

"Why?" She looked down. "I don't know. Just because. Seemed like something to do." She stood up, brushing grass from her shorts and legs as she did. Some bits of it fell onto the corpse of her latest victim, which we had been ignoring as we talked. I stood up, too.

"Here," she said, beckoning me to follow her. She walked slowly, then stopped, groaning. "Oh!" she said, holding her belly. "I think I might actually be full."

"About time," I said, trying to get things back to a joking mood, but I didn't really feel that way.

She began walking again, heading towards one of the other people lying in the grass, and for the first time, I noticed that one of them was moving, but slowly. The other was still.

"Don't bother with her," Carolyn said, pointing at the motionless body of a girl lying face down near the front door of the house. "I already finished that one."

We reached the other body, a small, blonde girl. She was struggling along on her stomach, her small hands clawing at the grass. She was making little whimpering sounds that matched her movements, and Carolyn knelt down beside her, grabbing her behind the neck and on the lower part of her back. The little girl froze, then let out a quiet whine.

Carolyn then reached for her shoulder, pulling and flipping her over. As she did, she scooped the young girl up onto her knees, cupping her with her arms. I could see that the girl had already been bitten by Carolyn, too wounded and weak to get away.

"Here you go," Carolyn said to me, smiling. "I saved her for you."

I knelt down in the grass. The wound on the little girl's neck was on the side nearest to me, and I felt drawn to the two little holes, which were streaming red. I started to bend down towards them, and the girl shifted, letting out a whimper that sounded like she was trying to tell me no. As she did, she screwed shut her eyes, which I had noticed were wide, pale, and blue.

I stopped. I looked again at the girl, noticing the white nightgown she was wearing, which had a cutesy design of a cartoon sheep on the front. There was a slipper on one of her feet, and farther across the lawn, I could see where the other one had fallen off. The girl couldn't have been more than five years old, if that.

"I don't…" was all I could manage to say. I didn't want to kill her. I didn't want her to exist. Her presence was breaking my heart. I felt sorry for her, but I also felt angry at myself for that. I was supposed to be a vampire, after all, tough and uncaring and powerful. I wasn't supposed to have sympathy for these people that we killed.

"Do it," Carolyn said firmly. "You have to."

She was right, though I didn't really understand why. I knew that this girl was in pain, and it was within my power to make that pain end. She was also scared. For some reason, so was I.

Finally I forced my head down to her neck, stopping for a moment to whisper into her ear, "This won't hurt a bit." It was a stupid thing to say, and a complete lie, but it seemed appropriate to try to comfort her. I had been told that lie before by doctors just before they jabbed a painful needle into my arm, so maybe this was no different. I tried to tell myself that, anyway.

As I lowered my head to her neck, I noticed the smell of her thin, straight hair, and I recognized it immediately. I got a quick flash in my head of myself, several years younger, my mother holding my head under the bathroom sink as she rinsed out my hair. I had continued to use that same brand of baby shampoo for a few years afterwards, and this girl must have still been using it, too. For a second, I wondered if she was old enough to wash her own hair yet, or if, like the version of me in that brief memory, she was still having to have her mother do it for her.

I bit down, trying to find the same two holes that Carolyn had made earlier and line my teeth up with them, thinking that might hurt less. Apparently it didn't, as the girl let out a noise that was sort of like a scream, but it was more like what a scream would sound like if her mouth were covered up. I began to drink from her, the salty blood feeling so warm that it almost burned my throat as it went down. And as her scream-like noise then began to break up into rhythmic spasms, I knew she was crying.

Thinking that it might distract me from what was going on, I began wondering again about the girl's life, again picturing her mother washing her hair for her in a sink. Then I wondered where the girls' parents actually were. Were they in the house, asleep? Maybe Carolyn had already killed them, too. This line of thought only made me feel worse. Soon, the girl would be dead, another of our victims. Each swallow of her blood was like liquid guilt. I hated what I was having to do, and by the time it was all over, I hated myself.

I stopped drinking as soon as I felt the girl's heartbeat stop, and I leaned back from her, practically throwing myself backwards onto the ground. I didn't even realize at first that I was crying.

After she laid the girl's body onto the ground, Carolyn got up and walked over and knelt down beside me, putting her arms around me. I cried into her chest.

"Shh," she said. "It's okay." It wasn't. "I shouldn't have made you do that. I'm sorry."

I stopped crying for a moment, then started up again. I no longer wanted to be a vampire, and I certainly didn't want to kill my own sister. But the plan was in motion, and I didn't know what to do.

Carolyn pulled back from me, then said with authority, "Come on. We should get back to the house. The last thing we want is for someone to drive by and see us."

Instead of flying, we walked the two blocks back to our house, saying very little. Carolyn said that she felt too full to fly, and because I was still upset and recovering from my bout of crying earlier, I didn't feel like flying, either. As we walked, I wasn't sure what to say to her, and I was caught up in my own thoughts, confused and afraid. I considered telling her what the others — what *we* — had been planning, but I was scared that doing so would make things even worse. If I betrayed the rest of them, what would happen then? They would probably turn on me, too.

Carolyn's attitude confused me. Even though she had been the one who wanted for us to stop being vampires initially, now she seemed to be enjoying it more than any of us. Maybe the plan wasn't necessary anymore. I certainly didn't feel the same abhorrence towards her that I had over the past couple of days. Perhaps I could convince the others to feel the same way.

But there was also the fact that I was tired of the whole thing, too. It had been fun for a while, being vampires and all that, but this entire night had been pretty horrible. Seeing Carolyn turn into some monstrous killing machine was upsetting enough, and having to kill that young girl myself just kind of did me in. And yet, I had already seen what the rest of the group did when one of us suggested changing back to human.

By the time we got home, I made sure that I had regained enough composure so that the others couldn't tell that I'd been crying. I had already asked Carolyn not to tell anyone what had happened, and she understood. She and I were getting along better than we had been for days, and that just made me feel even more guilty.

The front door was locked, which meant that we had to ring the doorbell and be let in by Susanna, who was not happy. This was another one of those times when she seemed like a third parent, just as stern and disapproving as our mother and father might have been, angry at us for disobeying her.

However, Susanna only had a few seconds to look at us angrily and belt out an indignant "Where the hell have you been?" before Carolyn suddenly pushed me to one side, staggered past Susanna, and ran loudly and clumsily to the bathroom. Shortly afterwards, I heard the sound of the toilet lid being thrown back, followed by another unmistakable sound, that of Carolyn throwing up.

Susanna and I ran to catch up with her and stopped at the bathroom door, and Tim and Carl soon joined us. Carolyn was kneeling down and bending over the toilet, vomiting blood in spurts. She gasped heavily between each effort.

"Are you okay?" I asked, immediately feeling stupid. Obviously, she wasn't.

Carolyn spluttered and gasped, then croaked out, "Leave me alone!" She held up a hand and motioned me away when I started to approach, then threw up again.

"Must be all that blood she drank," Carl said.

"Please, just go away!" Carolyn shouted, not looking up, still facing into the toilet. She continued to breathe heavily, but her vomiting seemed to be tapering off. "I'll be… I'll be okay in a… *mmmph…*" Once again, her cheeks swelled and she closed her eyes, another shower of reddish-clear fluid shooting out of her mouth and splattering into the bowl.

"Guys, really, just go," Susanna said to me and my friends. Reluctantly, I followed Carl and Tim into the den, hearing Susanna as she continued to talk to Carolyn, her voice more calm and comforting than when we had first arrived.

"Well that was kinda funny," Carl said.

"No it wasn't," I said, giving him an angry look. "Have you ever thrown up like that before?" I recalled a time two years earlier when Susanna, Carolyn, and I had all contracted the same stomach bug, which had us vomiting several times for a couple of days.

"Well, no, I just…" He shrugged. "What's your problem?"

"Nothing."

Tim started to speak, but we were distracted by Susanna's voice as she called out to Carolyn, who was heading down the hall and to her bedroom. She was saying something to her about the garbage bags needing to be put back up on the windows, and she was making her way into the den to talk to the rest of us. Mostly, though, she seemed to want to talk to me.

After being questioned by her and the others about where Carolyn and I had been and what had happened, I began to feel defensive, which turned out to be a good thing. The vulnerability and sadness I had felt over the past couple of hours evaporated, and I felt the need to stand up for myself. It didn't take much to convince everyone that I was still on board with the plan and that I had not revealed any of it to Carolyn, which Tim subtly accused me of doing, but he did not come right out and say so. Things seemed to settle down after a while, and the antagonism lessened.

"So," Tim began, "I guess it's safe to say that giving her the cure didn't work?"

"Sure looks like it," I said.

"Because she took it while eating that food," Carl said, looking thoughtful. "Does that mean we don't get to kill her?" As soon as the words left his mouth, he froze, his eyes going wide. "I mean… um…"

"Damn it, Carl!" Tim said. It was the first time I had heard him swear.

I froze as well, wishing that I could somehow wind back time and make it so that Susanna had already left the room when Carl had let that slip.

"It's okay, Carl," she said. "I'd pretty much come to the same conclusion myself."

I turned to her, surprised but trying to hide my disbelief. "Really? You want to kill her, too?"

She looked down at me, and I wasn't sure how to read her expression. "It's not a matter of 'want,'" she said. "If the antidote —

'the cure' as you keep calling it — were to take effect, and she were to suddenly be human in our presence, well…"

"We'd have to kill her," Tim said, nodding his head. I held back from expressing my disgust at the leering grin he had.

"I guess there's a small chance that it might still take effect," Susanna said. "So we should probably keep our eyes open just in case. But anyway, it's probably a moot point." She seemed resigned, and as she spoke, she never actually looked at any of us, just up in the air and around the room. Then she sighed and said she was going upstairs.

"Don't forget to pack the kitchen sink!" Tim said with a laugh.

Susanna looked at him, barely managing a sneer. "I'm done."

As she left the room, I noticed that she just seemed weary, perhaps tired of dealing with everything, my friends, and the whole vampire business. I had heard of the expression of overstaying one's welcome before, but it wasn't until this moment that I truly understood what that meant. This week had started off fun, my two best friends coming over and spending a few nights, practicing for the race, playing games, and having a good time. The vampire aspect of it was an unexpected surprise, and it had been surreal and amazing, but by this point, it was all wearing thin. I began to wonder just how we might wind this whole thing up, to send my friends on their way and have everything go back to normal.

As sunrise approached, I continued to have similar thoughts, a feeling of being trapped by the situation. I didn't dare express any of this to Tim or Carl, though, as they would probably have just seen me as weak. We settled down to sleep in my room as usual, the garbage bags still in place on my windows to block out the impending sunlight.

Carolyn had stayed in her bedroom the rest of the night after her unfortunate experience in the bathroom, and just a few minutes before sunrise, I heard Susanna walk down the hall, presumably to check on Carolyn. I didn't hear either of them speak, but by then, I was already starting to drift off. It had been an exhausting night, both physically and emotionally. I hoped that the following night might be more calm and routine, but that certainly was not the case.

"Hey, you know what might be cool?" Carl said as we gathered in the den the next evening. Carolyn was still in the kitchen where we had found her upon getting up, and Susanna had just come downstairs.

"No, what?" I asked.

"Instead of going outside first and changing into bats, why don't we fly out through the chimney?" It sounded like an interesting idea, I thought.

"You can't do that," Susanna said, pointing at the fireplace. "This one's blocked off." Because our house had two dens, one of which had been added on after the house was built, it also had two chimneys, but only one of them was functional, the one in the red den. She explained this to Carl and Tim, so then Tim suggested using that one instead.

"The flue is closed on that one," Carolyn said. "It's summer, you know."

"Well open it, then!" Tim said.

Carolyn huffed. "Do we really have to? I don't see anything cool about flying up a dirty old chimney. That just sounds dumb."

The rest of us disagreed, that is, the boys did. Susanna didn't seem to have an opinion.

"Fine," Carolyn said, looking annoyed.

"Awesome!" Carl said, and he changed into a bat. Tim and I did the same.

"Are you two coming?" Tim asked squeakily.

Susanna changed into her bat form as well, but Carolyn hesitated. "Well, someone has to open the vent first." She turned toward the door to the den, then stopped by the sink. "Actually, can I just let you guys out? I don't feel like going out tonight. I'm still feeling kind of sick."

"Oh, come on!" Carl whined. "Don't start getting all soft on us again. We all go out together!" We had been hovering in place, and then we flapped our way into the kitchen. Carolyn seemed to flinch for some reason.

"Really, no," she said, suddenly looking nervous. "I… I just don't want to."

I realized what was going on, and the others must have, too.

"What's wrong, Carolyn?" Tim said, a smile in his voice. "Don't you want to come with us?"

"Yeah," Carl began with a similarly taunting tone. "Why don't you go ahead and change into a bat? I'll open the vent instead."

We flew slightly closer to her, lining up in a semi-circle. She was human. The cure had worked. And while I had changed my mind the previous night about wanting to kill her, I couldn't help but think about the blood that was inside her.

"Is something wrong?" Tim asked, almost laughing.

"You're damn right it is," she said, turning around and reaching for the sink. She quickly grabbed the sprayer, yanking it out by its hose, which made an odd *vvvwwoot* sound. She pointed the nozzle at each of us in turn, her other hand on the faucet, ready to turn it on. "Back off," she said with confidence.

"Ha! Nice try!" Carl said. "You can't hurt us with that! The water isn't even on!"

"Carolyn," Susanna said as she flapped in the air next to me. She was on my left, and Carl and Tim were to my right. Things were still for just a second or two, and I suddenly noticed a faint hissing sound. Too late, I realized what it was.

With a determined look on her face, Carolyn slammed the faucet knob on as she aimed the sprayer, nailing Susanna with a stream of running water.

"Run!" I shouted, realizing after I said it that "Fly!" would have made more sense, but it was a gut reaction.

Carl, Tim, and I quickly flew back into the yellow den, then stopped and looked back. Things had happened so fast that I had not yet digested the implications of them, and I was further surprised by what I saw. Susanna was standing next to Carolyn, shaking her head but quickly regaining her composure. She grabbed Carolyn's arm and pulled her towards the doorway, and they ran through the house.

"Quick! After them!" Tim said, and we flew back through the kitchen and into the dining room. By then, they had made it through the living room and to the base of the stairs, and I heard them pounding their way up and away from us. By the time we reached the stairs, we saw them slamming Susanna's bedroom door, which they then locked.

We changed back into our person forms, and I led Tim and Carl up the stairs, slowly and as silently as possible. As I got closer to the door, I saw that it was different than before. Painted on it was a large, black cross.

"Keep back," I said to the others. "It's a cross."

"No shit," Carl said. "But how the hell did it get there?"

"Carolyn must have painted it on there while we were asleep," Tim said. "Who knows how long she was up before we were!"

I was still trying to process everything. The best I could do was try to be tough and in control.

"Carolyn! Susanna!" I called out, my voice echoing loudly in the small stairwell. "What's going on?"

"Ray, just stop," I heard Carolyn say from the other side of the door. "All of you, just touch the cross and this can all be over with."

"What are you talking about?"

"I told you there was more than one antidote to the potion, Ray," Susanna said. Her voice was muffled slightly by the door, but she was annunciating more, wanting me to understand her. "There's the chemical one, the one that takes a long time to work…" Carolyn said something at that point, but I couldn't make it out. "And then the other, more risky route to take is using the things that normally are supposed to kill vampires. Running water, garlic, crosses, stuff like that."

"What?" Carl shrieked. "You mean those things don't actually kill us? They just turn us back into regular people?"

"So all you three have to do is reach up and touch the cross on the door, and you'll change back," she continued.

"Hell no!" Carl said. Tim agreed.

"How about you just open the door and let us come in and kill you?" Tim asked. It was a joke, but a cruel one. What he really meant was that her asking us to voluntarily give up our vampire status was about as ridiculous of a request.

"Yeah, or wait until we find another way in!" Carl said.

"You really don't want to do that," Susanna said calmly.

Carolyn whispered something, a question to Susanna, which she quietly responded to with a quick "No. Not yet."

I wasn't sure what I felt. Part of me was angry and wanted nothing more than to somehow break down that door and force our way in there, killing and drinking them before they had a chance to fight back. I could see us doing it, but that also made me feel strange. Another part of me was reminiscent of the night before, feeling guilty and not wanting to kill my sisters, to somehow let this entire thing be over. But I couldn't say that to Tim or Carl, who were likely only feeling the blood thirst. I turned to look at them.

"What do we do now?" Carl whispered.

"I don't know," I whispered back.

"Let's regroup downstairs and figure something out," Tim said, and we followed him back down to the living room.

We spoke in hushed tones, occasionally stopping and listening when we heard talking or other noises coming from upstairs. It was a standoff, and we wanted desperately to come out on top. We also wanted to drink blood, and there were two ripe sources of it just a dozen or so feet away.

Tim suggested that we try making our way outside and over to the other side of the house, attacking Susanna's bedroom window as bats. We might be able to throw a rock through the window and make an opening for ourselves, then fly in and attack. This plan failed when we found that none of us were strong enough in our bat forms to lift a big enough rock, much less lob it accurately. A brief attempt at throwing a rock from the patio while we were in our person forms was cut short when King began barking at us furiously and jumping at the gate. How much of an actual threat he was to us was unclear, but none of us was willing to risk a real confrontation with him. I had never heard him growl and snarl like that before, either.

We still hovered at the window for a little while afterwards, though, trying to peer in through the blinds but unable to see much. The garbage bags Susanna had put up before were gone, and in their place were several makeshift wooden crosses, some of which were popsicle sticks tied together with string. They may have been crude, but they were enough of a deterrent.

"Is there some other way we could get into her room?" Tim asked as we flew away from the window and up to the roof. I couldn't think of one. "What about through the air conditioner vents?"

"Yeah, that might work!" Carl said.

"But how can we get into the vents?" I asked. No one knew of a way.

But then I remembered that there was in fact another door to Susanna's room. Our house was not in fact what could be considered a two-story one; the upper part of the house was just a large attic, and Susanna's bedroom was adjoined to it. There had been a fold-away ladder in the hall ceiling that led up to the attic, but this was sealed off by construction workers when they built the extra room and the staircase. Since then, the only way to get into the attic was through a door in Susanna's room, which was similar to the other doors in our house, but it was a little bit smaller and, as I began to realize as I explained everything to Tim and Carl, somewhat lighter weight and flimsier. We just might be able to make our way in through there, if only we could find another way into the attic.

"The chimney!" Carl suggested. "Does that lead into the attic?"

I actually didn't know, but Tim did. "No, Carl," he said. "or else they would burn the house down every winter when they lit a fire." I pictured the attic filling up with smoke, then fire, grateful that such a thing had never happened. But then something else clicked.

"There is a way in!" I said, the squeaking in my bat voice rising in pitch. "I remember Mom saying something about squirrels getting in there."

"So there must be a hole," Tim reasoned. "We just have to find it."

"And fast," Carl added. "I want to get them." He meant Susanna and Carolyn, and I still wasn't sure where I stood on that issue. In a sense, I was just playing along.

After flying around the roof for a little while, we eventually spotted a small, uneven hole on the same side of the house as the basement door. It was just barely wide enough for us to squeeze through, but we managed it. It was completely dark in there, so we had to use our glowing eyes to see where we were going. We flapped along, making our way among the various boxes and piles of old clothes, toys, and other things that our family had decided over the years were no longer needed in our daily lives but were not yet ready to be thrown away.

We made our way along what was the upstairs equivalent of Carolyn's bedroom, then my bedroom, then the hallway. Occasionally, we whispered to each other, then urged each other to keep quiet. We had to have the element of surprise if this were to work.

As we reached the door that led to Susanna's room, we saw that our moves had been anticipated. Just like the other door, this one was painted with a large cross.

Carl changed into his person form, slamming his feet down onto the wooden floor as he did so. "You stupid bitches!" he shrieked. "Let us in!" He balled up his fists and then lifted up his foot, preparing to kick at the door.

I quickly changed form and pulled him back by his arms, causing the two of us to topple back onto a pile of old encyclopedias. He struggled against me for a bit, and I told him to calm down. He stopped fighting me and settled down, but he was still quite angry. Tim, meanwhile, turned on the light using a switch by the door.

The attic was small and cramped, and there wasn't a lot of room to move around. All around us were unpainted wooden beams, some of them with exposed nails that had not been hammered all the way in. Scant electrical fixtures were scattered throughout the attic, providing minimal light. The ceiling, such as it was, was sloped and closer to our heads than a normal one, but we were still short enough to fit into the small space more comfortably than an adult might. Nevertheless, it still felt imposing and somewhat claustrophobic, which wasn't helping any of our moods.

A noise came from the door, a small scraping sound. I saw a small, metal tube as it began to poke out through the crack at the bottom of the door. I wasn't sure what it was, but somehow, I knew it was dangerous. I called for the others to get back, pushing them in the direction from which we had come. From behind us, I heard another strange sound, a repetitive sort of puffing. We looked back and saw what looked like a cloud of thick dust filling the area near the door.

"What the shit is that?" Carl asked.

"Garlic powder," Tim said simply. "We have to get out of here."

Outside and on the ground outside the basement door, Carl continued to express his rage at my sisters, and I felt some of it, too. Even at the best of times, I hated it when they had me at a disadvantage, but I wasn't really myself at the moment. None of us were. We needed to feed, and soon.

I led them away from the house to find victims, this time feeling more confident in my ability to find my way around. Although I had gotten lost the night before, I at least knew the way back to the main road, the one that would eventually lead to our school. Surely there would be some people along there, I thought.

After a while, we spotted three people on the sidewalk, and I directed Tim and Carl to attack them as bats. The sooner we could get back to the house, the better. I also found that I liked being in charge, which seemed to have happened by default.

There was one woman in the group, which Tim took, and Carl and I killed the two men. Killing one of the men instead of the woman was a conscious decision on my part; I wanted to be reminded of last night's killing of that girl as little as possible. Drinking in bat form instead of person form seemed to help with that, too.

Getting the blood we needed also had the desired effect of helping us feel less agitated, so now we could think more clearly. Before going back to the house, we perched in a pine tree to try to work out some plan of attack. Unfortunately, we were not really the military geniuses we liked to pretend. Seeing bad guys — or good guys, for that matter — come up with brilliant plans on TV was one thing, but the truth was that we were still just kids. We wanted to believe that we could outsmart my older sisters and find some way to beat them, to win this final stage of the game, but we just were not capable of coming up with anything sufficient.

The best idea I could muster was to sneak back into the house, at which point I would make my way to the fuse box and turn off the electricity.

"Great idea!" Carl said.

"But what good will that do?" Tim asked.

"It... um..." I realized I wasn't sure just what that would accomplish. "Well it will probably scare them, for one thing."

"Yeah, and make them feel more helpless!" Carl said.

"I guess," Tim said.

"Plus we'll have the advantage of being able to see in the dark when they can't," Carl added.

"Yeah, but it still doesn't solve the problem of how to get them to come out of that room," Tim said.

"Maybe they'll come out to try and turn the power back on," I said. I knew that I was grasping at straws, but I tried to remain optimistic.

"Yeah!" Carl said, his bat voice screeching higher than usual. "And then when they come down the stairs, boom! We get them!"

"It's worth a try," I said, but deep down, I wondered. It wasn't just that I was doubting our chances of success; I was also unsure of whether or not I really wanted us to succeed.

I continued to ponder these feelings as we flew back, not daring to mention them to Tim or Carl. Once I had been satiated by the earlier kill, the more rational side of my mind resurfaced, and I was again questioning the idea of killing my sisters. Plotting to kill just Carolyn had been more simple, but even that was something I had become unsure about because of more recent events. And with Susanna also being on the other side, the stakes seemed higher. For the very first time, I wondered what might happen when our parents got back, if we succeeded, that is.

The thought of that made me freeze inside, and I suddenly began to seriously doubt what we were doing. But I still didn't know a way out. Any weakness shown on my part would make Tim and Carl turn against me, and then I would be all alone.

As we got closer to the house, we went over our plan again, what there was of it. Hopefully, the front door would still be unlocked, and we could sneak back inside through there, cut off the electricity, then wait as bats on the stairwell for when Susanna and Carolyn came out.

We descended over the front lawn as usual, preparing to land on the porch. But before that could happen, I was distracted by a sudden hissing sound. It took me a couple of seconds to recognize what it was: Someone had turned on the sprinklers.

Jets of water spewed through the air at us, and we did our best to dodge them, but only Tim and I managed to. A few feet from the ground, Carl was caught by a stream of running water, and the vampire potion within him was immediately cancelled out. With a quick flash of light, what was once a bat was now a human boy, tumbling from the air and onto the ground. He rolled as he landed, and I wondered if he had broken any bones.

More importantly, I wondered if I could manage to escape the sprinklers. Despite my misgivings about the overall plan, there still seemed to be some survival instinct driving me. I spotted Carolyn crouched down in the bushes outside my bedroom window, which was where the valve controlling the sprinklers was located. Susanna was coming out from behind another bush and running over toward Carl, who was lying on the ground. I had an urge to go after her, the vampire in me still wanting to win this battle. But because the sprinklers oscillated and were spraying water around in ways I could not predict, I feared that I too might be nailed at any second.

I spotted Tim flapping randomly around and trying to avoid getting hit as well. I called out to him, "Quick! Get to the driveway!"

"Fly up first!" he shouted back, and I realized he was right. If we could just get high enough into the air, we could avoid the sprinklers altogether.

We met above the house and hovered in the air, unsure what to do next. I looked back down at the lawn and saw the sprinklers continuing to spray away, alternating between putting out steady streams of water and ticking repeatedly, sending out small spurts. It had been a brilliant move by Susanna and Carolyn, who had by then reached Carl and were helping him off the ground. They were also occasionally getting blasted by the sprinklers, but they didn't seem to care.

"All right, we're not beaten yet," Tim said. "While they're distracted, let's break in through one of the windows on the side of the house. Then we'll hide for a while, letting them think we're gone. When they least expect it, we'll get them."

While part of me was impressed by his sudden initiative, something about it bothered me, too. I wasn't even sure why. Maybe it was because I was supposed to be the leader, even though there were only two of us left. Or maybe I really was just ready for this whole thing to be over. We were outnumbered, so maybe it was time to give up. All we would really have to do would be to fly back down to those sprinklers and let ourselves get hit, but I could tell from Tim's bloodthirsty tone that he wasn't going to go for such an idea.

After thinking this through, I said, "Okay, good idea. Follow me." I led him over to the side of the house where the driveway was, well out of the range of the sprinklers.

"Okay," he whispered, "now we just have to find a window to bust in that they won't notice, and then we can slip in."

"This way," I whispered, leading him towards the kitchen window.

"No!" he hissed. "They might see that one!"

"Trust me," I said, and the irony of those words was not lost on me.

Beneath the kitchen window was a faucet that was occasionally used, most often with a hose for washing cars or watering plants. But one time, Carolyn had played a trick on me using this faucet, a time when the hose wasn't hooked up.

"What we need to do is this," I said quietly, beckoning him to come closer so he could hear me.

Once he had leaned in closely enough, I quickly reached for the faucet and turned it on, holding two fingers tightly over the opening so that the water sprayed up and onto both of us. Suddenly, I felt like a cool rush of water had passed over my entire body, a wave of peace and relief rushing through me, the feeling passing after only a few seconds. But I knew what it meant: The vampire potion had been neutralized, and I was a regular human being again.

Tim was cured as well, and he laughed. "You…" was all he could manage to get out. Then he just sighed and laughed again, taking off his glasses and wiping the water off of them with his shirt. "Well, whatever. Are you going to leave that running or what?"

"Oh," I said, laughing. No longer able to see in the dark, I had to fumble around for a bit before finding the faucet again, which I then turned off.

We walked back over to the driveway, not very far from the carport and the backyard. All of a sudden, King was barking at us through the fence, having heard us. Susanna, Carolyn, and Carl came running up the driveway toward us, and I saw that they were each carrying crosses. Carolyn also had a small canister in one of her hands, which I would later learn contained garlic powder.

"It's okay," I said to them, holding up my hands in surrender. "We're done."

Back inside, there was an overall feeling of relief among the group. Despite the fact that we had been trying to kill each other all that time, no one seemed to harbor any bad feelings or major resentments.

"Yeah, um, sorry about… all of that," Carl said. He was rubbing his wrist from time to time, his only injury from the fall he had taken when he was changed back.

"Don't worry about it," Susanna said. "Under the influence of the potion, you couldn't really help it. None of us could."

"We're lucky things turned out as well as they did, though," Carolyn said. Out of the entire group, she seemed like the most likely candidate for holding a grudge, but she didn't appear to. Like the rest of us, she just seemed glad that it was all over. By the end of the night, which came early this time because we were exhausted, we were joking and laughing about the whole thing.

We took some time to clean up a bit, which included taking down the garbage bags from the windows. While Tim and Carl were in another part of the house doing that, Susanna, Carolyn, and I went upstairs, where I saw some of the anti-vampire weapons they had stockpiled to defend themselves. Mostly these were homemade crosses, though there were also a couple of wooden stakes.

Carolyn made it a point to show me the bellows, which normally resided in the red den by the fireplace. Instead, she had filled them with garlic powder.

"Pretty cool idea, huh?" she said. "I mean, aside from the fact that it didn't really work."

I laughed. "Well, it kinda did! We just got out of the way in time."

"Yeah, Carolyn," Susanna said from the other side of the room, where she was gathering up all of the vampire potion ingredients and putting them away. "You might want to make sure to get all of that powder out of there. Otherwise, good luck explaining to Dad this winter why the fire smells like garlic."

Carolyn frowned, then said she would do it tomorrow and needed to go to bed soon. "And I'll get these doors repainted then, too, to hide the crosses," she said.

"I don't know, I kind of like them!" Susanna said.

"Really?" I asked.

"No." We laughed. Things were quickly getting back to normal.

Falling asleep that night was not very difficult, though I was still kind of wound up from everything. Fortunately, fatigue won out. As I drifted off, I focused mainly on the fun aspects of the previous week, the camaraderie we felt, the amazing abilities we had, and how we had gotten away with it all. It felt like something spectacular, not that we had committed horrible atrocities that we would later regret. The scale of my comprehension just wasn't big enough for that, not yet.

The following day was Saturday, and it was time for Tim and Carl to go home. It had been an amazing week, and we were still talking about it.

"All right, you two," Susanna began. We were in the living room, waiting for their parents to arrive. "And this goes for you too, Ray. I do hope I don't have to tell you that you're sworn to secrecy. No bragging to anyone else about all of this."

"We know," Tim said, a tinge of regret in his voice, but it was mostly playful.

"But it was still really cool," Carl said. I agreed.

Carolyn had just walked into the room and sat down, wanting to put in her two cents. "Yeah. If anyone ever finds out what we did, well, to say that we would be in huge trouble is the understatement of the year."

We talked about various other things, and even though we still had about two months left of summer, we found ourselves talking about the upcoming school year. Susanna would soon be leaving for Charleston, and Carolyn would be starting ninth grade in the fall.

"What do you think fourth grade is going to be like?" I asked.

"Probably the same old crap, I'd say," Carl said.

"Yeah, except you're not going to be in our class this year!" Tim pointed out. The grades were divided into two classes each, and we already knew which ones we would be in and who our teachers would be.

"Do you think Mrs. Holloway will be a bitch?" Carl asked.

"Carl, I've told you about cussing," Carolyn said.

"What about it?" Carl puffed himself up, but again, we were all mostly joking.

"Keep it up and you'll end up going to… to, um…"

"To where, Carolyn?" I asked, smiling.

She paused, then took on a mock serious expression and leaned forward, saying, "You'll go to *BEEEEP!!*" We laughed.

"Hey," I said, "maybe that's what you should do instead of cussing, Carl! Just say 'BEEP!' all the time instead." He just rolled his eyes.

"But, speaking of school," Tim said, bringing us back on topic, "well, I kind of wonder about something."

"What?" I asked.

"What do we do if the teacher tells us to write an essay called 'How I Spent My Summer Vacation?'"

PART TWO

It was pretty much inevitable that we would use the potion again to become vampires, which we did two years later. We had gotten away with it once already, and that felt like a big accomplishment. The five of us had a secret, and that also felt really neat. As far as the bad things that went on that first summer were concerned, none of us dwelled on those very much. Instead, we only seemed to remember the good parts and the fun stuff, when we remembered it at all, that is.

It wasn't like we each went around day to day with this weighing on our minds, or at least, that wasn't the case for me. Over time, recalling specific details of that week became more difficult, kind of like trying to recall a really good dream. The killing and brutality aspects of it all seemed to slip through the cracks in my mind, but I was still aware of the need for secrecy.

There was one major difference when we got together to become vampires again in 1985, though: Carl was not part of the group. Over the two intervening years, he and I had drifted apart and were no longer friends, or at least, we certainly were not as close as we had been before. The reasons for this varied, and most of them might seem pretty trivial by adult standards. But when we were kids, small things could happen over time, things that would cause one to turn against their friends and declare them enemies instead.

Probably the first thing to drive Carl and me apart was the fact that we were in separate classes in fourth grade. We had known about this ahead of time and had talked about it over the summer, but we thought we would remain friends anyway. I saw both him and Tim a few more times before school started, including on my birthday, which was in July, about a week before Susanna's.

When the school year began, things were fine between me, Carl, and Tim, but it did not take very long for things to change. The separation of the students between the two classes — referred to as 4-A and 4-B — was very pronounced. The only time the two groups mixed was at recess. Even at lunch, the classes were still separated, and we were all assigned seats just as we were in the classroom. Class itself was almost entirely spent in the same room day after day with most of the various subjects being taught by our homeroom teacher, Mrs. Patterson.

After a while, it just felt natural to regard the kids of 4-B, Mrs. Holloway's class, as different from us. It's not like we were specifically taught this separatism or told to think this way; it just developed. This would happen every school year as the students were juggled and mixed up, presumably arbitrarily, and everyone's friendships changed and shifted as a result.

New kids, those who had just started at the school, had things even worse. It seemed like they were part of neither group, and it was not unusual for a student to be referred to as "new" for the entire school year, not being accepted as legitimate until the following year. By then, if they were lucky, there were more new kids to be ostracized, and those would have to make their own attempts at fitting in. It didn't help that we were just naturally mean anyway, each of us struggling to be cool and accepted, forming our little groups and cliques based on whatever somewhat arbitrary boundaries we came up with: what people looked like, what clothes they wore, songs or TV shows they liked, how funny or strange they were, and so on.

There was one new kid in particular whom I singled out for ridicule, but I can't rationally say why. He was new, different, and therefore the enemy, and I did my best to make his life hell every chance I got. This wasn't an all-day affair; since he was in 4-B, I only encountered him at recess. His name was Dennis Williams, and I didn't like him.

He was kind of fat and awkward, very pale, and spoke with a lisp. Because of this, I began taunting him by calling him "Dennith Williamth." He hated that, which of course just egged me on. He also had red hair, something else I would point out. It wasn't like there was anything all that unusual about red hair, but the key to picking on someone was to point out any little thing you could, then insist that it was worthy of ridicule. I could just have easily have pointed out that he was wearing blue shoes with Velcro straps on them, a style that had been popular the previous year. So I did.

All of this made sense to me at the time, or perhaps it's more honest to say that I didn't really think about it this thoroughly at that age. It was just fun to be mean. Perhaps my efforts to belittle Dennis were an attempt to assert myself as an alpha male, or maybe it felt empowering to act like a jerk. My efforts in that realm were not just focused on classmates I didn't like; I also mouthed off to my teachers plenty of times, seeing myself as much more clever than them. This may have been typical behavior for a fourth grader, but it was probably enhanced by my previous experience with the vampire potion.

That was my big secret, and even when other people, adult or my own age, thought they had me at a disadvantage, I knew that deep down, I always had something hidden within that they couldn't touch. *You think you're so bad for telling me off and making me miss recess for talking back to you, Mrs. Patterson? Well, what you don't know is that my friends and I were vampires last summer, we killed people, and we got away with it.* Thoughts like that sometimes ran through my head on my darker days, but I didn't dare say them aloud (nor even that articulately in my own head). As naive as I was, I was still smart enough to know that to do so would be suicide. I still didn't have a clue about the enormity of our crimes, nor was I capable of comprehending the larger consequences of what we had done. Moreover, I also had no idea how much worse things were going to get in the years to come; that would happen later.

For now, I was content to be a young, sarcastic boy with a big secret and perhaps an even bigger attitude. So I entertained myself with that as much as I saw fit, but I still did my schoolwork as assigned. I wasn't a complete delinquent. In fact, I tended to make fairly good grades, though usually not as good as Tim's. He was the brain of the class, but this was still early enough in our school careers before such smart kids would start being branded as "nerds" and seen as contemptible. Our standards for hate were still primitive. They barely even made sense, really, which goes back to my hatred for Dennis.

Dennis wasn't the only new kid in our grade that year. There was a girl in 4-A, my class, who didn't even make it through her first day. This wasn't specifically because of anything I did, though.

Our teacher asked us that first school day about our summer vacations, which prompted me to look over at Tim. He peered at me over his glasses, giving me a look that seemed to say, *Don't you dare say a word,* but with a smile.

Various children in the class raised their hands and talked about trips to the beach, visiting relatives, funny things that happened to them, and the like. The teacher prompted us with more questions whenever there was an extended silence, and then she ended up calling on me.

"Oh, not much," I said, giving off an air of boredom. "Tim and Carl came over to my house and played video games a few times. It was fun."

"Tim and who?" Mrs. Patterson asked.

"Carl Hendricks. He's in 4-B." I said it like she was the dumbest person in the world for not knowing that.

"Oh, I see," she said, being perfectly polite. By the end of the school year, she would be completely sick of my sarcastic attitude, and she would make no attempt to hide that. "Anything else anyone wants to share?" she asked, looking eagerly around the room.

"What about all those vampires?" a boy called out from the back of the room, his hand reaching for the ceiling. It was David, a goofy, rather dumb kid I had never really liked. Even so, my heart jumped a little due to what he had said.

"Oh, like whatever," a girl next to him said. "That wasn't real." This was Laura, a girl I had also never liked, mostly because she was a snobby little brat, the kind of girl who would be the first to point at you and tattle if you did something wrong. She had gotten me into trouble more than once in the past.

"Yeah it was!" David insisted. "All these people died!"

The class began to get riled up, and the teacher tried to hush everyone with a vertical motion of her hands.

"I really don't think…" she began, "What's your name again?"

"Um, Bob," David said, which prompted several giggles from the rest of us. I may not have liked David very much, but this was a joke that got played on new teachers several times over the years, trying to trick them into calling us by the wrong names. I found it funny, and I looked over at Tim, expecting him to also be laughing. He wasn't.

"Well, Bob," Mrs. Patterson said, either not getting the joke or choosing to ignore it, "I don't think that's an appropriate topic of conversation for this class."

"Why not?" David continued defiantly. "I think it's pretty interesting!"

"Interesting?" Laura asked. "Are you kidding? I heard that a bunch of wild animals got loose. And yeah, some people got killed. But it wasn't something stupid like vampires. There's no such thing."

"Oh yeah?" David blurted back.

The debate might have continued further, but everyone was distracted by a strange sound from the corner of the classroom, something like a short screech. Everyone got quiet, and then I heard what sounded like very quick breathing. Eventually, all of the students directed their attention to the source of the noise: the new girl. She was leaning forward, her head almost touching her desk, and her face was partly hidden by a tightly balled fist. It didn't take me long to realize what was happening: She was crying.

The teacher walked quickly over to the girl, then asked her something I couldn't quite hear, putting a hand on her shoulder. The girl just shook her head, her hands spreading from fists into palms to further cover her face. Mrs. Patterson squatted down and continued speaking very softly, and the girl responded in an inaudible whisper.

After a few moments, the girl was being led out of the classroom by the hand, her other hand covering her face as she fought back more tears and possibly embarrassment, too. She and Mrs. Patterson talked just outside the door for a minute or two, but I still couldn't make out what they were saying.

"What's that all about?" one of the students asked a friend.

"Yeah, who's the new crybaby?" another said. Some of the other kids laughed.

I didn't know what to make of this, either. I had barely noticed the girl or cared who she was when the teacher introduced her to the class that morning, and as far as I was concerned, she was just some kind of weirdo. Weren't we getting too old to be crying over stupid things?

Eventually, Mrs. Patterson came back inside, but without the girl. She told us that she was being sent home, though at first she didn't say why. When the class prompted her with more questions, she paused, choosing her words carefully before continuing.

"Her father passed away this summer. She's still very upset about it. So all of that talk about killing and vampires was not, as I said, appropriate for classroom discussion." Her face was serious, a sharp contrast from the eager, somewhat fake smile she had worn earlier.

I looked over at Tim, but he was looking down at his desk, avoiding eye contact with anyone. I then looked back at David, who looked more confused than ashamed. He didn't appear to think he had done anything wrong.

At recess, I talked to Tim and Carl about the incident, but away from the rest of the children, making sure no one heard us. I wondered if the reason the girl's father had died was because of us, if he had been one of our victims when we were vampires.

"Not necessarily," Tim said. "He might have died some other way, and then the mention of people dying might have set her off crying. Who knows?"

"Sounds like a typical wimpy girl to me," Carl said. "Always so prissy and delicate, you know…"

I laughed a little in agreement. I didn't like girls; we were still a couple of years away from the point when puberty would set in and we would start to find them intriguing as opposed to repulsive or annoying. "Yeah," I said. "I mean, lots of people die all the time. What gives her the right to make such a big deal about it?"

It was then that I spotted Dennis for the first time, and I asked Carl who he was.

"Some new kid," he said. "I think his sister is in sixth or seventh grade."

"Man, check out the cool outfit!" Tim said sarcastically. His clothes were slightly different from what the rest of us usually wore. We didn't have school uniforms, but most of the boys wore blue jeans and collared, knit shirts. That was a recurring theme at our school: If you wore something different, you were weird.

"We should go say hello," Carl said, grinning.

And so began a year-long rivalry with the new kid Dennis, my friends and I being cruel to him for no good reason. He tried to shrug it off in the beginning, but soon enough, he started to fight back, coming up with insults of his own. Sometimes, our confrontations culminated into physical ones, but not often. Mostly it was just a contest of trying to out-attitude each other, so to speak. Had I actually had any classes with him, I would have picked on him more often, but we were limited to the times we encountered each other at recess or in the hallways between classes. Whether we avoided each other or intentionally looked for confrontation varied.

The crying girl, by the way, never came back to school after that first day, though at the time of the incident, I had figured that she would be back in class the following day. Instead, I never saw her again. It was just as well for her, really, given how thin-skinned she appeared to be. She probably wouldn't have survived the harsh treatment the rest of us heaped onto each other.

Over the course of the school year, Dennis managed to make a couple of friends, which meant that they were also my enemies and deserving of my contempt. Tim sometimes joined me in my taunting of them, but he wasn't all that into it. Carl certainly was, but as time went on, he and I also started to clash.

At first, it was over little disagreements, silly things that we would find to argue about, like my opinion of his trying to learn how to breakdance or do Michael Jackson's famous moonwalk. He insisted that it was cool, but I thought he just looked stupid, and I found myself embarrassed to be around him when he demonstrated his attempts. Dennis also picked on Carl for this once at recess, and it bothered me that for a moment, I felt like I was on his side, not Carl's. This led Carl to tell us both off, his usual swearing included.

That was another thing that changed over time, his swearing. His teacher, Mrs. Holloway, was very strict, and Carl got into trouble enough times that he eventually learned to curb his foul mouth, substituting other words for curses whenever he could remember to. This led me to ridicule him further, as I thought he just sounded like an idiot when he would say things like "dag" instead of "damn," "aspirin" instead of "ass," and another one that never really made sense to me: "Oh, foot!"

Overall, he became more and more like a stranger to me, someone I used to like but no longer wanted to be around. Sometimes, we would sort of get along when we both picked on Dennis, but that also tapered off. We may have had our dislike of him in common, but by the end of the year, we disliked each other just as much.

Something odd happened when fifth grade began. I was in 5-B this year, and so was Dennis. By some cruel twist of fate, not only were he and I stuck in the same class together, but we were also assigned desks right next to each other.

When we first sat down and discovered this, we both groaned dramatically and said, almost in unison, "Oh, no!"

"Is there a problem, boys?" our new teacher, Ms. Barnwell, asked.

"Can't I sit somewhere else?" I asked. "I don't want to sit next to Dennis. He smells." He didn't, but it was a standard insult, plus it was a set-up that I was hoping he would fall for.

"I don't smell!" he said, his lisp making it sound like he said, "I don't thmell."

"Then what else do you do with your nose?"

He faltered, realizing I'd gotten him. He narrowed his eyes at me, which were already pretty small to begin with, a feature further magnified by his pudgy face. When he squinted, his eyes practically disappeared.

"That's enough, you two," Ms. Barnwell said. "I'm sorry, but the seats are assigned as they are for a reason."

"What reason?" I asked.

She pursed her lips. "I'll explain later. But the point is that you two are just going to have to learn to get along."

The strange thing was that we did, and very quickly, too. While we picked at each other initially, by the end of the first week of school, we were cracking jokes and getting along, though reluctantly. It turned out that we had more in common than we had ever bothered to find out.

We liked a lot of the same music and TV shows, plus Dennis seemed to be a bit mysterious at times, which I found intriguing. He would hint occasionally at having some kind of secret, then change the subject if I pried too closely. I wasn't sure if he actually did have something to hide or if he just acted that way so people would think he was more interesting. And while we did still occasionally pick on each other, sometimes bringing up old fights from the previous year, for the most part, we were pretty good friends as the weeks and months progressed.

Carl was also in our class, but he sat on the other side of the room. That didn't stop him from occasionally blurting out mean things either about me or about Dennis, whom he still hated. He probably hated him even more once Dennis and I became friends, as that might have seemed like even more of a betrayal. He especially liked to pick on him for his lisp, which I eventually stopped doing when he confided to me that it was something that really bothered him, something he couldn't help and was embarrassed about, though he didn't like to admit it. Sometimes, when Carl did say or do mean things to Dennis, he would end up getting in trouble, which Dennis and I liked seeing.

Tim had sort of bounced between me and Carl throughout fourth grade in terms of loyalty, but by fifth grade, he tended to stick by me, joining me in my disdain for Carl. Sometimes, he tried to play the mediator and encourage everyone to calm down and be nice, but that never really worked. Either Carl or I would start hurling insults, and arguments would ensue, sometimes leading to physical fights. These usually only lasted a few seconds at most, quickly broken apart by other students. Any physical conflict that lasted longer than that would attract the attention of our teachers, which would lead to disciplinary action. As much as we all disagreed with each other and liked to fight, there seemed to be this unspoken agreement that everyone wanted to stay out of trouble. These interactions usually happened at recess or at lunch, which this year did not have assigned seating, leaving us to sit where we chose to.

Tim and I of course still shared the vampire secret, but we didn't talk about it often. It was more like a silent bond between us, something we knew that no one else was allowed to, which itself was kind of fun.

But there was also the fact that Carl knew about it, and the more he and I butted heads, the more I feared that he might betray the rest of us and blab everything to the world out of spite.

This came to a head during the height of what we would later refer to as "The Club Wars," something that happened during the second half of fifth grade. Tim, Dennis, and I decided to form a club, but there wasn't really much of a purpose to it other than to say that we were a club and could include or exclude other kids as we saw fit. Carl, along with anyone else we didn't like, was not allowed to be in it. I was the leader, and it was up to me to decide who could or could not join.

In response, Carl formed his own club, its sole purpose being to rival ours. Initially, he did it mostly to make fun of us, saying that it was stupid for us to have a club that didn't really do anything. But very quickly, the rivalry between the two groups became intense, and it became a competition to see which side could recruit the most members. This included both boys and girls, even though prior to this, the boys and the girls tended to stay separate from each other. The girls who did get involved in this conflict tended to be somewhat tomboyish, while the ones into more girly things avoided the situation altogether.

After a few weeks, more than half of the entire fifth grade was involved, and once physical confrontations began to occur, the teachers stepped in and forbade us to have clubs, and that was the end of that.

At one point before this enforced dissolution occurred, I wound up alone in the boys' restroom with Carl, which was awkward given our dislike for each other. Even so, it provided a rare opportunity for us to speak privately about the state of things.

At first, we gave each other dirty looks and were annoyed to have happened to have ended up in the same room. After taking care of our reasons for being in the restroom in the first place, we each made our way to the sinks.

"Dork-head," Carl said to me as he washed his hands. This insult had become Carl's standard, an epithet he used so often that other people, including me, sometimes hurled it back at him while imitating the way he said it. He tended to hold out the second syllable for an extended period of time, sounding goofier than the person he was trying to ridicule. My gut reaction was to do so now, to make fun of him, but I held back.

As he pulled a paper towel from the dispenser on the wall and wiped his hands, his back to me, I said, "Look." He turned around, still holding the paper towel. "As much as we keep fighting and all, I hope you're not going to tell anyone about the whole vampire thing from a couple of years ago." I half expected him to lash out at me and tell me that he had already told half the class.

Instead, his face lit up with a smile, which was unexpected. "Oh, hell no! Are you kidding?" He giggled, but then he caught himself, trying to appear tough. "Don't worry. I'm not that stupid."

"Well, good," I said. Then I couldn't resist the temptation and asked, "How stupid are you?"

Rather than getting mad, he just rolled his eyes and laughed. "Not half as dumb as you," he said, smiling slyly. He was taller than me, and he liked to bear down on me whenever we had these stand-offs, which were usually in the presence of other kids. He assumed the same stance as usual, but rather than feeling threatened or defiant, I was amused.

I started to say something mean, but then I just laughed. "You know, this whole thing, these clubs and all…" I trailed off, not sure how to articulate what I was thinking. But he got it.

"It's kind of fun!" he said. For a moment, it seemed like we were back in 1983, two friends enjoying being bad together. Still, despite briefly getting along at this moment, once we were back out among our friends again, we were at each other's throats. We were used to that by then, and our friends expected it.

But he was right about it being fun. Before the teachers made us dissolve the clubs, part of the enjoyment was having these two warring groups of kids being so mean to each other day after day. The other part of the fun was that our teachers had no idea what we were doing, why so many of the children stopped playing normal games at recess and started gathering in increasingly larger groups on the far side of the playground. Everyone involved on both sides liked being secretive about what we were up to. In truth, what we had formed weren't really clubs but gangs. But all of that came to an end once the grown-ups stepped in.

My bringing up the vampire incident with Carl that day was a rare thing. Keeping things quiet about what happened that summer was paramount, and not talking about it had become the norm. This meant that it sometimes faded from our minds completely. On the rare occasions when I did think about it, I mostly just thought of the supernatural abilities we had and how fun it was to get away with being so bad.

The Club Wars also brought out that feeling in me, and they were a reminder of how cool it was to feel separate and yet more powerful, much as we had when we were vampires. That started me toying with the idea of getting everyone together and taking the potion again. It would be so cool to do it, I thought, but there was a problem. I didn't want Carl to be part of the group this time, but he knew about the potion. And while Dennis didn't know about the potion because I hadn't told him, I wondered if maybe he could be part of the group this time instead.

I struggled with the idea for a while, weighing the pros and cons in my head. Could Dennis handle it? Probably. In terms of all of the blood and killing involved, he seemed to have no qualms with that. For his birthday in November, he'd had a slumber party, and part of that involved watching videotapes of some of the *Friday the 13th* movies, which he liked. All of the boys at the party, which included Tim and myself, were supposed to be too young to watch horror movies like that, but Dennis's father was okay with renting the videotapes and letting us watch them.

I had been nervous about this, having developed a sort of second-hand fear of horror movies through Carolyn. When she watched them with her friends, she got so scared that she made me sleep in her room with her, afraid that she would have bad dreams. I adopted this attitude from her, as I did with many of her tastes and opinions, seeing her as older and wiser, someone to look up to. I was afraid that if I watched such scary, R-rated movies, I too might have bad dreams. But letting on about my fear of this to the other boys at the party would have branded me a wimp, so I kept it private.

As it turned out, the movies weren't terribly frightening. We got caught up in them and had fun being scared, but for the most part, we knew they were fake. Dennis saw them as something to be laughed at, not afraid of. His outlook spread to the rest of us that night, and his father, who stayed in the room with us and held the remote control, laughed along with us, encouraging us to have fun. Because these films were geared toward older teenagers, there were occasional references to sex, even scenes vaguely depicting intercourse itself, but Dennis's father was careful to fast-forward the tape whenever things got too graphic in that realm. As kids, we didn't really care or feel deprived. We were slightly aware of the existence of sex and that it was something that older people did, but for the most part, we weren't interested. Our minds and bodies weren't ready for that kind of thing yet, so we just glossed over it. We were much more interested in the next time that the masked, ax-wielding Jason would claim another victim, some dumb teenager walking around in the dark amidst spooky music, their gruesome fate awaiting them in whatever form the filmmakers could come up with. After a while, some of us (especially Dennis) were rooting for the murderer, joking about how we wanted the stupid kids in the movie to get killed.

"Don't go in there, you idiot!" one of us would shout at the screen.

"Why don't you just run and not call out, 'Is someone there?' like, 'Hey, bad guy! Come kill me!'" Tim remarked at one point.

"She's in there, Jason! Get her!" I joked.

"God, what a bunch of dumb-asses!" Dennis said one time, and I held back from making fun of how it sounded like he said "dumb-athith." I was more concerned that he might get in trouble with his father for saying that, and he did get a stern look from him, but that was it.

Once we got to where we were laughing at and enjoying the movies, most of us were even cheering whenever a murder would happen. When it did, often there was blood spraying all over the place, and there was a part of me that reacted, remembering the real killings the others and I had done just over a year before. What happened on the TV screen was over the top and ridiculous, and I knew that things didn't really happen like that. But I couldn't say so for fear of letting on just how or why I might know that, instead going along with the screams and laughs of the rest of the boys as they reacted to the movie.

Another movie we tried to watch that night was one that Dennis's father insisted on, some old one from the 1960s or '70s. "If you're going to watch these Jason movies," he said, "you should at least see one of the classics." He wanted to get in on the joke of laughing at and enjoying horror movies along with the rest of us, but for the most part, I resented his presence and intrusion. The movie he showed us was just cheesy and dumb, full of weird looking people in out of date fashions, and the overacting was terrible.

"What, you don't like Hammer Horror films?" he asked, trying to joke around with us, but we just didn't get it. I thought he was using the word "hammer" as an adjective or outdated slang word, not knowing that he was in fact describing a particular genre of film. Instead, he just seemed like another example of an adult trying too hard to connect with people our age, something I had seen other parents and teachers do from time to time.

Dennis protested more than the rest of us, clearly embarrassed by all of this, and eventually, his dad relented and stopped the tape. Just a few minutes before this happened, it became clear that the movie was about vampires, but the pacing of the movie was so slow that it seemed to take forever to get to that point. About twenty minutes seemed to be wasted on men with weird coifs and women with thick eyelashes and straight hair talking melodramatically about nothing. Once the vampire aspect became apparent, I was slightly interested, and Tim and I exchanged knowing looks. But the movie was just too stupid for us to sit through.

Still, a seed was planted in my mind that night, eventually leading me to want to get Dennis to be part of the vampire group once I thought about getting it together again. I was still unsure, though, given that Carl and I were no longer friends.

"Well, why don't you just ask Dennis and not tell Carl?" Carolyn said. "Doesn't seem like a big deal to me."

"But what if he tells someone?" I asked. "If we start going around as vampires again and he sees that on the news, well…?"

Carolyn sighed, looking impatient. "He already said he wasn't going to tell anyone. And do you think he wants to get in trouble, too? Even if he's not with us this time, he's still culpable for his actions last time." I had never heard the word "culpable" before, but I figured out its meaning from the context.

"I guess," I said.

This was one of the many things Carolyn and I discussed when I brought up the idea to her of taking the potion again. Because of the way things had gone in 1983, she was the first person I approached. I half expected her to say no, then was surprised when she didn't. If she had, I probably would have dropped the notion altogether.

Instead, she seemed rather nonchalant about the whole thing, sitting in the yellow den with our cat, Crowley, in her lap. As she stroked him, he kept his eyes closed most of the time, occasionally halfway opening them to peer at me from across the room. He was a plain looking white cat, but he had an air of mystery about him that was sometimes unnerving. My mistrust of him probably also had to do with the small scar on my cheek, one put there by another white cat many years ago. But in time, I grew to like him just fine.

He was new to our family, a cat Carolyn had taken in after a friend of hers had been forced to give him up in January. The girl's family had moved overseas, and her parents wouldn't let her keep Crowley, so we ended up with him. King had in fact come to us in much the same way a few years earlier, with another friend of Carolyn's moving into a smaller home, the family being forced to admit that there just wasn't room in their new place for a huge, lumbering St. Bernard.

King, unfortunately, had to be put down several months prior to this conversation. It was a decision our father had made, and not one that I forgave him for very quickly. King was already old when we got him, and he began to develop a problem with his hip that caused him a lot of pain. This led to him becoming even more aggressive than before, so much that he lunged at my father one afternoon during a thunderstorm, teeth bared. The only thing that stopped him was the fact that he was in his pen at the time. Thunder had always frightened him and put him on edge, but with this added arthritic pain, he was beginning to lose his self control.

Fearing that the dog might turn on me or Carolyn and injure one of us (or worse), our father had King put to sleep despite our objections. I was angry at him for weeks because of this, and Carolyn and I both refused his offer to get a new puppy to make up for it. Part of that was just to spite him, but I also felt like doing so would be a betrayal of King's memory. I eventually got over it, just as I had with the loss of previous pets, but King was the one I had cared about the most so far in my life, so it took time to heal.

Still, the presence of Crowley in our lives provided an opportunity for me and Carolyn to become closer, something that became necessary once she and I had begun to drift apart. When she started high school in 1983, the year I started fourth grade, she began to change, becoming more grown up and more girly than I was used to. Prior to that, she had mostly been a tomboy, sort of like the older brother I never got to have. For her, ninth grade brought about a feminine phase with her becoming more like Susanna, interested in things like clothes and hair and make-up. These things were all foreign to me, and I didn't like how she changed. It wasn't just fashion; she also began to hang out with her friends at school more, which for some reason caused her to develop more of an attitude, a sense of separatism from me. We had always clashed from time to time as any siblings did, but I got an increasing sense from her that she felt like she was too grown up for me, that I was the little brother that she needed to distance herself from. Not surprisingly, I countered this with hostility, so we grew apart.

Other times, she was more like her old self, and we got along fine. Those times were just less frequent than they had been before. After a while, I got used to this new version of her, even if I didn't really understand it. This prissy phase of hers would eventually taper off by the time she reached the end of high school, but there was still no doubt that she and I were both growing and changing. Our evolving relationship was not all that different from the way things developed between me and Carl — or perhaps even me and Dennis — and I was beginning to learn that the older one got, the more things changed. It was like the rules of life itself kept changing, and what you knew before no longer applied, so you had to adapt and play the game differently. That had certainly happened when I discovered the vampire potion.

I liked Carolyn better when Crowley was around, though. He seemed to bring her back down to earth, to force her to be less pretentious and snooty. While she had otherwise begun to have a tendency to turn her nose up at everything and be highly critical of whatever she could, including me, something about having a purring mass of calmness to shower affection onto curbed that. She seemed more natural and more like her old self in his presence.

In terms of becoming vampires again, I was surprised by Carolyn's acceptance of my proposal, and I said so.

"Why?" she asked.

"Well…" I suddenly felt uncomfortable. I'd felt that way earlier when I first brought things up, afraid that someone might be listening to us. But our parents were in the other end of the house, so I figured we were safe. But now, I was feeling uneasy once again. "You know. All of the… um…"

Carolyn narrowed her eyes at me. "Say it."

"Trying to, you know, kill you and all." I avoided eye contact as I said it.

Surprisingly, she just laughed, but it was a fake laugh I had noticed that she'd recently adopted, one I would hear her use while talking on the phone to her friends. "Ray, really, it wasn't that big of a deal."

I looked back up at her. "Really?"

"Really." She had the same haughty grin, then looked up at the ceiling as she continued to stroke Crowley, who had begun to stretch out in her lap, yawning. I tried to suppress the nervousness I felt, both at the menacing way that a cat's mouth could look when baring all its teeth like that and at Carolyn's superior attitude. I expected her to rip into me any second now and tell me what a horrible person I was for what my friends and I had tried to do to her. But she surprised me again with her next revelation: "Susanna was on to you guys the entire time. She knew what you were planning."

"What?"

"She knew what the potion was doing to all of us, like bringing out the urge to kill and all. So she figured out that the only way to get us all out of it safely was to change us back with running water and garlic and crosses and all that. The cure took forever to work on me, so we went with a more direct route… well, kinda." She seemed to lose her train of thought here, looking away from me again, maybe trying to collect her thoughts or just caught up in remembering.

"I don't get it," I said, trying to take in what she had been saying.

She seemed to come back to herself and regained her composure. "You know, what's funny is that I didn't even think the vampire potion was real. Like, when you guys told me you wanted to do it."

This surprised me, too. "Well then why did you go along with it?"

She was still stroking Crowley, who had almost fallen asleep but stirred again when she let out another almost fake laugh. "Just to do it, I guess. I thought it was a game, another one of Susanna's pranks. You remember the things she used to do to me when we were little."

I did, though I only knew them anecdotally. Carolyn had told me stories of the tricks Susanna used to play on her when they were much younger, some of which had happened before I was born. One in particular that always stuck out in my mind was how Susanna managed to convince Carolyn that she was secretly a witch, and the closet of the room they shared had a hidden door in it. According to the story, Susanna would — when Carolyn wasn't looking, naturally— slip out through this trapdoor and fly away on a broom. This led Carolyn to search for the hidden door whenever Susanna wasn't around. There were other stories like this where Susanna outright lied to Carolyn and had her believing all kinds of things, but this was the one I thought of the most often, and I brought it up during this conversation.

"Yeah," Carolyn said, looking perturbed. "So I figured that this vampire thing was another load of crap. But at the same time, I kinda thought it was a neat idea."

I did my best to process this new information, but I felt like I didn't have all of the facts yet. "So what was that about her being on to us?"

"Oh, that," Carolyn said, laughing again and looking down at Crowley, who was now mostly asleep and either snoring or purring; I wasn't sure which. "She let me know what was up and what to do to prepare for the night when we changed you all back." She fixed me with a proud look and said, "Really, you guys never stood a chance."

I was dumbfounded, but I tried to keep from showing it. I was also beginning to feel angry, mostly at Susanna. But once I re-examined this later, I knew that she had done the right thing; it wouldn't have been good had Tim, Carl, and I succeeded and actually managed to kill my sisters that night.

Carolyn seemed to be enjoying telling me all this, probably seeing through my attempts to hide my disappointment. I hadn't realized just how on top of things she and Susanna had been during that confrontation, plus I hadn't thought about the details of it for quite a while. And when I tried to remember exactly what had happened, I found that I could no longer accurately recall things, so I was mostly dependent on Carolyn's recollection to fill in the gaps. I remembered that certain things had happened, just not exactly what I was thinking at the time. Those particular memories were lost to me for some reason.

Trying to salvage the conversation, I sighed and repeated my original question to her, which was whether or not she was okay with us taking the potion and becoming vampires again that summer.

"Sure, if you want to," she said, sounding bored, or maybe just trying to sound that way. She was harder for me to read these days. "But only if we can do it right this time."

"Right?"

"You know, like not getting all stupid and turning on each other."

If only it had gone that way.

Now that it was decided that Dennis would be part of the group, the next step was to ask him if he was interested. I was nervous bringing this up with him, though I wasn't entirely sure why. Perhaps I worried that he might not go along with it and then might tell someone else, which would be a disaster. Instead, the first hurdle to overcome was not so much convincing him to join us, but that I wasn't lying to him.

"Oh, yeah, right," he said to me. We were at recess, hanging out away from everyone else by a large oak tree. At first, he had seemed intrigued that I wanted to ask him about something in secret, but then he just seemed annoyed.

"No, I'm serious!" I said. "You remember the summer before you started going here? All those vampire killings and stuff? That was us!"

Dennis wasn't buying it. "Right. You're a vampire." He rolled his eyes and added sarcastically, "And I'm a supervillain with psychic powers."

I was starting to get angry. This wasn't what I had expected. I had spent more than a year and a half keeping this entire thing a secret, and now that I was going out on a limb and trying to share it with somebody I liked and trusted, I was being laughed at. "Well, if you were, you could read my mind and know that I was telling the truth," I said snidely.

His face changed slightly, but I couldn't quite read the expression. I wasn't sure if he was smarting from my comeback or was starting to come around.

"And if you're such a bad-ass vampire, how come you're not on fire right now?" He pointed up at the sky. "There's the sun, genius."

My rising anger made it harder for me to fight the urge to make fun of his lisp, but I was also distracted by his last question, not just the way he'd pronounced it. "What? The sun doesn't set vampires on fire. It just, um… kills them."

"See, you don't even know what you're talking about." He huffed. "The point is, if you were a vampire, you wouldn't be out in the sun. The end."

"It wasn't a permanent thing," I said. "It was a potion my sister made. It turned us into vampires for a week, and then we changed back to normal people again." He just looked at me, still unconvinced. "Look, I'm telling you this because it's something big, something real, and it's cool. And I want you to take part in it when we get together this summer. We did it two years ago, me, my sisters, Tim, Carl…"

"What? Are you serious? You really think I want to hang out with Carl all summer?"

"No!" I said, realizing how loud we had gotten. I quickly looked around to make sure that no one, particularly Carl, had started paying attention to us. Lowering my voice again, I explained that I wasn't planning on including Carl this time.

"Well, maybe he'd be dumb enough to believe you," Dennis said, but I could see that he was beginning to listen, if only just.

"He was there," I said firmly, then sighed. "But it's not like he would admit to it. Like I said, it was a secret. And it's not like he and I are friends anymore. I wouldn't want him to be around for it this time."

Dennis seemed to soften a bit, but I could tell that he still wasn't sold. "You are serious, aren't you? Or crazier than I ever thought."

"Maybe both," I said, trying to sound clever.

He thought for a moment. "I still don't believe you."

"But if you did, would you want to do it?"

"I… I guess. Kind of. I don't know." After a pause, he continued, "All of that stuff a couple of years ago…?"

He still wasn't sure whether or not to believe me, but at least I had him interested. I knew he was into spooky and mysterious stuff, so I had figured that he would leap at the opportunity to be involved in something like this. I hadn't counted on his skepticism. It took Tim's corroboration of my story to finally get him to take me seriously.

"You told him?" Tim whispered loudly at me, his teeth clenched and eyes wide.Dennis, who had been standing with his arms folded after I called Tim over to us, also went wide-eyed. "Whoa…" he said, then whispered, "Really?"

"Absolutely," I said with an evil smile. Finally, he was getting it.

The rest of recess was spent with the two of us telling Dennis as much as we could recall about the summer of 1983, the potion, and how cool it was to be vampires. Dennis still expressed some disbelief occasionally, but I could tell that he was on board for the most part. As I said, he was already drawn to dark things, and it didn't seem like much of a stretch for him to go from liking horror movies to wanting to be in a real-life one.

After the bell rang, everyone began heading toward the school building for lunch. Still caught up in the excitement of everything, Dennis said to me and Tim, "So, just when is this vampire club going to get together this summer?"

I turned to him sharply and said, almost involuntarily, "Shh!"

"What? A vampire club?" a boy's voice said from behind us. It was Gary, one of the boys in 5-A whom I really didn't like. He was a jerk, and one of the kids who sided with Carl during the Club Wars earlier that year. His expression wasn't one of shock, just derision. He went on, "Y'all are gonna have a vampire club? That's so gay."

"No we're not!" I snapped back. "We were just…"

"Just seeing if you'd believe us and go off telling people we were trying to make another club," Tim said. It seemed like a plausible enough story.

Gary just laughed. "Sure, whatever. You know we're not allowed to have stupid clubs anymore. You'll get in trouble."

"That's why we were just making it up," I said, adopting Tim's lie. "You gonna go around and tell everybody and then look like an idiot when we don't do anything?"

Gary just gave me a dirty look, then pushed his way in front of us on the way to the lunchroom. He said something else about us being stupid, but I couldn't quite make it out.

Once he was out of earshot, I turned to Dennis and whispered harshly, "Dennis! Don't ever say anything else like that again!"

"We can't let anyone know about this," Tim also whispered, looking more stern than I was used to seeing him be.

"Okay, okay," Dennis said quietly. "Sorry."

"I had a feeling you'd come up with something like that sooner or later," Susanna said to me over the phone. She sounded irritated, but less antagonistic than I had feared she might be.

She was in her second year of college in Charleston, which was about a three-hour drive from Augusta. Her visits home were infrequent, and I missed her sometimes. Because of the age difference between us, we had never been all that close, but still, it felt weird once she left for school and was no longer around. Part of me was just fine with that, my bossy and sometimes condescending sister being out of the house. Even so, I felt like the vampire experience that summer had meant something, that maybe it brought us closer in a way that we hadn't been before. Whether she felt the same way or not, I wasn't quite sure. As it was with the others, we had the secret in common, but we rarely talked about it.

And it wasn't like we had all that much else in common, either. The shift in the relationship I'd had with Carolyn as she got older was unsettling, but with Susanna, it felt like that gulf had always been there. I just didn't get most of the things she was into, like her cheerleading, which she had continued to do at college. She was an English major, and I barely understood what that even was, just that it had something to do with reading a lot of books for school. I wasn't all that big into reading myself, really, and only did it when I had to for assignments.

As had been the case when I talked to Carolyn about the idea of taking the potion again, I feared that Susanna might say no, but she also seemed interested, though she sounded somewhat disdainful. I mentioned that, but she clarified that she had also occasionally thought of doing it again.

"No, I think it would be interesting to do it," she said. "We just have to be more careful this time."

"Yeah, Carolyn said something like that."

"Hmm?"

"You know, like not turning on each other, you scheming behind our backs to get us all turned back, stuff like that." I had been waiting to spring that on her ever since Carolyn had told me about it. I resented the fact that she had been so manipulative, and I thought that once I brought it up, she would be surprised that I'd found out. Instead, she barely reacted and just kept on talking.

"Well, yeah, but this time, we need to change back using what your friend Carl called the 'vampire killers,' garlic or crosses or running water, something like that."

"I… um… why?" I managed to say. I was thrown by her non-reaction to my revelation, but there wasn't really any way to say so without seeming too obvious.

"Because of how the antidote worked on Carolyn last time. It took way too long, and it made her all unstable and weird. The things that just eliminate the potion's effects in us are quicker and more reliable. So I'm thinking we just do it, have some fun with it for a while, then change back all at the same time."

"You mean like we all gather around the sink and run the water and… *ping!* We all change back?" I pictured the scenario in my head as I spoke.

"Yeah, something like that. Or garlic, or crosses. I'm not sure. But I think it would be safer that way." I agreed.

"By the way," I said, "I've still never heard anything from anywhere else about water being something that's used against vampires." Since the summer of 1983, I had paid a lot more attention to vampire lore whenever I happened to be exposed to it, though I didn't actively seek it out. Water, running or otherwise, never seemed to come up.

"Oh, it's part of the legend all right," Susanna assured me.

"But I've never heard anyone else mention it," I insisted.

"That doesn't mean that it isn't true," she said sternly. "Maybe you're just too young to understand that."

"Fine, whatever," I said, annoyed that she'd once again brought up my age. "Oh, and another thing, I'm not friends with Carl anymore. He's just… I don't know… stupid. So I asked my friend Dennis to be vampires with us this time instead."

"You told someone else," she said flatly.

"Well, yeah… I mean… Don't worry; he's cool." Susanna didn't respond. "And Carolyn said that Carl shouldn't be a problem anyway. Even if we don't include him this year, he won't tell anyone about us. He'd be too scared of getting the chair, she said. Whatever that means."

Susanna paused for a while. "So you've already talked to Carolyn about it."

"Yeah. And she's fine with it."

She sighed. "Okay then, I guess we'll do it. We just need to be careful not to get caught or found out."

"Or to Mace ourselves," I joked, referring to an incident that had happened the previous Christmas. Susanna had been given a can of Mace, some spray-type stuff that was supposed to ward off criminals. She'd wanted to test it to make sure it worked, so she'd sprayed a small amount of it in the bathroom. I didn't know this at first; I was across the hall in my bedroom minding my own business when I heard her coughing. And then, moments later, I felt something making me want to choke, and I began coughing as well, as did Carolyn when she came up the hall to find out what was going on. Apparently, the cloud of Mace had travelled more than Susanna had expected.

"You're never going to stop bringing that up, are you," she said.

"Nope."

The rest of the conversation was brief, and even though I thought I might mention it, I decided on the fly not to bring up the fact that Gary had overheard me, Dennis, and Tim talking about vampires a few days earlier. I didn't want her to think that we might be in danger of exposure, a concept I was beginning to become more familiar with. If she knew about that, she might back out. We still had about a month to go in the school year, so my hope was that Gary would just forget about what he heard that day and that it wouldn't be that big of a deal.

That proved not to be the case. On the last day of school, everyone was of course excited about summer vacation beginning, and many of us talked about what we planned to do over the next few months. Some kids had plans for family trips or other interesting things, but I was looking forward to our second stint as vampires. I couldn't say so, though, so I just vaguely hinted at having something cool planned.

I had occasionally thought about how Gary had overheard us talking about a "vampire club" before, and I worried about the implications of that. What if, once we were vampires again and starting killing around town, he remembered that? Would he think we were actually involved and tell someone?

These thoughts were running through my head on and off, and then, at the end of the day when everyone was gathered in the parking lot waiting to be picked up by our parents, Gary said to me, "Hey, have fun with your gay little vampire club this summer, Ray." He said it with his usual sneer, looking down at me with what I called his "bloodhound eyes." He was a rather ugly boy, tall and with a large mouth, big and kind of saggy-looking eyes, and an ego that bugged the hell out of me. Like Carl, he was one of the more athletic boys in the class, and he seemed to think that this made him cool and important. As far as his referring to mine and my friends' interest in vampires as "gay," that was just an insult that had become standard in our lives at that time. We barely knew what the word meant.

"Shut up, Gary," I said to him. "We're not even doing that." I hoped he believed me.

"Yeah, whatever," he said, and the argument might have continued had not his mother honked the horn from her station wagon nearby and waved to him through the windshield to get into the car.

I stood there, glad to see him go. But inside, I worried.

"There," Susanna said, having drawn a big "V" in pencil on the calendar in the kitchen. "Friday the 12th is when we'll change back to human. That gives us a day to get everything cleaned up and ready before Mom and Dad get back."

"Won't your mom wonder why there's a big 'V' on that day?" Tim asked.

"That's why it's in pencil," she said impatiently.

Dennis and Tim had arrived shortly before this, not long after our parents left for the ALA conference, which this year was in Chicago. I did my best to hide my eagerness for them to leave, but I wasn't sure I did a very good job. I was just so excited about the chance to become vampires again. Two years ago, I had also expected to have a good time with my friends staying over for a week, but I'd had no idea just how intense of an experience it would turn out to be. This time, I had some idea of what to expect, so my anticipation was greater. That was mixed with a feeling of apprehension, a hope that things would go well this time, too, and that we would get away with all of our wrongdoing as flawlessly as we had before. Well, almost.

When our parents got back from their trip in 1983, they hadn't had a clue about what we had gotten up to while they were gone. As far as the panic we had caused around town, that died down once our attacks stopped, and it was old news soon enough. No one knew just what we had done or how. The closest any of us got to being found out happened a few months later when my father went to the storage shed and was surprised to find that the wood that was supposed to be in there was gone. That was because we had used it to try to make coffins that summer, and when that failed, we threw it away. When asked about it, I quickly had to come up with a lie about Carolyn trying to build some bookshelves with it while they were gone, but they fell apart and so she got rid of the wood. My dad seemed to buy it, and I had to go tell Carolyn the story immediately so she would corroborate it if asked.

Another thing I worried about was the weather. It had been more unstable the previous week, particularly in terms of thunderstorms. The July 4th fireworks show that we usually attended had been rained out that year, and I wondered if that might affect our time as vampires as well. Susanna had told us before that rain would work on us the same way that running water did, so I was afraid we might get caught by a freak thunderstorm one night and get changed back unexpectedly. At the very least, we might get stuck inside due to the rain, especially if it went on all night.

Still, aside from these worries, I was mostly in a good mood and glad to have everyone together. It felt a little weird to be doing it all without Carl, though. He and I had in fact managed to patch things up some by the end of the school year, having been forced to work together on a project in our Science class during the final month of fifth grade. We had balked at being paired together, and I think that our teacher enjoyed the unease we felt. Or maybe she was hoping that having to work together would help us become friends again, which it kind of did. We weren't all "buddy-buddy" afterwards, but we seemed to have at least stopped loathing each other as much as we had over the past year or so.

It did occur to me at that point to try to include Carl in the vampire gathering that summer after all, but I was still much closer to Dennis, and I knew he wouldn't like that. Also, I had already told Susanna that it would just be the five of us and not Carl, so I thought it best to stick to the plan.

Another thing that occurred to me was that Susanna might go ahead and make the potion ahead of time and bring it with her to Augusta. If so, I knew she would only make enough for five people, not six. If I sprang it on her at the last minute that Carl was showing up after all, that could complicate things. I'm not sure why I thought she might do that; it was just a scenario that ran through my head as I was picturing how things might go in anticipation of the actual event.

As it turned out, she didn't make it ahead of time, and so things ended up being much like they were two years before. The rest of us had to kill time during the afternoon while she made the potion upstairs in her old bedroom, which she still stayed in whenever she visited. There was something nice about having her there again whenever she did come home (the Mace incident notwithstanding), even if we hadn't been all that close while growing up.

Carolyn, despite the alienation I sometimes felt from her, also seemed eager to get back into some of the same routine from before. She was still snide to me and my friends at times and played the whole *I'm older and you dumb young kids don't know any better* card, but overall, we got along. In a lot of ways, she seemed more like her younger self, which I liked. This included her joining us in playing games in the backyard.

"You want to play Ghost in the Graveyard again?" I asked everyone.

"No, that's stupid," Carolyn said.

"I don't even know what that is," Dennis said.

Tim started to explain the rules, but Carolyn cut him off. "How about Freeze Tag?" she said. "You guys know how to play that, right?" We did; we had played it at school plenty of times before.

"Okay, but someone has to be 'it' first," I said.

Carolyn smiled as she slapped my hand with hers and said, "You're it!" and ran off. Dennis and Tim quickly caught on and ran away as well.

My surprise at this meant that everyone had a good head start on me, but eventually, I caught up to Dennis, tagging him and "freezing" him. I next went after Carolyn, but once she led me far enough away from where Dennis was left standing, Tim was able to run up to him and tag him, "defrosting" him and allowing him to run free.

The game continued for a long time. According to the rules, once anyone got frozen three times, they then became "it" and had to chase the other players around trying to freeze them. All four of us had our turns being it, being frozen, and being defrosted. Sometimes I was the pursuer, sometimes I was being pursued, and sometimes I needed to be rescued by others. It was fun, a cyclical game that could go on forever if we wanted it to. We took occasional breaks, but we kept playing until it was time for dinner.

While we were eating, we talked excitedly about becoming vampires again. Dennis of course hadn't been one yet, so a lot of the conversation was focused on explaining various things to him, how we could turn into bats and fly, the glowing eyes that allowed us to see in the dark, and the various things we had to avoid that could change us back to regular human beings if we came into contact with them.

"So those things don't kill us?" Dennis asked.

"No," I said. "Instead, we just get changed back into regular people. It's like… I don't know…" I looked to Susanna, wondering if she had a more thorough explanation.

"Those specific things eliminate the effects of the vampire potion within us, turning us back to normal."

"Oh," I said. "Why?"

"That's just the way it is," Susanna said simply. "Crowley, get down."

Crowley had been prowling around the kitchen table throughout dinner, occasionally jumping up on the sides of our chairs, hoping for a handout. Susanna was his latest target. She batted at him with her hand, which caused him to squint angrily and slink back to the floor.

"Don't give him anything," Carolyn said, "or else he won't leave you alone."

"Okay," Tim said. "So, that spice rack over there," he said, pointing at the wall behind Carolyn, "I guess that has garlic in it? And we'll use that to turn back to human when this is all done?"

"I think there's still some there," Carolyn said as she turned and looked behind her. As she did, Tim quickly tore off a piece of his fried chicken and slipped it down to Crowley, who was waiting at his feet. I fought back a laugh.

"I think running water is the best way to go," Susanna said, ignoring the situation with the cat. "We can do the same thing as before where we turn off the water flow under the sinks, and then when next Friday comes, we can turn it back on again, gather around the kitchen sink or wherever, and then that's that."

"No!" Tim said in a sing-song kind of voice, leaning over and looking down at Crowley. "I don't have anything for you!" Crowley jumped up against the side of his chair again, mewing quietly.

"Crap," Carolyn said. "So we're going to have to do that thing again where we don't bathe for however long? Ew." She scrunched up her nose, stuck her tongue out while sneering, then went back to eating.

"I got wipes for us again," Susanna assured her. "It'll be fine."

Further explanation of this was needed for Dennis's sake, but he seemed okay with it. Even though I was a couple of years older than the last time we had done this, I still didn't have a problem with not showering or bathing for a few days. In fact, I liked the idea of not having to bother with that for a while; it seemed like an unnecessary chore to me.

By the time dinner was done, the sun was set, and it was time to take the potion. This time, instead of walking into the kitchen with a tray of cups, Susanna came in with a large beaker, took some plastic cups from the cabinet, and proceeded to fill those with the potion.

I suddenly felt apprehensive. I had been looking forward to becoming vampires again for months, but the sight of those cups filled me with an unexpected dread. I began to realize that the next thing I would have to do was actually drink that stuff.

It was the same as before, a brown fizzy liquid that gave off some kind of salty smell. But what was bothering me was the idea of going through the transformation again, the weird, scary experience that the potion had put me through last time. That transition, the bizarre feeling of my heart pounding, feeling dizzy, my vision going all strange, and just overall tension and fear, was one of my most vivid memories of what I went through two years earlier. I remembered the experience more clearly than I liked, including the very end of it. Aside from the rushing sound in my ears that sounded like horses galloping, there was that strange sort of boom at the very end, followed by what sounded like some old man laughing. In my mind, it sounded very much like Vincent Price's laugh at the end of Michael Jackson's song "Thriller," not the loud cackling part of it, just that final *"uh huh huh huh huh huh"* thing he did at the very end. It creeped me out whenever I thought of it, and I was not looking forward to going through that again, no matter how much I wanted to be a vampire.

"You okay?" Dennis asked me.

"Hmm?" I said, remembering my surroundings. "Yeah, fine." I did my best to look brave.

Once Susanna had finished pouring the potion, she set the beaker down and brought the cups over to the kitchen table. "Okay," she said, "here we go again."

"Any last words?" Tim asked, smiling.

"Just that there's no going back from here," Susanna said, also beginning to smile.

"Cool," Dennis said, an eager gleam in his eyes. Any doubts he might have had before seemed to be gone, or at least I knew they would be in a couple of minutes. "So it's time for the vampire club to start up again."

"Vampire club?" Carolyn said mockingly.

"Oh, that's just what Dennis called it before," Tim said. "Right when that jerk Gary was listening…" He stopped, noticing the look I had given him.

Susanna, who had already picked up her cup, set it down again quickly. "What?"

"This boy at school," Dennis said. "Real jerk. He overheard us talking about vampires, then made fun of us."

"We told him we were just making it up," I said, fearing what Susanna might say next.

She was silent for a moment, then fixed me with an angry glare and said slowly, "I *told* you *not* to tell anyone else about this, Ray."

"I know! I know! Sorry."

"He didn't believe us!" Tim said. "We told him it was just a joke."

"Yeah, it'll be fine," I said. "Let's just take the potion." Suddenly, my fear of that was eclipsed by my fear of Susanna, or more specifically, the idea that she might change her mind at the last second and say that we couldn't become vampires after all.

She continued to look at me angrily, then just sighed heavily. "I hope you're right." She picked up her cup again, now in much less of a good mood. I could see the doubt on her face, and she was probably thinking of abandoning the plan. But we had gotten this far already. "Come on, everyone."

As she drank her cup down, the rest of us did the same. A few moments after we set them back onto the table, the transformation began. As before, it began with heavy breathing and a feeling of dizziness. Out of the corner of my eye, I noticed that Crowley suddenly ran out of the room toward the red den, but that was one of the last things I was aware of externally. I was soon far too focused on myself, scared but knowing I needed to ride this out. The tunnel vision began, and I closed my eyes, feeling my heart pounding, and the sound of blood rushing in my ears. That was what it was; I hadn't realized that when it happened to me before. It still sounded like horses running faster and faster, which I began to picture in my head, and the image frightened me. I wanted to say something, but by then, my arms, legs, and face had gone numb, and I could barely move. All I could do was continue to breathe more and more heavily while I gripped the side of the table. My eyes were screwed shut, my vision nothing but a mass of black mixed with strange starburst patterns of bright green and red.

Finally, the sensations culminated in that loud "boom" sound in my head, and the change was complete. It felt like it had taken longer this time, but I wasn't entirely sure. Maybe it was just so hard to endure that it felt like longer. One thing that was different was that I didn't hear that spooky laughter in my head this time. Maybe that had all been my imagination, something I had made up over the years when I remembered how traumatic the transformation was. I only thought about this for a couple of seconds, though, because I was beginning to feel better and also excited, knowing what this meant. We were finally vampires again.

I looked around at the others, who had also recovered. Dennis was the first one to reach up and feel that he had fangs. I did the same, and it made me so happy to feel them there again. I'd missed them.

"Whoa," Dennis said, then smiled. "Holy shit."

Carolyn rolled her eyes and let out a sort of combination sigh and groan. "So you're going to be the one cussing all the time now?"

"What?"

"Oh, never mind," I said. "She's talking about Carl. He kept cussing a lot last time we got together, and it got on her nerves."

Dennis frowned at the mention of Carl. "Well, at least I didn't say something stupid like 'holy squid.'" Tim and I laughed, and so did he. Carolyn and Susanna didn't know about Carl's more recent method of substitute swearing, so they didn't get the joke.

"So," Susanna said, "looks like we're back." It had been a while since I had seen her with fangs, but there they were just as before, only slightly visible as she spoke. "Now, about this Gary kid."

As we flew through the night, I was full of anticipation. It felt wonderful to be able to turn into a bat again, to fly high above the trees and the streets. Even though I had been looking forward to experiencing this again, it wasn't until it was actually happening that I remembered how cool all of it was. And it barely took any time at all to settle back into the old feelings and abilities; it was the typical "like riding a bike" cliché, only this bike was small, black, and furry with wings.

We were on our way to Gary's house, which was not very far from my own. Susanna was still uncomfortable with the idea of someone possibly knowing about us, which she made clear back at the house. It was then that Dennis suggested that we show up at his house and scare him.

"Yeah, that will work out really well, I'm sure," Carolyn said.

"What do you mean?" Dennis asked.

"That was what we tried to do last time," Tim said. "Our plan was just to scare those people at the YMCA who made us mad. Things kind of got out of hand."

"Yeah, just a bit," Carolyn said, still sarcastic.

As Tim and Carolyn spoke, I began picturing our first attack in 1983. In fact, it was the first time in two years that I had been able to remember it this clearly.

"Well, they're not going to this time," Susanna said. "We know what we're doing and can handle ourselves. No killing this time around. At least, not someone you know."

Part of me wanted to argue. Now that I was a vampire again, I had little to no qualms about killing people, and I had always hated Gary. But something else in me knew that she was right. The people we had killed before were strangers, so they seemed to matter less to me. The idea of actually murdering someone I had known for a few years actually bothered me. "So what do we do?" I asked.

And so we came up with a plan that we hoped would work, something that would scare Gary enough to shut him up. That was the idea, anyway. We talked some about the plan at the house, then more on the way, again having those squeaky, small-sounding bat versions of our regular voices. Dennis found this especially entertaining, and he occasionally made high-pitched squeaks for no real reason. I joined in, as did Tim. By the time we reached Gary's house, Susanna told us to keep quiet, and we tried to find a way to set our plan in motion.

I knew from things Gary had said at school that he had an upstairs bedroom; his family's house was bigger than ours and had two full stories. I worried that figuring out just which room was his might be a problem, but it ended up only taking a minute or two. He was in his room, the lights on and curtains open, sitting in a light green beanbag and watching TV. I was instantly jealous upon seeing this; not many kids had their own TVs in their bedrooms.

"Okay," Susanna said, "that tree over there should work." It was the one nearest to Gary's window. We flew into it, then perched on the branches. "Your turn, Tim."

Tim exited the tree and hovered outside Gary's window, and he began squeaking loudly. I could see Gary from my vantage point, and he hadn't moved. Tim began flapping around more and more furiously, eventually slamming himself up against the window a few times.

Finally, Gary turned toward the window, looking confused, and he got up from where he was sitting. He turned the TV volume down, then walked over to the window. Tim had gone back to hovering in place.

As Gary put his hands up to the glass and peered out, Tim squeaked again, then lunged forward. Gary leapt back, saying something, and Tim hovered again, squeaking a little more. Gary looked outside again, this time more cautiously, and Tim flapped around some more, doing a little dance in the air. As we had hoped, this made Gary curious enough to leave his room and head downstairs.

"Cool," I said. "It's working."

"Okay, now remember," Susanna said, "just chase after him, but don't catch him." By then, Tim had rejoined us in the tree.

Gary came outside through the door nearest to our hiding place, and we all began squeaking at once. This lured him closer, though he stepped tentatively. He was also looking up at his bedroom window, wondering if anything was there.

When I thought he was close enough to the tree, I shot out of it and circled around toward him, and the others flew out as well.

"What in the…?" Gary said, not seeming as frightened as I would have liked, just confused. I then buzzed past his head, and he let out a small scream. Just for a moment, I pictured myself back at the racetrack, flying close to that other boy's head. A feeling began to well up inside me.

The other bats had now begun flying closer to Gary as well, squeaking loudly, and he ran back to the house. Before he could make it to the door, one of us, I think Tim, flew in front of it and hovered, blocking his way. I squeaked again as the rest of us zoomed in closer, and Gary ran in another direction, heading for the street. Just before he did that, he called out, "Mom!" I looked back to the door as we remained stationary in the air for a few moments, wondering if anyone might come out, but no one did. He was on his own.

"Phase two?" Tim asked.

"Phase two," Susanna said. "See if you can get ahead of him without him seeing you. Carolyn and I will be nearby."

"Got it," I said, and I led Tim and Dennis in the direction Gary had run.

"This is awesome!" Dennis said as we flew. I wasn't sure if his bat form also had a lisp; it was hard to tell through the squeakiness.

"Shh!" Tim said. "Don't let him hear you. Not yet."

After a few moments, we had caught up, but too high for him to see. He had stopped running and had slowed to a sort of stagger, looking behind him and up at the sky in random places, trying to see if he was being pursued. Then he stopped, still looking around and panting.

"Okay, this will work," I said softly. "Follow me."

I led the others farther up the street and to a telephone pole, where we landed and changed into our human forms. A bright purple streetlight shone down from above, making our faces look weird in the shadows. I then leaned against the pole casually and began talking loudly to Tim and Dennis.

"So I was thinking that would be pretty cool!"

"That what would… oh," Dennis began, catching on and raising his voice. "Yeah, we should do that!"

"Totally!" Tim said, almost shouting.

"Do you think it would really work, though?" Dennis said. "I mean it might be kind of difficult to squeeze a penguin into such a small space."

This threw me for a loop. We were supposed to be talking about nothing in particular, but I hadn't expected something so random. The bizarre image made me laugh, and the others did the same, again being more loud than we needed to be.

"Hey!" Gary's voice called out from nearby, and I turned to see him running toward us. "There's… Oh, it's you." His tone shifted from urgency to disgust. Because he and I only lived a couple of blocks apart, it wasn't unusual for us to occasionally run into each other in the neighborhood. But this wasn't a usual night.

"What are you jerk-offs doing here?" he asked, adopting his usual tough stance, though he was still visibly shaken from his earlier experience.

"Just hanging out," I said. "You?"

"Yeah, well, y'all might want to keep a lookout. I just saw a whole bunch of bats flying around. Might be something your stupid little vampire club might be interested in." He jeered at us and quickly came back to his old self, defiant and smug. But he looked different to me. He may have been bigger than me physically, but he just looked somehow… small. Vulnerable.

"You think there are vampires around?" Tim said with exaggerated shock. "Really?"

"Might be some closer than you think," I said.

"What are you talking about?" Gary said, still defiant but glancing up again at the sky.

Dennis suddenly bared his fangs at him and hissed in a cat-like manner, like something out of a typical vampire movie.

"What the hell?" Gary said, again seeming more confused than actually afraid.

Then, there were menacing squeaks from above, and I knew that Susanna and Carolyn were about to fly in. Mimicking Dennis's gesture, I also showed my fangs, as did Tim, and we raised our arms threateningly.

Gary stumbled over himself and began running back down the street away from us, and we took to the air to pursue him. He was heading back to his house, and it would have been so easy to catch him had we really wanted to. Instead of lunging straight for his neck and taking him down — which I pictured myself doing more than once as I flew — I occasionally led the group higher up into the air and then back down again, basically stalling in order to give him enough headway to escape us. Susanna and Carolyn swooped close to his head a couple of times, calling out his name. One of them said something else to him, but I couldn't quite make it out.

He eventually made it to the door to his house, getting through it so quickly that it was almost cartoonish the way he seemed to burst through. I could hear the rattling sounds as he hurriedly locked the door behind him.

"So is that it?" Dennis asked, hovering by the door. "We just let him go?"

"Follow me," Susanna said. She led us around to a nearby window, where we could see Gary talking to his mother in the kitchen, looking frantic. We had to get close to the glass to hear what was being said.

"Yes I did!" Gary shrieked.

"Gary, calm down," his mother said. "You probably just got too close to a bird's nest, and the mama bird came out after you."

"No! It was bats! Like, vampire bats! They were after me!"

"There's no such thing. You just…"

"They were squeaking at me and everything like *beeeep beeeep beeeep!* And..."

"Birds chirp, not squeak. Will you please calm down?" She had leaned in closer to him, holding his shoulders with both hands.

"But one *talked* to me, Mom," he insisted. "I could have sworn it said, 'We've come for you.'"

His mother huffed. "Now you're just being ridiculous. I can understand your being scared by that mother bird flying after you. She probably had some baby birds in the nest, and..."

"But then I saw Ray Young, and... and Dennis Williams and Tim Donnelly from school! And they all had fangs! Like vampires!"

Gary's mother, who had been trying to be sympathetic and understanding up until this point, straightened up and became stern. "Oh, your story just keeps getting bigger and better, doesn't it?"

"I'm not lying!" he shouted, his voice cracking.

"Don't you talk to me like that! I've had enough of this, young man. Go to your room."

"But...!"

"Now!" She snapped her fingers, extended her arm, and pointed to the stairs, all in one gesture. The finality of her tone shut Gary up, and he stomped away angrily. His mother sighed and shook her head, then went back to what she had been doing at the table, putting leftover food into containers.

We flew away from the window, hovering a few feet away.

I laughed. "That was hilarious! I've never seen him so... I don't know..."

"Put in his place?" Tim offered.

"Yeah, I guess," I said.

"Come on," Carolyn said. "We should check and see what he's doing in his room."

We flew back up to his bedroom window, and I was surprised by what I saw. Gary was lying face down on his bed, gripping a pillow with both hands. From the motion of his upper body, I could tell he was crying. I'd never seen him do that before. In a way, this felt like more of a victory than catching and killing him would ever have been.

Back at the house, we gathered in the kitchen and began talking about everything that had happened so far.

"Okay, hold on, everybody," Susanna said, holding up her hand. "One more thing to take care of."

"What do you mean?" I asked.

"What's Gary's last name?"

I had to think for a second, but Dennis beat me to it. "Bertram," he said.

"Okay then," Susanna said, reaching for the phone book on the counter by the kitchen table. She spread it open, then began running her finger up and down the listings. "Bernard… Bellamy… Ber… *Bertram.* And…" She made a few more singing tones under her breath, this time reading out street names, finally settling on what must have been Gary's address. "There." She picked up the phone and began dialing, her fingers cranking the wheel in rapid succession. After a few seconds, she said, "Hello, may I please speak to Mrs. Bertram?"

Very quickly, I made my way to the other end of the house to my parents' bedroom, followed by Dennis and Tim. From time to time, I had listened in on some of Carolyn's telephone conversations with her friends, and I had learned how to pick up the other phone discreetly. I placed my finger on the small white pegs under the receiver, carefully lifted it to my ear, then released the pegs and opened the connection, motioning to the other boys to keep it down.

"…sounded the way he described it that your son was pretty upset," Susanna was saying, "and I just wanted to make sure that everything was okay. Ray and his friends can get kind of out of control, and…" — she paused and let out a fake laugh — "well, since I'm supposed to be the responsible adult put in charge of them while our parents are away, I just feel kind of bad about what happened."

"Oh, it's okay," Gary's mother said over the line. "He'll be okay after I make him some cheese toast and hot chocolate. Always makes him feel better. I'm sure he just got worked up over nothing. You know how little boys are."

Susanna fake-laughed again. "Yes, ma'am. Ray can be quite the little handful, too." I grimaced at that. How old did she think I was? "I think he and his friends just thought that putting on fake vampire fangs and scaring Gary would be a fun thing to do, and I'm sorry that it got so out of hand. I really don't think they meant any harm."

"Yes, yes, I'm sure. Well you just tell those boys to behave themselves, and good luck babysitting them yourself."

"Yes, ma'am. Thank you for being so understanding about all this."

"Of course. Thank you for calling."

Click.

The receiver made a few quiet gurgling sounds as the line disconnected, followed by Susanna's voice: "Okay, Ray, you can come back to the kitchen now."

"Crap," I said involuntarily. I hated it when I got caught listening in.

Back in the kitchen, Susanna was filling Carolyn in on the parts of the conversation she hadn't been able to hear.

"So we're okay?" Carolyn asked her.

"I think so," Susanna said, pleased with herself.

"And that," Carolyn said, turning to me and my friends as we walked in, "is how you do a good cover-up."

"Hmm?" I said.

"Just saying that the older you get, the more you'll learn the importance of that." She turned to Susanna, and they gave each other a knowing look.

Fearing that the next thing to come out of either of their mouths was something along the lines of how I was too young to understand something or other, I tried to salvage the situation: "So can we please go out and get some real victims tonight?"

Susanna led us downtown, insisting that our first kill should be far away from our house, or more importantly, far from Gary's house. Once the bodies started piling up, she said, it would be best if they were nowhere near where we lived. That minimized our chances of being implicated.

We reached our destination, soon finding a group of five people isolated enough for us to attack. I was looking forward to making my first kill of the summer, and I was also eager to see how Dennis handled himself. The rest of us had done this before, but this was new to him.

The people we targeted were all teenagers, possibly Carolyn's age or maybe a little bit older. They had just parked their car and had gotten out, and I could hear them talking, something to do with where they were planning on going.

"Should we attack them as bats or as people?" I asked Susanna.

"Hmm… I'm not sure."

"Let's do it as people," Tim said. "Dennis should get to experience his first bite that way. Right, Dennis?"

"Sure, I guess," he said.

And so we repeated a move we had done two years earlier, flying down and landing around them in a circle, changing into our person forms as we did so. This shocked and surprised them, and before the teenagers had time to fully understand what was happening, we were upon them.

My victim was not much taller than me, a preppy, well-dressed girl who reminded me of one of Carolyn's friends. I leapt up onto her and bit down into the side of her neck as she screamed, and I heard the other people call out as they too were taken down. I drank and drank from the girl, loving every second of it, feeling her limply struggle against me and quickly lose strength. The power of it, the taste of the warm, salty blood, and the joy I felt at being this way again was incredible. I was irritated by the smell of the girl's overly styled hair — which reminded me of the times I had walked past the bathroom at home when Carolyn had the door open and was dousing her own hair in tons of stinky chemicals — but the pleasure of the kill overwhelmed that feeling.

Once I was done, I stood up and looked down at the girl's lifeless body, then over at the others, who were also finishing up. I also looked around to see if anyone else was nearby, but we were alone.

"So, Dennis," I said to him, "how'd you like it?"

He was standing over his prey, an older boy with short, spiky black hair. He smiled broadly, his fangs showing and his eyes wide, or as wide as his pudgy face would let them be. Then he laughed. "That was…" He seemed at a loss for words. "Can we do it again?"

Later on at the house, we talked for a little while. Dennis was amazed at how cool all of this was, and he was very glad that I had asked him to take part. I was happy, too, and it was fun showing the ropes to somebody new. It made me feel like a mentor.

"Okay, so now you all know what time it is!" Dennis said excitedly.

"What?" I asked.

"11:32 p.m.," Tim said, looking at his watch, though he said it with a confused tone, not sure what Dennis was getting at.

"Time to watch *Friday the 13th!*" he said. "You did get them, right?" Because the movies were R-rated, we had to rely on Susanna to rent them for us from the video store, and she had agreed to do so.

She huffed, but it was all in fun. "Yes, Dennis, I got you your movies. I think they're still upstairs in my room, though. Hang on." She got up and left the room.

"Y'all are going to watch horror movies?" Carolyn said.

"Yeah," Dennis said. "They're cool."

"Scared?" I asked her, suddenly feeling superior.

"What? Well, no, I mean… Well, kinda."

"Come on, Carolyn!" Tim said. "They're really not that bad. They're more funny than they are scary. And now that we're vampires, we can watch them differently, being on the side of the bad guy. It's fun to root for him and hope he catches the dumb kids!"

Carolyn thought for a moment. "Well, maybe. I'll give it a shot."

Susanna came back downstairs with a paper bag full of videocassettes, which she handed to me. I laid the tapes out on the yellow den floor.

"I wasn't able to get every single one of the movies, though," Susanna said. "They were out of some of them. They had them in VHS, but not Beta."

"Yeah, I still wish Dad had gotten a VHS instead of a Betamax," Carolyn said. "Every time you go to the video store, there's always more VHSes than Betas."

"Well, I read somewhere that Betamax has better picture quality," Tim said.

Carolyn looked at him, then said slowly, "And every time you go to the video store, they have more VHS movies than Beta."

"Whatever," Tim said.

Crowley had by then leapt up into Carolyn's lap, and she began petting him, ignoring the rest of us. The fact that we were vampires didn't seem to bother him, either.

"So do we want to start with number one?" I asked Dennis. By then, the franchise had gotten up to *Friday the 13th: Part V.*

"No, let's do number three!" he said. "It's in 3-D!"

"But we don't have any 3-D glasses," Tim said.

"Oh, it's fine," Dennis insisted. "The special effects are still really cool. I've seen it before."

Before I could put the tape into the VCR, I had to eject one of Carolyn's tapes, which was still inside. We both had our own little collections, which we filled up with recorded TV shows we wanted to save and watch later, or we used the VCR's timer to record things that aired when we weren't there to watch them. All of this was very new to us, the idea of being able to control just when we viewed things on TV. Prior to that, we either had to catch things when they were on, or else we simply missed them.

I remembered as I ejected the tape that Carolyn had used the timer to record *Miami Vice* earlier that night; we were out killing while it was on. I liked the show, and so did she; it was one of the few things we had in common. I enjoyed it because of the fast cars, speedboats, and action sequences, while she was more into it because she liked the music and thought that one of the lead actors was "hot," as she put it. While I wouldn't have minded watching it at this point, I knew that Dennis was eager to see the movies Susanna had rented for us, so I didn't say anything, hoping Carolyn might not notice.

"Oh yeah," she said. "That's my tape of *Miami Vice* from earlier tonight."

I flinched, thinking for a second that maybe I could have been more surreptitious, and maybe she wouldn't have thought of that. "Do you want to watch it now?" I asked, hoping she would say no.

"No, it's fine," she said. "It's a rerun anyway. We can watch it later."

We watched the movie, my friends and I again enjoying the ridiculous, over-the-top violence and gore. Carolyn was less than thrilled, but at least she gave it a chance. Susanna mentioned that she had also seen the movie before, but in the theater. She told us how every time one of the 3-D effects happened, appearing to shove something scary at the audience, everyone would scream, then laugh at themselves for getting so scared.

But some of the effects were just obnoxious, almost arbitrary. Even though we weren't experiencing things quite the same way that one would in a theater with the special glasses on — which I had never done, so I had to take Susanna's word on this — it was still pretty easy to tell from the way things looked on our TV where things were being intentionally thrown at the screen. When it was the killer throwing a spear or thrusting his knife at someone, that made sense, but there were other times when something as innocuous as an apple lunged forward, which just seemed stupid.

I might not have been as cynical about all of this if it weren't for Carolyn, who kept pointing out these and other flaws whenever she could. She kind of spoiled things for us, constantly criticizing everything and becoming more unpleasant as the movie went on. One particularly funny moment was when Crowley, who had left the room for a while, came back and jumped into Carolyn's lap, startling her during one of the more tense moments in the movie. The parts that were actually scary often weren't the supposedly shocking bits when the murderous Jason killed yet another person, but the bits leading up to that, a soon-to-be victim walking along slowly amidst eerie music saying something like, "Who's there?" It was the tension that was hardest to get through.

Crowley's surprise attack on Carolyn and her subsequent scream made the rest of us laugh, which just made her even more mad.

"Damn it, Crowley!" she shouted at him, trying to regain her composure.

"See?" Tim said. "That's what Susanna was talking about. You get scared, get over it because it was nothing, then laugh about it."

Carolyn glared at him. "Yeah, hilarious."

Another thing that seemed to get on Carolyn's nerves was something that Dennis and I kept doing, but we weren't doing it on purpose. It just kept happening. Several times throughout the movie, we each kept thinking the same things. Either I would think of something to say about the film and then he would blurt it out before I got the chance, or it would be the other way around, where I would say something I thought was clever only to have Dennis say, "I was just about to say that!" It happened over and over to the point where Carolyn told us to shut up about it and that it was just coincidence.

The final straw for her was when Dennis took the remote control and started rewinding some of the murder scenes. In order to be shocking, the parts where the kids in the movie got killed were often very quick, and sometimes it was hard to tell exactly what had happened. So Dennis rewound the tape to see the murders again, then found it funny to see the action zipping backwards, joking that the people were being "unkilled, then killed again."

Carolyn was annoyed enough at having to see the murders repeated backwards and forward, but one particularly gory one was just too much for her. About an hour into the film, Jason killed a man by crushing his head with his bare hands, resulting in a gratuitous 3-D shot of the man's eyeball popping out and toward the screen. Dennis found this hilarious, laughing at how fake it looked. He kept rewinding the segment back and forth, laughing hysterically as the victim's eyeball popped out, got sucked back in, then popped out again, over and over.

"All right, that's enough for me!" Carolyn said, standing up suddenly and walking out of the room in a huff. Crowley bounded after her. The rest of us called out to her to come back and keep watching, but the only answer we got was the slamming of her bedroom door.

We finished up the movie, and by the end of it, I felt a sense of accomplishment. I hadn't been scared at all, and that made me feel superior to Carolyn. There was also this feeling of getting away with something, the fact that my friends and I really had no business watching such a bad movie, but we had done it anyway. Aside from all of the violence in it, there was also a lot of swearing, which made me miss Carl a little bit.

I did feel kind of bad for Carolyn, though, and while Dennis and Susanna remained in the den talking about some of the other horror movies they had seen, Tim and I went down the hall to Carolyn's room to see how she was doing. I knocked on the door and waited for her to say we could come in, then found her on her bed, reading through a music magazine.

"How's Duran Duran doing?" I asked, figuring she was probably reading about her favorite band.

"What?" she asked, apparently still not in a good mood.

"Um, nothing, just…" I was unsure how to get out what I wanted to say. "Are you okay?"

"Sure, fine, whatever."

"I mean, I know you don't like scary movies and all, but was it really that bad?"

She sighed. "I don't know. Kind of. It's…" She shrugged.

"No, I get it," Tim said. "It's not just the movie; it's how you feel afterwards. Like once it's all over, you still keep thinking about it."

"Right!" Carolyn said. "Like whenever I walk down the hall, I keep thinking that that stupid hockey-masked guy is going to jump out at me with a big knife. I know it's not really going to happen, but…" She sighed. "I don't know."

"But think about it!" Tim continued. "Imagine if that did really happen right now. You're a vampire! If some dumb killer guy with a knife came after you, all you'd have to do is bite him on the neck, and *boom!* He's down."

Carolyn thought about this for a moment, then gave a weak smile. "Hmm. I guess so."

"Wow, Jason versus the vampires," I said, suddenly inspired. "Now that would make a cool movie."

Carolyn gave me a disdainful look, then softened. "Yeah, it might."

"Are you going to be okay going to bed tonight?" I asked.

"This morning," Tim corrected.

"Yeah, yeah," I said.

"I… I think so. Maybe I'll feel better imagining the scary movie guy getting his ass kicked by all of us as vampires." She smiled, then picked up her magazine. I could tell that this was our cue to leave.

The mention of bed prompted me to ask Susanna how we were going to handle our sleeping arrangements this time, if we were going to do the same thing as before with blocking out all of the windows with black garbage bags. She said that we would, but with one major modification.

"This time, we're just going to blot out the windows on the western side of the house, the ones not visible from the street," she said.

"Why?"

"Well, it might look kind of weird to the neighbors. I didn't even really think about that last time, but given the entire thing that happened with Gary…"

"Oh," Tim said. "You're afraid that if he happens to walk by the house and sees that, he'll tell someone about it."

"But what if he comes in the backyard and sees those windows?" I asked.

"I don't think he'll do that," Susanna said. "If I'm right, his mother will convince him to leave us alone and that you kids were just performing a particularly nasty joke on him. And eventually, he'll convince himself that that's true."

"Yeah, I remember my mom telling me that people don't like to believe things they can't understand," Tim added.

I hoped that they were right.

For the next hour or so, everyone set about placing the plastic bags over the windows, holding them in place with masking tape as before. Prior to this, we worked out just who would be sleeping in which room. Both mine and Carolyn's rooms were on the front, east-facing side of the house, so sleeping in there during the day wouldn't be possible. Instead, Carolyn would be sleeping in our parents' room, Susanna in her own room upstairs, and my friends and I would be in the yellow den using a combination of sleeping bags, the couch, and the mattress from my bed.

At one point, Dennis and I were alone in my parents' room as we were putting the bags over the windows in there, and he said that he wanted to tell me something, but I needed to keep it a secret.

Unsure what was coming, I said, "Okay," but it came out more like a question than a statement.

"Well, I'm psychic," he said simply. "Like, for real."

I began to laugh, then immediately stopped when I saw his expression. "Wait, are you serious?"

"Yes," he said, still frowning at me. "You remember how that kept happening tonight during the movie? When we kept saying things the other was thinking?"

"Well, yeah, but…"

"I've been doing stuff like that all my life." He almost sounded sad about it. "I can't really help it."

"Well, sure, but I do it too sometimes. Carolyn said it's just coincidence. I remember one time a few summers ago at my aunt and uncle's, and there were these couple of days where I kept doing that to Carolyn, saying stuff she was just about to, stuff like that…"

"Maybe you are too, then!" Dennis said. "That would be pretty cool."

I had to admit that he was right. I had always liked science fiction and had seen shows about psychics and telepathic people, but I was torn on whether or not any of that was real. I had seen one program, a documentary about a man who claimed to be psychic and to have telekinetic powers, but the show ended up proving that the man was a fraud and was just using subtle conjuring tricks to fool people. So I kind of had it in my head that that was all there was to people who claimed to be psychic. But then again, I hadn't really believed in vampires until a couple of years ago, either.

"Okay, what am I thinking of right now?" I said, picturing a playing card, the ace of spades, in my head.

"It doesn't work like that. It's more… um… accidental."

"Sure."

"No, I'm serious! Like, remember that bit near the beginning of the movie when the girl got her leg sliced open, and all that blood went everywhere, and I said, 'Tasty!' and you said you were just about to say it?"

"Yeah…"

"Well, it's not like I was sitting there trying to look inside your mind and saying, 'What's Ray thinking right now?' It just… kind of happened."

I still wasn't convinced. The idea sounded cool, but I still didn't know whether to give it any serious consideration.

Dennis seemed to pick up on this, and he looked disappointed. "Look, never mind. It's… Just don't tell anyone else, okay? You let me in on this vampire thing, so I thought it might be cool to tell you one of my secrets, too. But don't go blabbing it to everyone else." I said I wouldn't. "I mean it. I made the mistake of telling my sister about it a while back, and all she did was make fun of me for it. I later had to tell her that I was just kidding, but I don't think she believed me."

"Okay, don't worry," I said. "I mean, if you are, then cool. I just don't know if I can believe in that."

"I'm not sure if I can believe in vampires, then," he said with a wicked smile. For the majority of this conversation, we had stopped our work and just stood there talking, Dennis standing on a stepladder and holding a garbage bag in place over the top of one of the windows, and me holding a roll of tape and some scissors. "Come on," he said, looking more serious. "The others might need the ladder soon."

"You guys done with the ladder yet?" Carolyn called from the hallway.

Dennis grinned at me again.

The following night, I was woken by the alarm on my digital watch, and I soon heard both Tim's and Dennis's going off as well. Sleeping on my mattress in a different room had felt kind of odd, but it wasn't intolerable. It was different and therefore interesting.

Once Susanna was up, she opened the front door and retrieved the newspaper, repeating her practice from before. "Hmm," she said, looking through the pages.

"What?" I asked.

"No mention of our attacks last night at all. That's a little weird."

It wasn't until she said this that I realized that we had completely forgotten to check the TV news the night before after getting home, something we did regularly two years earlier. Then I remembered that doing so had usually been Carl's idea. He always liked seeing us, or mentions of us anyway, in the news. I did too; it made it feel like we were some sort of local celebrities, but evil ones.

"Why not?" Tim asked.

"Who knows," Carolyn said. "You wanna call them up and ask?" She stuck out her fingers and mimed putting a phone up to her head, saying, "'Hello, newspaper people? How come you didn't tell everyone about us being vampires?'"

"Oh, shut up," Tim said.

"Whatever; who cares," I said. "Let's just go out and get some blood."

"Yeah," Dennis agreed.

Not long afterwards, we made our way to a neighborhood pretty far from our own, somewhere between our house and downtown. Unfortunately, there weren't very many people around, at least, not a large enough group for all of us to attack at once.

This meant that Dennis and I had to break off from the others while they went after a group of three people on one street, and he and I killed two other people on another. I again enjoyed the kill and loved the taste of the blood, and I thought once more about how new all of this was to Dennis, hoping he was enjoying it.

He clearly was, as evidenced by the huge grin on his face as he stood over his victim and wiped his mouth, laughing. I couldn't help but do the same. We had attacked them as bats, then each changed into our person forms to finish them off.

"That was good," I said.

"Yeah, it was," Dennis said, looking down at the body of the young man he had just killed.

"We should get back to the others," I said. "What are you doing?"

He had bent down and was pulling at the man's side, then rolled him over onto his stomach. He reached into the man's back pocket and pulled out a wallet, which he placed onto the sidewalk. "Your turn," he said to me.

"What?"

"Get his, too," he said, pointing at the guy I had just killed.

"Why?"

"Come on, just do it."

I went along with what he was saying, uncertain what he was up to. The man I had killed had fallen face down when I bit him, so I didn't have to roll his body over. Reluctantly following Dennis's instructions, I removed the wallet and placed it next to the other one.

"Now," Dennis said, kneeling down in front of the two wallets. He held out his hand, fingers straight, palm flat. He hovered his hand over each wallet.

"What are you doing?"

"Trying to guess which one has more money in it." Finally I understood; this was related to the psychic stuff he had told me about the night before. After a few moments, he picked up the wallet on the left and opened it, then began counting the money. "Fifteen... twenty. Okay, now you get the other one."

I realized that Dennis's intention was for us to keep the money, which bugged me for some reason. "So we're thieves now, too?"

"Ray, we just killed them. I really don't think they need their money anymore."

"Yeah, I suppose you're right," I said, bending down and picking up the wallet. I thumbed through it, catching a glimpse of the man's driver's license. He looked completely different in his photo than he had earlier when Dennis and I descended upon him and his friend, and the sight of him still alive in that picture unnerved me. I quickly flipped past the license and found the money, which I counted. The wallet had almost forty dollars in it.

"Crap," Dennis said.

"Way to go, Mr. Psychic," I said.

"Well, it doesn't work all the time," he said, dejected. "But sometimes I can do it. It's called clairvoyance."

"Fine," I said, suddenly feeling exposed and nervous. We had been hanging around next to our victims for way too long. "We need to get out of here before someone spots us." I almost felt like someone may have already, or maybe I was just feeling guilty about stealing the dead men's wallets.

Back home, everyone talked about what we had done while we were out. Dennis didn't mention how he and I had robbed our victims after killing them, so I kept quiet about it as well, thinking that Susanna or Carolyn might disapprove.

As we talked, Crowley moved about the den, occasionally sniffing or rubbing up against each of us. He had been wary of my friends when they had first come over the day before, but he became comfortable with them soon enough. Tim asked about what had happened to King and how we had come to have a cat instead of a dog, and Carolyn and I told him the details.

"So how did you come up with the name Crowley?" he asked.

"Oh, I didn't name him," Carolyn said. "That was Sondra, the girl I got him from. She was kind of weird, but cool."

"Kind of weird how?" Dennis asked.

"Well, she was into witchcraft and all this occult kind of stuff."

"Really?" Dennis seemed intrigued.

"Yeah. And I think she said that she named the cat after an Ozzy Osbourne song."

"So now we have a satanic kitty," Susanna said, smiling.

"He's not satanic," Carolyn said angrily. "But he can be kind of strange sometimes. Like, I swear he understands English."

Carolyn and I had talked about this before, and I had seen what she meant, so I chimed in. "Yeah! Like sometimes you'll say to him, 'Crowley, put that down,' and he'll..." Crowley, who had been slowly creeping over to Dennis, stopped suddenly and looked over at me, seeming confused. "No, I don't mean now!" I laughed, and so did Carolyn.

"My dad said that witchcraft and Satanism aren't really the same thing," Dennis said. I knew bits and pieces about Dennis's father and the rest of his family, including the fact that his father used to be an Episcopalian priest, but he had left the church for some reason, possibly something to do with divorcing Dennis's mother, whom I had only met a couple of times. I didn't really understand all of the details, nor did I know much about divorce. My parents were, as far as I knew, happily married, and that was good enough for me.

Crowley had resumed his approach to Dennis, who bent down in his chair and reached out his hand, saying in an exaggeratedly enthusiastic voice, "And you're not a Satanist, are you, little...?"

Without warning, Crowley let out a little snarl and leapt up at Dennis's hand, scratching him. I immediately remembered the time that Susanna's old cat, Muffin, had scratched my face when I was much younger. Dennis's manner had been very similar to my own when my particular incident had occurred; I had bent down and thought I was just being friendly to the cat, only to have it leap up into my face and claw my left cheek, leaving me bleeding and crying.

"Ow!" Dennis shouted, jumping back. Crowley immediately ran from him and across the room. "You little shit!" He shook his hand and then held it tightly, wincing at the pain. "I'm going to bite you and drain every last drop of blood out of you!" His fangs showed more prominently than usual as he ranted.

"Dennis, calm down!" Susanna said.

"If you lay a finger on him, I'll rip your damn throat out!" Carolyn shouted at him, shooting up from her chair. While Dennis had seemed threatening in his anger, Carolyn looked about ten times as fierce. I wanted to somehow fix the situation, but I was too surprised by how quickly everything had happened.

"Whoa, whoa, whoa!" Tim said, also standing up and holding his hands out. "Calm down, everybody! We're all friends here! Really, Dennis, it was just a little scratch, right?"

"Says you," Dennis said after sucking at his wound briefly and looking at it with a pained expression. Then he looked at it again more calmly. "Hmm," he said, then brought his hand to his mouth again and began sucking at it.

"Dennis, stop that," Susanna said.

"What?" Dennis said, stopping what he was doing. "Tastes good, you know."

"Don't drink your own blood," she said. "That's gross."

"Why?" he asked, but Susanna only responded with an angry stare. "Fine," he said, folding his arms. "Sorry about yelling at your cat, Carolyn."

For a moment, I was reminded of the time that Carolyn had angrily confronted Carl two years before when he called her a bitch. Dennis had similarly gone from angry to submissive after seeing her darker side, but this confrontation had felt a lot less comical. I hadn't even been sure how to react, which is why I remained still, waiting to see what would happen.

"Yeah, sorry too," she said, walking over to the side of the room where Crowley was. As she walked, she caught her leg on the coffee table and tripped, which I involuntarily laughed at. I clammed up immediately when she glared at me. She then joined Crowley on the floor, petting him and asking him if he was okay.

"Okay, okay, everyone," Susanna said. "It's almost eleven o'clock. Let's check the news and see if they said anything about us this time."

Surprisingly, there were still no mentions of our attacks. Back in 1983, there were constant reports both on TV and in the newspaper about what we had done, but no one ever figured out exactly what had happened. As far as the rest of the city was concerned, people were mysteriously being killed, and that may or may not have been due to vampires, or it might have just been some vicious bats on the loose. Susanna had tried to explain to us one night that everyone had been in denial, going on a long and boring explanation about how people tended to do that, and also trying to explain to us how the city of Augusta was run by those who wanted to keep the status quo. Neither Carolyn nor my young friends and I really got what she was saying at the time.

She picked up on this theme again the following night after reading through the paper, still not finding any stories about vampire activity.

"See, the thing about Augusta is that it's all old money."

"What does that mean?" I asked, more aggravated than curious.

"The same rich white people run everything, passing down their wealth from generation to generation, so the same families stay in charge over the years."

"What's wrong with that?" I asked.

"Because it means that minorities, poor people, black people, and so on… They never get a chance to have any real power in this city. So nothing ever really changes."

I barely understood what she was talking about, nor did I see what this had to do with our attacks not being reported. I had never given much thought to things like politics and race, but part of that was a symptom of what Susanna was describing. I did not have very much exposure to black people, or really any other races than my own, aside from what I saw of them on TV. There was only a handful of black children at my school, which was a private, Episcopalian school populated mostly by the sons and daughters of the wealthy. My parents, and likely many of my friends' parents, were well off mainly because they inherited so much from their own parents.

My friends and I weren't prejudiced against other races, or at least, we didn't think we were. None of us harbored any extreme hatred towards blacks; one of the first people that Dennis made friends with when he came to our school in fourth grade was the only black kid in our grade, a boy named Antonio. But truth be told, us well-off white people were indeed the majority, which was just what we were used to. When Dennis and I were still at odds during his first year at the school, some of the other boys and I would insult Antonio for being black, but to us, that was no different than making fun of what he was wearing or any other aspect of him, just as I would ridicule Dennis for having red hair. And once Dennis and I became friends in fifth grade, I warmed up to Antonio as well, and the color of his skin was more or less a non-issue as far as I was concerned. I was aware that he was different, but I no longer considered that a bad thing.

It would be several years before I began to understand the bigger picture, though, and I expressed my confusion to Susanna over what this racial stuff she was going on about had to do with us at the moment.

"Well, I don't exactly mean it's a racial thing," she said.

"You're losing 'em, Susanna," Carolyn said with a sneer.

Susanna got a pained look, realizing that a group of ten- and eleven-year-olds and a sarcastic teenager probably wasn't the best audience for this kind of talk. She sighed. "I guess what I'm getting at is that the powers that be, the authorities I guess you could say, don't want people to know about our attacks as vampires because they don't want people to get into a panic. So they're covering it up."

"Seriously?" Carolyn said. "Come on."

"No, I mean it. And…" She paused, looking thoughtful, and her mouth dropped open as her eyebrows went upward. "I think I just figured something out. Give me a sec." She rushed back over to the newspaper, which was still spread open on the kitchen table. After scanning a few articles, she said triumphantly, "A-*ha,*" and firmly pressed her finger down on the page.

"What?" Tim asked.

"I didn't see it at first because I was just looking for reports of people being killed. And while there aren't any of those, there are some stories about people going missing instead. There were some in yesterday's paper, too, and if you remember, they talked about that on the news last night."

She was right, but I still didn't see what this had to do with us, and I said so.

"Because the places they're saying the people were last seen are very close to the same places we've been killing each night."

"So…" Tim said pensively, "the police are… Wait. I still don't get it. Why would the police hide the bodies?"

"I didn't say they were," Susanna said. "Just that they're not telling anyone what happened to the people." She seemed to waver as she said this, possibly doubting her own explanation.

"I don't buy it," Carolyn said.

"And I don't really care," I added. "I'm thirsty. Can we come up with weird ideas some other time and just go out and feed already?"

Susanna sighed again. "Fine. But I still think something's up. And I think it's political."

"Whatever!" Dennis said. "Let's just go!"

Susanna led us out through the front door. As we walked, I felt impatient with her attitude, the way she seemed to think that her idea was too much for us to handle, where I just saw it as pointless and improbable. It also surprised me that she didn't berate me and my friends for being too young to understand what she was saying.

Just before turning into a bat and flying up into the air, Susanna said under her breath, "This is what I get for hanging out all week with a bunch of kids half my age."

We killed that night in the area of town known informally as South Augusta, though really it was just the southern part of the city. There was in fact an actual town across the river called North Augusta, but that was somewhere my family didn't often go. Perhaps because of the existence of the city of North Augusta, people were led to create a sort of fictional "South Augusta" to differentiate it from the central part of the city, where the majority of the population resided. It may also have even been another symptom of the separatism and political stuff that Susanna had unsuccessfully tried to educate us on earlier in the night, but this didn't really concern me.

Still, once my head was clear after having fed and I was flying back home with the others, I began to think more about what Susanna had said, the idea of there being some kind of cover-up by the police. We had just killed five people, and I tried to picture in my head what would happen if she were right, that a bunch of cops in uniform would soon show up and stealthily shuffle the bodies away in order to dissuade panic. But then a major flaw in the idea popped into my head.

"Susanna," I said, "if what you're saying is true, well, what about the people who called the police in the first place? I mean, isn't that what usually happens? We kill some people, someone finds the bodies, and then they call the police? What about them? Wouldn't they talk to the news people, too? Tell them they found all these bodies drained of blood?"

She seemed to ponder this for a few moments. "I don't know. Maybe." I expected more of an argument from her, but none came. Then she said, "Look, down there."

There was a man walking alone on the sidewalk, oblivious to the five vampire bats high above him. Without another word, Susanna broke off from the group and flew down to him, latching onto his neck and bringing him down to the ground. I found this unusual, and I hovered in place with the others, who also watched her.

"What did she do that for?" Dennis asked.

"Still hungry, I guess," Carolyn said. "So am I, come to think of it." All of a sudden, she too flew off and toward the ground, zooming in on another solitary victim, a woman who had been far enough away from Susanna and her prey not to have been aware of them. Carolyn bit the woman and continued drinking from her after she fell.

"That looks good," Dennis said.

"Yeah, it does," Tim agreed.

I felt strange. I was jealous that Susanna and Carolyn had gotten to kill again. "Well, if they get to have dessert, so do I." I looked around, hoping to spot another victim for myself. We were high enough up in the air to be able to see several streets at once, and I soon spotted a group of three people walking along one of the roads. "Come on," I said to Tim and Dennis.

I led them to the group, and we each chose and brought down our victims. The one I killed, a short man somewhat older than I was used to killing, tasted better than my previous kill that night. Maybe it was because I had jokingly called him "dessert." Whatever the reason, I relished the kill more than usual.

When I finished drinking, I fluttered up from the body and looked around, seeing the bodies Tim and Dennis had left behind, but not Tim and Dennis themselves. I was alone, and I began to feel scared. I remembered the time I went out on my own to search for Carolyn two years earlier, how I had thought at the time that I could navigate the city, only to get lost for a while. Because we were in South Augusta, I knew that I needed to head north, but I wasn't sure which way that was.

As I tried to remember exactly where I was in relation to the direction we had been heading before Susanna had suddenly broken away from us, I was distracted, this time by a scream from a woman who had stumbled upon our newly created crime scene.

I was on her neck before she had managed to run more than a few feet, and I drank her dry, no longer concerned with finding my way home. She was a black woman, the first I had ever killed, I realized once I was done. That made me think back to Susanna's talk about race and politics earlier.

Reminded that I needed to get home somehow, I wondered where the other vampires were, if they had already made it back to the house without me, or maybe they were looking for me instead. I resumed my course to what I was pretty sure was north, only to be distracted yet again by a potential victim. This one wasn't alone; there were two of them, a man and a woman who were standing and looking around, the woman saying something about hearing screams.

I took the man first, and the woman ran away as I drank from him. After just a few moments, though, she made her way back to us, crying and shouting "No!" over and over. I reasoned that the man was probably her boyfriend or something, and she was upset that I was killing him. Maybe she stupidly thought that she could help him. I proved her wrong by flying straight from the dead man's neck to her own, enjoying her shriek as I bit down and took her life as well.

This went on for a while, so much that I lost count of how many people I killed as I slowly tried to make my way home. I just felt compelled to keep doing it over and over, and when I tried to think about why this was happening and how I couldn't stop, those thoughts were shoved aside whenever I spotted another person, another meal. I wanted blood, tons and tons of it, and getting it felt like the right thing to do. I was a vampire. This was what I was. Despite how much I was drinking, I never felt full, nor was I satisfied. The killing became almost mechanical. It felt sometimes like someone was watching me, and I was expected to fulfill my role, to do what needed to be done.

And then, with no explanation, the compulsion to keep killing left me. I realized that I had been doing it over and over, that this wasn't normal behavior. Usually, the group went out and killed once, maybe twice, often together but occasionally separated up, but nothing like this had ever happened. Now I was all alone with no idea where I was. I flew up into the night sky and then hovered, looking around with my special light-up night vision eyes, hoping to see a friendly bat somewhere in the distance. But there was no one.

Fighting the urge to panic, I looked back down at the streets below me, hoping to spot something that looked familiar. Throughout my repeatedly interrupted journey, I had still flown north, as far as I knew. I tried to remember how to find the North Star, then realized that I had no idea how to do so, wishing I had paid more attention in Science class the previous year when we had gone over astronomy.

Finally, I spotted an area that looked familiar, a patch of darkness with long strips of light on it, the small airport next to the Daniel Village shopping center. This was the area I had tried to find my way to while searching for Carolyn in 1983, and ever since then, I had made it a point to pay attention to the route between it and my house. Following the streets the same way I would have had I been riding in a car, I flew home, glad that the scary events of the night were almost over.

I landed on the front porch, hoping that the others were already home. I tried the doorknob and was relieved to find that the door was unlocked, but this disturbed me as well. It wasn't common practice in our family to leave the front door unlocked. I walked in tentatively, then called out, "Hello?"

"In here, Ray!" I heard Carolyn call from the yellow den. Relieved, I shut the door behind me and walked into the den, where I found Susanna, Carolyn, and Tim waiting for me, but not Dennis.

"Where's Dennis?" I asked.

"Hopefully he'll be back soon," Susanna said.

"Are you okay?" Carolyn asked.

"I guess," I said. I realized suddenly that I felt guilty over how out of control I had gotten earlier, but I also wondered if the others had done the same thing. "Are you all… um…"

"Yes, we all had something weird happen to us tonight," Susanna said. "Let me guess, you kept stopping over and over and killing on your way here?"

"Yes!" I said, feeling less guilty, even redeemed. I could tell from her tone that she was implying that the same thing had indeed happened to everyone else, not just me. "What the hell was that?" I caught myself, realizing that I didn't usually swear around my sisters, even if I did occasionally do it with my friends.

Susanna ignored this, though, and just said, "I don't know. I really don't." There was something odd about her demeanor, and I couldn't quite tell what it was.

"I think I do," Tim said, also with a strange tone. He seemed tense, kind of reserved, almost like he was angry about something.

We were all a bit shaken up, but I was curious as to what he might have come up with, so I asked him what he thought.

"I don't want to say yet," he said. "Wait until Dennis comes back. If he does."

I got the implications of what he was saying, the notion that, unlike the rest of us, Dennis might not be able to find his way back to the house, that the same weird compulsion to keep killing had driven him too far off track. But almost immediately, there was a knock at the front door, and I jumped up and ran to it, letting Dennis in. He too looked freaked out, but glad to see me.

"Man, what the hell was all that?" he asked in almost a whisper. "I mean, I was into the vampire thing and all, and I thought it was cool, but I didn't think it would be like that!"

"It isn't usually," I said, leading him into the den. "Tim says he thinks he knows what happened."

As Dennis settled down, still somewhat shaken, Tim said with a smug look on his face, "Yeah, I think I do." He then turned to Susanna and said sharply, "So, Susanna, when did you slip all of us the cure?"

Susanna, sitting in her wicker chair, straightened up and looked at Tim with shock. "What? No! Why would I do that?"

I began to realize what Tim was getting at, and I immediately felt suspicious.

"This impulse to kill over and over. We all felt it tonight. Like we couldn't help it. The same thing happened to Carolyn before when you gave her the cure and it took all that time to work." Tim seemed very sure of himself, and he was drilling my sister the same way his father might do so to a witness in a courtroom, if the TV shows I'd seen were any indication.

My mind flashed back to Carolyn's behavior two years before when the antidote to the potion seemed to make her go crazy, causing her to kill several times in one night. In fact, this was the first time since then that I was able to recall that so clearly, including the remorse that I had over us betraying her and the pain I felt when I finished off one of her victims for her. I hadn't thought of that little girl for ages. And as far as what had happened to me earlier in the night was concerned, I didn't like the way I had felt so forced into doing those repeated killings this night, and it felt like a violation to have lost my own sense of control.

"No, I didn't, I swear!" Susanna said to Tim, then looked around at the rest of us. She seemed genuinely upset and surprised, which was not something I was used to. I could see where Tim was coming from and feared that he was right. "I swear, you guys," she continued, almost frantic. "I didn't do anything like that."

"She's right," Carolyn said calmly. "It wasn't like that. I mean, what I went through before wasn't like what tonight was like."

"What do you mean?" I asked.

"I mean... I'm not sure," Carolyn continued. "Tonight was different. Back then, I think what happened was that once the antidote was working in me, the vampire inside of me knew it was dying. It was like she knew that, and she had to get in as many kills as possible. So there was that big killing spree, and then, well, the next night, nothing. I was human again." She looked ashamed, and despite the air of suspicion and accusation in the room, I believed her. I began to believe that Susanna was innocent of wrongdoing, too.

"I didn't know about all that," Dennis said, and I realized that I had never told him about Carolyn's weird behavior those last few nights. "But as far as I was concerned, tonight I mean, it felt like something was driving me on. I almost heard a voice, I thought, like someone saying to me, 'That one.' 'Yes.' 'Go on.' Stuff like that."

"Yeah, kind of like that," Carolyn said, then shook her head. "Tonight wasn't like two years ago."

I hadn't heard anyone speaking to me, but I still empathized with what Dennis and Carolyn were saying. The urge for me to kill was similar, like I was supposed to keep doing it, and I told myself that it was the right thing to do. "So then what was it? Did you maybe get the potion wrong somehow this time?" I directed this last question to Susanna.

"I don't know," she said, still looking bewildered. "I mean, I'm certain I mixed it the same way as before..." She sighed, looking around the room at no one in particular. "I really, really just don't know." Again, she seemed genuinely confused and somewhat scared, which led me to believe that she was telling the truth.

"Okay, okay," Tim said. "Sorry. I was just trying to figure this whole thing out." He looked pensive. "Well, hey, why don't we check the news?"

"Yeah, let's see what they say," I said, checking my watch. "Whoa! It's already 2:32 in the morning!"

"Guess we missed it, then," Carolyn said.

"No, I set the timer earlier tonight," Tim said.

I was impressed by the way that Tim had managed to figure out our VCR's timer on his own without any prompting from me; the procedure for making that thing work was pretty complicated. But even though he had a different brand of VCR at his house, he apparently had little trouble learning how to work ours.

We watched the videotaped recording of the 11:00 news, and this time, there were indeed mentions of vampire attacks, but they were speculative. People had called in and reported sightings of both bats and dead bodies, but what was interesting was that the police had found no evidence when arriving on the scene.

"See?" Susanna said, pointing at the TV. "I told you! They're lying!"

"Shh!" I said, still trying to listen to the report.

Not much else was said other than a vague warning against panic and urging people to stay indoors. Mention was also made of the mysterious attacks two years earlier, and the reporter emphasized the fact that no concrete evidence of vampires was ever found back then.

The following story was about a sharp increase in the number of missing persons that was occurring, but no connection seemed to be made to the "alleged" vampires. I found this odd, but maybe I was too close to what was actually happening to understand why anyone else wouldn't see the correlation immediately. Dennis, however, came up with yet another possibility that hadn't even crossed my mind, which he brought up once we turned the tape off.

"I bet you I know what's going on!" he said. "Our victims! The people we're killing!"

"What about them?" I asked.

"Well, isn't it supposed to be that when someone gets killed by a vampire, then they come back to life as a vampire too? That's what's happening! They're getting up and flying away after we leave!"

Susanna laughed slightly. "No, Dennis. That's not how it works with us."

"Huh?"

"Yeah, it's true," I said. "Our victims don't come back. Susanna explained it to us before, I mean, last time, when you weren't here."

"Right," Tim said. "Something to do with how we were turned into vampires by a potion, not by dying and coming back to life like regular vampires. So our victims don't, either."

"Oh," Dennis said, looking genuinely disappointed.

"No, I really do think that this is some big conspiracy by the authorities," Susanna said. None of us had any better suggestions to offer.

We were uneasy the rest of the night, and the five of us stayed together as we tried to distract ourselves by watching TV. While some stations were off the air, there were still plenty of cable channels that showed various programs, most of them pretty boring. I looked through the *TV Guide* hoping to find something interesting, and I wasn't disappointed.

"Hey, look!" I said excitedly. "There's a movie coming on at four called *Vampire Circus!*"

"What?" Carolyn asked. "Vampires in a circus?"

"That's what it says," I told her. "Something about an evil circus coming to town. Maybe the performers are vampires and kill a bunch of people or something."

"Oh great," Carolyn said. "More horror movies. Lovely."

"Sounds cool to me!" Dennis said. Tim nodded in agreement.

"Oh, come on," I said to Carolyn. "It says it's from 1972. It's probably not all that scary. Hey, Dennis, maybe it's one of those cheesy 'sledgehammer' movies your dad likes!"

He groaned comically. "Oh, God, I hope not. In that case, never mind."

"No, let's watch it!" Tim said. "It might be cool."

Susanna agreed, saying that if nothing else, it might be good for a laugh.

As it turned out, the movie did seem pretty cool at the beginning. It was set sometime in the past, and we rooted for the vampire as he battled several angry villagers who wanted to put a stop to his evil. We cheered whenever he bit and killed someone, then booed when he was killed by a stake through the heart.

But after about fifteen or twenty minutes, the movie suddenly became boring. The people in their weird costumes and British accents started droning on and on about nothing at all, and I quickly lost interest, as did Dennis and Tim. We gave up about half an hour into the film, but Susanna said she wanted to keep watching it. Surprisingly, so did Carolyn.

My friends and I went into the red den and watched TV in there instead, desperately trying to find something good on. After a while, Carolyn joined us, saying she'd had enough of the movie.

"Too stupid, huh?" I asked her.

"No, too disturbing. I mean, it wasn't really all that bad of a story, but... um..."

"What?" Tim asked.

"I don't know... Like there was this midget clown guy who was all creepy and stuff. And the rest of it..." She shuddered. "Forget it. I don't want to talk about it. Susanna wants to finish watching it, so whatever. More power to her, I guess."

"Scaaaaredy, scaaaaredy..." Dennis sang quietly, grinning.

"Oh, shut up. It's not so much the scariness as it is the... goriness, if that's even a word. All blood and guts flying everywhere... It's just not my thing. And, like, we've done plenty of killing of our own, and we know it's not like that in real life. I don't mind a scary story, I mean, you're talking to a girl who reads Edgar Allan Poe sometimes just for fun."

"You still do that?" I asked. I remembered a while back when she had gotten interested in his writing, first being assigned to read some of his short stories for school, then later getting a book of his work and reading it at home. I had thought that she'd given that up after a short time, particularly as she grew up and became more feminine.

"Sure," she said. "I picked it up again recently, I guess trying to psyche myself up for all this vampire stuff again. And I can handle the printed page okay. It's the images on TV, actually seeing it, that I just don't like."

"Well, the other thing is the music," Tim said. "Half the time, if I actually jump or get scared or anything during a movie, it's because of that, the music making it all scary." He started imitating the music he was talking about: *"Dmmmmm.... dmmmmm.... dmm dmm DMMMMM!"* As he did so, he held his fingers up in a crooked gesture and waved his hands back and forth.

"Oh, I know," Carolyn said. "I really hate it when it's all quiet and then something jumps out and there's this *BOOMP!!* sound." She thrust her hands out quickly as she imitated the music cue. "Makes me crap my pants every time."

I laughed, then pretended I was sniffing the air as I leaned towards her. "Really?"

Carolyn rolled her eyes, but Dennis and Tim laughed. She sighed dramatically. "Boys…"

We managed to get through the rest of the night distracting ourselves with the television and with conversation, but when it came time to go to bed before sunrise, I found it difficult to get to sleep. What had happened to me earlier that night, the unexpected compulsion to keep killing, was still bugging me, mostly because it was unexplained. I was afraid that the same thing might happen again the following night, and I wondered if maybe we should stay home instead of going out.

When we got up that night, though, I was once again craving blood, but not any more than usual. I felt more or less normal, or at least the "normal" that I had gotten used to when under the influence of the vampire potion.

Tim had again set the timer to record the 6:00 news, and we watched it before leaving the house, hoping to see some mention of our attacks and the mysterious disappearances. There was quite a bit of talk about both, and finally, people were starting to make a connection, speculating that the fact — or fiction, as Susanna sarcastically pointed out — that so many people were disappearing might have something to do with the recent sightings of vampire bats and reports of drained bodies being found. A policeman who was interviewed also made the suggestion that the entire thing might be a hoax, "some stunt to drum up fear or garner attention," as he put it.

"Yeah, bullshit," Carolyn said. "I think you're right, Susanna. The police are doing this, aren't they? Trying to be in control of everything. I thought you were full of it last night going on about conspiracy theories and all, but now I'm not so sure."

"Why, thank you," Susanna said condescendingly. "Glad you approve."

"No, I'm serious!" she said, somewhat apologetically. "It goes back to what you said about people being in denial when they don't want to believe something. I mean, two years ago, back when people were all worried about what we were doing and suspecting it was vampires, well, take your parents, for example," she said, turning to Tim.

"What about them?"

"Well, I remember both you and Carl talking to your parents on the phone that week, and there's all this talk on the news of vampires and people being killed and all that, but did they ever bring that up? Did they say, 'Hey, kids, come home! There are vampires on the loose!'"

"No. They never even brought it up." Tim thought for a moment. "Glad they didn't, though."

"Actually, I should probably call home just to check in," Dennis said. "Maybe Tim should, too."

"That's probably a good idea," I said. "Just don't say anything about the news or anything. You wouldn't want to give them some excuse to tell you to come home early."

I waited impatiently for Tim and Dennis to make their phone calls, neither of which took very long, and nothing interesting came of that. I was eager to get out and kill, but at the same time, I was nervous, still afraid that what happened the previous night might happen again. As it turned out, none of us ever felt that intense desire to continuously kill the entire night, but there was a new problem to deal with.

Our actions the night before, though involuntary, had consequences. Lots of people had been killed, and there was no denying that, even if people weren't sure just how. As a result, the police were everywhere.

No matter where we went, we saw parked patrol cars, the police apparently poised to confront any potential killers, vampire or otherwise. I began to wonder about Susanna's conspiracy theory again, picturing policemen springing out of their cars to confront us should we attack. I had seen plenty of action-adventure shows on TV where the cops courageously fought the bad guys, and suddenly, I realized that we were the bad guys and that the cops might turn their firepower on us. Then again, I had seen Carolyn kill a policeman back in 1983, and the thought of that made me wonder if I really needed to be worried at all. Enforcers of the law or not, they were still just ordinary humans, and we were vampires.

Patrol cars were all over the place, sometimes in seemingly random areas, but Susanna also led us to a couple of places where we had previously killed, and we saw more cars there. At one point, I didn't think there were any police cars and only saw plain, ordinary looking cars below, but Carolyn pointed out that those were likely unmarked vehicles.

"Okay," Susanna said, "enough of this. We need to find somewhere to feed, and it doesn't look like we're going to find it anywhere around here. Follow me."

"Are you feeling okay?" I asked her. "I mean…"

"I know what you mean," she snapped, then said, "Sorry. But yes. I don't feel like I did last night. Does anyone else?" No one spoke up. "Good."

"Let's hope it stays that way," Carolyn said. "Maybe last night was just a fluke."

Susanna led us to an area west of Augusta called Evans, somewhere I had heard of more than actually been to. My only real experience with the place was riding through it in the car on the way to Appling, the town where my aunt and uncle lived. Appling was definitely small and "out in the country," as people often described it, but Evans was sort of in between. There were far fewer houses than in the city, many of them situated on large properties with lots of open fields, which were visible from the main road. I had heard Carolyn describe the area before as "rural," a word I'd learned in school a year or two earlier that basically meant "out in the country." When Carolyn said the word, she did so with an exaggerated southern accent, so it came out sounding like *"roo*-rul." This was her way of describing not just the area but also its inhabitants.

We were used to hunting in the city, where there were plenty of people, enough random strangers wandering around outside at night for us to find an unlucky few and prey on them. But this was entirely different. The only people we saw were the ones driving on the road below us in cars, and those were infrequent. Dennis suggested trying to flag down a car so we could then kill the people in it, but Susanna vetoed the idea, saying that it wouldn't work.

Finally, we lucked out as we spotted a tent in the yard behind a house. The tent was dimly lit from within, and as we got closer, I figured out that this was because of a flashlight one of the occupants was holding. Once we were within range, I was able to hear a boy's voice. We approached the tent, then hovered in the air, trying to listen to what was being said.

"Really?" a young boy's voice said in response to what the other had been saying.

"Yeah, Daddy told me about it after he was lookin' at the news tonight." The way the boy pronounced "Daddy" sounded more like "Diddy." I was immediately reminded of the two mean boys who had cheated Carl at the race at the YMCA, two of our first victims. Maybe they had been from Evans, too, I thought.

"There's all these vampires," the older boy continued, "and they're goin' around killin' people." I could just barely make out their shadows on the wall of the tent; mostly they were vague dark forms on the vinyl, shifting from side to side as the boy holding the flashlight moved around slightly. "But what's really creepy is that after the people get killed, when the police get there, there aren't any bodies. It's like they just up and leave, like after they're dead."

"But how?" the younger boy said.

"Because," the older boy said, pausing dramatically, "if a vampire bites you and you die, then you come back to life as a vampire yourself. And then you kill people, too."

"Nuh-*uhhh!*" the younger boy said.

At the same time, Dennis muttered, "Told you so." This prompted a quick shushing noise from Susanna.

"What?" the younger boy said.

After a few seconds of silence, the older boy said softly, "Nothing. I thought I heard something." We flapped in place, not saying a word. After a few moments, the boy continued telling what I assumed was his younger brother about the scary vampire menace in the city, all the while not knowing that it was much closer than he realized.

"Daddy knew somebody who got killed back two years ago, too. So when he saw on the news that the vampires are back, he got real worked up. Says he's gonna take the fight to them and blow their asses away." The little boy giggled. "Don't tell Mama I said that," the older brother added.

"Okay," he said.

"Okay," Carolyn repeated, mocking the little boy's accent, which had made the word sound more like "oh-ky-ee."

The boys in the tent became still again, and the flashlight stopped moving around. "Did you hear that?" one of them whispered.

"No!" Carolyn whispered. I couldn't resist letting out a small laugh, which I then tried to hold back.

"What *was* that?" one of the boys rasped. When they were whispering, I couldn't tell their voices apart and wasn't sure which one was speaking.

"Nothing!" I said in a loud whisper. Tim and Dennis were beginning to let out stifled snickers as well.

"There's someone out there!" one of the boys said quietly.

"No there isn't!" Dennis said, also quietly.

"And even if we were, we definitely wouldn't be vampires!" Tim said, joining in on the fun. "Nope, not at all. Promise."

The boys shuffled in their tent, the flashlight moving about wildly.

"Guys," Susanna said, disapproval in her tone. And then, after a pause, she said with a smile, "Don't play with your food."

We all burst out laughing, and I noticed that the strange squeaking effect that our voices had as bats was more pronounced the louder we got. Our laughter died down, and we waited to see what happened next.

"Okay, I have this," the older boy said, but I didn't know what he meant. "When I open the tent, run straight for the house and don't look back. Ready?"

Knowing that they were about to make a run for it, I led the others over to the front of the tent and waited. The flap was unzipped quickly, and I started to lunge forward, then lurched back immediately. The older boy, whom I was seeing for the first time, was holding a large wooden cross. He thrust it out and waved it around, and we flew back from it while the younger of the two boys sprinted from the tent. The other quickly followed, still holding the cross high above his head. As he ran, he looked behind him several times, but I wasn't sure if he could actually see us. We pursued, but none of us got close enough to bite him, still afraid of coming into contact with the cross. The boys made it to the house and were yelling various pleas to their father to come help them as they tumbled inside. I heard the door lock behind them.

"Well, that didn't work," Dennis said as we hovered by the door.

There was a lot of yelling inside of the house for a few moments, and I heard heavy footsteps approaching the door. Some extremely bright floodlights suddenly came on, and after a sharp click from the lock, the door flew open. A large, bearded man stood in the doorway, and he looked around quickly as he pointed his rifle in various directions.

"Shit!" I involuntarily exclaimed. "Everyone get away!"

We flew back from the door, and the man began firing into the air. The sound of the gunshots was deafening, and I was terrified. Almost without thinking, I flew over the top of the house and to the other side of it, trying to get away from that doorway as fast as I could. I heard Susanna calling out "This way!" to the rest of us from nearby, and I realized that she had flown in the same direction I had.

After a few seconds, all of us had managed to reach the far side of the house. My heart was pounding, and for the first time, I found myself very aware of the fact that it was a tiny bat heart in a tiny bat's chest. For the moment, I was just grateful to still be alive and in one piece. I was panting heavily as I hovered, as were the others.

The gunshots had stopped, but I could hear the man yelling out various obscenities and threats, referring to us as "vampire pieces of shit" and "fucking trash." The sound of his voice began to change and become louder, and I realized that this was because he was walking around the house and in our direction.

"Let's get out of here!" I said, and we flew straight up into the air. I hoped that the altitude would be enough protection, that the man with the gun wouldn't be able to spot us once we were high enough, at which point we could get our bearings and get as far away from that house as possible.

Susanna led us away, and as we flew farther to the east, the sound of the father and his two sons yelling after us quickly faded, but I was still scared. Even when we were well out of range, I got this creepy feeling that the man with the gun could still see us. I had noticed a small scope on his rifle, and I pictured myself in the crosshairs, fearing that at any second, another shot might sound and a bullet would hit me. It took me a minute or two to feel satisfied that we were far enough away to no longer be seen, but I was still unnerved.

As we flew back to Augusta, I kept running what had happened over and over in my head. I quickly went from scared to angry, both at the father who had shot at us and at myself for being so afraid. I wasn't used to losing when it came to confrontations with humans.

The nearer we got to the city, the more dense the population became, and we managed to find five people to prey on at a newly built gas station. But the satisfaction of the kill was spoiled by my disappointment over the night's earlier events. I then thought about previous kills we had made as vampires, ones that had been successful, maybe trying to comfort myself.

I wasn't sure why, but my mind also drifted back to the Club Wars at school. I thought about some of the fights we'd had back then, both ones in which my group seemed to come out on top and others when Carl's side seemed to win out. Really, while we tried to pretend that those "battles" were a big deal at the time, nearly all of it was simply pretend violence. Most of the time, we just sniped at each other with insults and threats; it was more a war of intimidation than anything else. By the end of it all, the number of kids on Carl's side outnumbered the ones in our club, and that was because he had done something I wasn't willing to do, which was get some of the girls in the class involved.

I didn't like most girls; a lot of them still seemed prissy and rather stupid to me. But there were some who were more tomboyish and didn't mind getting their hands dirty, so Carl had no qualms about involving them in our little gang war if it meant his side would win, whatever that meant. None of us ever really had a clear picture just what we were trying to accomplish or how one side might actually defeat the other. We just liked the conflict.

Things came to a head with that last big battle, which did become physical and violent. It began when Antonio, one of the boys on my side, found a large box of tennis balls outside the door to the gym, which was adjacent to the playground. We began throwing these at Carl's group, who retaliated by throwing them back, sometimes hitting us. It was fun, but things escalated when other children began throwing large sticks, then small rocks. Once people started actually getting hurt by this, some of the kids began to fight hand to hand, knocking each other to the ground and sometimes wrestling. All of this happened over the span of just a few minutes, and our teachers were too far away to see what was really going on. To them, it probably looked like we were simply playing.

I wanted a chance to confront Carl directly, but before that could happen, a cry rang out from elsewhere in the crowd, followed by a sudden drop in the noise level as most — though not all — of the kids stopped to see what had happened. We gathered around a boy who was lying on the ground and clutching his ear, rocking back and forth and moaning in pain. It was Bryan, one of Carl's group, and on the ground next to him was a fruit from a magnolia tree. These were similar in shape to pine cones, but because they were more dense and weighed more, they were easier to throw at people, which we had done on previous occasions (but never on this scale before). I liked using them as weapons particularly because the stems on them were easily detachable, so it was fun to pretend that they were actually hand grenades, and one could imagine themselves first pulling out the "grenade's" pin before lobbing it at somebody. It had never occurred to me that someone could be seriously injured by them, but apparently this one had been thrown with enough force to do some damage.

Bryan was usually quite a tough boy and a jerk, and the sight of him lying on the ground near to tears amused me at first. I was still riding the high of the battle. His wavy brown hair was full of sand, and he had carved little patterns in the dirt with his limbs as he flailed around. But it quickly became apparent that this was serious, particularly when I spotted the blood leaking through his fingers as he held his hand to his ear.

After a visit to the school nurse and some patching up, Bryan turned out to be okay, but this was the end as far as the Club Wars went. Perhaps trying to deflect blame from themselves, many of the students were more than willing to spill the beans to our teachers about what we had been doing. For a little while, I feared that both Carl and I would get into trouble since we were the leaders of our rival clubs, but because so many kids were involved, it wasn't easy to place the blame on just one or two people. Instead, a blanket punishment of no recess for a week for the entire grade — including those who had not taken part — was imposed, and we were forbidden to form clubs from that point on.

Still, once time had passed and Carl and I had settled our differences, he and I were able to think back on that period more fondly, even joke about it. Despite the abrupt and violent end, overall it had been a fun time, and we were each able to develop a grudging respect for how the other person handled it. Carl admitted that he liked how I kept my group going despite being so outnumbered by his, and I was impressed — though bothered — by how he had managed to recruit so many members, particularly the girls.

As I continued to fly, it struck me as odd how much of a contrast there was between these past events and the very real violence we had just encountered, to say nothing of the violence we inflicted on people every night. Thinking about the Club Wars just felt a little comforting, a memory of when things were simpler and less serious.

At home, I found that the others felt more or less the same way I did: first scared, relieved to get away, then angry that a family of ordinary people had managed to get the better of us.

"Those stupid rednecks," Carolyn said, scowling.

"Yeah!" Dennis said. "Who do they think they are?"

"Well, I wouldn't be surprised if one of them was named Billy Bob," Carolyn joked, but her tone was still angry. "All a-shootin' with his big ole gun and stuff," she added with her Evans accent.

"You know what really bugs me?" Susanna said.

"The fact that that entire family's IQ combined is probably less than Crowley's?" Carolyn said, petting him while he sat in her lap. He looked up at her sharply.

"I'm not sure we were ever in any real danger back there."

"What?" I asked her. "Are you kidding?"

"Yeah!" Dennis said. "That big guy meant business!"

"Oh…" Tim said, his eyebrows rising as he nodded. He looked over at Susanna. "I think I see what you're getting at."

"What do you mean?" I asked.

"Well, think about it, Ray," he said. "What are the things that can kill vampires?"

Bored and still not seeing his point, I rattled them off: "Sunlight, garlic, crosses, running water, fire, wooden stakes."

"And are bullets anywhere on that list?" Susanna asked.

Suddenly, I got it. "Wait… You're saying that we wouldn't be hurt by that? That we're invulnerable?"

"That's how it works in the movies," Dennis said, catching on. "Remember last night on TV? The big vampire guy got stabbed, but not in the right place, so his wound just healed right up. I've seen that happen with vampires getting shot in other movies, too."

"So," Tim said, smiling, "aside from the other abilities we have as vampires, not being able to be killed is on that list, too."

Susanna smiled. "Yes."

"Holy crap," I said. "That's… That's kind of cool." Very quickly, an idea began to form in my mind.

"So," Dennis began, "if Mr. Big Shot back there in the country can't hurt us with his gun…"

"Hang on, hang on, hang on," Carolyn said, waving her hands about and shaking her head. Crowley jumped out of her lap as she sat up. "If you're thinking what I think you're thinking, then stop."

Our return trip to Evans was different than the previous one. Before, we had been aimlessly searching for victims to feed on, but this time, we had a specific destination. I only hoped we could find the same house again. Now that we felt more confident in our chances of survival, we wanted another shot at these people. It didn't feel right that they had bested us in the first place.

"There it is," Susanna said, and I looked below and saw that she was right. The tent in the backyard was no longer occupied, but the lights were still on in the house. I noticed some details I hadn't before, mainly because I had been too busy flying for my life. Mounted on the front of the house was a large Confederate flag, blowing gently in the wind. Next to it was a smaller, white flag, one I wasn't familiar with. Out of curiosity, I flew closer to it, all the while keeping an eye out for anyone who might be outside and waiting for us.

A gentle breeze caught the smaller flag in just the right way, and I was able to see that it was a homemade one, a white piece of cloth with the words *VAMPIRE KILLERS* written on it in black marker. Although I hadn't seen it earlier in the night, I had no doubt that the Confederate flag was a regular fixture on the house; many southerners displayed such flags on their homes, their cars, or even their clothing. My aunt and uncle out in the country had such a flag on their house, which my father always jeered at. Both he and my mother felt that such displays, while meant to be an evocation of southern pride, were also derogatory to black people.

I didn't really care about that; it wasn't something that affected me directly. But I did find the *VAMPIRE KILLERS* flag both insulting and amusing. I had no way to know for sure, but I got the idea that it had just been put up, that the boys or their father, perhaps both, had made it by hand and put it up shortly after chasing us off earlier. It may have been meant to intimidate us, or maybe it had been put there to impress the neighbors.

"Hey!" I said quietly to the others. "Get a load of this!"

They fluttered over to me, and Tim laughed. "Oh, nice. Well, we'll just see about that." He flew onto the flag and began biting at it, shredding it as he went. Dennis and I joined in.

After a few moments, the flag was in tatters, and one final pull at its remains left it clattering to the ground, a mess of rags on a stick. Almost immediately, I heard a voice from inside the house call out. Those same booming footsteps approached the front door, and I knew that Billy Bob the gun-toter was about to make another appearance. This time, I was ready for him. As soon as he opened the door, I'd go straight for his neck.

Unfortunately, he was more prepared than I'd expected. Flinging the door open, he again aimed with his rifle, hoping to spot a target. He looked around wildly upon seeing all of us, then pulled the trigger. As before, the noise shook my entire body, and I felt less confident than I had a few moments earlier. No one had been hit as far as I knew, and if Susanna and Tim were correct, it wouldn't have mattered anyway. But what threw off our plan was that in addition to being armed with a gun, the father also had a string of garlic cloves around his neck. There was no way for me to bite him.

As he swung his rifle around to aim again, the rest of the vampires and I scattered, unsure what to do. As long as the garlic around the man's neck didn't come into contact with us, we were fine, and hopefully the bullets from his gun wouldn't do any damage, either. But then the two boys came running up behind him, one holding garlic cloves, the older with a cross in one hand a wooden stake in the other. As they scampered up, scowling at us with their scrunched up faces, I managed to catch a glimpse through the doorway of a woman farther inside the house, presumably their mother. She was calling out to the boys frantically and telling them to get away from the door.

Things weren't going according to plan. These rednecks, as Carolyn called them, were a lot more prepared to defend themselves than any of us had expected. "This way!" Susanna called out, and we followed her around the corner of the house. Another gunshot went off in our direction, but it missed. I could hear the man and the two boys yelling as they chased after us.

I wasn't sure if Susanna had a plan or was just winging it. As we made a full counterclockwise circuit of the house, she then veered to the left and in through the front door, where we found the woman I had seen earlier in the dining room.

The mother, who had a large, bouffant hairdo, gasped and put her hands to her mouth, trembling. She was like a frightened animal, and I began to relish her terror. We hovered in place for a few moments as we took in our surroundings. The living room, which was adjacent to the dining room just as it was in my own house, was lined with hunting trophies, including several mounted deer heads. I had never understood the appeal of keeping a dead stuffed animal in one's home, but this wasn't the first time I had seen such things. Some of my friends at school had them, too, but I had never seen a collection as big as this one.

Delaying our attack on the mother turned out to be a mistake. Though scared at first, she quickly regained her composure and ran over to a wooden chest situated near the threshold of the dining room and living room. It was open, and I saw its contents as she pulled out another large clove of garlic. Inside the chest were all sorts of weapons, that is, weapons to be used against vampires: garlic, crosses, and wooden stakes. The woman held the clove out towards us, but she didn't look very confident. "Keep back," she said as firmly as she could.

The man and the two sons caught up and came rushing in through the doorway, and I wasn't sure what we should do. All four family members were armed against us, and while the man's gun probably wasn't a threat, I was still nervous about it. Prior to this night, no one had ever pointed a gun at me before.

The most vulnerable person in the room seemed to be the mother, and just as I thought of that, Susanna flew closer to her. The rest of us instinctually followed her.

"Y'all pieces of shit vampires get the hell away from my wife!" the man screamed, raising his gun to his shoulder.

I quickly picked up on what Susanna was trying to do, and the trick was to get close enough to the woman without getting near enough for her to touch us with the garlic. We flew closer to her in small increments. "I said get away!" the man screamed.

"Yeah!" one of the boys added.

The mother was once again terrified and trembling. But we were all cautious as well. Any number of things could happen. One of us might manage to actually bite her, but she might also get lucky and get one of us with the garlic. She had been clutching it tightly and seemed to be thinking about throwing it, but if she did that, she might miss, or she might only hit one of us, then be defenseless. As for the father, I was banking on him being too afraid of accidentally shooting his wife if he tried firing at us. No one spoke for several moments, but I got the feeling that everyone, like me, was weighing all of these options and trying to decide what to do, which chance to take. It reminded me a lot of the situations I would see on TV when cops were confronting a bad guy in a hostage situation, only with much less dialogue. There was no tense background music, and no one was saying something like, *Come on, Charlie, put the gun down. It isn't worth it.*

"So I guess the question is…" Susanna began calmly, only to be interrupted by a quick yelp from the mother just below us. Obviously she wasn't used to seeing a talking bat in her dining room. She cowered, still holding the garlic above her. Susanna finished her sentence: "How good of a shot are you?"

All of a sudden, one of the bats broke off from the group and zoomed towards the living room window, which was about halfway between us and the father. The bat thudded against the glass and dropped to the floor, and at the same time, the father fired, aiming for the bat but missing, his shot hitting the wall just beside the window instead.

"Outside! Now!" Susanna shouted, and without thinking, the rest of us zipped past the man and out the front door. There was a lot of incoherent yelling and running around on the part of the humans, but the rest of us managed to get away.

A quick roll call as we hovered a dozen or so feet above the front of the house established that it was Dennis who had flown into the window, and I wondered why he had done it. It had given us the necessary distraction to make it out of the house, which seemed to be the only option given the stalemate we had all reached. But Dennis was still in there, and I began to get worried.

A scream rang out from below, that of a young boy, and I feared the worst. I started to fly back down to the house, but Carolyn called out to me to stop. I ignored her, and within a few seconds, Dennis flew outside and up towards me, and we quickly rejoined the others.

"Are you okay?" Tim asked.

"Yeah, fine," Dennis said.

"That scream…" I began, but Susanna cut me off.

"Talk later! We're leaving."

Flying back to Augusta felt much the same as it had earlier in the night. Again, I was disappointed about losing the fight, angry at the family, and mad at myself for not managing to kill anyone. I had thought that the scream I heard coming from the house was Dennis, but then when I saw him escape, I wondered if he had managed to bite one of the boys. He told me that he had tried to go after one of them, which is why the boy screamed. But Dennis realized at the last second that he was outnumbered and probably wouldn't survive, so he flew off.

"So what was the deal with flying into the window?" Carolyn asked him.

"Oh, that. I was trying to break through it. You know, like they do in the movies. I thought we could all get out that way. Didn't really work, though."

"No, it didn't," I said, and I would have laughed had I been in a better mood. "Glad you're okay, though."

Back at the house, we still weren't satisfied. There had to be a way to finally defeat this "Vampire Killers" family.

"I think I can come up with some ideas," Susanna said. "Our main problem is that this family, *roo-rul* though they are, as Carolyn would say, aren't stupid. They're organized and ready for an attack. We need to undermine that, to catch them off guard."

"How do we do that?" I asked.

"Well, now that I've gotten a good look around their house and the rest of their property, I think I can draw up some kind of plan. It needs to be a more coordinated attack."

"We're going back there again?" Carolyn asked. "Come on, can't we just let it go?"

"No," Susanna said firmly. "I don't like being beaten."

This wasn't a side of her I was used to seeing. More often, she seemed pretty laid back. "Wow," I said. "You're really getting into this, aren't you?"

"I just don't..." she began, her voice raised, but then she stopped. "No, Carolyn, we're not going back tonight. But tomorrow night, we're going to finish them off."

"So how do we come up with this plan?" Dennis asked.

"'We' don't," Susanna said. "It's better if I do it myself. Too many cooks and all that."

"Huh?" he said.

"She means that if we all try to come up with different ideas, it won't work as well," Tim said. Susanna nodded. I was starting to resent her, the way she was being so controlling. "But I might be able to help a little," Tim continued. "I was able to get a view of the kitchen and another room off of the dining room."

"Okay," Susanna said. "You can help me out some. I've got some paper and stuff up in my room. Come on."

"And what do the rest of us do?" I asked as they began to leave the den.

"Probably watch TV, I would guess," Susanna said.

As it turned out, that was exactly what Dennis, Carolyn, and I did the rest of the night. We still had the tape of *Miami Vice* from the other night, which Carolyn suggested we watch at almost the same time I remembered it and was about to bring it up. I had in fact been thinking about the show earlier; it had been on my mind on our way home from the second confrontation with that family.

The stand-off inside the house reminded me of similar scenarios I had seen on this and other shows, and I recalled a particular episode I had seen earlier in the year. In it, several teenage boys had acquired some pretty powerful guns and got into a hostage situation with the police. Although we had not had any direct conflicts with the police so far this year, I wondered if we might, much like the boys in that episode. When Carolyn and I had watched it, she commented on how sad it was, saying something about the boys getting in over their heads. I didn't really get the more deep issues the show was trying to address; I was more interested in the action and the gunfights, plus I thought that the incidental music was pretty cool.

The episode we watched this night was a rerun from the previous year, but it was one I hadn't seen. I must have missed it, or it may have been one that aired before Carolyn got me interested in the show. And while I liked it overall, the opening sequence of the story unnerved me. In it, the cops got into a gun battle with some criminals, and I found myself involuntarily flinching when shots were fired. I had never had this reaction before, but prior to this night, I had never been shot at before, either. I hoped that neither Carolyn nor Dennis noticed my reaction, and then I felt mad at myself for getting worked up over something that was just made up and on TV. The tension was relieved just before the opening credits, when Tubbs, one of the main characters, went on a rant to his colleagues after the danger was past. His delivery was somewhat comical, and the three of us laughed at what he said, which helped me relax more. I also reminded myself that guns couldn't actually hurt us, which also made me feel more calm and able to enjoy the show.

Later on, I was able to share a laugh with Carolyn when one of the female characters was on screen, prompting Carolyn to let out a short cackle and say, "Oh my God! What is she wearing?" This was a recurring thing with her, making fun of people on TV, even on shows she liked. She enjoyed pointing out the over-the-top fashions and ridiculous things people sometimes wore, like the dress this particular woman was wearing. It had huge shoulder pads that stuck out very far, and it just looked silly, or at least, it did once Carolyn pointed it out.

Dennis was not a fan of the series; he preferred things with a more supernatural or science fiction bent to them. As a result, he was mostly bored while we were watching it, which he mentioned a couple of times. But he did get in on mine and Carolyn's ridiculing of the characters and their weird fashions, which led into a conversation we had once the tape was finished.

"It's, um… I don't know," he began. "I mean, who really dresses like that?"

"People on TV," Carolyn said with a smirk. "But yeah, I know what you mean. I've seen people at school who sometimes try to dress like that or what you see in videos and stuff, and when they do, we just laugh at them. It's just so obvious that they're trying to copy something they've seen, and it just ends up looking stupid."

"Yeah!" Dennis said. "People at our school do it, too. Ray, you remember that time that Antonio came to school wearing that Michael Jackson jacket?"

I laughed. "Oh, yeah. That was hilarious."

"A Michael Jackson jacket?" Carolyn said, smiling broadly. Her fangs showed as she did.

"Yeah!" I said. "Straight out of the 'Thriller' video. Red and black stripes and all, with that 'V' shape down the back…"

Dennis laughed hysterically, rolling over onto his side. Crowley bounded over to him as he did so, apparently thinking this was an invitation to play. Dennis was still a little suspicious of him, though, because of the scratch he had gotten a couple of nights before.

"Well, he only wore it that one day, after we all picked on him for it," I said.

"See, that just makes me wonder," Carolyn said, still grinning but looking more thoughtful.

"About what?" Dennis asked, sitting upright again, still eyeballing Crowley as he petted him.

"Well, like, what are people going to say in twenty, maybe thirty years, when they see all this stuff on TV? Are they going to think we all dressed in poofy shoulder pad dresses and torn jeans, stupid looking crap, everyone hopping into the backs of convertibles and zooming around while synthesizer music goes *'dee-deet-dee-deet-dee-doo...'* She smiled and bopped her hands around in a silly way.

I laughed, but I knew what she was getting at. I was reminded of a conversation she and I had with our parents a while back. "Yeah, you're right. I mean, no one really does all that crap in real life, right? But people in the future might think that that's all we did. It's like Mom and Dad when they were going on about how things in the '50s weren't really like what we see nowadays."

"Right," Carolyn said. "Like how not every guy back then dressed like the Fonz or those people in *Grease,* and the girls didn't all wear poodle skirts and ponytails. It's just a popular image all these years later."

"Oh, I see what you're saying," Dennis said, nodding. "My dad grew up in the '60s, and he told me and my sister that he and my mom weren't hippies or flower children and all that." He held up his hand and made the "peace" symbol as he said this. "We didn't believe him, though." Carolyn laughed. "But yeah, I guess you're right. Maybe someday, people will think we all went around with pink hair and torn jeans and all, but we didn't, you know?"

"See, I knew you were a smart kid," Carolyn said to him, smiling. "Aside from the fact that you're friends with Ray."

"Hey!" I said, smacking her arm lightly with my hand.

Our conversation was interrupted by Susanna, who called us into the kitchen. As we walked in, we saw her and Tim spreading out some large pieces of paper onto the kitchen table. The two of them had been busy, and while everything looked pretty impressive, I again resented how the others and I had been left out of the planning process. But as it turned out, what they had come up with looked pretty good.

There were a few drawings of the house, some just showing the outline and others depicting the interior, like a floor plan. Tim pointed out almost immediately that the interior drawings were speculative and based on what he had managed to work out from what we saw while we were inside. He sounded apologetic about this, but I was still impressed by what he and Susanna had managed to do. I also remembered that Tim was something of an amateur cartoonist; I'd seen plenty of his drawings at school. He had obviously applied this talent to the plans.

Sounding very official, Susanna explained to each of us what our roles would be during the attack, what our goals were, possible contingencies, and what to do if things went wrong. On each of the diagrams were cartoon depictions of us as bats and also in human form, stick figures with lines and arrows drawn to indicate our movements. Overall, our plan was to lure the family out of the house and try to split them up, taking them down one by one. My job in particular, along with Tim, was to get to the chest full of anti-vampire weapons and hide it while the family was distracted. That way, they would have a limited supply of weapons. Other parts of the plan involved disarming each of them, and Susanna had given herself the particularly dangerous task of trying to get the father's rifle from him, possibly threatening him with it. We weren't certain exactly how things would go, but after reviewing everything, we felt pretty sure that we could win this time.

It was almost sunrise by this point, and as everyone left the room to go to bed, I walked over to the switch on the kitchen wall to turn off the light. Next to it was the calendar, and I happened to glance at the big "V" Susanna had drawn in pencil on Friday's date. I had noticed it a couple of times already since it had been put there, knowing that it indicated when we would have to change back to being regular humans. I hated the thought of that, but I knew it was necessary. But for the moment, I was going to enjoy being a vampire for as long as I could. I was looking forward to the following night's confrontation. It was us versus the humans, and we were going to beat them.

Getting to sleep was difficult, and I was probably awake well past sunrise, though the others and I were shielded from the sunlight on our blacked-out side of the house. I was just too excited to sleep. I kept picturing the upcoming battle, how our carefully planned attack on the family was going to play out.

As I envisioned everything that might happen, I began to think of us being in our own action-adventure show like *Miami Vice,* and I also thought of other shows I liked to watch, particularly *Knight Rider* and *The A-Team.* Even though we as the vampires were technically the villains in this story, I still saw us as the main characters. I began to drift off slightly, which led to my thoughts becoming more scattered, but whenever I could concentrate enough, I kept thinking about us as action heroes.

In my imagination, we went after not only the family of vampire killers but also our regular victims night after night, which we did so accompanied by cool music and carefully shot camera angles and action sequences. It was a neat idea, and I started putting together in my head the opening title sequence and theme song for a TV series called *The Vampires.*

Like most programs of the time, the opening was a fast-paced montage of clips accompanied by a catchy theme tune that suggested force, determination, and heroism. Shots of exciting things happening were interspersed with close-ups of each of the main characters, and at regular intervals, the actors' names were displayed in big letters over a particularly impressive action shot of them doing something cool. I could clearly picture this, images of us flying around as bats, attacking people, running from people chasing after us with vampire-repelling weapons and getting away, and so on. I kept turning this idea over and over in my head, revising it each time to make it more interesting. It was a fun fantasy, something to think about as I tried to fall asleep.

I ran the loop through again, imagining the title sequence from start to finish, first with various depictions of things that had actually happened to us in real life, but portrayed very dramatically. I heard the theme song: *doon, doon, doooon, doooon, dooooon,* a low-pitched, sinister kind of tune, but fast-paced and accompanied by a synthesized drum beat. *THE VAMPIRES,* the title shown in white letters over an overhead view of Augusta at night. Quick sequences, only a few seconds each, showed us running along the sidewalk outside the pizza place as we fled after killing our victims, changing into bats in our driveway and flying up into the air, killing some teenagers near their campfire by the lake, and being shot at by the big scary man with the gun out in Evans.

The sequence continued with an overlay of the word in smaller letters: *STARRING.* Then each of us was depicted doing things individually, starting with me. The words *RAY YOUNG* were displayed over well-directed shots of me laughing at the TV with Dennis and Carolyn earlier that night, then me baring my fangs as I lunged at one of my victims, and another view of me giving a thoughtful smirk after saying something clever. Next, *SUSANNA YOUNG* was shown at the bottom of the screen while she sat at her desk mixing potions, stood in the kitchen and told us what to do, and led us as we chased Gary at his house. Carolyn's sequence showed her petting Crowley as she sat in the wicker chair in the den, sneering as she made some snide remark at me and my friends, and comically glowering at the mirror in the bathroom as she tried to fuss with her hair and found that she had no reflection.

Next, Tim was shown adjusting his glasses and giving a cute smile to someone while looking sure of himself, then drawing a complicated diagram on a large piece of paper, all the while with the words *TIM DONNELLY* displayed. Then came footage of a tall, skinny boy running as fast as he could, arms pumping by his sides as he gave it his all, accompanied by the words *CARL HENDRICKS.*

I started awake. I hadn't even realized that I was halfway asleep, somewhere on that weird borderline between waking and dreaming. But the fact that I had imagined Carl being in this TV version of our story caught me off guard, and it made me realize something that I had been in denial about for a few days: I missed him. In fact, as much as I liked having Dennis around for all of this instead of him, it felt wrong deep down for Carl not to be taking part. He had been a jerk to me for a couple of years, but we had since patched things up, and I regretted his not being a part of the fun we'd had so far this time.

As I had done many times recently, I again reminisced about the Club Wars and how all of that went, how it was actually fun pitting my group against Carl's. He had been a worthy opponent, and going farther back to when he was part of the vampire group in 1983, he had been a great ally. It didn't take long for me to start wondering if there might be a way to bring him back into the group this time around, but there was the problem of Dennis.

While Carl and I had become uneasy friends again by the end of the school year, he and Dennis still didn't get along. Tim was more or less neutral; he neither despised Carl nor went out of his way to be nice to him. He probably wouldn't object to my getting Carl to join up, but I knew that Dennis would. But then, it wasn't like Dennis and I always got along perfectly well, either. There were times during the Club Wars when he got on my nerves, overstepping his authority in a way.

I was the leader of our club, and whenever we let in a new member, we would refer to it as "hiring" them. And if there was some reason to kick someone out, which happened from time to time, then they were "fired." I was supposed to be the one in charge of that, but sometimes Dennis would take it upon himself to declare someone "hired" or "fired." He got particularly obnoxious about it one time with a boy named Kevin, saying to him, "You're fired! Okay, now you're hired again. Now you're fired!" This escalated into him saying rapidly, "You're hired, you're fired, you're hired, you're fired..." until Kevin finally flipped him the bird and told all of us off, then joined Carl's club.

This angered me, so I ended up firing Dennis. Dennis tried to join Carl's club to spite me, but Carl wouldn't take him in. Not long after, he came back to me wanting to join us again, claiming that he only tried to get into Carl's group to spy on them and act as a double agent. I wasn't sure if I believed him, but I took him back anyway. He was, after all, my friend. But I made the stipulation that he could only be in our club again if he promised to leave all of the hiring and firing to me. Petty skirmishes like this were common during the Club Wars. In some ways, we were just doing our best impression of what we thought more official and grown up organizations were like.

Once I recalled this incident, I felt a sense of gratification. I was the one in charge of the club, and it was established that I could say who came and who had to go. It wasn't really all that different with the vampires, so if I wanted Carl in, he was going to be whether Dennis liked it or not. That is, if Carl wanted to do it. But how could he not? He had probably already seen the news reports about our activity and known what we were up to, and it wouldn't have surprised me at all if he had felt left out. I also realized that adding another member to the team would increase our chances of success at defeating the Vampire Killers family.

So as far as I was concerned, it was decided. I was going to bring Carl into the group. But there was another hurdle to consider, which was whether or not Susanna would allow it. Despite my feelings of superiority towards Dennis and my notion that I was mostly in charge of our "vampire club" — it had been my idea for us to get together like this in the first place, after all — Susanna was still the oldest and also held a position of authority. I knew I would need to convince her of the value of adding Carl.

The first thing we did the next night after checking the tape of the 6:00 news (which didn't tell us anything new) was to go out and find some victims. This was in fact part of the overall plan to attack the family; Susanna insisted that we kill elsewhere first in order to get our strength up and not feel distracted or too eager to kill during the actual battle.

In order to avoid the police, who were still out in force but not quite as heavily as the night before, we flew to the Augusta Mall, a place we had never killed at before. Finding five vulnerable people in the mall's extremely large parking lot wasn't difficult, and we each managed to make our kills and get away before anyone knew what was happening. Police would undoubtedly start patrolling that area after this night, but that just meant that we wouldn't go back there and could keep them guessing.

Back home, Susanna and I met upstairs in her room. At the mall, she and I had killed a man and a woman who were just about to get into a car, and as we flew up from the bodies, I told her that I had something I wanted to ask her about once we got back to the house.

"Why not just ask me now?" she said as we reached the prearranged meeting spot on the mall roof, waiting for the rest of the vampires to show up.

"Just... Let's just wait till we're back home." I couldn't really come up with a good reason for delaying, at least not one I wanted to say.

In her room later on, I told her my idea about contacting Carl and asking him to join us. "It would help, right? We could work him into the plan to attack the Vampire Killers family. I'm sure he'd want to. I feel kind of bad about leaving him out of things this time, too."

Susanna pondered this for a moment. "Sure, I guess. I mean, you said before that you two weren't friends anymore, so…"

"No, no, that was just me being stupid. We were enemies for a little bit in fifth grade, but that's all over now. The truth is that I should have included him in our plans all along. I was just, I don't know…"

"Being stupid?" Susanna said with an evil smile. "It's okay. I understand. Friendships come and go, and they can be kind of weird."

I felt very relieved. "So can you make some more of the potion, just a little bit, you know, for him?"

She laughed, which I didn't expect. "Funny you should say that," she said, turning around in her desk chair and reaching for a small beaker with a cork in it. "As it turns out, I made a little bit too much of the potion this time, and I was trying to figure out what to do with it."

"Really?" This was an unexpected coincidence, but not an unwelcome one. I started to ask her why she didn't just dump it down the sink, but I was too excited by what this meant. I'd assumed that she would have to take a few hours to make the extra potion for Carl, which might also delay our plans to attack the family.

"Yeah," she said. "So this works out pretty well. Are the others okay with it?"

I froze for a moment, then decided to lie. "Yeah. They're fine." I hadn't mentioned the idea of Carl to any of them, especially Dennis. I wanted Susanna's cooperation first. "Is… um… is the potion okay?"

"Hmm?"

"I mean, will it still work? That bit of it must have been sitting on your desk for days."

"Hmm, that's a good point," she said, holding the beaker up in front of her face and peering at it. "I think so. It looks pretty much the same."

"Maybe you should do some tests or something to make sure it's okay," I suggested. I didn't even know what kinds of tests she could run on it, but it sounded like a good idea at the time.

"Maybe so," she said, rolling the beaker back and forth and watching the liquid as it moved around. "Really, it's probably fine." She turned her eyes to me. "Shouldn't you go call Carl?"

I went downstairs and to my parents' bedroom, avoiding the others. This was where I would go whenever I wanted to use the phone but not be overheard by anyone; the room was at the far end of the house and mostly private. I surprised myself by remembering Carl's phone number without looking it up, but I hesitated before dialing. The feeling was similar to how I felt when I first told Dennis about the potion.

Pushing that aside, I called Carl's house and waited for someone to pick up. There was some strange commotion when the call went through, something that sounded like a struggle coupled with high-pitched laughter. After a few seconds, that calmed down, and I heard Carl say, out of breath, "Hello?"

"Um, Carl? What was all that?"

"Sorry, that was just Karen fighting for the phone. Who's this?"

"It's Ray."

"Oh! Hi!" He sounded genuinely happy to hear from me, and I realized that what had been making me so nervous before was the fear that he might not, that he would resent my calling him instead. He then said away from the phone to his older sister, "No, it's not for you. You can go away now."

Karen said something snide in response that was too faint for me to make out, to which Carl responded with a sarcastic, "Ha, ha." After a few seconds, Carl said into the phone almost in a whisper, "Y'all have been busy, haven't you?"

I laughed, then went on to tell him that yes, we had gotten together and taken the potion again. "Don't tell anyone, though."

"Are you kidding? Like who would flipping believe me anyway?" After a pause, he added, "To be honest, I've been keeping garlic around my window every night ever since they started talking about vampires in the news again. I was afraid you guys might come after me!"

"What? No!" I laughed again. "Actually the reason I called was to see if you wanted to join up with us after all. Sorry about not including you before; I just... I don't know... I wasn't sure if you would want to." That was a lie; I had excluded him on purpose.

"Well, I mean... I guess."

"It's just that, well, some of the others were asking about you, so I thought 'why not?'" As long as I was lying, I might as well stay on a roll. I told him that we only had a few more days before my parents got back, but if he wanted to have some fun for the last few days, it would be great to have him along.

"Well, yeah! Sure!"

"Will your parents be okay with it?" This was actually the first time I had considered the possibility that they might not let him come over, plus I glanced at the clock in the bedroom and realized that it was pretty late to be calling.

"Oh, they're out of town," Carl said. "It's just me and Karen. And she was wanting to hang out at her friend Brandi's house this week anyway, so I bet she'll be glad to get rid of me. Hang on and let me check, okay?"

I heard him put the phone down and run out of the room, calling out to his sister. He clearly seemed excited, which made me happy. The minute or two I had alone with my thoughts, though, gave me time to realize that there were a couple of problems. The first one was how Dennis would react, but I hoped I could talk him into being okay with Carl's presence. Even if the two of them fought, I figured it would be kind of like Mr. T's character and Murdock from *The A-Team*. Sure, they didn't get along, but they were all part of the same team, and the rest of the group would keep them together.

The other problem occurred to me as I began to picture Carl arriving at our house later, how the rest of us would react to him. We were already fully entrenched in the whole vampires versus humans thing, and Carl was human. What if one of us, particularly Dennis, couldn't restrain themselves and killed him as soon as he arrived? What if Dennis did it out of spite?

During all of this, Crowley had come into the room and jumped up onto my parents' bed, where he sat, looking at me with his wide, green eyes. "What?" I said to him. "Don't look at me like that." I began to get a strange, guilty feeling, so I looked away from him.

Shortly after that, Carl returned to the phone sounding eager and excited. "Okay, Karen's fine with it. She's going over to Brandi's, and I can just ride my bike to your house. This is going to be so cool!"

"Carl, I just realized something."

"What?"

"Well, do you remember how strong the craving was when you were a vampire before? Like, for blood I mean?"

"Yeah, sure," he said. "Kind of. I remember doing it and all…"

"What I mean is that I'm not entirely sure that all of us can hold back if you come over. Like, if the urge to kill is too strong."

"Oh, right," he said. "Like when Carolyn and Susanna changed back before the rest of us did. I remember that. Sort of."

"But there's got to be a way to get…" Halfway through my sentence, I realized the solution. "Okay, I've got it. What we can do is just leave the potion out on the front porch for you. We'll all stay inside until you've taken it."

"That works, I guess." He paused for a few seconds. "You're not inviting me over just so you can kill me, are you?"

Convincing Carl to join up and that he would be safe wasn't nearly as difficult as what came next. I expected Dennis to object, not to blow up at me like he did.

"You said he wasn't going to be in it this year!" he shouted. "I don't want to have to put up with Carl! I thought we had a good enough thing going on here without him!"

"Dennis, calm down," Tim said.

"No! I don't want to calm down! I hate that guy! I always have!"

"He's not really all that bad," Carolyn said. "I haven't seen him for a couple of years, but still…"

"Then you don't know what he's like now," Dennis said, folding his arms and turning away.

"Come on, Dennis," I said. "It won't be that bad. Maybe this will be a chance for you two to learn to get along!"

"Who said I wanted a chance to get along?"

Susanna came downstairs in the middle of this, and she was holding the beaker of the potion. She looked around, confused as to why everyone seemed so worked up.

Trying to distract her from the situation, I turned to her and said, "Oh, good, you've brought the potion. I was talking to Carl on the phone, and we realized that the safest thing to do is leave that on the porch for him to take first. That way none of us will be tempted to bite him while he's still human." As I spoke, I walked toward her, hoping to encourage her to go to the front door and away from everyone else.

She nodded, but she was still looking past me and at the others. "What's going on?"

"Oh, Dennis is just upset about the idea of Carl coming over," Carolyn said. "Apparently they don't like each other or something."

"I thought you said everyone was okay with this," Susanna said to me.

"We are!" I insisted. "Right, guys?"

Carolyn and Tim nodded, though not with certainty. Dennis just looked at the rest of us angrily.

"Look, he's already on his way over," I said. "Let's just make the most of this and try to get along."

Dennis just scowled and left the room.

After placing the beaker outside the front door, Susanna and I sat at the bottom of the stairs, which faced the door. Carolyn, Tim, and Dennis were in the red den, and I could hear them talking, but I couldn't make out what they were saying. The gist of the discussion seemed to center around Dennis's dismay about Carl joining the group and the others' attempts to get him to see reason.

"Well," I said after a few moments of awkward silence between me and Susanna, "at least with Carl in the group, we'll stand a better chance against the Vampire Killers family, right?"

Susanna waited for a bit. "Probably."

"Sorry. I really thought everyone would be okay with this."

We heard something outside, which I figured was Carl arriving on his bike. As I listened, I tried to picture what he was doing, first arriving, setting his bike down, picking up the beaker, and then reading the note we had left with it. As I envisioned it, he uncorked the beaker and threw his head back as he downed the potion, then waited for it to take effect. Sure enough, I heard the sounds of his labored breathing through the door, and I felt a pang of sympathy, knowing how difficult the transformation process was to get through.

All the while, I was also listening for signs of life from the den. I had wondered earlier if Dennis might make some attempt to attack Carl as he arrived, which was why I was glad to hear him still talking with Carolyn and Tim. My thoughts were interrupted by a knock at the door, and I eagerly sprang up, followed by Susanna. I unlocked the door and opened it, and there was Carl, smiling his big goofy grin, which was punctuated by two fangs. He was one of us again.

"Time to party!" he said, then laughed, as did I.

"Hey, Carl," Susanna said. "You've grown."

Carl shrugged. "Yeah, well, like my mom says, 'That's what happens when you keep feeding them!'"

Susanna and I laughed, and then she called out in the direction of the den, "Hey guys! He's here!"

As Carl came inside and looked around the foyer, he said, "Wow, been a long time since I was in here."

Carolyn and the others made their way from the red den through the dining room and living room, and Carl's face fell as he saw Dennis, who also looked less than thrilled.

"What?" he said. "You didn't tell me about him being here!"

"Carl, it's okay," I said. "We're all friends here."

"Well, maybe, but I didn't know that this would include that dork-head!"

"Dennis is my friend, too," I said.

"Don't worry about it, Carl," Dennis said with a calmness that surprised me. "I'm leaving anyway."

"What?" I asked.

"I said I'm leaving. I don't want to be in the group if he's going to be in. And you seem to have made up your mind about that."

"Well, good," Carl said. "Doesn't bother me."

"No!" I insisted. "Come on, Dennis! We can all stay!"

"I said I'm leaving," he repeated firmly.

Susanna stepped in, saying, "Okay, then, if that's what you want to do, Dennis."

"What? No!" I said.

"No, Ray," she said, ramping up her authoritative stance. "If he wants to leave, then we have to accept that. There's the garlic powder on the spice rack in the kitchen if you want to use that," she said, turning back to Dennis.

"I didn't say I wanted to stop being a vampire," he said confidently. "I said I wanted to leave."

"Well don't let any of us stop you..." Carl said, but Susanna cut him off with an angry motion of her hand.

"You can't do that," she said.

"Yes I can," Dennis said. "I'll be fine."

"I'm leaving, too," Tim said, which shocked me further.

"What?" Susanna and I said together.

"Yeah, I think so," Tim said. "You really should have asked the rest of us first, Ray."

The conversation went back and forth for a while with lots of stubbornness and calls for each side to see reason, but what it boiled down to was that Carl was staying, and Dennis and Tim were leaving. They would go off on their own as vampires, and Carl would continue to stay with me and my sisters as our own separate group. I was surprised when Susanna agreed to this, but when I thought about it later, I realized that there wasn't actually a way for her to force Dennis and Tim to change back to human just because she said so. Insisting on that might have developed into a confrontation much like the one we had in 1983 when we were all trying to force the "vampire killers" on each other, resulting in all of us being changed back to human.

So, reluctantly, we let Tim and Dennis leave, and they flew away leaving the four of us standing on the front porch.

"Well, that kind of sucks," Carolyn said. I was too angry to respond.

"Well, whatever!" Carl said enthusiastically. "We've still got each other! Let's go out and have fun without those party poopers!"

"Actually, we were in the middle of something," Susanna said.

On the way out to Evans, we stopped to let Carl have his first kill in two years, which he seemed to very eager to do. Susanna pointed out a solitary person on the street below, directing Carl to take them. Just before he dove down away from me, he said, "I've always wanted to try this," but I didn't know what he meant.

He flew down very quickly, and just before he reached his intended target, he changed into his person form and tackled the man to the ground. It was interesting from a physics perspective: He used the speed he was able to fly at as a bat and combined it with the sudden increase in mass as a person to knock the unsuspecting man to the ground. It was a neat effect, one that I hoped to recreate myself when I got the chance. Maybe I would even be able to incorporate that move into our attack on the Vampire Killers family, I thought.

I was also glad to have him back in the fold, almost feeling proud of him as I watched him drink his prey dry and then fly back up to us. For a few moments, it felt like old times. But in the old times, Tim was with us. And I had hoped that Dennis would still be with us too, but now all of that was out the window.

While I was mad at Dennis for leaving, in a more general sense, I just felt sad. Things hadn't worked out anything like I had hoped, nor had I expected them to go as badly as they had. Dennis's objection to Carl was understandable, but I thought I'd be able to talk him into being okay with things or at the very least have the majority overrule him and have him grudgingly accept things. And while that technically did happen, Tim's decision to also leave was a complete surprise. I knew he wasn't terribly close with Carl, but I didn't think he actively hated him this much. Thinking this through made angry at him, too. Because the two of them hadn't been able to accept not getting their way, we were now a group of four, not six, and we no longer outnumbered the family we were on our way to attack.

"You okay?" Carolyn asked after flying up beside me. Susanna and Carl were farther above us in the air, and I had been aware of the rest of the group talking as we flew, but I hadn't been paying much attention. I was too busy brooding. I wondered what this meant for the future of my friendship with both Dennis and Tim, if we were done from this point on. I felt betrayed and let down. I even tried to convince myself that I had never really liked Dennis to begin with and would be glad to be done with him, but that wasn't really true.

"I don't know," was all I could say.

"Sorry things went so crappy," she said. "Friendships can be stupid sometimes."

"Yeah, Susanna said something like that before." I didn't feel comforted, nor did I really want to.

"Tim didn't really want to leave, by the way," she told me.

"What?" I was getting tired of surprises.

"He told me in private just before he and Dennis left. He did it to keep an eye on Dennis, to make sure he'd be okay. Letting him go off on his own would have been a mistake."

I pondered this, then felt a little better. So Tim wasn't a total jerk, after all. He was doing his best to keep the peace, to make sure everyone was taken care of. Perhaps for the first time, I realized that this was something he often did.

"Well, I just hope they stay out of trouble," I said finally.

"Since when do any of us do that?" Carolyn joked.

After this conversation, she and I rejoined Carl and Susanna in flight. Although we had gone over the diagrams and the plan with Carl before leaving, Susanna was telling him more details about the house and what to expect when we got there.

Carl seemed a little nervous but also excited, and I brought up the Club Wars with him, which we reminisced about. We talked about a few specific confrontations we had been through during all of that, both ones where his club came out on top and ones when mine got the better of his. I mentioned the thing about him getting some of the girls in the class to join up with him, and he pointed out that one or two girls also joined my side, which I had forgotten about until he said it. That was near the very end of things, just a day or two before the big confrontation that led to us getting in trouble and the clubs being disbanded. All the while, I thought about Tim and Dennis also being in my club, then got sad again when I remembered that they were no longer in this one.

Still, we had more important things to think about, as Susanna reminded us when we got close to the house in Evans. I felt nervous as we approached, but even so, we had our plan, and I was eager to carry it out. Even with the abrupt changes that had occurred recently, I felt confident that we could win.

The house was below us, and the lights were on. I wondered if perhaps the family had replaced their homemade *VAMPIRE KILLERS* flag in a further attempt to intimidate us, but when I looked to see if it was there, I noticed something else. The front door was open, and light from inside the house spilled out from it.

"Oh, no!" Carolyn said. "Look out!"

"What?" I asked.

"Police!"

I hadn't even spotted the car until she mentioned it, but there it was, a patrol car parked in the driveway. Something about it was strange, though. It wasn't directly lined up with the gravel path from the street but was slightly askew.

"Hold on, everybody," Susanna said. "Let me go check."

She flew down to the car as the rest of us waited, unsure what to do. After a few seconds, she flew back up to us. "It's empty," she said.

Something else caught my attention, and I made my eyes glow in order to see better in the dark. It was the boys' tent in the backyard, the place where we had first confronted them. But it looked different.

"Hang on," I said, and flew toward it, ignoring a whispered warning from Susanna to wait.

I didn't have to get very close to see that the tent was crushed, like something heavy had fallen onto it. I squeaked at the others, a signal for them to come over. They understood, then saw what I had seen.

"What happened here?" Carl asked. "Did a tree fall on their tent or something?"

"No," I said. "It wasn't like this before."

We flew closer and saw no signs of life, but it was certainly odd. It looked like something had forcefully knocked the tent over, but no one had bothered to set it back up.

"This is strange," Susanna said.

"No duh," Carl said. "So what do we do?"

"Give me a second," Susanna said impatiently, still keeping her voice down. Then she said, "Follow me."

We flew to one of the windows and looked in, seeing the living room where our encounter with the family had occurred the night before. Nothing looked too unusual, but then Susanna gasped.

Without a word, she zipped around to the open front door, and the rest of us followed. We flew inside, and I expected to be confronted by the big man with the gun, but the place was eerily quiet. It was then that I noticed how much of a mess the house was.

One of the chairs in the living room was turned over on its front, and some of the animal heads that had been mounted on the walls were on the floor, some partly crushed. The table in the dining room had been smashed into a nearby china cabinet, and broken glass and dishes were strewn about the floor. In sharp contrast, the trunk full of anti-vampire weapons was closed and unmoved from the spot where I had seen it the night before.

"What the hell?" Carl said in a hushed tone.

"This isn't..." Susanna began, but didn't finish her sentence. "Wait here." She flew out of the dining room and in a circle around the interior of the house, rejoining us after about half a minute.

"Well?" I asked, an idea beginning to form.

"They're gone. The whole family is gone."

"What happened to them?" Carl asked.

"Look over by the window," Susanna said gravely.

Next to the window was a large black spot, which I had vaguely been aware of the night before after the father's rifle went off in his attempt to shoot at Dennis. But next to that was something more interesting, a red arc that I immediately recognized as blood. Once I noticed this, I spotted a few other patches of blood around the rest of the room, including one on the carpet next to the overturned chair I had seen earlier.

"I don't understand," Carolyn said. "What happened here?"

"I do," I said. "It was Dennis and Tim! They got here before us!"

"What?" she asked.

"Oh," Carl said. "I get it. Those two little shits got here first and killed the family before we got a chance to!"

"I think you're right," Susanna said, sounding both disappointed and concerned.

We each digested this for a while, hovering in place as bats. The plan we had devised required us to stay in bat mode during the first part of our attack, the logic being that we were smaller and more stealthy in that form. But now the plan was completely useless, and we were uncertain of what to do.

Carl asked the obvious question that the rest of us had gotten used to ignoring. "Wait, what about the bodies? Where are they?"

"Good question," I said, though I was partly being sarcastic. This night had been one disappointment after another, and I was worn out by this point.

"The police car outside," Carolyn said. "I think that pretty much proves what you were saying before."

"Yes," Susanna said. "I guess they left that car behind for some reason." She didn't sound very sure of herself. "But see? They did another cleanup operation to try to get rid of the evidence."

"But why?" Carl asked.

"Let's go," she said, not answering his question.

"I think we made a huge mistake," Susanna said in the yellow den, sitting in the wicker chair and not looking at anyone in particular.

"What do you mean?" Carolyn asked, stroking Crowley in her lap. He was eyeballing Carl suspiciously, unsure of the new arrival in our house.

"Dennis and Tim," she said. "We need to get them back. This whole idea of two separate groups just isn't going to work."

"Why not?" Carl asked with exasperation. "We don't need them!"

"Carl, please," Susanna said impatiently. "I know you don't like them or whatever. It's not about that. It's about a separate group of vampires out there on the loose doing whatever they want, and I'm not okay with that."

I could see her point. At first, once I had gotten past my anger and the feeling of betrayal, I had settled on being okay with Dennis and Tim being off on their own and doing whatever they wanted. The rest of us could still have our fun with Carl in the group.

"Yeah, me neither," I said. "I don't know how they managed to pull that off, just the two of them, but they apparently did their own good job of taking care of that Vampire Killers family without us. Who knows what else they're capable of!"

"Right," Susanna said, looking up at me.

"So…" Carolyn said uncertainly. "What do we do? Try to find them again?"

"We have to," Susanna said.

"But how?" I asked. "Who knows where they've gone!"

"I know, I know!" Susanna said.

"And who the fart cares anyway?" Carl said snidely.

Susanna gave him a withering look and said, "Carl, if you don't shut it right now…" She didn't have to finish her sentence. Carl barely spoke for the rest of the night.

We went around the city for a while, hoping to find Dennis and Tim again and convince them to get back together with our group, but that never happened. The idea was to tell them that we all needed to stick together in the face of this conspiracy that the police seemed to be propagating, regardless of how they felt about Carl. But we never got a chance to pitch that to them since we never encountered them.

Carolyn suggested revisiting some of the places we had killed earlier in the week, but that didn't work, either. Doing that also reminded me of the night when we all got out of control and kept killing over and over, barely even aware of where we were, which wasn't a pleasant thought to revisit.

We eventually had to resign ourselves to giving up but renewing our efforts the following night. I wondered what Tim and Dennis were up to, but there wasn't even a chance of getting some secondhand account of what other vampire activity might have occurred around town given that none of us had remembered to set the VCR to catch the news. Too much else had been going on.

All the while, I knew that Carl was resenting this emphasis on getting our old team members back, and I tried to placate him.

"I know it bothers you, but…"

"No it doesn't bother me!" he snapped. "Okay, yeah, maybe a little. I just don't know why they had to be such whiny babies and stomp out just because I arrived. I wouldn't have picked on them that much. I'm just fine with Tim, and Dennis, well… I could have put up with him, I guess."

"I know. But Susanna's right. Having them off on their own makes it more like a competition. I mean, it's almost like another Club Wars, this time with vampires. Well, kind of. Not really."

"You sure about that?" Carl said with a grin. He was lying on his side with one hand propping himself up, the other stroking Crowley, who had finally accepted him and was purring up a storm.

"I don't know," I said.

"So, this thing about the police. I don't get it. Why would they be trying to cover things up?"

"Susanna seems to think it's something to do with politics, or race, or… something. I don't entirely get it either."

"Hmm?" Susanna said, walking into the den and having heard her name.

"Oh, we were just talking about the police cover-up thing," I said. "I'm still not sure that that makes sense."

"And you have a better idea?" she asked with a sneer.

"No, I didn't say I did. Just that some things don't add up."

"Like what." Again, she used that flat tone that tried to dissuade any argument. I wasn't sure how to respond.

"Well, like that police car at the house tonight!" Carl said. "Why would they leave it there? You know, if they were trying to be all secretive."

Susanna frowned. "I don't know. Mistake?"

"Or a warning," Carolyn said as she returned from the kitchen. "Kind of like trying to put a decoy to warn us off."

"That doesn't make much sense, either," I said. "What about Dennis's other theory?"

"Which one?" Carolyn asked, sitting down next to Crowley and beginning to draw his attention away from Carl.

"About the bodies of our victims coming back to life as vampires."

"Ray, I've told you," Susanna said with a sigh. "It doesn't work like that with us. Yes, I know, in the movies and legends and stuff, vampires' victims come back to life. But, well, if you want to look at this way, we're not real vampires. We're artificial ones created by a potion."

"That sounds kind of… I don't know, disappointing," Carl said.

"Well, it's the truth. Back when we made the original potion in high school, we used it on mice, and none of the mice that were bitten by the little vampire mice were resurrected. They just stayed dead. End of story. Now, if we had somehow worked it in that the potion's effects were contagious and could be transmitted, that would be one thing. But the fact of the matter is: We didn't. The potion we've taken isn't any different. So neither are the effects."

"Hmm," I said. "I guess you're right."

"So do you think we'll be able to find Tim and Dennis tomorrow?" Carolyn asked.

We never got the chance to try. The following night, there was a huge thunderstorm that lasted for hours. It began just after we got up in the evening, and we were very upset. Susanna had warned us before that rain would have the same effect on us as running water, that it would change us from vampires back to normal humans, so all we could do was stay inside and hope to wait the storm out.

Not being able to go out and feed was maddening, and it was not a fun night. We could still eat other food, but blood was what we wanted more than anything. This resulted in tempers flaring and a few unkind words being said, but things were patched up after a few apologies. After a while, everyone avoided each other to keep from getting into fights.

We gathered in the yellow den at 11:00 to watch the news, which reported on both the thunderstorm and the latest developments in the ongoing vampire scare. Not surprisingly, nothing related to that had happened this night. I suspected that Tim and Dennis were huddled away somewhere also hiding from the rain, if they were still okay at all. For all I knew, they had been caught by the rain and were human again, but I had no way of knowing this. I had wondered if the news might reveal anything about their activities the night before, and I realized that I was very curious as to what they might be getting up to, not being able to keep an eye on them myself.

The news was still speculative when it came to any mentions of vampires, but it did report on more unexplained disappearances, including some out in Evans. As the reporter put it, the phenomenon seemed to be spreading outside the city limits, but so far there was no satisfactory explanation. I found it interesting that very little was said about the police department's take on the matter.

The rain let up around 2:00, but Susanna insisted that we still stay in. Carolyn, Carl, and I objected to this very strongly, but she was adamant, saying that summer thunderstorms were very unpredictable and could pop up at any time.

Finally, around 5:00, we couldn't take it anymore and had to take our chances and go out. It hadn't rained for a few hours, and the sky seemed to have cleared up enough, though it was still cloudy in some places. Finding people to kill at that time of the night was difficult, and we finally settled on a 24-hour gas station near Daniel Village.

We had to wait a while for anyone to show up, but once they did, we drained the two occupants of the car of every drop of blood we could get.

We then raced home, fearing the oncoming sunrise.

The next night, the weather was clear, and we made sure to check the newspaper's forecast to see if there was any threat of rain. There wasn't, so we renewed our efforts to find Tim and Dennis, plus we needed to do our usual killing of the night.

The police were still out in force, but not quite as much as they had been recently. This made it easier to find people to kill, which we did this time closer to downtown.

My victim for the night was a young woman with short, permed hair, the smell of which bothered me. But I barely cared; I just needed to feed. I was also annoyed by the long, dangling earrings she was wearing, which got in the way when I was first trying to bite her. As I finished her off and stood up from her body, I noticed that she was also wearing a thin white blouse with large shoulder pads, which reminded me of the conversation that Carolyn, Dennis, and I had a couple of nights earlier about fashion.

This got me thinking about Dennis again, and I wondered where he and Tim might be, making their own kills somewhere else in town. I also got this notion that maybe they were nearby, hiding and watching us, but I didn't know what made me think that. As we flew away from the bodies below, I asked Susanna what might happen if we never managed to find them.

"I don't know," she said. "But we have to. It's not safe for them to be out on their own."

"And what about the deadline?" Carolyn asked, and I asked what she meant. "Well, we had all agreed to change back by Friday. What if they don't do that? Their parents will be expecting them back on Saturday, so…"

We pondered this as we flew. She was right. The simple truth was that we had to get the entire group back together if for no other reason than practicality. We should never have allowed it to splinter the way it had. While I was glad to have Carl around again, I was beginning to regret asking him to join up with us in the first place. Things would have been simpler if I hadn't, but I kept this to myself. And if he were aware of how much his presence had screwed things up, he also said nothing.

As we returned home, I was planning on telling everyone that we needed to make some kind of stronger effort to find Dennis and Tim. I had no idea how we might do that, but I hoped that saying something along those lines would prompt a conversation that would eventually lead to a solution. I was distracted, though, by a small detail that I just happened to notice as we approached the house: The basement door was open.

"Susanna," I began.

"I see it, too!" she said.

"What?" Carl asked.

"The basement door!" I said. "It's wide open!"

"Do you think somebody broke in?" Carolyn asked.

"If they did, they're in for a nasty surprise," Carl said. "We'll have ourselves a little dessert."

"Unless they've already come and gone," Carolyn said, sounding worried.

"Or maybe it's Dennis and Tim!" I said.

"Maybe," Susanna said. "Let's sneak in, but stay as bats."

We fluttered down to the open basement door and flew in, but there didn't appear to be anyone inside. After only a few moments, I looked back to the stairs and saw Susanna landing and changing form, after which she pulled the cord that turned on the light. The rest of us changed as well and looked around, but we didn't see or hear anything suspicious.

"Do you think they're here?" Carl whispered.

"I don't know," I said. "Doesn't look like it."

"Guys," Susanna said gravely. "There's something here." She was standing by one of the walls, the one that ran parallel to the back side of the house. In the wall was a large opening, roughly the size and shape of a doorway.

"Where did that come from?" I asked.

"Did Dad put in a new storage closet or something?" Susanna asked.

"No," Carolyn said, tentatively placing her hand near the edge of the opening. "There's no door. And… something else…"

"Are you sure this wasn't here before?" Carl asked.

"No, Carl," Carolyn said angrily. "No one in the family ever noticed a big-ass hole in the wall in our basement."

Carl was taken aback, but then he smiled. "A big… what?"

"Shut up," Carolyn said, then turned back to the strange doorway. "The edges… They're like, I don't know, smooth. Sort of shiny. Or slimy."

"Don't touch it," Susanna said. She poked her head into the opening and used her glowing eyes to see more clearly. "It's as if… No way…"

"What?" I asked impatiently.

She pulled her head back but continued to face away from us. "I think it's a tunnel."

"A tunnel?" I asked. "To where?"

"And how the hell did it get there?" Carl asked.

None of us had any idea. I realized that it had been a long time, several months if not longer, since I had been in the basement, which I mentioned. Carolyn said that she had been in here just a few weeks ago looking for something, and she was sure she would have spotted this. I wondered if this might somehow have something to do with Tim and Dennis, but I didn't see how it could. Regardless, it was a mystery we needed to solve.

First, Susanna insisted on checking the house. Carolyn agreed, wanting to check on Crowley. While they flew up there, Carl and I stayed behind and kept an eye on the tunnel.

"Here," Carl said, picking up a couple of flashlights he spotted on a nearby shelf. "We should probably take these."

"We don't really need them, though, do we? I mean, we've got the glowing eyes thing and all."

"Yeah, but that gets tiring after a while. At least it does for me. If I do it for too long, I start to feel kind of dizzy."

"Yeah, me too," I said. "And we have no idea how long this thing goes on for. So you're probably right."

Carl looked at the doorway again. "Where do you think it leads?"

"No idea. Hey, it's like we're in *Scooby Doo!* 'Hey look, guys! A secret passage!'"

"'Ruh roh!'" Carl said, imitating the famous cartoon dog. We laughed.

By then, Carolyn and Susanna had come back, saying that the house was locked and no one was inside. They were also carrying flashlights.

"Oh, I see you brought some, too," Carl said. "Ray didn't think we needed them, but I figured it would be better if we…"

"Yes, yes, good thinking," Susanna said impatiently.

"Batteries okay?" I asked everyone. As it turned out, the flashlights Carl had found were almost dead, but the ones Carolyn and Susanna brought were just fine.

"Oh well," Carl said, putting them back on the shelf.

"This should be fine," Susanna said. "Everyone ready?"

We indicated that we were, but Carolyn added, "I have a bad feeling about this."

We stepped into the tunnel, Susanna in front with her flashlight and Carolyn in the back with hers. Although the initial passageway was only the size of a regular door, the tunnel quickly widened to where we could walk two by two along it. The flashlights were shone around as we walked, and I saw that the walls, ceiling, and floor were made of dirt and rock. But they also looked shiny, like they were coated with something.

I reached out to one of the walls and touched it, wondering what it felt like. I expected it to either be smooth like glass or slimy, as Carolyn had described the entrance earlier. To my surprise, the spot I touched suddenly gave way and crumbled, letting a small amount of reddish brown dirt tumble free. I drew my hand back suddenly and let out a small exclamation.

"What?" Susanna asked, and everyone stopped.

I explained what had happened. Out of curiosity, I touched another spot on the wall, this time just with my finger. A much smaller area dissolved, prompting reactions from the others.

"That's really freaky," Carl said. "What is it?"

"I guess," Susanna said, shining her light around the walls and ceiling, "it's what's holding this tunnel in place."

"But how?" Carolyn asked.

"Magic!" Carl joked. No one laughed.

"Don't touch the roof, then," Carolyn said.

Almost without thinking, I jumped up and tapped the ceiling above me, which I could just barely reach. I was greeted by a bunch of dirt in my face, causing me to cough and brush it out of my eyes and hair.

"Told you," she said.

"Come on," Susanna said. "We need to figure this thing out."

As we continued walking, we kept our voices down as we speculated a lot about what this meant, who may have made the tunnel, and how. While she had accepted that this weird shiny substance was somehow holding the dirt in place, Susanna couldn't see how someone could have managed to dig a tunnel underneath our house without anyone hearing it. I wondered whether or not the tunnel had been made to our house from elsewhere, or maybe it was the other way around, that someone had dug it from our house to somewhere else. Maybe that was why the basement door was open: Something made its way inside, then tunneled out to escape. Carolyn commented that it all seemed like something out of Edgar Allan Poe. Carl repeated my mention of *Scooby Doo* from before, but by this point, we weren't in a joking mood.

The tunnel had first turned to the right when we left the basement, and while it occasionally veered slightly from left to right, for the most part, it felt like we were walking in a straight line. The farther we went, the more surreal the entire thing was. Everything felt so strange, almost dreamlike. I was simultaneously intrigued, curious, and scared. I was also angry. Whoever built this mysterious tunnel had invaded my family's personal space, and that was not a feeling I was used to or comfortable with.

"Hey, are there any footprints?" Carl asked after we had been walking silently for a while. "I just thought about what Ray said about whether or not someone dug this tunnel to or from the house."

"Hmm," Susanna said as she shone her light down at the floor. "No, there aren't. I hadn't even thought to look. But no. No footprints."

"Wait," I said, touching Carolyn's arm. "Shine the light back there again," I said, pointing behind us.

"Why?"

"Just do it. I'm curious about something."

"Okay," she said with a sigh, then pointed her flashlight back down the tunnel. It looked nearly identical to the view ahead of us, almost eerily so. I looked more closely at the ground, then grabbed Carolyn's hand to aim the flashlight.

"What are you doing?" she asked.

"Where are our footprints?" I asked.

She leaned down and looked. "Hmm. You're right. You'd think we would at least have left some kind of trail." She stomped her foot down on the ground, then stepped back, holding the beam in place. Her shoe had left a print, but after a few seconds, the shiny coated floor moved back into place, looking undisturbed. "That's really weird," she said quietly.

"It's not important," Susanna said. "Let's just go."

After about half an hour's worth of walking, we finally came to something interesting. The tunnel split into a fork, two passages leading right and left.

"Which way?" Carl asked.

"Both?" I suggested. "Let's split up."

"I don't like that idea," Carolyn said.

"No, it's fine," Susanna said. "But just for a little bit. Ray, you and Carolyn go that way, and we'll take this one. If you don't find anything in five minutes, come back here."

That sounded reasonable, so Carolyn and I took the tunnel to the right. But after only a few yards, the tunnel came to a dead end, or so it seemed. "Look, up there," Carolyn said, pointing her flashlight at the ceiling. There was a round hole about a foot in diameter. "I wonder what that's for."

"Wait, what's this?" I asked, prompting her to shine the light at the far wall. "Another hole." We could see this one more clearly, and upon further inspection, it appeared that this was a smaller tunnel, but far too small for anyone to get inside. "This doesn't make any sense," I said. "Is it like a drain or something?"

"Maybe," Carolyn said. "Let's go find Susanna and Carl."

We almost bumped into them as we met up at the junction, and we told each other what we had found. While our discovery had just been confusing, what Susanna and Carl had found seemed more practical, and they led us to what amounted to a steep ramp. This led to a platform with a few steps leading into the wall, and above this, a large metal door in the roof of the chamber.

"A trapdoor?" Carolyn said.

"That would be my guess," Susanna said, pointing. "It's got a handle and everything. Give me a hand."

Resisting the urge to make the old joke where I would start clapping instead of helping — something Carolyn would do if I ever used that phrase — I joined Carl in helping her push the door open. It creaked on its hinges as we did so, but it wasn't very difficult to move. Fresh air flooded in as we managed to open it fully, and the door flopped neatly onto the ground beside it. The steps led us out onto some grass, and we looked around trying to make sense of our surroundings.

We appeared to be in a field. There were trees off to the right, and as I made my eyes glow in order to see in the dark more clearly, I was immediately reminded of the fields on my aunt and uncle's property in Appling. There was no way we were that far out in the country, though, given that we had only walked for about half an hour. But the place felt kind of like that, or like the Vampire Killers' house out in Evans.

Then, over to the left, I saw the house. It was huge, bigger than any I had seen before, at least in real life. It was three stories high and looked very impressive, with floodlights all around illuminating both the house and its surrounding yards. My first impression was that it looked like some of the rich people's homes I'd seen depicted on *Miami Vice.*

"What the hell?" Carolyn said. "Where are we?"

"Whose house is this?" I asked. "Are they the ones that dug the tunnel?" My recollection of *Miami Vice* put a weird image in my head, that suddenly Crockett and Tubbs were about to jump out from nowhere with their guns pointed at us and shout, *Freeze!* The only thing that made sense to me was that this was somehow related to Susanna's big police conspiracy, that maybe the tunnel had been a trap to lure us here. The scenario continued in my mind, the cops holding us at gunpoint and saying, *You're under arrest for the murders of...* How many people?

"Holy shit, this place is huge," Carl said almost in a whisper. "Seriously, what is this?"

"It's certainly big," Susanna said, more calm than the rest of us. "But I have no idea where we are. Maybe some new subdivision that's being built up?"

"Whoever it is must be really well off," I said.

"Old money, maybe?" Carolyn offered.

"Maybe," Susanna continued, "but I don't see what this could possibly have to do with us."

"Well, this is interesting," Carl said from behind us, and I turned to see what he was referring to. He had closed the trapdoor part of the way, and he was brushing the lid of it with his hand. "Grass," he said. "So it blends in with the rest of the yard." He closed it all the way, and the door seemed to disappear. He then grabbed a seemingly invisible handle and pulled the door open again, then closed it.

"Wow," I said. "You can barely see it."

"Leave it open for now, Carl," Susanna said.

"Okay then," he said, opening it again and placing the heavy lid back onto the ground.

"So, that should mean…" Susanna began, but she didn't finish. She walked back to the door Carl had left open, looked down into the ground, then around in another direction, pointing as she turned. "Should be…" She continued to point as she walked, her arm falling as she went. She was looking at the ground. Finally she said, "Here."

"What?" I asked.

She knelt down and picked up something round and flat. It was like a manhole cover, but from the way she was holding it as she stood back up, it didn't appear to be as heavy. One side of it was covered with grass.

"That's the other hole we found!" Carolyn said. "The one in the roof of the tunnel!"

"So…" Carl said, then suddenly changed into a bat and flew down into the open trapdoor. It took me a second, but I realized what he was doing and turned back to the spot where Susanna was holding the round lid. Carl came flying up through the smaller tunnel, then landed next to it and changed back to his regular self. "We can fit through the smaller tunnels as bats!"

None of this seemed to make a whole lot of sense, but it was intriguing. "So what about the other tunnel?" I asked. "The one Carolyn and I found down below?"

"I guess we should find out," Susanna said.

"But wait!" Carolyn said. "Just what the hell is going on here? Tunnels? A big house? Trapdoors? This is all just kind of insane."

"I have a theory about what's going on," Susanna said, "but I want to figure out a few more things to be sure." While Carolyn appeared to feel threatened by all of this, and Carl and I were the most curious, Susanna seemed to have settled on a slightly amused attitude. I wasn't sure why this was, but it helped comfort me. If she wasn't afraid, I felt no reason to be. She clipped her flashlight to a belt loop on her shorts, then said, "So, down the rabbit hole?"

This invoked in my mind a particularly disturbing scene I remembered from the animated movie *Watership Down,* in which a bunch of rabbits were trapped underground in a tunnel, all crammed together and looking desperate. "You mean bat hole," I corrected, hoping to shake the image.

"So wait," Carl said, pointing. "How are you going to keep the flashlight with you when you change into a bat?"

Susanna frowned at him. "The same way the rest of my clothes stay with me whenever I do."

This had never occurred to me, but it was an interesting point. How exactly…

The whole world seemed to tip to one side, and everything just felt wrong. My mind clouded, and I felt disconnected. I couldn't remember where I was, or even who I was. And then, just as quickly, the weird feeling went away, and we were all standing in the yard next to the entrance to the bat-sized tunnel. I completely forgot what we had been talking about, and I also quickly forgot the strange feeling I had just experienced. It was like it never happened.

Susanna led us as bats down into the small tunnel, which immediately opened up into the larger chamber Carolyn and I had found. Judging from the position of the other small opening in the wall, I guessed that it led to the huge house we had seen. As we flew along the passageway, I wondered what all of this was for. Was someone using these tunnels to sneak into other people's houses? Was this really leading to somewhere, or were we about to end up in a sewer or something? It felt like we were flying too fast, and I was worried about slamming into a wall if the tunnel made any sharp turns. But it didn't, and I saw a light up ahead sooner than I expected. Perhaps this was another underground chamber, I thought, but it seemed too well lit.

As we reached the new area, we found that it was brightly colored stone, not the strange, coated dirt and rock that composed the tunnels we had seen so far. It wasn't very large, maybe the size of a walk-in closet, but more cramped. Susanna changed back to her regular form, so the rest of us did the same. There were strange, iron bars on the floor, and they were arranged in angular patterns that seemed familiar but didn't quite make sense to me.

"Now where are we?" Carolyn asked.

"Shh!" Susanna said, holding up a finger behind her. Beyond her, I could see what looked like a room with red carpet and furniture, but I couldn't get a good look.

All of a sudden, there was a noise like sliding metal, similar to the sound of a jail cell door being slammed shut. Bars came down in front of us, blocking our path, and I instinctively looked behind me to the tunnel we had just left. It was blocked, too, not by bars, but by a large metal sheet covering the opening.

"What the fart?" Carl said. "We're trapped!"

"No shit, Sherlock," Carolyn said.

"Calm down," Susanna said.

"What do you…" I began, but Susanna cut me off with a loud shushing sound. I didn't understand why until I heard what had gotten her attention, a rapid clicking noise. It reminded me of a ticking watch, only much louder. There was also a more subtle sound, something like wind blowing.

"Quick!" Susanna shouted, which echoed painfully in the small stone chamber. "Change into bats and squeeze through the bars!"

I didn't bother to argue; her urgent tone left no room for that. Within seconds, we had escaped through the bars as bats, then settled onto a carpeted floor a few feet from our recent prison. We changed back to our person forms again. Almost immediately, the ticking noise I had been hearing was cut off by a heavy *whoosh!* as blue and orange flames filled the area we had just left. After an initial burst, the flames became smaller and remained near the bottom of the framed area, which I realized was a very large fireplace.

I took in the rest of our surroundings, a vast, ornate living room, presumably inside the house we had seen earlier. The ceilings were high, and there were several pieces of expensive looking furniture around the room. The walls were off-white and decorated with fancy paintings, and a huge gold chandelier hung from the ceiling, its light bulbs made to look like candles.

"What… the… hell…" Carl managed to say. "We could have been in that." He was staring at the fireplace, which was still blazing away.

I looked back to Susanna, who was gasping for breath. We all were. She looked confused, then thoughtful. "But why would they…" she said quietly. "Unless it was some kind of…" She stopped again.

"All right, cut the crap, Susanna," Carolyn snapped. "If you know what's going on, spill it." As she said this, she stood up, brushing herself off. Carl and I did the same, but Susanna stood up more slowly, looking around her.

"I'm not… I'm still not sure."

"Well can you at least give us a hint or something?" I hadn't seen Carolyn this angry in a while. "I'm getting kind of tired of all this melodramatic bullshit. Secret tunnels, a big mansion in the middle of who knows where, traps in the fireplace…"

"The tunnels are the biggest clue," Susanna said, trying to regain her usual air of authority. "Think about it. Bat-sized tunnels? Who else could make that? You know, besides…"

"Other vampires," I said, suddenly figuring it out.

"Wait, are you freaking kidding me?" Carl asked. "You think those dork-heads Dennis and Tim did all this?"

"No," Susanna said.

"*Other* vampires," I said, this time more pointedly.

"Oh." Carl's expression went from confused to intrigued. "Oh! But… Wait. Is this a good thing or a bad thing?"

I was also intrigued. If there were in fact other vampires than us, this could be very interesting. But another notion began to creep into my mind, a much less pleasant one.

Before I had time to complete the thought, I heard something that distracted me. The others heard it, too, and we turned as a group to a doorway at the far corner of the room. It was a shuffling sound, like someone dragging their feet, but very slowly. As it grew louder, it began to sound like more than one person, then more and more. The effect was repeated from another doorway, this one in another corner of the room, the one on the same wall as the fireplace.

It was this far doorway that revealed the source of the noise first. A man shuffled in slowly, followed by a woman, then more people. The flow increased as the procession continued, and I soon noticed what was so odd about the way they walked. They were moving slowly, almost like zombies. I immediately thought of the undead people in Michael Jackson's "Thriller" video, but these weren't decaying, rotted corpses. They looked mostly normal, aside from their gait. At least, they did until I looked more closely at their faces.

Each person had a dead expression, in keeping with my first impression of them as zombies. Their eyes seemed almost emotionless, but they were also looking at us. In fact, they never took their increasingly creepy eyes off of us as they walked, though they didn't walk directly toward us. Instead, they seemed to be lining up along the far wall, not exactly in formation but at least in some semblance of a crowd. There were dozens of them, some of which began to spill in from the other doorway farther down the wall. As unsettling as their manner of walking, their eyes, and general demeanor was, the final detail that sent a chill down my spine was their open, gaping mouths. Each mouth sported a pair of long, curved fangs.

"Not possible," Susanna said, almost whispering. "Not… possible." She was more firm the second time.

I didn't quite know what she meant until one particular detail of a woman in the group caught my eye. As she shuffled along and gazed at me and the others with the same blankness, I noticed that her white blouse had some rather prominent shoulder pads. Her hair was permed, and she had long, dangling earrings. I recognized her. I had killed her earlier that same night.

"Susanna," Carl said sternly, "you said our victims didn't come back to life as vampires."

"They don't," she said, but I could tell that she was just as terrified as the rest of us.

"Well maybe they don't realize that," Carolyn said, also frightened but angry as well.

But here they were, filing into the room one after another, every person we had killed over the past week. I saw the black woman I had taken down during that mysterious rampage we went on Sunday night, the man whose wallet I had emptied when prompted to by Dennis, the boy with spiky black hair whom Dennis had so gleefully killed his first night as a vampire, and several others I didn't recognize. Presumably, these were other victims my sisters and friends had killed whom I hadn't taken much notice of at the time. As the crowd seemed to settle and become complete, I guessed that there were close to a hundred of them.

For a while, they just stood there, and we couldn't do much else but look at them and wonder what was going on. There was a strange stillness in the room, the only sounds being the roar from the fireplace and the much more subtle, but somehow more menacing, sound of a hundred blank-eyed vampires breathing, but not doing anything else.

I wanted to ask Susanna what we should do next, but I just stood there, afraid that breaking the silence would cause something bad to happen. Instead, I just looked at these vampires more, seeing which ones I recognized. There was a policeman among them, and I wasn't sure where he had come from. I should have made the connection when I saw the handful of people next to him, but their appearance shocked me too much. The large man's beard was the first thing I noticed. Had he been carrying a shotgun, the picture would have been more complete. Next to him was the rest of his family, the mother and the two young boys, the so-called Vampire Killers. Now they were here, vampires themselves. We hadn't killed them, but presumably Dennis and Tim had.

After what felt like several minutes of this stand-off, the vampires started walking toward us, slowly and then more quickly, more or less in unison. This built up into a light run, and finally, I realized that we needed to get out of there. I turned to flee in the opposite direction, having no idea where I might be headed.

"Over here!" Carl called out, pointing to a door next to a staircase I hadn't noticed before. At first I thought he had been directing us to the stairs, but instead he reached the front door at amazing speed, then flung it open and ran out into the night. Susanna, Carolyn, and I quickly followed.

We found ourselves on a large porch illuminated by several lights, and a wide, stone staircase led down to the front lawn. I looked back and saw the other vampires chasing after us, moving more slowly than I had initially feared.

"What do we do?" I cried.

"Only thing we can do!" Susanna shouted. She changed into a bat, and we followed her up into the air.

What happened next reminded me of the times I had been at the beach and would play around in the ocean. Some of the beaches in

South Carolina had particularly large waves, and from time to time, I would get swept up in one as I tried to make my way back to land, temporarily losing all control and being at the mercy of the water. After a few seconds, the wave would pass, and I would recover. The effect was both frightening and fun, at least once it was over.

The force of dozens of bats whipping around our group as they overtook us felt similar. It was disorienting and scary, though just as it was at the beach, the wave of bats passed, and it took a moment to figure out which way was up and if I had survived. I had, as had the others, but we had stopped flying and were hovering in place as we tried to get our bearings.

There was no way we were flying out of there. The enemy vampire bats filled the sky above us in a huge black crescent, blocking any chance of escape. I wondered if we might be able to find our way back to the tunnel, which I suggested to the others.

"I doubt we'd make it," Carolyn said. "I'm not even sure where it is."

"Somewhere off to the left, I think," Susanna said. "But you're right." She flew back toward the ground, and the other vampires did the same, but still keeping the same distance between us.

We landed, then changed form. To my surprise, several of the vampire bats in the air also changed into person form, which made them plummet several feet to the ground, each landing with a thud. They remained motionless for a few seconds, then slowly got up, apparently unharmed. Meanwhile, the rest of the bats carefully flapped their way to ground level, then also changed.

"What the hell happened there?" Carl asked.

"I'm not sure," Susanna said.

Carl changed back into his bat form. I was about to call out to him to wait, but then I noticed that about half of the vampires had changed back to bats as well. The rest of them were slowly making their way toward us on foot, but they didn't seem to be in much of a hurry.

Carl once again transformed to his regular shape, and the other bats followed his lead.

"Wait," Carolyn said. She walked a few paces to the right. Most of the vampires did the same, matching her steps. She then carefully stepped back to her original spot, and those same vampires also walked back in the same direction. As a group, they were still approaching us, but very slowly. Carolyn turned to face me, and I noticed that a few, but not many, of the vampires also turned around, facing in the opposite direction.

"Berzerk," she whispered to me. I understood immediately. One of the video games we had gotten for our Atari back in 1982 was *Berzerk,* which pitted a lone human against a bunch of evil robots. The playing field consisted of a vaguely maze-like area, and the walls were lethal to both the human and the enemy robots. One strategy, aside from just shooting them, was to manipulate the robots into walking into the electrified walls, which was easy to do because the robots would often mimic the moves the player made. Although it had been a while, Carolyn and I had played this game quite a bit back in the day, and Carl was familiar with it, too.

"What?" Susanna asked.

"Oh, shit," Carl said. "She's right."

"There's a pool over behind the house," Carolyn said, keeping her voice low as she turned back to the slowly approaching vampires. "I saw it when we were in the air before. If we can make it to that, we could jump in, and the vampires would follow us and be destroyed."

"That's brilliant!" I said.

"No it isn't," Susanna said. "A pool won't do us any good. It has to be running water, remember?"

"Crap," Carl said. The vampires were getting uncomfortably close.

"Would a hot tub work, then?" Carolyn asked, one eyebrow raised. "That's got running water in it, with the jets and all."

Susanna thought for a moment. "Well, probably, but…"

"Then come on!" Carolyn said, quickly changing into a bat and flying toward the corner of the house.

There wasn't time to argue, so the rest of us flew after her, hoping that the other vampires wouldn't catch up. We stayed at ground level as we went, rounding the house counterclockwise. Susanna began shouting something as we got to the back of the house, but I couldn't quite make it out. She managed to catch up to Carolyn, and instead of flying all the way to the extremely large in-ground pool which I was seeing for the first time, they settled behind a shrubbery close to it. Carl and I zipped in closely behind them, and the four of us stayed as bats, hiding on the ground. Carolyn and Susanna had already been arguing by the time we arrived, Susanna whispering sharply.

"The Jacuzzi is probably too small for all of us to fit in there at once, and besides, we'd be changed back to human then!"

"Good!" Carolyn hissed back. "As long as it means that we don't get torn to pieces by these monster vampire things!"

Susanna retorted, "And if it didn't work, they'd get us…"

PLOOP! PLOOP PLOOP SPLASHHHH!

We peered out from our hiding place to see that some of the bats were flying straight into the pool, while others were landing safely around it. Some changed to person form, while others hovered at ground level. So far, Carolyn's theory seemed sound, but then I noticed that the bats that had landed in the pool were transforming to their person forms and clambering out along the edges.

"Told you so," Susanna whispered.

"Still, not very bright, are they?" I said. I was beginning to feel more confident, like we might actually survive this after all.

A few more splashes were followed by horrible shrieks as several of the less coordinated bats managed to end up in the hot tub, which was adjacent to the pool. The steam from it had caught my eye a few moments before, but then the air above it filled with much thicker smoke as the vampires within went from bats to vaguely humanoid shapes, screaming and then dissolving into the churning water, clothes and all. I was reminded of something else, the movie *Gremlins,* in which the evil monsters were destroyed in bubbling puddles of ooze.

"Told you so, too," Carolyn said.

"Well if you have some brilliant idea as to how to get the other eight thousand of them into that little pool, I'm all for it," Susanna said with a sneer. At least, it sounded like a sneer, but she was still a bat.

"Over here!" Carl called from the edge of the house. I hadn't even noticed he'd left us. He was standing against one of the outer walls of the house and holding a hose. "Get behind me!"

The vampires had seen him, too, and they were beginning to make their way toward him, so we only had seconds to get there. As we flew, I saw him doing something to a spot on the wall, and once we arrived and stood behind him, I realized that he was turning on a faucet. The end of the hose he was holding, meanwhile, had one of those nozzles that acted like a high-powered squirt gun.

"Running water, right?" he said to Susanna with a grin. Without waiting for an answer, he let loose the high pressure stream of water onto the first vampire he saw, a short, heavyset, balding man who was lumbering toward us with fangs bared and his arms raised. The vampire shrieked in pain as the water hit him, then quickly dissolved into a puddle of slime. It was a horrible sight to see, but at the same time, it was a relief.

Carl continued his deadly spray of water across the approaching army of vampires, and one by one, they each succumbed and were destroyed. They kept coming, one after the other, not once seeming to figure out that if they just stopped approaching and ran or flew away to safety, they could have escaped. It was like their only purpose was to trap and attack us, and they couldn't get past their programming, much like the robots in the video game.

After several minutes, it was all over, and there was nothing left of the vampires. Carl dropped the hose, exhausted, and I turned back to the wall and shut off the water flow. We had done it. We had survived.

In the aftermath of all that had happened, we made our way back around to the side of the house, eager to get away from the soaked battlefield. While we were relieved to have made it through the ordeal, something still didn't feel right.

"Okay, so, these vampires," Carolyn said, "these people who came back to life even though you told us I don't know how many times that that wouldn't happen…"

"I don't know," Susanna said angrily. "I honestly don't. It doesn't make any sense to me, either."

"Oh, who cares?" I said. "We made it, didn't we? Let's just go home. Where's the tunnel back to the house, anyway?" I looked off to my left, having a vague idea of where it probably was.

"No," Susanna said firmly. "Not yet. Something about all of this still doesn't add up."

"Oh, come on," Carl said. "Ray's right. Can't we just get out of here? This whole thing totally sucked." We walked a little farther. "Though I did like getting all Rambo on those stupid vampire robots, or whatever they were."

I couldn't help but laugh at this, but neither of my sisters were amused. They walked in front, and Carl and I followed, not sure where they were headed. It soon became clear that Susanna was taking us back to the stairs that led to the front door of the house.

We made our way up, and I noticed once more how amazingly fancy the whole place was. It reminded me a little of a hotel my siblings and I had been dragged to during one of our parents' conferences, some overly rich looking place that was more intimidating than welcoming. Still, I had to admit that Susanna was right, that even though we had wiped out all of those weird and scary vampires, something felt wrong.

The porch we ended up on, which I hadn't had much time to examine earlier when we were being chased by a huge horde of mindless monsters, was equally fancy and unnecessarily impressive. There were electric lights all over, seemingly arranged to highlight how wonderful of a place this was, so much that I heard an imaginary *tah-dahhhh!* in my head as I looked at them. It felt more like we were on a stage than a front porch. Next to the door, there was a golden plaque with words on it stark capital letters: *THE TRUEBLOODS.*

Carolyn spotted this, too. "Oh, look! 'The Truebloods.' I guess that's the name of the people who live here."

"What?" Susanna almost shouted. She stopped and looked at the plaque, touching it lightly. She then drew back. "We have to get out of here," she said firmly, but her voice was almost a whisper.

This confused me. "What do you mean? I thought you were all eager to solve the big mystery. Maybe these..." "I said we have to go!" she snarled, which made me jump. "Back to..." She stopped, then looked at me strangely. She seemed confused. Her head moved forward slightly, like she was going to speak but then wasn't able to. Her head tilted to one side, and her eyebrows went up. It was a look I had seen our dog King make back when he was still alive, an expression he got when he heard something that confused him, like the beeping of my watch's alarm. He also got this look whenever he first heard a thunderstorm approaching.

I started to ask her what was wrong, but nothing happened. It was like I had forgotten how to talk. I wanted to look around at either Carolyn or Carl, but my neck didn't move. The rest of my body had suddenly stopped responding to my thoughts, too.

"We should go inside," Susanna said, but her voice didn't sound like it usually did. It was flat, emotionless.

I wanted to protest, but I couldn't. I couldn't do anything but stand there, breathe, and think. No one else said anything, either. It seemed like the doorway started somehow moving toward us, but then I realized that we were walking. I wasn't meaning to; I was just doing it. I could hear Carolyn and Carl behind me, and as we entered the house, all I could see at first was Susanna's back. We were walking single file, and I couldn't turn my head to see anything else in the room.

It was when we turned and headed toward the center of the room that I saw them for the first time. There were two of them, a man and a woman, dressed in fancy evening clothes. Their skin was quite pale, and they were smiling broadly, and I was immediately afraid of them. As we got closer, I realized that they were younger than I had initially thought; their clothes made them look older. In fact, they were probably somewhere between Susanna's and Carolyn's age, but I couldn't be certain. What I was sure of was that they were the ones who were controlling us like puppets, and I wanted more than anything else to get away from them. The other thing that I had no doubt about was that these were vampires, but not the brainless kind we had just gone up against. These two were the real thing.

We stopped in front of them, turning in unison like soldiers in formation. The pair continued to smile at us in their creepy manner. Finally, the young man, whom I noticed was quite tall, spoke.

"Welcome, everyone!" he said theatrically. I had half expected a dramatic *"Good eeeevening"* to come out of his mouth. "It's so nice to finally have you all here. Especially you, Susanna." I tried to turn and look at her, to ask her what he meant, but I couldn't.

"Aw, aren't they cute?" the girl said. Her voice was more high pitched than I expected. She had initially reminded me of Morticia from *The Addams Family,* long black dress and all, though she had red hair, not black. "Like little toy soldiers," she said, grinning at me with blood red lips. She was quite well styled, I noticed. While I didn't have any admiration for stuff like that, I had lived with older sisters long enough to appreciate — or at least recognize — when a girl was so carefully done up.

"Oh, don't be mean," he said with a grin, turning toward her briefly, then back to us. I felt a chill as our eyes met. "These are our honored guests. Please, everyone, sit." He held his arms open as he said this, and he and his cheerful companion sat down in two ornate chairs with soft, dark grey cushioning. I suddenly realized that I was sitting, too, presumably on a couch of the same design as the chairs, but I couldn't look down to be sure. I knew that Susanna was to my right, but I wasn't even sure whether it was Carolyn or Carl to my immediate left. I found that the one thing I could control was my eyes, able to move them up and down or left and right, but this still gave me a limited field of vision. I could blink, too, which I seemed to be doing a lot.

"So," he continued, "Introductions. My name is Robert, and this is my girlfriend, Jennifer."

"Pleased to meet you," Jennifer said sweetly, but there was a thinly veiled malevolence behind her ice blue eyes. I found it hard not to look at them, as they seemed to pierce right through to the back of my skull.

"For those of you who don't know, I am the one who, along with the lovely Susanna here," — he said this with a polite nod and a hand gesture — "created the vampire potion which all of you have been taking for the past two years."

Immediately, I flashed back to the night Susanna first told me about the potion, how she and a boy named Robert had developed it at school. I hadn't thought about that conversation for years, nor had I ever given much thought to this Robert guy. The way Susanna told it, he was freaked out after trying it and gave all the notes to Susanna as a way of safeguarding himself.

The tale Robert told us this night, however, was a different one. In his version, he had indeed been afraid of what the potion did to him initially, and he gave all of the notes for it to Susanna and told her to burn them. But once he realized that we had used the potion that first summer, he wanted to try it again, but Susanna refused any attempts he made at communication.

"As hard as I tried to get through, she wouldn't speak to me, return my calls, anything," Robert said. "It broke my heart." There was nothing in his tone to elicit sympathy, though. He mostly had a vain, sarcastic air to him, telling his story with the subtext that whatever had come before, tonight was his moment of triumph, and there was nothing we could do to stop him. All we could do was sit and listen. If I hadn't been so incredibly terrified, I would have been angry. Maybe there was room for both.

"How rude," Jennifer said, squinting her eyes slyly as she shook her head. Like Robert, she was all about the theatrics, also loving being in complete control. As I would soon learn, the two of them had been waiting for this night for a long time, and this was their big payoff. We made eye contact again, and she gave me a look of mock disbelief. "Can you believe her?" There was something almost musical about the way she spoke, very practiced and precise.

"I'm sorry, Robert," Susanna said, which startled me, but I was unable to actually jump. As before, her words were flat and without feeling. She wasn't really saying this; she was being forced to.

"Of course you are, dear," Robert said with a sick smile. He had narrow, dark eyes and both a pointed nose and pointed chin, but he didn't look particularly ugly or anything. He then went on to tell us how, over the next couple of years, he tried in vain to recreate the vampire potion, but he was never successful. He just couldn't do it without Susanna's help. I felt a strange pride in this, some small comfort that as powerful and clever as this guy seemed to be, he hadn't been able to achieve his goal without my big sister's assistance. But then again, here we all were.

The next turn in Robert's story was darker. When the chemical approach failed him, he took a different path, this time hoping to find a way to become a vampire through Satanism and devil worship. I knew a little bit about this sort of thing, just things I'd seen on TV and heard about second- or third-hand, secret cults around the country, hidden backwards messages in rock music that supposedly turned people evil, and the like. I wasn't sure how much I actually believed in all of that, but if anything was going to convince me, it was our current master of ceremonies.

"One night during one of our more successful rituals," Robert said with a nod toward Jennifer, who smiled knowingly, "the Prince of

Darkness himself answered my prayer, and a bolt of energy shot forth from the pentagram on the floor, killing us both. But not long after, we reawakened as vampires. It was the happiest night of my life."

"Or death," Jennifer said cutely, looking off to one side. Just for a second, I wanted to laugh, but then I felt mad at myself for that. Robert laughed, though.

"Yes. And so, after killing my parents, we took over this house." He went on to talk about what happened after that, but I got hung up on that last sentence. He just said it in such a matter-of-fact way, with no more gravity than if he had said, *So after that, we went to the grocery store and picked up some milk.* This guy was truly evil, I realized, and that just increased my fear.

I came back from my mental tangent and began listening again, and he was telling us how he and Jennifer had been spying on us for a while, months before we had even gotten together this time to take the potion. I wasn't clear on exactly how or when Jennifer had come into the picture, but there she was, beaming at us triumphantly and loving every minute of this. She didn't look like any girl I had ever seen in real life; she was more like someone I'd see on TV, or even one of the women in those cheesy Hammer Horror movies. There was an air of power about her that was both intriguing and repulsive.

Robert was similar in his demeanor, like some sort of fictional bad guy proudly spouting out his entire evil plan to the captured hero just before he executed his final move. In an actual story, this would precede his ultimate downfall, the hero saving the day at the last minute. But there was no way that was happening, I knew. I couldn't budge, let alone do anything to defeat him. None of us could. My eyes turned back to Jennifer again, who was still smiling away. Our eyes met, and for a moment, I wanted to somehow silently plead with her to let us go. She seemed to smile even more intensely then.

Robert's epic tale continued on as he told us how, once we had taken the potion and started killing, he and Jennifer had been sneaking around behind us and harvesting the bodies, resurrecting them as vampires. "Before then, we preyed on homeless people and hid their bodies, not wanting to cause a panic like your group did before. We decided to be more subtle. And then once you started leaving bodies around this time, we cleaned up after you, wanting to make use of the dead, not just waste them. But…" He paused. "Well, that didn't work as well as we'd hoped." As he said this, he tilted his head to one side and ran his fingers through his short, dark brown hair, looking almost apologetic. It was the first time I had seen him act the slightest bit humble.

"Well, it's not your fault," Jennifer said, reaching over and touching his knee. This made me want to flinch for some reason, but again, I couldn't move.

"Maybe," he said, shaking his head, but barely losing his grin. "I mean, it was a good idea. We wanted to build up this huge sort of vampire army." He looked back to us, catching my eye again, which led me to immediately avert my eyes to Jennifer. I regretted that; she was looking right at me. I looked down at my hands, which were neatly folded in my lap, though I hadn't put them there myself.

"That's why we made all of you kill so much a few nights back," Robert continued. Finally, that night made sense. It wasn't something that went wrong with the potion, nor was it Susanna slipping us the cure and giving us weird side effects. That night, I'd killed over and over because these two super-vampires were controlling my mind. I realized that there was a similar sensation in my head now that had been there that night, this weird sort of tingling feeling. It was much stronger tonight, and whenever I tried to move or speak, it was like a fist was clenched around my mind. I felt like a bug being held prisoner in the grasp of a child.

"But the mental energy it took to control them all was spread too thin," Robert said. "It just wasn't worth it. So we brought you four here instead. And you passed all of our tests!" He said this last bit with a fake clap of his hands, like some kindergarten schoolteacher congratulating a bunch of kids for getting their colors right. I hated him. "Mind you, the spell we used to create those tunnels was no small feat, but I must say I'm pleased with the results."

"Me too," Jennifer said. "Now we can start over with just the four of you, which is what we'd planned to do in the first place anyway!" She said this so brightly, like we should be as happy about it as they were.

"Yeah, I know," Robert said, again seeming uncharacteristically apologetic. "I guess the body harvesting idea was a bit too much of a stretch." He paused, looking pensive, then looked back up at Susanna. "But this really is better. It can be the way it was meant to be. All of us together, one big happy family."

I had assumed that they planned to kill us, but I was beginning to understand what they were really up to. My suspicions were confirmed when Robert explained that not only were they going to drain our bodies of blood, they would then bring us back to life as proper vampires, just like them. "You'll still be under our control, of course," he went on, "but hopefully not as dull and stupid as our earlier attempts were."

Hopefully? As brilliant as this guy thought he was, he wasn't even sure that we wouldn't end up as brainless undead slugs?

"It will be okay, Ray," Jennifer said to me soothingly. She actually seemed sincere for once, and I genuinely felt comforted for a moment, but that faded quickly. I went right back to being scared to death. Or worse.

"It's too bad that you couldn't have kept your little group together better, Susanna," Robert said. "It got to be too much trouble for us to keep track of both you and those other two… what were their names… The little red-headed pudgy one and the one with the glasses."

"Yes," Jennifer said with a pout. "They were kinda cute." She giggled. "Would have made nice pets." She flashed a more menacing grin than usual at me, and I felt my skin crawl. It became apparent that she, and probably Robert as well, was not very concerned about whether we ended up as articulate, "real" vampires like them or just vegetables, no more able to control our actions than we could at the moment. They had beaten us, and they could do whatever they wanted with us. I wanted to cry, but I wasn't even allowed to do that.

"All right, all right," Robert said, standing up. "Enough of all the talking. Sorry, I tend to go on a lot once I get on a roll."

"I'll say," Jennifer said, also standing up and smoothing out her long, black dress, not looking at anyone. She looked back to Robert, who was glaring at her angrily. It was the first time I had seen him look that way.

"I'll let that one slide," he said in a low tone. Jennifer seemed to wither, losing her usual composure, and I found myself feeling bad for her as well as extremely angry at Robert. I wasn't even sure why.

"Now," he said to Susanna, "come to me." Susanna stood up and walked slowly to Robert, who had his arms outstretched.

"And you," Jennifer said to me, pointing, and my heart leapt. I had thought for some reason that they might take the oldest of us first, then me and Carl. But no, this was it for me. No time left.

Without even trying, I stood up and seemed to glide toward her. I was tingling all over with fear, similar to how I felt the few times I was physically disciplined by either of my parents, that horrible anticipation before the spanking that was about to come. But this was much, much worse. If I had been allowed to, I would have been shaking. She was taller than me, but not by very much; she was about the same height as Carolyn or Susanna. Out of the corner of my eye, I noticed the height difference between Robert and Susanna, and I saw that he had grabbed her chin and was pointing her face up to his.

Jennifer didn't do this to me, though I imagined she might just for the effect, to show how in control of me she was. But she didn't need to. My eyes became locked onto hers, these intensely gorgeous, ice blue circles with wide, black pupils that I was feeling myself sucked into. She was powerful, amazing, and completely in control. I got this notion that her eyes could freeze fire if they wanted to, then realized that it was a rather poetic thought for me to have, not something I was used to thinking. But I was beginning to wonder how much of what was in my head was even my own, if my thoughts were mine or if she were putting them there. My defenses were falling away piece by piece, and I felt more and more okay with that.

She was beautiful. She was the prettiest thing I had ever seen. Her wide, amazing blue eyes were only a part of her absolute perfect beauty. I had never even been attracted to a girl before, but now all I could think about was her flawless rounded face, her dark arched eyebrows, her expertly feathered auburn hair that went past her shoulders. And then there was her mouth, that never-ending smile that widened and seemed to light up my entire soul, growing wider and wider until I saw — for the first time, I suddenly realized — her fangs.

They were the purest white, slightly curved, with points as sharp as razors, and I knew that any second now, those gorgeous teeth would be piercing my neck. I loved the idea. I wanted it to happen. I wanted to give every drop of my blood to her. There was no "me" anymore; I was hers.

I thought I heard or glimpsed something off to either side of me, but whatever it was, it didn't matter. Jennifer was all that existed in the entire world. If she had used some mental powers to make me feel this way about her, I didn't care. All I felt was what was happening right now, and I could forget the rest of my life up to this point. I was hers: mind, body, and soul.

An immense shriek suddenly rang out that echoed so painfully, it made my entire being quake, and the world went crazy. I couldn't see, think, or feel. I realized that it was my precious Jennifer crying out, and as I began to recover and could feel my limbs and then the rest of my body, I found that I was on the floor, my hands clawing at the dark red carpet. The screaming continued, now seeming to come not from within my own ears but in one direction, and I looked around and began to make sense of my surroundings again.

Both Jennifer and Robert were on the floor as well, on their backs. Standing near them were two people I didn't recognize at first, holding out wooden crosses toward the two vampires. Over to my left, Susanna was also sprawled on the floor, trying to get up and also brushing something white and powdery from her eyes.

"Stakes!" she screamed. "You have them! Use them!"

Almost simultaneously, Tim and Dennis ripped wooden stakes from their belt loops and leapt down, plunging the deadly weapons into the chests of Robert and Jennifer, who cried out horribly. I couldn't move. I was paralyzed, not by some psychic force, but by fear.

"Harder!" Susanna shouted, clambering over to Tim, who was trying to drive the stake into Robert's heart. "It has to go through!" Robert was fighting back as best as he could, but he was already weakening. She reached the two squirming figures and began helping Tim.

Dennis had managed to get his stake all the way through Jennifer's heart, and her pathetic wails died down immediately. I felt a tremendous sense of relief, and very quickly, I began to feel more like my real self again.

Susanna sighed as Robert died, and Tim picked up his cross from the floor nearby and tapped her on the forehead. "There you go," he said with a small smile.

"No need," she said, still out of breath. "You already got me with the garlic powder."

I quickly pieced together what had happened, and Dennis and I stood up. I was still a vampire, and Dennis looked at me doubtfully. "Go ahead," I said, holding my arms open in a non-threatening gesture. Dennis repeated Tim's earlier move and touched the cross to my forehead, which caused a familiar feeling to rush over me, like a strong, cool wind. The potion's effects were gone, and I was human again.

Carl and Carolyn still needed to be dealt with, but there was no struggle on their part, either. In fact, Carolyn jumped up from her place on the couch and said, "Give me that," grabbing the cross from Tim's hand. She instantly changed back.

Dennis cautiously approached Carl, probably wondering how this confrontation might play out, and I felt tense for a moment, too. But Carl just smiled at him and said, "Do it, dork-head." Dennis laughed, then tapped him on the head while making a little *boop!* sound effect, and we were all safe and human again.

At least, it seemed so, but then Carolyn staggered backwards onto the couch with a crestfallen look, flopping back to where she had been sitting and drawing her knees up to her chin. "Oh, God," she said, looking behind me.

"What?" I asked, starting to turn around.

"Don't!" Carolyn said loudly, then more softly: "Don't look at them."

But I couldn't help it, nor could Susanna and the rest of us. Once I comprehended what I was seeing, I wished I had followed Carolyn's advice. On the floor were the bodies of Robert and Jennifer, but they were horribly decomposed, mostly black but with some remnants of color on their faces and limbs. It was the most horrible thing I had ever seen. Just before I screwed my eyes shut, wishing I had never turned around, I caught a glimpse of Dennis doing the same thing.

Things eventually livened up as we made our way back through the tunnel to our house, and we talked about how relieved we were. It had been Carl who first speculated that the reason the bodies of the two vampires were so decayed was that they had in fact been dead for weeks, maybe months, and the way they looked when we had last seen them was how they would have looked had they never been vampires. That sounded reasonable, but Carolyn quickly requested that we change the subject.

Susanna asked Tim and Dennis what had happened to them after they broke off from our group a few nights ago. They'd had a fun night to begin with, breaking into a video arcade hoping to play some games for free, but that hadn't worked out. And then, once sunrise came, they weren't ready for it and had no safe place to hide, so they got changed back into humans.

"We really had to rough it for the next couple of days," Tim said, "or at least, we stayed in hiding. Our parents weren't expecting us back until the weekend, and we didn't want to tell them what was going on. You remember that tree house I used to have when I was little?" He directed this question to me, and I nodded, assuming he could see this in the dim light from the flashlights as we walked along the tunnel. "Well, it's still more or less intact, and so Dennis and I hid there the whole time, all the while not letting my parents see us."

"Yeah, that was kind of fun, I guess," Dennis said, "but nerve-wracking. I was thinking that any minute now, Tim's parents were going to find us hiding in their backyard and ask us what was up."

"And it's not like you could have said, 'Hey Mom and Dad! We're just hiding out from the rest of the vampires!'" Carl said, then laughed.

This was a tense moment for me; I expected Dennis to lash back at him with something mean. But he didn't. Instead, he just said, "Right!"

The story of their time apart from us continued, eventually leading up to their finding us at Robert's house and rescuing us. Dennis explained that it was Tim's description of what happened between us near the end of the 1983 session that led him to insist that they find us and change us back into regular people.

"I didn't know all the details of that," Dennis said, "where you first cured Carolyn, then everyone fought against each other, all that. So we figured that that might happen again."

"Yeah, we thought we were just going to have to sneak up on you and throw garlic on you or use crosses or whatever," Tim said, "but what we actually found…" He laughed. "Holy crap!"

Carl laughed too, adding with a bit of swagger, "What, you don't think we could've have handled those… you know…" He waited and then delivered his punch line: "Yeah, that was pretty damn scary and I'm glad you guys showed up when you did."

"You're welcome," Dennis said pointedly.

"Yeah, yeah, yeah," Carl said, adopting his usual attitude, but I could hear a smile in his voice.

We had to explain to Dennis and Tim exactly who Robert was, and I told them how he was a guy from Susanna's Chemistry class who helped her develop the potion. Susanna corrected me, saying that it was Biology they had together, not Chemistry. I shrugged, not knowing or really caring about the difference. As we continued to talk, it became apparent that by the time Dennis and Tim had arrived at our house, found the basement door open, and followed us to the other house, they had completely missed out on our encounter with the massive army of mindless vampires, instead only arriving in time to save us from Robert and Jennifer. I realized as this came up that I had already forgotten about that earlier confrontation, somehow letting it slip my mind and thinking only of that final showdown with the two.

"How the heck could I have forgotten that?" I asked, followed by a nervous laugh. It made me uneasy, the idea that I could so quickly forget such an epic battle, something that should have been important enough to remember.

"Probably the adrenaline," Carolyn said from behind me. She and Susanna were at the back of the group as we walked along the tunnel, while Dennis and I walked behind Carl and Tim, who were in front.

"The what?" I asked.

"Could be," Carl said. "It's something your body does to you when you're in a really tense situation. You get all strong and stuff, do what needs to be done, but then sometimes it's hard to remember what happened later on."

"Yeah, pretty much," Carolyn said. "Happens to athletes sometimes, I think."

I accepted this explanation uneasily, but I also knew that both Carolyn and Carl were more familiar than I was with athletics, so maybe they knew what they were talking about. But something was bugging me, something I had only barely noticed before and was beginning to feel again, this weird phenomenon of forgetting the details of what happened to us during the window of time that we were vampires. After the 1983 episode, I remembered some things that had happened, but not in any great detail. Now that our stint as vampires had ended this time around two years later, I found that I was already beginning to forget major things. It was like waking up from a dream, a particularly vivid and interesting one, and wanting to hold onto the details of it for as long as possible. It was an unsettling feeling, and I was afraid to tell the others about it. It was like the more I talked, the more I began to forget.

Things were silent for a while, and then Carolyn said to Susanna, "So, this Robert guy. Was he always, so… I don't know… hokey?"

Susanna laughed. "Yeah, a bit. I mean, I thought he was kinda neat and interesting when I was younger, but yeah, deep down he was kind of a cheeseball."

I had no idea what they were talking about. I hadn't found anything silly or laughable about the guy at all; he was terrifying as far as I was concerned. It even annoyed me that the two of them were able to make light of the situation. Or maybe I was already remembering it wrong. I became more uncomfortable as the two of them began talking about Jennifer's appearance, wondering how she could maintain herself so well without a reflection. Carolyn joked that maybe Robert did all of that for her, which set them off giggling. Wanting to get away from this conversation, I edged a little farther up the tunnel from them, hoping to talk to the other boys instead.

"Okay," I said to Tim, intentionally sounding irritated, "they're talking about girly crap now."

He and the others laughed, and I heard Susanna and Carolyn continue to talk behind us, more quietly, something to do with what they thought might happen to Robert's house. Tim then asked, "So how did it go with that family out in Evans, anyway?"

"What?" Carl asked. "We thought you guys took care of them!"

I then remembered that they had just gotten through telling us what they had done the night they left us, and I again kicked myself mentally for letting a detail like that slip through the cracks in my mind. This topic brought Susanna and Carolyn back into the main discussion, and we figured out that it was in fact Robert and Jennifer who had killed the family, presumably because their presence, or even the possibility that they might wipe us out instead, didn't fit in with their plans.

There was then some talk about Robert's mind control powers, which Susanna put down to his being a vampire, that somehow that had increased the psychic abilities he already had. According to her, he had demonstrated those to her in high school using something called Zener cards, which was another thing she found interesting about him at the time.

"Maybe his being a Satanist had something to do with it, too," Carolyn said. "I've heard about witches using spells to read people's minds and control them and all. Maybe he did pagan sacrifices and all, too!" She gave an exaggerated shudder.

"Well I told you what my dad said," Dennis said, "about pagans and witches and Satanists not being all the same…"

"Never mind," she interrupted. "I don't want to keep talking about him. I'm having a hard enough time getting that image out of my head." She didn't have to explain exactly which image; I too was trying to keep from remembering how horrible he and Jennifer looked once they were dead and decaying. Later on after we got home, Carolyn insisted that I sleep on the floor in her room that night, which I didn't mind at all, despite my friends ridiculing me about it at first. I insisted that it wasn't because I was scared, but that she was. It was mostly true.

We each got up at various times around or after noon on Friday, exhausted but recovering from the ordeal. The day was spent getting the house back in order before our parents arrived, which my friends helped with before eventually going home.

It was odd seeing how well Carl and Dennis got along at times, and it even bugged me a little, but I wasn't sure why. I figured it was just because I was so used to them being enemies, being torn between them, so to speak. Dennis even seemed a little suspicious of this, too, but Carl was perfectly polite, helping him and the rest of us as we took the garbage bags down from the windows and moved my mattress back into my bedroom.

Our other big project for the day was to rearrange the basement. This was made necessary due to something we had done upon arriving at the house the night (or morning) before, when we moved two large shelving units from one wall over onto the western one, covering up the entrance to the tunnel. Even though we had been exhausted by the time we arrived, Susanna insisted that we do it then. Her reason for us moving all of the other stuff around in the basement was for our parents' benefit: The story we would tell them was that we had decided while they were gone to rearrange everything, not just those two shelves, which would have looked too suspicious. I didn't like all of the manual labor, but the cover story seemed necessary.

After Tim and Dennis had been picked up by their parents and Carl had ridden back home on his bike, I went into the kitchen. I erased the large "V" Susanna had written on the calendar in pencil for this date, and I felt sad as I did so. Already, my memories were becoming fuzzy enough that I had forgotten most of the bad stuff that had happened, like the Vampire Killers family and the horrible things those other vampires had put us through. I hadn't forgotten them completely, just the details of how bad things were and how scared I was, choosing instead to focus on the more positive things. I even tried to gloss over the way that our group had fragmented and turned on itself; after all, we had reunited in the end, which was what wound up saving the day.

After we had covered up the tunnel with those shelves the night before, Carolyn said something about having had enough of vampires, and the thought of this disappointed me. Susanna gave some indication that we might try again someday, saying something about getting it right, which I found a little more encouraging. I wondered when we might use the potion again, if it would be possible to do it the following summer. That ended up not happening, but we did eventually take it one more time, which led to things turning out even worse than I could have possibly imagined.

PART THREE

The next time we got together and became vampires was two years later, which I started referring to as the "vampire reunion." Occasionally, my extended family on my mother's side would have family reunions out in Appling, during which I would meet distant cousins and other relatives. I would have no idea who they were, have it explained to me exactly what my relationship to them was, not particularly care, and then not see these people until the next reunion, once again having to be reminded who in the world they were. These were supposed to be fun occasions, but I mostly found them boring and pointless.

I came up with the idea of our own small version of a family reunion, but with vampires, mainly because I was disappointed over how things had somewhat deteriorated among the group during the 1985 gathering. I wanted to get all six of us together and actually have a good time, which seemed plausible given that Carl and Dennis had finally learned how to get along. They weren't best friends or anything, but it looked like I had managed to bring them together on some common ground, which I found encouraging. I had in fact hoped to have the reunion during the summer of 1986, but that didn't work out.

For one thing, once sixth grade began, our friendships continued to fluctuate. While Carl was friendly enough with Dennis at my house those couple of days in July, once we were back in school and around the other kids, he tended to pick on Dennis again, though maybe not as much as before. It seemed less cruel than it had been, but there was still some animosity there, and sometimes, I picked on him myself. Other times, I would instead turn on Carl and side with Dennis; I kind of bounced back and forth between the two.

Tim, meanwhile, was in the other class, 6-B, which meant that we didn't see him as much. However, unlike previous years at school, this year began to have the students from both classes mixed together more often, and we had a wider variety of teachers and subjects. So I wasn't quite as isolated from Tim as I might have been. Still, he ended up wanting to avoid the triangle of me, Dennis, and Carl, preferring to deal with us one on one, not when we were trying to pair off against each other. He wasn't hostile about this, but I did notice how he distanced himself from us over time.

Despite all of this, I still hoped that we would be able to get along as a small group in the summer and take the potion again, but Carolyn quashed those plans in the spring. She was dating a boy from her school named Paul, and when I approached her with the idea of becoming vampires again, she said no, that she would be busy doing stuff with him instead. I already didn't like Paul to begin with; he was this loud, arrogant guy who seemed to think that he was the coolest person in the world, and he was usually snide to me, which would lead Carolyn to act the same way when he was around. The fact that Carolyn refused to even consider becoming vampires because of him made me resent him even more.

As it turned out, the two of them had broken up by the time our parents' annual ALA conference came around at the end of June, but by then, I had already given up on the idea for that year. I didn't bother to bring it up to my friends, but Dennis did ask me about it during the last month of school. He was a little disappointed that we wouldn't get to do it, but not terribly.

One development that happened during the earlier half of sixth grade had to do with Dennis's psychic powers, which I still wasn't sure I believed in or not. Given what had happened with Robert and Jennifer and how they controlled our minds so effectively, I was at least open to the idea that vampires could have such powers, but I still wasn't convinced that normal people did. I also couldn't remember all of the details of what they had done to us, just that they had done it and that it had been a scary thing to go through. As far as regular, everyday people being psychics, I still had it in my head those who claimed to be were frauds, either clever illusionists or fortune tellers who just told people what they wanted to hear.

Tim had a similar attitude, which I found out when I noticed one day that he was carrying in his stack of schoolbooks a smaller book called *Powers of the Human Mind.* I wanted to ask him about it, but I was careful not to say anything about Dennis's claim earlier that year that he was psychic. Even though the conversation we'd had felt miles away in my head, I vaguely recalled it, and I remembered him telling me to keep it a secret, but I couldn't remember exactly why.

"What's that?" I asked Tim, pointing at the book. "'Powers of the mind?' Sounds a little weird."

"What? Oh, that," he said, setting the stack of books down on his desk. "Yeah, it kind of is," he said as he picked the book up and thumbed through it for a few moments. It was a small but thick paperback with a black cover that had some strange design on it. "But there's some interesting stuff in it, I guess. Probably most of it isn't true, but my mom was reading it, so I decided to take a look through it when she was done."

"Like what?"

"Oh, you know, telepathy, seeing into the future, psychokinesis, reincarnation, all that kinda stuff." He said it with a slight sneer, and I could tell that he wasn't taking the subject matter very seriously.

"Yeah, probably just a bunch of crap, right?" I laughed, and so did he.

I talked to Dennis later in the day, and I brought up the earlier conversation with Tim, how he was reading the book and didn't seem to think much of it. I wasn't sure exactly what I was after, whether I was trying to find out more about Dennis's supposed powers or just picking on him for believing in them.

"Well I would think that after what happened with those two vampires over the summer," he said, "he'd be a little more open-minded. There was definitely some serious mind control going on during that."

"Well, yeah, but they were vampires!" I caught myself, looking around to make sure that no one on the playground might be listening to us. There had already been some backlash from Gary over our successful attempt at scaring him during the summer: When we had gotten back to school at the end of August, I had initially hoped that we would be able to laugh at Gary for getting so afraid and upset over our little prank, but instead, he turned it back on us. He claimed that he wasn't really scared, his mother had told him about Susanna's phone call explaining everything, and that we were stupid and "gay" for having a vampire club and dressing up with fake fangs and everything. That was disappointing. Fortunately, not much was said about it after the first day of school.

But as far as the psychic thing went, Dennis insisted that it was true, plus he also began telling me that he thought I had powers of my own but hadn't realized it yet. He cited several instances of us having those "I was just about to say that!" coincidences, which I couldn't really deny. What's more, I had started to notice that sometimes in class, I would think of something clever to say, usually something making fun of what the teacher or another student said, only to have someone else say it before I got a chance to. Then they would get the laughs that I felt were rightfully mine. What was weird was that several times, the person saying what I'd been thinking wasn't usually the type of person to blurt out something like that, like when the normally goody two-shoes girl Laura made a particularly scathing, sarcastic remark to Carl over something he had said.

The more Dennis and I talked about these weird coincidences, the more I wondered if he might be right. We developed a non-verbal code whenever these incidents would occur, a gesture that he started doing with his eyebrows that, had it been in a cartoon, probably would have been accompanied by a tinkling sound effect. Rather than saying to me, "I was just about to say that," he would just move his eyebrows up and down quickly, usually with a smug expression. Soon, I started doing this back to him whenever I noticed the phenomenon happening.

Things came to a head one afternoon in November. By then, I was on less friendly terms with Carl and tending to side more with Dennis, and this was also before Tim had started drifting so far from me and the others. For the moment, he was loyal to me and Dennis.

We were getting to the age where the boys in our class liked to play more sports-like games at recess like kickball, football, or soccer. In previous years, those games were limited to P.E. class, things we were assigned to play. At recess, we could do whatever we wanted, which was usually more childlike playing, pretending to be good guys and bad guys, playing on the swings, or climbing on the monkey bars. There was also a geodesic dome on the playground, a large, metal structure similar to the monkey bars but in the shape of half a sphere. When I had first seen it as a child, I remarked on how it looked kind of like a giant brain sticking up out of the ground. During the Club Wars in fifth grade, my group had claimed this dome as our base, and the kids from Carl's club weren't allowed inside.

The transition from childish games to sports did not happen all at once, and not to everyone at the same time. Some of us, myself and Dennis included, saw the sports as too structured and boring, something one would do in P.E., not in our free time. The boys who wanted to play sports at recess were either more athletically inclined or just wanted to fit in with the boys who were. Carl was one of these, and it made me feel like I had less in common with him.

This particular afternoon, Dennis led me to the top of the geodome, as it was called. As we watched, the boys on the playground below played football.

"They think they're so grown-up and cool," Dennis said. "See how Gary tries to take over the whole game?" We watched as Gary ran around the designated area of the playground they had set aside as a mock football field, throwing the ball to Steven, another aspiring athlete.

"Okay, now watch," Dennis said pointedly, though I wasn't sure what he was up to.

The action on the playground had stopped between plays, and the boys lined up for the next one. Then they began running around, and one boy threw the ball. It sailed through the air toward Gary, who reached up for it.

"Miss it," Dennis said in a low voice. He didn't shout it out for anyone else to hear. Yelling something like that at a player to distract them was nothing unusual; we had all done that before. Gary did indeed miss the pass, and the ball tumbled to the ground. Gary looked annoyed.

I laughed, and Dennis just smiled.

"Okay, come on," I said. "Don't tell me you really did that. He just missed."

"Are you absolutely sure?" he asked me, raising his eyebrows.

On the next play of the game, Dennis repeated the demonstration, this time making David miss a pass. The next time, he said nothing as the ball was passed, and Bryan caught it. His track record wasn't perfect — sometimes he would say "miss it" and the player would in fact catch the ball — but it did seem like he had some influence over the game. He appeared to be successful more often than not, to the point where it became creepy, but intriguing.

"That's pretty cool," I eventually said, genuinely impressed.

"Now you try," he said, and I suddenly felt nervous.

"But how? What do you do to make it work?"

"Just do it. Think. Picture the ball bouncing out of their hands or flying past them completely."

The next time the ball was thrown — this time to Gary again — I said, "Miss it," and although he almost managed to intercept the pass, the ball fumbled from his hands and onto the ground.

It felt like my hair was standing up. Had I really done that? It was one thing for my spooky friend Dennis to have these magical powers, but did I really have them, too? After a few more attempts at making the boys mess up — not all of which worked, but many did — I was convinced that I did indeed have the same powers, or at least similar ones that were maybe not quite as powerful or advanced.

Dennis warned me not to brag about it or tell anyone else. In fact, we had to stop with our little lesson in telekinetic interference when Tim approached us, climbing up one side of the geodome toward us.

"Hey guys, what are we doing?" he asked in a friendly tone.

I started to tell him, but Dennis cut me off. "Nothing. Just watching the dumb-asses make fools of themselves."

His intrusion on mine and Dennis's experiment irritated me, and I could tell that Dennis didn't want him there, either. Normally he liked Tim just fine, but we were busy, and he didn't want to reveal his — now *our* — secret to him. But we also didn't want to indicate that he was intruding, or else that might seem suspicious.

As Tim started to settle down into a position on the bars beside us, he suddenly slipped, his hand missing one of the bars. His shoulder connected with the bar, but he wasn't hurt. His glasses, though, fell off his head and to the ground below, which fortunately was soft sand.

"Shoot!" Tim said, then made his way back down the bars and to the ground to retrieve his glasses. They weren't damaged. "Guess I'll stay down here, then," he said, resigned.

Later on, Dennis explained to me that what happened to Tim on the geodome was not a coincidence. He said that it was a side effect of his powers, something he couldn't really control. While he could make little things happen to people — like making them miss a football pass — other times, bad things would happen to them even when he didn't try. Almost every time, he said, it was because the person had made him mad, and the power within him seemed to lash out and do something to the offender.

This was intriguing, but it worried me. If I also had these powers, did this mean that I might accidentally hurt someone if they angered me? Petty disagreements were a part of everyday life, and I wondered what might happen if somebody made me mad.

Sure enough, over the next few weeks, I noticed that when people I didn't like — which sometimes included Carl — did something that angered me, something bad would happen to them, though it was never anything life-threatening. Usually, they just got yelled at by a teacher for something or got in trouble, or they would stumble and slightly injure themselves, usually within half an hour or so of the original offense. The same thing happened to anyone who crossed Dennis. While this was sometimes entertaining, it bothered me.

Things got even more disturbing to me when Dennis and I got into an argument one day at lunch, and as the class was making its way up the concrete staircase back to our classroom afterwards, I looked back at Dennis and saw him trip on the stairs, hurting his leg. He recovered and continued up the stairs, but I was immediately convinced that this had happened because I was angry at him.

We talked about it later after school, and we agreed to try to find a way to curb our powers, to keep them from getting out of hand in case we got to the point where we might hurt each other with them. By this point, it was kind of like we were making this up as we went along, defining things based on what we could come up with and imagine. But because these were psychic powers, that seemed to make sense. They were based in the mind, so if we could reimagine them, we could redefine them.

We found that by picturing barriers or shields around our bodies, we could cut back on the influence our powers seemed to have on other people. It worked: When we would do this, we were less likely to pick up on others' thoughts or experience the usual weird coincidences that had become so eerily common in our lives. When we took the barriers down, the weirdness picked up again.

How much of this was actually true and how much was just wishful thinking and the power of suggestion is hard to nail down when I look back on it. Dennis and I had both been into science fiction and the supernatural all our lives. As far back as the age of eight, I had learned that extraordinary things were possible, given my experiences with the vampire potion. It wasn't too much of a stretch for me to believe — given enough evidence, anyway — in other fantastic things like psychic powers.

Once I had accepted this, it felt like a new layer of secrecy, which I liked. I had already gotten used to the vampire secret, especially given our second round of using the potion in 1985. That was something I shared with a handful of people, and I trusted them. But this new secret, the telepathic powers that Dennis and I apparently had, was also fun because it was something that only he and I knew about. I accepted that his powers were probably stronger than mine, but I didn't mind. Within my own sphere of existence, I had two private worlds, the vampiric and the psychic. I had no idea how profoundly those two worlds would eventually collide.

As far as how the general public reacted to our activities in the summer of 1985, it wasn't all that different from how things went after our previous stint as vampires. There was some unrest and mild panic, but when it all came down to it, no one really knew what had happened. People disappeared and were never heard from again, and there were some sightings of bats and possibly vampires, but nothing could ever be proven. The authorities never offered a satisfactory explanation, and no one was ever able to mount a specific enough complaint or properly investigate the mystery. Once again, we had gotten away with murder, and we didn't see this as anything to be truly remorseful about. We were just glad to have escaped any blame.

Our parents also had no idea what had gone on during their absence, which was typical. My father didn't even notice that the basement had been rearranged until I mentioned it to him; I did so because I had been wondering for a while how he would react and how convincingly I might be able to pitch my lie to him that Susanna and the rest of us had worked on it as a special project. He looked around the area and seemed to approve, but for the most part, he barely seemed to care.

I didn't hear from Susanna as much after that summer, not as much as I was used to, anyway. When she had first gone away to college, we occasionally wrote letters to each other and talked on the phone, but this became less frequent as time went on. I assumed that this was because she was getting more caught up in college life, whatever that entailed. From time to time, she mentioned dating some guy or another, but by the next time I talked to her, things hadn't worked out for some reason, and she was either single again or dating someone else.

In the summer of 1986, she visited while our parents were away at their conference, which was in New York that year. But she didn't even stay at our house the entire time, nor did she come home for her birthday later in July as she had usually done. The way our parents had established things, there needed to be at least one person at the house while they were gone who was old enough to drive, and by this point, that included Carolyn, so there was no real reason for Susanna to be there during their absence.

Seventh grade began later that year, and what was interesting about that was the way everyone began to act toward each other by the end of the school year. Early on, things were more or less the same, everyone having their usual conflicts and exchanges, kids getting along or not, classes and teachers that we liked or disliked, and so on. Our school only went up to the seventh grade; after that, all of the kids graduated and went on to different schools around the city. While we were growing up, we were aware of this, but it wasn't until this final year of being together that we began to understand the implications.

We realized that even though some of us might end up at the same school as a few of our friends, for the most part, we were all being split up and might not see some of the people we had grown up with again. This was sad, but at the same time, it could also be a relief, the idea that certain people we didn't like might be gone from our lives altogether. But overall, there was a feeling of some sort of pre-enforced nostalgia, and it made everyone be a lot nicer to each other, even kids who had been at each other's throats for years.

But that didn't happen all at once. The first half of the school year was actually rather unpleasant for me in a few ways. For one thing, the concept of popularity began to come into play, something that none of us had ever thought much about. It was a word we heard older kids use, and as we got older ourselves, popularity — or a lack thereof — became more important.

When we were younger, how cool a person was considered was more simple. But starting around the end of sixth grade, things took on a more grown-up aspect. The athletic boys and the pretty girls, as well as those from the wealthier families — and often those groups closely overlapped, I noticed — began to have more power. Those of us who seemed more plain or ordinary got less attention and were looked down upon, both by classmates and by some of the teachers. Across the board, we were becoming more strong-willed and trying to establish our identities, and one of the ways in which I did this was to lash out with even more sarcasm and bitterness than I had previously.

My teachers had always disliked this trait of mine, but it eventually became apparent to me that quite a lot of the other children were getting sick of it, too. I didn't care, but after a while, I began to feel more isolated as fewer kids wanted to be around me or hear my quips in class. Dennis and I were both like this, and when things occasionally got to where he and I weren't getting along, we would be almost as nasty to each other as we were when we'd first met. Things fluctuated similarly with Carl for a while, too.

I began to have a problem with Tim as well, and I wasn't the only one. He had always been smart, but it wasn't until seventh grade that many people branded him a nerd and a teacher's pet. He wasn't particularly smug about his intelligence and didn't flaunt it all that much, but the teachers would often point out to the rest of us how good of a student he was and how we should try to be more like him and do better in our schoolwork. He wasn't the only kid in class like this, either; some of the girls were like that, too, and they were similarly loathed. Halfway through the year, Tim switched from wearing glasses to having contacts, probably hoping to shed his nerd image. It didn't work; he just went from being an annoyingly good student with glasses to a just as annoyingly good student who looked like he was squinting all the time.

Throughout all of this, I became friends with a new kid in school named Nick, who sat in the back of History class with me. New kids always had trouble fitting in at our school, but this was a particularly bad year for someone to be coming in right at the tail end of things. Most people didn't want to bother to get to know him. I didn't either, but as I began to find myself less popular with everyone else, I gravitated toward this misfit, deciding that I liked him. He was also very bitter and sarcastic, and we found common ground in ridiculing the other people around us, students and teachers alike.

Aside from just being new, Nick failed to fit in with most of the other kids mainly because he didn't want to. He was a punk, or at least, as punk as a 13-year-old boy could be in a town like Augusta. He wore strange, wild-looking clothes, and his black hair was so long that he was told by our homeroom teacher more than once that he needed to get it cut. His notebooks and book covers were scrawled with all sorts of weird drawings as well as anarchic symbols and sayings. I was intrigued by his stories of hanging out skateboarding with other delinquent kids, though he never invited me to join him in this. And while I didn't like most of the weird music he listened to, he did introduce me to a funny group called Beastie Boys, whom I liked for their harsh lyrics and antisocial attitudes. Their music videos were pretty funny, too. There was both anger and fun in their music, something I needed as my life took a lonelier turn.

For a while, Nick and I had our own little thing going, separate from just about everyone else, jeering at them from afar. He used the word "posers" to describe people whom he thought were fake and insincere, which was how I saw most of my peers. I was also bitter about the fact that any of the girls I became interested in didn't return my affection and always went for the jocks instead. That had begun near the end of sixth grade, and seventh grade didn't hold any better prospects so far. Nick told me not to worry about it, that I didn't need "any of these fake bitches." That didn't make me feel much better, but insulting people did provide a small amount of comfort, or at least a sense of power.

We also committed minor acts of vandalism, but nothing all that serious. One of the things he liked to do, which I started joining him in, was to take huge wads of toilet paper and soak them in the sink, hurl them at the bathroom walls or stalls, then leave them there. Often, we would find them still stuck in place days after the fact. Writing rude things on the walls in ballpoint pen was another favorite activity. A few times, he came over to my house, and one day, we explored some nearby woods together, stumbling across a small construction site that was adjacent to a park. He surprised me by whipping out a lighter, which he used to set small bits of trash on fire. He was the first kid I'd ever met who had a lighter, but he didn't smoke as far as I knew. He just liked lighting things on fire and seeing how different things burned in various ways, such as how paper burned cleanly while styrofoam cups melted and gave off a lot of thick smoke. The two of us weren't especially destructive; overall, these activities felt creative and fun, something else to get away with and avoid getting caught doing.

Undercutting all of this was the ongoing feeling of secrecy, which in previous years had been a source of strength. But when I began to feel so isolated, there was this sense of betrayal as well, like all that my friends and I had gone through before didn't really matter. There was the vampire secret with that small group, the psychic stuff with Dennis, and now this juvenile delinquent behavior with Nick, and while at times it was fun, it also reinforced this notion that no one truly understood me or knew what I was about.

But things began to look up after the Christmas holidays. It quickly sunk in that those of us who had known each other for years would soon be separated, and soon enough, everyone began to get along better. Everything wasn't all happiness and sunshine, but a lot of the old rivalries and snotty attitudes melted away as the last few months of the school year went along. Nick didn't really care about most of this, and as I reconnected with my older friends, he and I drifted apart somewhat, though never completely. He also became a little more integrated with some of us, particularly Dennis, who had recently developed quite a reputation as a class clown.

In fact, many of us who had previously cut up in class individually and had tended to pick on each other started to band together, turning our efforts to collectively annoying some of our teachers. One trick we would do was for someone to start humming when the class was quiet, like when we were supposed to be reading. Dennis was usually the one to start this: He would hum a single, steady note, but he would give no indication that he was the one doing it. To all appearances, he was, like everyone else, quietly reading his book. I would join in, followed by several other boys, and sometimes even a girl or two. Eventually the collective humming — which had minor fluctuations as some of us tried not to laugh or otherwise give ourselves away — would get loud enough that the teacher would get angry and tell us to stop.

A similar prank, which began in the spring as some of the students' allergies started kicking in, was for one kid to sniff loudly, then another, then another. Usually it started innocently, but then it would escalate into several of us doing it to be obnoxious. One time, this led to Dennis doing such an exaggerated snort that the rest of us cracked up, but our English teacher, Mrs. Warren, was not amused. She was one of our meanest teachers, prone to go off on huge tirades about how bad all of us were and how we needed to clean up our acts. She was known throughout the school as being horribly mean, and while some of the students liked her and claimed she was just trying to straighten us out for our own good, those of us who were less than model children just thought she was a hateful old woman.

When Dennis's epic nasal performance caused half the class to fall out laughing, Mrs. Warren decided to make an example of him. She called out, "Dennis Williams!" She always said the full names of any child in the class whom she didn't like. "You come up here to the front of the class right now!"

Dennis did so eagerly, smiling and still riding the high of making so many people laugh.

"Okay, now!" Mrs. Warren said in her excessive southern drawl. It wasn't a dumb sounding accent like I'd heard people from the country use, but there was still something grating about the way she spoke. She had a weird way of drawing out some of her words, which seemed to get longer the more angry she was. For example, the word "now" in this case somehow managed to have two syllables. "I want you all to take a good look at Dennis Williams here. Does everyone see him?" The class indicated that they did, some silently nodding, others verbally, but still smiling. "Now I want all of you to laugh at him, because apparently he isn't getting enough attention. Go on! Laugh!" There were a few small snickers, but most of us were just confused. "I said laugh!" she shouted, causing some of the kids in the front of the class to jump. Dennis also flinched. "Point at Mr. Funny Man and laugh! Anyone I see who isn't laughing is going to the office and getting a note sent home!"

And so we all laughed, pretending at first, but it didn't take long for the laughter to become genuine. There was something infectious about it, plus embarrassing a classmate was something we still took pleasure in. Dennis quickly went from wearing a defiant grin to looking genuinely uncomfortable, and after a solid minute of this, he looked pained. After Mrs. Warren had quieted the class down, she then barked, "Now I think that's all the laughs you need for the rest of the school year, Dennis Williams. You don't have to do anything else funny for the rest of us to see you. Now you apologize to the class for wasting everyone's time."

Normally, I would have said something under my breath about how it was in fact the teacher who had taken up class time with her elaborate punishment, but I was too busy noticing how Dennis, apparently hurt by all of this, just drooped his shoulders and sheepishly said, "Sorry." It sounded more like "thorry," which was unusual these days because he had somehow gotten over his characteristic lisp sometime between sixth and seventh grade. As he slunk back to his desk, I felt sorry for him, plus angry at Mrs. Warren for making such a big deal out of everything. If it had been Tim who made that loud snorting sound, I thought, she would have just chuckled and told him that he was a rascal and should stop.

We talked about the incident at recess, but by then, Dennis had recovered and was just angry, not wounded. Carl, who was in 7-A that year and not in the same class with me and Tim, had missed everything, so we caught him up. Although he laughed upon hearing that Dennis had gotten into trouble, he agreed that the teacher had gone overboard, especially over something so stupid.

"She sure is a bitch, isn't she?" Tim said. It was the first time I had heard him use the word. But lately, he had toughened up a bit, partly to try to get rid of his reputation as a goody-goody.

"Damn right she is," Dennis said.

"So what should we do to get back at her?" Nick asked.

"Sneak up behind her and go 'BOO!' and give her a heart attack," I joked.

"No, that's not cool," Antonio said. "Though I heard that she's really allergic to pollen. One of us could sneak into the room when she's not there and shake a pine tree branch over her desk!"

We all laughed at the idea, but Laura, who mainly hung out with this group because she was Bryan's girlfriend, spoke up and said that it was a terrible idea. "My mom has really bad allergies," she said. "She gets all swelled up and stuff. It's not funny." Bryan just nodded, having nothing else to add. Even though both he and Laura had gotten to the point where they seemed cool enough to hang out with us, I still didn't entirely trust her. For all I knew, if we tried anything, she might tell on us.

"We could set off a firecracker in her desk," Nick offered, and he seemed like he was sincerely trying to be helpful.

"No, no, it's not worth it," Dennis said. "She's just a dumb old biddy. Probably be dead next week, anyway."

We laughed, but Nick didn't. "Posers," he said, then walked off.

"What the hell does that mean?" Carl asked.

"Just… It's just one of his words," I said.

"I never liked that guy," Carl said.

"Yeah, me neither," Dennis said. "But he's okay sometimes, I guess."

This was typical of how we interacted these days: Normally, Dennis liked Nick just fine, but when someone said something bad about another person, the best way to get along with that person was to agree with them, to talk like you also didn't like someone they disliked. Slowly but surely, we were learning more about social interaction, becoming teenagers.

Later, when Dennis and I were alone, he said to me, "Man, you have no idea how hard it is trying to hold my powers back so they don't lash out and kill that stupid old bat."

"Yeah, I know what you mean," I said.

"When you said that thing about her having a heart attack, I got a little scared," he said.

"Oh, I didn't really mean it." I thought for a moment. "Besides, you're the one who said she'd be dead in a week."

"Stop it," he said firmly. "I was just talking shit for the others." I nodded. "So, barriers up?"

"Of course," I said, picturing a semi-transparent cube around my body. I imagined one around Dennis as well. We visualized them as being reflective, bouncing our powers back to us and not letting them break out. It seemed to work.

As far as the rest of all that went, we continued to develop our abilities in private. One day at his house, he did a test with these white cards that had symbols on them, each of us trying to guess which one the other was holding, or either of us trying to guess a card before it was turned over. We were both pretty good at it, and in time, I started getting more accurate results than he did. There were also times when we could intentionally mess the other person up, trying to project the wrong image into the other's head or just broadcast some kind of interference so they couldn't concentrate. Occasionally, I had successfully used this same technique on people in class when I wanted them to get a particular answer wrong. I made up a term for it, "brainstorming," not knowing that I was misusing an already existing word.

All of this experimentation went on as long as Dennis and I were friends, but when there were rifts between us, we stopped. The first big disagreement we had, by the way, centered around him being jealous that my powers seemed to have gotten stronger than his. I couldn't see why he was so upset about that; I'd expected him to be happy for me and impressed, given that he was the one who got me started on the whole thing in the first place.

Not long after the incident with Mrs. Warren and the conversation on the playground, the idea of the vampire reunion came back to me, and I mulled over the possibilities in my head. It occurred to me that it might be fun to include Nick in the group this time, but I still had the notion that I wanted to reunite everyone from the previous two summers when we had taken the potion. I wanted a chance for all of us to get along well this time, which seemed more possible given the camaraderie that sprang up among everyone as the school year wound down. Bringing Nick into it didn't really fit the idea of a reunion, I decided, so I didn't tell him about any of this and just left him out.

As for the rest of the guys, everyone seemed up for it. I had worried briefly that they might not be, and while Carl tried to be nonchalant about it in order to seem cool, I could tell as the weeks went on that he was looking forward to it. Dennis tried a similar tactic, but it was just as transparent. Tim, meanwhile, made no attempt to hide his eagerness to get the old crew together for one more fun summer of sneaking around and being bad.

Carolyn was another factor to consider, especially since she had yet another boyfriend who might interfere with my plans. This one, a guy named Damon, was the first boy she dated that I actually liked. But as it turned out, even though things were apparently going well between them, he wasn't going to be around during the part of the summer when we'd be able to take the potion.

"Oh, no, it's fine," Carolyn said when I talked to her about it. "His band will be going on tour." She said this with a smile, almost a glow, not so much because she was happy about being free to take part in the reunion, but because she was in love.

I could clearly recall the first night she came home after meeting Damon a couple of months earlier, giddy with excitement over this new boy in her life who seemed interested in her. He was apparently the hottest thing she had ever seen, and she had noticed him a few times at a club she and her friends liked to go to, a bar that let 18-year-olds in but didn't allow anyone under 21 to drink. She occasionally talked about this place to me, but not often, usually curtailing any stories she began with the "but you're too young" caveat. But the night she met Damon, she was so excited that she dropped all of that age-related snobbery and told me about how they started talking, how he looked like one of the members of Duran Duran, and how happy she was.

I tried to talk to her then about some of my crushes, the girls I had come to like at school that I wished would like me in return, but she quickly dismissed this. "Oh, it's really kinda stupid for people your age to try to date. I mean, you can't even go anywhere... Like, you have to have your parents take you somewhere... Whatever. Oh! And did I mention how cool his hair is? It's all styled up, I mean, not girly or anything, but really well done, sort of dark brown but with a little bit of blonde highlights..." She went on and on about this new guy, which annoyed me a great deal, first because she played the "you're too young" card once again, but also because she refused to acknowledge that my own romantic pursuits were real or worthy of discussion. Crowley, whom she was stroking in her lap as she rattled on, looked rather perturbed as well, squinting his eyes and flattening his ears whenever her voice got too loud.

But as it turned out, Damon was a really nice guy, and I liked him a lot. He was cool, funny, and not the least bit condescending to me. My parents had been suspicious of him because he was a little bit older than Carolyn, though not as old as Susanna. In time, he won them over, or at least my mother, and it wasn't long before he was coming over for dinner and getting along with everyone.

Aside from the reasons everybody else liked him, I thought it was pretty cool that he played guitar and sang in a band, just like the guys I would see on MTV. It would have been nice to have seen him play one of his shows, but I wasn't nearly old enough to go to any of the bars in town. So I had to rely on Carolyn's descriptions of what all of that was like. She admitted that she got jealous when other girls in the bar would go on about how cute and cool Damon and the other guys in the band were, but then she could feel pride in knowing that Damon was hers.

What probably made him seem the coolest in my mind was when he gave me his old Atari 5200. He felt that he had outgrown it, plus video games had started to become less popular over the past couple of years. I was delighted, though, and I spent a great deal of time playing it during the first few weeks of summer, leading all the way up to the vampire reunion.

An even better development was that this summer, our parents were going to be on vacation in San Francisco for a full three weeks. Aside from their usual routine of being out of town for a week for the annual conference, they had also made plans to stay with my father's aunt, who lived out there. Initially, it had been suggested that Susanna, Carolyn, and I join them for this trip, but the three of us had already settled on the idea of taking the potion, though of course we couldn't tell them that.

Instead, we each made up excuses for things we had to do during that time. Susanna claimed that she had things going on in Charleston that she couldn't get out of, and Carolyn had things to do with her friends, many of whom were leaving town for college. She had decided to stay in Augusta and go to a local college in the fall, but she was still going to move out, and she planned to take Crowley with her. I said as tactfully as possible that I didn't really like the idea of going on a long vacation with my parents without my sisters also coming along, plus I wanted to hang out with my friends before they all went off to their own schools around town later that year. Our parents accepted all of this, saying that we should do what we felt was right for us.

Susanna, meanwhile, didn't need any convincing from me when it came to the idea of getting together to become vampires. In fact, she was eager to do it, telling me that she had developed a new version of the potion that was a lot better, but she wouldn't give me many details and told me to be patient. That just made me more anxious for the final week of June to arrive.

I barely even cared about my graduation from St. Joseph's Episcopal School earlier in the month, which our parents, teachers, and classmates had made such a big deal over. Everyone talked about how this was the beginning of a new journey, that we should avoid feeling sad about missing our old friends and be excited about the new adventures ahead of us. They weren't entirely wrong, but then, they didn't know what our small group of murderous delinquents had in mind. The summer of 1987 was going to be the biggest adventure yet, and we were all looking forward to it.

"So, where do we put our stuff?" Tim asked.

"Oh, you're going to love this," Carolyn said, smiling broadly. "This way." She and I led him, Carl, and Dennis around the front of the house to the basement, which we'd spent quite a bit of time in since almost the second our parents had left the day before.

As we made our way down the stairs, Carl asked, "You mean we're staying down here the entire… Whoa!" He said this as Carolyn pulled the cord on the light, which instead of turning on just one bulb illuminated several that were festooned around the ceiling.

She, Susanna, and I had decided that instead of using garbage bags to block out the windows of the house this time, we would just sleep in the basement, which would be easier and less conspicuous. But rather than doing that on the hard floor in sleeping bags and waking up stiff and sore each night, we would make the place more comfortable and livable.

Most of this was done in secret, and what little our parents had seen of Carolyn and me gathering various items for this was under the pretense that we were preparing for Carolyn's upcoming move into her own apartment, temporarily storing things in the basement. In fact, we had rounded up a few extra mattresses, some rugs, fans, extension cords, and drop cord lights, which we then used to transform the basement into our own underground apartment. Some of these were things that we bought in thrift stores or at yard sales, and some we had been lucky enough to find near dumpsters or at the landfill. Once our parents left town, we started setting everything up.

"This is cool as hell!" Carl said.

"Yeah!" Dennis said. "It's like our own secret headquarters!"

"Oh, don't be such a dork-head," Carl said.

"Whatever, Chicken Legs." Recently, Dennis had learned from his sister Joanna, who occasionally hung out with Carl's sister Karen, that one of Carl's nicknames from when we was younger was "Chicken Legs." Apparently, this came about when Carl would run around practicing track, and Karen loved to taunt him with the name.

"Shut it," Carl said.

"Don't you two start again," Tim said. "We've got two weeks to get through, and I don't want to spend it listening to you two going at each other the whole time." While my parents were planning to be away for three weeks, it wasn't realistic to be able to get my friends to stay with us that entire time, so we had settled on two weeks of being vampires instead. It was still longer than we had ever gone before.

"All right, all right," Carolyn said. "Calm down. Come on, isn't this cool?" She gestured eagerly with her arm. "The Christmas lights were my idea. Ray didn't like them because he said it was stupid. 'It's not Christmas!'" she said in a mocking tone.

"Well it's not," I grumbled.

"No, it's fine!" Tim said. "I think it looks kinda neat."

"Yeah, kind of hippie-ish," Dennis added. He had become interested in 1960s pop culture and music over the past year. It wasn't something we had in common, though I had enjoyed the semi-recent reruns of *The Monkees* on TV and therefore had some exposure to the era. I actually did like their early, more pop-oriented music, but their later, more drug culture related stuff didn't appeal to me. Carolyn felt the same way about The Beatles and the way their style had changed over the years, and the next several days would include occasional debates between her and Dennis as to which group was superior. Carolyn felt that there was no contest and that the Beatles were better, but for some reason, Dennis kept wanting to argue with her about it.

As the boys picked out their mattresses and set their stuff down, Carl asked, "So, are we just going to hang out down here the whole time?"

"Well, no," I said. "I mean, there's the entire house upstairs. We'll do our usual stuff in there during the night, then sleep down here once the sun comes up."

"And…" Tim began, then squinted thoughtfully, trying to find the right words. "All of this was easier than just blacking out the windows?"

Carolyn laughed. "Not really, no. But once we got the idea, we kinda just went with it. It seemed like a fun thing to do."

It had been, and it was the first major project Carolyn and I had worked on together in years. I found that, while she had retained most of the femininity she had developed throughout high school, she had in some ways gone back to her more earthy self, the more practical girl I had grown up with and liked. Whether or not that was because of Damon, I wasn't sure, but the change had occurred in her not long after they had gotten together.

Back upstairs in the house, we tried to decide what to do next. Susanna was, as usual, up in her old room mixing together the potion, leaving the rest of us to kill time until she was done. Because of my idea of this being a reunion, I had it in my head that we should do many of the same things we had done before, like playing games to pass the time.

"Oh, like Ghost in the Backyard or whatever it is?" Carl said, jeering. "Seems a little, I don't know, dumb."

"Ghost in the Graveyard," I corrected him. "We don't necessarily have to play that. We played Freeze Tag last time."

"Yeah, but I don't really feel like that, either," Dennis said.

"I do have a Lazer Tag set," Tim said. "Well, at home I mean. Maybe I could get one of my parents to drop it off."

"No, let's not bother with that," Carolyn said. "Let's just see what's on TV."

There wasn't much on that was very interesting. After a while, Carolyn and I ended up showing the rest of the group some of our videotapes, things we had recorded off the TV and saved. She had some clips from *Late Night with David Letterman* and *Saturday Night Live* that she wanted to share with us, and I had a collection of episodes of *An Evening at the Improv* and other shows that had stand-up comics in them. Crowley hung out with us, getting along well with all of my friends and not spontaneously scratching any of them this time.

All of this helped pass the time, but for the majority of it, I was distracted, thinking a lot about taking the potion again. I was also curious as to what might be different about this one. Susanna wasn't very forthcoming about it so far, but she did say something about it providing "a more authentic vampire experience," whatever that might mean.

She surprised us by coming downstairs much earlier than expected, saying eagerly, "Okay! Potion time!" She was carrying a glass baking pan full of something dark.

"Is that... That's the potion?" Carolyn asked, stroking Crowley in her lap. He had been asleep, but he'd woken up suddenly when Susanna had come into the room.

"Yes," Susanna said with a proud grin. "I told you it would be different."

"But it's still light outside!" I said, standing up and following her into the kitchen. "We can't take it yet, or else the sun will get us!"

"Not this time," she said, setting the pan down onto the kitchen counter. "This potion is more slow-acting than the old one. Kind of a time-release thing. We'll take it now, and it will be a few hours before it fully takes effect."

"That's cool, I guess," Carl said as he and the others joined us. "Why, though?"

"Well, many reasons," Susanna said. "This is a new formula, so it's going to affect us differently. But it should be better." As she spoke, her back was to us, and she took several small plates out of the cabinet and set them beside the pan.

I moved up beside her and peered at it. Surprisingly, the potion wasn't liquid, but rather a black, spongy looking substance. Susanna began cutting it into squares and carefully distributing these among the plates.

"So, like, we're having vampire brownies this time?" Carl joked.

"No," Susanna said, sounding irritated. Then she brightened slightly. "Though I guess they are a bit like… Well, never mind." She continued her work. I could tell from the way she was cutting that the potion wasn't soft like brownies, but rather kind of rough and strong. It reminded me of charcoal, both in its consistency and the way it seemed to glisten in places, despite its otherwise dark color. Because the area she was working in was small, she moved the plates to the kitchen table two at a time, returning to the pan to continue dividing the potion up.

Carolyn, who had a dubious expression, arranged the plates around the table so that we could each have our portion. "So," she began, but then she stumbled. "Damn it, Crowley, knock it off." He had been weaving in and out of everyone's feet excitedly, apparently thinking that it was dinner time. He mewed up at Carolyn eagerly, curling his long white tail and hopping up at her leg. "You're not getting fed yet, young man!" she said firmly. This prompted another quick *"mrrrawr"* from him that sounded similarly perturbed.

"Come on," I said, bending down and pulling Crowley away from her feet. "Back into the den." I had gotten quite used to him over the years, and I liked him. In fact, since Carolyn had started dating

Damon and hadn't been home as much, I had found myself spending more time with Crowley and taking care of him. Even though he was technically Carolyn's cat, he felt more like mine recently, and I knew that I was going to miss him once she moved out and took him with her.

After I plopped Crowley down into the wicker chair, I headed back to the kitchen, where I saw Susanna looking at the baking pan with a strange expression. "Crap," she said, cocking her head to the side. She poked at the pan with the knife, looked at the plates on the counter, then turned toward the kitchen table. "One, two, three, four…" she counted softly, gesturing with the knife, then turning it back to the pan. "I could have sworn I did the proportions right."

"What?" I asked.

"I made too much of the potion," she said, looking disappointed. "There's enough for the six of us, but there's still some left over."

"Well, then just throw it out!" Dennis said.

"I don't think that's a good idea," Susanna said. "I can't just dump this stuff in the trash. The potion works on animals, too, not just people." She faced me. "Remember the tests I told you about with the mice."

"Right," I said, but I wasn't sure what else to offer.

"Oh," Tim said, "so if you just throw it away, then maybe some rats might eat it out of the trash, and then we'd get overrun with a bunch of vampire rats!" He laughed.

"That would suck," Carl said, smiling. "I mean, how do you deal with vampire rats? Well, I guess you could always stab them through the heart with a little toothpick."

I found this mental image funny, and I couldn't help but laugh. "Or you'd have to get them with a vampire cat!" I joked. Crowley, who had made his way back into the kitchen, meowed up at me. I bent down to him, then said comically, "Oh, Crowley! Would you like to be a vampire cat?" He blinked at me, then mewed.

"That would be kind of cool," Tim said.

"Yeah!" Dennis said. "He could come with us, flying around like a little bat and killing people too!"

"Guys…" Susanna began, sounding impatient, but then she softened. "I mean, that actually probably would work…" She turned to Carolyn, a curious smirk on her face. "What do you think?"

Carolyn wasn't sure. I half expected her to object strongly, but she also seemed to be considering the idea. "I… I don't know."

"Come on," Dennis said. "Let's do it. The vampires and their kitty sidekick. It'll be fun."

Carolyn shook her head, but she was smiling. "I… I guess so. You're sure it will be safe?"

"Sure," Susanna said, also smiling. This was an unexpected addition to our plan, but it sounded like a neat idea. I wondered if for some reason Crowley might be more difficult to keep under control as a vampire, but since I'd known him, he had always been remarkably calm, almost human in the way he carried himself and seemed to understand things. The idea of him being a part of our group of vampires, either as a sidekick or a mascot, was both funny and appealing. "Like I said," Susanna continued, "the potion works on other mammals, too. Not just humans. He should be fine."

"Well, okay, if you're certain," Carolyn said cautiously, bending down and rubbing Crowley's head. He rubbed her hand back, then shook his head vigorously, blinking and pretending he hadn't liked the attention.

"Can we just take the potion already?" I asked. But then something occurred to me. "Wait. So you said we'll take it now, and then it will kick in later on? How much later?"

"About four hours," Susanna said. "It's now five o'clock, so once the potion has fully taken effect, the sun will be down. Don't worry."

"But why?" Tim asked. "I mean, why is it so different this time? Last time, we just took the potion, and then, boom, that was it."

"Exactly," Susanna said. "And I don't know about you, but I always hated the way that happened. It was too sudden, too rushed."

"Oh," I said. "Yeah, I get it. That whole thing was pretty scary to go through. So this one won't do that?"

"Nope," she said with a grin.

"That's great!" I said. "So, let's get on with it!"

"Okay," she said, still smiling. She went back to the pan on the counter, scraped out the remaining solid potion for Crowley, and put it on a plate for him, which she set down onto the floor. She snapped her fingers, then said, "Come on!" to him. He bounded over, sniffed at the black substance, then began pawing at it. "No, hang on," Susanna said, pushing him away. She crushed the potion into pieces with her knife, holding Crowley at bay as she did so, then let him eat the smaller bits.

"Quickly," Tim said, picking up his black square from his plate on the table. "Remember, we all have to take it at the same time." He put the piece into his mouth and began chewing. It crunched quietly as he began to eat it.

The rest of us did the same, eagerly and almost like we were trying to race each other to get our portions down. The potion had a weird consistency, somehow both soft and also firm, hard to chew but then seeming to dissolve more quickly than regular food. After a few seconds, I was able to swallow it, and as it went down, I half expected the same scary transformation from the older potion to occur. But there was nothing.

"Everyone done?" Susanna asked. I looked down at Crowley, who was finishing up the last bits from his plate.

"Looks like it," I said. "So now what?"

Susanna sighed. "Okay, well," she said. "We should talk about the other differences in the potion."

"Like what?" Carl asked, his voice slightly raised for some reason.

"Well," Susanna said with a slightly apologetic tone, "we're not going to change into vampires immediately, but there will be some side effects."

"What?" I asked, almost shouting, surprised by how loud I had gotten. "What do you mean 'side effects?'"

"Yeah!" Dennis said angrily. "Is there something you're not telling us?"

"Oh, shut up, dork-head!" Carl said. "Be quiet and let her talk!"

I felt intensely angry at Carl all of a sudden, and I began to worry that he and Dennis were going to ruin everything this year by bickering the entire time and not getting along like I had hoped they would. "You shut up!" I shouted at him.

"You little shit…" He suddenly lunged at me, his hands reaching for my throat. I toppled over backwards as he took me down, fighting back as best as I could, vaguely aware of Dennis off to one side pulling violently at Carl to get him off of me. Everything was a blur, and I could hear lots of shouting, both male and female voices, as I was tossed about, flailing and swinging to defend myself as best as I could. One of the kitchen chairs fell into my field of vision as it clattered to the floor, and I involuntarily swung at it with a fist, sending it careering off in some direction away from me and into someone else.

My head was full of nothing but rage, and all I wanted to do was lash out at the next person or inanimate object I saw. I was vaguely aware of the other people in the room, all of them also shouting and hitting each other, and I had somehow ended up under the kitchen table. A couple of the chairs were still in their proper places, and I immediately wanted to punch at them and topple them over. But as I reached out and began to swing at one of them, I suddenly lost the strength to.

I crumpled to the floor, out of breath and feeling very weak. I was breathing heavily, and I wanted to get up, but I just couldn't manage to. Looking around, I saw that everyone else was similarly prone, struggling to move.

After about a minute, the fatigue passed, and I was able to get up on my hands and knees. I made my way out from under the table, and everyone seemed to be recovering as well. After a few more moments, we were all sitting on the kitchen floor, looking around at each other and wondering what was going on. I noticed that Crowley was over in one corner of the room, licking his paws and cleaning himself, though he was doing it more slowly than usual and occasionally stopping to look at the rest of us cautiously. Carolyn, meanwhile, was clutching her arm in pain, gripping it tightly where some red scratch marks had appeared.

"Susanna," she said, "what the *hell.*" She glowered at her angrily. "Side effects? Really?"

"Sorry!" Susanna said, seeming more vulnerable than usual. "I should have warned you all sooner. It's something to do with the potion." She was gasping and trying to sit up. Next to her, one of the kitchen chairs lay smashed almost in half. She turned and looked at it, saying, "Shit. Someone's going to have to fix that."

"I can probably manage that," Carolyn said angrily. "But not right now. Will you go on and tell us what the hell just happened?"

Apologetically, Susanna explained that the new potion she had developed, while it managed to bypass the extremely rapid and frightening transformation into vampires the previous one had put us through, spread things out over a longer period of time. Instead of zapping us into vampires all at once, as she put it, we would experience a more gradual change that was mostly painless but would still be punctuated by occasional mood swings and outbursts. These episodes would be followed by brief periods of exhaustion, but once everything was over and done with, we would be vampires, fully and completely. She finished up this explanation with a triumphant folding of her arms, as if she expected us to applaud.

"Couldn't you have warned us about all this ahead of time?" Carolyn asked. "Would have been nice."

"I know, I know," Susanna said. "I was going to. I didn't think that first burst of activity would happen so quickly."

"Well, as long as you know what you're doing," Carl said, looking around the kitchen. Some of the plates had been knocked to the floor and were broken. We set about cleaning things up.

Despite the still bleeding wound in her arm, Carolyn asked Crowley if he was okay, which he seemed to be. Presumably, the potion had affected him the same way as the rest of us, and he must have attacked Carolyn.

"You should take care of that," Susanna said, pointing at Carolyn's arm.

Carolyn reached for the sink, but then she hesitated. "Wait, can we still touch running water? Or will that mess things up…"

"No, it's fine," Susanna said. "We won't be vulnerable to those things until the potion has finished working."

The next time the potion affected us strangely was less violent, and I didn't even realize that it was happening at first. One by one, we became very thirsty, and it wasn't until we had each had four or five glasses of water, milk, orange juice, or anything else that was left in the refrigerator that we realized what was happening. Crowley also drained his water bowl three times, meowing loudly beside it each time it was empty. Once I saw that he was just as thirsty as the rest of us, I figured out that this was the next "burst of activity," as Susanna had described it.

As before, we suddenly found ourselves feeling very tired, not wanting to move at all for a few minutes.

"Blech…" Dennis said. "I'm not sure if this is better or worse than the older potion."

"I know," Tim said. "But, I guess, well, maybe…"

"You're sure about that, huh?" I joked. Feeling better, I tried to get up from my chair, but then I fell forward onto the carpet. I wasn't hurt, but it was kind of embarrassing. This recovery was taking longer than the previous one had.

Once we were feeling normal again, Carolyn asked, "So what other wonderful things do we have to look forward to, Susanna?"

"It won't be so bad," she assured everyone. "There will be a few more… episodes, and the last one should be a big burst of energy. Instead of feeling worn out after that one, we'll be vampires."

"If you say so," Carolyn said.

Then I remembered something. I'd been thinking about it leading up to the reunion, and I wasn't sure exactly when we would do it, but this seemed as good of a time as any to bring it up. "Hey, why don't we go to the other house?"

"What other house?" Susanna asked.

"You know, the one where we met those other vampires. The one the tunnel leads to." Over the past two years, I had occasionally thought about trying to go into the tunnel by myself, but the idea made me nervous. I also wasn't strong enough on my own to move the shelving units that were covering up the entrance.

"Why would we do that?" Carolyn asked. "I mean, what's the point?" "I don't know," I said, shrugging. "Just something to do, I guess. And besides, what if we have another outburst and start tearing things up again? We don't want to cause more damage than we already have."

"That's true," Tim said. "It might be safer to not be here when the next one hits."

"Yeah, and how much trouble can we get into in a tunnel?" Dennis offered.

"I guess that makes sense," Susanna said. "Sure, why not. Let's give it a shot."

"Sure is dark in there," Dennis said.

"It's a tunnel," Carl said. "They get like that."

"That's what these are for," I said, holding up two flashlights, which I turned on and shone in Carl's face. He squinted and tried to shield his eyes.

"Here," Susanna said, taking one of the flashlights from me. "You going in first, or do you want me to?"

"I'll go," I said, wanting not only to appear brave but also liking the idea of leading the group. Because of all of the extra things Carolyn and I had done to make the basement more livable recently, there wasn't room to pull the shelves very far from the wall. Instead, there was only a small gap for us to squeeze through, which we did one at a time, with me taking the lead.

Being back inside that tunnel after two years felt very strange. It smelled the same, this musty, earthy fragrance, plus the walls still glistened with the mysterious substance that held everything in place. I vaguely recalled that there was something magical about it, but I didn't quite understand it. I did know that touching the walls or roof with my hand would mean that the dirt would suddenly crumble free, so I resisted the urge to reach out.

"Crowley, come on!" I heard Carolyn say from the opening to the tunnel. Everyone except her and Susanna were in the tunnel now, and apparently Crowley was reluctant to go in, too. "It's okay!" There was some commotion, but eventually, I saw Carolyn making her way into the tunnel with Crowley in her arms.

Susanna came in after her, holding her flashlight. Carolyn put Crowley down, but he immediately began hopping around, letting out little meow-like yelps.

"What's he doing?" Dennis asked.

"I don't know!" Carolyn said worriedly. "It's like the floor... Crowley! Calm down!" She managed to grab him again, and she pulled him up to her chest, then rolled him over in her arms, examining his paws. "Did you step on something?"

"I don't think he's hurt," Susanna said, pointing her flashlight's beam at the floor. "I think he was just scared. Look." She pointed with her other hand at the spot where Crowley had been jumping.

We gathered around and looked. The floor was coated with the same weird material as the rest of the tunnel, but here, there were several small patches of dirt scattered around. Quickly, I realized what had happened: When Crowley's feet had touched the ground, it had the same effect as one of us touching it, causing the coating to disappear and letting the dirt loose. Susanna bent down and touched a portion of the ground with her finger, producing the same effect.

"Weird," Dennis said. "I wonder why it does that."

"Maybe it's body heat that does it," Carl suggested.

"Maybe," Susanna said. "I wondered about that, too. But, actually…" She didn't finish her sentence, but instead looked at her flashlight curiously. She then touched her finger to the front of it, pulling away quickly with a quiet "ow." Kneeling back down, she then shoved the flashlight down onto the ground, causing everything to get darker. After a couple of seconds, she pulled it back up and examined the area. The rest of us leaned in to see the result.

There was a circular indentation where the flashlight had been, but the surface remained shiny. After a few seconds, the ground moved back into place, leaving no trace of where the mark had been.

"So it isn't heat, but only when skin touches it," Susanna said. "Fascinating."

"Thank you, Mr. Spock," Carolyn said, still holding Crowley.

Susanna straightened up. "Okay, fine."

"So are we going or what?" I asked.

We then began our journey along the tunnel, talking about various things along the way. Carolyn wondered whether or not this was a good idea, speculating that maybe those vampires we encountered before might have survived and could be waiting for us.

"I don't think so," Susanna said. "Remember, those two were dead. I mean, really, really dead." As she said this, I recalled the horrible image of their decayed bodies, then immediately regretted doing so.

Carolyn let out an expression of disgust, obviously thinking the same thing. "Yeah, I remember."

"I mean, yes, I thought about that a couple of times later on, too," Susanna said. "Like what might happen if they somehow survived.

But I would think that if they had, they would have come after us again."

"Yeah, I guess," Carolyn said.

"Well, we kicked their asses anyway," Dennis said proudly.

We walked and talked for a while, though there were occasional lulls in the conversation. During one of these, I started thinking about some girls I had known at school, ones I'd had crushes on, and how disappointing it was that they hadn't returned my affection. There were two in particular, one at the end of sixth grade named Andrea, and then in seventh grade, a friend of hers named Valerie for whom I fell very hard.

At first, it seemed like they both liked me. They would laugh at the funny things I said in class, and after a while, I found that I could entertain them by reciting some of the routines I learned from the various stand-up comics I watched on TV. I interpreted this attention as actual romantic interest on their part, which led me to feel the same way about each of them, though not simultaneously. First, I was interested in Andrea, but then I decided that I liked Valerie better. The whole time, I was scared to just come out and say how I felt, afraid that they might reject me. I had already seen this happen to some of my other friends, how a girl would refuse their affection and instead start to be very mean to them. I didn't want that to happen to me, so I just kept my feelings secret.

Or at least, I tried to, but people noticed how much attention I paid to Valerie, and at times, I would get picked on for this. We were in a weird transition period, a sort of middle ground between still disliking girls, thinking of them as gross and stupid, and the looming teenage world of boys and girls pairing off and "going together," as it was called.

Valerie also started being mean to me to discourage my feelings, which hurt me a lot. It was one of the things that made the first half of seventh grade so miserable for me, and even when everyone started getting along during the second half of the year, things never got that much better between us. Worse still, she started going with Gary, which made me hate him even more than I had before. Andrea was also particularly cruel to me at times, which led me to hate her as well. Sometimes, my psychic powers seemed to make bad things happen to these people, which I simultaneously regretted and also took some twisted sort of comfort in.

There were a few times when I tried to use those same powers to somehow force Valerie to love me, but that never worked. It was frustrating, and at times it made me doubt that I had any powers at all. But the continued development and practicing of them with Dennis left me convinced that there was something there. Bitterly, I sometimes felt that the powers were completely useless if I couldn't make the things that I wanted happen.

While in the tunnel, I thought of Valerie, how pretty she was and how badly I had wanted her to be my girlfriend. She was a little taller than me, but I didn't mind, and she had long, wavy dark brown hair that was almost black. Truth be told, she wasn't even all that pretty, but once I made up my mind that she was the one I wanted, I had my heart set on making her mine. She had a shrewd sense of humor that I liked, and it was one of the reasons we had gotten along so well before things went wrong between us. Because I had seen it happen in movies and on TV, I had this notion that someday I could win her over and she would stop fighting me, that maybe if I could just kiss her one time, her defenses would crumble and she would realize how right we were for each other. I had pictured that happening many times and wished for it so much, but it never happened. Why I was thinking about this so much at this point, I wasn't sure.

It wasn't until Dennis spoke to me that I realized that none of us had been talking for quite a while. Very close to my ear, he whispered, "Hey, look, don't say anything, but… well… I've always thought your sister was pretty hot."

I let out a laugh, then caught myself. Assuming that he was talking about Carolyn and not Susanna, I whispered back to him, "She already has a boyfriend. And even if she didn't, I really don't think you'd stand a chance with her."

"You never know!" Dennis insisted.

"Yes, I do," I said, and I started to say something else but then heard a strange sound coming from behind me. "What's that?"

I realized that it was Crowley, who was doing some sort of combination of meowing and purring, repeatedly saying something that sounded like, *"rrrrrrow? rrrrrow?"*

"Shh, it's okay, Crowley," Carolyn said gently, nuzzling her head down to him as she continued to carry him.

"What's up with him?" Dennis asked.

"Sounds like he's horny to me!" Carl said, laughing. The rest of us boys laughed, but the girls didn't.

"Oh, is that what all of…" Tim began, but then he stopped and stood in place. "I need to sit down." He practically fell to the ground, and before I had a chance to ask him what was wrong, I suddenly felt extremely tired and also needed to lie down.

Everyone else did the same, collapsing onto the floor of the tunnel. I was exhausted, and I almost felt like curling up and going to sleep. But that didn't seem like a very good idea. Still, as we all lay there in silence, I figured out that the strong emotions that had been running through my head were the latest effects of the potion, and we were experiencing the exhausting aftereffects. It was probably about fifteen minutes before we were ready to start moving again, and as we stood up and brushed ourselves off, I noticed where some of the floor had crumbled where we had been touching it with our hands.

As we got nearer to the end of the tunnel, we began to wonder what we might find. Presumably, the house was still there, but we didn't know if it would be abandoned or if someone else might be living in it. Carolyn liked the idea of it being abandoned because she thought it would be neat to explore. Sneaking into places like that was something she had picked up from Damon, she explained, and she told us about an old hospital that they had briefly checked out a few weeks earlier.

"In fact," she said, "I wouldn't mind going back there again. We should do that sometime this week!" I liked the idea, as did the others.

"Maybe," Susanna said. "But as far as this house is concerned, if we see that anyone else is living there, we turn right back around and go home."

"What?" I said. "Then what's the point of us coming all this way in the first place?"

"To kill time," she said.

I started to argue more, but then I saw the fork in the tunnel that we had encountered before. I couldn't remember which way we were supposed to go in order to get to the house, though.

"Right," Carolyn said. "I think. Or is it left."

Eventually, we tried the right tunnel, but that led to the dead end that had the smaller, bat-sized tunnels leading from it, one to the surface and one to the house. I had forgotten about them until I saw them again. So we went back to the other tunnel, which then sloped up to the large trapdoor. Susanna tried to open it, but she couldn't get it to move very far.

Carl and Dennis came forward and pushed on it together with their shoulders, and after a few moments, the door gave way. They still had to fight to get it all the way open, and lots of dirt and grass fell as they pushed.

Finally, we were out on the surface again, and it felt good to be out of that gloomy tunnel. It was still light outside, and looking around, I saw the house again, which looked imposing even in the daytime. I could just barely recall how it looked at night when we had been here before, and as I spotted the pool off to one side, I got a brief flash in my mind of the enemy vampires flying into it. But I couldn't recall much more than that, only that we had eventually defeated them.

While it felt a bit scary to be there, not knowing if we should even be there at all, I also felt extremely happy to have arrived. I breathed in deeply, enjoying the fresh air. Everyone else looked fairly pleased with themselves, too. "So," I said with a smile, "here we are!"

"Yeah, but it looks like they've let the place go a bit, huh?" Carl said. All around us, the grass was tall and full of weeds. We walked a few paces toward the house, but it was difficult. The ground was tough to traverse, and I had to kick occasionally, knocking the unkempt grass aside as I went.

"Hey, what's this?" Tim said, bending down. He picked up an empty bottle from the ground. It was a weird shape, sort of flattened and curved.

Susanna laughed. "Looks like a liquor bottle. Careful; there might still be something left in it. We can't have you boozing it up or anything." Tim sneered, then dropped the bottle.

"There's another one!" Dennis said, pointing at the ground near Tim's feet. "Who's just been leaving empty bottles all over the place?" He let out a small laugh.

"Someone's been partying," Carolyn said with a smile, still holding Crowley in her arms. He was looking around curiously.

"Vagrants, maybe," Susanna offered.

"Hmm?" I asked.

"Like, homeless people," Carolyn said. "Sometimes they wind up drunk in places like this and leave their trash behind."

"If you say so," I said.

"Still wish I knew just where we are," Carolyn said, looking around at the sky and the trees. There was what looked like a forest off to the back side of the house, which I didn't remember from the last time we had been here. But that had been at night, so it may have escaped my notice altogether.

All of a sudden, Crowley leapt from Carolyn's arms and onto the grass, then crept around cautiously. He then started running, but he didn't go far. He stopped, looked around, poked his head up from the tall grass, and ran in another direction. He repeated this process several times, occasionally letting out little growls or yelps.

"What's up with him?" Dennis asked.

"Psycho kitty!" Tim said, then laughed loudly. I laughed, too, as did the others, but it wasn't a particularly funny joke.

"He's just playing," Carolyn said. She knelt down into the grass. "Crowley, will you come back here? Quit running around like a little crackhead."

That made us laugh again, this time more loudly than before. Susanna tried to shush us, but she was also fighting back laughter. "Quiet, everyone! We don't know yet whether anyone's spotted us. Anyone see a light on in the house?" We didn't, but it was still daylight.

"Anybody home?" Carl called out, prompting Susanna to shush him more loudly. He laughed, as did the rest of us.

"Knock it off, Carl!" Susanna said. "What time is it, anyway?"

"Time for you to get a watch!" Dennis joked. I couldn't help but laugh at this, too, even though I actually hated that joke. He had used it on me a few times at school before, and it always made me want to hit him. But for some reason, it seemed hilarious at the moment. "Just kidding," he said, looking up from his watch. "It's 7:40."

"Okay, smart-ass," she said. "So there should be less than an hour and a half before the potion has finished doing its work."

"What, the potion has a job now?" I joked. "It needs to work harder!"

Susanna didn't laugh at this one, but my friends did, and Dennis began singing tunelessly, *"Iiiiii've been working on the raaaaaailrooooooad!"* He held his arms open and danced around slowly as he sang, and the sight of it was ridiculously funny.

We tried to calm down, but things continued to get out of hand. "Hey, since you're such a good singer," Carl said sarcastically and with a wide grin, "why don't you go up to the front door and give them a singing telegram?" He then danced around and tried to make up a song about searching for vampires to the tune of "Yes, We Have No Bananas," but it didn't really work. Even so, we couldn't stop laughing.

"Oh! I get it!" Tim exclaimed. "This is the potion again, right? It's making us act like this! Good thing it's doing its job!" He fell onto his knees, laughing at his own joke.

I found this just as amusing as everything else around me, but for a moment, I was distracted by something far off to my right. There was something on the lawn, some small patch of white that wasn't moving. I began to walk toward it, but my legs suddenly gave way beneath me, and I fell to the ground. I tried to get up, gripping at the grass and dirt with my fingers, but it felt like I weighed a ton. I could hear the laughter of my friends quickly tapering off, followed by muffled thumps as they dropped where they stood. And then, I felt myself falling asleep, and the world was dark, quiet, and calm.

When I woke up, I was sitting up in a chair. This was strange; I couldn't recall ever falling asleep sitting up before. As my vision unclouded and I looked around me, I also tried to move my arm, and I found that it wouldn't budge. My other arm was the same way, and I looked down and saw that both arms were bound at the wrists with thick white ropes. Not only that, but my ankles were apparently similarly tied, as I couldn't move them, either. I began to understand the implications of this, then struggled, but it didn't do any good. I was tied to the chair, and I couldn't get out of it.

I looked around, and I saw that Susanna, Carolyn, and my friends were also tied to chairs, and they were waking up as well, too, discovering their predicaments individually.

"What the hell?" Dennis said. "Where are we?"

"Inside the house," Susanna said. I looked around some more and realized that she was right. We were in fact in the same living room where we had almost been killed by those two vampires before. I recognized the deep red carpet, and I spotted the gas fireplace on the far wall, though it wasn't lit, which made sense given that this was the middle of summer.

"How did we get here?" I asked, trying to keep from panicking. I had seen stuff like this on TV before, people being drugged, taken prisoner, and waking up tied to chairs, so I knew that whatever was going on, it couldn't be good.

"I'm not sure," Susanna said. "That last bout with the potion made us all pass out, and now here we are."

"Who cares how?" Carl shouted. "How do we get out of here?"

"I'm afraid you don't," a voice said from behind us. Instinctively, I tried to turn around to see who had spoken, but I couldn't turn far enough.

Two men came into my field of vision, both of them wearing what looked like lab coats. They also had on white button-up shirts and ties. They looked very pleased with themselves, and something about the way the taller of the two men smiled made me very uncomfortable.

"Let us go!" Tim shouted. "We haven't done anything to you!"

"Yeah, not yet, anyway," Carl said under his breath.

"Oh, he's feisty!" said the shorter of the two men. "I like him!"

Carl struggled against his ropes, giving the man a hateful look. "Fuck you," he said through clenched teeth.

"And so well mannered, too," the man said with a condescending smile.

The taller man laughed, then held out his arm toward the other man. "Please," he said, still with that same creepy grin. "I have to say, I'm so glad that all of you have come to join us tonight! It certainly is a helpful coincidence. We needed test subjects, and all this time, I thought we were going to have to kidnap them."

"What?" Carolyn shouted. "Oh, you have got to be kidding me."

"By the way, just to be formal," the taller man said, "I'm William, and this is my partner, Christopher." He said this with a broad smile, gesturing to his companion.

"So pleased to meet you," Christopher said.

"Mad scientists," Carolyn said disgustedly. "Seriously. That's what we're dealing with now?" She was right. Even though no explanation had been given to us yet, it was apparent that we were in a situation straight out of a mad scientist movie.

William looked hurt, but only in a comical way. "Oh, now that's not fair!"

"Certainly not," Christopher said. The two of them seemed to bounce off each other as they talked, like some old-time comedy duo.

"And I thought that guy Robert was cheesy," Carolyn said. Susanna turned and glared at her angrily, but it was too late.

"Robert?" William asked with surprise. "Are you friends of his?" He pondered for a moment. "No, you couldn't be. He died years ago, but... Oh! I think I see!" He paced back and forth, looking at us suspiciously. He then paused in front of Susanna's and Carolyn's chairs, then leaned down with his hands folded behind his back. "Which one of you is Susanna?"

"Let us go right now," Susanna said bravely, "or you're going to be really, really sorry."

William straightened up, then laughed. "Oh, this is just perfect."

"Wait," Christopher said. "This is *the* Susanna? The one from the notes?" He turned and looked at her, still leering. Susanna just glared back at him angrily.

"It would seem so," William said. "Little Miss Perfect, the one who wouldn't share the famous vampire potion." He sighed, but his sick smile never faded. "Poor Robert. Such a good little nephew, but boy could he ever get in over his head."

I was beginning to figure out some of what was going on. This man was apparently Robert's uncle, and he had moved into the house at some point after we had killed Robert and Jennifer, the two vampires. As I began to work this out, William then went on a detailed spiel about how he had inherited the house, found Robert's notes from when he had been trying to recreate the potion, and how his friend Christopher had later moved in with him to help continue the work.

Part of me was terrified, being at the mercy of these two crazy men, who had apparently tried to develop their own version of the potion, but with a significant change in direction. Rather than trying to turn people into vampires with it, they had decided to make werewolves instead. This sounded ridiculous to me, but then, if a vampire potion was possible, why not a werewolf one? I had never really cared much about or paid attention to werewolves as they appeared in popular culture, but prior to 1983, I hadn't given much thought to vampires, either.

The earlier mention of test subjects, coupled with what I knew scenes like this usually led to, made me nervous. Apparently, these guys were planning to use their special werewolf potion on us, and the idea of that was not the least bit appealing. Being turned into a vampire was one thing — something I liked — but changing into some hairy, bearded, howling thing with a black shiny nose seemed not only repugnant, but downright stupid.

I felt some comfort soon after catching sight of a large grandfather clock next to the fireplace. It ticked away, ominously it seemed at first, but once I noticed the time on the clock's face, I began to feel better. The time was 8:55, and if Susanna's estimates were right, we only had a few more minutes before our own potion kicked in and we became vampires. When that happened, we would make short work of these two corny rejects from an old black and white movie. All we had to do was hold out until then. I hoped that the others were thinking the same things I was, that they weren't too scared. Knowing Dennis, he was probably following along with my thoughts almost word for word, but I couldn't be sure about anyone else in the group.

"You two are so in for it," Carl began. I knew what he was about to say.

"Carl, shut up," I said. I couldn't quite see him; our six chairs were lined up side by side, and his was at the far right of the group, while mine was at the far left, next to Susanna.

"But..." he began, but Tim cut him off, hopefully also knowing that if Carl blurted out that we had already taken our potion and were about to become vampires, it would tip William and Christopher off, and who knows what might happen then. They might kill us first. They didn't seem any less capable of that than Robert, whom I suddenly remembered had told us that he'd killed his parents when he first became a vampire. This disturbed me even further.

"So what are you guys, anyway?" Tim asked in a defiant tone. "Satanists, or something else? Some kind of neo-pagan?"

I didn't know what that last word meant, but the older Tim got, the more used I got to him saying incomprehensible things like that. At least his interruption had stopped Carl from talking. I started to use my old "brainstorming" technique on Carl, visualizing a greyish, storm-like vortex rushing over his head, something like a cross between a small tornado and TV static. The idea was that this would somehow disrupt Carl's mind, to break up his train of thought.

"Oh, so this one sounds like the brains of the group," Christopher said, smiling at Tim. "No, we're not either of those things."

"It was Robert who decided to take the Satanic route when science failed him," William said, sounding somewhat sad but not losing his arrogance. "But we soldiered on, pursuing the inevitable conclusion that we knew science would lead us to."

Keep talking, I thought. *Just keep talking for as long as you can. Tell us everything about how great and superior you are.*

"So Robert just left all of his notes lying around?" Susanna asked. I couldn't tell if she was genuinely interested or if she was also stalling.

Everyone, keep them talking. I tried to direct my thoughts to my sisters and friends. *We're almost there. Just a few more minutes.* I didn't actually think that any of them could hear the words in my head, though. Dennis and I had tried to communicate that way several times, to use telepathy the same way we had seen it depicted on TV. But that never worked. However, concentrating on certain things sometimes resulted in the overall impression seeming to make its way through. I hoped that it was working this time.

William went on for a while longer, then stopped when the clock chimed. It was 9:00, four hours since we had first taken the potion. Why hadn't we turned into vampires yet? I looked over at the windows, which were to my right, and I could see that it was dark outside. To my left, I had also noticed one of the doorways leading out of the room, which those creepy, mindless vampires had come in through before. For the first time in almost two years, I could see them clearly in my mind, and I remembered how scared I had been that night.

"Ah, well," William said, breaking off in mid-sentence and turning to look at the chiming clock. "I'm sure that's enough talk."

"Yes," Christopher said. "Time for the real show." He walked around to the far side of the couch, which I remembered sitting on when Robert and Jennifer had us locked in a trance. He came back around to our side, wheeling a dark plastic cart that had some strange objects on it. The most prominent one was a large metal box with lots of knobs and dials on it, but I only caught a glimpse of those before he turned the cart to where just the back of the box was facing us. There was also a small, flat, black cone sticking up from one corner of the box.

"What is that?" I asked. I wanted to know, but I also wanted them to keep talking, to not actually do anything to us.

"Oh, this is the control box we will use to activate the werewolf potion in all of you," William said almost casually. "And it will allow us to control and train you using various ultrasonic and infrasonic frequencies. Through this speaker," he added, pointing at the protruding cone.

Next to the box were several small hypodermic needles. I realized what they must be for.

"Oh, hell no," Carolyn said, spotting them at the same time. "If that's the potion, you can forget it. I *hate* needles."

William and Christopher both chuckled. "Oh, sweetie, it's okay," Christopher said. "I understand. I'm the same way." He shuddered comically.

"But you don't need to worry," William said. "We already injected all of you with the potion while you were passed out."

"What?" I shouted involuntarily, suddenly noticing that my left arm felt sore as I tried once again to pull at the ropes holding me to the chair. I was immediately reminded of a tetanus shot I had gotten when I was five years old, how I screamed as I watched the nurse unexpectedly plunge the needle into my upper arm.

"And by the way," Christopher added, "aren't most of you too young to drink?" He said this with a slight wink, but I was confused.

"What?" I said again.

"I'm all about partying and being young and everything, but really. Sneaking onto someone else's property and intentionally wiping yourselves out. I thought we'd seen the last of that kind of thing months ago."

I didn't know what he was talking about. My heart was pounding in fear. I felt dizzy. These guys had gotten us, and any minute now, they were going to turn us into their werewolf slaves.

"Takes all kinds, dear," William said, reaching for the metal box on the cart.

I began to panic. I struggled against the ropes holding me down, and I noticed that Susanna was doing the same. The others probably were, too. I fought as hard as I could, but the ropes were just too strong and too tight. I couldn't break my arms free, and my legs were just as useless.

I screamed more loudly and more desperately than I ever had in my entire life. I heard something that sounded like more screams around me, but they were muffled. It felt like I was underwater, smacked by a wave but standing up in the middle of it, firmly fighting it off. The feeling rushed all around me, threatening to engulf me, but I stood firm. Something like a sonic boom went off, and it felt like a supernova had exploded around me, everything rushing out from within. It felt amazing, or actually, it felt like amazement itself, the very essence of the word, was suddenly pouring out from within me. It was the most incredible thing I had ever felt in my entire life. I was invincible.

Light and sound surrounded me, flaring out from within. Forms began to coalesce in my vision, and things started to feel more familiar. I was standing up. I had form. I was real. There was a chair behind me, and there were small bits of something lying near to it. Thin, white, cylindrical, with knots. Rope. I remembered that. I felt stronger than ever.

An unfamiliar sound, which I vaguely recognized as a human voice, rang out from somewhere nearby. It was forming words, something like, *"QUIT! ACT! IF! EIGHT!"* I wasn't sure if those were the actual words, but I knew that they were supposed to mean something to me.

And then everything went completely wrong. A shrill, piercing shriek flooded through my entire being, and it didn't stop. It was a very weird sound, something that was both very high pitched like a squeal and very low pitched like a deep hum, all at the same time. I had been standing up, but I quickly knelt to the floor, almost slamming my body down into that position. I was on my hands and knees, which suddenly felt like the right way to be.

My legs jutted out behind me, feeling like they were bending backwards. As this happened, both my pants and my shoes suddenly felt very uncomfortable and misshapen, and I struggled in them. It felt like my chest was stretching, and my arms had a strange sensation, too. I looked down and saw that they were becoming skinnier and were rapidly growing dark brown hair on them, and my fingers shrank into paws with long, thick claws on them. That was when I lost it. I tried to scream, but my voice was no longer human. Instead, what came out was a high-pitched wail, and the sound of it terrified me. It kept repeating involuntarily, and I heard similar noises around me. In between these cries for help, I panted heavily, completely frightened out of my mind.

After several moments of this terror, I became resigned to it, unable to fight what was happening to me. I was still aware of the changes and shifts in my physiology, but I cared less. It felt like my mouth was stretching out before me, and then I could see my snout growing outward before my eyes. I chomped at the air, my squealing replacing itself with deeper barks. The fear was beginning to give way to a new emotion: anger.

The strange fabric encasing me became increasingly irritating, and I rolled over to one side in an attempt to shake it off. I was partly successful, but my upper body was still trapped. I straightened back up on all fours, and then I noticed the others. I felt some sort of kinship with them, though they looked strange to me. They were wolves, or at least mostly wolves, and they too were struggling against the weird cloth that was partly enveloping them. They also seemed equally frightened, which comforted me somewhat. At least I wasn't alone.

I tried to say something to the one nearest to me, a wolf with dark brown fur. The bark I let out got her attention, and she stopped struggling for a moment, looking at me with her wide, brown eyes. She smelled familiar, which was also mildly comforting. The other wolves took notice of me, too, but then they went back to chewing at their bonds.

A sound came from nearby, and I looked to see where it had come from. There were two strange creatures standing not too far away, tall and pale. I hated them immediately. One of them continued to make its strange noises, which were sort of like barks but more complex. This irritated me further for some reason. The other of the two animals reached over and touched an object, and suddenly, a loud noise pierced my ears, causing me to yelp. The other wolves did so, too.

The dominant creature made another sound, and his companion touched the dark object again, producing another horrible ringing. This time, I began to growl. I bared my teeth, and I felt the fur on the back of my neck standing up. Whatever was going on, I didn't like it, and I needed to make it stop.

I began to creep toward the two of them, slowly and cautiously. I sniffed the air, hoping for some kind of information, but I wasn't sure just what. But then I got it, a change in the scent of one of the tall animals, a sort of salty smell. The closer I crept, the stronger it became. Fear. Vulnerability. That's what I was sensing.

When the third horrible, skull-piercing sound emitted from the box, which was clearly the fault of these creatures, I winced, then turned back to look at the rest of the wolves. A couple of them, including the brown-furred female, were starting to follow my lead, but the others were cowering. I directed a bark at them, then another, inviting them to join me. The second female, who had golden fur, responded with a growl, then a more friendly bark, which she repeated to the other males.

There were more strange vocalizations from the two animals, followed by more shrill sounds from that damned box of theirs. Some of these sounds were different, lower, but still just as annoying. I turned back to face them, letting out a steadily increasing growl. I then drew back, flattening myself to the ground, baring my teeth. The scent of their fear increased, which was exactly what I wanted. Part of me was still scared, too, but I needed to let that fuel me rather than hold me back.

The smaller of the two seemed a more achievable target, so I leapt through the air, landing on its chest and pulling it to the ground. It let out a strange yell as I did so, and I was vaguely aware of the strange object it had been torturing us with falling over as well. The creature struggled against me, but I was clearly stronger than it. It flailed at me with its limbs, but it was no use. A new feeling crept up inside me, or at least, I noticed it for the first time, realizing it had been there all along. I was hungry. And here was meat.

I clamped my jaw down as hard as I could onto the struggling animal's neck, and I felt its bones give way with a satisfying crunching sound. It continued to let out bizarre vocal sounds for a few more moments, but as I continued to bite and tear at it repeatedly, those sounds quickly ceased. I tore at the flesh with my teeth, ripping off bits of it and eagerly chewing, loving the taste of the meat and the blood. I had been more hungry than I'd realized.

Because I was so engrossed in my meal, I was only partly aware of the rest of the wolves as they joined the attack. I could hear some of them going after the other source of meat and taking it down; its shrieks and screams quickly died down as well. Two of the wolves, though, wanted some of my prey, and as they leapt onto it, they also dislodged me, sending me tumbling across the ground and into some strange object. It was somehow both hard and soft, sort of like a large tree trunk covered in fur. It probably served some function other than something for me to run into, but I had no idea what that might be. At least it had stopped me from tumbling.

I recovered, then looked back at my meal, which was being ripped at and torn apart by two of the male wolves, both of whom had dark brown fur. The third male, who had a strange, deep orange colored coat, was sharing the other source of meat with the two females. Things were still pretty chaotic, each of the wolves struggling to get as much to eat as possible, occasionally shoving each other out of the way. I bounded over to my prey and tried to eat some more, but the others tried to fight me off. I managed to get down a few more mouthfuls before I gave up, deciding that it wasn't worth the struggle. I was more or less sated by this point, anyway.

Wandering off to one side, I tried to make sense of my surroundings. Everything looked so strange. The ground was this weird, reddish substance. Like the object I had toppled into earlier, it was strange in that it was soft to the touch, but just beneath it was very firm and sturdy. I sniffed at it, hoping to learn more, but all I picked up were the scents of my fellow wolves, plus the smell of the animals we had just killed.

I wondered if there might be more of the same kind of animal nearby. I looked around for a while, but my search only led me to a vertical, wooden structure, a dead end of sorts. Near the base of it, I could feel a slight breeze, and there was the scent of fresh, nighttime air. I scratched at this area, hoping to somehow make it open up for me, but nothing happened. I let out a little wheeze of disappointment. Somehow I knew that beyond this wall, there was the real world, with real grass, real trees, and an open, dark sky. That was where I belonged, not trapped in this parody of the world. But there was nothing I could do for now.

Turning behind me, I noticed another strange structure. I walked up onto it, then found that it continued to go up. It would continue for just a very small way straight ahead, then straight up, then straight ahead again, over and over. I experimented with this weird thing for a few moments, finding that if I kept moving forward, I also moved up along it. As I got the hang of it, I found it kind of fun, but all of a sudden, the structure was behind me, and I was on flat ground again.

A long path lay on either side of me, and having nothing better to do, I picked a direction and began walking. The smells of those two dead creatures were up here, too, but the sensation was more faint. Very quickly, I came upon an opening on my right, which led into a darker, enclosed area. Seeing in the dark wasn't very difficult, so I went in to investigate.

There were several strange things in the place, none of which made any sense to me. I noticed an opening at the far end, through which I could see the outside world. I ran over to it eagerly, jumping up onto the edge of it with my front paws. I was so happy to see the sky, but then my nose bumped into something invisible, some barrier blocking my way. I beat against it with my head a couple more times, but it was no good. Despite being able to see out into the real world, I was still trapped. I hated this place, whatever it was.

Giving up, I jumped back down and looked around, wondering what else I might find. There was some shiny thing standing up in one corner, so I walked over to it, then leapt back as I saw another wolf heading towards me. The wolf jumped back at the same time, and then it stopped moving at the same time I did. This was confusing, but I was still curious. After a few moments, I realized that what I was seeing was not in fact another wolf, but myself, sort of like seeing my own shadow.

I wasn't displeased with what I saw. In fact, I quite liked it. My sleek, dark brown fur looked healthy, and the rest of my body was well proportioned. Behind me stood a tall, curved tail, its fur fanning out nicely. I had wide, brown eyes and a dignified expression, my long mouth held firmly clamped underneath my snout. There were a few flecks of blood and other bits of the animal I had eaten scattered about my fur, though, plus there was still that annoying tube of fabric draped around my upper half, and it was torn and shredded in a few places. If I worked at it, I could probably manage to get it off.

Just as I began to try, I heard a noise from outside the chamber, so I leapt up from the ground and went back out to the main path. To my surprise, there was another animal like the ones we had attacked earlier, but this one looked different. Like the others, it stood upright and had pale, hairless skin, but it also had a long mane of golden fur around its head, which the others hadn't had. It was also holding something in one of its paws, but I had no idea what it might be.

Still, I didn't care. If this was another one of those creatures, it probably meant me as much harm as they had. The thing it was holding might be another weapon like the box that made all of those horrible sounds before. I needed to defend myself, and I also realized that I wouldn't mind a second meal of that delicious meat. I growled, then hunched down, preparing to strike.

Something strange happened. The animal, which had been looking at me the whole time, did something weird with its eyes, which lit up and glowed brightly. They looked like tiny little suns, but then I realized that they were a deeper hue. A strange feeling crept through me, and I heard a sound, or at least, I thought I did. This wasn't like the grating, scraping shrieks that had hurt me before, but it did still feel like it was inside my head. And it was a soothing feeling, not a malevolent one. The sound I heard, if I heard it at all, was like a vague humming or whirring, and as I stared into those glowing orbs, I felt myself change.

My body shifted and altered, and most of the fur I had recently grown fell out and onto the floor, leaving my arms bare as they morphed back into human ones. I felt my face take shape, my ears shifting back down from the top of my head to the sides, and my upper and lower body went back to the way they were supposed to be. As my mind began to clear, I was relieved to understand that I was shifting back from being a wolf to being an actual person. I saw everything through a yellow haze as my eyes glowed in unison with my sister's. When my transformation was complete, her eyes stopped shining, as did mine. The world looked normal to me again.

I was crouched on the floor of a hallway with several doorways on each side, and I looked back to my right, seeing the dark room I had come out of a minute before. I then looked back at Carolyn, who quickly tossed something at me and turned her head away, covering her eyes. "Go on, hurry up," she said.

As my jeans and shoes landed in front of me, I suddenly became aware of the fact that I was naked from the waist down, but given the way I was positioned, my private parts were probably hidden from view. Nevertheless, it was embarrassing, and I quickly scrambled for my clothes and rushed to get them back on, which was a little difficult because they were quite ripped up and torn. At least my shoes had mostly survived intact.

"You done?" Carolyn called from her spot, and I looked and saw that she was still covering her eyes.

"Yeah," I said. "Thanks."

"Come on," she said, gesturing down the hallway behind her. "The others are downstairs."

I got up from the floor and followed her to another staircase, one at the far end of the hall, not the one I had come up earlier as a wolf. My clothes were wrecked, but for the most part, they served to cover me up as adequately as possible. I walked down the stairs behind Carolyn, holding back a laugh as I noticed that her shorts had a big split down the back of them.

"But how did he get inside?" I asked. We had just walked down the large stone staircase from the front of the house, heading out into the yard. The grass closer to the house was shorter and looked like it might have been mowed a few weeks earlier, but the farther out we went, the more rough and out of control the lawn was.

The others had explained to me that while they were still wolves and were chowing down on the bodies of the two scientists, Crowley had shown up in the room. As they started to turn on him, his eyes began to glow, and somehow, that changed all of them from wolves into people, or more specifically, vampires. Susanna said that the glowing eyes helped to activate our version of the potion, to assert it over the one we had been injected with. But as for how Crowley got there, she wasn't sure.

"That's just it," she said. "We don't know."

"I suppose one of them might have left a window open," Tim said. "And he came and found his way in."

"Maybe," Susanna said. "But you'd think they'd have been more cautious than that."

I figured that Crowley had gotten left outside, and the scientists had heard us laughing and carrying on before we passed out, then came outside, found us, and brought us inside. "And they didn't even see Crowley because he was hidden in the grass," I concluded.

"Or, you know, maybe they did find him!" Carolyn said. "But they didn't know what to do with him."

"Or maybe they even brought him inside, too," Dennis said. "Just left him in a room somewhere thinking he wasn't important."

"Well, I guess we'll never know," Susanna said. "I mean, you could always go back and ask them."

"No, thank you," Carolyn said firmly. We had left the two bodies behind in the den, what was left of them, anyway. It was a pretty horrible sight, but I found that it wasn't quite as disturbing to me as the way Robert and Jennifer's decayed bodies had looked two years earlier. "Crowley, why don't you tell us what happened?" she added with a smile. He was walking along beside us, working his way through the increasingly tall grass.

"Oh, you know, I just found the key under the mat and let myself in," someone said from behind me. I turned and saw that it was Dennis, speaking in a funny voice. The rest of us laughed. Going back to using his regular voice, he asked, "So where is the tunnel, anyway? It's hard to tell in all of these weeds."

Even though we could see in the dark, he was right. I had a vague idea of which direction the entrance to the tunnel was in, but it was impossible to be sure. One interesting thing about being able to see was that we didn't need to make our eyes glow in order to do it. We were just able to. I started to ask Susanna how this was possible, but I was cut off by Tim.

"It might be easier to spot it from the air," he said.

"He's right," Susanna said. "Let's go." It had been a while since I had turned into a bat, but I still remembered how to do it. What happened next, though, was a surprise.

Susanna stood with her arms straight out from her sides, looking like she was about to do some kind of ballet move. She said with a sly smile, "This is going to be a bit different. Watch." The previous two summers as vampires, our transformation into bats had looked like a magic trick, with a quick flash of light and a big puff of smoke. But as Susanna changed this time, there was no flash. Her entire body, clothes and all, quickly shrank into a winged form. As she did this, there was some smoke, but it poured out from her, almost like part of her was burning or steaming away. The smoke was also brownish orange, not dark grey like before. Within seconds, she was a bat, and she flapped in place for a few moments before shooting upwards.

"Wow," I said. "That *was* different!"

"And cool as shit!" Carl said. Immediately, he transformed as well, smoking and shrinking away into his bat form.

I started to do the same, but then I wondered about Crowley. Would he be able to do it, too? Would he even know how? But in fact, right after Carolyn changed, he did the same. It was pretty much the same type of effect, just on a smaller scale, and his bat form was smaller than ours, too. It was also white, like his fur when he was a cat.

I watched as he and Carolyn flew up from the ground. "Okay, now that's just cool," I said with a smile, then changed as well. It felt different than before, more gradual than the quick *POOF!* of the earlier kind of transformation. It only took about two seconds, but still, something about it felt more smooth and less jarring. I flew up to Susanna, who was hovering high above, waiting for everyone.

"Now what's up with that?" I asked her, flapping in the air beside her.

She laughed. "You like it? It's part of the new potion."

"That's pretty bad-ass!" Dennis said, joining us from below. "I like it better." Another thing that was different was our size. Before, our bat forms had been small, about the size of sparrows. But with this new formula, we were larger, closer to the size of crows. And our coloring was different: Instead of all of us being black and pretty much identical, we were each covered in fur the same color as our hair while in person mode. This meant that most of us were varying shades of brown, with Carolyn being golden colored and Dennis being reddish-orange. It was the same coloring we'd had during our brief time as wolves.

"There, I see it!" Tim said, flying down slightly and in the direction of the tunnel's entrance. He was right about it being easier to spot from above; being a couple of dozen feet up in the air gave us a much wider perspective.

"Do we really have to go all the way back through that?" Carl asked. "Why not just fly to the house from here?"

"And which way is that?" Susanna asked.

Carl paused. "Oh. Well, we could probably find it!"

"No, let's just go back the way we're sure of," I said.

"Fine," Carl said. "I guess you're right."

As we walked along the tunnel, we talked about various things, including how cool it felt to be vampires again. Carl was the first one to point out something the rest of us had somehow failed to notice: We didn't have fangs.

"What?" I said with surprise. "How can we not…?" I broke off, reaching up to my teeth with my right index finger. There wasn't a fang where I expected to find it. And there wasn't one on the other side of my mouth, either. "Susanna!"

"It's okay!" she said. "They only come out when we need them."

"Oh…" Dennis said. "I get it. Like when we're ready to actually make a kill."

"Right," she said.

I was beginning to get a sense of what Susanna had meant when she referred to this new potion giving us a more authentic vampire experience. This notion of not having fangs the entire time was akin to something I had seen occasionally in depictions of vampires on TV. The actor portraying the vampire would look normal most of the time, but then once he was about to kill someone, he'd bare his fangs. I hadn't really thought about it before, whether or not the fictional vampire was supposed to have fangs the entire time and they were just hidden, or if they only protruded when he wanted them to. In the past, we'd had them the entire time, which was simultaneously cool and problematic. More than once, I had accidentally bitten or at least scraped my tongue. It always healed quickly, but it was still a pain.

Apparently, I wouldn't have to worry about that anymore, but I still missed feeling them there. It didn't feel right without them. As we walked along, I concentrated, wondering if I could make my fangs present themselves at will. The correct two teeth on my upper jaw quickly sharpened, feeling just like they had before. I gently licked at them one at a time with my tongue, feeling the sharp, familiar points, then smiled. Once I relaxed, the fangs morphed back into normal teeth.

Dennis let out a small laugh, and I realized that he had probably just done the same thing, testing out his new fangs. "Pretty cool, huh?" I said to him quietly.

"Yeah," he said with a smile.

We continued along the tunnel, Carolyn holding Crowley in her arms as before. We talked a little more about those two men, including some supposition as to what might happen to the house now that they were dead. Carolyn suggested that it might end up abandoned if there weren't any more sick and twisted family members left to inherit it.

"You think they're all screwed up like that?" Carl asked.

"Who knows," Susanna said.

"God," he said, sounding exhausted. "I am so thirsty."

"Yeah, me too," I said. I regretted not going along with his suggestion to try finding our house via the air. At least we could have stopped along the way and done a proper kill. We still hadn't done that since becoming vampires, and I was craving that. The killing of those two scientists didn't seem to count.

"Sorry, guys," I said. "Guess I shouldn't have suggested we go to the house in the first place."

"No, it was a decent enough idea," Tim said. "We didn't know that Igor and Dr. Frankenstein would be hanging out there waiting for us. Things just got out of hand."

"I guess," I said.

"You know," Carl said, "we could get through this tunnel quicker if we flew."

"That's a good point," Carolyn said. "And I could stop carrying a certain someone who seems to keep getting heavier and heavier the further we go." Crowley looked up at her and meowed. "Yes, you," she said to him.

She stopped and set him down, and he again started hopping as the strange substance on the floor gave way and began turning into dirt. Carolyn changed into a bat, and he followed her lead immediately. The rest of us did the same. The new way of changing forms still took some getting used to, but I liked it. It just seemed cooler and more sophisticated, and I realized this time what it reminded me of: standing in a swimming pool, then putting out your arms and raising your feet to begin treading water, floating gently in place.

We didn't hang around at the house for very long; we were eager to get out into the city. I didn't really care where we went by then, either, just as long as there were fresh new victims. But Susanna insisted on a specific destination. Before she had a chance to explain exactly why or where she wanted us to go, I snapped at her, "Can we just go already?"

She scowled at me, but then her expression softened. "Okay, okay," she said. "I know. We're all hungry, Ray."

We went out the front door, changing into bats and flying up into the sky, just as we had so many times before. It felt familiar to be back in the same old routine again, but it still felt exciting as well. We were finally on our way downtown to attack some helpless victims again, and I felt very happy to have the group back together. Even Crowley, though he hadn't been a vampire before, felt like part of the team. He was family. We all were.

Our destination was a bridge somewhere near downtown Augusta, one that I recalled being driven over by both my parents and by Carolyn. I couldn't remember why we had been there on either occasion, though. Downtown wasn't somewhere we often went in my regular, day-to-day life, but it was certainly a place we had frequented as vampires before. Being back there in the middle of the night and looking for victims brought on a feeling of nostalgia and comfort. It was like revisiting an old vacation spot, remembering the good times and preparing to create new memories.

Still, what Susanna had planned for us was not what I expected. Instead of stalking regular, everyday people like we had done before, she explained, we were going to prey on the homeless people who slept under this particular bridge. I knew almost nothing about this particular demographic, but I had a vague idea of what they were probably like. I pictured them as adventurous, nomadic people who for some reason chose to live on the streets instead of in actual houses, outcasts and rebels, sort of like my friend Nick had described in his tales of his fellow punks who occasionally clashed with the police.

What we found was quite different. There was a lone middle-aged man huddled in an obscure corner where the concrete supports of the bridge met the ground, various piles of clothes next to him, plus a small radio that was just barely audible. Once the man saw us, he sat up quickly, then rushed to turn off his music, like we'd caught him doing something he wasn't supposed to do. He gathered a few sheets of newspaper from a nearby stack and held them close to his chest, looking at us with wild, strange eyes. He stood up, throwing the papers to the ground, then began pacing back and forth, not looking at us as we walked slowly towards him.

"Fuck! Fuck! Fuck!" he suddenly shouted, his hands clawing at the air, but he didn't run from us. I expected him to be scared, but he just seemed very angry. He was dressed in ragged, dirty clothes, including a flannel shirt that seemed like it would be too warm for the time of year. He also had red hair and a long, straight beard that protruded unevenly from his chin. After his profane outburst stopped, he went back to pacing back and forth, flailing his hands and muttering.

We stopped our approach. This was just confusing, nothing at all like the stealthy attacks we had done in the past. "Okay, seriously, what the hell," Carl said.

"HELL! FUCK! WHAT!" the man shouted, stopping his pacing and staring straight at my friend. Carl froze, as did I, unsure how to react. I had never seen anything like this before. I had heard of crazy people and had seen rather comic depictions of them on TV and in cartoons, but this was completely new to me. "This is the judgment, then, right?" he shouted. "Not what the son told me. I knew this was coming! I knew!"

"You knew what?" Tim asked, his voice very calm, almost soothing. "Why don't you tell…"

"WHY DON'T YOU!!!" the crazy man interrupted. He resumed his pacing for a few seconds, seeming almost apologetic for his outburst. Then he turned back to Tim, clenching his fist and looking angry, then sad, almost like he was about to cry. "I told them," he said gently. "I told them about the sons, the redemption, the coming of the dawn…" He trailed off, muttering a few words I couldn't make out.

"Okay, this is just pathetic," Carolyn said, sounding impatient. She opened her mouth wide, and I saw her fangs grow into place. At the same time, her eyes began to glow a deep yellow. But this was different from the way our eyes had glowed before. Rather than a sort of hazy, vague aura around her eyes, this was more concentrated, her eye sockets seeming to burn with light.

"The sons!" the man said, sounding inspired. Or had he said "suns" instead? I wasn't sure; nothing he said made any sense. "Like so many fireflies. Beautiful, and deadly. Trickle, trickle. Down, down, down…" He said this with a smile, almost like he was thrilled with what was happening. "They wouldn't listen. They kept stonewalling me."

Most of what this guy was saying was nonsense, but I had to admit that he was right about one thing: Carolyn's eyes did in fact look like fireflies lighting up. But while fireflies just flared briefly and went out, the glow of Carolyn's eyes was constant and steady. I remembered seeing her do this back at the other house where we had fought off the scientists, and I felt more confident. Almost involuntarily, I lit my eyes up as well, presuming that they looked the same way. I turned back to look at the homeless man, who was beginning to step back cautiously. My fangs began to grow.

"Careful," the man said. "The suns are coming. Rising in the east, rising in the west! Shad, rack! Me, shack! A bed, knee go!" I began to wonder if his words actually did mean something, like some kind of code.

"What?" Dennis whispered, sounding intrigued. "What's he saying?"

"Nothing," Carolyn said.

I wasn't sure what she meant; the entire experience was surreal. It felt for a moment like everyone was talking gibberish, and that somehow that was supposed to mean something. Maybe I just wasn't getting it. But Carolyn's next statement held more truth than I realized at the time.

"This is total bullshit," she said, and she ran and leapt onto the man, bringing him down to the ground as she latched onto his throat with her mouth. Surprisingly, he didn't scream, and Carolyn drank from him for several seconds. I was jealous that she had gotten to kill before I did, but I wasn't sure I wanted a taste of this weirdo.

Carolyn stood up and wiped her mouth with the back of her hand, then shook her head and let out a disgusted sound. "That tasted like shit," she said, then wrinkled her nose. "Or maybe it was just the smell."

"Actually," Tim said, "taste and smell are really part of the same sense, not two separate ones."

"Thank you, Dr. Science," Carolyn said sharply.

"Tim knows," Carl whispered to me. That was a catchphrase a few of us had developed at school once we began to get sick of Tim always knowing the answers in class. It was said in a sort of singing way, like the typical *ding-dong* of a doorbell. As far as we knew, Tim was never aware of this little private joke of ours.

"Crowley, do you want to…" Carolyn began, then looked down and said, "Oh."

Crowley had leapt onto the neck of the homeless man, whom I saw wasn't quite dead yet. It was weird watching a small white cat prey on a person like that, but I also got a small thrill from it, or at the very least, amusement. We had created our own little mini-killer.

"Okay, Susanna, seriously?" Carolyn continued. "Homeless people. You want us to go around picking off paranoid schizophrenics who haven't showered for weeks?"

"Fine, you're right," Susanna said, throwing up her arms. "I thought it would be a good idea. And I thought that there would be more of them. I figured it would be safer, that the police might not notice people off the radar."

"Oh, I get it," I said. "That's what that Robert guy said they did back in '85. They preyed on homeless people and hid the bodies."

Susanna nodded. "But now that I've seen what that's like, I don't know how they did it for so long."

"Can we please stop talking and find somewhere else to go?" Carl pleaded. "I'm starving."

The next place we went was Carolyn's suggestion, a spot along the Savannah River, which formed the border between Georgia and South Carolina. Carolyn explained as we flew that this area was being developed into a tourist spot, and soon, there would be new stores and other things built up, part of an effort to revitalize downtown Augusta. Along the river were some docks with various boats, and she said that it was likely that there would be some people around as well. Apparently, she and Damon had spent some time here, but she didn't go into any more detail.

Even before we arrived, I was pretty sure she was right about there being people there; I could picture them, four people on a boat that was arriving at one of the docks. Once we got there, I was a little surprised to find just that, almost exactly as I had pictured it: two men and two women on a medium-sized white boat, one of the men stepping out onto the dock with a rope, which he then started using to secure their craft in place. My premonition shouldn't have really surprised me, given that I had also pictured that lone crazy man under the bridge shortly before we found him. In both cases, it wasn't until after the fact that I realized I had foreseen what was coming. Still, I was far too hungry to give much thought to this.

We descended upon the boaters, changing into our person forms as we landed. I eagerly attacked my first victim, a taller, pale woman with freckled skin and bright red hair tied back in a short ponytail. I noticed how weak she seemed as I took her; she tried to fight back as I leapt at her, but I easily knocked her limbs back and was upon her neck in seconds. I loved the sound of her scream as I bit down on her almost white neck and began to drink, holding tight to her as she collapsed onto the deck. She tasted wonderful, so warm and salty and full of life. I had missed this feeling so much. I also noticed the scent of sunscreen on her, the smell of which usually bothered me. But this time, it was just another sensation to take in, part of this intoxicating experience.

Once I was done, I stood up and saw that Carl and Susanna had killed the other two people on the boat, and Tim had killed the man who had been on the dock. I could tell from their expressions that they were just as happy as I was to have finally killed again. I wasn't sure where Dennis, Carolyn, or Crowley were, and I looked around trying to find them. I then looked up, where I saw Carolyn and Crowley hovering high above us as bats. They were just barely visible, but once I made my eyes glow, they were easier to make out. Our night vision was different with this version of the potion: We could see pretty well in the dark the entire time, not just when we made an effort to. When needed, we could make our eyes light up with that creepy new effect, which made everything show up even more clearly, but with a yellowish hue. Like the different transformation into bats, this took some getting used to.

Finally, I spotted Dennis, who was on the shore, finishing up a man I hadn't noticed before. Maybe he'd heard the screams and come to help, only to be taken down by Dennis.

"Okay, let's dump the bodies," Susanna said.

"What?" I asked. "Oh, you mean into the river. Why?"

"Less evidence that way," she said with an evil smile. I agreed; if we wanted to avoid attracting attention this time, it would help if we didn't just leave our victims' bodies lying around. I wasn't sure how we could keep this up, though. I didn't like the idea of taking the time to bury people over and over for the next two weeks.

She picked up the corpse of the man she had killed and rolled it over the side of the boat, and it splashed down into the water. She flinched and drew back from the side of the boat, her arms held up and bent at the elbows. "Be careful not to splash," she said, squinting. "I'm not sure if splashing water counts as running water. It might."

Carl was more careful as he maneuvered the body of his victim — a tanned, bikini-clad blonde — over the side of the boat, then slid her slowly down. "Bye!" he said with a goofy grin and a wave.

I picked up the red-haired woman I had killed, and I was surprised by how light she was. It was the same feeling I remembered getting when I'd pick up a box or a suitcase that I thought was full, only to discover that it was empty. I repeated Carl's method and let the woman's body slide off the side of the boat rather than just tossing her into the water like a fish, which I briefly felt tempted to do. In the meantime, Dennis had seen what we were doing and had also carried the remnants of his meal to the dock, joining Tim in rolling the last evidence of our kills off and into the river.

"They might still wash up on shore," Tim pointed out. "But who knows if anyone will be able to tell by then that they were killed by vampires."

"Yeah, and who really cares, right?" Dennis said with a smile.

"So we're stronger now, too, huh?" Carl asked Susanna as we flew back home.

"Yes." I could hear a smile in her voice, and I noticed for the first time that when we talked as bats, we no longer sounded as squeaky as we had before. Our voices were more or less normal, but they were still smaller in a way, that is, they didn't carry as far as when we were in our person forms. That wasn't a change, though; it had been that way the previous two times we'd been vampires.

"Are there any more bits you're not telling us?" I asked. As interesting as the differences in this new formula were, I was beginning to get impatient over how Susanna seemed to be letting things out a little bit at a time. It would have been far better if she had just sat us down and outlined everything we needed to know ahead of time.

"No, I think that's pretty much it," she said. "And don't be mad. I thought it would be more fun to let the enhancements be a surprise."

"Yeah, maybe," I said.

"I think it's cool!" Tim said. "We're still vampires, but… different. It's neat."

"Yeah, I think so, too," Carl said.

I wondered if Carolyn might weigh in, or Dennis, but they were silent. Then I realized that they weren't even there. "Wait!" I said, stopping and hovering in place. Susanna, Tim, and Carl flew on ahead for a few seconds, then stopped and turned around. "Where are the others?"

I looked behind us and saw that Dennis and Carolyn were a little ways behind, but they quickly caught up. Resting on Carolyn's golden colored bat form was a smaller, white bat, Crowley.

"He was having trouble keeping up," Carolyn explained. "And it's a little tricky flying with someone else on your back." She wobbled a little as she continued on her way, passing me and Susanna, the tiny bat clinging to her back.

"Okay," my other sister said, "that's probably the cutest damn thing I've ever seen in my life."

Back home, we were all in pretty good moods. Despite the rough start we had gotten, our vampire summer finally seemed to be on the right track. Everyone was getting along, and things felt fun again. We were powerful, stealthy, and in control, and the excitement was just beginning.

Carl talked about the new features of the vampire potion, how much cooler everything was, and he also wondered if our glowing eyes might have a hypnotic quality to them. "Like, if a person looks into our eyes," he said, "we could make them stand still like zombies, just waiting for us to take them."

"Yeah, that would be cool," I said. "Susanna?" I gave her a pointed look.

She just smiled. "I guess you'll have to try it and see."

"Oh, come on!" I said. "Can't you just tell us and quit with the whole secretive bit?"

"No," she said, still smiling and looking pleased with herself. "Though I will go ahead and mention something else I forgot to earlier."

"What's that?" Tim asked.

"The antidote."

"Booooo!" Dennis said, cupping his hands around his mouth, leading some of the others to laugh, but I didn't.

"The what?" I asked, confused. "I thought we scrapped that idea because of all the problems with it before."

"Yeah, and we just change back with running water or garlic or crosses or whatever," Carl said.

"Um, yeah!" Carolyn said in a sarcastic tone, holding up her hand like she was in a classroom about to ask a question. "Not looking to go all crazy and screwed up again here!"

"No, don't worry," Susanna said. "The new antidote isn't like that. It works better, and it's instant. It will be better to change back that way. You know, when it's time."

"Is it some kind of chewy brownie thing, too?" Tim asked.

"No, it's a liquid. It's upstairs on my desk in a beaker. When the time comes, we'll all take it at once."

Already, I was beginning to dread that idea, but I took comfort in the fact that this time, we had two whole weeks to be vampires, not just one.

The entire group hung out together for a while, continuing to talk. Susanna asked Carolyn more about the revitalization going on downtown, but Carolyn didn't know a whole lot about it. They both agreed that there had never been much to do there, that once the malls and shopping centers in the western part of the city were built, downtown pretty much dried up. Carolyn also didn't think that the plan to get people interested in the area along the river was going to work, that people had already gotten used to thinking of it as a rundown, unsafe place, and there were better things to do elsewhere.

All of this talk quickly became boring to me and my friends, so we went into the red den to watch TV. It was pretty late by this point, and we had already missed *Saturday Night Live.* Because it was the summer, they were only showing reruns anyway, so I wasn't too disappointed.

Instead of settling on a particular show or movie to watch, we flicked through the channels, finding various things to poke fun at. Sometimes, we stopped paying attention to the TV and talked about other stuff, like what had happened earlier that night.

"That crazy guy was pretty fucked up!" Carl said.

"Yeah, I know," Dennis said. "It was kinda scary, even though he was the human and we were the vampires."

"I almost felt sorry for him, though," Tim said. "I mean, he probably had no idea what was going on."

"Well, I think he probably figured it out once Carolyn and Crowley were drinking from his neck," I said, smiling.

"What was up with all that weird shit he was saying, too?" Carl asked. "'Fuck fuck shit hell! Come shack knee fall Billy Bob!'" As he did his impression of the man, he waved his arms about, then laughed.

"Maybe he had turret syndrome," Tim said. "At least I think that's what it's called. It's this weird disease that makes you shout out cuss words all the time."

"Oh, is that what that is?" Dennis said with a big grin. "There's hope for you after all, Carl! Maybe there's a cure!"

"Fuck you," Carl said, but he wasn't really mad.

"Oh, gosh! Someone get this boy some help!" Dennis said. Everyone laughed.

"Maybe we should have one of those telethons!" I joked. "You know, with that guy... what's his name..."

"Jerry Lee Lewis?" Dennis offered.

"Yeah, that sounds right," I said.

We went on like this for a while, occasionally distracted by the TV. Eventually, we found a late night rerun of *An Evening at the Improv,* which kept us entertained for a while. I really liked stand-up comics, and I had found that repeating their jokes at school and passing them off as my own got me some attention, which had worked pretty well for me for a while. But over time, as my popularity declined during that first part of seventh grade, people seemed to get more sick of this than entertained by it, so I stopped.

I was particularly shunned by the snobbier members of the class, the ones from the wealthiest families, which included both Valerie's and Gary's. Dennis was also regarded with contempt by these kids, but within our "lower" circle of friends, people liked him for the most part. Sometimes, I would get a little jealous that he got laughs more often than I did, another factor that made our friendship fluctuate.

Still, none of that mattered anymore. I had my friends and my sisters — plus our cat — together once again. We were vampires, and everything was cool.

We woke up the following evening in our newly redecorated basement, and I was in a good mood. Everything was going well so far, even though the last minute addition of Crowley to our routine had been a little unsettling at first since it hadn't been part of the plan. But really, things weren't all that different with him as part of the group. He had slept on Carolyn's mattress next to her, and once we were upstairs in the house, he used his litter box at the same time that the rest of us were taking turns in the bathrooms. As before, we had to shut off the flow to the faucets to avoid any running water, but we kept the toilets turned on. It was weird getting used to not being able to see myself in the mirror again, but I did quickly enough.

I was eager to go out and kill again, but Susanna insisted that we do something else first. She gathered us in the kitchen, where she spread out a large map of the city on the table. Crowley jumped up and began walking around on it, sniffing and pawing at it until Carolyn picked him up and put him back down onto the floor, prompting a protesting *"mewww"* from him.

Susanna then went on a long spiel about how we were going to carefully plot out where we went to kill each time this summer, not just randomly fly around hoping to find people. This was so we could outmaneuver the police once the bodies started piling up.

That was something else we had decided upon late the previous night, that we weren't going to continue with Susanna's idea of hiding our victims' bodies. She had resisted this when I'd brought it up, but I'd insisted that it was going to be too much trouble, which the others agreed with. So she gave in, admitting that we were probably right. I mentioned this again while we were looking over the map, saying I was glad that we'd decided to do that.

"Yes, I know," Susanna said. "Still, I want us to keep track of things better this time. You can see where I've marked where we killed last night. Here, and here." She pointed to two red marks on the map, which I realized must have been both the bridge where we killed that crazy man and the docks along the river. The map looked strange to me, just a bunch of lines and colors that didn't really mean much. I knew that it was a representation of Augusta, but the scale of it just seemed weird. I was more used to looking at maps of the United States or the entire world, not individual cities. This confused me, but mostly, I was on edge because I wanted to drink.

"So," she continued, "what I'm going to do is mark in pencil where we're headed tonight. Of course, something might change, like we might not find anybody there, or we might kill somewhere else for some other reason. Once we get back, we'll mark on the map with the red pen just where we actually did kill." She scratched a little circle on the map, but I had no idea where in the city it was supposed to represent. I didn't care.

Dennis let out a loud, exaggerated yawn. "Are we done yet?"

Susanna scowled at him. "Fine. Come on."

"That's a high school?" I asked as we approached the imposing brick building.

"Yes," Susanna said, and there was some disdain in her voice.

"Sure doesn't look like yours and Carolyn's!" I said. Their school, which I had been to occasionally over the years, was a one-story, mostly light-colored building, not all that different looking from the school my friends and I had attended. This one was three or four stories high and very darkly colored. It reminded me more of a prison than a school.

"I think it used to be a college," Carolyn said, though I wasn't sure how this was any kind of satisfactory explanation. But I also didn't care. I suddenly got the feeling that there were people nearby, and I looked over to one side and saw that I was right.

"There," Susanna said, then flew in the direction of a large track next to the school. It reminded me quite a bit of the track at the YMCA where we had made our first attack, which suddenly felt like a very long time ago once I thought about it. There was no event happening this night, but there were a few people at various points along the track. They were walking, not running, and I wasn't sure just what it was they were up to.

"Oh," Dennis said. "They're exercising, I guess."

"Yeah," Carl said. "People do that, you know. Walking counts as exercise too."

"Hmm," Tim said, and I could hear a smile in his voice. "Maybe we should help them run instead." He zoomed toward the track, and the rest of us followed, spreading out as we picked our targets.

My meal for the night was a man who was older than the ones I was used to killing. He didn't see me coming, and because of the headphones he was wearing, he didn't hear the screams of the other people on the track as my friends reached them. He just continued walking briskly along the path, oblivious to his surroundings. I had seen this kind of thing before, people exercising to music while wearing their Walkmans, and I always wondered if they might get too distracted by their tapes and accidentally run out into traffic or something. It was a morbid fantasy, one that I probably should have felt guilty for picturing and laughing as I did so, but then, here I was bringing death upon some health-conscious person in quite a different way. The end result was the same.

As I flew up from the man's neck, my appetite satisfied, I noticed that his headphones had slipped off when he had fallen, and a rhythmic, tinny sound was coming from them. Apparently, his Walkman was still going, and I got curious as to what song might be playing, the last song this guy had ever heard. I flew close to the ground and leaned toward the headphones, hearing a faint rendition of "Another One Bites the Dust." I laughed at the odd coincidence, then flew up above the track, looking around as the others finished their meals and headed back into the sky.

Carolyn was gushing over Crowley, proud that he had made his first kill all on his own and without any help from her. When we had been at the school racetrack earlier, there had been seven people there, which matched up to the seven of us. We each talked about the people we had killed and how much we had enjoyed it, and while I had hoped that my story about the song playing on the middle-aged man's headphones would be particularly entertaining, it was cut off by Carl breaking in and bragging about the "hot redhead" he had taken down.

Just as she said she would, Susanna returned to the map on the kitchen table and drew a red dot on it where we had killed. It corresponded to the pencil mark she had made before we left. Tonight at least, we had attacked where she had planned. I looked at the other two spots on the map she had marked earlier, trying to get a sense of where they were.

"Okay, so where are we?" I asked. I said this defiantly, almost trying to imply that this map was useless because it didn't make any sense to me. The scale of everything was just not something I understood.

"Let me see," she said thoughtfully, moving her finger around for a few seconds. "Here." She pointed, and for the first time, I saw exactly where our house was on a map. It still looked weird to me, and it was hard to imagine the structure we were standing in as a place on this jumbled diagram. But I was beginning to get it.

"Oh, okay," Tim said. "I see it now. Wow. I didn't realize how far the school was from…" He trailed off, then pointed again eagerly. "There's my neighborhood!"

"And what's that?" Dennis asked, pointing at a large, strange pattern that looked sort of like a misshapen upside-down triangle.

"That's the airport," Carolyn said. "Not the main one, but…" She was interrupted by Crowley jumping up onto the table, wondering what all the excitement was about. He immediately walked onto the center of the map, sniffing around at where people had been pointing. Carolyn quickly picked him up and plopped him back down onto the floor.

Once I began to understand the map, it was pretty interesting looking over it and picking various things out. For the first time, I was getting a much better sense of how various locations in the city related to each other. Susanna and Carolyn got bored with this after a while, but my friends and I continued to go over the map, finding points of interest like our school, everyone else's houses, the mall, and Lake Olmstead, where we had killed four years earlier.

We were interrupted by Susanna calling to us from the yellow den as she told us that the news was on. Carl jumped up eagerly and ran to the TV, but I was less enthusiastic for some reason. As it turned out, I had good reason to be, as there were no mentions of our attacks whatsoever.

"Well, that was disappointing," Carl said.

"Not necessarily," Susanna said.

"What do you mean? Tim asked. "Do you think there's another cover-up going on?"

"No, not that," she said. "Just that maybe they didn't find the bodies yet, or they aren't reporting on it this early. It doesn't necessarily mean anything."

"Yeah," I said, "and remember, there wasn't really a cover-up last time. That was just your theory. It was because those two vampires were stealing the bodies, so no one ever found them."

"True," she said. "We should check the news again tomorrow morning. When does it come on? Six o'clock?"

I checked the *TV Guide,* and she was right. We realized we would have to set the timer on the VCR for it, though, because that was too close to sunrise.

Shortly afterwards, we watched a program called *The Young Ones,* a British comedy that I had never seen before. At school, Nick had told me about it, and he often quoted lines from the show. Taken out of context, the lines never struck me as all that funny, but really, his doing that was no different from my occasional quoting bits from my favorite comedians. I had spotted the show in the TV listings while looking for the news earlier, and I figured that I might as well give it a chance.

As it turned out, my friends and I all found it funny, as did Carolyn, but Susanna walked out early on. I had always liked British TV, partly because it seemed slightly exotic, these English-speaking but still foreign people with their weird, stuffy accents. They were similar to Americans in some ways, but they were also quite different, using interesting turns of phrase and just seeming overall to be more clever.

What I found particularly interesting about *The Young Ones* was that while I was used to British people being more proper and modest, the guys on this show were completely raunchy and over the top. They would hit each other, shout, and say terrible things, often with swear words, some of which were particular to "Brits," as Carolyn called them. Carl especially liked how the way they said the word "bastard" — and they said it often — sounded like "bah-stid," and he took to saying it that way over the next couple of days.

The show was definitely weird, sometimes so much that it was hard to understand. But something about that was appealing, too. I could certainly see why Nick liked it so much. These crass guys would go off on each other, break things for no good reason, even set things on fire. They reminded me of the Beastie Boys as well, whom I liked not only for their silliness but also their immaturity and recklessness.

By the time the show was over, I continued to think about Nick, and it occurred to me that it would have been cool to include him in our vampire group after all. But I suppressed that thought very quickly. This was supposed to be a reunion, and he hadn't been one of us before. Besides, the last time I brought someone into the group halfway through, we wound up splitting up. I definitely didn't want that to happen again.

Overall, the group got along well. In the beginning, we all hung out together, but as time went on, we tended to split off from each other more often. Sometimes it was just necessary to take a break from each other, but only for a little while. Carolyn, for example, occasionally sat on the roof of the house with Crowley, talking to him about what was on her mind. She wasn't, as far as I knew, aware that I also snuck up there and listened in sometimes, hiding on the other side of the chimney as a bat. Late Sunday night, after we had gotten back from exploring the abandoned Veteran Administrations Hospital, was one of the times I spied on her.

At first, she was quiet, letting out a sigh as she leaned back and stroked Crowley, who began purring. I couldn't actually see her from where I was, but I could picture the two of them. "So," she said softly, "having fun?" Crowley meowed. "Yeah, me too, I think. It's just… I don't know. This whole vampire thing is kind of weird. I mean, I guess I like it, but part of me doesn't want to." Crowley meowed again, this time more high pitched and drawn out, like he was asking a question. I knew deep down that he was just a cat and couldn't really speak or even understand what was being said, but he often seemed to. It was one of the things we liked about him.

"I like the special powers and all, the flying around and being strong and all that. But the killing…" She trailed off, remaining silent for a while. Crowley mewed a couple of times in the interim. "Yeah, okay, so maybe I do get off on it a little." I didn't know what that meant. "Really, I just miss Damon. I hope he's doing okay."

She talked a little more about him, and while I liked listening in on her, part of me felt a little guilty. But I was also amused because it was something I could get away with. But this was something that went way back with us, sneaking around and spying and such. It had started when I was in third grade, when she, Susanna, and my mother all watched the same soap opera. On it, one of the ongoing storylines involved this secret ring of spies, which led Carolyn to rope me into an ongoing game in which she and I pretended to be spies as well. She was in fact the first person to teach me the word for what I was doing right at the moment, eavesdropping, though for the longest time, I thought the word was "easedropping."

Some of this came into play in my life at school, too, and it was an integral part of the Club Wars. One of the things we liked to do was try to spy on each other, and I was particularly good at sneaking up on the place where Carl's group gathered, hoping to listen in on their plans. My friends and I also secretly passed notes to each other, either between classes or during them, almost always doing so without getting caught by our teachers. It was considered a big accomplishment to intercept a note from someone in the enemy club. I usually signed my notes *RAY* in all capitals, which I thought was cool because not only was that my name, but my initials.

There was also the added layer of secrecy between me and Dennis, the psychic powers that we didn't let anyone else know about. When he and I were alone in my bedroom later this same night, we talked about that some, though it started out as a conversation about something else. When we had been looking over the map earlier in the night and were pointing out various places, Dennis had spotted an area that he and Tim had ended up the night they had split off from the rest of us in 1985. We talked about this a little more, which led to how he and Tim had ended up rescuing us from the other vampires.

"Thank God you did," I said. "I still shudder when I think about what might have happened to us if you didn't."

"Yeah, well," he said. "Just glad we got there when we did."

"It's pretty amazing, though, how the two of you managed to sneak up on us, or them, I mean."

"Hmm?"

"Well, those two, what were their names… Robert and Jennifer. They were way more psychic than you and me. Really, really powerful. All they had to do was just look at us, and we were under their control. We couldn't move or anything."

"Yeah, I picked up on that," he said, something smug in his tone.

"No, what I mean is that if they were that psychic and all, it's just surprising that they didn't sense that you and Tim were coming.

Maybe it was because they were all kind of locked onto us mentally, sort of zoned out or something, not being able to see anything else. That's sure how I felt, I know." Dennis smiled at me knowingly, then waggled his eyebrows up and down, the gesture he did whenever he was indicating something to do with our psychic powers. "What?"

"Well, maybe." He looked down, then back up at me. "What I was doing at the time was trying to cloak us. Make us seem invisible. You know, like Mirage." He bent his arms at the elbows and held them close to his body, and I immediately knew what he was referring to: a character in the cartoon *The Transformers* who could turn himself invisible while making that same gesture. In my head, I heard the sound effect that accompanied this.

Dennis and I had both been fans of this show in sixth grade. It featured lots of robots who, in addition to their ability to change into cars, planes, and other machines, also had various unique traits, like Mirage's talent for turning invisible. As had started to be the case with many cartoons at the time, there was an accompanying line of action figures, which he and I also collected. I was aware of the criticism adults had of shows like this, calling them "half hour long toy commercials," but I never saw them that way. I genuinely liked the stories, the way everything was wrapped up by the end, everything very episodic and comforting. Even more exciting were the cliffhangers, the two-part stories that would end in the middle, usually on a scary note.

By this point in our lives, the show and the toys were considered childish by some of our classmates, so we mostly kept our interest in them to ourselves and a handful of others who were also into it. By seventh grade, any admission to being interested in Transformers was considered worthy of ridicule and a straight road to unpopularity, so Dennis and pretty much everyone else disavowed any liking of the franchise altogether. I did so as well, even though I secretly still liked to watch the show. One thing I especially liked was that most of the evil characters, the Decepticons, transformed from people-looking robots into jets and then flew around, which reminded me of our times as vampires when we could change into bats and fly. Also, as had been the case with most of the cartoons I liked when I was growing up, the bad guys were always more interesting and fun to watch than the noble, more boring good guys.

However, Dennis's revelation during this conversation — that he had somehow made himself and Tim invisible when they rescued us — seemed like too much of a stretch. Before I had a chance to say so, he elaborated: "I don't mean that we couldn't be seen. Just that I, you know, kind of shrouded us. Like, mentally. So they wouldn't notice us." He shrugged, seeming to doubt himself.

"No, I get it," I said. "I sometimes did that same thing when I was trying to sneak up on Carl and his group during the Club Wars. Like, I knew I wasn't physically unable to be seen, but if I could sort of cloak myself from their minds, then they might not think to look over at me."

"Exactly." He laughed a little and smiled. "In fact, I did the same thing just last night when we were down by the river."

"Really?"

He went on to explain that while the rest of us were attacking the people on that boat, he had spotted another man farther inland, whom he tried to sneak up on. "I did the same thing, picturing myself as invisible, willing the man not to see me or notice I was there. It seemed to work. And then, before he knew what hit him, I was on his neck." I got a small thrill picturing this, and I made a mental note to try to do the same thing soon.

I wanted to ask him if his powers had increased now that we were vampires, which mine certainly seemed to have done. Because our powers were secret, this wasn't something I could ask Susanna about, but I'd begun to suspect that not only had this new potion given us all these cool extra abilities that she had planned out for us, it had also given our psychic powers a boost. That would make sense, especially if being vampires had been why Robert and Jennifer were so psychically powerful.

Before I could put this idea to Dennis, Tim knocked on my door, telling us that it was almost time for sunrise, and we needed to get down to the basement. That was in fact the reason I had gone to my room in the first place, to get some sweat pants to sleep in before we all went down there.

Monday night, we scanned through the videotaped broadcasts of that morning's and evening's news, and we were pleased to find that once again, people were beginning to take notice of our attacks. The seven bodies we had left on the racetrack at Copeland High School had been found drained of blood, and no one was sure just what had happened. We were secretly notorious again, and we loved it.

Susanna surprised us by plotting out on the map that we would attack very near to the same spot this night. I had thought that her plan would be for us to go to very disparate places around the city to avoid detection. Instead, we found ourselves above the parking lot of a Chinese restaurant right down the street from that high school, where most of the group found fresh victims. I wasn't sure why we were killing somewhere so close to where we had been the night before, but when I questioned Susanna about this, all she said was, "Trust me."

I gave her the benefit of the doubt, not having much choice. Everyone else went along with her plan, so I had no reason not to. However, since there were only six people to prey upon in the parking lot, I took this as an opportunity to go off on my own.

"I think I saw someone a little further up the road," I told Susanna before she and the others descended on their prey, but this was a lie. I had not in fact seen anyone, but I wanted to find someone away from the group, to see if I could repeat the thing Dennis and I had talked about, cloaking myself so I could sneak up on them.

As I flew away, hearing a few screams and knowing that my friends and sisters were successfully getting their dinners, I smiled. Or at least, I smiled mentally, wondering for a moment if my bat form was even capable of doing that. Before I could ponder this further,

I sensed that a woman was somewhere nearby on one of the streets below, on the way to her car and getting her keys from her purse.

Soon after, I spotted a woman outside of a boxy, light blue colored car parked on the side of the road in a neighborhood a couple of blocks from the restaurant. As I flew nearer to her, I thought to myself, *Drop it.*

The woman dropped her keys as she was starting to put them into the door of her car, then cursed quietly. As she bent down to pick them up, I landed nearby, transforming into my person form. She didn't notice me.

I walked closer to her, slowly, all the time willing her not to see me. It seemed to work; she had picked her keys back up and was turning them in the door of her car, then opening it. If I didn't act quickly, she might get away.

I shot out a mental command to her, trying to get her to stand still. She did, just standing there with her car door open, not moving. I felt a thrill pass through me. Was this really happening? Could I do this to someone?

I crept closer, mentally telling the woman to turn around. I wanted her to face me as I killed her. Once she saw me, she jumped, startled. I made my eyes glow and my fangs grow, and she started to move back towards her car. *Be still,* I said in my mind. She seemed to relax, her arm drooping slightly. While she had looked terrified before, she began to look more serene, or maybe thoughtful. I liked having this much control over her, and I involuntarily smiled, walking slowly toward her.

Once I was almost upon her, she quickly reached into her purse, presumably for some kind of weapon, so I leapt up onto her and sunk my fangs into her neck. She slid down along the side of the car as I drank from her viciously, more violent than I was used to being. I was mad that my powers hadn't worked on her as effectively as I'd hoped, plus a glance off to one side once we were on the pavement revealed a small can of Mace rolling from her hand. Had I been just a little bit slower, she might have managed to catch me with that. I resented her, and I enjoyed the fact that I had still conquered her.

After finishing, I stood up and looked down at her drained body. Although my hunger was satisfied, I felt a little strange. I was glad that things had gone my way, even if not completely, but something was nagging at me. While part of me was disappointed that I hadn't been able to mentally control this woman completely, I knew that I had been at least partly successful. And something about that bugged me, but I wasn't sure why. It felt kind of like cheating, or at least, very different from the way I was used to killing. In the past, our kills had always been based around stealth or physically overpowering the person, sometimes both. Mentally controlling someone had felt weird, even though I'd thought I would like it.

At home, I considered telling Dennis about how all of that had gone, but I chose not to for some reason. It was easier to just go along with everyone else in conversation, to act like my kill had been as routine as all of theirs had been.

I asked Susanna why we had attacked so close to the high school this night, adding, "I thought we were supposed to be spreading things out so the police won't be able to track us." I had in fact spotted a couple of police cars in the neighborhood before we had left, but we never saw any actual policemen.

"Oh, we will," she said, "starting tomorrow night. This way, they'll think that all of the killings are being done in that small area, so tomorrow, we can go somewhere completely different and not have to worry about them."

"Oh, that makes sense," Tim said, then smiled. "Good plan."

"Thank you," Susanna said, smiling slyly.

Our attacks in that area had been more plentiful than expected, too, because once I rejoined the group in the sky above the Chinese restaurant, we had spotted a small group of people on the roof of a bar across the street. I hadn't even realized that it was a bar until

Carolyn pointed it out to me; it looked more like a house. But Carolyn explained that it was a popular place, that Damon and his band had played there a few times. I had heard loud music coming from the building, presumably another band doing their thing.

But what was interesting was the group of four people, three guys and one girl, who were on the roof and apparently trying to break into a room on the top floor. I found something about this endearing, perhaps admirable. They were delinquents, and so were we. They were in the middle of some complex move, two of the guys holding up a smaller one as they maneuvered him sideways through a gap in the window while the girl looked on, urging them to be careful.

The situation looked kind of amusing, so we couldn't resist descending upon them and attacking. Carolyn and Susanna took down the onlooking woman, which distracted the two men, who then dropped the guy they were trying to squeeze through the window. They were then killed by me and Dennis, and as I drank from my prey's neck, I heard Carl say, "Ew, gross!" He might have been referring to the other man, the one who had crashed through the lower half of the window when he had been dropped, but I barely cared. I was too busy drinking.

After I flew up from the body of the young man I had killed, I saw that Carl and Tim had finished off the guy from the window, who had been badly injured even before they had gotten to him. Crowley, meanwhile, was sipping on the ankle of the girl Carolyn and Susanna had gotten.

So we had definitely concentrated our kills in a small spot, including what we had done the night before. If Susanna was right, police would be all over this one neighborhood, leaving us to go anywhere we wanted the following evening.

Things seemed be going according to plan, at least initially. We went out and killed some people far from the previous night's location, close to Susanna and Carolyn's former high school. Back home, we checked the tape of that morning's news, which revealed that there was indeed a concentrated effort on the police's part to focus on the area near Copeland High.

A little later on, we watched the 11:00 news, which went into more detail, plus there was some speculation about possible vampire activity, but the reporters were very cautious about this. Nothing was said yet about our attack near Westlake High School, though there would be the following night. One thing surprised us: There was a handful of killings in another part of the city, and not very far from our house.

"Several bodies were also found in the Waverly Heights area earlier today," the reporter said, her brow furrowed and lips pursed, "but mostly those of animals, not people. However, the body of one young woman, whose name is being withheld pending notification of family, was found near an apartment building this morning. The animals, who appear to have been killed in a similar fashion, included a cat, a small dog, and several birds."

The screen cut to a police officer being interviewed who said pretty much the same thing the reporter had just said, but he added, "The coroner whom I spoke to noted that the wounds on young lady's neck appeared to be caused by an animal. It's our belief that whatever is doing all of this is either one or perhaps a series of rabid animals, not something ridiculous like vampires or what-have-you." He said this last sentence with a sneer, and I was annoyed at how cocky he acted.

The report finished up, and the program moved on to other stories. Tim fast-forwarded through the rest of the show, and there were no other mentions of vampire activity.

"Okay," Carl said once the tape was done. "So... um... What's that all about?"

"Yeah!" Tim said. "Other killings?"

"Does that mean there are other vampires again?" I asked.

"I'm not sure," Susanna said, looking concerned. She got up from the couch and went into the kitchen, looking at the map. She went over it with her red pen, then made a few marks. The rest of us joined her. I saw where she had marked a few spots where these mysterious killings were being made, and it was disturbing how close they were to our house. I was still getting used to the perspective of everything, how an inch on paper could in fact be several neighborhoods away, but these new red dots looked practically next door when compared to the other ones.

"As close as that is," Dennis said, "it's almost like…" I picked up on his thought, either telepathically or just by coming to the same conclusion.

"Like someone here could have done it," I said. "Has anyone been sneaking out on their own?" I looked around at everyone else, and they all seemed shocked at the suggestion.

"What?" Carl said. "No! I mean, I haven't!"

"Me neither," Tim said simply.

"I think I know," Carolyn said, her eyebrows raised and her head turning slowly toward the den. Crowley was sitting in there, looking off in no particular direction, but he was also looking over his shoulder at us periodically.

"What do you mean?" Carl asked. "Was it you?"

"No," she said, walking slowly toward the den. "Definitely not me." Her voice became more stern. I had heard her use this tone before, plus I had found myself using it on occasion. It was the voice we used when scolding Crowley, who had an uncanny knack for knowing when he was doing something wrong. When he was attempting something forbidden, like trying to sneak and jump up on something he wasn't allowed to, he would get a certain look, simultaneously avoiding eye contact while checking to see if we were watching him.

"You were gone for a long time last night, weren't you?" Carolyn said in her same scolding tone, reaching down and picking Crowley up. He started to run from her as she did, but as she caught him, he meowed at her pitifully. "And I thought you were just hiding again."

Crowley, like any cat, sometimes hid somewhere in the house for extended periods, so none of us thought anything of it. But once Carolyn said that, I realized that there had been a long stretch of time the previous night in which I hadn't seen him. Very quickly, we realized what had happened.

"Okay, that is not cool," Susanna said firmly. "We can't have him going off on his own and killing people."

"She's right, Carolyn," I said, then shrunk back from the angry look she shot at me. She was holding Crowley and scratching him under his chin, and he was purring away, acting like everything was normal. "I mean, if he does that, it messes up the thing about trying to spread our attacks out."

"Yeah," Dennis said. "He could end up leading the police right to us if we're not careful."

"You hear that?" Carolyn said to Crowley, who looked up at her and mewed again. She placed him back down onto the floor. He looked up at her as she continued, "You can't go out on your own again. It's not safe." He meowed at her once more, this time sounding more perturbed. "I mean it."

"Oh, come on," Carl said. "It's not like he understands English!"

"You'd be surprised," I said.

"Look, we can't have this kind of a liability," Susanna said. "He could end up exposing us."

"So what do you suggest we do?" Carolyn asked, then realized the answer. "Oh, no, give him a chance. We don't have to give him the cure. Let him have his fun!"

I could see it both ways. On the one hand, it wasn't a good idea to let him continue being a vampire if he was going to sneak out on his own and put the rest of us at risk. But it also seemed cruel to take the abilities away from him so quickly. I liked having him as truly part of the group, and I knew that the others did, too.

Carolyn knelt down to where Crowley was sitting. "Crowley, I'm serious. You cannot go out by yourself again. It's dangerous for all of us. Do you understand me?" He meowed in what sounded like agreement.

"Bullshit," Carl muttered, then clammed up when Carolyn looked up at him, her eyes lighting up with a harsh yellow glow for a split second. "Fine, fine," he said, putting his hands up.

Oddly enough, Crowley never did go out on his own again. Maybe he understood Carolyn's admonitions, or maybe he just decided not to do it for his own reasons. It was hard to tell how sentient he really was, how much he was actually capable of understanding. But as the next couple of nights went by, there were no more reports in the news of extraneous attacks. We continued to plot out our kills on the map and outmaneuver the police, and Susanna even admitted that Crowley's excursion had helped confuse things even more, maybe convincing people that animals, not people, were responsible for these deaths. Everything that happened was our doing, and we continued to get away with it, enjoying the power and the rush of the experience.

Things threatened to get complicated, though, when Tim's parents called our house, wanting him to come home early. They were concerned about what they had seen on the news, afraid that their son might be in danger. A quick phone call from Susanna was all it took to dissuade their fears, but there was an extra element to this that Susanna was, as far as I knew, unaware of.

When she called Tim's mother back (she had left a message during the day while we were asleep), Dennis and I went to my parents' room, where I listened in on the other phone. I kept quiet, but throughout the conversation, I used my psychic powers to help persuade Tim's mother to listen to what Susanna was saying. She did her best to convince her that we were safe and that everything would be fine, asking that Tim be allowed to stay since he was having such a good time with us. She emphasized that he and the other children were not without adult supervision; after all, both she and Carolyn were of age. All the while, I concentrated, feeling the familiar weird tingling in my scalp as I did my best to beam my thoughts over the phone line. Dennis also seemed to be doing the same, though he wasn't able to hear the conversation.

Tim's mother relented quickly, suddenly changing her tone from concern to embarrassment, saying that she had been overreacting and too swept up by the local news probably making a big deal out of nothing. Tim was allowed to stay.

We hadn't had an answering machine when we first got together as vampires in 1983, but we did have one by 1985. Both that year and this one, my own parents had left messages letting us know how they were during their trip. This year, they didn't even realize that Susanna was staying with us this entire time; she had lied to them about wanting to stay in Charleston instead. They had suggested, though not insisted, that she still come for a brief visit to Augusta to check in on Carolyn and me. What Susanna ended up doing on Wednesday night was calling them herself, letting them know that she had indeed stopped by and that everything was fine. Carolyn and I also spoke to them briefly, pretending that we were tired because it was so late at night in our time zone.

In private, Dennis and I talked about our powers, how we used them to try to manipulate the thoughts of others and how well it seemed to be working. I told him about my only partly successful attempt at controlling that woman the other night near the Chinese restaurant, and he admitted to trying the same thing, but with only limited success.

"It was like it kind of worked, but not really," he said. "I think I at least disoriented the guy, but it wasn't like I could just make him stand still like a zombie or anything."

"Yeah, that's what I was hoping for when I tried it," I said. "Remember what Carl said about our glowing eyes being hypnotic? Something like that."

"Yeah, he already mentioned that the other night."

"Huh?"

"I mean, he said he tried it. But it didn't work. Instead it just freaked the person out even more before he killed them."

I laughed at the thought of this, some victim of Carl's panicking as he advanced, eyes glowing and fangs bared. I acted it out, pointing and making silly, scared noises, which made Dennis laugh. Then I became more serious. "But aside from that, have your powers seemed stronger since we became vampires? Just in general, I mean?"

"Oh yeah, definitely," he said. "Certainly a lot cooler."

"I wish they could be stronger, though," I said. "Like as strong as those other vampires had a couple of years ago."

"Quick!" the harshly whispered word came from behind me. I had been so intent on watching what was happening in front of me that I hadn't even noticed that the woman had snuck up. I was irritated, both at how she had managed to do this and at how much I had jumped.

"Sorry," the woman whispered, kneeling down and reaching out to me. "I didn't mean to scare you. It's okay." She was a policewoman, I quickly realized, and my first instinct was to lunge at her, but I thought twice when I spotted the gun in her holster.

I had been hiding in some bushes beside the street, watching as Susanna, Carolyn, and Carl attacked a small group of people. Nearby, the other vampires were hiding as well, and our plan was to pick off the ones who escaped the initial assault. But this woman seemed to think that I was hiding for a different reason.

"It's not safe here!" she continued. Her manner seemed to be a combination of trying to comfort me and conveying a sense of urgency.

"I know," I said, smiling and baring my fangs. As I did, everything took on a yellowish hue as my eyes lit up, and the woman's own eyes went wide as she realized what was happening. She started to stand up, but I reached out with my mind, willing her to stay where she was.

As I crept closer to her, I either felt or just inferred that she was trying to struggle against my mental hold, so I concentrated more. I was still aware of her gun, wondering if she might suddenly reach for it, but she didn't.

A look of sadness washed over her face, and she began to stammer. "But… but…"

I moved in closer, slowly drawing toward her neck.

"You're just a *child!*" The last word was said with both amazement and sorrow.

As always, I loved the taste, the smell, the power. The woman let out a few whimpers as I drained her life away, soon going limp beneath me until she was dead. Once I was done, I stood up and looked down at her body. Part of me felt proud, glad that I had finally been able to use my psychic powers to subdue someone like I'd hoped to. I wasn't sure why it had worked this time and not a few nights earlier, and I wondered if maybe my ability to control varied from person to person.

I also wasn't sure if I liked it or not. The kill had been satisfying, but I felt a bit silly, figuring that it probably would have been easier just to take the woman down quickly and simply, not go through the complicated process of trying to clamp down on her mind first. Then another thought pushed this one aside, a more angry one.

"I am *not* a child," I said to her, then went off to join the others.

Later, I told Dennis about my success, and he was intrigued. He also seemed annoyed with how I had been able to control someone so powerfully while he wasn't able to, but he didn't come out and say so.

"Don't worry," I said. "I can teach you how to do it. It's just a matter of concentration and control."

"Well, I thought I had a good enough handle on that already," he said, again barely hiding his resentment.

"You can do it!" I assured him. "You just need more practice."

"Maybe. But then, maybe it's different from person to person. Like, some people are more vulnerable to our powers than others."

I started to tell him that I had been thinking the same thing earlier, but I was interrupted by an urgent call from the yellow den. Carl was shouting, "You guys! Come in here, quick!"

It sounded important, so Dennis and I joined the others in the room, nearly bumping into Carolyn as she and Crowley came up the hall from her bedroom. I also almost tripped over Crowley as he stepped between my feet.

"This could be some serious shit, guys," Carl said, pointing at the TV. On it was a frozen image of a news reporter, the videotape of that night's news broadcast having been put on pause while everyone gathered to see what the big deal was.

I involuntarily laughed at the picture on the screen, as the normally composed and professional newsman had been caught in the middle of speaking, his eyes half-closed and his mouth hanging open stupidly.

Dennis also laughed, pointing at the screen like Carl had done. "Oh my God! This *is* serious! Britt Henson is retarded!"

Susanna cut us off, telling Carl to "un-pause" the tape. She looked angry, which made me wonder if there really was something important going on.

The picture unfroze, and it took half a second for the sound to kick in. "…itt Henson for Channel Four Action News. While reports of vampires have been flapping up lately…"

Carolyn immediately broke out into fake laughter, which caused Crowley to run from her and into the kitchen, startled by such a loud outburst. This wasn't her fake social laugh, though; she did this particular one to make fun of corny things. She had used it on me several times in the past, and the effect was diminishing, that is, whenever I said something that I thought was funny and she instead thought it was stupid, her exaggerated laugh immediately made me feel like an idiot. I had adopted this technique from her, sometimes using it on teachers at school when they tried to be clever and I wanted to take them down a notch. For a while, my classmates found this funny, but once I did it too many times, people got tired of it, especially the teachers.

Susanna was also not amused, and after Carolyn's performance and my own genuine laughing had run their course, she said, "Carl, rewind it again. And you guys shut up for once."

This angered me, but I let her have her way. The videotape silently wound back for a few seconds in fast motion while covered with bars of static, then jerked back to almost the same spot where Carl had started it before.

"…apping up lately," the newscaster repeated, "speculation still runs high as to the true nature of these mysterious deaths in the greater Augusta area. While some maintain that vampires are indeed the cause, the official word from authorities is that some as yet unknown animals are to blame."

"Blah blah blah," I said, which prompted a harsh shush from Susanna.

"However, one man who plans to visit the Garden City has other ideas." I never understood why Augusta was sometimes referred to as "The Garden City." If Augusta was known for anything, it was golf and the yearly Masters tournament, not gardens. Neither topic interested me. In fact, my friends, family, and I were all pretty cynical about the Masters, seeing it as an aggravating annual occurrence in which tons of tourists came from out of town to clog up the city and make traffic unbearable. Local businesses would start airing ads aimed at strangers, alienating those of us who had lived here all our lives. It was like the city, or at least those in charge of it, put on a mask every spring and tried to make things seem more impressive than they actually were. Once the golf tournament was over and everyone left town, things went back to normal.

"A self proclaimed 'vampire hunter' has expressed interest in the recent happenings around the city," the reporter continued. "Alexander Shelling, who contacted Channel Four Action News earlier today, says he wishes to, quote: 'rid this city of the foul creatures which have beset it.'"

The screen cut to a still image of a large tape recorder, one of those old-fashioned ones with the big metal reels on it. I was used to smaller cassette players and stereos like the ones my sisters and I owned, but I had seen this other kind on TV. A caption in yellow letters at the bottom of the screen read: *voice of ALEXANDER SHELLING (recorded earlier).*

The voice was slightly distorted, apparently a recording of a telephone conversation, but that wasn't the only thing that made it hard to understand. The man speaking had some kind of foreign accent, but it wasn't one I was familiar with. "I come to Augusta," the man said slowly, "because it interest me. If there indeed be vampires at work in your fair city, I pledge to do all that can be to destroy this threat. I arrive by the plane tomorrow and will start my work at once."

The reporter was then shown again, and he added, "No word yet on whether Mr. Shelling will be aiding the police in their efforts. Be sure to tune in tomorrow evening to Channel Four Action News at Six, where our own Walter Rhodes will have an exclusive interview with Mr. Shelling." There was something flippant in Britt Henson's attitude, and I felt the same way.

"Okay, what is up with that guy's accent?" I asked the group with a smile. I then tried to do my best impression of him: "I arrive by dee plane and do all that can be!" I expected a big laugh, but none came.

"Ray, this could be a problem," Susanna said. "Just because the guy has an accent doesn't mean he's stupid."

"Or maybe it's nothing!" I said. "Just some crazy guy who thinks he can stop us. What makes him so special?"

"Well, he's a vampire hunter, for one thing," Carolyn said. "Maybe he really knows his stuff."

I still didn't want to believe it. "Yeah, or maybe not!" I meant to follow that up with something more clever, but nothing came to mind.

"So what do we do?" Tim asked. "Just hide out and hope he doesn't find us?"

"Nah, I say we take the fight to him!" Carl said. "We can take his stupid ass down. We've been through worse. And hey, we're famous now! Enough that someone from out of town wants to come visit!"

"And that's a good thing?" Tim asked rhetorically.

The conversation went back and forth for a long time, and the more we talked, the more worried everyone got, including me. Even though we knew next to nothing about this mysterious man apart from his name, his weird way of speaking, and that he was a vampire hunter, it didn't take long for our imaginations to build him up into a serious threat. The turning point for me was when I tried to encourage everyone that this wasn't a big issue because we had gone up against a hunter before and come out of it just fine.

"Oh, really?" Carolyn asked angrily. "If I recall correctly, that guy chased us away three or four times with his gun, and we never managed to get the better of him. It was those other two vampires who ended up killing him, Robert and… what's-her-name." My heart sank as I realized she was right.

"Yeah, and that guy wasn't even a vampire hunter, just a regular hunter!" Tim said. "This Alexander Shelling guy probably has all kinds of vampire-specific weaponry, like crossbows with wooden stakes in them, or…"

"Maybe garlic bullets!" Dennis offered.

"Don't get carried away," Susanna said. She then threw up her arms, saying, "And maybe Ray's right! Maybe he is just some quack who doesn't know anything."

Dennis let out a quiet *"quack"* sound effect, and I fought back a laugh despite myself.

As the night went on, we got ourselves more worked up, alternating between thinking that this wasn't that big of a deal and that this man's upcoming visit was a major problem. The more we talked about the subject, the less I liked it, and in time, we splintered off and tried to busy ourselves with other things. Eventually, I ended up on the roof with Carolyn and Crowley, but this time, I sat with them instead of hiding and eavesdropping.

"Do you really think we need to be worried?" I asked her.

She sighed. "I don't know. Maybe. Like Susanna said, maybe he's a threat; maybe he isn't. It's the whole not knowing thing that bugs me."

"Yeah, me too." There was silence, and I reached down and petted Crowley, who rubbed his head up against my hand. "I'd feel better if we had some kind of plan." I began thinking about the big, intricate one that we drew up before to attack the "Vampire Killers" family, then tried to shove the thought down when I was reminded of the earlier conversation. That had just been a family of country bumpkins, and we hadn't managed to kill them, so what hope did we have against a professional vampire hunter? I suddenly had a very clear memory of the terrifyingly loud blasts from that other hunter's shotgun, and I shook my head, trying to somehow erase the thoughts.

"You okay?" Carolyn asked.

"Kind of." I was feeling more scared than I wanted to admit.

"Well, look," she said, sounding more sympathetic than I was used to. "I think the best we can do is just calm down for tonight. We'll set the timer for the news and watch it when we get up tomorrow, then figure it out from there. I mean, Carl's probably right. We've been through worse shit than this, right?"

I smiled. "Was that an exact quote?"

She laughed. "Might as well be." We sat silently for a little while, looking up at the night sky. It seemed peaceful enough, but once I noticed that, a feeling of anxiety started to creep up in me again, this notion that something bad was coming.

We talked for a little while longer, but I began to get distracted by another idea, one that I couldn't tell her about. I wondered about my powers, how they seemed to have been getting stronger lately, and if they might be an effective weapon against this new menace.

"That's an idea," Dennis said. After I had left Carolyn and Crowley on the roof and joined the others inside, it took a while to get Dennis alone so I could talk to him about this. Finally, we had gone down to the basement together, pretending that we needed to check on something. "Especially if we both go after him at once. Mentally, I mean."

"Hmm?"

"Well, I saw on this show one time how these psychic people ended up being more powerful if they sort of combined their powers, like focused on the same thing. Somehow it makes them stronger. There was a special name for it, but I can't remember what it was."

"That's cool," I said, wondering if this might work. I pictured the two of us bearing down on the vampire hunter, who in my mind now resembled some jungle warrior with lots of weapons strapped to his body. We could concentrate our powers, eyes glowing and all, and maybe cripple him so he couldn't resist us. That way, killing him wouldn't be difficult at all.

As everyone went to bed at the end of the night, I found comfort in this, hoping that we really would have the advantage over this guy after all. I was still worried, but I did my best not to be. I ran over various scenarios in my head, trying to suppress the more unsettling ones, like when I pictured him finding us at the house and killing us with wooden stakes. In order to get to sleep, I had to fantasize instead that Dennis and I were able to subdue him with our powers, we were able to attack and kill him successfully, and everything turned out okay.

"Walter Rhodes, on location for Channel Four Action News."

I hated this guy. He was the station's "man on the street" reporter, which for some reason seemed to give him a kind of special status, but for the most part, he was just annoying. Slightly overweight and with a pinched face fixed in an arrogant expression, he looked, as Carl described him, "like he's always in the middle of taking a dump." Worst of all was his voice, this shrill, nasally drone that was about as pleasant as listening to fingernails scraping down a chalkboard while getting one's teeth drilled. The attitude he tried to convey was one of superiority and wry humor, but really, he just seemed like a jerk. I had seen him on TV from time to time over the years, and he was so intolerable that I usually had to turn the station whenever his fat, goofy face popped up on the screen. Unfortunately, we had to watch him this time and sit through his interview with our newest nemesis.

"I'm here with Professor Alexander Shelling," Rhodes screeched on, "self-proclaimed vampire hunter and scholar."

The camera pulled back to reveal Shelling, slowly framing the two men as they spoke to each other, while Rhodes held his microphone and turned away from the camera to face his latest subject. The fact that the "roving reporter" was interviewing him was telling, I realized. Almost always, Walter Rhodes interviewed strange people around Augusta and its outlying rural areas, usually quirky, weird people. Carolyn explained to me once that these were called "human interest stories," but she also joked that they were really "nobody gives a crap stories" or "slow news day stories." I remembered an interview he did a year or so earlier with a woman who raised and kept pet squirrels after they fell out of their mothers' nests as babies, plus another story about a man who rode his lawnmower to work, claiming it saved him gas money.

Recalling all of this as soon as Whiny Roads (as I liked to call him) showed up on screen made me relax for a moment, thinking that this supposed vampire hunter was probably nothing of the sort, just some nobody who wanted attention and managed to get some on-air time. That feeling was reinforced when I saw how old this Shelling character was; he wasn't some fierce warrior-looking type, but what looked at first like some cranky old man. He had a weird haircut that was brushed back from his forehead, a strange mix of grey hair with streaks of red. He also had a big, beak-like nose and tightly pursed lips.

"Mr. Shelling," Rhodes began, only to be cut off almost at once.

"*Doctor* Shelling," the man said impatiently, his wide eyes suddenly narrowing. Something about him reminded me of a vulture.

"Excuse me, *Doctor* Shelling," Rhodes said, but he over-emphasized the word "doctor" in such a way that suggested condescension rather than respect. "I take it that you believe in vampires."

"Of course I believe," he said, still sounding tetchy. "Why else would I be the one to hunt them?" His voice was more clear in this live interview than it had been on the previous night's recording, and I again wondered about his accent. It wasn't British; I had gotten pretty good at spotting that early on in life, but I still sometimes confused English or Scottish accents with Australian ones. I had occasionally heard French and German characters speak on various TV shows as well and could recognize them, but this guy sounded altogether different.

"Of course, of course," Rhodes continued. "And how many vampires have you hunted?"

"Oh, many." For the first time, Shelling smiled, giving a sort of dismissive gesture.

At that moment, some guy appeared in the side of the frame, shouting, "Hi, Mom!" He was quickly rushed away by someone else, presumably one of the camera crew.

"God, I hate it when people do that," Carolyn said. "'Hi, Mom!' It's what everyone says when they see a camera, and they think they're so damn funny."

Susanna shushed her, as by then, Rhodes had recovered from the interruption and was continuing to interview Shelling. "Many, you say. Could you be more specific? And am I correct in assuming that these were in Europe, where you're from?"

Shelling's eyes narrowed again, and his massive eyebrows seemed to scrunch together into one huge eyebrow. "You may well assume, dear boy. But I do not speak of my exact exploit over many years. Yes, you may think that I say this because I not speak the truth. But you will be wrong." He pointed as he said this, reminding me of someone's grandfather speaking to an ignorant child. The more he spoke, the more uncertain I was about him. He may have been old and had a funny way of talking, but he was starting to come across as a little frightening.

Walter Rhodes, meanwhile, seemed oblivious to this. "I have to say, Dr. Shelling, that I'm not entirely convinced. You have stated that you've come to Augusta to take care of its supposed vampire problem, but if you can't provide proof of your credentials…"

"You think I jest?" Shelling barked at him. For once, Rhodes looked taken aback. "I do not. I hunt the vampire, I kill him. Even if you do not take him seriously, know that I do my work, whether you believe or not. This is serious problem, and I solve it."

"You say 'him,'" Rhodes said. "Do you think that the killings in this town are being done by one man?"

"No, I do not. When I say him, I mean it as a… how do you say… expression. The sheer number of killing suggest that it is more than one. One or many, it matters not."

"Well, I must say that you sound very sure of yourself, mister… I mean, Dr. Shelling."

"Aye, and with good reason. I once destroy a group of four vampires at once. And no, before you ask, I cannot tell you just how. My method must be concealed. But if any vampire watches us now as we speak, I say to him, be warned." He glanced at the camera.

I suddenly felt very cold. Despite my contempt for Walter Rhodes and how I liked seeing someone tell him off, I was not enjoying this one bit. Shelling, even though he was nothing like what I expected, was turning out to be very intimidating nonetheless. Even through his muddled accent, he sounded like he knew what he was talking about.

"Words of wisdom, no doubt," Rhodes said, still sounding sarcastic. "I wish you the best in your search, Professor Shelling." He then turned to the camera and concluded the interview, signing off in his usual arrogant manner.

Once it became clear that nothing else was going to be said about vampires, Susanna said, "Okay, Carl, you can turn it down now. Carolyn, did you recognize it?"

"Yep," she said. "That was Washington Road in the background. I recognized the view from the parking lot."

"Which hotel?" Susanna asked.

"Westchester Suites."

"You could tell that from that interview?" Dennis asked.

"Certainly," she said, looking proud of herself. "I've been there before."

I had no idea how Carolyn had so much familiarity with that particular part of the city, but there was no reason to doubt her, especially since she seemed so certain. This tied in to something she and Susanna had come up with the night before as a sort of preliminary plan, but we'd had no idea at the time whether or not it would play out this way. There had been a few other pseudo-plans tossed about, but as it turned out, this was the one that seemed to fit. The notion was that if we could determine where Shelling was staying in town, we could, as Carl had put it, take the fight to him.

She and Susanna went into the kitchen, and the rest of us followed. "Okay, let's see…" Susanna said quietly. She scanned over the map, motioning Carolyn to move in closer, and they began to work out precisely where this hotel was. I leaned in, too. Very quickly, we managed to come up with a more concise plan.

Flying to the hotel, I was filled with a mixture of anticipation and fear. I was definitely scared of this mysterious vampire hunter, but at the same time, I hoped that we had the advantage. For one thing, there were seven of us and only one of him, and I also liked how we were in fact hunting him, rather than the other way around. The way we had things planned, though, was to let him chase us, to lull him into a false sense of security and then turn the tables on him.

I was also looking forward to drinking from someone who didn't taste so bad. When we had first gotten up that night, we'd gone to an abandoned store downtown, one that, according to Carolyn, was known for being a squatting site for homeless people. While we had dropped Susanna's idea of preying on the homeless before, it made a lot of sense to go back to that temporarily. If we had killed in a more public area like we usually did, Shelling might very well find out about it, then go there to try to track us down. Killing people no one would miss was safer, Susanna explained, and we all agreed. Even if the police did find those bodies, it wouldn't be for a while, and definitely not in time to lure Shelling away from his hotel. We wanted him in one place, somewhere we could find him.

We arrived at the Westchester Suites hotel, which was a two-story building along Washington Road, one of the busiest streets in Augusta. Once we got there, we landed in the parking lot but stayed in our bat forms, figuring that we were less visible that way. We had let Carolyn and Crowley lead the group so she could try to figure out the exact spot where the news crew had shot its interview with Shelling.

"Okay, yeah, this looks about right," she said. She hovered in the air at about the same level her head would have been had she been in her person form, turning around in a circle as she got her bearings. Crowley, in his small, white bat form, flew around her, seeming a little confused. Carolyn ignored him, saying, "So… then… hmm."

"What?" I asked.

"Well, I mean, yeah, sure, we know that this is the right hotel, but then, how do we find out just which room he's in?"

"If he hasn't already left," Dennis pointed out.

I reached out with my mind, trying to psychically scan the building. Almost immediately, I got a mental image of Shelling in one of the rooms. Focusing further, I was able to pinpoint his location to a single room on the second floor, and I found myself staring straight at it. But this was tricky; I couldn't just tell the others that I knew this. "No, I'm pretty sure he's still here," I said.

"How do you know?" Carl asked.

"Just a feeling." I wanted to waggle my eyebrows at Dennis so at least he would see the signal and know that I had been using my powers, but in my bat form, that wasn't possible.

"Yeah, okay," Dennis said. "So, assuming he is, how to we find him?"

"Maybe we could sneak in and look at the hotel registry," Carl suggested.

"No," Susanna said. "Too risky. They probably have security cameras. And I don't think the employees would react very calmly if we just flew in to take a look."

"I think I know a way," Tim said. "Look up there." A woman was moving along the walkway outside the rooms on the second level. "If we kill somebody, then maybe this Shelling guy will hear the scream and then come out to help."

"That's a good idea," Carl said. "Wait here, and I'll go get her."

"No, not yet," Tim said. "We should surround the hotel first, then see which room he comes out of."

"Good plan," I said, but I was partly just playing along. I knew exactly which room Shelling was in, or at least, I was pretty sure. "So, once we get him outside, we lure him to the park as planned."

"Are we still doing the two teams thing?" Carolyn asked.

"Yes," Susanna said. "You, Crowley, and I will hang back and let the boys get his attention. Carl..."

"Well, she's gone now," he said, meaning the woman we had seen earlier. "We'll have to wait for someone else to show up."

Susanna and her group flew up above the center of the hotel, and the remaining four of us surrounded the place. It felt for a moment like we were cops sneakily surrounding somewhere before storming in after the bad guy, but then, we were the true bad guys. Fairly certain which room Shelling would emerge from, I stayed on that side of the building.

Time passed, and no one went by. Our plan was already failing, or at least it wasn't moving quickly enough for me. I began to wonder if I might be able to use my psychic powers again, this time to get someone to come out of their room so one of the others could attack them. Fortunately, that wasn't necessary, as someone finally did come out of his room, and Dennis flew in for the kill.

Just as we'd predicted, a few seconds after the man screamed, the door to Shelling's room flew open, and I saw him in person for the first time. He was looking around wildly, a large wooden stake held high. Spotting the prone man on the walkway several doors down, he began to creep slowly towards him. I wasn't sure if he could actually see Dennis from his vantage point or not.

Surprising myself, I bravely zoomed forward, stopping and hovering just a few feet in the air in front of him. He stopped in his tracks and drew back, letting out a sort of backwards hiss, grimacing and catching his breath.

"Mine got!" he whispered harshly, but that didn't make sense to me, if that was what he'd said at all. I wondered if it was some foreign expression; I was accustomed to British people using odd turns of phrase even though they used English words. He stared at me intently, his stake rotating slightly as he watched. I wasn't scared, as I reasoned that he wouldn't actually be able to use it on me when I was so small.

"Nice to meet you, Mr. Shelling," I said.

His eyes went wide, and then he did that same expression I had seen on TV where his huge, bushy eyebrows seemed to squish into one. *"Doctor* Shelling!" he insisted. "Prepare for your end!" He reached for his chest, where a large, metal cross hung from a thin rope around his neck. He thrust it out toward me, and I instinctively flew back.

Leaving him on the balcony, I was relieved to see Dennis joining me as we flew out into the open air above the parking lot, but there didn't seem to have been enough time for him to have drained the man he'd taken down. Shelling ran back to his hotel room, and for a moment, I thought we might have to chase him in there. As Carl and Tim joined us, though, Shelling quickly made his way back out of the room. The door slammed behind him as he rushed toward the nearest staircase, this time wearing a backpack. It looked kind of odd on him, contrasting with the rest of his clothing, which was more old-fashioned and almost formal. Once he had arrived on the ground below us, we put our plan into motion, which was to lead him to a less crowded area away from the hotel.

It was a little tricky getting him to follow us; we could have easily lost him if we'd wanted to. But we had to stay in sight and get him to follow us to the park, which was on a side street a few blocks away from Washington Road. In addition to flying more slowly than usual, we occasionally stopped and flew back down toward him, giving him a chance to wave his stake at us. In time, he also produced yet another cross from his backpack, which I assumed was full of similar anti-vampire weapons. Still, we never got close enough for him to do us any real harm.

We arrived at the park, and I began to wish that we had scouted it out on the way to the hotel rather than just flying over it briefly. If we had, we could have planned some specific tactics against Shelling. Instead, we were just improvising. Presumably, he was doing the same thing, but I realized that we would have had more of an advantage had we been prepared to lure him into a specific trap. I looked around the area, spotting various playground equipment, and I wondered if it might be possible to lure him on top of this large wooden structure, something normally used by children for climbing and playing. But then I couldn't think of what that would accomplish.

Shelling had stopped, looking around and up into the air, apparently having lost sight of us. There were fewer lights in the park than there had been along the road, and our tiny dark forms must have eluded him.

"Do not think you have escape!" he shouted. "I shall find you, vermin!"

"Guys, come on," I said to the others. I led them to the ground several yards behind Shelling, where we changed form. We stood in a line, side by side and facing our attacker. "Or perhaps we shall find you first!" I said. As the words came out, I realized that I was speaking kind of like he did, but without the funny accent.

He turned around quickly, eyes blazing and stake held high. He had an extremely fierce expression, but it immediately changed to confusion. In fact, he hadn't even made eye contact at first, instead aiming his vision slightly higher than us, then correcting himself as he realized how short we were. He did that same shocked sucking in of breath and gritted his teeth, but there was also something sad in his eyes.

"Children!" he said, almost disbelieving. "You are all just children!"

"That's what you think," I said. I liked that he had been caught off guard; I always enjoyed catching adults and authority figures by surprise.

Shelling's face hardened. "Devil children," he said.

"Yes!" I said, smiling. "13-year-olds, in fact! How lucky for us, right?" I was not in fact 13 yet, but I would be in a few weeks.

"You think to mock me?" Shelling said angrily, stepping forward. "Young or not, you are still vampire, and I shall rid the world of your foul presence!"

"'Foul presence?'" Dennis said, mimicking his accent. "Carl, did you fart again?" The four of us, even Carl, couldn't help but laugh at that one.

"Wasn't me!" Carl said with a smile. "Must be old Grandpa here!"

Shelling grew more angry, and he continued to step slowly toward us, stake in hand. I wasn't frightened of him anymore. He was just another stupid adult who thought he was superior because he was older.

"No," I said as deeply as I could with my prepubescent voice. I made my eyes light up, then felt that strange tingle in my forehead as I ramped up my psychic powers and used them to reach out to the old man's mind. He froze.

"Submit to us, Alexander Shelling," Dennis said in an equally grave tone.

"So it does work!" Carl said quietly.

"Shh," Tim whispered. "Just do it."

Although I hadn't turned to look at the others, I knew that everyone was now transfixing our prey with our glowing eyes, but I had a pretty good idea that it was only mine and Dennis's that were having any real effect. We were the ones with the psychic powers, after all. But it added to the overall display to have Carl and Tim lighting up their eyes as well.

Just as I began to think to myself, *Some "master vampire hunter" this guy is,* Shelling reached for the shiny metal cross that hung from his neck. He quickly rotated it, and it caught the glow from our eyes, reflecting it back to each of us in turn. The glowing image of the cross seemed to burn into my skull, and I fell backwards, clutching at my eyes in pain. I heard the others cry out and fall down as well, but for the moment, I couldn't see them. The feeling passed in just a few seconds, and my vision cleared just in time to see Shelling barreling toward us.

"Run!" I shouted. Everyone scrambled to their feet and fled. According to the plan, we were supposed to stick together as a group at this point rather than scattering, but then I noticed that Carl was no longer beside me. I looked back, seeing that Shelling had already overtaken him, and Carl was rolling over in the grass, holding up an arm to try to fight off the vampire hunter. Shelling leaned down and had his stake raised high, looking ready to plunge it right into Carl.

I stopped running and shouted, "Carl! Change into a bat!"

Immediately, he did, quickly escaping to join the rest of us. Shelling pursued, and we all changed form and joined Carl, who was already heading back up into the sky. Below, we heard various threats and insults being hurled at us.

"That was close," Tim said.

"I know," Carl said. "I'm sorry. I panicked. There's something strange about that man."

"You mean aside from the fact that he almost killed you?" Dennis quipped.

"No, I mean… It's just… He moves pretty damn fast for such an old geezer."

I couldn't argue with that, but I hadn't really noticed how odd it was until Carl pointed it out. "Hmm, that's true. Well, there's still four of us and only one of him. We should be able to take him."

"You first," Tim said.

"No, it has to be a group thing." Just for a moment, I had forgotten that Susanna, Carolyn, and Crowley were somewhere nearby, waiting for us to implement phase two of our plan. There was something nice about it being just us four, like it was at school, only now with the power to kill.

"It would help if we could get that damn cross from around his neck," Carl said. "It almost hit me in the face when he leaned down over me."

It was only then that the true logistics of this confrontation hit me. If any of us managed to get touched by that cross or any other vampire killer, that person would be changed back to human. Shelling probably didn't know that, being used to fighting more traditional, "real" vampires. If that happened, would he spare them because they were human? Truth be told, given our track record, they would then be in danger from the rest of us instead.

"Okay," I said. "Let's try for another run. This time, we'll surround him."

We landed around him in a square, once again changing to our person forms. I held my hands out, and the others did the same, almost daring him to try to move in any direction. We maintained a safe distance, but if he made a break for it, any two of us could nab him. He looked around, weighing his options.

"A clever move," he said slowly. "But it matters not. You are all evil, which will be defeat in the end."

"Dude, speak English already!" Dennis said.

Although he had been temporarily calm, Shelling again became angry, and he thrust forward a cross at Dennis, shouting something foreign that I couldn't even make out. Whatever the words were, it didn't matter, as his suddenly aggressive move was enough to make Dennis falter and stagger back. His back now to me, I tried to advance on him, but he swung the cross back in my direction. Tim and Carl were similarly repelled as he quickly moved back and forth, holding the cross at arm's length. The other one on the rope around his neck dangled wildly, occasionally reflecting the few lights in the park and making me want to avoid looking at it.

I decided to put an end to this stand-off, so it was time for phase two. Standing up straight, I shouted at the sky, "Ambush!"

Shelling stopped his movements and looked up and around him, surprised. But nothing happened.

"Ambush!" I repeated, trying to sound distressed, but this was, in fact, part of the plan.

"So," Shelling said with a sly smile. "There are others like yourself. It would appear that they are not foolish as you, and will stay away from this battle. No matter. I shall find them, too, when time comes."

Without warning, the small forms of Susanna, Carolyn, and Crowley zipped out of the sky and circled Shelling's head several times, causing him to drop both the cross and the stake he was carrying. He batted at his head like someone being attacked by a swarm of bees, again shouting in some unknown language. They then flew back up into the air, and I noticed that at least one of them had managed to get a small bite in, as there was a little trickle of blood coming from his cheek, just below his left eye.

The sight of the blood energized me, and I started to leap forward, wanting to clamp down on his neck and drink the rest of him. But that cross was still hanging there, and it made me resist the urge. Instead, I changed and flew up to Susanna and the others, and my friends did the same.

"Well, that almost worked," I said once we were all together in the sky.

"Uh-oh," Carolyn said, and while she couldn't exactly point while in her current form, I knew that she was indicating something happening on the ground below. I looked and saw that Shelling had taken from his backpack a small crossbow, which he was loading. He aimed it at the sky, looking around and trying to spot us.

"I'm betting that's a wooden arrow," Susanna said. "Probably works just as well as a wooden stake."

"You know," I said, "it just occurred to me that, well, you know how all of the vampire killers that we've learned to avoid just change us back into human…"

"I know," Susanna said. "We can't let him change even one of us back. That would be a disaster."

"No, there's something else! Think about it. Sunlight or garlic or whatever just turns us back to a regular person. But a wooden stake through the heart?"

"Oh," Tim said. "I get it. Even if all that supposedly did was change you back into a human, well, then you're a human with a big wooden stake through your heart."

"Dead," Carl added.

"Oh," Dennis added unnecessarily. "Shit."

The battle with Shelling continued, and neither side seemed to tire. We could attack in brief bursts and then fly away after being repelled by his weaponry, resting before the next seemingly pointless attack. A couple of times, he fired wooden arrows into the sky after us, but those missed. Trying to get close enough to bite him never seemed to work, even with us outnumbering him seven to one.

Dennis suggested spiraling down toward him from the air in an attempt to make him dizzy, but that plan was foiled by him hurling a large clove of garlic up at us, which fortunately missed. Had it made contact with any of us, that person would have plummeted to the ground as a human, probably dying in the process or at the very least getting seriously injured.

Tim pointed out that we should get Shelling's backpack off of him somehow, to separate him from his arsenal, which led to an abortive attempt that didn't accomplish much. Tim had landed on the backpack and changed into his person form, only to have Shelling swing wildly and leave Tim sprawling on the ground. As the rest of us tried to take advantage of the distraction and move in, we were driven away by Shelling's quick reaction and yet another arrow from his crossbow, which almost caught me in the wing.

Throughout all of this, we worked our way around the park, not once encountering any other people. It occurred to me that someone else might stumble across this battle, either police or just innocent bystanders, and that might complicate things. It was well after dark, though, so presumably most people were at home by then. But when we happened to end up near the official entrance to the park, I noticed something that probably explained why there was no foot traffic in this area.

An orange *UNDER CONSTRUCTION* sign stood next to a newly built larger, wooden sign that bore the official name of the park. It was designed to look primitive, carved letters in the wood and all, but everything was freshly painted and was obviously quite new. For the first time, I noticed that an unpaved driveway leading into the park was cordoned off with plastic yellow and black *CAUTION* tape. Whatever this place had been before, it was now being built into a park, but it wasn't complete yet. No one came here, which made it an ideal place to battle this mysterious vampire hunter, away from the prying eyes of the police or the general public. I wondered if Carolyn already knew this; she was the one who suggested that we lure Shelling here to fight him.

Shelling, as usual, advanced on us whenever we got to ground level, whether in bat form or person form. I had advised Susanna and Carolyn on how taunting and mocking him seemed to work so well, and they had joined in on that front, angering him further.

Finding the entrance to the park helped give me a reference point, and I realized that it would be helpful to explore the boundaries of this place and figure out what our options might be. I again thought about somehow trying to use the playground equipment against Shelling, but I couldn't come up with anything, not even an idea good enough to run by the others. But I did tell them that I wanted to try circling the entire park, and no one objected.

Susanna insisted that I not go on my own, so Tim accompanied me while the others stayed behind to continue the fight. As we flew around the perimeter, I noted where the trees began, and I vaguely remembered riding past this area a few years before and seeing that it was all trees. Apparently, this lot had been cleared out, but I had no idea how recently. There was still some development going on, as evidenced by the construction equipment we came across. A chain-link fence was being built along the park's border, but only part of it was up. Several metal posts were in the ground in a line where the rest of the fence material would eventually go, and not long after those stopped, there was something intriguing.

Almost directly opposite to the entrance where we had left the others, there was a large pile of orange dirt. A thin, rust-colored pole was stuck into it, and more *CAUTION* tape was strung between that and the last fence post. The trees had tapered off and were farther away by this point, but between us and them, there was a deep ditch. I flew over it and saw that there was a steep drop-off just on the other side of the pile of dirt. Several feet below the ground level, there were lots of large, white rocks that looked like they had been placed there.

Somewhere nearby, I could hear the trickle of running water. As near as I could figure out, this was some kind of artificially created ditch, probably having been dug by the construction equipment nearby. A plan began to form in my head.

"Are you thinking what I think you're thinking?" Tim said with a smile.

"Depends," I said, feeling inspired. "Owen Raforth?"

Owen was the only other new kid besides Nick to come to our school in seventh grade, and he never fit in. There was just something weird about him, this vibe that made everyone uncomfortable. He was kind of a geek, and while Tim had always been the big nerd in our class growing up, he'd eventually begun to shed that image the older he got, though not entirely. Owen's presence probably helped Tim somewhat in this respect: Suddenly, he wasn't the goofiest boy around. And even when my own popularity had gotten to its lowest that year, I never considered befriending this guy.

Tim let out a small chuckle, and I knew that he was also remembering the prank some of us had played on Owen at recess not long before the end of the school year. "Got it in one," he said. "Let's go tell the others."

We flew straight across the park and back toward the entrance, but by then, the battle had moved and was no longer where we had left it. Once we found everyone again, I saw that there had been at least one interesting development. Shelling was no longer wearing his backpack; it looked like someone had finally managed to wrest it from him, causing its contents to spill all over the ground. There were stakes, garlic, crosses, more wooden arrows, and even a spare crossbow lying around, and Shelling stood close to the pile, using various items from it to ward off the attacking vampires.

"Guys!" I shouted to the group, which was hovering several feet above the ground and dodging yet another clove of garlic that was hurled into the air. I led them farther up and out of range, then told them about what Tim and I had found and how we thought we could adapt the Owen Raforth prank. That time, Dennis had lured Owen to a spot in the playground where there was a large puddle of mud, and I had knelt down on the ground behind him without him noticing. Dennis then shoved Owen and caused him to topple backwards over me and into the mud. I got splashed a little, but Owen was completely soaked, and everyone who had gathered around (including Tim and Carl) had a good laugh at his expense. We got in trouble for it, of course, but we felt that it was worth it.

We worked out how we would use a similar strategy on Shelling, this time in a much more violent way. I then flew back to the area Tim and I had discovered, where I tore away the *CAUTION* tape and hid it. Next, I sat on the ground in my bat form, hoping that I was virtually invisible to anyone approaching on foot. I found sitting there and waiting to be difficult; I wanted this whole thing to be over with, and I was eager to see this plan work. From far away, I could hear the sounds of the battle, mostly Shelling shouting at the vampires and occasional taunts back at him.

Finally, the sounds got louder, and I heard what I presumed to be Carl running toward me. I could just barely make out the sounds of heavy breathing as his hurried stomps approached. I pictured him doing his signature over-the-top athletic exertion as he ran, and once he was in range, I saw him doing just that, occasionally looking over his shoulder as Shelling ran behind him and kept up.

As I watched, Carl's eyes lit up, enhancing his night vision, and I saw him spot me on the ground, waiting. He smiled briefly as he continued to accelerate, and it looked like he was going to run right over me. What happened next seemed perfectly choreographed, and it worked like a charm.

In the span of just a few seconds, Carl jumped over me, then changed into a bat and flew in order to avoid dropping into the abyss. Shelling was right behind him and moving just as quickly, unable to stop. I changed into my person form and held my knees under me with my arms, transforming myself into a stumbling block. I willed myself to stay in position, even when Shelling's legs slammed into me. I was pushed over onto my side, but it was Shelling who toppled over me and into the open air, screaming as he fell toward the rocks at the bottom of the ditch. I heard him hit the ground as I recovered from the impact and straightened up, still lying down. I then peered over the edge.

He lay there unmoving, his body twisted in a weird way. He was lying face down on the rocks, and his arms and legs looked kind of wrong, like they weren't supposed to fit into his body the way I was seeing them. The stake he had been carrying had fallen a few feet away from his body. The idea had been to incapacitate him and then go in for the kill, but I began to wonder if the job had already been done.

I stood up and brushed myself off, glancing behind me briefly to see the rest of the group running up. I looked back down to the bottom of the ditch, lighting up my eyes to get a better look. Carl flew down to Shelling and then back up to the rest of us, then changed form and landed next to me.

"Is he dead?" I asked.

"Sure looks that way," Carl said with a triumphant grin.

Everyone else looked over the edge of the cliff, and I heard Carolyn let out a sigh of relief. Crowley rubbed up against her leg and let out a small *"mrrrow."*

"Aww," Dennis said. "I was hoping we could actually bite him!"

"You could always go down there and drink from his corpse," Carolyn said.

"No," Susanna said. "That probably wouldn't taste right."

"Hmm," I said, "I guess you're right." I sighed too, glad that this was all over.

"So," Tim said in a cheerful tone, "back to the house?"

"Sure," I said.

As we walked across the park, we talked about the various tactics we had tried against the vampire hunter, what had worked and what hadn't, and how cool it was that we had managed to defeat him. There was a lot of bragging to go around, but I felt a certain amount of pride in coming up with the plan that ultimately worked. Crowley walked alongside us at a leisurely pace, but then suddenly, he stopped.

"You okay, Crowley?" I asked, still smiling and sharing everyone's good mood.

He turned around and faced behind us, his long white tail standing straight up and becoming bushy. He let out a meow that sounded like a question, then walked slowly in the direction from which we'd come.

"What?" Carolyn asked him. "Crowley, come here."

He ignored her and continued to creep along, then suddenly darted in the opposite direction, running away from us.

"Crowley!" Carolyn called after him. "Come back here!"

"Oh my God," Carl said. "That's impossible."

Before I had a chance to ask him what he meant, I saw Shelling walking toward us, wooden stake in hand. He was moving quickly and had a crazed, angry look, sort of limping but speeding up as he went.

"I… will not… be defeated… so easily…" he said, his voice rough and threatening. His face was scratched and his hair in disarray, and his clothes were torn and covered in dirt. His button-up shirt and vest were a mess, making him look more like a homeless man than the cultured European we had spent the entire night fighting. Despite that, he still looked extremely scary as he approached.

"Run!" I shouted. Everyone ran, but as I looked back, I saw Shelling break into a sprint after us.

I ran as fast as I could, and for some reason, the idea of changing into a bat and flying to safety escaped me. I was just too freaked out by Shelling's supposed resurrection to do anything else. But then I heard a strange noise behind me, so I turned around to see what was happening.

The cross Shelling had worn around his neck this entire time was now right up against his throat, and he was clawing at it with his hands, choking for breath. Behind him, I saw Carl, and I realized that he had grabbed the cord from behind and was now using it and the cross to strangle Shelling. With a great deal of effort, Shelling grabbed at the rope that was bearing down into the sides of his neck, then tore it from him. The cross toppled to the ground while Carl ran away.

I was torn between the urge to lunge at Shelling at this point or just run away, and during that time, he picked up the cross and held it out at us defiantly. All of a sudden, a bat flew at his arm and latched onto it, causing him to scream and drop the cross. He fell to his knees, then slammed his arm onto the ground, which caused the bat biting him to transform into Carolyn. She was dazed and trying to recover, but before she could, Shelling put his hand around her throat and picked up the wooden stake lying next to him.

I was just about to intervene when Crowley appeared from nowhere, snarling and leaping onto Shelling's neck, causing him to cry out in pain. He then angrily grabbed Crowley by the back of the neck and tore him away, slamming him onto the ground next to him. In less than a second, he had plunged the wooden stake straight through Crowley and into the ground.

The sounds that filled my ears in that moment will never, ever be erased from my memory. I screamed, Carolyn screamed Crowley's name, and some of the others called out as well. But worst of all was the monstrous shriek that Crowley himself made as he was killed. I had never heard anything like it before. For years, just thinking about that sound was enough to give me chills and bring me to tears at the same time.

Carolyn leapt from the ground and threw herself onto Shelling, biting into his neck. The impact caused him to roll over onto his back, and he tried to struggle as he screamed. Within seconds, I also jumped onto him and bit the other side of his neck, Carolyn and I pinning him down. I drank, but there was no pleasure in it, only white-hot anger.

This creepy old bastard had just killed our cat, and I wanted nothing more in the entire world than to destroy him completely. The kill didn't seem to take as long as others I had done, and once I leaned back and looked around, I saw why. The four remaining vampires had also helped us drain Shelling, each of them biting down on his arms and legs.

Once we were done with him, he was pale and completely emptied of blood. As I stood up, I noticed a strange look on his dead face, one of complete bewilderment, like he hadn't known where he was or how this had happened. I had a strong urge to kick him right in the face, but I was distracted by Carolyn scrambling over to Crowley, still impaled on the stake. She was crying, calling out his name over and over in a desperate, pleading tone. I fought back tears, not wanting to let my friends see me cry. Susanna looked similarly pained, though also completely shocked.

Carolyn pounded on the ground and wailed, and I knelt down beside her, putting my hand on her back. I felt her shuddering as she cried silently for a few seconds, breathing rapidly through clenched teeth. Finally, she turned away from Crowley and toward me, and our eyes met. Her face was covered in tears, and she looked more fragile than I could ever remember seeing her. After a moment, she buried her head in my chest, shaking and crying some more. I held her to me, hoping I was of some comfort to her.

The rest of the night was a mix of emotions: mostly grief, guilt, and anger. No one really wanted to talk about what had happened to Crowley, especially not when Carolyn was around. Any attempt at conversation broke down in tears, usually hers. I allowed for some sniffling on my part, and at times, my voice cracked from the emotion. Dennis and Carl did that a couple of times, too, but as boys, we had it ingrained in us to be tough and level-headed, to not be too emotional. Susanna, meanwhile, took charge as the responsible adult, but I could tell that she was also fighting back certain feelings.

She flew back to the house to get her car while the rest of us stayed at the park with Crowley's body. Carolyn wanted to bury him in the small pet cemetery at our house. We couldn't fly back carrying him, so it was necessary for Susanna to go get her car so we could transport him that way.

Not wanting to hang around near Shelling's drained body, we had opted to move Crowley's farther away, but still in the park. So Carolyn wouldn't have to deal with it, I took on the gruesome task of removing the stake from Crowley and carrying him to our new spot, which was over by that large wooden structure I had noticed when we first arrived. The others joined me, and we sat on the ground.

"I hope no one else comes by while we're waiting," Dennis said. "We wouldn't want to have to explain why we're all sitting here with a… um…." He broke off, realizing how heartless what he was about to say would have sounded.

I wanted to change the subject, so I said bravely, "If they do, we'll deal with them, just like we did with that old piece of shit over there." Then I wondered if that was just as insensitive, and I clammed up. We may have killed Shelling, but as for how well we dealt with him, there was a dead white cat on the ground next to us that seemed to suggest that we could have done a better job.

Running over everything in my mind, I kept wishing that it had gone differently. I questioned it all, imagining scenarios that would have resulted in Crowley still being alive. We should have made him stay home, I thought, rather than have him be a part of this big battle with the super-powerful vampire hunter. But then again, I had been torn between thinking of him as a serious threat and just some kind of joke. And if we had left Crowley at home, he might have gone out on his own again and killed people near our house, raising suspicion. Even so, I would have preferred that over him winding up dead.

I also wondered if this incident would make Carolyn suggest that we change back to regular humans, if she'd had enough and wanted to give it up. I didn't want that, but I wouldn't have been surprised if she had suggested it. As it turned out — though I wouldn't realize this until the following night — Carolyn wanted no such thing. After her initial period of mourning, she went from being sad and crying alone in her room to being very bitter and angry. Instead of wanting to stop being a vampire, she seemed to feel that the best revenge for Crowley's death was to keep on killing. When I had asked her after Crowley's burial if there was anything I could do for her, all she said was, "Is it possible to kill that fucking Shelling guy again?" I was surprised by this and didn't know how to respond, but when I saw how she acted the following night, I understood. She became brutal and extremely vicious in her killing, and I wondered if she was imagining that each new victim was in fact Shelling himself.

The night Crowley was killed, we left Carolyn in her room to grieve; she had told us she wanted to be left alone. At this point, I was still wondering if she might want to change back, and I didn't like how her isolation from the group reminded me of the summer four years earlier.

The guys were unsure how to handle everything, I could tell. Honestly, I wasn't sure what to do with myself, either. We defaulted to watching TV, but it was hard to settle on anything. We didn't want to watch anything funny because we weren't in the mood for it, but anything serious or sad would just be depressing. Eventually, Susanna called me from the red den and told me that she needed my help with something.

"It was an idea Carolyn and I came up with back at the hotel," she said, "but given what's happened, I don't want to bother her with it now."

"What is it?"

"She suggested that we sneak into Shelling's hotel room and go through his things. I'm especially curious about anything that has to do with us, you know, what he might have known about us. Evidence, maps, something like that."

"Yeah, that makes sense, I guess. We'll have to be careful, though, if he has any vampire killer stuff in there. Well, *had.*"

Susanna frowned, and I picked up on the fact that she was reminded that not only did we have to talk about Shelling in the past tense, but Crowley as well. We should have been celebrating one death, but it was spoiled by another. She sighed and said, "Yes, you're right. I'm thinking we should take my car again, just in case we find something worth bringing back."

I agreed, and we told the others — including Carolyn — where we were going. The guys wanted to go with us, but Susanna insisted that it would be better for just a couple of us to break into the hotel room, not a large group. She also didn't want to leave Carolyn at the house by herself, even if she had insisted on being left alone.

As we settled down into her car, I glanced at the back seat. Earlier in the night, I had ridden back there with Carolyn, Crowley's body wrapped in a towel on my lap. The others followed us as bats as Susanna drove, turning us into some weird sort of funeral procession. Everyone in the car kept quiet, so at the time, I hadn't bothered to ask Susanna about the large coil of yellow nylon rope I'd had to move from the seat to the floorboard in order to make room for us to sit down. Now that it was just me and her, I asked.

"Oh, that? That was just from last night, you know, when we were tossing around various ideas. Carolyn got the rope out of the storage shed and put it in my car after I said that it might be good to kidnap Shelling and tie him up, you know, interrogate him and all. Then we could find out what he knew. But I decided that it was probably too dangerous."

"Yeah," I said. "Given how long it took us to even get close to him, I can't imagine trying to tackle him and tie him up or something." Again, there was that feeling of regret, wishing that we had played it differently, that somehow we could have kept Crowley from getting killed.

We drove in silence for a while, and I figured that she was thinking along the same lines I was. After a while, I said, "Do you think we'll be able to get into his hotel room?"

"Hmm? Oh, I'm sure we can break in. Our added strength should take care of that."

"But what if someone hears us?"

"You know what to do," she said, smiling. I smiled, too, then felt guilty. It didn't seem right to be having evil, murderous thoughts so soon after what had happened. I sighed again.

"Look," Susanna said, "I know it sucks about what happened to Crowley. I didn't know him all that well, but you and Carolyn did, and it's okay to be sad. But let's try to salvage what we can from the situation."

I nodded, knowing that she was right. I thought she might have more to say on the subject, but then she got distracted by something on her dashboard.

"Aw, crap, I'm almost out of gas. We'll have to stop somewhere on the way."

I had a strange notion, that it seemed really inefficient to travel by car. Traveling as bats seemed much more convenient and faster. Despite everything that had happened, I still enjoyed being a vampire and wanted to stay this way.

There wasn't very much of interest in Shelling's hotel room. An open suitcase on the bed had some clothes in it, and as I expected, more anti-vampire weapons, including some garlic that was thankfully sealed up in plastic bags. I was careful not to touch either those or the crosses I saw, though I was disappointed that there wasn't another crossbow around. I would have liked to have had one of those, just to play with it and see if it was something I could learn to use.

But as far as Susanna's idea that Shelling might have somehow tracked us down, had maps leading to our house, or whatever, there was no evidence of that. There was also nothing to indicate who he was or where he'd come from, which I found frustrating. The more Susanna talked about trying to figure this guy out, the more I wanted to know about him, too.

There was one interesting item in his suitcase, however, a book with a yellowish-orange cover that caught my eye. Pulling it out from underneath some clothes, I saw in large, bright red letters: *DRACULA,* and underneath that, *By Bram Stoker.*

"Oh, cool!" I said, getting Susanna's attention; she had been snooping around the rest of the room. "Man, this looks old." The cover was worn and cracked in a few places, and the pages of the fragile book were sort of tan colored, particularly around the edges. I immediately thought of our father, given that he was a librarian. "Dad would love this." I held it up and showed the cover to Susanna.

She grinned, then nodded her head. "Aha," she said knowingly. "I wondered. That explains a lot."

"It does? How?"

"I'll explain later. We should go. I think we've found all we're going to in here."

Back in her car, I asked her what she meant. I had taken the book with me, thinking that we should at least get some kind of souvenir, something to justify our trip back to the hotel.

"Here," she said, holding out her hands as she sat in the driver's seat. We were still in the parking lot, and she had just started up the car, but she seemed to be ignoring the chiming that was reminding her to put on her seatbelt. I handed her the book, and she thumbed through it. "Have you ever read *Dracula?"*

"No," I said. "I mean, I've seen him on TV and stuff, but he always seemed a bit corny to me. You know, all 'Bluh! Bluh! I vant to drink your blooood!'"

She laughed, but she also gave me a disappointed look. "A smart boy like you," she said, but she didn't finish her thought and continued to look through the pages. "Hmm. Well. I can't find a particularly telling passage, but here. Take a look at this bit." She handed the book back to me, then pointed to a paragraph. "Read that. Notice anything?"

The typeface seemed kind of weird and old-fashioned to me, but I was able to read it just fine:

Presently she woke, and I gave her food, as Van Helsing had prescribed. She took but a little, and that languidly. There did not seem to be with her now the unconscious struggle for life and strength that had hitherto so marked her illness. It struck me as curious that the moment she became conscious she pressed the garlic flowers close to her.

The wording was a bit strange and hard to understand, but I got the gist of what was being said. It also intrigued me that the passage mentioned garlic, which began to make me think that this could turn out to be a sort of vampire guidebook. Dracula was, as far as I knew, the oldest vampire in the world. I got excited about the idea of reading this book later at home, thinking that I might learn some interesting things from it. But as far as what Susanna was trying to point out to me, I still didn't get it.

"What?" I asked her.

"Here," she said, pointing a little farther down the page. "Read that one. Out loud this time."

I began to feel annoyed; she was reminding me of a teacher. "'At six o'clock Van Helsing came to relieve me,'" I began reading, and then she cut me off.

"That name," she said with a smile. "Recognize it?"

"No."

"Who did we spend all night fighting?"

"A vampire hunter named Alexander Shelling."

"And that's spelled…?"

"Will you just get to the point already?"

She shook her head. "S-H-E-L-I-N-G."

"Oh. I thought it had two L's." I recalled the newscast from the night before, picturing the caption onscreen when they played the recording of Shelling's — or Sheling's — phone call. I was certain that they had spelled his name with two L's. Or maybe they just got it wrong? It wouldn't be the first time I'd seen them do something like that. Finally, it clicked. I looked back down at the page. *Helsing.*

Susanna could tell from the look on my face that the penny had dropped. "Same guy," she said triumphantly. I looked back up at her, then saw her expression change. "Or maybe just some weirdo pretending to be the same guy. I guess it could be either way."

On the way home, she explained things a little more, that Van Helsing was, in the book, the man who hunted down and killed Dracula. It had been a while since she had read the story, but she recalled that Van Helsing also spoke in broken English. "I can't believe I didn't spot it before," she said, sounding both amused and irritated with herself.

I continued to look through the book randomly, trying to find more mentions of him, maybe even passages of dialogue. It was difficult to read because of the intermittent streetlights as we drove along, but my night vision mostly compensated for that. About three quarters of the way through the book, I happened across this part:

> *Van Helsing says that our chance will be to get on the boat between sunrise and sunset. The Count, even if he takes the form of a bat, cannot cross the running water of his own volition, and so cannot leave the ship.*

"Holy crap!" I said. "You were right!"

"About what?"

"Running water! I just spotted a bit that talks about that."

"Well, given what happened to us the last two times we were like this, I thought that would be pretty obvious."

"I know, I know. But there was the time when I told you that I'd never heard of running water being part of the whole vampire thing, and you insisted it was. So you were right, and I was wrong. Fine." I wasn't mad, just intrigued.

"One of these days, you'll learn to trust me," she said, but I could tell she was mostly playing around.

I started reading some more, but then I was overcome by a strange feeling. In my mind, I pictured a car speeding toward us, its headlights blazing into our car's windshield. The vision passed quickly, but as we approached a sharp curve in the road, I couldn't stop myself from speaking up. "Susanna, be careful going around this corner. There's a car coming."

"How could you possibly…" She didn't have time to finish her sentence and instead put all of her effort into steering out of the way of a car that came speeding around the curve toward us, swerving into our lane and just barely missing us. Everything looked just like it had in my mind a few seconds earlier. Susanna and I both swore at the same time, even with the same word. There hadn't even been time for her to honk her horn at the other driver. Once the danger was past, she pulled off onto a side street and stopped the car, breathing heavily, her eyes like saucers. I probably looked the same, and I was also suddenly very aware of my pulse. I could feel it pounding along the sides of my neck, a sensation that passed after about half a minute.

Once we had calmed down, I said to her, "Okay, so, yeah. There's something I've never told you."

Surprisingly, Susanna fully accepted my telling her that Dennis and I were psychic, and not just because she had seen it demonstrated so dramatically. That was in fact the first true premonition I could remember having, but I also told her about the other things, how I would think things and other people would say them, the way Dennis and I could sometimes influence events, and the way that our powers seemed to have increased recently after having taken the potion. Susanna said that she had in fact noticed this about me for a long time, even back when I was little. She even cited a couple of examples I had completely forgotten about.

I felt weird admitting this to her, even if she was accepting of it. It had been a secret for so long, so I was used to that. Also, Dennis had made me promise to keep quiet about it, and I was having to break that promise.

Back at the house, she gathered everyone but Carolyn into the red den, having told me in the car that Dennis and I needed to share this with the rest of the group. I wasn't comfortable with this idea at first, but there was another part of me that felt relieved. Not having to be so secretive about it anymore might make things easier, I reasoned. I wasn't sure if Dennis would feel the same way, and I wasn't all that surprised by the other boys' reactions.

"You told her?" Dennis said angrily.

"I had to! I got this vision of a car that was going to crash into us, then had to warn her. We could have been killed otherwise!"

"Car crashes aren't fatal to vampires," Tim said simply. "Well, maybe, if the car caught fire."

"That's not the point," Susanna said.

"No, the point is that you're full of shit!" Carl said.

"Look, I know what I saw," Susanna said, "and I believe what Ray told me." She turned to Dennis with a pointed look.

"Fine, yeah, sure," Dennis said, throwing up his arms.

Carl rolled his eyes and let out a sarcastic *"pfft"* sound. Tim just seemed kind of amused, not really wanting to get drawn into the argument.

"My bigger point," Susanna said, "is that it was wrong of you two to keep something like this from the rest of the group, particularly when it could have been such an important advantage."

"What?" Dennis asked.

"Well, for example, if you really can control your victims like Ray said you can, we could have used that against Sheling tonight."

"No," I said, "we tried. It didn't work. The powers don't seem to work all the time."

"Yeah, I'll bet they don't," Carl said. "If you're so psychic, then tell me, what am I thinking right now?"

I peered at him. "You're thinking, 'There's no way you can read my mind.'" Carl's eyes became huge, and his mouth gaped open. "Okay, I admit it, that was just a guess."

"Or just reasoning," Tim offered. He was right. I knew Carl well enough to know that that's what he would think at a time like this; I hadn't had to use my powers for that.

"Look, you want a real demonstration?" Dennis said angrily. "How about this?" He turned to face Carl. "Ray, help me out here." I was about to ask him what he wanted me to do, but then I didn't have to. Dennis pointed. "You, there, sitting in your chair."

"Hey, that rhymed!" Carl said, having gone back to sneering.

"Why don't you try standing up?"

I willed Carl to be unable to stand, and I knew that Dennis was doing the same. Carl put his hands on either side of the recliner and began to get up, but then he couldn't budge. His eyes went wide again, and he quickly looked more panicked as he began to struggle. It was like he was glued to his chair.

"Okay," he said. "Okay! Stop! I believe you!"

Dennis and I released our mental hold on him, and he shot up out of the chair, still looking frightened. He looked back at the chair, then back at us.

"Wow," Tim said. "Impressive."

"Yes, maybe so," Susanna said. "Carl, it's okay. Calm down."

"Sorry, guys," he said, still freaked out. "Just please don't ever do that shit again."

"I agree," Susanna said. "We're establishing a ground rule right now. If this is something you two can use against our enemies, then fine. I guess it's an unexpected effect of the potion. But do not use it against anyone else in the group."

I nodded, and Dennis did the same, saying, "Fine."

"So," Carl began, looking back at the recliner before sitting back down in it, "if you can be all psychic and stuff, did you see Crowley's death coming?"

That stung. "No, I didn't. Like I said, it doesn't work all the time. And sometimes, I don't even realize that it's worked until after the fact."

"Yeah," Dennis said. "Like something will happen, and then you'll realize that you had a premonition about it earlier."

"What happened tonight with the car, though," I said, "that was new. And pretty freaky, too. I wonder if it will happen again."

When I later looked back over what happened the next few days, I remembered that I got a sense this night, though not necessarily an actual vision, that something extremely dark was on the horizon. It felt like an oncoming storm, the coming of something very, very bad.

The following night, there was a report on the news about Sheling's body being found, and the police were again being reluctant to admit that vampires were actually involved. A new possibility was put forth that there might be some kind of cult behind all of this, which I found slightly amusing. I had never thought of us as satanic or cult-like before; the tales I'd heard of people like that involved sacrificing babies or animals. Then my amusement quickly evaporated when the idea of animals being sacrificed reminded me of Crowley.

Carolyn, meanwhile, was pretty quiet. When asked how she was doing, she just shrugged and said she was okay, and she didn't seem overly sad, just withdrawn. She surprised me by being so eager to go out and kill, which turned out to be problematic this night.

The news report about Sheling's death was overshadowed by lots of speculative weather forecasting, the reporters fearing that thunderstorms might end up raining out the planned July 4th fireworks. It was also uncertain whether or not the fireworks display would be rescheduled for a later night or just cancelled, which would leave lots of patriotic locals disappointed.

We were also bothered by this for a couple of reasons. For one, Tim had suggested attacking the July 4th event just for the fun of it, turning what was supposed to be a happy occasion into a tragedy. That sounded like nice, cruel fun, and we had been looking forward to it for a few days. But the bigger worry was whether or not the rain would actually come. If it did, the last thing we wanted was to get caught in it.

Instead, we decided not to risk going all the way to the mall for the event and just killed relatively close to our house, which was when I noticed how Carolyn seemed to be coping with Crowley's death by being as vicious as possible. It bothered me a little, but I wasn't sure why.

In the kitchen, I watched as Susanna marked on the map where we had killed that night, and she also drew a big *S* on another spot.

"What's that?" I asked.

"That's more or less where we fought Sheling," she said, her voice low.

"Oh," I said. "Where's the park?"

"Roughly here," she said, pointing at the bottom loop of the *S*. "I guess it's not on the map because it hadn't been built when this was printed."

"Hmm," I said. "Sounds reasonable." I paused. "So, what did you think about Carolyn?"

"What?"

"I mean, how she attacked that man tonight. It was pretty brutal. I thought she was going to tear his head off when she jumped on him."

"So?"

"Just seemed unusual, I guess. For her, I mean."

"Ray, she's going through a lot. Her cat's just died, her boyfriend's out of town, we're doing all this vampire stuff, which you know she wasn't always so keen on…"

"I know, I know. But that's what I mean. I half expected her to say she wanted us to change back to humans again because of what happened."

"Do you want to?" she asked, eyebrows raised.

"Me? No!"

Susanna smiled flatly. "Then why do you think she wants to."

"I… I don't know, I just…" I couldn't think of anything else to say.

"Look, if staying a vampire and being more brutal about it is what she needs to do in order to cope with this, then I don't see a problem with that. Do you?"

"No, I don't suppose I… No." I barely understood what we were arguing about. I suddenly got the impression that this conversation was going to head into the "you're too young" territory or maybe something else I couldn't understand, so I just wanted to drop it.

We were distracted by Carolyn, who called to me from the yellow den. "Ray! There were a couple of messages on the answering machine, including one for you. Some guy named Nick. Do you want me to save it?"

"What did he say?" I asked.

"Just that he wanted you to call him back."

"Oh." I thought about it, then wasn't sure if I wanted to. I liked Nick just fine, and we had talked a couple of times since graduation, but I wasn't sure what I could say to him while the rest of us were all caught up in being vampires. *"So, what are you up to?" "Listening to punk music. What about you?" "Killing lots of people around town."*

I told Carolyn to go ahead and erase the message, then asked her who the other one was from, wondering if it was from our parents. "Oh, it was just Damon again," she said. He had occasionally been checking in while he and his band were on the road, and Carolyn had talked to him once or twice. Usually, he called during the day while we were asleep, and Carolyn had trouble getting in touch with him after dark.

"Are you going to call him back?" I asked.

Carolyn shrugged. "No, I don't think so. Not tonight." She sighed. "Actually, I think I'm going to go hang out up on the roof. Just... I don't know. Just because." She looked sad, and I felt sorry for her.

"Want me to come, too?" I asked.

"Not this time," she said, surprising me by smiling. "Need some alone time."

"Okay," I said, trying to convey my sympathy in my tone.

"If you see any lightning," Susanna said, "you come back inside. Okay?"

"Yeah, sure," she said. "I will."

After she left, Susanna asked me, "And how are you doing?"

"Me? Fine. I mean, I'm sad and all, but more or less okay I guess."

"You sure?"

"Yes," I said firmly. "He was more Carolyn's cat than anything." That was true, but I didn't like how my emotions were beginning to build up inside. Very quickly, I dropped out of the conversation and went to join the other boys in the red den.

It turned out that there never were any big thunderstorms Saturday night, which was disappointing because it meant that we probably could have gone to the fireworks event at the mall after all. Sunday night was a different story. We had barely made it out of the basement and into the house before a huge storm rolled in, and it lasted almost the entire night. Even when it let up for a while and we thought things were okay, the skies remained cloudy, and the wind never died down. Another bout of heavy rain would start, accompanied by lots of lightning and thunder, and the cycle kept repeating.

Thunderstorms had always frightened Carolyn, and at times, she seemed so much younger than she actually was, even screaming a couple of times when there were some particularly bright flashes of lightning followed almost immediately by huge claps of thunder.

Susanna assured us that we were okay as long as we stayed inside, but we were still aggravated by the fact that we couldn't go out and kill.

As had been the case before, we could in fact eat regular food and drink normal things, so it wasn't like this storm was going to cause us to starve to death. But there was something odd that we realized early on about this particular summer: Even though we could consume things other than blood, we found that we didn't want to. Blood was enough to satisfy our hunger each night, and normal food just had no appeal.

This led to us being very cranky about not being able to go out and feed, but Susanna had planned ahead this time. I was surprised when she brought out from the refrigerator three oddly shaped plastic bags filled with blood, and I was extremely relieved once I realized what they were. She divided up the portions among six glasses, heated them up in the microwave for several seconds, then distributed them around the table.

It was strange to be drinking blood from a glass and not from a person's neck, and it wasn't nearly as satisfying, but I was grateful for it nonetheless. By the time we had done this, it was well into the night, so everyone's craving for blood had been mounting for a while. There wasn't much room for complaining.

"Well that was interesting," Carl said. "Not as good as drinking right from the source, though."

"I was just thinking that," I said. I turned to Dennis, who smiled and wiggled his eyebrows.

"Of course you were," Carl said with a strange look. He seemed a little mad, but not terribly.

"I think we all were," Carolyn said. She had been told about mine and Dennis's psychic powers the night after we revealed them to everyone else, but she hadn't acted overly impressed or concerned. And even though she had been doubtful of their existence before, she accepted them once Susanna told her more details of how we had demonstrated them. "I'd much rather have done an actual killing tonight," she continued. "But thank you, Susanna. That was good thinking."

"Wasn't it?" she said, looking pleased with herself.

"So," Tim asked with a sort of sing-song tone, "where did you get the handy sacks of blood?"

"It's a secret," Susanna said, grinning. "I have my ways."

"Oh, come on!" I said.

"Nope," she said, acting more playful than I was used to seeing.

"Maybe she hijacked a bloodmobile," Dennis said with a laugh, holding up his finger in the shape of a gun.

Carolyn laughed, too, which was nice to see. "Or maybe…"

She was interrupted by a shattering burst of thunder, and the lights flickered but didn't go completely out. She screamed at almost the same time, but then recovered and laughed again, this time at herself.

Aside from the ongoing storm, the night was mostly uneventful. We watched TV and the occasional news reports about the weather, and it occurred to me that I never really seemed to care about the news unless we were being vampires. At school, our teachers were always complaining about us watching too much TV and how it was "dumbing down" our generation, but I always found that idea laughable. They also tried to encourage us, sometimes even assign us, to read the newspaper, which I found boring and also unwieldy. I didn't like how the pages were arranged, all big and bulky and not even in an order that made much sense to me, always falling over and getting crumpled. When asked by Mrs. Warren what might make the paper more interesting and make me to want to read it, I joked, "Well, you could try putting it on a TV screen."

But the news broadcasts were pretty dull to me as well. Being able to videotape the programs was great, as it meant that we could just watch the bits we cared about and fast-forward through the rest. Usually, what we considered relevant was vampire-related, but on this and some other nights, the weather was also important. In terms of just sitting down and watching adults ramble on about whatever was happening around the city or the rest of the world, that was just tiresome for me. I liked actual stories, fiction, and people acting out real-life situations. I wanted to be entertained.

We ended up watching *The Young Ones* again this night, which wasn't as good as the previous week's episode. It was still funny at times, but it was also kind of boring. That may have been due to everyone's bad mood, though; it wasn't until later in the night that Susanna surprised us with the secret stash of refrigerated blood. Still, watching the show again reminded me of Nick, and I thought about returning his call from the other night. But it was too late by then to call anyway, and I forgot about it by the following evening.

Things began to get strange by Tuesday. On Monday, the weather had cleared up again, and everything was more or less back to normal, though we still missed Crowley. Carolyn was still a bit sad and quiet at times, and she continued to attack very violently, her targets almost always being older men.

This night, we attacked people on a golf course, one that teenagers would sneak onto after dark so they could make out or just explore the place for fun. Carolyn mentioned that she and Damon had been there before, and I got the impression that Susanna might have been there back when she still lived in Augusta, too.

Being able to kill as usual that night had all of us feeling better, and we found ourselves not wanting to stay home, probably because we had been cooped up the entire night before. There was one of those Hammer Horror movies on TV just after midnight that Susanna wanted to watch, but the rest of us didn't want to bother. Instead, we talked her into coming out with the rest of us. We didn't even feel like killing again; we just wanted to get out and do something interesting. We ended up wandering around the city, some of us occasionally pointing out places we might want to attack on subsequent nights.

Toward the end of the night, we explored that abandoned veterans' hospital again, which Susanna and Carolyn referred to as simply "the V.A." I liked the place; it was fun to look around, seeing what was left behind and imagining what might have gone on there. I didn't know much of anything about what veterans were other than the definition: people who had fought in wars. In a way, I felt like we were waging our own war on the city.

And there was something that was fun about being in the building when we knew we weren't supposed to. The fact that it was old and derelict made it creepy, but in an exciting way. But from time to time, I felt just a little too overwhelmed by that feeling, like something bad was going to happen. I also began to wonder if the place might be haunted, but I didn't say anything to the others for fear of sounding scared or weak.

The first sign of something unusual Tuesday night came from the news, which we watched the tape of once we had gotten up. The fact that we had killed the night before was mentioned, but there was something new: Several people had been reported missing. While there was no implication that these disappearances were connected with the "supposed vampire killings," as they were beginning to be called, the fact that the story on them ran right afterwards was telling. It was also worrying.

"I don't like the sound of that," I said. "Reminds me too much of what happened last time." I looked at Susanna, who was frowning.

"Maybe," she said. "Except then, remember, it was our victims who were disappearing, and they just now reported on the people we killed last night. It might just be a coincidence." She didn't sound very convinced of what she was saying.

"But what if it isn't?" Tim asked. "What if it's those same vampires again?"

"I really don't think so," Susanna said.

"Me neither," Carolyn said with a shudder. "Remember how they looked, you know, afterwards. I'd say they were definitely dead."

"Right. And like I said before, I really think that if Robert had survived, he'd have come after us a long time ago. He never did know when to quit."

"Yeah, but…" Dennis began, then stopped.

"What?" I asked.

"I don't know. Probably nothing."

"Don't keep us in suspense," Carl said, irritated.

Dennis sighed. "Well… What if it's some other vampires? You know, doing the same thing. Snatching people up and turning them into real vampires."

"Then we'll beat their asses the same way we did before," Carl said. "Can we just hurry up and go out and kill?"

"Yes," Susanna said, standing up from her chair. "And don't any of you go jumping to conclusions. It really may be nothing at all."

"I hope you're right," I said, almost certain that she wasn't. "But maybe we should check. They said the people disappeared near 5th Street, so let's go kill down there and see if we spot anything weird." As I said this, I headed into the kitchen and looked at the map, trying to figure out where 5th Street was. I was, however, looking in the wrong place until Tim joined me and pointed out where we needed to go.

"Okay, fine," Susanna said. "I guess it's worth a look."

Nothing seemed out of the ordinary when we arrived downtown, and killing went as routinely as ever. There were occasional police cars here and there, but we easily avoided them. I had a weird feeling overall, but I didn't know whether to count that as some psychic thing or just nervousness, wondering if something bad really was going on.

"So what are we looking for, anyway?" Carl asked.

"I don't know," I admitted. "Something… unusual?"

"Thanks for clearing that up," Dennis said.

"Look, I don't really know," I said. "I guess just look around and see if you spot anything suspicious."

"Well, there's a group of talking bats hovering above 5th Street and Broad," Carolyn said wryly.

"Oh, shut up," I said, then felt guilty for getting mad at her. Less and less had been said about Crowley since his death, but I still felt bad about him, and I wondered just how much pain Carolyn was covering up. I was also beginning to feel foolish, having brought the group all the way downtown with no idea what to even look for.

"Look," Susanna said, "how about we split up for a little bit, fly around and see if we spot anything, then meet back here."

"Where's here?" Dennis asked.

"Corner of 5th and Broad," Carolyn repeated.

"Oh. Right."

"Why don't we just meet back at the house?" Tim suggested. "We could cover more ground that way."

"Hmm, I guess so," I said. "Everyone know how to find their way back from here?" They did. Unlike previous years, I — and apparently the others, too — had gotten much more used to the layout of the city and navigating it by air. Becoming familiar with the map probably helped, too. We each headed in our own directions, and I went northeast, closer to the river.

Being on my own was an interesting feeling, a combination of independence and nervousness. For the most part, I liked it, but I also wondered what I would do if I actually found something. I looked down at the streets below, spotting various people, but not many, and there didn't seem to be any evidence of anything unusual.

After several minutes, I concluded that there was nothing to find, and I got my bearings and began my journey back to the house. I was uncertain of my exact location, though, and had to fly down a few times to look at street signs before I figured out where I was.

But I worked it out pretty quickly and headed home with renewed confidence in myself.

From the air, I recognized the spot where the group had separated earlier, which I also felt proud of. I was getting the hang of things. Not far from there, I spotted another bat in the air ahead of me, but I wasn't sure which one of us it was. This bat seemed more darkly colored than any of us, but I thought that maybe that was just because it was so far away.

The bat flew down to a crowd of three people on the street below, and I expected it to latch on to one of them. We had already fed earlier in the night, but it wasn't unusual for us to get in a bonus kill or two from time to time. Because of the bat's dark fur, I assumed that this was either Carl, Tim, or Susanna, but I couldn't be sure. I also found it odd that whoever it was would be going after a group of three, but all I could do was watch and see what happened. Maybe I'd even join in on the attack.

All of a sudden, two very narrow red beams of light shot out from the front of the bat and struck one of the three people on the street. It looked like something out of a sci-fi show, like a spaceship or a ray gun firing on someone. I even heard a little high-pitched *zeeeep* sound as it happened, and I was completely bewildered. Even more bizarre was what the man who was hit by the beams did next.

As the other two people in the group continued walking, the third one stopped. In just under two seconds, his skin went pale, and he seemed to shrink inward slightly, his shoulders shrugging and his arms drawing up at his sides. I flew in closer but still kept high up in the air, further examining the changed man. On his hands were long, sharp fingernails, almost like claws, and his eyes seemed to glow red, though not exactly luminescent like ours did when we chose to make them do so. What I noticed next was barely even a surprise to me given what I had seen so far: His mouth drooped open to reveal fangs. He was a vampire.

Meanwhile, the other two people had noticed their friend's absence and turned back to face him. The woman drew one hand up to her mouth and screamed, and the man looked equally scared. The new vampire, meanwhile, seemed ready to pounce. The man shouted at the woman to run, and as they turned around, the vampire leapt at the woman's back and carried her to the pavement with his momentum, biting down on her neck as she screamed again. A part of me felt envious for a second, but I was also aware that what I was witnessing was a pretty big deal.

The man had started to flee but then turned back to try to rescue the woman, who was being drained by this new vampire. He shouted something, and the vampire looked up from the woman's neck. She had stopped moving and was facedown on the pavement, her long, straight blonde hair partly covered in blood, as was the vampire's mouth. The man drew back at the sight, unsure what to do, and was struck with two laser-like beams from the vampire's eyes.

The blast lasted only a second or two, and then this man also turned into a vampire, his features immediately changing just as the previous man's had. He stood there for a moment, baring his fangs, and the first vampire bent down and continued drinking from the woman he was killing. Her limbs twitched as he sunk his teeth back into her, and I could just barely make out her muffled crying.

The newest vampire, whom I thought might join in on the meal, instead looked up into the sky, but not in my direction. It occurred to me that I had completely lost track of the first bat I saw, presumably also one of these vampires, and I looked around trying to spot it but couldn't. I looked back down and saw the third member of the party change into a bat, then fly up into the sky and away. I was too freaked out by what I was seeing to take note of which direction he was flying, but when I thought about it later, I was pretty sure it was to the east.

Back on the ground, the feeding vampire had sat back and was done drinking, and he rolled the woman over onto her back. She was still just barely alive, her breathing faint and her eyes staring up at nothing. I continued to hover overhead, wondering what would happen next. The vampire shot his red beams into her eyes, and then she also changed, becoming a vampire as well. She was just as pale and had the same red eyes, which I realized looked a lot like the effect in photographs when the camera's flash made people's pupils look like they were lit up. She grimaced, her mouth full of fangs, then suddenly changed into a bat and flew away. The vampire who had changed her also turned into a bat and flew off, but in a completely different direction. Their transformation was more like the kind we used to have during previous summers than our current one; they would let off a quick puff of nearly black smoke as they changed, and the bat form flapped out from inside.

I sped back to the house, trying to digest everything. Besides being intrigued by what I had seen and realizing its relevance to the recent news reports about people disappearing, I also began to worry. Were these new vampires a threat to us? Did they know or even care that we existed? Where had they come from? Why were they here now? All of these questions raced through my head, and I hoped that Susanna might have some kind of explanation or at least an idea of what was going on. For all I knew, she and maybe some of the others had also encountered these vampires.

I wondered if maybe I could use my psychic powers to figure out what was happening with all of them, and I tried to picture what they were doing. But I couldn't be certain if what I was imagining was actually true or just what I thought might be happening. Once home, I realized that I had been right, more or less.

"Okay, this is some really heavy shit," Carl said, looking scared. On my way home, I had gotten a vision of him hiding in a tree with Tim as they watched a similar episode to the one I had seen, people being changed by these mysterious vampires and then flying away. "What does it all mean?"

"I don't know," I said. "Any idea, Susanna?"

She sighed, pensively looking straight ahead and not at any of us. "Not really. We don't know a thing about them." She had been the first to arrive at the house earlier, and she hadn't even encountered the new vampires. This was also something I saw in my mind when I reached out with it, her arriving safely. Carolyn, meanwhile, had also managed to avoid seeing them, plus she had stopped on the way and killed a man, though she didn't say anything about this. But as everyone else described what had happened to them, I realized that my visions had been correct.

While that should have been a comfort, it was instead even more worrying, as I could not get a read on Dennis at all. When I tried to see him in my mind, there was just a blank. "I'm really worried about Dennis, you guys," I said.

"Oh, he's probably just running late," Carl said. "He'll be fine."

"No, I don't think so. I've been trying to find him with my psychic powers, and there's nothing." Carolyn rolled her eyes. Before she had a chance to say something dismissive, I asked her pointedly, "How was that man you killed on the way home tonight, Carolyn?" She froze, then looked at me, frightened.

"I thought I said no more using your powers on the rest of the group, Ray," Susanna said.

"I wasn't… I mean… I wasn't trying to spy on everyone or anything. I was just worried! And I was able to picture what all of you were doing, just little flashes of it. Except for Dennis. For him it's just… nothing."

"That's not good," Tim said. "Do you think he's… you know…"

"I can think of only two things that could mean," Susanna said. "Well, three. The first could be that your powers aren't working, Ray, but I think you've already proven that they are. So…" She paused. "I'd say that either Dennis has been killed somehow, or else one of these new vampires got him and turned him into one of them."

Everyone let this sink in for a few moments. I didn't even want to think about the possibility that Dennis might be dead, so I considered the other option. "Is that even possible? We're already vampires. What would be the point of changing us again, you know, even if they could?"

"To make us more like them?" Carolyn offered. "I mean, they sure do sound like a different kind of vampire."

"That's what I was thinking," Tim said. "They don't seem to even care about each other. They just zap people, change them, and fly off in opposite directions. Sometimes they fed, and sometimes they didn't. And there wasn't any verbal communication at all, almost like they were following some kind of instinct."

"And did you notice how sloppy they were when they fed?" Carl said to Tim. "All messy and stuff. Their fangs were different, too. Like, all curvy instead of straight like ours." He held two fingers up to his mouth as he said this. I again pictured the blonde woman I had seen attacked and then changed earlier, her own blood smeared onto one side of her head.

We talked some more, trying to outline everything that we knew, but it wasn't very helpful. Dennis was still missing. I tried once more to reach out with my powers to see if I could find out what was happening to him, but it didn't do any good.

"So, what do you think's going on?" Carl asked me. He and I were flying back downtown to search for Dennis, while Susanna, Carolyn, and Tim were doing the same elsewhere.

"I have no idea," I said, frustrated. "I just wish I knew where these things started coming from all of a sudden."

"Hmm, how about Transylvania?" Carl said this with a smile in his voice, but I didn't find it funny. "Is that even a real place?"

"I think so," I said. "I remember Tim telling me one time that it was now called Romania, but I have no idea where that is. Probably Europe."

"Like where that Sheling guy came from."

Finally, something clicked. "Oh my God, Carl," I said, suddenly stopping my flight and hovering in place.

He turned around and maneuvered back to my position. "What's up?"

"I think I just realized something. Maybe killing Sheling wasn't such a great thing to do."

"What do you mean? He was a vampire hunter! He was going to kill us! Don't tell me you're getting all pussy on me, Ray."

"No, I mean, well, look at what's happened! We kill this big famous vampire hunter guy, and now…"

"Ohhh," Carl said. "And now Augusta gets overrun by vampires. Maybe they knew he was dead and thought this would be a good place to come!"

"Right." We hovered and pondered this for a few seconds.

"Well, fuck that shit," Carl said. "This is our town. They can damn well find another."

"Always so poetic, aren't you?" I joked, surprising myself. I wasn't in a joking mood, but that just came out. Honestly, I was getting more and more frightened at the implications of everything. Had we brought on our own destruction by killing Van Helsing?

Before I had a chance to think about this further, Carl said, "Look! A bat!" I turned in the direction he had been facing, and I saw it. Like the one I had seen before, this one was black, which disappointed me. For a second, I had hoped to see the familiar reddish-orange of Dennis's bat form.

"Don't get too close," I warned Carl. "We don't want to get zapped."

"I think we're probably okay like this," he whispered. "We more or less look like them. It's only in our people forms that we look different."

"Probably," I also whispered. "What's it doing?"

The bat seemed to be circling, like it was unsure what to do. Then it dove off to one side in a weird arc, heading for the ground below.

We followed it, and I saw a man walking, not realizing at first what was strange about him.

"What the hell is he wearing?" Carl asked quietly. "Did someone forget to tell him it's the middle of summer?" I then saw what he meant: The man was wearing a long, grey coat, and it looked out of place. I couldn't see his face from our vantage point, but judging by his hair style, he was probably fairly young, maybe around Carolyn's age. His hair was dark and long, kind of puffed up on top and hanging down the back of his neck, a style similar to Damon's, I realized.

The bat was approaching the man from behind, but rather than just blast him with red eyebeams from above, he landed and changed into his "people form," as Carl had called it. I realized that it was the first time I had seen one of these vampires do that. As with the opposite transformation, there was an accompanying cloud of black smoke, but almost no noise. The vampire crept up behind the man, arms raised and talons bared.

Nearby, a woman screamed, "Look out!" I hadn't even seen her; she was hidden from my view by some nearby trees.

The man spun around and saw the vampire behind him, who prepared to attack. But all of a sudden, the man's coat flew open with a quick motion of his arms, and he snatched out a long string of garlic cloves. The vampire immediately recoiled, and the man began to advance on him confidently. With another quick motion, the man pulled out a small wooden cross from another pocket in his coat, also holding this out toward the vampire.

Although he was starting to cower, the vampire didn't seem ready to give up yet. His eyes flashed red, and the two glowing beams shot forward. But instead of hitting the man and transforming him into yet another vampire, the beams veered off to one side and seemed to be absorbed by the cross. The shock of this apparently surprised the man, who jumped slightly and dropped the cross, which clattered to the sidewalk. The vampire regained some confidence and began to stand up, only to be slammed in the face by the rope of garlic as this new vampire hunter slung it at him.

The vampire clutched at his face and screamed horribly, and a small amount of smoke came from his skin where the garlic had touched it. He fell onto his back, and at the same time, the man pulled yet another weapon from his long coat: a wooden stake. He leapt onto the prone vampire and plunged the stake into its heart with both hands, immediately jumping back and standing up as the vampire continued to scream and writhe in pain. More smoke poured out from the center of its chest, and after a short time, it lay there motionless.

Carl and I continued to hover in the air, taking all of this in. I wanted to say something to Carl, but I was afraid to speak. The man walked slowly over to where the garlic cloves had landed, but all of a sudden, another vampire bat zoomed in from nowhere and shot him with its eyebeams. Immediately, the man was transformed into a vampire himself, and he quickly drew back from the garlic on the ground. He then threw off his coat, which crumpled to the pavement and spilled out a few more anti-vampire weapons. He looked around for a few seconds, pale and with a mouth full of fangs, eyes red and glowing. Then he looked up at the sky, changed into a bat, and flew off. The other bat was nowhere to be seen.

I also heard the footsteps of someone running away, presumably the woman whose voice I had heard earlier. I was a little bit curious as to who she might be, but by this point, I was too freaked out by everything to even think about chasing after her.

"Carl," I said, "this is getting bad."

"Very bad," he agreed.

The rest of the night was filled with more uncertainty. Everyone made their way back to the house eventually, everyone except for Dennis, that is. We were all fairly certain that he had fallen prey to these new vampires. Susanna, meanwhile, wanted to share something that had occurred to her now that she and Carolyn had been able to see these vampires firsthand.

"I kept thinking about what Tim said earlier about them seeming to just be following their instincts, not even communicating with each other. And that *almost* makes sense."

"What do you mean?" I asked.

"It has to do with how they would sometimes bite people and drink, but sometimes, they wouldn't. They'd just hit them with those beams from their eyes and move on. As far as instincts go, the primary drive should be to kill, or at the very least to drink blood. But for some reason, that seems secondary."

I thought about this, and she was right. "Secondary to what, though?"

"It's like the eyebeams thing comes first," Tim broke in, "like they're more interested in spreading vampirism than anything else."

"Almost like a disease," Carl said thoughtfully.

"Or a plague," Susanna said. "This could get out of hand very, very fast."

"You know what I wonder," Carolyn said after a few moments, "is what's going to happen when the sun comes up. Will they all know to hide from it?"

"I would guess so," Susanna said, then pointed vaguely in my direction. "Ray said that the vampires they saw avoided garlic and crosses, so presumably, they'd know to stay away from the sun, too. Again, instincts."

"And what about Dennis?" I asked. "What's going to happen to him?"

Susanna looked down, then back up at me. "I really don't know. We'll just have to keep hoping that he'll be okay. Maybe we can find him and change him back somehow."

"If he's not already dead," I said gravely, turning away from her.

"He's not," Tim said. "We have to keep telling ourselves that. Hey, for all we know, he could show up at the door any second now and be perfectly fine."

"He's not fine," I said. "I'd be able to sense him if he was."

Getting to sleep as the sun came up was difficult, to say the least. It wasn't helped by the fact that the mattress Dennis normally slept on in our basement hideaway was right next to mine, and its emptiness seemed to glare at me, keeping me awake. I rolled over to face away from it, but I could still feel the void behind me. I was worried about Dennis, about these vampires, about everything. My mind raced, not allowing me to fall asleep. What if he actually were dead, or if there were no way to get him back? What would we tell his father? Sometimes, I was so exhausted and worried that I felt like crying, but I didn't want to do that with everyone else in the room.

Another thought occurred to me, this notion of vampirism being spread, and whether or not we could stop it. For all I knew, we could all fall victim to this new threat, changed into these strange, more powerful vampires, no longer even being ourselves: silent, pale, and menacing. Maybe that's what real vampires were like; we were just artificial ones created by a potion, after all. I also remembered that, unlike us, most vampires I'd heard or read about turned their victims into vampires as well. I had sort of forgotten that over the years, having been used to our particular method of doing things. We just killed people and left them there, never to rise again. These vampires obviously had other plans.

The one small comfort I was able to settle on was that maybe this was all just temporary, that, like us, these vampires were just as likely to be changed back to normal by the rising sun, something Carolyn had mentioned. I had temporarily forgotten about the way that vampire earlier in the night had reacted to garlic and then ended up being staked and killed, which was just as well. The small hope that things might all be better in the morning — or for us, the evening

— was just enough to calm me down and let myself sleep, even if it wasn't true.

We got up the following evening and immediately checked the videotape of the 6:00 news to find out what, if anything, had been said about the latest developments. As it turned out, there was quite a lot of vampire-related news.

Many more disappearances had occurred, which was not surprising. The scale of it was so massive that not even the police could deny that something major was happening, but there was still no official admission from them that vampires were involved. I wondered just how much they actually knew, plus how many people might have been changed so far.

"In a very grim development," the news reporter said, "the bodies of nine people were found early this morning at various locations downtown. In every case, the bodies appeared to have been burned right out in the open."

"The ones who didn't make it in from the sun, I'll bet," Tim said.

"Shh!" I said, wanting to hear the rest.

"...of them even had what appeared to be large sticks of wood in their chests," the reporter continued. I was about to insist that the tape be rewound to hear the earlier part of that sentence, but then I realized what the woman was indicating. Those were the vampires who had been killed with wooden stakes, presumably by that man Carl and I had encountered the night before. I briefly wondered if he, whoever he was, might be able to keep these new vampires at bay, then remembered that he had already been turned into one as well.

The report ended with the predictable generic warnings from police for people to stay indoors, followed by concerned platitudes from the reporters themselves and some mild speculation before moving on to the weather forecast. Everything was supposed to be clear and free of rain, which I was glad to hear, but that was a small comfort considering everything else that was going on. For all I knew, one of those charred bodies that had been found was all that was left of Dennis.

We needed to go out and kill, so we did that closer to South Augusta, an area of town we hadn't yet been to that summer. As far as we could tell from the news reports, the other vampires had been mostly confined to downtown, so we were pretty sure we were safe. It was a quick hit-and-run attack, each of us flying down to the necks of our victims at a gas station on Gordon Highway, then heading straight back to the house. All the while, I kept an eye out for Dennis, disappointed but not surprised when I didn't see him.

Back home, we talked, worried, and speculated some more. By default, everyone held out hope that Dennis was still alive and that there was some way to change him back from what he must have become.

"I wonder if the same thing could happen to the rest of the people, too," Carl said. "Getting changed back, I mean. Maybe there's a cure."

"That would be my guess," Susanna said. "Their transformation was so instantaneous, not all that different from how quickly the older version of the potion worked. So that could mean that the condition is reversible. Or maybe not. We just don't know enough about them to be sure."

Carolyn let out a small laugh, but her expression was still sad. "Well, this is a little ironic."

"What's that?" I asked.

"Just, you know, this talk of changing those people back to normal now that they're vampires. Saving them somehow. All this time, we've been going around killing them."

"Yeah, but this is different!" Tim said. "We're just doing a handful a night, a few people here and there. We've been a lot more subtle. This is a much bigger deal!"

"I know, I know. Still, it seems like a bit of a double standard."

"Maybe so," Susanna said. "But there's nothing we can do about that."

I sighed. "Isn't there any way we can fight back?"

"How?" Susanna asked. "It's not like we can fight them by traditional means. That guy you saw last night, and Sheling for that matter, were using crosses and garlic and such, but we can't do that. If we try to, we'd just be changed back to human."

"Well, maybe we should!" Carl said. I looked at him, surprised. "I'm not saying I don't like what we've been doing. But maybe we'd be able to fight them if we could use regular vampire killers!"

"Just us?" Susanna asked. "Against all of them? We don't even know how many there are now."

"You're right," I said.

"But what about running water?" Carl said. "Maybe we could trap them somewhere, like a football field, then turn on the sprinklers. Or get the fire department involved, and they could squirt them with big hoses…" His face fell as he talked, and his voice got quieter. "Yeah, okay, so that probably wouldn't work."

"We stand a much better chance of surviving if we stay like we are," Susanna said.

We went on like this for a while, never coming up with anything useful. While Tim had expressed a small hope that things might blow over and the vampires could end up leaving town somehow, the 11:00 news shattered any chance of that. In the few hours since the last broadcast, things had gotten much worse.

"A frightening development in the increase of the report… that is, an increase of purported vampire activity, rather, in the Augusta area has the mayor considering declaring a state of emergency, officials say," the reporter said. I noticed that she was hosting the show on her own this time, and I wondered where her male co-anchor was. Another thing that was interesting was that, rather that her usual seemingly fake concern about things, she seemed genuinely nervous, blinking a lot and almost scowling.

She went on to report that possibly hundreds of people were now missing and that both the police and the news stations around town had been flooded with calls. People had reported seeing the vampires, both in bat and person forms, throughout the downtown area. The reporter did her best to keep things vague, official, and detached, not giving in to actually admitting that all of this was truly supernatural, but there was no way to deny that something, however implausible, was happening.

"Whatever the explanation, the bizarre activity seems to be spreading at an alarming rate," she continued, and the camera cut away from her to show a computer-generated map of the city. I recognized it as what was normally used for the weather map, but instead of various shades of green depicting predicted rainfall, there was instead a red-colored blob covering a small area downtown. "This map shows the area where both disappearances and supposable... supposed, rather, vampire sightings were reported twenty-four hours ago." The red blob changed, its size jumping to include a much larger span. "The reported activity then increased to this amount by six o'clock this morning. As of this hour..." The blob almost doubled in size.

"Good Lord!" Carl shouted. "That's insane!"

"This area seems to be affected," the reporter continued. Although she tried to maintain her professionalism, I could hear a slight quiver in her voice. "The phenomenal... phenomenon, rather, excuse me... seems to show no signs of abating."

As the woman went on with her report, Susanna jumped up from her chair and ran to the kitchen, then leaned over the map. As I watched her, I saw her look from the map to the TV, then back to the map again, pointing at it with her finger.

"We have to get out of here," she said. "Ray, turn that down." She pointed at the TV as she said this, and I picked up the remote, then hesitated.

"Hang on," I said. "There might be something else." I looked back to the TV, watching the woman give her report.

"It doesn't matter," Susanna said. "Turn it off now."

Tim stood up from his spot on the floor and turned the TV off with its own button, not waiting for me to comply. "She's right," he said.

"But..."

"According to that map," Susanna said firmly, "those vampires have spread so much that they're almost here."

"Here?" Carolyn said. "You mean to our house?"

"Yes. If they start swarming around here, we won't stand a chance. We have to go right now." She walked quickly from the kitchen back into the den.

"But where are we going?" I asked.

"West," she said simply. "That's all I can think of for now. That map on the TV showed that the vampires were spreading to the west. We have to stay ahead of them."

I didn't like this idea. Whatever else had gone on throughout the years, whatever threats we'd had to deal with, our house was always our point of origin, our safe place. To abandon ship seemed too scary. "But even if we do get away," I said, "where do we go? Where are we going to sleep when the sun comes up?"

"I... I don't know," Susanna said, clearly frustrated. "We'll just have to figure something out." I didn't like seeing her frightened and uncertain.

"Hold on," Tim said, his face brightening. "I think I know!"

"What?" I asked.

"The house. The other house. The one that the tunnel leads to! Let's go there!" "That's not a bad idea," Carolyn said, standing up. "Maybe we can escape that way."

"But we don't even know where that house is," Susanna said. She thought for a moment. "But I suppose you're right, Tim. It's as good of an idea as any."

After a hurried check to make sure all the other doors were locked, Susanna led us out through the front door, which she also locked behind us. I still didn't like the idea of leaving our house behind, and I was worried about Dennis, what might have happened to him, to say nothing of what might happen to us. I pictured his father, the goofy guy at the slumber party who tried to make us watch crappy old horror movies, and I again worried about what explanation we might have to give to him if Dennis ended up dead. But given how bad things seemed to be getting, maybe it didn't even matter. If the vampires continued to spread and we weren't able to stop them, the entire city, Dennis's father included, could wind up dead, or maybe undead.

These thoughts were running through my head while we gathered on the front porch. Susanna led us down the small steps to the front yard, and we started to make our way around to the side of the house and toward the basement door. All of a sudden, a black bat flew in front of us.

"What the…" Carl managed to say, then stopped short as the bat changed itself into Dennis, who stood there looking at us.

This wasn't the Dennis I was used to, though. He was pale and looked a little bit confused, not the usually confident and joking guy I knew. Back when I first met him, he had always seemed like some dumb fat kid that I felt the need to make fun of, stupid-sounding lisp and all. He had changed over the years as we had become friends, losing some of his extra weight and learning to conquer his speech impediment. He was a good friend, which was why seeing him this way was so difficult.

Like the other vampires, he had those glowing red pupils, and his mouth hung open to show those strange, curved fangs. This was the closest look I'd gotten at these vampires' fangs so far, and I noticed that the front teeth, the ones between the two main fangs, were also smaller, straight fangs. Overall, there was a much more threatening look to them. He also held his arms out from his sides, his fingernails having become sharp claws.

"Dennis?" I almost whispered. "Are you…?" I wasn't sure what to say.

"Come on," Carolyn said gently. "Let us help you." She stepped forward slowly.

"No, don't," Susanna said.

Without warning, Dennis's eyes lit up a bright red, and he shot his eyebeams at Carolyn. She had ducked away at the last second, and her head was turned toward me when the beams struck her. She screamed briefly, then stopped, her eyes opening and her mouth gaping as she changed. Within seconds, she had become one of them, her eyes now red and her fangs just like Dennis's. She straightened up and faced me directly.

I felt a hand clamp down on my shoulder, then heard Carl shouting, "Quick! Take off!" He pulled me backwards, but I just fell onto the ground, in shock over what I had just seen happen to my sister.

Carolyn began to move toward me, and I was vaguely aware of Dennis doing something behind her, but she suddenly stopped. She looked around quickly, first in one direction and then the other, like she'd heard something. Dennis was doing this, too, but I couldn't hear anything. And then, seeming to have forgotten about us, they both changed into bats and flew up into the sky. While their coloring as bats usually matched the color of their hair in human form, they were instead black like all of the other rogue vampires we'd encountered.

"What happened?" Tim asked.

"Oh my God." Carl pointed at the sky. "Look."

I saw what appeared to be a column of smoke arcing across the sky, its boundaries seeming to shift back and forth. I could also hear a faint bleeping sound, but there was no real pattern to it. Finally I realized that I was looking at a swarm of bats flying overhead, and Dennis and Carolyn had just joined it. There were hundreds of them.

Recovering, I stood up and asked, "Where are they all going?" Almost as soon as I said it, I realized the answer, and Susanna's words echoed my thoughts.

"To whoever's controlling them."

"What?" Carl asked. "Someone's in charge of all this?"

"You saw it," Susanna said. "Somebody was calling them. That's why they stopped attacking."

"But I didn't hear anything," Carl said.

"It was a telepathic call, I would guess," Susanna said. "Did you hear anything, Ray?"

"No. We should go after them. Maybe if we can find out who's behind all this, we can finally do something about it." I got ready to change form, but Susanna held up her hand.

"No. Not yet. Wait until they've passed overhead, and then we can follow them. We don't want to get caught in the middle."

It took a couple of minutes, but eventually, the swarm tapered off, and the four of us began to follow it.

It was a very long flight, but the pace was steady, so I didn't get too tired. That was one thing about being a bat that was interesting, that I very rarely if ever got tired when flying. I mentioned this to Carl one night, and he said that it might have had to do with the fact that we were smaller and weighed less, so there was less exertion involved. It seemed like a decent enough explanation, and I didn't have a reason to challenge it.

We flew a safe distance behind the bats, and I worried at first that one or more of them might spot us and come after us, but that never happened. They seemed to have only one agenda: to get to wherever it was they were going. I noticed that we flew over several people as we were leaving the city, and not once did any of the vampires swoop down to attack or convert any of them.

I had no idea where we were going, but I had noticed when we left the house that we were heading west, or maybe southwest. We went out farther than I had ever been in this direction, and I was amazed by just how unpopulated everything was. The few towns we passed over were small, not unlike Appling where my aunt and uncle lived. We were definitely out in the country and far from civilization.

None of us said anything to each other the entire journey, again afraid of alerting the other vampires. We just flew, which left me lots of time alone with my thoughts. I was still freaked out by seeing Dennis and Carolyn looking so different and scary, and I hoped that there was some way to get them back. If that were so, then it would presumably apply to the rest of the people who had been changed, and we could save them, too.

I also wondered who it was that had called them away, who was behind everything. I wondered if someone had created these new vampires as an experiment, perhaps with some different kind of potion. I thought of both Robert and his uncle, how they had tried similar things in order to make their own vampires or werewolves, creatures that they could control and use to kill other people. The actual answer wasn't too far off in terms of intention, but as for who it was, I kicked myself for not figuring it out sooner.

We finally arrived at our destination, another small town out in the middle of nowhere. We happened to fly past a bank that had a large, illuminated clock on it, and I saw that it was almost 12:45 a.m., which meant that we had been flying for about an hour and a half. How far away from Augusta we were, I had no idea.

We followed the bats to a large, run-down building that looked abandoned, as did some of the other buildings around it. The place might have been a school at some point, but I was never sure. Whatever it was, it had seen better days, and there were lots of holes in the windows, doors, and even in the roof. The bats poured into the structure via several of these holes, and we hovered in place and waited for them to finish going inside.

"Okay, now what?" I whispered once all the bats were gone. "Do we go in, too?"

"Yes," Susanna said, "but we need to stay hidden. Just be careful, everyone. And keep quiet."

She led us in through one of the holes in the roof, and we ended up perching on the rafters over what turned out to be an old auditorium. There were no seats, but I could see some spots on the floor where there used to be some. All of the vampires were in their person forms and standing, every one of them facing in the same direction. They looked like an army in formation, silent and unmoving. At the far end of the room was a stage, and on it were dozens of lit candles. As far as I could tell, the place had no electricity, so the only illumination was coming from the candlelight and from the streetlights outside. In the middle of the stage stood a man, his arms held open and a broad smile on his face. He was wearing what looked like a tuxedo, only with a black shirt instead of a white one.

"Welcome to you all!" he said in a strange voice. Like Sheling, he was old and had a weird accent, but it wasn't the same one. "I trust that your journey was a pleasant one." He laughed slightly and looked down at his chest, clasping his hands before it. Then he looked up again, still smiling. "But alas, I mostly say that in jest, as I know that your minds are not quite whole at the moment. But no matter; that will change over time as you continue to consume the living.

"But, for the sake of formality, I speak to you now to mark this momentous occasion. You are here because I have called you to this faraway place, though soon, we will return to that city from whence you came and sweep destruction upon it, conquering every small village along the way." He continued to smile as he said this, his fangs showing the entire time. This man was clearly a vampire, but he wasn't like the ones in the auditorium below. Like us, he looked mostly normal aside from his fangs, but he was much older. He had curly grey hair and a slightly receding hairline, plus a moustache that was almost white. Almost never did he lose his continuous grin; obviously he was quite pleased with himself.

"I am not quite clear if it is necessary, given the state of your young, primitive minds, but I will introduce myself to you nonetheless. I have been known by many names throughout the years, but the most recent one is Dracula." When he spoke his name, I didn't quite understand it at first because of his accent; it sounded more like "Droh-*cool*-yah." But as he said it, I heard a tiny gasp come from Susanna, who was perched beside me. In that moment, the wheels clicked in my head, and I realized what had been said. Part of me felt thrilled, almost like a fan getting a first glimpse of his favorite rock star. But that was quickly crushed by the enormity of the situation, and I was aware that this was not a good thing.

Another thought that went through my mind was, *Of course. Dracula.* We had already battled Van Helsing, so why not be faced with the world's most famous vampire next? But then I was confused: Susanna had told me back when I found that book at the hotel that Van Helsing had killed Dracula, so what was he doing here? I wanted to put this question to Susanna, but I didn't dare speak. Another thing that had me confused was his appearance. He looked nothing like the typical portrayals of Dracula I had seen before, all slicked-back hair, wild-eyed, and flapping around in a long black cloak. This guy was an elderly man with a moustache, and it occurred to me that he looked more like Colonel Sanders than Count Dracula.

All of this wondering distracted me for a few seconds, so I lost track of what was being said. I picked up the monologue a few sentences later; Dracula was explaining to the crowd what had happened to him in the past.

"...when I was tracked down," he was saying, "then killed by a group of people in my home country of Transylvania. They drove a knife through my heart, and I died, though only for the moment. I was reborn at the next sunset, but then that foolhardy Van Helsing found me once more." He said the name with an angry snarl, and for the first time, he lost his ongoing smile. "He was able to trap me in my coffin with a wild rose, one of those many seemingly arbitrary talismans which can have such adverse effects upon a vampire." I had never heard of that one before, but I wasn't about to speak up and question him. I then wished that I had taken the time to read the copy of *Dracula* I had found once I had gotten it home, but I had only skimmed over a few parts before getting bored and putting it away.

"But his efforts did not end there. The rose was only a brief solution, and this man sought a more permanent way to imprison me, to keep me from this world which is rightfully mine." Dracula went on to explain that Van Helsing found a spell that somehow bound the two of them together, making it so that as long as he was alive, Dracula would remain dormant. Not only that, but Van Helsing in a way stole Dracula's power of immortality, never growing older, though not actually a vampire himself. All of this was explained to Dracula by Van Helsing just before he impaled him once more, saying to him, "The hell of immortality is to be the price I pay to rid the world of the evil of you!" Dracula's voice changed slightly as he spoke this line, and I almost smiled as I realized that he was doing a pretty accurate impression of the man we had recently killed.

"And so I died yet again, lying dormant for almost a century, until Van Helsing met his end. Upon my resurrection, I came to the city of Augusta to find out how." He mispronounced the name as if it sounded like the month of August, which both annoyed and amused me. "The nature of the spell was such that he may only die by the bite of a vampire, and if there are indeed vampires in that city, then I would know them."

I began to get a chill, wondering if he might be able to sense us psychically. Remembering what Dennis had told me before, I tried to imagine myself and the others with me as invisible, hoping that might cloak us from him somehow. I then thought that if he had been able to find us in that way, then presumably, he already would have. Maybe he was just as unable to detect us as I had been to find Dennis and Carolyn with my mind. I had tried that both on the way out to this mysterious place and again once we were hiding above the crowd, and it wasn't working. I also hadn't been able to hear Dracula calling to them initially, so it seemed sort of like we were both psychic, but on different channels or frequencies.

"And there is so much to know about this new world!" Dracula said, again spreading his arms out dramatically and smiling. "Nations have changed names, and machinery seems to be everywhere. Mankind has achieved so much in the years I have slept, and I wish to learn more. Even I seem to have changed, perhaps a reflection of this new age. Never before has it been so easy for me to transfer my way of being to so many. And now, it is time for you to repay to me the gift I have given you." He spread out his arms yet again, this time as far as they would go, his palms flat. I noticed for the first time that his fingernails were sharp and pointed, much like those of the assembled vampires, who had remained motionless and unspeaking this entire time. "Cast your blood-rays upon me, that I might gain from you the life you have gathered thus far."

I wasn't sure what he meant by this, but all at once, the vampires shot their red eyebeams at Dracula. When I had witnessed this happening individually, the beams had made a faint little zapping sound, but the noise of hundreds of them at once was huge. It was a drilling, piercing sound, and I fought back the urge to let out an exclamation. Dracula, meanwhile, didn't even flinch, instead welcoming the glowing red rays as they converged. A luminescent cloud seemed to grow around him, and after a while, I couldn't even see him. After several seconds, the beams ceased, but not all at the same time; some lasted longer than others. Once all of them had stopped, the illuminated aura around Dracula diminished, and he seemed to absorb it into himself.

He had changed. His evil-looking smile was even more intense, and he had a maniacal look in his eyes, which glowed in the same way that the other vampires' eyes had. This faded after a few seconds once he began speaking again, but I barely noticed because I was distracted by how different the rest of him looked. His hair and moustache had changed, having gone from grey and white to jet black, and he no longer looked like he was losing his hair around the temples. In short, he looked younger, and when he spoke, his voice had lost the scratchy quality it had possessed before.

"That… was… wonderful!" he said. "Truly amazing! And…" He gasped, seeming genuinely surprised. "It's not just the blood energy. It's the knowledge, too! I now know everything that you do. Your thoughts have been transmitted to me through some sort of telepathic exchange. Though I suppose it was that way in the past as well. But this was just so… immediate!" He paced back and forth across the stage very quickly, his hands held behind his back, ignoring the crowd for a moment. "I need a little bit of time to process this." I realized that his speech patterns had changed; he'd begun to sound more like a modern-day person, not some hokey weird guy from a hundred years ago.

He stopped his movement and threw back his head with a dramatic laugh, then turned to face the crowd again to speak some more. It struck me as odd how he continued to talk to these apparently mindless vampires, and I wondered how much they actually understood him. It was sort of like a regular person speaking to a pet, or in this case, hundreds of pets. Maybe he was only doing it for his own benefit. "This is truly a time of wonders! So much change, so many new things to know! Oh, I've been away too long! The population of this world has increased… so much… blood… And what is this 'AIDS' that people are so concerned about? Something to do with blood… yes… but a disease… fatal, even… Could it harm me? Ha! What do I care for some trifling disease? I am Vlad Dracula! I am invulnerable!"

He continued to throw his arms out to his sides, occasionally looking up to the ceiling. Suddenly, his arms fell, and he jerked his head toward the assembled vampires. I noticed that they all looked thinner, more emaciated than they had before. Somehow, the transfer of energy to Dracula had drained them. They didn't act any differently, though, still standing there and looking at their master with dull expressions.

"Oh, but this is too good," he said, smiling more broadly than ever. "Not only were there already vampires in nearby Augusta —" I noticed that he pronounced it correctly this time — "but two of them are already here and under my power! Come to me, my new friends!" He held a hand out to the crowd, and there was a ripple of activity in it. For the first time, I was able to spot Carolyn and Dennis in the huge mass of vampires.

They approached from about one-third of the way from the back of the group toward the stage, the others stepping aside slightly to let them through. No one even turned to look at them as they did so; they just moved over when needed, then continued to stand in place. Once the two of them reached Dracula on the stage, they stopped at the same time, looking up at him blankly. He was quite tall, something I hadn't been able to discern until then.

He was facing them, but from where I was, I couldn't see his face anymore. As he spoke, though, I could hear that same smile in his voice. "So young! So very, very young! And yet, you were already vampires! How fascinating." There was a pause, and then he exclaimed, "Artificial! Not properly undead at all! Oh, but that's brilliant. Can it be that the scientists of this age have found a way to create vampires at will?" There was more silence. "Yes, I would very much like to meet her. And the other young ones, as well! Unless…" He began to look around, his eyebrows arched. "Unless perhaps they have already followed you here?"

I froze. I didn't dare to breathe. I concentrated harder on imagining us as invisible, hoping against all else that it was working. *Don't look up, don't look up,* I began to say in my mind, then tried to stop thinking even that, fearing that it might somehow have the opposite effect.

"No. Not here." I relaxed, but only barely. "They were preparing to run. But we shall find them. Come, you two. You will show me where this house is." He turned back to face the mute assembly. "The rest of you will remain here until my return." Then he, Carolyn, and Dennis changed into black bats, his form being larger. They flew over the crowd and to the other end of the auditorium, and as they did, the vampires turned to watch them go, their faces still expressionless and open-mouthed.

"Okay, seriously," Carl said quietly, "what the hell?" We had gathered outside of the building after Dracula had left, first sneaking outside to watch from the roof as he went. "Dracula? For real?"

"Sure looks like it," I said. I then turned to see Tim running lightly over to us, having just had a quick peek in through the door, part of which was missing.

"They're just sort of milling around in there," he said, "not really doing anything. Some aren't moving at all. Kind of reminds me of the cows out at your uncle's place, Ray."

"Probably a pretty good analogy," Susanna said absently.

"So what are we going to do?" I asked. "Is there some way we can beat him?"

"I'd still like to know what a fictional character is doing running around turning the whole damn city into vampires," Carl said.

"Not entirely fictional," Tim said. "Dracula was based on a real person."

"Well, apparently Dracula *is* a real person," I said angrily. "We all saw him, and we've seen what he can do."

"At least we've got some time now," Susanna said. "He's wasting his time going back to Augusta to look for us. I wonder why he couldn't detect us in there, though."

"Oh, I was hoping he wouldn't," I said. "It may have been a psychic thing, maybe not. But you know like when you're hiding from someone, and you try to sort of will them not to look over at you? Like that."

"Well, sure," Carl said. "Any little kid who's ever played hide-and-go-seek has done that. But whatever. I don't care. We just need to figure this thing out somehow."

"Hmm," Tim said, squinting. "Do you think that if we managed to kill Dracula, that might change all the other vampires back to normal?"

"Maybe," Susanna said. "I'm trying to remember how it went in the original book." She was quiet for a few seconds, then shook her head, frowning. "Won't work."

"What won't?" I asked.

"They got him because he was asleep during the day."

"So we can't…" Carl began. "Not unless we… Crap."

We went on like this for a while, not really coming up with any kind of plan. My hope was that since we had been able to kill Sheling, we would also be able to handle Dracula. We just needed to outmaneuver him somehow. But we still didn't know how to deal with the army of vampires that was uncomfortably close by. Before getting a chance to discuss that part of the problem further, we were interrupted.

"Look out!" Tim shouted, pointing at the building. He immediately regretted raising his voice, as that got the attention of the lone vampire who had wandered outside. Had we stayed quiet, we might have gotten away without being noticed.

It began running toward us, fangs bared and eyes red. I told everyone to run, but all of a sudden, the vampire shot his eyebeams at Carl, who immediately changed. The rest of us scattered, unsure what to do. Carl, now one of the enemy vampires, began to advance on me, and I decided to try to use my powers to control him.

"Carl," I said as bravely as I could, and I concentrated my powers on him. As I did, I made my eyes glow, hoping they might have a hypnotic effect. Carl immediately stopped running and looked confused, his lips frowning over the curvy teeth. His eyes lit up red, but then their color changed to match the glowing yellow of my own. As quickly as he had changed just a few moments earlier, he reverted to our kind of vampire, back to his old self.

"What?" he said.

"It's like what happened when we got turned into werewolves!" Tim said from behind me, which startled me. I hadn't realized he was

there; I had been too caught up in dealing with Carl. "Then I'll bet..."
He broke off and ran over to where the other vampire was shooting
his eyebeams up into the sky at Susanna, who was trying to avoid
getting hit.

Tim shouted to get the vampire's attention, and once it turned to
him, Tim lit up his eyes. The man's eyes flared red briefly, and then
he changed. Like Carl, he went from being pale and skinny to normal-
looking in just a few seconds, and he also looked quite bewildered. I
had no idea who he might be; he was just some random person who
had gotten caught and transformed by the other vampires.

"What?" he asked. "Who are you?" He looked around, trying to
figure out what had happened to him.

"Never mind," Tim said. "You need to get out of here."

"What are you talking about? Where's 'here?'" The man was
quickly going from confused to angry.

"There are vampires here, and you don't want to stick around," I
said.

"Not if you know what's good for you," Carl added.

The mention of vampires seemed to make an impression. I quickly
realized that this man didn't seem to have any memory of being a
vampire himself, but he must have had a frightening encounter with
some of them before he was changed. Susanna swooped down near
the man's head, and for a second, I thought she was going to kill him.
Instead, the man just screamed and swatted at his head, then turned
and almost fell over as he ran away. Susanna landed next to us and
changed form, watching the man flee.

"So that's how we'll do it," she said confidently. It was good to
hear that tone in her voice again.

Changing the entire crowd of vampires back to human proved
more difficult, though. Susanna wasn't exactly sure why our glowing
yellow eyes were able to counteract Dracula's effects on them, but
it worked, so none of us felt the need to argue. Initially, we thought

we could just stand on the stage and make our eyes light up, turning the whole group back at once. But Susanna pointed out the danger of someone recognizing us. After all, we had no idea just who might be in this crowd; there might be people who would know who we were once they were back to normal again. We couldn't risk that.

So instead, we sneakily made our way to the backstage area first, where we were lucky enough to find an old woolen blanket. Susanna draped it over herself, then said, "Oh, man, this thing stinks." With a pained expression, she bundled it up so that it covered her head and most of her face, the rest of it draping over her upper body. She looked a bit like some pictures I had seen of people in countries in the Middle East, or maybe some twisted version of the Virgin Mary in some low-budget Christmas play. "Okay, here we go," she said, heading for the stage. The rest of us watched from the side, just out of sight of the assembled vampires.

"Attention, everyone!" she shouted with authority. I was able to see a small portion of the crowd from where we were hiding, and they all turned to face her. The sound of so many people turning around but not saying anything was an eerie combination of muffled noise and absolute quiet, and just for a moment, I wondered if one of the vampires might zap her before she had a chance to carry out her plan.

I couldn't see her eyes from where I was standing, but the effect from her lighting them up and turning the entire vampire army back to regular humans was immediately apparent. What few of them I could see had their features fill out to normal, and almost as quickly, the faces went from dull and lifeless to animated and confused. In addition, what had once been a mostly silent auditorium quickly became a room full of discordant voices, everyone suddenly finding themselves in a strange place with no idea how they had gotten there.

"Please!" Susanna shouted, raising her arms, which were partly covered by the blanket. The crowd's volume diminished, but not by much. "You must all leave this place immediately!" she continued. The confused people continued to babble and shout, but there was another sound, that of lots of shushing permeating the room. At least some people were ready to listen.

"It's not safe here!" Susanna shouted. "You have to go!"

"Who are you?" a voice called out. Several people shouted in agreement. Other questions like "How did we get here?" and "What do you mean?" were also thrown out, each one adding more confusion and panic to the situation.

"Everybody, try to stay calm!" Susanna yelled over the noise.

"You said she used to be a cheerleader, right?" Carl said to me. "She's not doing a very good job of working the crowd."

"The vampires will be coming back!" she screamed, and that at least got some of the people to shut up for a few seconds. I knew that she was right. Dracula had a link with his vampires, so he might very well know that something had happened to them. More questions were shouted back to the stage, everyone more interested in interrogating Susanna than leaving.

"These idiots!" I said. "Don't they see we're trying to help them?"

"Well, I think it's time for a less sympathetic approach," Tim said. He changed into his bat form and flew out from the backstage area, and Carl and I quickly followed. We circled in the air above the stage, our eyes glowing for maximum effect.

People in the crowd began to scream and point, and Susanna looked up and saw what we were doing. "They're here!" she shouted, then ran off the other side of the stage.

I watched as the people reacted to us, but aside from a few at the far end of the auditorium who were running out, the majority of them just stood and watched us, still not sure what to do.

"Told you so," I heard Tim say, and he dove down to the front row of people, latching onto a man's neck.

"Now you're talking," Carl said, repeating the move on a woman farther back toward the middle of the group.

Terror blazed through the room as it finally dawned on everyone that they were in real danger. As I flew to make my own persuasive kill, I saw Susanna flying from backstage to join us. My victim was a rather plain-looking brunette with glasses, which had just been knocked from her head by a frantic person next to her. She had bent down to look for them, and I caught a glimpse of their crushed form on the floor just before landing on her neck and drinking from her.

Once I was done, I flew up and circled above the chaos, seeing that Susanna and the others were doing the same. Our plan, improvised though it was, had finally worked, and everyone was fighting to make their way outside. We gathered in the center of the room, hovering as we watched.

"Okay, I think they got the message," I said.

"Let's go, then," Susanna said. "I don't think we need to hang around and wait on them anymore."

I had thought that we were going to wait for Dracula and the others to return, possibly ambushing them somehow, but Susanna had decided that it would be better to go ahead and fly back to Augusta. "It will take a while for all those people to actually make their way out of town," she said as we flew, "and the last thing we need is for Dracula to come back and have fresh cannon fodder to turn into vampires again."

"Yeah," Carl said. "At least now, we outnumber him and the others."

Almost as soon as he said that, two red beams came out of nowhere and struck Susanna, and she veered wildly off to one side, her small bat eyes turning red as she recovered from the blast.

"Shit!" Carl exclaimed.

"Down there!" I shouted, having spotted a barn on the ground below. More red beams shot through the air, a pair of them just missing my wing. I led Tim and Carl to the barn, which was also in disrepair like the auditorium we had just left. We weren't all that far from the town, but we were a little farther east, having just reached an even less populated area.

We made our way in through a hole in the side of the upper half of the barn, then landed on the floor and changed our forms. "Now what?" Tim asked.

I wasn't sure. All I could think to do was hide, and I looked around the inside of the place. There were some old hay bales at various points as well as several pieces of farm equipment. On the far wall, I saw what must have once been a loft that had crashed to the floor sometime in the past. That seemed as good of a place to hide as any, but as I started to head toward it, I looked up as I heard the sound of flapping wings.

"No!" I screamed as the zapping sound flooded my ears and the red beams hit me. I crouched down and screwed my eyes shut, trying to will myself not to change. But it was too late. All I could see was a red haze, and my head was filled with intense pain. I was vaguely aware of strange noises around me, but everything sounded muffled. I fell to my knees and opened my eyes, but I still couldn't see anything but red light. My breathing was heavy, and my heart was pounding. I was afraid that at any second, I would completely forget who I was and begin attacking my friends, and I didn't want that to happen.

The red I saw changed to bright green, and a high-pitched whining sound filled my head. It was like when my ears would sometimes ring, only louder, but then it died down after a few seconds. The sounds around me began to become clearer. I heard shouting and various things being said, but I couldn't make them out at first. The green glow began to fade, and I heard someone say, "Blast him again!" This was followed by a faint zapping sound, then a deep-throated scream.

My vision mostly cleared, but I still saw everything through a greenish fog. Dennis, apparently having been changed back into a regular vampire, shot two yellow eyebeams at Dracula, who held up his arms and screamed, trying to shield himself. Tim also shot the same colored rays at him, causing him to stagger back some more. The beams were just like the ones Dracula's vampires had been using all this time, but they seemed to be coming from the yellowish glow our eyes usually had when we wanted them to.

Carolyn, also back to normal, ran over to me and knelt down. I was shaking, and my head still hurt. "Are you okay?" she asked me.

"Yes," I said, "but I don't see how." Her face was full of concern, but I turned away, more interested in what was happening with everyone else.

Susanna had joined the others in blasting Dracula with short bursts of yellow energy, and the effect on him was crippling. I glanced over at Carl, who had just picked up an old pitchfork. He steadied the metal end of it on the ground, then jumped and kicked at its center, causing it to break in half.

Dracula, meanwhile, was on his knees, still screaming and trying to resist the effects of the blasts being poured down on him. As my vision fully cleared, I noticed something strange about his face. Most of the time, it looked normal, much like I had seen him back at the auditorium, though twisted in pain. But whenever a short burst of energy from the vampires hit him, his faced abruptly changed and looked more savage, almost identical to the emaciated features of the people he had changed into vampires before. His eyes glowed red, his skin was paler, and his mouth had those same ghastly, curved fangs. As soon as a burst stopped, his face looked more human. Then another energy blast would make him look more frightening. The effect reminded me of switching back and forth rapidly between two TV channels.

Seconds after Carl had made his impromptu and rather substantial wooden stake, he ran up to Dracula and kicked him right in the face, sending him sprawling to the floor and onto his back. The others broke off their assault of yellow eyebeams, and Carl slammed the stake straight down into the vampire's chest, giving it a few more thrusts as Dracula shrieked in pain. Smoke poured out from the wound, and then there was a bright flash of what looked like lightning, only indoors.

Where Dracula had been, there was nothing left but an empty suit filled with ashes.

Carl stood still for a moment, then raised the stake up, streams of dust falling out of the sleeves, legs, and neck of the black tuxedo. He turned back to us, holding the stake and clothing up triumphantly, but he looked more baffled than heroic, at least at first. Susanna, Tim, and Dennis cheered and clapped, and Carl's face broke out in a wide grin. Still kneeling next to me with her hand on my back, Carolyn let out a gasp, but it was a happy one. Carl then got a stern and proud look on his face and slammed the stake to the ground, throwing one arm up in a celebratory gesture. I wanted to shout out my own congratulations, but my head was still filled with pain.

The headache continued for the rest of the night, and I still didn't know exactly what had happened. Flying home was difficult, but I managed it, mostly because I knew I had to. Everyone wanted to talk about the adventure after we left that abandoned farm, but Susanna advised them to wait until we got back home. She seemed to understand that I also wanted to talk about everything, but I wasn't yet up to it.

We stopped a little less than halfway there, then again once we got to Evans, so that Carolyn and Dennis could feed. Because of what Dracula had done to them, they were quite drained of blood and needed to replenish themselves. While they fed, I waited on the ground with the others and watched. The first time we stopped, I considered joining in on the kill, but I just didn't feel well enough to. Mostly, I was just grateful for the break in flying.

While Susanna, Carolyn, and I kept mostly quiet the rest of the way home, my friends occasionally talked. Most of the time, I didn't bother to listen to them; I was too caught up in my thoughts about everything that we'd been through. But one small thing early on caught my ear, which was Carl saying to Dennis, "Hey. Glad you didn't wind up getting killed or anything, dork-head."

"Yeah, thanks, Chicken Wings."

"Hey! Wait. What?"

"Well, you're a bat right now, so it's 'Chicken Wings' instead of 'Chicken Legs.'"

"Fine. I take it back." They both laughed. It was still a little weird for me whenever Carl and Dennis got along and joked around, but I liked it for the most part. In fact, what Carl said initially echoed my own thoughts. It was good to have everyone back together again, to have survived yet another big challenge.

All I wanted to do was lie down on my mattress in the basement even though there were still a few hours until sunrise. But Susanna didn't like that idea. "I really think it's better that you stay here with the rest of us so we can keep an eye on you," she said as I lay on the couch in the red den.

Carolyn, who was standing next to me, suddenly shoved her face onto my shoulder. "What are you doing?" I asked, anticipating the punch line.

"Keeping my eye on you," she said in a silly voice. I recognized the gag; it was from an old episode of *Mork & Mindy,* a show we had liked when we were younger. I laughed, but then I forced myself to stop because it made my head hurt more.

I was also reminded of something funny Dennis had done in class one day, when the teacher had warned the class, "I'm keeping my eye on you!" Dennis had jumped up in his desk and made an *"ew!"* sound as he frantically batted at his shoulder, trying to flick the imaginary eyeball away. That time, the teacher had ignored him. I thought of this and looked over at him, and he just smiled knowingly. Tim laughed, too, remembering the joke and then acting it out for old times' sake.

"So," I said to Dennis, "that thing with the yellowish eyebeams. How did you do that?"

"Just by thinking I could, really," he said. "Once I was normal again, I figured that if Dracula's vampires could do it, then so could we."

"Were you conscious of anything at all when you were one of them?" Susanna asked.

"A little. It kind of came and went. When I was aware of what was going on, I couldn't control it. I kept wanting to fight back but just couldn't manage it."

"Not me," Carolyn said. "It was like I blacked out. I guess I did. For me, it was like everything just jumped from the time you changed me to when we were all in the barn. Suddenly I was surrounded by everyone blasting these weird yellow things from their eyes and some strange guy screaming and all that. I didn't know what to do."

"And you, Ray," Susanna said, "you were pretty lucky, it seems."

"Still don't know how," I said.

"You don't?" Dennis asked. "Come on."

"Oh…" Carl said, turning from Dennis to me with a fascinated expression.

"Your powers shielded you. Yours are stronger than mine, remember?"

It made sense once I thought about it, but then just for a moment, my headache flared, and I winced. I closed my eyes, but all I could picture was Dracula's face, distorted and full of agony as he was dying. My eyes shot back open, trying to avoid the image.

"So, yeah," Tim said. "This whole thing was pretty weird. In a way, it almost seemed too easy." Carl asked what he meant, so he continued, "I don't know. I mean, I'm not complaining, but it seems kind of funny how we took big bad Dracula out so quickly."

"But it took forever to bring down Van Helsing," I said.

"Who?" Carl asked.

I left it to Susanna to explain about Sheling actually being Van Helsing and the copy of *Dracula* that we found at the hotel room. Tim went on to tell us what he knew about Vlad Tepes, the man Bram

Stoker supposedly based the character of Dracula on, which led to some speculation over just how much of the novel was actually true. My theory was that maybe the entire thing had been real, and Bram Stoker was just a pen name that Van Helsing had used back when the book came out. Susanna and Tim both doubted this. All I could say to defend my position was, "Well, Dracula was real. We all saw him."

"And what was up with how he looked?" Carl asked. "He didn't look a thing like Dracula. I always thought he was supposed to have white make-up on, slicked-back black hair, red lips, you know."

"No, that's Pee-wee Herman," Dennis quipped. "Pretty sure he's not a vampire."

"You never know!" Tim said with a smile.

"Well, if he shows up next, we'll kill him, too," Carl said, then laughed. "But yeah, we're pretty bad-ass, aren't we? We just managed to wipe out the world's biggest vampire hunter and then the world's scariest vampire. I'd say that makes us pretty cool."

As we wound down the night and settled in the basement, I was mostly feeling better, and I was glad to have Dennis back. I was still a little weirded out by how things had gone, though. For a moment, I got this notion that this could be a good stopping point, that maybe things had gone far enough and it was time to change back to regular humans. I didn't say so to the others, afraid of what they might think of me, maybe viewing me as weak or scared by everything that had happened. By the following night, I dismissed the thought entirely, writing it off as a side effect of being worn out and not feeling well.

Getting to sleep wasn't that difficult, though a few times early on, I kept picturing Dracula's face in my mind. I could see him on that stage in whatever small country town that might have been, all arrogant and self-satisfied, only to be killed by us roughly an hour later. I even felt a little jealous of Carl for having been the one who killed him; I would rather have done it myself.

The news programs that we watched the next evening took a while to get through because we had set the timer to record not just the 6:00 show, but two earlier ones from the same day. By the lunchtime broadcast, reports had started coming in about the missing people turning up in a place called Warren County, which I had never heard of but assumed was where we had been the night before. Several of the people in that group had turned out to be policemen, and they were able to organize things and get everyone back to Augusta, mostly in buses.

"Though almost everyone escaped without injury," the reporter explained, "nearly all of the victims of this bizarre displacement appeared to be in ill health. The nearly one thousand people are being transported to various hospitals around the city. More on this story as it develops."

The evening news had more details, stating that the people had been examined at the local hospitals and all needed blood transfusions. Appeals were made to citizens to donate blood, but no one knew yet if that would fully restore these people to health. The explanation that the doctors seemed to be settling on was that this was some unknown disease that caused anemia and memory loss, and there was speculation that it might be highly contagious. Still, no new cases had been reported, so they hoped that this was just a brief fluke.

There was no explanation for why every single victim of this supposed outbreak ended up in the same small town so many miles away, none of them remembering how they had gotten there. And while the news attempted to dance around the obvious link between the event and the sudden spike in vampire sightings and reports, there was also the testimony of the people themselves to consider.

Many of them spoke of the mysterious woman who had warned everyone to escape, though there were differing testimonies. One eyewitness claimed that the woman was killed by the vampires when they returned, but of course that wasn't true; Susanna had just run offstage when the others and I attacked the crowd. Another man left out any mention of the bats that attacked at all and just said that everyone panicked, but the police had managed to settle everyone down and get them to safety. One woman even claimed that it was the Virgin Mary who appeared to everyone and appealed to them to leave before they got hurt. This prompted a few jokes from us at Susanna's expense.

"Oh, please!" she said. "It just shows you how hard people will try to believe something just because they want to."

"It's how people cope with things they don't understand," Carolyn said. "Some people will probably repress the experience altogether."

Carl started to ask her something about that, but Susanna shushed him as the next news report began.

"While the debate appears to still be out as to whether or not vampires truly exist and have been responsible for recent events, one local group has decided to take these claims very seriously. A representative from a newly formed organization calling itself 'Life Force' contacted Channel Four Action News today to announce its intention to, quote: 'provide support for survivors and family members impacted by this new and very real threat. We have grown tired of law enforcement's lack of concern for this city's well being and wish to take steps to ensure the safety and comfort of its people.'" The reporter looked up from the paper she had been reading this quote from, then said, "Anyone with information regarding alleged vampire activity is asked to call the telephone number shown on your screen." No phone number appeared, which prompted a laugh from me.

"Typical," I said. I always found it funny whenever the local news messed things up; it seemed in direct contrast to their authoritarian and official stance on things, to say nothing of their faked sincerity. I was in a much better mood, feeling mostly recovered from my ordeal the night before. I still had a rather odd feeling in the back of my mind, though, something strange that I couldn't quite figure out. Mostly, I was just glad to be rid of that awful headache.

Once we were done with the news, it was time to go out. "So, where to now?" Tim asked.

"Let me see," Susanna said, heading to the kitchen to look at the map again. Usually, I followed her when she did this, but I didn't this time. "I'm going to mark off the area they reported last night that all of Dracula's vampires had spread to. We should probably just consider that part of the city off-limits for now. The police now have a defined area that they can search, so good for them. There are plenty of other places we can go."

"Hey, why don't we go to one of those hospitals?" Tim suggested. "What they said about getting all those people to donate blood…"

"Yeah!" Dennis said. "That sounds like a free buffet! Everyone lined up, just waiting to give. We can help!"

"No," Susanna said sternly, but she was also smiling. "Those places will be too crowded, maybe even guarded. We need to go somewhere more simple."

A thought entered my mind, and I said, "Hang on a second, everyone. I need to go check on something." I wasn't even sure what that was. It was like I had forgotten, but I had no idea just what I'd forgotten.

"Okay," Susanna said from the kitchen. "But hurry back. We need to go out."

"Sure," I said, still unclear about what I was doing. I first walked toward my bedroom, but I paused by the stairs that led up to Susanna's room, looking at the front door. *Outside,* I thought. There was something out there that I needed to do.

I walked to the front door and unlocked it, being very quiet but not knowing why. I also opened the door very slowly, not wanting the others to hear me. After closing it behind me and slowly releasing the handle, I walked as quietly as I could through the front yard and toward the driveway. Then I stopped. Why had I stopped? What was it I was supposed to be looking for?

The weather was clear, but there was mist on the driveway, the kind I would see sometimes just after a thunderstorm when the sun had come back out. But it was night, and I could tell from the lack of dampness that it hadn't rained. Nevertheless, there was that mist, which was traveling along the driveway slowly. I should have realized that something was odd when the mist began to build up and move more quickly, but I just stood there and watched, not really thinking anything at all.

The mist thickened into fog and began swirling around quickly and soundlessly, growing into a sort of pillar in front of me. It stopped growing when it reached about six feet high, but it continued to spin in place, growing more and more dense. A glowing red light appeared near the top of the column, and it looked familiar, but I couldn't remember why. The light became oblong, then split into two small, separate globes side-by-side. The spinning column of smoke shrank in on itself at various points and formed curves, the glowing orbs becoming the eyes of a man. Moments later, Dracula stood before me, and I could do nothing but stand there and stare at him.

He was smiling, but his expression abruptly changed to rage, and he thrust his hand at my throat. His grip felt strange, not like that of a normal man. It was like being touched by a mannequin, the skin not exactly cold but certainly not warm like a living person's. His fingernails, or claws, dug into the flesh of my neck. The pain was immense, and I began to choke, finally coming back to my senses and realizing what was happening. I tried to struggle and beat at Dracula's arm with both hands, but it did me no good.

"You impudent child!" he said in a harsh whisper. "How dare you attempt to meddle with me!" I wanted to call for help, but I could barely breathe, let alone cry out. My face began to feel hot and tingly, and tears involuntarily welled up in my eyes. "Did you really think that you and your fledgling friends could destroy me? I, who have lived for over five centuries, conquering the weak, enslaving the poor, and feeding on all that lives?" He was beginning to speak more loudly, but at the same time, my ears felt like they were closing up, and my vision was getting cloudier.

He jerked me to one side, throwing me to the ground. I gasped and choked for air, dizzy and trying to clutch at my throat with one hand while trying to hold myself up with the other. It was too much effort, and I collapsed, feeling the dirt and grass on my face.

As I rolled over to one side, I saw him stepping towards me as he continued to speak. "I know what you are," he said gravely, "and I know of those powers inside you. You stole the power I intended to use to make you mine, and you think to use that power against me! Not so, you little animal, not so!"

I was looking up at him from the ground, and he seemed impossibly tall, bigger and more frightening than anything I had ever seen. I was in more agony than I had ever felt in my life, too much to even move. Once or twice I tried to start crawling away, but I knew that it was hopeless. My mind raced to find some way out of this, and finally it hit me: I could fight him with the same yellow eyebeams that the others had used the night before. But when I tried to make my eyes glow, I couldn't even do that. I couldn't concentrate enough; there was just too much pain.

"So, then," Dracula said, "if you will not be mine the way I intended, then we shall have to resort to more traditional means."

I had no idea what he meant, but then I was distracted by the sound of Susanna and Carolyn calling to me from across the yard. I had been completely disoriented up until that point, but once I reasoned that they were at the front door of the house, I got my bearings and realized just where I was. I rolled over again, this time facing the house, and I saw them coming in our direction, still calling out my name. Part of me wanted them to rescue me, but I also wanted to warn them to stay away, which was impossible in my condition.

"Oh my God," Susanna said once she got close enough to see Dracula. She froze in place, as did Carolyn. Then Carolyn looked down and saw me sprawled on the ground at his feet, and she called out my name again. She and Susanna began running toward me, but after a few steps, they both stopped simultaneously and just stood there. Their expressions went from frightened and concerned to completely blank, and I heard Dracula chuckle triumphantly.

They began walking slowly, their eyes fixed on Dracula, whom I heard behind me moving over a few paces. Their heads turned in sync to match his position, but I still couldn't quite see him. With great pain, I managed to reposition my head so I could see what was happening, even though part of me didn't want to. I just wanted all of this to stop, for everything to go away, but I also couldn't stand not seeing what was going on.

Dracula, whose eyes had that same red-eye photograph look to them I had seen before, was smiling and holding his arms wide, just as I had seen him do several times at the theater. "Yes, my lovely ones," he said, "come to me." They stopped a couple of feet in front of him, and Dracula smiled even more evilly, reaching with both hands for the black bow tie around his neck. He unfastened it quickly, then unbuttoned his shirt, his chest slowly becoming exposed as the shirt opened more and more. He then pulled it wide open, baring his chest. From my vantage point on the ground, I could see him perfectly positioned between the backs of Susanna and Carolyn, and I wondered later if he had done that on purpose so I could see every gory detail.

Using one of his perfectly pointed fingernails, he carefully tore open a small, horizontal gash above his left nipple, then did the same over his right one. Blood began to trickle out slowly, and though I wondered if this might be hurting him, I then noticed that his expression remained mostly unchanged. He was still smiling as diabolically as ever, maybe even more as he continued this bizarre behavior.

"Now, my young beauties," he said in a low voice, "become one with me, blood of my blood, flesh of my flesh." Carolyn and Susanna stepped forward and right up to his bleeding chest, the backs of their heads now obscuring my view of the wounds he had made. He grabbed the backs of both of their necks and pulled them right up against him, and I saw their bodies go limp, held up only by his powerful grasp.

Dracula threw back his head and sighed dramatically, and then there was silence for a moment. I heard, very faintly, a weird sort of slurping sound, and it reminded me of scenes I had seen in movies or TV shows when a man and a woman kissed, a sort of obnoxious smacking sound that had always grossed me out. Usually, that was accompanied by the actors making these supposedly pleasant high-pitched *"mmmm"* noises to each other, but there was none of that here. There was just that weird smacking sound, which I realized was accompanied by the sounds of someone swallowing. I was horrified once I realized just what was happening: Dracula was feeding his own blood to my sisters.

Some of my strength returned, but I was still in tremendous pain. I managed to maneuver myself up from the ground with my arms, mostly still prone on the ground. If I could manage to stand up, maybe I could pull them away from Dracula, saving them somehow. But then, things got even worse.

While I struggled, my sisters went from being motionless to more animated as they drank, their bodies moving back and forth and side to side in a strange way. It was almost like they were dancing, their hips going left to right slowly and rhythmically, and they had begun reaching for his chest and around his back with their hands. He released his grip on them, putting his arms at his sides, and they stood back, also putting their arms at their sides and becoming still. They then turned around in unison, and the sight of them was one of the most horrifying things I had ever seen.

My two sisters, whom I had spent my entire life simultaneously looking up to as role models and also despising whenever we happened to get into a fight over something petty, now looked completely foreign to me. There was no more bossy, condescending oldest sister whom I was forced to having a grudging respect for because I knew she was probably right most of the time. Gone was the sometimes hilarious, sometimes infuriating tomboy-turned-glamour puss that I struggled between admiring and hating, depending on how well we happened to be getting along from moment to moment. In their place and wearing their faces were two terrible creatures, pale and menacing, curvy fangs bared and the lower half of their faces smeared with blood. Their eyes were the same glowing red ones I had seen on those countless, nearly mindless vampires from the past couple of nights, but even then, they looked different.

Those vampires, the ones who had rapidly spread their condition by means of those quick and convenient eyebeams, had seemed more or less vacant, not much more intelligent than apes or chimpanzees. They were sort of human, but not really. Carolyn and Susanna, while obviously under the control of the monster standing behind them, seemed much more alive, though this was only conveyed by their body language. Like the other vampires we'd encountered before, they were mute and seemingly subordinate, but there was something new. Their eyes and facial expressions were more animated, and I felt like they actually knew who I was. When I thought about them a bit later on, I realized that I was very glad that they didn't speak, as they might have said some truly horrible things.

"And now you see, young one," Dracula said, looking down at me with that same infuriating sneer. "You cannot stop me. They are mine."

The vampires that had once been my sisters smiled and laughed, but it was this weird, fake laughter that seemed more about mocking me than laughing at what their master had just said. It wasn't even like the fake, social laughter I had heard them both use when they were human and talking with their friends. I almost wished it had been; that at least would have been familiar.

"Now, my beautiful ones, it is time to reward your brother for his interference in my plans." Susanna and Carolyn, smiling in much the same way Dracula was, walked over to me and knelt down, then picked me up from the ground. This didn't seem to require any effort at all on their part, and it was a very weird sensation because it reminded me of when I was much younger, a small child who could gently and easily be picked up from the floor by a grown-up. Each of them was on either side of me, Carolyn slightly more facing my front, Susanna just out of my field of vision. Carolyn opened her mouth wide, fangs bared, and then she and Susanna simultaneously lowered their heads onto either side of my neck.

I tried to scream as they bit into me, but all that came out was a series of quick, soundless hisses. I felt their lips on my skin, and I could hear them drinking my blood as it poured down their throats. Very quickly, I began to feel weaker and weaker, and I knew that there was nothing I could do to stop this.

"Ray!" I heard Carl calling from the house. "Where is everybody?"

I was suddenly dropped onto the ground, and I heard my sisters move away from me, but I couldn't see what was going on. I could barely move or even think. Dennis's and Tim's voices entered earshot, and I was aware of lots of shouting and more of those now familiar zapping noises.

After a few moments, things settled down, and I was aware of someone sitting down next to me on the ground. I was then rolled over onto my back by Carl.

"Holy shit!" he said. "Look at his neck!"

Tim and Dennis also knelt down and examined me, and while I was glad that they had arrived, I didn't like the looks on their faces. I tried to ask them what had happened, but only a faint croak came out at first. I concentrated, then managed to get the question out.

"Looks like Dracula came back," Dennis said. "And he got Susanna and Carolyn. But what got you?"

"Susanna and Carolyn," I managed to say. "He… did something to them. Then they got me."

"We tried to get them with our eyebeams," Tim said, "but they flew away too fast."

"Let's get him inside," Carl said.

"But what about Carolyn and Susanna?" Dennis asked. "Shouldn't we go after them, try and change them back?"

Carl wiped at the wound on the left side of my neck, and I winced, expecting more pain. Surprisingly, there wasn't any. "The bleeding's stopped," he said. He then tilted my head to look at the other side of my neck. "There, too. Looks like you're healing already."

"It's because he's a vampire," Tim said.

I began to feel a little bit better, but not much. "Fine," I said, my voice slightly closer to normal. "I'll recover. You guys go on and go after them."

"We can't just leave you here!" Tim said.

"Yes you can," I said, suddenly feeling heroic. "Did you see which way they went?"

"West," Tim said. "Maybe they're heading back to Warren County again. You really want us to just leave you here?"

"Yes," I said. "I'll recover in a little while, then try to catch up with you. Please, just go." Aside from the urgency of the situation, there was another reason I wanted them to hurry up and leave, but I didn't want to let on as to what that was.

Once they had flown away, I lay on my back in the grass, running everything through my head. When I got to the point where I was picturing Carolyn and Susanna getting changed so horribly by Dracula, I cried, which I knew I would do. My whole body shook, which just made everything hurt more. And while I had started to feel stronger once I'd been told that I was healing, that stopped once the others were gone. I felt weaker again, dizzy, and unable to move. I was alone and scared, wishing the others hadn't left. I felt an unfamiliar sense of dread, and I wanted to will the others to come back, to help me somehow.

I tried to reach out with my psychic powers, and for a moment, I could see my three friends flying through the air. The vision was cut short as a terrible pain shot through my head, and I saw what looked like a greenish flash of lightning. Then I felt even worse, still regretting telling them to go. I wondered if I might die, but then, how could I? I was a vampire. I was supposed to be invulnerable as long as the potion was working and doing its thing. But I'd had all that blood drained from me, so was that an issue? That thought made me picture the evil, transformed Carolyn and Susanna as they bit my neck and drank from me, and I screwed my eyes shut, trying to make the memory disappear. It didn't work.

Reaching out with my mind again, I saw Tim and the others flying up from a group of three people they had just killed, but that same terrible pain filled my head, and I again saw that green flash. It was like my powers were damaged, and using them made me hurt. I realized that my friends had stopped to kill, presumably to get their strength up, and then I was aware of the fact that I hadn't yet taken any blood that night. Not only that, but I'd had mine drained, so I was even weaker as a result. Could that mean that, even as a vampire, I might die after all? Wasn't the whole point of vampires that they needed blood to survive?

I lay there, getting more and more scared. I closed my eyes, and my mind started falling apart. Thoughts and images ran through my brain, seemingly random and disjointed. I even pictured my brain inside my skull, green arcs of lightning pulsing wildly through it, like some computer in a sci-fi movie exploding after being given an impossible logic problem to solve. I grew more frightened, unable to comprehend what was happening to me. Nothing made sense anymore, and I suddenly forgot who I was, what anything was. I realized that I had been hearing myself breathe heavily through my nose, each time with increased effort. I breathed in deeply once more, then didn't exhale. Everything went black.

When I awoke, I had no idea where I was or what was happening. There was a strange humming, which I quickly recognized as the sound of a moving car. The vibration all around me was a familiar sensation, and as I became aware of the feeling of cloth on my skin, I realized that I was lying down in the back seat of a car. I was on my back, and I began to feel around with my hands, trying to figure out my surroundings.

I must have made some kind of vocal noise when I regained consciousness, as it got the attention of one of the people in the front seat, a young woman who turned around and looked at me with wide, brown eyes and a concerned look on her face. "Hi," she said to me in a cooing voice.

"Where…" I managed to get out, but she cut me off, holding her hand up.

"It's okay," she said in that same tone. There was definitely something calming about it. "We found you in the yard in front of someone's house. It looks like some vampires got you. But don't worry. We're taking you to the hospital. Just lie back down and relax."

I did as she said, still feeling terribly weak. But I still felt unsafe, disoriented, and confused. I didn't know who this woman was, and I couldn't see the driver. "Who are you?" I asked.

"Life Force," a man's voice said from the driver's seat. "We're here to help."

"Don't worry," the woman said. "It's okay. Do you remember what happened to you?"

I did, but I wasn't about to tell these two strangers. "No," I said as I sat back up, managing to maneuver myself around to the other side of the back of the car so I could get a look at the man who was driving. There was nothing all that remarkable about him aside from the confident manner in which he spoke. He went on to explain how he and the woman had been driving along and happened to spot me on the ground, then stopped and got out to help. I tried to pay attention to what he said, but I was distracted by two things: a strange, unpleasant smell coming from somewhere, and the overwhelming need to drink the blood from these two unwitting good Samaritans.

The car slowed to a halt, at which point the woman said, "Oh, go on, run the red light! There's no one around."

"There might be a cop hiding somewhere," he said in his deep, authoritative voice. "The last thing we need is to get pulled over and have them give us a hard time. They're great at giving out tickets, even if they totally suck when it comes to handling the vampire situation."

Somehow, the mention of the word "vampire" made me involuntarily spring into action. That word was at the core of my being, it was who I was, and within it lay the remedy to how weak and vulnerable I was feeling. I needed to feed. Before I knew what I was doing, I had lunged forward from the back seat and was drinking from the neck of the driver, who screamed briefly. The woman also screamed, this piercing, grating whistle pouring down my right ear, and almost as a reflex, I punched her face with my right arm, not even looking as I did it. The shrill scream abruptly stopped, and I continued to drink from the man, soaking up every drop I possibly could.

Several seconds later, I turned away from the drained man's neck and looked over to the woman, who was sitting in the passenger seat completely motionless, her head turned away at a weird angle. I realized that she was dead; apparently, I had hit her so hard that I'd broken her neck. I didn't care, though, because there was another source of the precious blood I so desperately needed. It was a weird feeling to be drinking from someone whose heart had already stopped beating, but I took in the nourishment just the same. By the time I was done with her, I was finally starting to feel better, or at least closer to normal.

I also realized that the car was moving, something I had been only vaguely aware of the whole time I had been feeding on these two. It was creeping along slowly and beginning to veer off the road, the steering wheel turning on its own. I needed to get out of there, so I reached over the body of the dead woman and frantically pushed down on the switch in the car door, the window humming as it opened. I then changed into a bat and shot out of the car, escaping just before it slammed into a telephone pole on the side of the road. Hovering, I looked back just after the impact happened, expecting the car to explode and burst into flames like on TV. Instead, it just sat there, a strange ticking sound coming from the car's engine.

I changed back into my person form, looking around to see if anyone else was nearby. But there was only me, the wrecked car, and nothing else. The air was full of familiar sounds and smells, the chirping of katydids mixed with the smoke from the car's exhaust. I also realized that a particularly pungent smell I had been sensing before was gone, the scent of garlic. I looked back again at the unmoving car, piecing together that it had come from there.

Gathering my wits, I realized that none of this mattered. I needed to find my friends. I also had absolutely no idea where I was.

On the way to find everyone, I stopped to kill one more time, still needing more blood in order to feel whole again. Once I had gotten that, I sped toward the area where everyone was, thinking about what had happened. My psychic powers still seemed to be damaged, which was troublesome. Ever since Dracula had blasted me with his eyebeams the night before, it hurt like hell whenever I tried to use them. They had increased over the years and seemed to have really taken off recently, but what was the point if every time I tried to concentrate and make them work, it felt like someone was jabbing an ice pick through my head?

Still, I managed to clairvoyantly figure out where the main action was, briefly enduring the severe pain just to find that out. Though crippled, it was like my powers had become even more precise, and I was able to use them sort of like a compass to determine which direction I should fly in order to catch up with everybody. When I first began flying, I assumed that I was going west and out into the country again, then was surprised to find that I was instead heading back into the city.

As I neared the location, I had to suffer through using my powers again in brief bursts in order to figure out exactly where to find everyone. The closer I got, the more I recognized the area, even though I hadn't flown this exact route before. An even bigger surprise for me was arriving at my old school, which was apparently where everybody had ended up. I had no idea why, but that's how things had gone.

On the roof of the main building, I spotted Tim and Dennis, who were creeping along quietly and partly hunched over. I waited until I was close, then whispered as loudly as I could, "Hey!" Startled, they both looked up quickly, and their eyes glowed yellow. "It's me, Ray!" I said, realizing that they were about to shoot me with their beams. I had no idea if that would have any effect on me, but it didn't matter. They relaxed and looked relieved as I landed.

"You're okay!" Dennis said, keeping his voice down.

"Yeah, told you I'd get better," I said. "What's going on?"

"Dracula and the others are around here somewhere, but we're not sure exactly where," Tim said. "We thought we saw them fly up here, but now there's nothing."

"Where's Carl?" I asked.

"They got him," Dennis said. "He's one of them now. Or, again."

"Yeah," Tim said, "we've all pretty much been doing this weird cat-and-mouse game of zapping each other back and forth. One of us will get blasted and changed into Dracula's type of vampire, and then another of us zaps them back with the yellow beams, or just seeing the glow is enough to do it. It kept going on and on while we were in the air, and then we sort of accidentally ended up here at the school."

"There was some fighting and stuff down on the playground for a little while," Dennis said, "but then they all flew up here."

"I wonder why," I said.

"There's something else, too, Ray," Tim said gravely.

I started to ask him what, but then I heard something, and I held up a finger to silence everyone. I looked around, trying to figure out what the noise was, and I also took in my surroundings. It felt weird to be on the roof of my school; I had heard some of my classmates, including Nick, talk about how they had sometimes snuck onto the school grounds at night and been able to climb up onto the roof. No one had ever told me just how they had done it, but now here we were, having flown up there ourselves. It felt like a forbidden space, somewhere we knew we shouldn't be, and there was a small thrill in that. But for the moment, there was something much more urgent to think about. The strange noise sounded kind of like paper rattling, and there was also a weird bleeping sound. I was reminded of the sound the swarm of bats had made the night before, but this wasn't quite the same.

"Um…" Dennis said, but then kept quiet.

"What?" I asked.

"You remember what Nick said about the time he came up here? About the rats?"

"Yeah, but that was ages ago," I said.

"And I heard that they were going to treat the whole building for them this summer," Tim added.

"I don't think they got around to it," Dennis said, pointing to the far end of the roof.

There was something dark along its edge, like a long, black cloud, but at floor level. A hundred or more tiny little red lights seemed to be dancing around inside it, almost like Christmas lights, but smaller. All of a sudden, the mass began to move toward us very quickly, the lights pairing up to form the eyes of scampering rats.

"Shit!" Dennis exclaimed. "Let's get out of here!" We started to run, but then I realized something. I didn't know a whole lot about rats, but I was pretty sure that they didn't normally have eyes that lit up like little red LEDs. "They're under Dracula's control!" I said. "Blast them with your eyes!"

Tim and Dennis began to shoot their eyebeams into the oncoming pack, but when I tried to do so, I only saw that same green glare, and my head hurt again. I winced, but then I looked back up, seeing that the rats had broken off and were running away, some off to the sides and some back in the direction from which they'd come. My idea had worked, but my glowing eyes hadn't.

"Were they vampires?" Dennis asked.

"No, I don't think so," Tim said. "Just animals under his control. The legend is that…"

He stopped speaking when two red beams came from behind, turning him into a Dracula-vampire. He turned toward me with his glowing red eyes, and in defense, I made my eyes light up. They were still green, and using them caused me that same pain, but I endured it long enough to see Tim's eyes change to a glowing yellow, and he was back to his old self again.

"Well, that's different," he said simply. He turned around and shot his own beams at Carl, who was approaching on foot and was then changed back into his regular self as well. He looked around and tried to figure out where he was, then ran over to us.

"Ray!" he said. "You're back!"

"And apparently with fancy green eyes instead of yellow," Tim said with a curious smile. "Is that something to do with what happened to you last night?"

"Yeah," I said. "I think so. Ever since then, my powers have been all strange. They don't seem to be working right."

"Maybe they were damaged when you absorbed that blast," Dennis said.

"That's what I was thinking, but at the same time, well, whenever they actually do work, they're really precise. That's how I found you guys. But it also hurts whenever I use them, like this really bad headache. Same with making my eyes glow."

"Well hurry up and get over it," Carl said, having turned around and looked behind him. "Here they come again."

Dracula, Susanna, and Carolyn were walking along the roof toward us, and then Carolyn shot Dennis with her red rays. He changed, but in just under two seconds, Tim turned and shot him again, and he changed back. I could tell that before I had arrived a little earlier, they had gone through this routine so many times that it was a very rapid thing, almost like playing a game of tag. It kind of seemed pointless.

"Okay," I said, "now change the rest of them back!"

"Oh," Dennis said, a strange tone in his voice.

"What?"

"We'll have to show him," Tim said. He and Dennis shot their eyebeams at Carolyn and Susanna, who were walking along either side of Dracula. They screamed and held up their arms much the same way he had done the night before, but once they recovered, they were still the same. Our beams weren't changing them back to normal. They continued to advance on us slowly, looking both angry and triumphant at the same time. Dracula had the same smug look.

"It isn't working!" I said. "How do we change them back?"

"We could try this," Tim said, and he shot his beams not at my sisters, but at Dracula himself, who cried out in pain. At the same time, Carolyn and Susanna also screamed, acting like they had been blasted as well. They then recovered at the same time Dracula did.

"You cannot win," Dracula said through clenched teeth. "These two are mine. Make it easy on yourselves and surrender. Become mine as well." As he said this, his pupils lit up with that same hypnotic glow, and for a moment, I thought about doing as he said.

"No!" I shouted, my eyes lighting up green and the headache flaring up again. Both Dracula and my sisters turned away, shielding their eyes. "Come on!" I said to the others, changing into a bat and flying up. "Follow me!"

"Do you have a plan?" Dennis asked me. We had made our way to the ground level and had gathered under a covered walkway next to the playground.

"No, not really. But I keep feeling like there's something I'm missing, something I've forgotten."

"Like what?"

"What I don't understand is how Dracula is here in the first place," Carl said. "I killed him. You all saw it."

"Van Helsing killed him, too," I said. "And he still came back." I explained to them how he had reconstituted himself out of that strange mist in front of me earlier. "I'm not sure if we really can kill him."

"Remember what he said?" Tim asked. "Last night out at that place. Sheling, Helsing… *Whoever* had to keep him imprisoned. Killing him wasn't enough."

"Does that mean we're going to have to do the same thing?" Carl asked. "Stay alive forever and make sure he stays locked up?"

"Let's worry about actually killing him first," Dennis said, then sighed. "But how? And what about Carolyn and Susanna?"

"Ah, yes, what indeed?" Dracula said from nearby. We turned and saw him and my sisters slowly walking along the concrete path toward us. "Why do you fight what must be? This struggle is so unnecessary. We could rule this city together, and then the world!"

The sinister trio stepped closer, their faces illuminated by one of the electric lights along the walkway. I couldn't stand to look at Susanna and Carolyn, who were some perverted mixture of their real selves and Dracula's vacant, zombie-like vampires. They leered and grinned at us in the most horrible way, and they giggled in this sinister manner that made my skin crawl.

"Please," Dracula said, holding out his arms in that same formal gesture I had seen him use so many times. "There is no need for us to be at odds!" His pupils lit up that same familiar red, and something started trying to get inside of my head. "We can share in this power." He smiled broadly, his fangs showing.

Finally, something clicked. "Oh no you don't!" I shouted, enduring the pain of making my eyes glow. He and the girls once again shielded their eyes with their hands, and I said to my friends, "Blast him! Not them, just him!"

My vision went back to normal as the pain subsided, and I saw that everyone had concentrated their beams on Dracula. Three simultaneous pairs of yellow, laser-like beams were enough to bring him to his knees, and Carolyn and Susanna also screamed, mimicking his movements. I hated seeing them in so much pain, but I had finally figured out what needed to be done. Back at the house, Dracula had hinted at it, but I had been too busy being choked to death by him to pay attention. At last, I had managed to recall what he'd said.

The others had stopped their assault, and Dracula and my sisters were beginning to recover, but I said, "No! Do it again! Hold your beams on him!" They did as I said, and he continued to cry out in agony, his face doing that same strange thing where it seemed to switch back and forth between a human-looking one and a more savage, beastly look. At the same time, Carolyn and Susanna cried out in this shrill siren, holding their hands to the sides of their heads, their eyes switching between glowing red and glowing yellow. Dracula had also been holding his hands to his head, but then he pulled his arms to his sides, his chest bulging out like he was trying to exert all his strength and somehow force the energy back. I knew that this was the moment to strike.

I concentrated, making the power build up in my head. It hurt terribly, but I knew I had to keep going. The green glow filled my eyes, and then it brightened, becoming almost white. The pain intensified, and I began to cry out. But then, as I had hoped, the piercing feeling in my head suddenly dropped away, and I envisioned all of the energy that had built up inside of me shooting forward and right at Dracula's chest. I saw it rush forward from me, an intense white-green blast going straight from my eyes and right through his heart, blasting a baseball-sized hole right through him.

Everyone stopped their assault, and just for a second, Dracula looked human again, an utterly stunned look on his face. And then, just like the night before, he immediately crumbled into dust, his clothes flopping to the ground in a heap. Carolyn and Susanna, meanwhile, had finally stopped screaming, which was a great relief. I began running over to them, expecting any moment to feel more pain or dizziness, but there was none. I finally felt like myself again.

They both looked up at me as I approached, and I could tell that they too had gone back to normal. Susanna smiled at me and let out a short laugh of relief, then turned to look at what was left of Dracula. I knelt down and hugged Carolyn, who said to me very softly, "Thank you. I'm so sorry for earlier."

I pulled back and looked at her. "You remember what happened?"

"Yes," she said, looking down. She seemed ashamed. "I couldn't help it. I couldn't do anything."

"Neither of us could," Susanna said, getting up and brushing herself off. "Don't beat yourself up over it."

By then, the others had joined us, and I felt a hand patting me on my shoulder. "That was the coolest thing I've ever fucking seen!" Carl said. I turned back and watched as he made a gesture like his fist was punching through his right hand. "Boom! Right through the chest!"

I felt a sense of pride, but mostly, I was just glad that it was all over and that my sisters were okay. But then I realized something. "It's not over yet."

"Right," Tim said. "Unless we do something, Mr. Ashes-to-Ashes here is going to just get right back up and come after us again tomorrow night."

"So what do we do?" Dennis asked. "Scoop his remains up and lock them up somehow?"

"That's exactly what we should do," Susanna said, seeming a little shaken up but slowly returning to her old self.

"Careful," Susanna said to Carl. "Don't let it touch you."

"I know, I know," he said impatiently, his gloved hands carefully maneuvering the solitary rose over the box.

"Gently now," I said as he began to lower it.

He paused, then said through clenched teeth, "I *know*. Let me freakin' concentrate."

"Sorry."

In contrast to his slow, deliberate movements, once the flower was safely inside the metal box, Carl slammed the lid down quickly and fastened the two silver-colored latches. He beat a sideways fist down on the lid for good measure, then said triumphantly, "Yes! And that's how it's done, ladies and gentlemen!" He jumped up from the ground, fists held high above his head like he'd just scored a touchdown.

"Very good, Carl," Carolyn said with a smile, being somehow both condescending and genuinely congratulatory. She patted her hands together in a quiet clapping gesture.

"There we go," Susanna said, picking up the box and looking at it proudly. "One desiccated vampire, imprisoned in his coffin by a wild rose."

"Pretty small coffin," Dennis said. He was right; the strongbox we had found in the janitor's closet at the school was only about a foot wide and six inches deep, but it had been just the right size to hold the vacuum cleaner bag that now contained Dracula's remains.

While Carolyn had been sucking the ashes up with the vacuum cleaner earlier, Tim wondered aloud what Mr. Walker, the school janitor, would say when he returned to work and found that the bag and box were missing.

"Probably something like, 'Ee weh blaggum mah blarbum gloh…'" Dennis said, which made the rest of us laugh. Mr. Walker was a nice enough guy, we thought, but a running joke was that we could almost never understand a word he was saying.

When Susanna had first proposed this, I questioned whether or not it would work. But she reminded me that Dracula himself had mentioned the night before that this was the same way, more or less, that Van Helsing had imprisoned him a hundred years ago. And while the notion of a rose being used against a vampire was new to me, I accepted that there were some things about the legend I just did not know, much like I had previously not known about the effects of running water.

From that point, our plan had been to take the box home with us on foot; none of us wanted to risk trying to fly with it and end up dropping it, releasing Dracula's remains. Once home, we would get a rose from our mother's garden and use it to keep him imprisoned, but Susanna warned that this might only be a temporary fix. Once the rose had fully died after being cut, Dracula might be able to escape.

As it turned out, less than halfway into our journey back to the house, we happened upon a small, pink rose growing next to a fence by the side of the road, and the opportunity seemed too good to pass up. One thing we were uncertain of, though, was whether or not it would be safe to touch. For all we knew, it could have the same effects of any of the other "vampire killers" and end up changing whoever touched it back to human, which would have been a very bad thing for them.

Instead, we had to resort to kicking at the base of the plant and trying to dig it out with our feet. Eventually, we decided against this and figured that it would be easier, if not quicker, to just wait until we got home and could use proper gardening equipment.

So we did, and Susanna and Carl had used gloves to protect themselves while they selected the rose, cut it, then carefully put it into the box containing Dracula. As we headed back into the house, I asked Susanna what we could do in the long term.

"Well, I'd say that mixing in some garlic and maybe even some of the potion's antidote with the ashes might be a good way to completely destroy him. But I can't do anything like that without risking getting changed back."

"And you don't want to do that yet?" I asked, sounding more hopeful than I meant to.

"No. Why, do you?"

"No! No. I was just asking."

"I'd think that the rose would last long enough," Tim said. "Until we go back to being human again, I mean."

"Right," Susanna said.

Unfortunately, the next night, we realized that time had gotten away from us. It was Friday, almost exactly two weeks since we had gotten together for the summer, and the plan had been for all of us to take the antidote at that point. My friends were expected to go back home the next day.

"It can't be that soon already!" Carl said. "I know what they say about 'time flies when you're having fun,' but…" He trailed off, looking sad.

I felt the same way. As she had done two years ago, Susanna had drawn a "V" in pencil on the calendar in the kitchen to mark this day, but I had gotten into the habit of avoiding looking at the calendar for that very reason. I didn't want this day to come.

"It's time, though," Susanna said, also looking disappointed.

"Yeah, I guess we have to stick to the plan," I said.

"It sucks, though," Dennis said. "This has been a lot of fun! I mean, aside from some of the really bad stuff. You know." He deliberately avoided looking at Carolyn, instead fixing his gaze on me. While it had been only a few days since Crowley had died, there had been little to no mention of him once we had gotten caught up in the Dracula situation. We had been too busy fighting for our lives.

Carolyn, meanwhile, seemed resigned, but also kind of down. "Yeah, I know. Some things have been bad, but not all of it. It kind of felt like we were just hitting our stride. Getting over the big obstacles, you know what I mean?"

"You're not sick of it this time?" Tim asked with a small grin.

Carolyn rolled her eyes. "God, am I ever going to live that down? That was years ago. I was a kid then, not much older than you. To be perfectly honest, I was scared, okay? But I'm not scared anymore."

"Sorry!" Tim said, but he was laughing about it. Then he stopped, looking off to one side and sighing. "I guess we've all gotten pretty used to this, huh? But maybe…" He was beginning to get that sly look of his again.

"What?" I asked.

"Maybe we could convince our parents to let us stay a little longer. Just a few more days. Your parents aren't coming back for another week, right?"

"True," Susanna said, looking thoughtful. Then she shook her head. "No. No. We really do just need to quit after tonight."

"He's right, though!" I said. "Come on, Susanna. Let's just stick with it for a little longer if we can. I'll bet we can convince everyone's parents to let them stay. In fact…" I looked over at Dennis, who was grinning wildly. He wiggled his eyebrows. "In fact, it worked on Tim's mom just fine last week."

"What?" Tim asked. Then he got it. "Oh, you're good."

And so we set about having Tim, Carl, and Dennis call home, each time with me sitting silently with the other phone and using my powers to psychically control each of their parents. It was tricky because I couldn't have the phone off the hook when they called, or else the phone wouldn't dial properly. We had to time things so I picked up the phone in my parents' room just after they'd dialed but before the other line had picked up. My psychic powers helped with this, too, as I could see everyone in the kitchen in my mind.

What had happened to my powers was a surprise, but certainly one that I liked. Having recovered from the weird effects of Dracula's influence the night before, my powers had in fact not been damaged, but enhanced. Dennis and I talked about this some, figuring out that the reason I had been getting those headaches and was having trouble getting everything to work right wasn't because I had been incapacitated; it was growing pains. Somehow, I had absorbed a great deal of Dracula's own powers, which was what he had tried to tell me while choking me out in the driveway that night. It just took my mind a while to catch up and be able to use them. Once I had, they were more finely tuned, stronger than ever.

This meant that little to no persuasion was needed with my friends' parents once we had them on the phone. The conversations were comically short, which we joked about later. Basically, they went like this: "Can I stay at Ray's house for another week?" I would concentrate, feeling that tingle in my forehead, willing the person to say yes. And then they would, almost no questions asked. It was quite a rush, first surprising me and then making me feel rather cocky.

As far as my own parents were concerned, we had occasionally gotten answering machine messages from them over the past two weeks, but they were pretty generic, most of them along the lines of either my mom or dad saying that they were calling to check in to make sure everything was okay, and we could call them back if we needed anything. The most recent one we had gotten said that they might be heading to Hawaii for a few days with our aunt before returning to San Francisco and then back to Augusta, which was fine with me. I had this fear that what had been happening in town might end up making the national news, which might make them concerned and insist on hearing from us to make sure we were okay. That never happened, or at least, they never called to ask about any of it. That was also fine, because even though it wouldn't have been hard to lie to them and tell them that we had no idea what was going on, I just found the idea of doing that kind of tiring, almost trite. I was used to keeping them in the dark by this point.

Once all of the phone calls had been made and I joined everyone back in the kitchen, the air was full of excitement. Instead of the earlier feeling of disappointment over having to stop being vampires before we were ready, we felt a sort of wicked glee, a renewed sense of freedom. We could keep being bad, having fun, and doing whatever we wanted. Susanna still tried to keep everything in check and warned us not to get too over the top, but we couldn't help it. We felt invincible. We had been breaking society's rules for ages, and now we were beginning to break our own.

We didn't even watch the videotape of the news before heading out to kill. "Why bother?" Carl asked when it was brought up. "It's not like they'll have anything new to say. 'Some people got killed,'" he said, putting on an official-sounding voice. "'We have no idea why. Tune in next time.'"

Dennis laughed, then adopted the same demeanor. "'Janitor's closet found broken into at local school. Police deny everything.'"

"'Can vacuum cleaners be used as a new weapon against the vampires we're pretending don't exist?'" Carolyn said, doing an eerily accurate impression of Channel Four's female news anchor. She even had the fake concerned look down perfectly.

We again flew to South Augusta to kill that night, avoiding the inner city and the area where we assumed the police would be concentrating their efforts. Because we were less familiar with this part of the city despite our occasional visits in the past, we didn't have a specific destination in mind and just wandered, hoping to find a group of people to prey upon.

"That looks promising," Tim said, and I saw two cars parked in the middle of a field below. We had happened upon a less populated part of town, which were more common the farther away one traveled from the city in any direction. Even though there were two cars, one of which was a pick-up truck, the only people we saw at first were a boy and a girl who were sitting in the back of the truck. They were both smoking, and I could just barely make out the guy's voice, which was unusually deep. He said something, and the girl laughed. She leaned up against him affectionately for a moment, then straightened up and drank from a bottle she'd been holding by her side.

"I wonder if they're old enough to be drinking," Carolyn said with a smile.

"Who cares," I said. *"We* are." No one seemed to get the joke. "Blood, I mean. Oh, forget it."

"Is it just the two of them?" Susanna asked, sounding disappointed.

"No, there are two more in the back of that other car," Dennis said. He was right; I could sense them. I assumed that he was doing the same thing, as I couldn't see any indication of the other boy and girl visually, but I knew they were there just the same.

"Guess we'll have to share," Tim said.

"First come, first served," Carl said, then zoomed downward without waiting for the rest of us.

"Oh, that asshole," Dennis said, then followed. Within seconds, he and Carl had landed on the people in the back of the truck and were drinking from them.

"Well, crap," Carolyn said. "Do we have to fight over the rest?"

Susanna laughed. "How about you and I go off and find our own. Ray, you and Tim can go have the others. We'll meet back at the house. You can find your way back, right?"

"Yes," I said impatiently. "Go on. We'll see you later."

While she and Carolyn flew away, Tim and I made our way toward the ground. When the first two people had been attacked, they had of course screamed, which had led the guy in the other car to get out and see what was happening. He slammed the door to the backseat behind him, then ran over to the truck, only to see his two friends being killed.

He swore and looked around, unsure what to do. He didn't have much time to do anything, though, before Tim landed on him, changing into his person form as he did and toppling the guy to the ground. Stunned, he was unable to fight back enough before Tim had sunk his teeth into him.

I knew that the one remaining girl was still hiding in the car, and rather than going in after her, I decided to perch myself on the roof and wait. I could feel her in there, terrified and bewildered. I then projected a thought into her mind: *Escape.*

The car door opened slowly, and I flapped my wings a little to bounce myself over to the edge of the top of the car, watching with amusement as the girl crawled out onto the ground and looked around, trying to sneak away. She let out a small, stifled cry as she saw her boyfriend being killed by Tim, but her urge to survive surpassed everything. If she could just be quiet enough, she might get away. I could tell what she was thinking; it almost felt like I was thinking it myself.

I let her get several feet from the car, then flew and pounced on her, changing form. She cried out pitifully, but I just relished the moment, knowing that I had already won. She struggled, but then I subdued her telepathically. Her legs no longer worked, and she flailed about with her arms, still trying to pull herself along while I straddled her back. She wailed again, the last few moments of her life having become a waking nightmare.

"Don't cry, Mandy," I said to her quietly, having learned her name by reading her mind. I wasn't saying that to be kind, but to mock her. A confused little squeak from her was followed by some silent sobbing, and I felt a little bit sorry for her, but that passed. I bent down and pulled her hair back from her neck, which was a little difficult because it was so heavily styled that it was pretty stiff. I had known of girls, including my sisters, who had done their hair like this occasionally for whatever reason that girls did that sort of thing, but this was different from anything I had encountered before. The hair felt more like plastic than anything else, and I wondered for a moment if perhaps it was a wig instead.

Still, getting to her neck wasn't difficult once I willed the girl to be still and turn her head to one side, giving me better access. I leaned down and bit into her, and she let out another little yelp as I did, then went quiet. As I swallowed over and over, loving the taste of her hot, precious blood, random images and thoughts flowed into me.

There was a much younger version of Mandy riding down a driveway on a blue bike with training wheels on it. Why hadn't Daddy gotten her a pink bike like she'd asked for? Then I saw another memory, her father yelling at her mother as he stood up from the dinner table, his chair flying back behind him as it crashed into the wall. There was the high school prom, and she was stuck there with a boy she barely even liked, all the time resenting the guy who was supposed to go with her instead. She and Sharon were talking about which boys they liked in junior high. Sharon was laughing at her along with Holly, that bitch. She was staying after school as punishment for something she didn't do, and Dale didn't even thank her for covering for him. Her tenth birthday was one of the happiest ones of her life. John was a jerk who would one day be sorry for breaking her heart. She wasn't sure about going out to the Hill tonight, but everyone insisted that it would be okay. She looked down at her grandmother's gravestone, regretting the fact that she'd never thanked her for everything. Andrew was trying to talk her into giving it up for him, that it would be okay because he really loved her. Her friends were screaming. A vampire was jumping onto her back and pinning her down. Her life was over.

I straightened up and looked down at her drained body, a little shaken by the experience. I hadn't meant to read all of those thoughts of hers at first; it just seemed to start on its own, and they kept coming as I drank. It was interesting, but a little disconcerting as well. I had heard of the phenomenon of someone's life flashing before their eyes just before they died, but to actually experience that, even if it were someone else's life, felt weird.

A chuckle came from behind me, and I turned around to see Dennis looking down, his arms folded. "Man, you have got to teach me how to do that." Apparently, his own powers had picked up on what mine had been doing.

Standing up, I said, "I don't know. I mean, I don't know if I even want to do it again. It was neat, but also kind of freaky."

I started to explain more, but then I looked behind Dennis and saw Carl bending down toward the ground doing something strange while Tim watched. I could hear a hissing sound, and as Dennis and I got closer, I saw that Carl had a can of hairspray in his hand and was spraying it onto the grass.

"What the hell are you doing?" Dennis asked.

"You'll see. It's cool, trust me."

"Where did you get that?" I asked.

"The girl in the truck had it in her extremely huge purse," Tim said.

"Okay," Carl said, straightening up and setting the can down on the truck's tailgate. "Now, let's see…" He picked up something else from the back of the truck, and I stepped closer, seeing that it was a lighter.

"Wait!" Tim shouted. "Don't. That'll make a spark on your thumb, and you might get burned. Remember what fire does to us."

"Oh," Carl said, looking at the lighter like it was a loaded gun. "Well, crap. I wanted to show you something cool."

"If one of them had any matches, though, that might be safe," Tim said, hopping up into the truck's bed. He searched through the dead girl's purse. "Aha! Here we go."

After jumping back to the ground, he held up a matchbox to Carl with a proud look. "Now, watch closely. The trick is to not let the flame touch your fingers."

"Oh, so you've seen this trick before," Carl said.

"Yes, but with another kind of aerosol, actually."

"What are you talking about?" I asked impatiently. "What trick?"

"Just watch," Tim said, grinning. He pulled out a match and carefully struck it, then dropped it onto the ground where Carl had been spraying. All of a sudden, a big flame shot up from the ground, then quickly looped around and formed a glowing ring of blue and orange.

"Whoa!" Dennis said. I was similarly impressed.

"That's the hairspray?" I asked. This reminded me of some of the times that Nick and I had hung out together and lit things on fire for fun, but we'd never done anything this cool before.

"Yep," Carl said. "Be sure to keep back."

"That's really cool looking," Dennis said. The fire wobbled back and forth about an inch off the ground, and after a minute or so, it sputtered silently and disappeared.

"Do it again!" I said.

"Okay," Carl said, letting a small, evil giggle. "Let's see." He sprayed the ground again, this time running and zigzagging as he went.

Tim repeated the process, creating another brilliant flaming pattern along the ground. It was beautiful, but the biggest thrill came from knowing how dangerous it was. Nick certainly would have appreciated it, but there was the added aspect of how careful we had to be not to let the flames touch us, even more than would normally be the case. If the fire came into contact with any one of us, that person would be changed from a vampire back to a human, finding themselves in a great deal of danger from everyone else.

We kept at this for a few minutes, each time trying to get more creative with the patterns. Tim insisted that Carl never be allowed to light any of the matches, fearing that he might have gotten some of the hairspray on his hands and could end up lighting himself on fire. Dennis was scared that he might burn himself while trying to light one of the matches, so Tim and I ended up taking turns with them, all of us enjoying the gorgeous and deadly art we found ourselves making. It was a fun and surreal moment, the beauty of the flames even eclipsing the rather breathtaking view of South Augusta from the hill we were on. I realized that it must have been the view that lured those teenagers here, a cool place for them to hang out. I hadn't even noticed it until that point since I had gotten so used to seeing spectacular vistas like that from the air.

"Here, let's try something else," Carl said. "I saw this in a movie once. Someone light another match, then hold it out as far as you can." Tim did so. "Now hold still." He held the top of the spray can right up to the burning match, then pressed the button, which resulted in a huge jet of fire pouring forth from it. Tim jumped back and dropped the match, falling backwards and onto the ground, then laughed. Carl continued to wave the can around, his makeshift flamethrower blasting away. Dennis and I looked on in awe.

"That is so damn cool!" I said.

"Careful!" Dennis warned. "Don't use it all up!"

Carl stopped, looking quite pleased with himself. I realized that the other girl, the one I had killed, might also have had a can of hairspray in her purse, which was presumably in the car. I ran over to check, glancing over at her prone body as I went. I found nothing in the backseat, but there was another large, denim purse in the front of the car containing yet another can of flammable fun.

I brought it back to the group, smiling as I held it up. "We're not done yet! What else can we do?"

"I've got an idea," Carl said, "but I'm not sure if it will work. Let's see." He put down his can, then leapt up into the back of the truck. "No, hang on. This will be better."

"What are you trying to do?" I asked.

Carl relayed a story to us that his sister Karen had told him about a girl she had seen in the cafeteria at her college. The girl had been trying to light a cigarette, but the flame from her lighter flared up and set her hair on fire. The girl ended up being okay, but the way Karen had told it, it was really funny the way she had freaked out when it happened. So Carl wanted to try to recreate that same incident again. He picked up the can of hairspray and drew a trail along the bed of the truck, up the side of the girl's body, and right up to her shoulder. Both her body and the boy's were still propped up in a sitting position, their backs against the truck's cab.

"That's never going to work," Dennis said cynically as we watched.

"It might," Tim said.

"Okay, someone give me a light," Carl said, standing above the newly flammable girl and her recently killed boyfriend.

"Get out of the truck first, stupid," I said.

Carl looked down. "Oh. Right." He walked onto the tailgate and jumped back down onto the grass.

Tim stepped forward. "Where did you...? Never mind, I see it." He lit another match, dropped it onto the beginning of the hairspray trail, then immediately turned around and shouted, "Run!"

We ran a few yards away, then looked back. The fire had traveled quickly, making its way up the girl's body and then to her hair, which suddenly burst into a huge fireball. The image was extremely morbid and hilarious at the same time, and we laughed hysterically as we watched.

The flames eventually died down, and the air was full of a horrible, acrid smell, but we didn't care. What we were doing was extremely wrong and forbidden, and that was why we loved it. Once this particular bit of fun had dissipated, the only thing we could think to do was to top it.

I wanted to set the entire truck on fire, hopefully igniting its gas tank and making it blow up in a huge explosion. Carl did as I instructed, picking up the other girl's body from the ground and carrying her over to the side of the truck. It still weirded me out a bit whenever I saw one of us using the increased strength the vampire potion gave us; the ease with which Carl carried and maneuvered the girl's body made it look more like he was a regular person carrying a large, lightweight stuffed animal.

He propped the girl up, her legs straight and together along the ground, and her head not far below the opening to the truck's gas tank, which Dennis had uncapped and left exposed. Since he had already declared that he wasn't going to be lighting any matches himself, he felt safe using the other can of hairspray to repeat Carl's earlier experiment and make a trail along the grass, up the girl's body, and up to her hair. As everyone stood back and waited for the fireworks, I lit the match and dropped it onto the ground.

As before, the bluish orange flame traveled quickly along the ground and to its target, and the girl's stiff hairspray sculpture burst into flames as expected. This did not, however, result in the truck's gas tank also catching fire, which was disappointing.

"Aww," Carl said dramatically. "I was really hoping that would work."

"What the hell do you think you're doing?" a voice shrieked. I turned around and saw my sisters, who had flown in behind us unseen. Susanna's voice got louder and more fierce as she approached on foot. "Are you out of your fucking minds?"

"We were just fooling around!" Carl said.

"'Fooling around' my ass!" she snarled. "Back to the house! Now!"

As we flew, she continued to rail at us. She was in utter disbelief that we had been so reckless, literally playing with fire and risking not only our physical safety but also our status as vampires. I knew she was right, but at the same time, I resented her being so authoritative and parental. I tried to defend what we had done, insisting that we had been very careful, but she refused to listen.

Once home, I continued to defy her. "What were you and Carolyn doing there anyway? You said you'd meet us back here."

"That's not the point," she said angrily.

"Yeah, what were you doing, spying on us?" Carl jeered.

"No, we weren't spying on you," she answered with extreme condescension. "Carolyn and I were… Where did she go?" She looked around the room, as did I, but our sibling had apparently left without anyone noticing, perhaps wanting to avoid the conflict. "It doesn't matter. We had flown farther away from the house after we left you, and we were on our way back when we spotted you making complete fools of yourselves."

"Come on!" Tim said. "It's not that big of a deal! No one got hurt! Well, aside from those other kids…" He fought back a laugh, as did I, knowing that this wasn't a good time to be joking around.

"If any of you little shits pull anything like that again," Susanna said, "I'm making you take the antidote and sending you straight home."

"Oh yeah?" I said. "What about me? I'm already home."

Susanna began to respond, but then Carolyn came back into the room from the hallway with a worried look. "Guys, we've got a problem. Everyone just make up and be nice. Ray, tell Susanna that you'll all be good and not do it again. Susanna, stop overreacting."

Susanna and I both began to protest, but Carolyn held up her hand.

"What problem?" Tim asked.

"I just checked the answering machine. Damon called, and he's on his way back to Augusta right now. He might already be in town."

"What?" I said. "I thought he was going to be out of town for a few more weeks! You know, all on tour with his band and everything." As I said this, I mimed playing a guitar.

"He was," Carolyn said anxiously, "but their tour got cancelled. Or really, they cancelled it. Their stupid slack drummer decided to quit the band half-way through the trip, so now everyone is heading home."

I remembered a conversation I'd had with Damon earlier in the year when I was getting to know him, back when he and Carolyn were first dating. I was curious about what being in a band was like, and Damon talked like it was great fun, but also sometimes frustrating.

"It's kind of like a family," he had told me. "Or maybe more like being in a big relationship with four other guys. When you get along, it's great, and you can do really cool things. But sometimes you fight and you don't get along, and you want to kick the other person out because you're sick of their crap. And then you wonder if you can find someone better to replace them, get scared that you can't, then end up compromising." I didn't fully understand everything he was talking about, but I did know that their band, which was called Clandestiny, had gone through a series of different drummers over the years. For some reason, that position in the band had always been unstable. They had just gotten this latest drummer, whom they were pretty optimistic about, when he and I were having this conversation back in March.

"Well, crap!" I said. "What are we going to do? Does this mean we have to change back after all?"

"I don't know!" Carolyn said. "His message was from sometime earlier in the day, and I think they had gotten up to Virginia so far, so…"

"So if he's driving back," Susanna said, "it's possible that he's already back in Augusta." She looked down, then back up at Carolyn. "So what do you want to do?"

"I don't…" She paused, then looked down as well. "Let me think."

"I can let you take the antidote and go be with him if you want," Susanna said.

"I know! I…" She broke off again, not looking at anyone. When she lifted her head, she was smiling, and for a second, her look reminded me of the one Tim sometimes got. "I know what I really want to do," she said, her eyes meeting mine.

The idea of adding Damon to the group, to make him a vampire as well, was exciting and very intriguing. I had always liked him, and as soon as Carolyn brought up the idea, I immediately began picturing him as one of us, doing all of the same cool things we had been doing for so long. It also opened the door to an idea I had been casually tossing around in my head since we had first gotten together this summer: I wanted Nick to be one of us, too.

When we had first been making our plans, I'd decided that this was supposed to be a reunion of the vampires, both groups from 1983 and 1985, and I closed myself off to the possibility of adding anyone new. At the time, Nick was the only person from school that I would have even considered including, but my tendency to be a control freak sort of painted me into a corner, making me insist that no one new be allowed in. It was strictly a reunion, and that was that. I had briefly wondered if Carolyn's involvement with Damon might end up meaning that she couldn't take part, but once I knew that Damon would be out of town for the entire time we were planning to be vampires, things seemed more or less perfect, and I was content with that. Almost.

Deep down, I knew that Nick would fit in with us just fine, that he would enjoy being a vampire and that I should give him the chance to, just as I had brought Dennis in back in 1985. My stubbornness kept me from allowing for the possibility, though, so I planned things out as I did, getting all of the former vampires together this summer and insisting on things being that way.

But once Susanna and the others agreed with Carolyn's suggestion of adding Damon to our group, I couldn't deny that it would be great. Damon was a really cool guy, and so was Nick, so I brought up the idea of also including him. Susanna was initially suspicious, but she warmed up soon enough when both Dennis and Tim spoke up and said that Nick would be a good addition as well. Dennis even asked me at this point why I hadn't brought him into the group in the first place, which led me to waffle a bit and give an apologetic explanation, realizing as I spoke that I had been rather silly about the whole thing all along.

Carolyn was on the phone with Damon for a long time, presumably having to first explain things to him, convince him that she was telling the truth, and then talk him into taking part. I had gone through something similar with Dennis two years earlier, and I realized that I would have to do the same with Nick, which made me nervous.

"God, what's taking them so long?" Carl asked. Carolyn was in our parents' bedroom talking privately, which meant that we had to wait for her to be done before I could call Nick. It was already getting pretty late, almost time for the news, but I had talked to him on the phone late on Friday nights a couple of times before. My parents hadn't been happy that he had called me so late one time, but for whatever reason, his parents didn't consider it a problem if I called him at that hour. Still, I was getting impatient.

"Maybe they're getting all lovey and kissy on the phone because they haven't seen each other in so long," Dennis said in a sing-song tone.

"We could always listen in on the other phone," Tim suggested evilly.

"Or I could probably listen in telepathically," I said.

"No," Susanna said. "I told you, Ray: No using your powers on anyone else in the group."

I considered pushing back on this, but I didn't want to get into another argument with her. The earlier one had been uncomfortable enough, and I was grateful for the distraction Damon's impending arrival had caused. So I just dropped it.

Finally, Carolyn came up the hall and into the yellow den, a big smile on her face. I asked her how it went, and she laughed. "Oh, he's a little freaked out! But mostly in a good way. I think he thought I was crazy at first."

"But he's going to do it?" Susanna asked. "He's on his way here?"

"Yes," Carolyn said, looking very happy. She folded her arms, then hugged herself and bounced up and down a couple of times. "This is going to be so cool."

"Okay, okay," I said. "Now it's my turn."

"You're going to call your boyfriend and get all giddy and stupid, too?" Dennis joked.

"Ha, ha," I said, sneering at him. Carolyn gave him a dirty look as she did a gesture that was almost the same as flipping the bird, but with her ring finger instead of her middle one. It was something she had started doing as a joke several months earlier, kind of like she was censoring herself by using the incorrect finger. But really, it meant the same thing.

In my parents' room, I began to hesitate. How exactly was I going to approach Nick about this? What if he didn't believe me? I pushed those fears aside and forced myself to think about how I had been able to convince Dennis before, so this wasn't a big deal.

"Hey, man!" he said over the phone. "What's up? I called you a few days ago, but you didn't call me back, you dweeb."

"Yeah, yeah, I know. Sorry. Just been really busy with stuff." I paused, unsure how to segue into the vampire topic. "So, what have you been up to?"

"Not a whole lot. Just hanging out. My parents are out of town this weekend, so I've just kinda been chilling out on my own."

"Oh, yeah, my parents are still out of town, too."

"You should come hang out! I've been listening to this new tape I got, but it may be a little too punk for you."

"Which band is it?"

"Bleeding Toenails. It's pretty cool."

The music groups Nick was into always had weird and sometimes violent sounding names, but this was a new one on me. My first thought was something along the lines of *That's disgusting, even if I am a vampire.* But then, my stomach growled. That just made me laugh.

Thinking that I was just laughing at the funny name, Nick continued talking. "Yeah, well, maybe it's not your thing. But I think they're pretty rad." He sometimes used slang words I wasn't familiar with, and really, he probably enjoyed it when I asked him to explain what they meant. He liked being different and not like everyone else, which was one of the things I thought was cool about him.

"Yeah, probably," I said dismissively. "So, have you been watching the news lately?"

"The what? No, not really. I don't bother with boring crap like that."

"Oh. I just meant, you know, all of the supposed vampire stuff that's been going on lately."

"Oh, yeah, I've seen that! That shit's pretty cool! Like total anarchy all the way." Nick had, in fact, been the person who first introduced me to that word, which came about because I spotted a weird symbol he'd drawn on one of his book covers at school. He liked to heavily decorate those with lots of graffiti and weird phrases, and the symbol for anarchy caught my eye because at first glance, it looked like a pentagram to me. This made me wonder if he might in fact be a Satanist, but he insisted that he was an atheist instead. The concept of anarchy as he explained it really appealed to me, and it was one of the main things that cemented our friendship, but I still had to keep from him the details of all of the bad things I had done in the past. Instead, we indulged our desire to be defiant in more tame things like minor vandalism and amateur pyromania.

Nick went on to say that he wished he could meet up with the vampires himself. "I mean, I don't know if they're real or not, but everyone seems to think they are. I'd love to get in on some of that action and cause some real trouble!"

"You think you'd make a good vampire?" I asked, keeping my tone light.

"Oh, hell yeah!" he laughed.

"Well, then you're in luck," I said, suddenly feeling like a game show host. "It just so happens that my sisters and some of the guys from school are the vampires, and we're hoping you could join us." Nick went quiet. "Did you hear me?"

"Are you fucking serious?"

"Yes," I said, faltering. I immediately realized that Nick wasn't the kind of guy who would suddenly jump up and down and squeal with delight after being offered something like this.

"Dude, that's just…"

"No, no, no!" I said, trying to recover. "I'm serious. For real."

"Get out."

"No, really, I mean it. My oldest sister has this potion that turns people into vampires. That's what's been going on all this time! It's us! We've taken the potion, turned ourselves into vampires temporarily, and gone around killing people." For the first time in ages, I realized how implausible the entire thing sounded. I'd known that it was true for years, but all of a sudden, I was having to convince someone new.

"Dude, what have you been smoking?" He laughed at his own joke, then got quiet again.

"Okay, look," I said, realizing what I needed to do. "What time is it now?"

"What? Um, like almost eleven o'clock."

"Good. I'm going to come over to your house, and I'll prove that I'm telling the truth."

"Whatever, Ray. You're not a vampire. Maybe you wish you could be, but that's just bullshit. I wish I could be one, too, but that's not going to make it happen."

"No, really, just trust me." I knew that he wouldn't, but what I had planned would probably fix that. "Turn on Channel Four and watch the news when it comes on. There will probably be a story about a bunch of people who got set on fire somewhere in South Augusta."

"What? Ray, I'm a little worried about you."

"Shut up. You'll see what I'm talking about."

A few moments later, I was hurrying up the hallway, and I told everyone in the den that I had to fly to Nick's house in order to convince him to join up. It was a very rushed thing, and timing was the key. Susanna didn't object and seemed to understand, for which I was grateful.

"Is Damon still on his way?" I asked Carolyn.

"Yes, he is," she said to me, walking with me as I quickly made my way to the front door. "Don't worry, Ray. I'm not entirely sure that he believed me either, but we'll get both of them in soon." She smiled at me broadly, and that gave me some comfort. As much as she wanted her precious boyfriend to join us, I wanted Nick to as well. I just had to handle things right.

I flew to his house, which was only a few blocks from mine. I could fly about thirty miles per hour, which was something that Tim figured out. After our encounter with Dracula out in Warrenton, he calculated how far we had flown and how long it had taken us, which turned out to be that speed. Also, flying in a straight line from one place to another, rather than following the streets like a car would, was something that we were getting better at and more comfortable with, so it meant that I would make it to Nick's house in just a couple of minutes.

He was, as planned, surprised when he opened the door to his house and saw me standing there, and his normally squinty eyes went as wide as they could. "How…?" I just smiled proudly. "What, did someone drive you here?" He pushed past me and walked out onto the porch, looking up and down the street, hoping to spot a car.

"Nope," I said.

"Oh, let me guess. You turned into a bat and flew here, is that it?"

"Yep."

"Ray! Come on!"

I heard that the TV was on inside, and the theme music for the news was playing. "Hey, the news is coming on," I said calmly. "We should go watch it." Not waiting for him to follow me, I let myself inside and settled down in his living room.

Still confused, Nick followed me in and shut the front door. He had a nice house, and I knew that his parents were pretty well off. I had met them before, and they seemed pretty laid back, not all that different from my own parents. The couch I sat on was large and comfortable, and their TV was one of those obnoxiously huge big screen ones, which were pretty rare. As impressive at it was supposed to be, though, I found that the picture looked weird and distorted, slightly fuzzy.

"Our top story tonight," the reporter began after the usual introduction, "concerns a brutal slaying that occurred in South Augusta sometime earlier tonight."

"This is it," I said, pointing at the screen. Nick, meanwhile, was still standing, his arms folded.

The screen cut to a shot of some police, the lights on their cars flashing away as official people stood around looking important and talking to each other. In the background were cars I recognized, the ones belonging to the teenagers we had killed. There was black and yellow *CAUTION* tape strewn about the scene, and I saw a white sheet draped over the side of the truck, presumably to cover the body of the girl we had tried to use to ignite the gas tank.

"The bodies of four teenagers were found in a field near the Hillcrest area off Deans Bridge Road. While this appears to have been another alleged vampire killing, a new, disturbing twist reveals that in addition to the bodies being found drained of blood, the victims were also set on fire."

I turned to look at Nick, who had been watching the screen. He stepped backwards, then looked over at me. I sat there, my eyes glowing green and my fangs bared. Nick jumped back, toppling to the floor as he tripped over a large wooden stool carved in the shape of an elephant. He recovered quickly, then stood up, eyeing me cautiously.

"So," I asked, dimming my eyes but keeping my fangs out, "you still want to get in on the action?"

"Holy crap," he said. "You weren't lying." I could tell that he was scared, but he was doing his best to play it cool.

"No," I said, remaining seated. "So do you?"

"How the hell can you be a vampire?" he asked. "I've seen you during the day plenty of times."

"I told you. It's temporary." I relaxed, and my fangs went back to being normal teeth. "The potion my sister makes turns you into a vampire for a while, and then you can go back to being a normal human again. It's scientific, not some cheesy legend."

"But what... I mean... Why?"

"Why what?"

"I mean, what for?" It was a practical enough question, one that had never really occurred to me.

"I don't know," I said simply. "Because it's fun?"

Nick tried to process everything. It was interesting seeing him so unsure of himself; usually he was the one who was trying to impress me with his tales of rebelliousness, the worst of which would usually amount to things like skateboarding along the walkways of Daniel Village and flipping off a cop who told him to stop.

"I'd been wanting to bring you into the group for a while," I said, "but the others needed convincing. I spoke up for you and said you'd be a good candidate."

"And all that stuff they just said on the news," he said, glancing back at the TV, "that was you?"

"Sure," I said. "You and I have set lots of stuff on fire, so we decided to do something like that tonight, too. I guess it made me kind of miss you!"

"Gee, thanks," he said, getting some of his sarcastic edge back.

"You still haven't answered my question. Do you want to join up with us or not?"

"I don't know, I... Kind of, I guess."

"You really should," I said, standing up. It suddenly occurred to me that if he ended up refusing, I would have to kill him. I couldn't just tell him about this and then go home without him, or else he might tell someone about us.

"Or what? You'll bite me?" I gave him a pointed look. "No, no, wait. Don't do that, dude. I was just kidding."

Stepping closer to him, I repeated, this time more slowly, "You really should. Trust me. You'll like it a lot. Don't be scared."

"I'm not scared, man!" he practically shouted. "But... Well, how long are we going to do it for? Just tonight? A couple of days?"

"A few more days," I said. "We're not really sure. My parents get back in about a week, so we have to stop by then. What about yours?"

"Oh, them? They'll be back sometime Sunday." That was disappointing; I didn't want Nick to only be with us for a couple of days. "But I can leave them a note! They won't mind if I hang out at yours for a while. I'm sure of it." He still seemed afraid of me, and I found that I loved that. It would be so easy to just go ahead and kill him; there would be no way he could stop me. But he was my friend, so I fought that urge back down.

"So you're in?" I asked.

"Yeah. Yeah! Why the hell not?"

"Good," I said, relaxing inside. It was only then that I realized how much I was wanting to bite him. It wasn't even that I was hungry or felt threatened by him; I just knew that I could, and I might have to if he'd continued to argue and refused to give in.

On the way back to my house, I flew while he skated along on the street below, occasionally looking up at my bat form, which had also freaked him out the first time he'd seen it. We didn't talk on the way, which gave me a few minutes alone with my thoughts.

Although I didn't like admitting it, part of me wished I had killed him. But again, that was more of a power thing than any actual need or desire. I then remembered how Susanna had warned us against killing anyone we knew, like when we went after Gary that time. I thought about that, realizing that it would feel strange to take the life of someone I had known all this time. But killing strangers didn't bother me at all; I usually enjoyed it.

"Are you sure that stuff's still going to be good?" Carl asked, pointing at the small Tupperware container Susanna had just handed to Damon. "It's been a few days, you know."

"Oh, it'll last a lot longer than that," she said. "It's got quite a shelf life."

Inside the container was a new, smaller batch of the vampire potion, but it wasn't something that Susanna had hurriedly whipped up that night. She had in fact made it a few nights before when we decided as a group that we were tired of reeking from not being able to take proper baths. Because we were all more or less on the same level of filthiness, we didn't often notice the smell for a while. We had the bowls of water that we occasionally — and very carefully — refilled, plus the baby wipes, but even then, we eventually felt gross. Carolyn was, not surprisingly, the first one who complained about this, and I found myself agreeing with her.

Showers were out of the question, but we came up with a complicated procedure for baths. The trickiest part was running the water and resisting the habit of touching it to check its temperature. Once the tub was full, one could safely slip in, wash off our bodies and our hair, then get out. Still, we were realistic, knowing that at least one of us might slip up and accidentally change ourselves back.

So Susanna made a little more of the potion just in case. Each person would take this with them into the bathroom, and if they messed up and ended up human again, they would take the potion. Because it would take four hours for it to take effect, the person would also slip a pre-written note under the bathroom door that said, *LEAVE NOW.* We knew that if a defenseless human being, even if we were normally friends, were locked up in that bathroom, the rest of us would be very tempted to break in and drink them. The note, once spotted by someone outside, would be a cue for the vampires to leave the house for a few hours to avoid the temptation, giving the other person time for the potion to change them again.

As it turned out, everything went smoothly, and no one got accidentally changed. Everyone felt better once we were clean, and the Wet Naps and baby wipes seemed sufficient to get us through the last few days of being vampires. That was before we had decided to extend our time another week, and it was likely that we would feel the need to repeat the process at least one more time. But it also gave us some idea of how to handle the presence of Damon and Nick.

Once Susanna had given the plastic container to Damon, she said, "Okay, you two need to get down to the basement. Fast."

Damon, who normally had an almost permanent happy-go-lucky expression, instead looked rather pensive. "Okay," he said. "And all that stuff you said was going to happen to us, the behavioral weirdness and all…"

"Just ride it out," Carolyn said. "You'll be fine. I promise." She leaned over and kissed his cheek. Then she drew back quickly, a strange look on her face. She had screwed her eyes shut, and she looked a little frightened. "Okay, yes, she's right. Get down there now. I'll see you soon, honey."

I knew what was going through her head; it was the same feeling we were all experiencing. It was very unusual for us to be in the presence of two ordinary humans and not be drinking their blood, so the safest thing to do was to lock them away while they took the potion and waited for it to take effect.

As we shut the door behind them, Dennis called out, "Good luck, honey!" The boys and I laughed.

"So now we've got, what, four hours to kill?" Carl asked.

"Looks that way," I said.

"I hope Damon and your friend don't get too bored down there," Carolyn said. "That's a long time to be cooped up."

"Oh, I'm sure they'll be fine," Tim said. "And hey, soon we'll have two new vampires!"

The time went by slowly, and we did various things like watching TV and playing video games while we waited. It had occurred to me earlier that we hadn't played with the Atari 5200 that much since we'd gotten together this summer, which I felt a little bad about once I realized that Damon would be coming over. After all, he had been the one who had given me this newer model, and I had played on it quite a lot earlier in the year. But for some reason, my friends weren't that interested in it.

Occasionally, I reached out with my mind and spied on what Damon and Nick were getting up to, but then I stopped that, as I found that picturing two vulnerable humans in our basement was a bit too much for me. It wouldn't be good to invite them over to take the potion, only to turn around and kill them because I couldn't keep my hunger in check. When we had planned this out, we figured that the entrance to the basement was far enough away that we wouldn't be tempted to sneak down there for a quick bite, so to speak. It wasn't working out that way, not for me or for any of the others. So, taking a cue from the plans we had drawn up for the bathing scenario, we left the house and ended up flying around the city for a while as a distraction.

Finally, the long wait was over, and we met Damon and Nick down in the basement, finding them newly transformed and part of the group at last.

"Can you feel it?" Carolyn asked Damon, putting her arms around his neck and looking up at him lovingly. "The thirst?"

"Yes," he said slyly, then leaned forward and kissed her.

"Oh, barf," Dennis muttered.

"Yeah, can we just get out of here already?" Nick asked. "Oh, and, um, sorry about the table." He pointed over to a corner of the basement, where an old table lay in pieces.

"Got too violent and out of control, huh?" Carl asked.

"Yeah," he said. "I know you guys warned us and all, but still, that was some trippy shit to go through."

"It's fine," Susanna said. "We can either fix it or throw it out. It's not a big deal. Now, I think it's time that we took you two out and showed you how things are done."

So we did, splitting into two groups. Carl, Dennis, and I took Nick to a gas station near Daniel Village to make his first kill. It was very late at night by then, so finding prey was more difficult, which was why we decided to split up. Soon enough, we spotted a lone car pulling up to the station, and when the driver got out, we landed around him.

The man realized what was happening and started to get back into his car, but I willed him to be still. His hand dropped to his side once he'd started to reach for the car door, and then he just stood there, looking anxious and confused. "Okay, Nick," I said. "Go for it."

"I, um…" He seemed unsure for a moment, but then he grinned. I knew that look well: It was the one he got just before he did something he knew was wrong. "Yeah, okay."

He walked forward and effortlessly bit down into the man's neck, and I realized that I probably shouldn't have subdued the man telepathically like that. If Nick were going to learn how to kill properly, he'd need to be able to pin someone down as they struggled against him. But by the time I thought all of this through, Nick was already halfway done with his meal.

Once the body was emptied, Nick stood up and looked around at the rest of us, a goofy, bloody smile on his face. "That was totally radical," he said. He seemed to be out of breath.

"Yeah, it's not usually that easy," Carl said. "But Ray and Dennis have these extra powers, so sometimes they can just kind of stun someone into standing there like an idiot so you can take them down easily."

"No shit, really?" Nick asked. I wondered if convincing him of that might be a problem, but he seemed to have seen enough already to have gotten past the threshold of cynical skepticism.

"Yeah," Dennis said. "It doesn't always work right, though. But even if you do have to fight to take a victim down, it's not all that hard since we're stronger than regular people."

"Yeah, I can kind of feel that," Nick said, looking down at his arm and flexing his fingers.

"Hey!" a man's voice called out from nearby. "Stop!"

We looked up, and a man with bright blond hair was running toward us, a cross in one of his hands. He was holding it out as he approached, and he looked like he meant business.

"Uh oh, time to go!" Dennis said.

"Wait!" Nick said. "Maybe we can take him!"

"No," I said. "Not if he's armed. It's not worth the risk."

We changed into bats and flew away, the man shouting at us as he stood by the body of Nick's first victim.

"Does that happen a lot?" Nick asked me as we flew home.

"What, you mean people like that guy with the cross? Not often."

"It does seem to be happening a lot more lately, though," Carl said pensively.

I was going to mention this to Susanna and the others once they got back to the house as well, but they had a more interesting story to tell as soon as they arrived.

"Tim got shot!" Carolyn said, but she sounded more excited than worried.

"What?" I asked Tim. "Are you okay?"

"Yeah, I'm fine," he said, smiling. "It hurt like hell when it happened, but once I changed into a bat, I was okay again. And then once I was back in my regular form, you couldn't even tell it had happened. Well, except for this." He pointed at a dime-sized hole in the right shoulder of his shirt, then stuck his finger through it playfully.

"Wow," Carl said. "What was it like?"

"It was weird. Like, at first I didn't even know what happened. I just felt this sharp pain, and then half a second later, I heard this loud *BANG!* Once I looked at my shoulder and saw that it was bleeding, I started to get scared. But then Susanna grabbed my other shoulder and screamed in my ear."

"I wasn't just screaming in your ear," she insisted. "I was telling you to change into a bat."

"I know, I know."

"So, if we get hurt, even shot, we can still be okay?" Nick asked.

"Yeah, pretty much," Carl said. "Something kind of like that happened to Ray, too."

I wasn't sure what he meant. "It did?"

"Yeah! No wounds on your neck," he said, pointing to either side of his own neck as he spoke.

"Oh," I said, realizing what he meant. It hadn't even occurred to me to check to see if I still had any marks or scars from when Susanna and Carolyn had bitten me while under Dracula's influence, and it wasn't like I could use a mirror to look for that anyway. But apparently, the injuries I had suffered that night had completely vanished once I had been able to change form. We talked about this a little more, establishing that the potion somehow made us default to a pre-injured state whenever we changed from one form to the other.

"Man, this is a lot to take in," Damon said. "But it's cool."

"Sure is," Nick said. "You okay with joining up now?" He directed this joke to Damon, who just laughed and flashed his usual charming smile.

The rest of the night was mostly spent catching Damon and Nick up on everything that had happened, not just the past couple of weeks but also the more interesting highlights of what we had done the previous two summers as vampires. They remained intrigued and asked a lot of questions, and I could tell that they were glad to be included despite their initial reluctance. I hadn't seen much of Damon's firsthand, but I suspected that it was similar to the resistance I got from Nick. And as I expected, once they were in on everything, they were enjoying it.

Another thing we needed to do was to update the map, which we had slacked off on doing the past couple of nights because of all that had been going on. In fact, I had completely forgotten about Susanna declaring the "Dracula zone" off-limits when I had led my friends to that gas station earlier. She chided me for this, but then she admitted that she had made a similar mistake by taking Damon to the very same gas station on Gordon Highway where we had killed a few nights before, which was how Tim ended up getting shot by a policeman who was staked out nearby.

"It wasn't a big deal," Tim insisted. In fact, he seemed a little proud of himself for having survived.

"Yeah," Nick said. "The police don't know all that much, those pigs."

"Maybe," Susanna said, "but one of the main reasons we've been doing this with the map all this time is that I'm guessing that 'the pigs' are doing the same thing, and we need to be careful to outmaneuver them. Going to the same places over and over is dangerous."

"Well, they can't be everywhere at once," I offered.

"And the longer we do this, plus the bigger our group gets," Tim said, "we may just have to accept some overlap here and there. I think Ray's right. There's only so much ground the police can cover. We should just be more careful about scouting out an area before we actually make a kill."

"I suppose," Susanna said with a slight sigh.

"Plus it's not just the police," Carl said. "We keep seeing other people trying to fight back with crosses and stakes and stuff." We finally got around to telling her about the man we had encountered that night.

"I'm hoping that's not as big of a problem," Susanna said. "But you're right, I guess. We should keep an eye out for people like that, too."

We got back to looking over the map, each of us trying to recall exactly where we had killed recently. Sometimes, we knew the exact location, but others were more difficult to pin down, like the couple I killed in their car when they were taking me to the hospital. Susanna marked our defeat of Dracula with a big red *D* over the location of our old school, then realized that it wasn't really necessary since it wasn't like the cops would have found a body there.

"And, let's see," Susanna said, pointing her marker at the map. "I guess I'll put another little dot here where Damon did his first… Now where's he gone?"

"Oh, he and Carolyn are making out in the living room," Carl said loudly.

A faint "I heard that!" from Damon came from around the corner, and Carl laughed.

Dennis rolled his eyes. "Great. Are we going to have to put up with them getting like that the whole time?"

"Probably," Susanna said dismissively, not looking up from the map.

I hadn't noticed it at first, but once I did, I asked Dennis once he and I were alone if he had a problem with Damon. I knew the answer already, but I wanted to get him to admit it.

"What?" he asked, screwing his face up in mock confusion. "No? No! Why would I?" I just stood there and looked at him. "Fine. Maybe a little."

"I remember what you said back in the tunnel. So you're jealous?"

"No… I mean… kinda… It's stupid. Yeah, I think Carolyn's hot and all. But it's not like she'd go with me anyway."

"True. But it bugs you seeing her with someone else. I know; I had to go through crap like that with Valerie back at school. Seeing her getting all cutesy and 'aww' over Gary made me want to puke."

"Don't say anything, okay?"

"I won't. It probably would be a good idea to put up your shields, though, so your powers don't end up making something bad happen to them."

"Oh, yeah, that's a good point." He thought for a moment. "God, especially now, since the potion has been making them stronger! I'm glad you thought of that. Hang on." He closed his eyes, and I could see in my mind how he was visualizing a clear, oval-shaped bubble surrounding his body. "There."

"All better now?" I asked, grinning.

"Well, the poofy-haired prick is still here, but I'll live with it."

We laughed, and then I said, "He's not a bad guy. Just give him a chance."

"I know, I know. And it's cool to have more people now. I'm glad Nick's around. He seems like he was made for this kind of thing. But there's also… I don't know."

"What?"

"I… I just keep getting this weird feeling. I don't even know what it is."

"Something bad?"

"Like I said, I don't know. Maybe. Something looming. That's the only way I can describe it."

"I had something like that a few days ago. But then I pretty much forgot about it. Hopefully it's nothing. Maybe it's just part of your bad feelings about…"

"Hey, dweebs," Nick said from my bedroom doorway. "What's going on in here?"

"Hmm?" I said. "Oh, nothing. Just talking about stuff."

"Susanna said we need to get the mattress from in here and take it down to the basement so I'll have somewhere to sleep."

"Why my mattress?" I asked. "Can't we get one from one of the other beds?"

"Hey, man, don't yell at me; that's just what she said to tell you."

My mattress was the only one left in the house that was a twin size, and there was only room enough for that downstairs. Floor space had already been a bit scarce in the basement, so adding another "bed" in there was tricky enough as it was.

Carolyn and Damon, meanwhile, shared the mattress she'd been sleeping on, which I was sure didn't thrill Dennis. It didn't make me terribly happy, either, not because I objected on any moral grounds, but because they kept me awake being all snuggly and squirmy with each other for a while.

The following night, we gathered in the kitchen as usual, though we now had our two new members to consider. With there being so many of us, we realized that the possibility of finding eight victims in one place each night was going to be slim.

"So I'm thinking that, like last night, we should split up into groups of four," Susanna said. "And I suppose we might even split those up further if necessary. Let's just see how it goes tonight."

"So where are we going?" I asked.

"You know what we should do," Tim said, "is kill in two very different locations. That will confuse the police even more."

Susanna nodded. "Good thinking."

Dennis, who was standing behind me, let out a little two-toned hum, the same tune we used when announcing *"Tim knows"* to each other whenever he showed off his brainy nature. I stifled a laugh and caught Carl's eye, and he just smiled at me knowingly. I couldn't remember if I had ever let Nick in on that joke.

"This is another thing we should get back to doing," Susanna said, picking up a pencil and pointing it around various spots on the map. She was referring to how we had originally marked places in pencil before leaving the house, then erased those upon our return and dotted in red where we had actually killed. We had dropped this practice after a while because it seemed redundant, as we almost always killed where we'd planned. But Susanna said that things might change now given how we were splitting up more and might end up having to improvise.

"So, let's see," she said, making a mark over a small green area. "Ray, how about you and the same boys from last night go here, to this park."

"Isn't that inside the Dracula zone?" I asked, pointing to the red line denoting that area.

"Yes, but it's somewhere we haven't been before. And so then the rest of us can go way over here." She moved her pencil in an exaggerated arc to a place farther north on the map, well outside of the red loop. "That should keep them guessing."

"Oh, so we have to go all that way?" Carolyn complained.

"We'll change it around tomorrow night," Susanna said.

"Yeah, and we should mix up the groups some, too," I said, "so it's not always the same."

"Can we just hurry up and go?" Damon said, being uncharacteristically crabby. "I'm starving!"

Carolyn pulled him to her briefly. "Aw, see? He's fitting in already."

Dennis, Carl, Nick, and I arrived at the park and immediately spotted a man and a woman walking along one of the concrete paths. They seemed to be arguing about something, but we were too high up to hear what was being said. After some more walking and speaking in raised voices, they settled onto a bench by the walkway and quieted down. The man was speaking urgently but softly, and the woman was avoiding his eyes, looking down at the ground.

"This could be fun," I said to the guys as we hovered overhead. "Let me try something." I reached out with my mind, envisioning it as an outstretched arm that went from my head down to the woman below. Once the invisible arm reached her, I pictured a fist closing around her head. The man kept talking, and I picked up on some of what he was saying, something about apologizing but not thinking he really needed to.

With a psychic prompt from me, the woman suddenly straightened up and turned towards the man, swiping at his face with her hand. Her long fingernails left four bloody gashes in the man's cheek, and he stood up quickly, crying out, "Bitch! What the hell is wrong with you?" She just sat there and looked at him blankly.

"Dude, that's messed up," Nick said.

"It's Ray making her do it," Dennis said gravely. "Come on, let's just kill them."

Ignoring them, I made the woman stand up while the man clutched at his cheek and continued to berate her. I was about to make her jump onto the man and start beating the hell out of him, but then Carl said, "To hell with this!" and zoomed down to the feuding couple. He latched onto the woman's neck and began drinking from her, and for a moment, I considered making her keep going as if Carl wasn't there. But that seemed like too much trouble, so I released my hold on her mind and just watched as she crumpled to the ground, her life being drained away.

The man, meanwhile, was bewildered and confused, torn between trying to help the woman or just running for his life. "Go get him, Nick," I said.

Nick reached the man and bit into him, and within seconds, there were two more dead bodies on the ground.

Once they were done, Carl and Nick rejoined us in the air. "Okay, that was pretty cool," Nick said. "This whole bat thing is kind of freaky to me, but I'm pretty sure I like it."

"You get used to it," Carl said.

"Still hungry over here," Dennis said impatiently. "Can we keep looking?"

We found our next victims not too far way, a younger couple who were sitting on top of an old army tank in the middle of the park. It looked out of place, and its presence confused me.

"What the hell is that doing here?" Carl asked.

"It's just for display," Nick said. "Probably came from Fort Gordon. My parents used to take me here when I was a kid."

"Oh, so it's, like, for climbing on?" Dennis asked. The tank was situated next to some more traditional playground equipment, so then it seemed to make more sense.

"Yeah," Nick said. "Like those two are doing. Still hungry?"

Dennis laughed. "Oh, definitely." He and I flew down and killed the boy and the girl, leaving their bodies sprawled on top of the tank.

"So what now?" Nick asked. "Do we just go back to the house?"

"That's usually what we do," I said, "but we don't really have to. What do you want to do?"

"Let's just hang out around here for a while!" he suggested. "Maybe there are some more people we can get." I liked that he was getting into it and enjoying being a vampire, just as I knew he would.

We walked away from the playground and toward a small brick building, and Carl asked Nick if he knew what it was. Nick shrugged and said he wasn't sure, that maybe it was the restrooms. Before we could speculate further, a man's voice distracted us.

"Hey! What are you kids doing?" We spotted the source of the gruff voice, and at first, I thought he was a policeman. He was wearing a dark-colored uniform that looked kind of like a cop's, but as he quickly walked toward us, I realized that he was just some kind of security guard.

"What's it to you?" Nick yelled back.

"Y'all kids better not be thinking of doing any vandalism on this wall," he said. "We just now got it cleaned from the last time some of you went and spray-painted it."

"What are you talking about?" I asked angrily. By then, he had reached us, and I could see his face more clearly. He was older and had a round head with a wrinkled, fat face and a moustache. "We didn't do anything to your precious wall."

"Don't you talk back to me, young man!" He reached for his belt and pulled a walkie-talkie to his ear.

"Drop it," Dennis said, and the man did, looking confused.

"I'll show you how we're going to mess up your damn wall," Carl said, stepping forward and grabbing the man by the throat, pushing him backwards. Carl was almost as tall as he was, though he was also probably less than half this man's weight. Again, there was that weird disconnect in my mind when I saw how easily his strength enabled him to propel the much bigger man.

He slammed the guard against the wall with his right hand, and the man looked too bewildered to fight back. As Carl drew back his left arm, the man's expression grew more fearful. Then, with the palm of his flattened hand, Carl smashed right through the man's head from below, splattering his skull all over the bricks in a fantastic arc of blood, brains, and bits of bone. It was simultaneously one of the most disgusting and most amazing things I had ever seen.

"Holy shit!" Nick shouted. "That was… Man! I don't even know what that was!"

Carl, meanwhile, seemed almost as surprised as the rest of us, and he let the man's mostly headless body slide to the pavement below. He looked back at us, wide-eyed and breathing heavily. He was grinning, but he also looked baffled. "Guess I don't know my own strength!" he said, then gasped. He looked down at his gore-covered hand and shook it, bits of the man's remains flying off of it. Carl got a thoughtful look and licked his lips, and I could tell that he was about to lick some of the bloody bits off his hand. But then he shook his head as if to clear it, instead choosing to wipe his hand off as best as he could along the side of the wall.

"Ewww!" Dennis said, but he was laughing about it. Once we had recovered from the shock, the rest of us also laughed.

"I saw these four vampires looming over the man," the blond-haired man on TV said. "I tried to intervene and save his life, but it was too late. But I was able to drive them away with a cross. If I ever see them again, you can bet I'll deal with them properly." He had this weird, fanatical look in his eyes, and the reporter holding the microphone seemed to flinch, like he really didn't want to be interviewing this weirdo.

"That's the man you saw?" Damon asked, referring to our encounter at the gas station the previous night. I nodded. "I really don't like the look of him. Seems kind of crazy."

The news story was about Life Force, whom we had heard a little bit about already, but we didn't know very much. So far, we had encountered a handful of their members, but as the report stated, the group was growing in number and was determined to rid Augusta of the vampire threat. Susanna hadn't taken them very seriously before, but she hadn't actually seen one of them until just then.

"He certainly seems like it," she said. "I wonder how many of them there are."

"Does it matter?" I asked.

"Well, it might be helpful to know."

"If we knew where they were based," Dennis said, "then maybe we could attack them and wipe them out."

"Or they might be a really big group," Carolyn said. "Like, bigger than us. That's a little different than one small family of rednecks with a 'Vampire Killers' flag stuck on the side of their house."

Susanna looked unhappy and was staring off, not making eye contact with anyone. "Between them and the police, I almost wonder if it might be safer to…" She stopped mid-sentence, then just sat there.

"Might what?" I asked her. She didn't respond; she just kept staring ahead. "Susanna?"

"Hmm?" she said, looking over at me. "Sorry, I guess I spaced out there for a little bit. What were we talking about?"

"These Life Force people," Carolyn said.

"Oh. Right. Let's just watch some more of the news and see if they say anything important."

Not much else was said. There was an earlier report that, as we had predicted, mentioned that there were two separate vampire killings in different areas of the city. Following the story on Life Force, it was noted that the police were not affiliated with them and did not condone people trying to take the law into their own hands. This worried Damon, who said that if those people were willing to act like vigilantes, we should be careful of them.

The other worrying thing was the weather forecast, which predicted thunderstorms the following night. We didn't want to be trapped inside the house all night again and be unable to go out and feed, and the supply of blood Susanna had gotten for us the week before had been mostly depleted.

"So I guess we need to stock up on some more!" I said. "Where do we get it from?"

"A hospital," Susanna said. "We'll have to sneak into one and find where they keep the blood saved for patients."

"Yeah!" Carl said. "Remember how they said the other night that all those people were supposed to be donating blood? I bet there's tons of it for us to take."

"We don't need tons," Susanna said. "Just enough to get by."

"So let's find a hospital and go there!" I said.

We looked over the map, and once I knew that the little red plus signs on it designated hospitals, I knew how to spot them. "How about this one?" I said, pointing.

"Careful," Carolyn said, brushing my hand aside. "For all we know, that counts as a cross and you could get changed back."

"Whoa," I said. "Right. But anyway, there's one. It's pretty far out of the city, so maybe it's a good place to go."

Damon peered over my shoulder. "Oh, no. Not there."

"Why not?"

"That's on Fort Gordon, the Army base. That's where my dad was stationed."

"Oh, so you think he might be there?"

"No, that's not what I mean. There will be lots of soldiers. Dudes with guns. Not a good idea."

"What does that matter?" Carl asked. "Guns can't hurt us. Or at least, they can't kill us."

"I'm not really keen on the idea of getting shot again, Carl," Tim said. "Yeah, I survived it, but it still hurt."

"What I mean," Damon said firmly, "is that if we were to go there and end up killing some Army guys, that could stir up a lot more trouble. The FBI might get involved."

"So?" Dennis asked. "Let them! We'll kill them, too!"

"No," Susanna said. "He's right. That's just another complication we don't need."

"Here's one," Tim said, pointing with a pencil. "Garden City Medical. Why don't we just keep it simple and go there?"

"That sounds good," Susanna said. "It's nearby, and besides, we're going to need to drive there. Whose car do we want to take?"

The raid went surprisingly well. No one even noticed us as we flitted about from ceiling to ceiling as we snuck around trying to find the hospital's supply of blood. Everyone who worked there seemed far too absorbed in what they were doing as they rushed around, not one of them ever bothering to look up and spot us. We thought we might have to kill a few people in order to get out of there, plus there was the added temptation of all of those regular humans sitting around in their beds just ready for us to prey upon.

But that was another interesting thing. As Susanna, Carl, Tim, and I made our way through the hospital, I would occasionally spot a person and get the urge to bite them. This included the doctors, nurses, and other staff, and also the various patients. Sometimes, I would spot someone on a bed through a doorway, or I would see a person wheeling somebody along on their way from one place to another, and a weird feeling would come over me. Somehow, I knew that certain people I saw had diseases, and it was like they had something wrong with their blood. I then had no desire whatsoever to bite them, and I was even repulsed. Once I realized that this was happening, I figured that it must have been because of my psychic powers, but once we were back home and everyone was talking, I realized I was wrong.

It turned out that all of the other vampires had similar things happen to them. We figured out from this discussion that we had yet another unexpected ability given to us by the potion, the power to detect and avoid people who had diseases. It made a weird sort of sense, given that we fed on blood. If we drank the blood of someone with an illness, then that might affect us, or at the very least, it might just taste bad. We wondered if this had been happening all along, if the reason we had occasionally passed over potential victims was due to this same phenomenon, and we only noticed it this night because there were so many sick people around.

Carl mentioned something else I had noticed while we were at the hospital, that there were flyers on various bulletin boards that were like informal advertisements for Life Force. I took the time to look one over when we happened to be in an unoccupied hallway, noticing that it was a photocopied, handwritten screed that echoed some of the same things we had already heard on the news from these people. The only contact information was a phone number, and I got a little laugh from the idea of calling them up and threatening them, but there didn't seem to be much point in that.

Susanna reasoned that Life Force had probably put those flyers up in hospitals hoping to recruit some of the people who had been taken there for transfusions after they had been bussed in from Warren County. It was certainly possible that some of those people might have been angered by the experience and had at least some notion of it being vampire-related, so they might be eager to join up with a group that was dedicated to getting rid of that threat. This made us speculate further as to just how much of a danger this group might be for us.

Throughout this discussion, Susanna, Carolyn, and Damon seemed to have the most insight into the bigger picture, and I found it interesting how having another adult around changed things. Damon wasn't like most of the older, more boring grown-ups that I knew, but still, having him there made things feel slightly different, almost like his presence made me feel more adult as well. I wasn't used to having an older guy to look up to.

On the other hand, having Nick in the mix also appealed to my juvenile delinquent side. The other boys also seemed to be enjoying being even more decadent than before, which just added to the fun. Nick, who sometimes shunned any kind of group activity while we were in school, appeared to be fitting in well with the rest of my friends and family, which was nice to see.

An interesting balance was found the following night when everyone except Susanna gathered in the red den to watch that night's episode of *The Young Ones,* which I enjoyed a lot more than the previous week's. This one was mostly funny throughout, and everyone liked it, even Carolyn, who restrained herself from objecting to some of the gross-out humor that the show often employed. This may have been due to Damon's also being a fan of the program, though one of the things he liked about it was the main thing I disliked, that halfway through each episode, a musical group would show up from nowhere and interrupt the story, play a weird song, and then disappear with no explanation. Nick and some of the others were fine with this, putting it down to just another aspect of the show's bizarre appeal.

Nick also had a habit of reciting some of the jokes from the program, as he had seen it several times already. There were only twelve episodes, he explained, and MTV aired them over and over. So there were times when Nick would blurt something out ahead of time, spoiling the joke. He did this several times until Carolyn pointed out how annoying it was, echoing my own thoughts.

But all of that was later on Sunday night; what happened earlier in the evening was much more interesting.

We woke up in the basement as usual, eager to go out and kill. We checked the news and found nothing all that interesting aside from the fact that the weather forecast had changed, and there were no longer any thunderstorms expected that night. While that made things more convenient, it also pissed us off because of all the effort spent the night before stocking up on blood.

Wanting to keep all eight of us together this time, Susanna made a mark on the map in pencil and announced to everyone that we would be attacking the parking lot of Regency Mall, which was another location in South Augusta where we'd never killed before. Before heading out, everyone took care of any last minute stuff they needed to do, which for me was setting the VCR to record the news in case we didn't get back in time for it. I was getting increasingly curious about Life Force, and I wondered if we might be able to find out anything else about them.

I got more than I bargained for when, after we made our kills in various parts of the mall's vast parking lot and regrouped, we suddenly became aware of the sound of lots of people shouting and screaming.

"What is that?" Tim asked.

"Sounds like some people at a concert," Damon said, standing up from the body of the woman he had just finished killing. Two other bodies were on the pavement nearby, the ones Tim and I had left behind. "Or quite possibly an angry mob."

"You're not kidding!" Dennis said, pointing. "Look!"

At least two dozen people were running toward us and shouting, and I could make out various things being said like "There they are!" and "Vampires!" and "Kill them!" Every single person in the group had at least one anti-vampire weapon, and they ran toward us, their crosses, wooden stakes, garlic, and crossbows held aloft. One of them even had a flaming torch, and I felt a sudden chill as I pictured that being hurled at me if the crowd got any closer.

"Quick!" I shouted. "Let's fly!"

We did, and we got away easily, though a few cloves of garlic and other paraphernalia were thrown up into the air in our direction. The experience was disturbingly reminiscent of our confrontation with Van Helsing, only multiplied at least twenty times over.

"It was another one of those flyers for Life Force," Carl said, referring to one that he'd seen on a telephone pole not long after we had safely gotten away from the mall. He had briefly broken formation to fly down and get a better look at it, then explained what he was up to later on.

"Well, I guess it's like I was always telling the band," Damon said. "Good promotion is important."

"I really don't think that's relevant," Susanna said.

"What I mean is that they're getting the word out, so people are joining their group."

"Like they did at the hospital," I said. Damon nodded.

"I noticed that guy from the news in the crowd," Carolyn said with a small shudder. "He looks even more crazy in person." I hadn't even bothered to look to see if he was among the mob; I was more concerned with getting out of there in one piece.

"They all did," Nick said. "We should have wiped them all out."

"No," Susanna said. "Not with all those weapons they had. I'm sure if we'd tried to fight back, they'd have gotten at least some of us."

"How did they know how to find us?" Dennis asked.

"Probably just dumb luck, I'd think," Susanna said. "Maybe they're based in South Augusta. If we just stay away from that area, then we'll probably be okay."

"But what if they have more than one… I don't know… faction?" Dennis asked. "There might be a whole bunch of them around the city!"

"I don't know about that," Damon said. "There was that same guy from the news there tonight, after all. It's probably not a huge group."

"Besides, most people wouldn't go so far as to take up arms and all that," Carolyn said. "They're more inclined to sit back and hope that someone else will take care of things."

"But we don't know that for certain," I said.

"I kept getting flashbacks to the night we fought against Sheling," Dennis said.

"Yeah, but he was a professional vampire hunter," Tim said. "These are just regular people. That's something to consider."

"I guess," I said, shrugging. "Still, there's a lot of them. A lot more than us."

"Maybe we could split them up somehow," Carl offered. "You know, even the odds a little more."

"I'd rather just avoid them altogether," Susanna said.

We went around in circles like this for a while, no one able to come up with anything truly useful. If Susanna was right and our encounter with them this night had just been a fluke, then we probably didn't have anything to really worry about. Unfortunately, she wasn't right.

Monday night, it was cloudy. I noticed as we flew downtown how everything seemed just a little bit brighter on cloudy nights, the sky a sort of vaguely bluish haze. It had in fact rained late the night before, despite the revised forecast having predicted otherwise, which made me uneasy. This night was also supposed to be free of rain, but then, if the forecast kept being so unreliable, what was the point of it?

Susanna had decided again to keep the entire group together, saying that if we did run into Life Force again, we would be safer that way. I disagreed with this, thinking that smaller groups would be a better way to avoid detection, but she ignored me. So we ended up heading for a spot right in the middle of downtown, the idea being that we hadn't killed there for a while, so it was unlikely that the police or anyone else would be looking for us there.

We approached an area that had a handful of bars, restaurants, and stores, some of which were still open. There were lots of people around, and I asked Susanna what we were doing there.

"Meaning?" she asked flatly.

"We usually attack people in out-of-the-way places, not in crowds."

"Not always. Remember the YMCA?" I pictured the night of my first kill all those years ago, how we picked individual victims from the panicked crowd, repeating the process over and over. I could see it in my mind as clearly as if it had happened the night before.

"So, we're going for a more classic approach tonight?" I asked.

"Always best to keep the enemy guessing," she said slyly.

"You know what you could do," Carl said, flying up beside me. "Use those fancy-shmancy powers of yours and find out if those Life Force guys are lurking around somewhere."

This sounded like a good idea at first, but then I worried about what might happen. Casting my mind out to listen in on the thoughts of individuals was one thing, but I suddenly got this fear that trying to scan an entire crowd would be overwhelming. I was reminded of a time when I was little and our family had gone to church for the Easter service. Everyone was making their way to the exit afterwards, people towering over me on all sides, all of them having loud conversations simultaneously. Their voices echoed in what felt like an intimidating and huge space, and I felt claustrophobic. The words blurred in my ears and sounded like a bunch of people asynchronously saying "audie-eddie, audie-eddie, audie-eddie" over and over. The experience freaked me out, so much that the memory stayed with me over the years.

I didn't want to bring this up to everyone, both because it was an unpleasant recollection and because it would take too long to explain. So instead, I lied, pretending to scan the crowd and then telling them that I couldn't detect anything.

I was going to ask Dennis if he had picked up on any danger, but then Nick interrupted. "Oh, who cares, you guys! Let's just go!" With that, he flew down to a group of people on the sidewalk, and Tim went straight after him. While I liked how quickly both he and Damon had embraced this new lifestyle, it bugged me that Nick had been the one to initiate the attack. But really, that was just me being a control freak again.

People began screaming and running around, and we began picking out victims and pursuing them. I saw a group of three people run into an alleyway next to a record store, an older boy and a girl, the latter of which was pulling another, shorter girl alongside her. They were trying to hide, so I couldn't resist going after them. Carolyn and Damon were still hovering next to me, so I invited them along.

Trapping the teenagers in the alley was easy. Carolyn and Damon landed farther along the narrow passage and cornered the two older kids, and I landed in front of the younger girl. She looked strange to me, her clothes mostly black and her hair, which was also black, was cut in a short, weirdly shaped style. She wore fishnet-patterned tights which led down to black high-top tennis shoes, the same brand Damon wore, I noticed. I found her slightly attractive, but just a little bit too bizarre, like she was trying too hard to look different and interesting.

But the strangest thing about her was her demeanor. I had expected her to be terrified, but instead, she looked much more calm. Her friends screamed as Carolyn and Damon bit into them and took them down, and she looked over at them for a second, a vaguely sad expression on her face as she turned back to me. Then she held out her arms, kind of like the gesture I had seen Dracula do several times.

"Come on," she said in a high, soft voice. "Let's get this over with."

This confused me, but I still stepped closer to her, unsure what was happening. I lit my eyes up and bared my fangs, thinking that this might send her into a panic, and then I would have to chase her down. Instead, her eyes lit up as well, but only figuratively. Really, she just looked very surprised, even happy. She already had wide, round brown eyes, their shape enhanced by thick, black eyeliner. She was very pale, and it occurred to me that she looked a bit like a vampire, though not a real one. She was more like someone dressed up for Halloween, but given that her two friends had been dressed similarly, I figured that this must have just been their style. Once I realized this, it kind of got on my nerves.

"Please," she continued. "I want to be like you!"

"Whatever," I said, jumping forward and grabbing her, then biting down into her neck. She let out a little wail, but it wasn't like the screams I was used to. She sounded pleased, and I was surprised to feel her hand on the back of my head, like she was trying to hold me onto her neck. There was no need for that, as I would have drunk from her regardless, but it was still a very unfamiliar sensation. I drank her blood the same as I always did from any other victim, but this was the first time I had ever had a willing one. Her breathing increased and became very rapid, and I tried to peer into her mind to find out just where all of this bizarre behavior was coming from, but for some reason, I couldn't. Still, the time I spent draining her life gave me some time to think, and once I was done, I figured it out.

I stood up, leaving her lifeless body on the pavement, and I noticed the pleased look on her dead face. This girl had apparently believed that if she got killed by a vampire, she would become one as well, which she had wanted. I felt a little bit sorry for her since I knew that wouldn't actually happen, but at least now that she was dead, she wouldn't get the chance to be disappointed. But then a more sadistic thought went through my mind, and I joked to myself that I wished that more of my victims were like her.

The humans who had managed to get away had fled the area, and the street was deserted, at least for the moment. Everyone gathered on the sidewalk, trying to decide what to do next.

"Should we go back to the house or hang around and get a few more victims?" Nick asked.

"Not full yet?" Damon asked him.

"Well, maybe, but I wouldn't mind a little more…" All of a sudden, a familiar sound came into earshot. "Shit! Again?" The noise of angry shouting was coming from around the corner, and I knew that at any second, we would be confronted by Life Force.

"Quick!" Susanna hissed. "Everyone change into bats and perch up there." She pointed to a large, illuminated sign hanging at an angle over the entrance to the record store. We did as she said, hiding and peering over the edge of the metal sign, which I noticed was quite hot from the electric lights inside. We couldn't stay there very long.

As expected, the vigilantes came rushing around the corner, weapons in hand. It was a little hard to see them over the glare from the sign, but I could mostly make them out. Some of the ones in front stopped, and a few people bumped into each other and then regained their composure.

"Why don't we just get out of here?" Tim whispered.

"Shh," Susanna said. "Not yet."

"Where did they go?" a young woman said. "I swear, they were right here!"

"You're sure?" the blond man said coldly.

"Well, they're not here now."

Another person from the crowd spoke up. "But they were definitely in this area! We saw the bodies!"

"Then we were too late," the man said dramatically. "At least this proves that our contact was telling the truth." He led the disappointed mob back the way they had come, disappearing around the corner. Relieved, I flapped my wings and hovered up from the sign, which was almost burning me by that point. The others did the same.

"What did he mean by that?" Carolyn asked.

"I don't know," Susanna said. She was lying.

As soon as we got back, Susanna walked silently and determinedly to the kitchen, picking up the red marker and designating our most recent attack site on the map. The rest of us followed, but Damon and Carolyn stayed in the adjacent yellow den. Susanna then slammed the marker down onto the table.

"All right," she said firmly. "Which one of you is it."

"Which one of you is it who?" Dennis said with a laugh, but his face fell when he saw the seriousness in Susanna's expression. She hadn't spoken the entire way home, and when I'd tried to engage her in conversation once, she'd just said, "Later." I could tell she was angry, but I wasn't sure why.

"That man downtown mentioned a contact. Someone told that group where to find us. Last night, I wanted to believe it was a coincidence. But not two nights in a row."

I realized what she was implying. "You mean," I said, pausing as things continued to sink in, "someone here is a traitor?"

"That's exactly what I mean." I hadn't seen her look this angry in a long time. "So," she continued, folding her arms and raising her eyebrows, "anybody want to fess up?"

Everyone was silent and began looking around at each other cautiously. Could this really be true? Would someone actually go so far as to turn on the rest of us and betray us to these vampire killers?

I jumped when Dennis spoke up, afraid that he was about to admit to it. Instead, he was about to be the first to point a finger. "I know it's not me," he said in a sly tone, "but I do think that it's interesting that almost as soon as we have two new people join up, there's a traitor." He looked meaningfully at Damon and Carolyn, who were sitting on the couch.

"What?" Damon asked, sitting up straight. "You think I would do something like that?"

"That's my boyfriend you're accusing, you little shit," Carolyn said, narrowing her eyes and remaining still, her arms also folded.

"I'm not a little thit!" Dennis shot back, momentarily forgetting to control his lisp. He then clammed up, embarrassed.

"And I'm not a narc!" Nick said, almost shouting. More quietly, he added, "That's just great. Invite me into your secret little vampire club, then accuse me of stabbing you in the back. Fuck you people."

"Nick, calm down," I said, holding up a hand. I couldn't argue with Dennis's logic, though. But I didn't want to believe that Nick was the traitor, nor Damon, nor anyone. I didn't want to believe that any of this was happening. "No one's accusing you of anything."

"I am," Dennis said.

"Yeah, well, who says that you're not the one, piss-face?" Nick said to him. He had a point, but I couldn't really picture Dennis doing something like that. Then again, he and I had occasionally turned on each other in the past, particularly during our last year of school. For all I knew, he was doing something similar again.

"Guys," Susanna said, trying to get things under control.

"'Guys' what?" Dennis shouted. "How do we know it's not you?"

"Me?" She let out a haughty laugh. "Don't be stupid."

"You did get pretty sneaky in the past," Tim said, "like when you conspired against us to change us back along with… Well, there's a thought." He then turned to Carolyn, a smug look on his face.

"Don't even start," Carolyn said. "I'm not a 'narc,' either." She said the word with exaggerated sarcasm, mimicking Nick's voice. Nick just rolled his eyes and looked away from her.

"Hang on, hang on," Carl said, holding up his hands. Everyone looked at him, and he flinched. "What? No, I'm not the mysterious bad guy, either. But I know how we can find out." He looked at me. "Ray? Mr. Psychic? Surely you can read everyone's mind and find out the truth."

"Yeah, well," I said, "about that…" I was going to cite Susanna's rule that I wasn't supposed to use my powers on any of the other vampires. But then I figured that, given the heightened suspicion in the room, I should just admit to everyone what was happening. I had tried to use my powers on that strange girl I had killed earlier in the night, but nothing had happened. I told myself at the time that it was just a weird coincidence, or maybe the fact that she was a willing victim had screwed things up somehow. But then later, when we were spying on Life Force, I tried to reach out to at least one or two people in the crowd with my mind, and again, there was nothing. "My powers don't seem to be working anymore," I said, feeling defeated.

"What?" Carolyn said. "Since when? I thought you were all powerful and scary now, ever since Dracula did… whatever he did to you."

"I was. But at least as far back as when we were downtown tonight, well, something's gone wrong. It's like they're just not there anymore." I hated admitting this, partly because doing so made me feel suddenly vulnerable, even scared. It was like going blind or deaf, and it made me feel helpless and small, particularly given this latest crisis. "I don't understand it, and it bugs me. Maybe Dracula only boosted my powers temporarily, and now there's been some kind of retro effect." I looked over at Dennis, but he was looking at the floor, so we didn't make eye contact.

"So you can't read anyone's mind?" Carl asked. "Now, that's kind of convenient."

"What do you mean?"

"Well, what gets you off the hook?" He stepped slightly closer to me as he spoke. "Who's to say that you're not the one behind all this?"

"He's got a point," Tim said.

"No he doesn't!" was all I could think to say back. I knew I wasn't the traitor, so it seemed ridiculous for anyone to suggest that I was.

"It's not just you, Ray," Dennis said in a somber tone. "My powers have crapped out, too. I didn't want to say anything, but, yeah, they have. I thought it was just me."

"Wait, wait, wait," Carolyn said, standing up from the couch and shaking her hands in a weird gesture, her eyes closing as she shook her head. "Tell me how this makes any sense at all."

"It doesn't," Tim said. "But I agree with Carl; it's quite a coincidence that this is supposedly happening and then, all of a sudden, you two guys can't work your psychic mumbo-jumbo and figure it all out."

"Look, everyone," Susanna said. "I don't really care. Your superpowers can do whatever the hell they want as far as I'm concerned. What matters here is that someone has taken it upon themselves to sell us out to these Life Force people, and that's bullshit. Whoever it is needs to confess right now and find some way to redeem themselves, like telling us where Life Force has its base, headquarters, whatever, so we can go wipe them out. If you do that, then we'll just say all is forgiven and let it go." She looked around the room. Everyone remained silent.

No progress was made, and we stopped the endless and pointless questioning of each other at 11:00 to watch the news. There was a story about our attack downtown, which was followed by a brief mention of Life Force and their continued efforts, which the police still didn't endorse. Most of the time, we watched the news with a sense of amusement, knowing that we were always a step ahead of the authorities, and we liked making fun of the news anchors and their occasional blunders on the air. But this time, everyone sat quiet and still, our eyes fixed on the screen. It wasn't fun this time.

When the relevant part of the broadcast was over, everybody was still uneasy, and I didn't like the feeling in the room. I also didn't like this recent loss of my powers, and the fact that Dennis's weren't working bugged me, too. I went to the back door and unlocked it, which prompted Susanna to ask me where I was going.

"Out," I said simply, echoing a stereotypical angry teenager from a TV show.

"That's not good enough," she said.

"I'm going up to the roof for a while, okay? I just need some fresh air. Come up and chaperone me if you don't believe me."

She gave me a sort of weak, sympathetic look, which surprised me. But I knew that it indicated consent, so I went outside, flew up to the roof, then changed back to my person form and settled next to the defunct chimney directly above the yellow den. It felt good to be on my own for once, away from the bickering group downstairs. Things were just getting too intense.

I sat for a while and tried to work out my thoughts. The first thing I did was let go of the resentment I felt for Susanna over that most recent confrontation. I hated it when she got all authoritative on me, acting more like a parent than a sister. But I realized that she was right to question me, just as I would have questioned anyone else if they had suddenly announced that they were leaving the house for no reason. Given what was apparently happening with this whole traitor business, anyone who did that would look suspicious, maybe sneaking away to contact Life Force. Once I figured all of that out, I regretted what I was doing, knowing how it looked. But then, I knew that I wasn't the traitor, so what did I have to prove?

I ran over every aspect of the situation in my head, trying to make sense of it and maybe even figure out who the traitor was. Nick and Damon seemed like the most obvious possibilities, but that bothered me as well, how simple it was. It was just as likely that whoever it was took their arrival as an opportunity, letting them be the scapegoats. I didn't like that thought, either, that one of my friends or sisters — if it was indeed only one person, that is — could have been planning to turn on us for a while.

As for Nick, I could see him pulling something like this, given how he was such a troublemaker. Normally, I liked that about him, but not if it meant that he was putting the rest of us at risk. I'd also only known him for a year, so maybe he was more untrustworthy than I'd realized.

The same could be said for Damon; I had only known him for a few months, and even then, I mostly knew him through Carolyn. He and I did talk by ourselves from time to time, but usually, she was nearby if not in the same room. Was he maybe not into being a vampire as much as we'd hoped? Did he think that this was actually something horrible, that it was his duty to save his precious Carolyn from it? If that were the case, then he was sadly mistaken. Those Life Force guys weren't playing around, and if things went badly, one or more of us could end up dead.

That got me thinking about Crowley. His death was still looming over us, but with everything else that had happened since then, there wasn't time to think about him all that often. When I did, I would just get sad, particularly when I would picture him in my mind. *He was just a sweet little white cat,* I said to myself. *He never hurt anybody. Well, okay, so that's not true.*

I thought of the times he and Carolyn had sat up here on the roof, including the times I spied on them or joined them. Then I began to picture him, like a ghost cat sidling up next to me, rubbing on my legs as I held my knees up near to my chin. *Hey, little guy,* I thought. *I'm really sorry. I didn't know that Sheling was going to kill you.*

Well, he did, I imagined him saying back to me. *And if you don't hurry up and turn this thing around, there are going to be a lot more deaths than just one little cat.*

This was just upsetting me more, so I went back to running down the list of suspects. Thinking back to Damon and his possible motivation, I considered the flip side of that. Maybe it was Carolyn who didn't want Damon caught up in all of this evil nastiness, so she was trying to find a way out for him. But that didn't really make sense; she had been the one to suggest bringing him into the group.

Then there was Susanna, who, as Tim pointed out, had turned on us before and conspired against us. I also wondered if she might have something to do with why mine and Dennis's powers weren't working. Had she somehow slipped us something similar to the potion, neutralizing our powers somehow so we couldn't detect her? But how could she do that? Apart from what we told her, she knew very little about psychic powers, at least as far as I knew.

Honestly, I could think of a possible motivation for everyone in the group if I tried to. Maybe Dennis was more jealous of Damon than I realized, or maybe he resented my bringing Nick in, just as he did when he seceded from the group when I brought Carl in last time. Maybe Carl had some latent resentment for not being included initially that time, or this could be some kind of residual hostility from the Club Wars or one of the many other rifts we'd had over the years. Tim had been less popular at school in recent years, so maybe he resented being thought of as a nerd and looked down on.

The more I pondered, the more frustrated I got, because I couldn't figure it out on my own. If I just had my powers working right, I could reach out with my mind and solve this mystery right away. I tried to use them again, but still there was nothing, or at least, almost nothing. I still felt that familiar tingle in my head. Closing my eyes, I tried to visualize my powers as greenish light, like an aura in my brain. I tried to push the glow outward, and it started to happen, but then it stopped short. The range wouldn't extend beyond my head. Something was blocking them.

It was kind of like when Dennis or I would put up shields to keep our powers from accidentally harming people, but this was different. Or was it? Had I accidentally put up a barrier on myself? Our powers were based in thought, after all, so maybe I had subconsciously blocked them somehow. I knew a little bit about the conscious and subconscious from Carolyn, who occasionally told me things she had learned in the Psychology class she had taken during her senior year of high school. The idea of a separate, inner, unknown mind fascinated me. Had I perhaps done this to myself without realizing it?

With that in mind, I tried to picture the shell around me, then willed it to disappear. I made my powers flare again, but they still felt blocked. I then concentrated and tried as hard as I could to smash through the barrier, but that didn't work, either. Frustrated, I tried again. Still nothing.

Suddenly, I was distracted by the faint sound of flapping wings. Susanna landed next to me and changed form, then asked me how I was doing.

"I don't know," I said. "Angry, mostly."

"Yeah, I know. Me too. Did you manage to figure anything out?" She was being much more amiable than she had been earlier in the house, which — like everything else I gave any thought to — made me suspicious.

"How did you know I was doing that? You must be psychic," I said sarcastically.

"I wish," she said with a faint smile. "But that's supposed to be your department."

"And I wish it still was," I said bitterly. I started to tell her about the barrier I'd been trying to break through, but then I remembered my other idea, that maybe she had somehow made it happen through some kind of secret potion. I was afraid that mentioning this to her would somehow put me in danger, so instead I said, "I just don't know what's gone wrong."

"Well, you did say something downstairs about them being damaged by Dracula. Maybe that's it? And who knows, maybe they'll heal and come back."

"Maybe. But then, what about Dennis?"

"Dracula got him too, remember. Or at least, one of his vampires did."

"That's true." I had forgotten that part. We were quiet for a little while, looking up at the sky. It was still cloudy, but there were gaps in the clouds, the whole sky looking like three-dimensional bluish-grey pavement with cracks in it. Here and there, larger gaps managed to let a few stars through. To the west, a brighter haze indicated the moon, itself shrouded but trying to peek out.

"So who do you think it is," Susanna asked in her usual flat tone.

I sighed. "Well, I know it's not me."

She laughed a little. "Me too. I mean, I don't think it's you, either. I've seen you do a lot of stupid things in your time…"

"Gee, thanks."

"Oh, shut up. I meant that even though you've done a lot of dumb things, I couldn't really see you doing something to break us up. You're the one who gets everyone together, after all."

I thought about that, how I liked to consider this my group, but I was never really sure just how much I was in charge. When I was younger, it always seemed like Susanna ran things because she was the oldest, and besides, she was the one with the potion. But as I got older, particularly after all that happened with the clubs in fifth grade, I found that I liked being the leader. It was fun to have people depend on me to tell them what to do. Susanna's statement seemed to validate that status, that maybe this really was my vampire group, not hers. Or maybe it was better to think of it as ours.

We talked some more, bouncing ideas off each other. Despite the obviousness of it, her top two suspects were still Damon and Nick, mostly because they were new to the whole thing and maybe didn't understand it. She had also picked up on Nick's predilection for stirring up trouble, but she pointed out that Damon was kind of the same way.

"He seems like a nice enough guy and all," she said, "but I don't fully trust him. He's got a little too much of that bad boy rock star thing going on, which I know Carolyn likes, but still. People like that can be unstable." I took her word for this, accepting that she knew more about the inner workings of people her own age.

I put forth that if anyone wanted out, they should just say so, and we could give them the antidote and let them go on their way. "And maybe if they had some info on Life Force, we could forgive and forget, like you offered earlier."

"Oh, that was just a ploy," she said. "I think we're beyond forgiveness. You don't come in here and endanger my family and get away with it." I understood what she meant, and while the thought disturbed me, I realized that I agreed with her.

The rest of the night was pretty uncomfortable. After Susanna and I went back inside, we found that everyone was mostly keeping to themselves aside from Carolyn and Damon, who still stayed close. Nick was watching TV with Carl in the red den, but from what I could tell, they weren't really talking to each other. Dennis was watching the other TV in the yellow den, and Tim was in the living room reading. The house just felt dull and lifeless, not fun anymore. I almost wondered what we were still doing together.

Sunrise approached, and Susanna and I corralled everybody as usual and told them that it was time to go to the basement to sleep. After everyone had gone, I noticed that Susanna was still standing at the front door, facing the eastern sky as it started to brighten.

"What's up?" I asked her.

"You know, just for a second there, I had half a mind to just tell everybody to stand here and wait for the sun to come up. But I still don't want to change back. Do you?" I didn't like the pointed way she asked me that.

"No," I said, turning my back to her. I walked to the basement door, resentment building up again. Despite all that we had talked about on the roof, somewhere deep down, she still suspected me.

As we settled down to go to sleep, she made one more ominous announcement: "Whoever it was who tried to sell us out to those Life Force people, I'm just going to say this one time. Let it go and don't do anything else to betray us. We'll all be okay if no one does anything stupid."

"And to all, a good night," Dennis whispered sarcastically. Any other time, I might have laughed.

The next night wasn't much better as far as morale went. We still felt committed to staying together and being vampires, but the mystery was still there. I wanted so much to know who the traitor might be, but at the same time, I hoped that whoever it was might have heeded Susanna's warning. Maybe this could all just go away.

Changing things up, Susanna announced that she was adapting my idea from the previous night — splitting up to avoid detection — by having us go out not in two separate groups, but four pairs. In a sense, we were each going out with an escort, but she didn't actually say this outright. But I knew that this meant that everyone was supposed to keep an eye on each other to make sure that no one got up to any wrongdoing, letting Life Force know where to find and attack us.

It worked; we didn't encounter the vigilante vampire hunters at all that night. I was paired with Nick, who assured me once we were alone that he wasn't the traitor. He seemed genuinely concerned that the others might suspect him, but I acted like it wasn't a big deal. Really, I was keeping things light between us because I hoped to catch him off guard somehow. Despite my scattered suspicions and the wish that none of my friends or family might do something so horrible, I still saw him as the most likely candidate.

Later on in the night, I wound up having private discussions like this with all of the other vampires, and in each case, there were the same three main points. Everyone said that they weren't the traitor, they had their reasons for suspecting one or more of the others, and they assured me that they didn't believe I was behind it. After a while, I realized how pointless all of this was, how no one in their right mind would actually confess to any wrongdoing, and any one of them could be lying. What's more, they were probably thinking the exact same thing, suspecting me just as much as anyone else.

Most of those informal interrogations happened later in the night, though. Earlier, we saw on the news that Life Force was still a threat, and not just to us.

"The group reportedly attacked the old Sky City building downtown around 9:30 tonight," the news reporter said. The picture cut to a dimly lit storefront that had been boarded up, graffiti decorating it in various places. I recognized it immediately; we had killed there about a week earlier before going after Sheling at his hotel.

But it looked different. One of the boards looked like it had been busted inward on one corner, and I could tell that some parts of the building had been set on fire but had since been put out. There were several people consoling each other while others were being carried along stretchers to waiting ambulances. Lights flashed from the vehicles of medical personnel, firemen, and law enforcement.

Over this chilling scene, the reporter continued, "According to Augusta police, the place has been known as an unofficial gathering place for homeless people and other area vagrants. But until tonight, it had remained virtually trouble-free. Those calling themselves Life Force apparently believed that the building was instead rife with vampire activity, leading them to attack several unarmed people, including a number of social workers who were visiting the area in hopes of spreading the word about new assistance programs. At least three people were killed, and many others suffered both minor and serious injuries, some of them requiring hospitalization."

The camera then cut to a heavyset policeman with reddish blonde hair, a matching moustache, and large eyeglasses. He spoke to an interviewer just off camera, droning on in a southern accented monotone. "We arrived at the scene just as the altercation was coming to a close, and unfortunately, the perpetrators escaped. We talked to the various eyewitnesses and sent for ambulances and what have you..." There was a rough edit to a close-up of a broken window, and then the officer spoke again. When the camera went back to him, his already frowning face had gone a little more harsh. "There was no evidence of vampires or anything of that nature, and we... uh... We've now decided that this Life Force nonsense has gotten too far out of control, and we're... uh... We're going to bring them to justice." He said this last bit with a decisive nod.

Back in the studio, the reporter added that if anyone had any information on Life Force, they should contact the police. The next story mentioned the various killings we had done ourselves.

"So, is that a good thing or a bad thing?" Dennis asked. "If the police are after them, does that mean they won't be coming after us?"

"Not necessarily," Susanna said.

"Sounds more like some kind of gang warfare to me," Damon said grimly.

"Normally I'd say that sounds kinda cool," Nick said, "but not now. Things could get ugly."

"Worse than they already are?" I asked.

"Yes," Susanna said. "Much worse. But I guess you could be right, Dennis. Maybe if Life Force gets preoccupied with hiding from the police, they won't be as keen on hunting us." She paused. "I know, that's not exactly what you said. But the principle is kind of the same."

"Or the opposite could be true," Carolyn said, frowning. "The police could catch them, then be led straight to us. Depending on how much they know, that is."

"But maybe they don't know anything!" Tim offered. "If they did, they wouldn't have attacked an abandoned store that has nothing to do with us. Maybe they really are just guessing!"

"You're forgetting how they 'guessed' pretty accurately two nights in a row," I told him.

"They were way the hell off tonight," Carl said. "Lucky for us."

"But not so lucky for those innocent people," Susanna said. "Honestly, I think what really needs to happen is for us to just wipe these Life Force people out completely."

There was some debate as to how we might do that, which eventually degenerated into too much speculation and not enough decisive thought. Susanna changed the subject by going ahead and penciling in another location for us to attack the following night, this time as a large group. It wasn't very far from the Sky City building, so I guessed that she was hoping to lure Life Force there, perhaps with a plan to take them out. By the following night, though, she seemed to have changed her tune completely.

"You know what?" she asked, addressing everyone in the yellow den not long after we had gotten up. "I think I've been making a huge mistake, and I'm sorry for ruining everything for everybody. I think that Life Force got me so freaked out that I blew one little thing out of proportion, misinterpreting what that one guy said."

"What are you talking about?" I asked.

"I mean that maybe I was wrong about there being a traitor."

"What?" Carolyn asked. "Are you kidding me?"

Damon raised his hand, saying, "I second that!" It was nice to see his more fun-loving side emerging again.

Susanna laughed apologetically. "I know, I know. Things have been pretty crappy the past couple of nights, and it's my fault. I've been so caught up in trying to accuse everyone, and suspect everyone, when really, I know it's probably all been a bunch of stupidity on my part."

"So, you don't think there's a traitor anymore?" Carl asked.

"No. I think I finally figured it out."

"But what about what that guy said about there being an informant?" Tim asked. "That sounded pretty conclusive to me."

"No, the word he used was 'contact.' And it was when I went back and thought about that a little more that I realized what might be happening." She turned to me and Dennis. "I'm assuming that your powers are still blocked off?"

"Yes," we said simultaneously, then looked at each other, eyebrows raised.

"See, I think what he meant when he said they had a contact was that there's a psychic helping them. Someone in their group. Someone who can not only predict where we're going, but can also block you two so you can't do anything."

This sort of made sense, and I liked the sound of it for one reason in particular: It got Dennis off the hook. After I had realized that the barrier around my mind was like the shields he and I had used in the past, I'd begun to wonder if maybe he was in fact the traitor, and he had somehow managed to cut my powers off using a similar method. He could then just as easily lie about his own powers not working, all the while going behind everyone's back and contacting Life Force.

"I suppose so," Dennis said.

"I did some reading last night," Susanna said, gesturing to the slightly outdated set of encyclopedias on the shelf behind me, which I turned and glanced at. "One of the theories about psychic powers is that they're stronger if two or more people combine them, working together towards a certain goal. So I'm thinking that if you two try really hard to break down the walls together, it will work."

"That might work," I said, but I wasn't entirely sure. I also wondered just where she had read that, because I had long since read all of the extremely limited ESP-related articles in that encyclopedia, and I couldn't recall any of them mentioning this combining thing. Dennis had brought it up before, though.

"And then," she continued enthusiastically, "you can track down this other psychic that Life Force is using. Use them against themselves, so to speak."

"That's..." Tim began. "That's pretty brilliant. You ripped off the idea from *Dracula,* though." Susanna smiled at him knowingly.

"Wait, what has Dracula got to...?" I started to ask. "Oh, you mean the book?"

"Right," Tim said. Once again, I regretted not having taken the time to sit down and read the thing.

"So if we can get our powers working again, we then use them to sort of home in on whoever is spying on us telepathically?" I asked. "Yeah, okay. I like that idea."

"Why not do it now?" Dennis asked, turning towards me.

"No, let's go out and kill first," Susanna said. "We'll get some blood, get our strength up, and then once we're back here, we can take care of that part of the plan."

"Hear, hear!" Carl said, raising a fist. "Seriously, you guys, we've got to stop these long, drawn out meetings before going out to eat. I'm freakin' starving."

Susanna was up to something, I was sure of it. In fact, she was acting so out of character that the only thing I could think was that she must have been fully convinced that either Nick or Damon was the traitor. Carolyn and I knew her better than anyone else, and my other friends had also gotten to know her over the past four years, but at least those other two might be inexperienced enough to fall for her overly apologetic and enthusiastic act. She had been so eager at the house that I half expected her to kick one of her legs up and throw out her arms, fists extended, letting out a cheerful *"Woo!"* at some point. Her cheerleading background meant that she was at least a passable actress, but I saw through what she was doing.

I thought of leading her away from the flock for a moment to tell her that I was on to her, but I didn't want to alert the traitor. I also realized that another big giveaway was the misdirection she was employing, changing our intended destination at the last minute. The night before, she had told everyone that we would attack somewhere downtown, but she flippantly announced instead that we would be flying out to Martinez, a suburb of Augusta that was in the opposite direction. Presumably, this was another ploy to outmaneuver the traitor, perhaps even to force his hand.

Once we got to Martinez, we found that there weren't any big enough groups to attack all at once, so Susanna directed us to split up. "Go in pairs if you want to," she said, "but it doesn't really matter. I'm going this way." With that, she broke off and headed in a random direction, shouting back, "See everyone back at the house!"

"Okay," Carolyn said, sounding confused.

"What is she on?" Damon asked.

"I don't know," she said, "but there's a couple down there. Shall we?"

"Of course," he said with a smile, and the two of them sped away.

I finally realized what Susanna was planning or at least hoping for, so I said, "Yeah, I think I'll go this way," and flew off farther west. I heard someone calling out to me to wait, but I ignored them.

I ended up in the parking lot of a small shopping center called Columbia Square. There was a movie theater there, and even though I hadn't been to this place before, I realized that it was kind of like a smaller version of Daniel Village, which also had its own theater. Lined up outside were people of various ages waiting to buy their tickets, and I hovered overhead for a few moments, picking out my prey.

The girl I killed had dyed black hair, the same as the willing victim I'd taken a couple of nights before. There was that same strange smell to her hair, sort of like burnt rubber, which I didn't find all that unpleasant given that it was mixed with the taste of her warm, salty blood. She was at the back of the line, and while she tried to cry out as I flew in and clamped down on her neck, the people in front of her didn't even notice as she collapsed to the pavement, her life being slowly drained away.

My meal was interrupted by a scream from a woman who finally noticed what was happening, and I flew away, looking back for a moment to see everyone shouting and running. I hadn't been able to drink from the girl for as long as I would have liked, and for all I knew, she might have survived. But that didn't matter to me. Something far more important was about to happen.

While having my psychic powers taken away from me had been disconcerting, that was nothing compared to the shock I got when they suddenly came rushing back. My brain flared with intense energy, and a huge wave of images crashed through my mind, disorienting me. I had to land immediately, half-crashing to the pavement, fortunate to have made it far enough away from the crowd at the theater not to be noticed.

Still in my bat form, I tried to steady myself as the power swept through my head, confusing images passing before my mind's eye. I got an image of Nick rushing toward me to attack, mouth wide and fangs at the ready. There was a blur, lots of unclear movement that occasionally looked like an arm or a leg flashing about. It reminded me of old news footage I had seen of riots in which the camera rushed around shakily, the frame jerking back and forth and sometimes even turning on its side if the camera were hit or knocked over.

The strange movie in my mind ceased, but I still got this impression of fear from someone. Was it Dennis? Had his powers returned as well? Whoever it was needed help, and I was able to use my "radar" to determine which direction I needed to go.

My destination turned out to be yet another shopping center, one called West Town. At the corner of the outermost store, there was a pay phone, and someone was lying on the ground beneath it. I thought it might be a victim that one of the other vampires had left behind, but once I saw that the person was moving, my mind immediately zeroed in on theirs. It was Nick, lying on his back, one knee up and his lower arms flailing as he struggled. As I sped toward him, I saw another bat heading in from the opposite direction. Dennis and I landed in almost the same spot by Nick's feet and changed form.

"Nick!" I called. He tried to raise his head, but all he could do was groan. There was blood on his neck and on his arms, and his skin was extremely pale. Dennis and I knelt on either side of him, and then I heard another voice from nearby, getting louder as it approached.

"Hey, you guys!" Carl called out. "Dennis, what's up? You just sped off all of a sudden…"

"It's Nick!" Dennis said. "He's really hurt."

Carl caught up to us and knelt down, saying in almost a whisper, "Oh, no." He leaned down and looked at Nick's neck, then back up at me. "This wasn't Life Force. It was a vampire."

"Nick, who was it?" I asked urgently. "Who attacked you?" He tried to speak, then let his head drop back to the pavement as he stared off into space.

"We've got to help him!" Carl said. "He needs blood. Could we, like, give him some of ours? Like a transfusion?"

"He might not be able to stop drinking if we do that," I said. "Then one of us might end up just as bad."

"Help might be on the way," Dennis said, looking up and out towards the parking lot.

Hearing an approaching car, I looked up as well, then began to worry once I realized that it was a police car. But I got an idea. I ran out toward the car, waving my arms to get the driver's attention. "Hey!" I called.

The car stopped and a policeman got out quickly, first looking at me and then behind me where the others were. "What's the problem here?" the man asked.

"My friend's been hurt. You've got to help him!"

The man rushed past me and over to Nick and the others. Dennis and Carl stood up quickly, and I could tell that they were instinctively nervous being in the presence of the police. After all of our run-ins with them, it felt very strange to be letting one of them approach voluntarily.

The policeman knelt down beside Nick. As he did, Nick's eyes came alive, and he let out a growl as he bared his fangs and tried to grab at the man with his weak arms. Anticipating this, I used my powers to prevent the man from standing up to get away, and he looked around, surprised. Nick was still too weak, and he fell back to the pavement once more, letting out a painful whine.

"Dennis, a little help here," I said, still concentrating on the policeman. Although it felt great to have my powers again, I was a little out of practice.

"Sure," he said. We both focused our energies, and the cop's face went blank. Looking vaguely confused, he knelt down closer to Nick until his head was right over him. Carl rushed back to Nick's side and lifted up his head, guiding him to the man's neck.

The man didn't even cry out as Nick eagerly chomped down into his flesh. There was the sound of rapid swallowing, and as I felt the man get weaker, I loosened my grip on his mind. Carl let go of Nick as he continued to drink, then caught the man's body a few moments later as it almost collapsed on top of our friend.

While Carl dragged the body away, I knelt down again beside Nick, who still looked very weak. His neck was still bleeding, but then it stopped, the wounds beginning to heal. "Nick?" I asked. "Who did this? Was it the traitor?"

"Yes," he said weakly. "It was Tim. I… I saw him at the pay phone. Calling Life Force. Told them the address."

"The what?" Carl asked.

"What address?" I asked.

He started to speak, then winced, obviously still in a lot of pain. "Yours," he managed to say.

"He told them where the house is?" Dennis almost shouted.

"Holy shit," Carl said.

"We've got to warn the others!" Dennis said. "They're on their way back there!"

"But we can't just leave Nick here," Carl said.

"I know," I said, knowing all too well what Nick was going through. At the same time, I was trying to process the fact that Tim was actually the traitor. My mind was in a whirl. Turning my thoughts back to Nick, I said, "We need to nurse him back to health with more victims."

"No time…" Nick said. "He got away. Don't know where…"

"Does anyone have any money?" Dennis asked. "We could call the house and let them know."

Unfortunately, no one did, and as Nick had pointed out, time was a factor. Susanna, Carolyn, and Damon were presumably on their way to the house, and if Nick was right, so was Life Force. As for Tim, I had no idea.

"One of us needs to get back there," Dennis said. "I'll go."

This bugged me. I felt that since it was my house that was going to be under attack, to say nothing of my sisters, I should be the one to go. I said so, but Carl objected.

"No! You and I need to stay here and help Nick. We need to lure in some more victims, and you're better at that than Dennis." He was right. Reluctantly, I nodded at Dennis, and he flew away as fast as he could.

It had taken at least half an hour, maybe more, to psychically subdue enough victims to get Nick strong enough to be able to change into a bat, fully heal, and fly back with us. There were occasional lulls when he was busy feeding, during which Carl and I managed to get in little snippets of conversation. As Nick began to feel better, he joined in, adding his input.

"I still can't believe it's Tim," Carl said. "He was always just... I don't know... just *Tim.*"

"Maybe that was the problem," I said, though as it came out, I didn't think it made much sense. Honestly, I couldn't understand it either.

In a later mini-conversation, after I'd had more time to think, I expressed my own disbelief, adding, "He was always the nice guy, the one wanting everyone to get along."

"Maybe *that* was the problem," Carl said wryly. "What is it they always say about the quiet ones? The guy you least suspect..."

I knew what he meant, but it still wasn't a satisfactory explanation. Why had this boy I had known practically all my life gone this far to stab us all in the back, to betray us like this? The more I thought about it, the more angry I got.

Carl, meanwhile, went from sarcastic detachment to anger as well, particularly once Nick was almost healed. One crisis was averted, so it was time to deal with the bigger one. "I'm going to kill that fucking dork-head," he said just before we took flight.

As Nick had gotten better, he was able to fill us in on more details as to precisely what happened when he confronted Tim, and then once we were in the air, the three of us pieced everything together. He told us how he'd spotted Tim at the pay phone, then snuck up on him to listen in. As soon as he figured out that he was telling Life Force where the house was, he pounced on him, but Tim was able to fight him off. Nick still wasn't used to the increased strength we had as vampires, so he wasn't expecting this skinny, nerdy guy to be able to fight back so strongly. Once he recovered from the surprise of this and was trying to use his own might to overpower Tim, he ran into another unexpected difficulty.

"His eyes lit up, you know, that same yellow glowing thing, but there was something else. It was like I went limp, and I couldn't fight him anymore. That gave him time to take the advantage and bite me, and after that, it was all over. He won."

"But our glowing eyes alone don't…" Carl began, then gasped. "Whoa, shit."

I got it, too. Tim was psychic, just as Dennis and I were, but he had somehow managed to keep it hidden from us all these years. The thought sent a chill through my small bat body, the implications of this hitting me one by one. Stopping the conversation and telling Carl and Nick to hold on for a moment, I concentrated and reached out with my mind, trying to find out just where Tim was at the moment. I couldn't do it. My powers were still working, but it was like Tim didn't exist. Finding him was impossible. He could somehow cloak himself, which could mean that he was more powerful than either me or Dennis.

I shared this latest disturbing revelation with the others, which left them quiet for a few moments as we continued to speed toward my house. "Let's just hope we get there in time," Carl said gravely.

"We will, we will," Nick said, being uncharacteristically reassuring. "And we'll find that dweeb and knock his beady little eyes down his throat when we do." I almost laughed, but the situation was too grim for that.

"By the way," Nick said with a bit of a smile, "you totally thought it was me, didn't you?" I didn't answer. Part of that was because I wasn't in the mood for joking, but also, I felt kind of guilty now that I knew he was innocent. "It's okay. We're cool. I totally thought it was *you,* anyway."

The sight that greeted us at the house was completely not what I expected. As we were making our way there, I had a terrible feeling that I would find the house under violent attack, windows bashed in and half of the place on fire. The more I worried, the worse my imagination got, and I had to force myself to stop picturing things when I began to think of Susanna and Carolyn impaled on wooden stakes.

As we approached, my pulse quickened as I noticed the flashing lights of police cars along the street in front of my house, but I was still too far away to tell what was happening. I expected to hear a lot of shouting, maybe even gunshots, but things were eerily quiet. Once we were almost above the property, I saw that things were, surprisingly, downright calm and orderly.

People, some of whom I recognized from our earlier encounters with Life Force, were being ushered into the backs of police cars, the policemen doing that thing I had seen on TV where they held the person's head to keep it from bumping into the roof of the car. Those who weren't already in handcuffs were being fitted with them, and while a couple of the people struggled and needed to be put onto the ground by force, most of them seemed resigned. I spotted at least a dozen cars, one of which was already driving away.

The most surprising thing of all, though, was seeing Susanna, Carolyn, and Damon on the front porch talking to a policeman. Carolyn seemed upset and was clinging close to Damon, and this made me concerned. There was a little bit of damage to the shutters outside my bedroom window, and it looked like one of the windows to the living room had been cracked but not broken all the way through.

Carolyn's demeanor made me wonder if something might have happened to Dennis, whom I hadn't yet seen. I reached out with my mind, then was drawn to the roof just above the front door, where

Dennis was hiding as a bat. I led Nick and Carl to this spot, then perched next to him.

We listened as Susanna and the others continued to talk to the police. From where we were sitting, I could no longer see them, but I could still see the various cops milling around the front yard. Some of them were busy holding Life Force members while they waited for their turn for a ride downtown, and others were picking up anti-vampire weapons from various spots on the lawn.

From what I could gather, the police had come to the house and arrested everyone, and I would soon learn that it was Susanna who had called them. I also realized that Carolyn's distressed act was just that: She was playing up the idea of being upset and confused, having no idea why these crazy people started attacking our house and shouting things about vampires. Susanna and Damon went along with this, successfully passing themselves off as human.

I could sense that Dennis was doing something with his powers, influencing the mind of the policeman as he talked, and I reasoned that he must be trying to convince the man to swallow their story. There weren't any vampires here, and this had all just been a big misunderstanding. Not wanting to get too involved with the police, Susanna said something about not pressing charges, but the cop said that the entire group would still be taken in for questioning.

Once everyone was gone, we regrouped inside and caught each other up on everything. Dennis had arrived at the house in time and warned everyone about Life Force's impending arrival, something Susanna had thought might happen. She had successfully tricked Tim into exposing himself, then turned the tables on Life Force by letting the police be the ones to fight them, not us.

Also, Dennis didn't have to work very hard to psychically influence the policeman that Susanna and the others had talked to. Their helpless victim act was convincing enough, but this man in particular also didn't believe in vampires to begin with. He was in fact very disdainful of the idea and considered the members of Life Force deluded and just looking for an excuse to cause trouble. Even more unfortunate for them was the fact that the man's daughter was one of the social workers who had been injured in the previous night's attack on the Sky City building, so he was already eager to find the group and bring them in. Aside from that, they were also wanted for murder.

I was quite impressed with Susanna's cunning and how successful she and the others had been, but there was still another problem to deal with: No one had seen Tim since we had split up in Martinez. I told those who didn't yet know about him being secretly psychic, how he had managed to keep that hidden from everyone, including me and Dennis.

"Yeah, that really bugs me," Dennis said. "How could we not have picked up on that?"

"Well, the two of you kept it secret from us for a long time, too," Susanna said pointedly.

"I know, I know," I said. "But it just seems like one of *us* should have been able to sense it." I indicated me and Dennis as I said this.

"Maybe that's what he was afraid of," Carolyn pointed out, "especially with your powers getting stronger recently."

"Yeah, maybe," I said. "Or he was just blocking us so we couldn't pick up on the fact that he was planning on betraying everyone."

"And then when Nick found him and attacked him," Dennis said, "that must have broken his concentration enough to where we were able to break through his barriers. I guess you got the same flash from his mind?" I nodded.

"Can you figure out where he is now?" Susanna asked.

"I tried earlier, but it's like he's made himself invisible. I can't sense him anywhere. Same for you?"

"Yeah," Dennis said. "We could try doing what Susanna said earlier, though, combining our powers."

I reached out for his mind, and I could feel his power reaching back to me. It was an odd feeling, but it did seem to be working, or at least doing something. We weren't able to find Tim, but I did get a small impression of him, like he was on his own and very far away. But much nearer, I felt someone else, and I could tell that Dennis did, too, our eyes opening and meeting as the sensation hit us.

"Cassie," the frightened young woman answered after Susanna calmly asked what her name was. "Please, don't hurt me. I just want to go home."

"And would you like to tell us why you're hiding in our basement?"

"I… The police came. I didn't want to get caught. I told Phil… that's my boyfriend… um… I didn't want to get involved in all this!" She was cowering in the far corner of the basement, not far from the table that Nick and Damon had accidentally smashed when they were suffering the side effects of the potion.

"So you're a member of Life Force," I said in a matter-of-fact way. She nodded, still looking scared.

"But not really, I mean, I never wanted to… I just went along with Phil to try to… Oh, God…" She bit her lower lip and shook her head, tears welling up in her eyes. A few strands of her straight, light brown hair stuck to her face, which was drenched with sweat. "You really are vampires," she whispered.

"Don't worry," Susanna said, stepping toward her slowly. "Just tell us what we need to know. When did the person from our group first contact you?"

"What? Um… I'm not sure. Three nights ago, I think."

She turned out to be a good little informant, her cooperation stemming from the faint hope that we would let her go if she told us everything she knew. In time, she grew slightly more relaxed, but I could still sense how scared she was. We learned a little bit more about how Tim had been calling them and telling them where to find us, leading up to this night when he had given them the address to our house. She swore that she wouldn't tell anyone else about us, and I knew that this was true, but not because she'd said so.

To help defuse her fear, each of us had settled down and sat on our mattresses one by one. The less threatening we appeared, the more forthcoming she became. By the time we had learned all that we could from her, she was much more calm, and I almost felt bad for her, knowing what would come next. The thought of actually letting her go did cross my mind; she seemed like a nice enough person, and there was something kind of sweet and pretty about her. She reminded me a bit of Valerie, but older, nicer, and without the snobby refusal to return my affection. She was too old for me, though. I wondered for a moment if I could somehow use my powers to wipe her memory, sending her on her way, unable to remember us or where to find our house.

That was an extension of something I had done just as the police and everyone else were leaving, when I sent out a sort of wave from my mind that encompassed the entire area, an instruction to be embedded into their minds: *There are no vampires here.* I hoped that it would stick, that is, if any of the police or the other people got the idea to try to come back to our house later on, this command would be somewhere in their subconscious and deter them.

As for this Cassie girl, she seemed to be warming up to us, or at least trying to win us over and somehow survive the night. Any remote possibility of that happening ended with the next thing she said.

"Hey, aren't you that guy?" she asked, pointing to Damon. "I thought I recognized you."

"What?" he asked.

"You're in that band, right? I can't remember the name. But I know I've been to a couple of your shows." She was smiling for the first time since I'd met her, and she seemed more relaxed than ever. "There's that song y'all do." She began singing tunelessly, *"I don't know why, I can't explaaaaain... why the clearest pictures come out in the raaaaaain..."*

"Aw," Carolyn said, nudging Damon with her elbow and smiling. "You've got a fan." Her tone became harsher by the end of her sentence.

"Yes," Damon said. "I guess so."

"You guys are really good!" Cassie said enthusiastically, nodding. "I had a boyfriend who was in a band once, but they sucked. But I couldn't tell them that." She laughed nervously. Damon stood up, and Carolyn did the same. Cassie eyed them with uncertainty.

"It's always good to be supportive," Carolyn said vaguely.

Knowing what was about to happen, I turned to Susanna and asked, "So, have we learned everything we can?"

She nodded, sitting on her mattress and staring at the wall. "Mm-hmm," she said, looking contemplative.

"Good," I said, turning back to Damon and Carolyn, who had sat down on the floor on either side of Cassie, both of them acting friendly and eager, like they wanted to continue talking to her. She looked over at Damon, then moved her head quickly to look at Carolyn.

"Please," she said, almost whispering, something tearful in her voice. "Please don't."

While Damon and Carolyn were taking the girl's body to somewhere that was a safe distance from the house, I thought about the fact that my friends and I had become more cruel and brutal in recent days. It seemed like the longer we stayed vampires, the worse we got, but I loved every minute of it. Up until this point, I hadn't realized that the same thing had also been happening to my sisters, and Damon seemed to be doing a pretty good job of keeping up.

Carolyn had also changed since Damon's arrival, and there was something both sweet and menacing about the way they acted. Watching the two of them drink from both sides of that girl's neck was like seeing some bizarre, evil version of two smitten lovebirds sipping on straws out of the same milkshake.

"We need to find Tim," Susanna said, standing up from where she'd been sitting. Her words snapped me out of my daydreaming and brought me back to the current situation.

"I can't," I said. "Whenever I try to look for him with my mind, he's just not there."

"Ahem," Carl said, exaggeratingly clearing his throat. He was standing by a set of shelves on the western wall of the basement, and for the first time, I noticed that it was slightly out of place.

"So that's where he's gone," I said. Carl pulled the shelves farther away from the wall, revealing the opening to the tunnel. Normally, when we were human, it took more than one of us to do that, but he moved it easily.

"That's the tunnel to that other house?" Nick asked.

"Yes," I said, standing up. "We should go after him."

"I agree," Susanna said, "but we have to wait for Carolyn and Damon to get back."

I noticed for the first time that, because it turned sharply to the right almost as soon as we were in it, the tunnel led to somewhere north of our house. It occasionally veered to the left or right and even sloped up and down in places, but for the most part, it felt like we were going straight. I started to look for evidence that Tim had come this way, but then I remembered that any footprints he might have left would have disappeared almost immediately.

The closer we got to the other house, I started getting little flashes in my mind of Tim. He was definitely there, but it was hard to pinpoint him. I asked Dennis if he had been getting these impressions as well, and he had.

"His control is breaking down," he said. "He's afraid, so he keeps losing his concentration. That's when we can sense him."

"I can't wait to catch up to that little twat and show him what's what," Damon said. I had never heard that term before, but I knew a swear word when I heard it. "I never really liked him, anyway. You remember how he laughed at me that night?" He had directed this question at Carolyn.

"Well, you had just slammed your hand into the door frame by accident," she said with a smile. "And right after you'd insulted him."

"What?" I asked. "I don't remember that."

"You weren't there," she said. "Damon said something mean to him…"

"Just a joke," he said quietly.

"I know. But it was something about him being all bookwormy and stuff. And then, like a second or two later, he turned to leave the kitchen and smacked his hand right into the door. *Whack!*"

"It hurt!" he said, halfway laughing. "Besides, I have to be careful about my hands. If I mess those up, I can't play guitar, and that affects the band." He paused. "Not that that matters much right now, now that we've lost another drummer."

"Wait," Dennis said. "So you made Tim mad, and then something bad happened to you?"

"Well, yeah. Just a coincidence, really, but it still pissed me off, especially the way he laughed."

"You brought it on yourself," Carolyn said, grinning.

"Did not."

I kept quiet, but there wasn't really any need to. It wasn't like I was keeping the facts surrounding mine and Dennis's — and apparently Tim's — powers from everyone anymore. But I noticed that Dennis also didn't say anything, even though I knew that he must be thinking the exact same thing I was. If either of us had been in the room the night that had happened, we might have noticed that Tim had the same powers we did, including the ability to either consciously or unconsciously make bad things happen to the people that made us angry. As the silence went on, I realized that I liked how both Dennis and I decided at the same time not to reveal this to the others. It was like we still had one or two things left that were secret, things only he and I knew.

Finally, we arrived at the house. By then, Dennis and I had decided to try our own bit of invisibility and keep Tim from being able to sense us, though we wondered if we had thought of that too late in the game. He probably already knew that we were coming. But just in case, and hopefully to give us some kind of advantage, we pictured a field of invisibility around not just ourselves, but the entire group. We weren't sure if this would work, but we figured it was worth a try.

I half-expected the trapdoor leading out of the tunnel to be blocked somehow, like a bunch of bricks or something being placed on top to prevent us from pushing it open. But there was nothing like that. Had Tim actually not expected us to follow him?

Using my mind to scan for him, I was surprised to find that I could clearly pick him up again. Apparently, he had chosen to discard his psychic camouflage, knowing that we had arrived. He was standing near the pool behind the huge house, looking up at the sky and waiting for us.

"Come on," I said to the others. "I've found him." I changed into a bat, and the others did the same and followed me around the side of the house. Just as I had seen in my mind, there was Tim, standing by the wall next to the pool. Nearby, the Jacuzzi was bubbling away. Tim held up his hands as we approached, his demeanor somewhere between surrender and defiance.

"Guys!" he shouted as we flew toward him. "Just hear me out!"

I had half a mind to just launch myself at him and drain every last bit of blood from his worthless neck, but I at least wanted to hear what he had to say. I landed several feet in front of him, and the others followed my lead. We surrounded him in an arc, not leaving an avenue of escape. I realized that he still had the option of flying away, but I was pretty confident that at least one of us could catch him if he did. I also wondered how difficult it might be to bite him if he were in his bat form.

"All right, Tim," I said angrily. "Tell us *why.*" I had been practicing that line in my head almost the entire way from the house; it was lifted from a cartoon I remembered seeing a couple of years before in which a character confronted an old friend who had betrayed him.

"Look, I'm sorry about the whole traitor business. But I had to! Things were getting out of hand!"

"What are you talking about?" Susanna asked. "The only one getting out of hand was you, selling us out to be slaughtered."

Tim looked slightly hurt by this. "It wasn't like that! Really! I just knew that things had gone too far, that we weren't going to be able to change ourselves back when the time came."

"So you tried to get us killed?" she shouted back.

"No! I just wanted those people to change us back."

"And do you really think they would have just let us go then? Tim, I always thought you were one of the smartest of Ray's friends, but now I see that you're just an idiot."

"I am not," he said. This time, he looked very angry, his eyes narrowing at my sister.

"Then why do something so incredibly stupid?" I asked. "Even if they had just changed us back, we…"

Without warning, a jet of water slammed into Tim's side, coming somewhere from his left. I looked and saw that Carl was holding the same hose and sprayer he had used two years ago to defeat the zombie-like vampires, only this time, he had used it on Tim.

There was an arrogant look of accomplishment on his face, and then he said to no one in particular, "Sorry. I just got sick of all the bullshitting."

I turned back to Tim, who had dropped to his knees. I knew that the blast of running water must have changed him back to human, but there was something else happening. He was clutching at his stomach and groaning, and then his groans grew into screams of pain. His hands moved from his torso to his head, which he began clutching with his upper arms. His eyes were screwed shut, and he continued to cry out for several seconds.

"What's wrong with him?" Carolyn asked.

"Oh yeah," Susanna said simply. "You know how I kept forgetting to tell you guys about the new effects of the potion?"

"Yes…?" I asked with uncertainty.

"Well, if we get changed back to human instead of taking the actual antidote, it hurts. A lot. Now you know."

This certainly was a change. In the past, changing from vampire to human actually felt very nice, like a cool breeze and a feeling of immense tranquility rushing in. If this new transformation was as painful as it looked, I wasn't looking forward to experiencing it myself anytime soon.

"Gee," Dennis said. "Thanks for the heads-up."

Tim seemed to have mostly recovered, having ended up on his hands and knees. He was breathing heavily, and as he looked up at us, I could see tears on his cheeks. He stood up shakily, falling halfway against the brick wall behind him.

"Oh, God…" he said between deep breaths, "I'm sorry… really, really sorry… please…" His eyes got bigger for a brief moment, and he seemed to be looking above our heads, like he didn't even know that we were there. "No!" he shouted. "I… So sorry… I…" He seemed to come back to his immediate surroundings, and he looked around at us. His eyes were strange and darting about, and he swallowed heavily. More tears began to well up, and he said faintly, "Please, everyone, don't."

Carl had left a gap in the line of us surrounding Tim, so he took advantage of that, running clumsily through it. A quick mental command from me caused him to momentarily lose control of his legs, and he tumbled to the pavement near Carl's feet. Carl then reached down and yanked him up from the ground by his left arm, causing him to cry out in pain.

"So!" he said brightly. "Gather around, everyone! Let's each pick a spot. Like we did with Sheling. Everybody gets a limb!" He eyed Tim up and down hungrily as he spoke, and Tim could do nothing but struggle in his grip.

"No, I think we should all take turns," Dennis said, stepping closer.

"Hmm," Carl said with a sick smile. "It would take longer that way. A prolonged execution of the traitor. That sounds good to me."

I agreed. I hated Tim immensely; his betrayal of the group — of me — was beyond unforgivable. He deserved to suffer. The others expressed similar sentiments, their words echoing my unspoken thoughts.

"Please, stop!" Tim shrieked, still squirming. "The Jacuzzi… right there…" He pointed with his free arm. "All you have to do is… I turned it on for…" His breathing was getting heavier, and he swallowed hard.

"I don't think so," Damon said. He stepped over to the control panel next to the pool and pushed a button, and the bubbling of the water ceased.

"I think I should get the first bite, don't you?" Nick said, stepping closer to Carl. "Payback and all that."

"Okay, but don't go hogging it all for yourself. Probably best not to get him in the neck, either. He might bleed to death before we all get our turns." Tim began sobbing as Carl shoved his arm up to Nick's mouth.

Grinning evilly, Nick bit down into the flesh of Tim's forearm, and Tim, not surprisingly, screamed even louder. After a few seconds, Nick drew back, wiping the excess blood from his mouth.

"Who's next?" Carl asked eagerly.

"Me!" I said, bounding forward. I hoped that I could exercise the same restraint as Nick; it would be difficult to stop drinking once I'd started. I looked at Tim with the most contempt I could ever remember feeling toward anyone. He looked so small and helpless, and I loved the fact that we had beaten him. He'd always thought he was so smart, better than the rest of us, and it was time to show him otherwise.

Something strange began happening. Tim squinted tightly, and his breathing became extremely deep. He seemed to be gasping for breath, almost like he was trying to keep from suffocating. But no one had gone near his throat yet or tried to choke him, so I was confused. Carl, also confused, looked down as Tim's legs gave way and he fell to the ground limply.

The others gathered around, and Carolyn said, "Carl, let him go for a second." He did, and rather than making any attempt to run away, Tim just lay there on the ground, partly supporting himself with his hands and knees. Blood poured from the wound Nick had left, but I couldn't see how that could be causing whatever it was we were seeing.

Tim clutched at his chest for a moment, then pulled his hand away, peering at it strangely. His hand was shaking, and it looked like he was trying to make a fist but couldn't quite manage it. He continued to breathe more heavily, the gasps turning into groans, and his eyes began rolling back into his head.

"Is he having a heart attack?" Dennis asked.

"That, or maybe a seizure," Susanna said. "Is he epileptic?" None of us knew. I knew that Dennis's sister had epilepsy, but I had never heard Tim say that he had it.

"Could be asthma," Carolyn suggested. "Should we try to help him?"

All of a sudden, the labored breathing reached its peak, and then it stopped, Tim collapsing to the pavement. Everyone was still for what felt like ages. Finally, Damon squatted next to Tim and rolled him over onto his back, then leaned down toward his head. For a moment, I thought he was going to bite him.

"He's still breathing," he said, straightening up. "Just passed out. I think it was a panic attack."

"A what?" I asked.

"Panic attack. My mom used to have them. So did Mike, the drummer from our band. The little pussy couldn't stand all the pressures of being on the road, so he freaked the hell out and then decided he didn't want to be in the band anymore. I've never actually seen anybody pass out from one before, but I guess it's possible."

"Well, that's unfortunate," Carolyn said.

"Can you wake him up?" I asked.

"I don't know." He patted the sides of Tim's face gently, but nothing happened.

"Well, shit!" Carl said. "That's no fun! He didn't even give the rest of us a chance!"

I had hoped that Tim would regain consciousness quickly, but it became apparent over the next few hours that he wasn't going to, at least not anytime soon. This disappointed everyone greatly, the consensus being that we wanted him to be fully awake and aware when we executed him. Carl even went so far as to bandage up the wound on his arm using a first aid kit he had found in one of the bathrooms of the house. We didn't want him to bleed to death while in a coma. If he was going to die, we wanted to be directly responsible for it.

Tim was right about one thing: Things had gone too far. But we didn't see that as a bad thing. Aside from the fact that we were more than prepared, even eager to kill one of our oldest friends, there was another step we found ourselves taking that at the time seemed perfectly reasonable.

"So once we do kill him," Dennis asked, "what do we end up telling his parents?"

"We don't tell them anything," Susanna said simply.

"Maybe we should kill them, too!" I suggested. Carl and Nick liked this idea, but the others weren't so sure.

"And what about our own parents?" Susanna asked me with a raised eyebrow. "Or everyone else's?" I could tell that she wasn't actually wanting to do this; she was questioning my line of thinking. "You need to think about the bigger picture, where we go from here."

She was right. Things felt different for some reason. The conclusion that everyone came to, which Susanna sort of walked us through, was that we weren't going to take the antidote and change back into humans, not at the end of the week as planned, not ever. We were in this for the long haul. We had beaten humans, rival vampires, and even one of our own when he tried to betray us. We were invincible.

As far as our lives up to his point were concerned, we didn't care about them anymore. There was no need to go back to school or to our families; we had our own family of vampires. Our parents would come home to find the house deserted, and as for my friends and Damon, their families would never hear from them again. In essence, we were all running away from home, but it felt more important than that. We had a chance for a new start, and we had a new house in which to do it.

The first thing we did was move Tim's unconscious body into the living room, settling him on one of the large, plush couches. Because we had no idea when or if he might wake up, someone had to stand watch over him at all times. We did this in shifts, Nick taking the first.

There was also the issue of cleaning up after our most recent adventure there, the encounter with the scientists who tried to turn us into werewolves. What was left of their bodies was still decaying on the floor, and Carolyn did her best to clean the carpet while Susanna and I were left with the rather gruesome task of burying their remains in the yard. I had suggested just sealing them up in the secret compartment behind the obnoxiously large gas fireplace, but Susanna insisted that burying them was the better option, as the smell of decomposition might filter out into the room.

Their bizarre scientific equipment would also need to be put away at some point, but we had so much else to do that we decided to deal with that later. We did find a use for the discarded ropes that had been used to tie us down before, though: Tim's body was tied up with them just in case he regained consciousness and tried to escape.

"What do we do if someone shows up looking for those two scientists?" Dennis asked.

"We kill them," I said. "Doesn't sound that hard."

"That probably will happen eventually," Susanna said, distributing black garbage bags along the large living room wall. She had found some in the kitchen, and Damon and Carolyn were already on their way back to our old house to get some more, plus we were waiting on them to bring back some tape. As we had done in the past, we planned to block out the windows so we could sleep inside safe from the sunlight. Because we had only ever been to the house after sundown (or close to it), no one knew which way was east or west, so we didn't know which direction to expect the sunrise to come from. As we later found out, we weren't able to gather up enough bags to cover every window in the house, so we had to skip using them in the living room and instead put them on the windows of the various bedrooms we took over upstairs.

"I got the impression that they were pretty reclusive," Susanna continued, "but sure, sooner or later, someone might notice that they're missing. In fact…" She looked around, then let out a sigh, her cheeks puffing out and deflating as she did so. "We're going to need to figure out some way to keep this place running, bill-wise."

"Who's Bill?" Nick joked.

"Ha, ha. You know what I mean. At some point, the gas and electricity and everything is probably going to get cut off. Someone has to pay for it, after all." That hadn't even occurred to me, but then, I wasn't used to having to worry about such things.

"That's true," Carl said. He looked thoughtful. "I hope the water is still on. We'll need it for the toilets and stuff. Oh! And we should probably cut the flows to the sinks off, too." He got up from his chair and left the room, heading for the kitchen.

Taking over this new house was fun, but it was also pretty tiring. I had always lived in the same place growing up, so this was a new experience for me. After a while, we decided to join Damon and

Carolyn at the other house and gather up some personal belongings. Nick was relieved of duty, and Dennis and Carl stayed behind to watch over Tim. I warned them not to give in to any urges to go ahead and kill him before we got back, even if he did happen to wake up.

As Susanna, Nick, and I made our way out the front door, she paused for a moment and turned back to the outer wall. "I don't think this needs to be here anymore," she said haughtily, reaching for the golden plaque with the printed words *THE TRUEBLOODS*. She pried at it with her fingers, and it came away easily. Then she casually let it clatter to the pavement, saying that we could clean it up later.

On our return to the basement, we found that it had changed. Many of the modifications Carolyn and I had made to it had been undone, and the mattresses were stacked in two piles near the base of the stairs. Sometime over the next night or two, we would need to throw those away and remove all evidence of us having converted the basement into a temporary apartment. We didn't want to leave any clues for our parents to find, anything that might lead them to us.

Getting rid of the mattresses would involve using Susanna's, Carolyn's, and Damon's cars, another detail we would need to iron out, but not yet. We also needed to get their cars to our new house, but we still didn't know how to get there. I had some vague notion that it was somewhere to the north, but beyond that, the only way we knew how to get there was via the underground tunnel.

All of this was discussed, but we knew that we couldn't get it done in one night. That was fine; we had a couple of days before our parents got back. Still, I felt impatient, frustrated at all of the things that kept coming up that needed to be dealt with. What I really wanted was to be back at the new house, and more importantly, for Tim to wake up so we could torture and kill him.

I ended up in the bathroom, the larger one with its big counter by the sink. Normally, it was filled with all of Susanna's and Carolyn's make-up and stinky hair products and such, but they had already gathered those up, leaving the counter mostly bare. I wondered how many bathrooms there were in the other place, hoping that things could be more separated up and that we wouldn't have to share as much space.

This thought was interrupted by something I saw in the sink, a wet sheen that looked kind of like someone had run the faucet recently, but that shouldn't have been possible. Very carefully, I turned one of the knobs, and nothing came out, which left me more confused. I realized what had happened once I spotted something else next to the sink, and I hadn't even realized what it was when I first glanced at it. It was one of Susanna's glass beakers, the kind she used for making the potion. This one was fairly large, and I recognized it from the few times I had been upstairs in her room this summer. Normally, it had a black, rubber stopper on its top, but that was lying next to it, and the beaker itself was empty. It used to contain the antidote to the vampire potion.

I was anxious when we got back to the house, but there really wasn't any reason to be. Even before we had gotten there, each of us carrying various belongings, I had reached out with my mind to look in on events there and find out if maybe Tim had woken up and anything had happened. It hadn't; we returned to find Dennis and Carl sitting in the living room talking, Tim still tied up and unmoving.

As exciting as this new step in our lives was supposed to be, I found it difficult to enjoy. Moving into one place from another was quite a lot of effort, and I was much more eager to deal with Tim if he would ever have the decency to just wake up and let us kill him. Back at our old house, I hadn't even bothered to get any of my own stuff, but I had promised to bring Carl and Dennis some of theirs since they hadn't been able to come with us. Sometime over the next couple of nights, we would finish moving everything we needed, but I was already feeling worn out by the whole process. Tim's things, as far as I was concerned, could be thrown away.

"We really should get our cars to do all this," Damon said, dumping a pile of clothes onto the living room floor. "All this walking kind of sucks." Earlier, we had flown as bats through the tunnel from the new house back to our old one, but that wasn't possible on the return journey.

"It will be worth it in the end," Carolyn said, dropping her load next to his, then collapsing into a well-padded velvet chair.

"Any sign of life from our traitor friend?" I asked Dennis and Carl.

"Nope," Dennis said. "Not a peep."

"Though while you were gone," Carl said with a grin, "we tried to come up with a list of things we can do to him once he does wake up. I'm thinking broken bones would be a good start." I liked that thought, and I smiled at Carl evilly, who beamed back at me proudly.

"I really do hope he recovers soon," Carolyn said, and for a moment, I resented her for saying this because she sounded genuinely concerned for his well-being. "If he keeps being unconscious, well, he can't eat! We don't want him to starve to death. That wouldn't be any fun."

Damon sat down on the arm of her chair. "I suppose we could always get some fast food for him, like some cheeseburgers or something. Then when he wakes up, we shove them down his throat!" As he said this, he mimed doing the same thing to Carolyn. She giggled and looked up at him, then reached for him, pulling him down into the chair.

"That's an idea," Dennis said thoughtfully, "or maybe… Susanna?"

"Hmm?" she said, not looking up from the things she was sorting through on the floor.

"Did you happen to bring that blood we got from the hospital?"

She looked up, then got an angry look, though it wasn't Dennis she was mad at. "Damn. I really need to remember to bring that next time."

"I was thinking that we could force Tim to drink that," he said. "He'd probably really hate that since he decided to wimp out on us and not be a vampire anymore."

"That's a really sick thought, Dennis," Susanna said. Then she smiled. "I'm proud of you." Everyone laughed. "But no. We should save that stash in case we need it."

"Yeah," I said. "Raiding the hospital might have to become a regular thing!"

Dennis and Carl rattled off a few more sadistic ideas they had come up with during our absence, which led Nick to say, "Man, you guys are something else. And you're making me wish I'd brought some of my firecrackers from home."

After a brief rest, we explored some more, finding that the house was big enough that everyone would be able to have their own bedroom (except for Damon and Carolyn, who chose to share one). We then decided to also explore the surrounding area. Up until then, the house had always been this mysterious place at the end of a magical tunnel, but we knew that it must still be somewhere in Augusta, roads leading away from it and probably with other houses nearby. Initially, I had pictured it being fairly isolated and on a large property much like my aunt and uncle's place in the country.

We flew along the wide, brick driveway and out to the street, past an ornate gateway I had never noticed before. Everything about the place seemed fancy and opulent, and Carl made a comment about how well off Robert's family must have been. "I guess that's why you were all into him," he said to Susanna suggestively.

If it were possible for a bat to roll its eyes, she probably did, judging by her condescending sigh. "No. In fact, when I was with him, his family didn't live in this house. Believe me, I'd have remembered that. It must have been built sometime after I stopped talking to him."

We flew along the road, not seeing any other houses at first. There was nothing but trees around. Eventually, we came to an intersection, and Susanna fluttered over to a sign on the corner. She came back to us, saying that she didn't recognize the street name.

As we continued to fly, we started to spot more houses, and these were almost as big and impressive as the former Trueblood residence. Like that one, they were situated on expansive properties which were surrounded by undeveloped land. It sort of reminded me of Appling, but not exactly. The place where my mother had grown up did have houses that were spread this far apart, but those were smaller, more ordinary looking homes on large farms, the trees much less dense than what we were seeing here.

"Seriously," Susanna said after checking a couple more street signs, "I have no idea where we are. This is weird."

"Well, maybe it's just somewhere you never went when you lived here," I said. "You know, something new." I was reminded of a particular incident that happened the previous summer when I was riding with her in her car: She, Carolyn, and I were driving along on a road we had traveled many times. A little less than a year before that, a new traffic light had been installed above an intersection that previously hadn't had one, and my parents and Carolyn had learned to adjust their driving habits to stop for it when necessary.

Susanna, meanwhile, no longer lived in town, and neither Carolyn nor I had thought to warn her about the new light, which by then we were both used to. All of a sudden, Susanna called out, *"Whoa!"* and slammed on her brakes, caught off guard by an unexpected red light. That was the day that I learned exactly how seatbelts worked. No one was hurt, but we were all pretty freaked out by the incident.

We wound up at a gas station and killed some people there, mostly for fun. We weren't particularly hungry at the time, but once we were there, we decided to do it just for the hell of it. On our way back to the house, Susanna pointed out that it was probably a good thing, that doing so would stave off any temptation we might feel to feed on Tim. I realized that she was right, and I also thought about how strange it was going to be going to sleep that morning with a perfectly vulnerable and tasty human tied up in our new living room.

Carolyn and Damon had been on guard duty, so once we were back, we sent them out to do their own killing while we wrapped things up for the night and prepared to go to bed. Susanna, meanwhile, was pouring over the city map and looking quite perturbed.

"I just don't get this," she said. "I can't even find the street names I saw when we were out."

"Maybe they're not on the map yet," I offered, "like that park where we killed Sheling-Van-Helsing-dude."

"Maybe," she said. "Or maybe I just read them wrong. This is so frustrating. I hate not being able to figure this out."

For a brief moment, I expected Tim to pipe up with some kind of brilliant suggestion. Then I mentally kicked myself for missing him. I curbed this feeling by reminding myself of what a despicable piece of shit he was and how much I was looking forward to drinking him. But if he wouldn't wake up from his coma, what then? Maybe we could pass ourselves off as humans and take him to a hospital, get the doctors to nurse him back to health, and then kill him. It was a clumsy but plausible idea, one that I ran through my head as I was falling asleep in my new bed.

I felt disoriented when I woke up, not sure where I was, but I remembered quickly enough. Downstairs, I found the others gathered in the living room. I looked around at our new, expensively decorated living room, and a good feeling swept through me. All of this was ours, and our new life was just beginning.

Meanwhile, Tim was still out cold and on the couch, lying on his back with the white nylon ropes wrapped around him. His hands were folded over his chest, much like someone in a coffin, though his wrists were bound. I wondered for a moment if he might be dead after all.

"He's still alive," Dennis said to me from across the room.

"Yeah," Carl said. "He'd better wake up soon. I'm getting tired of waiting."

Once Carolyn and Damon had come downstairs, Susanna asked him about something he had mentioned the night before. The two of them had gotten home just before sunrise, saying that it took a long time to find people to kill. Damon also had something he wanted to talk to her about, but he said it could wait until the next night.

"Oh, right," he said, walking over to her. "Have you got the map?"

"Sure," she said, "just over here." It was on the floor next to a pile of stuff she had brought from the old house; we hadn't yet had time to get things truly organized. "In fact, let me bring it in here so we can all look at it."

She picked the map up and led us into the kitchen, which was much more modern and fancy than the one I was used to. There were shiny white countertops, and along some parts of the wall, black and white checker patterned tiles. Large utensils and cooking implements hung neatly above the stove, which was also shiny and looked brand new. A festive, foot-wide strip of wallpaper in some kind of garden-themed pattern surrounded the tops of the walls, its dark green border meeting the ceiling. Lights that looked like small floodlights hung from the ceiling near what looked like an old wooden chest holding big bottles. Near that, there was a large, round, neatly polished wooden table with chairs that had ornate patterns carved into their backs. It was still taking me a while get used to all of this, how elegant our new home was.

Susanna spread the map out onto the table, and we gathered around. This was our old ritual, but it felt weird to be doing it in a different place. Susanna began looking over the map again, pointing her finger around it. "I still can't figure out where we are," she said, annoyed.

"That's because you're looking in the wrong place," Damon said. He then pointed at a green-colored section of the map that was much farther up from where Susanna had been looking. "Here. This is where we are. I figured it out last night while we were out."

"What?" she exclaimed. "That's impossible."

"Why is it impossible?" I asked.

"But…" She looked closer at the area Damon had indicated, then gasped. "That's the street. We're more or less here." She waved her finger back and forth over a small section. There was a red dot near it, which I recognized as a place that she and the others had gone to kill a few nights earlier while my friends and I attacked the park in town. "I don't understand."

"What's the big deal?" Carl asked. "So we know where this place is now. That's good, right?"

"But look at how far it is on the map," she said, pointing back to where our old house was. Weeks before, she had indicated it with a large, circular blob in pencil, designating that entire area as a no-kill zone. "How could we have walked that far?"

"Wait," Dennis said, looking more closely. "You're right. That's a long way. I mean, we could fly it in… No. Wow. Okay, that's really weird."

I was beginning to see the problem. The distance between our old home and our new one was several inches on the map, as was the distance from there to downtown, South Augusta, or many of the other somewhat faraway places we had attacked. I wasn't clear on the exact difference between our flying speed versus walking, but I knew that there had to be some. Walking all the way from our old school with Dracula's remains, for example, took a lot longer than I thought it would at the time, even though it looked like a short distance on the map.

"Well, we did go through an underground tunnel," I said. "Maybe it was a shortcut. Like, we didn't have to wind around all those roads and stuff, so maybe it…" I trailed off, no longer convinced by my own argument.

Susanna shook her head slowly, her eyes not leaving the map. "I really just don't get it." She didn't sound overly distressed by this, just bewildered.

"Hey!" Dennis said. "I know. Well, maybe. But maybe it's like that video game. You know, the one where you go under and in those tunnels and it's..."

"This isn't a video game, Dennis," Carolyn said.

"I know, but..."

"Can we just go, please?" Nick almost shouted. "I'm starving, and I really don't care if the map is wrong or Damon's full of crap or whatever! I just want to eat something!" Everyone glared at him for his outburst. "Someone," he corrected with a weak smile.

I was left on my own to guard Tim's body, which annoyed me, but it was my turn. Everyone was just as eager as Nick to go out and make their kills, and Susanna also wanted to confirm Damon's findings and try to figure out how we could possibly be so far away from where she'd expected.

While I normally might have been quite intrigued by that mystery, at the moment, I really didn't care. I wanted everyone to get back soon so I could go out and kill, plus I was preoccupied with Tim's condition. I looked over at him from my chair, trying to will him to wake up. I considered talking to him like I had seen people do to coma patients on TV, but those scenes always seemed so heartfelt and tender, which was the direct opposite of what I was feeling towards this worthless traitor.

My resentment built up further, and I began to wonder what he would taste like. I suppressed the thought, knowing that I would have to wait. But then another idea came to me. Maybe I could somehow use my psychic powers to reach into his mind and force him awake, or at the very least, I might be able to peer in and find out what his sleeping thoughts were.

I tried to sense him, but there was almost nothing there. I felt a brief spark, something tiny that seemed to be inside his head, but no actual consciousness. Was he already too far gone? I stood up and walked over to him, looking down at his prone body. It would be so easy to just bend down and drink from his neck. Maybe I could sneak a little taste before the others got back.

Another thought occurred to me. I wanted to go outside, perhaps to wait at the front door for the others to return so I could leave immediately once they did. But there was something more to it than that. Abandoning my post, I went out the door and left Tim unguarded on the couch, knowing that I wasn't supposed to be doing it. But something was driving me on, some vague sensation that I needed to do something important.

I walked down the large stone steps to the yard, looking around and trying to figure things out. I wasn't even sure what I was looking for, but I kept getting this feeling that I wasn't in the right place, that something was wrong. Before I knew it, I was on the other side of the house and by the swimming pool, the same spot where we had changed Tim back to human and started to kill him. I looked over at the Jacuzzi, then at its control panel. Was there some clue here to discover? That was what it felt like.

I leaned down and pressed the *ON* button, causing the hot tub to begin bubbling away. There was something almost hypnotic about the repetitive sound of the rushing, lapping water, and the steam that rose from the small pool brushed up against my face. It stung slightly, but I didn't mind. Then I stepped forward, falling into the water.

Immediately, I came back to my senses and realized what I had done, but it was too late. The painful transformation from vampire back to human had begun, and it was excruciating. My first instinct was to bend over in pain, and as I did, my head went beneath the surface. Water shot into my mouth and nose, and I began to panic. I was immediately reminded of a time at the beach a few years back when a huge wave had caught me at just the right angle and tumbled my body over and over until it released me, leaving me unharmed but freaked out.

This time, the memory of that event was enough to force me into action, to do what needed in order to survive. I straightened up, still in pain from the transformation, but I managed to get the water out of my mouth and nose with a forced cough. I was shaking, but I managed to clamber out of the Jacuzzi and onto the pavement, my head throbbing with intense pain. I could feel my heart pounding relentlessly, and with each beat, my head pounded along with it. I tried to scream, but it only came out between gasps for breath as I lay there on my hands and knees. Water dripped onto the pavement from my body, changing it to a darker grey in random patterns that seemed oddly fascinating and comforting to me, something to focus on until the agony subsided.

It did, but then something else happened. I was acutely aware of the fact that I was human again, vulnerable to the rest of the vampires if they should come back and find me. I wondered if I might be able to talk them out of killing me, escape, or survive some other way. If they did catch me, they might very well bite me and drink my blood, and then I would die, the same way that all of those people I had killed had done.

All of those people.

For the first time in my life, the enormity of what I had done hit me. It was like a speeding car slamming into the side of my psyche, this sudden, unexpected realization. I had killed tons of people, ended their lives. I had done it for fun. Sometimes it had been for survival, to protect myself or those I cared about, but I finally knew the truth: I was a murderer, countless times over. And it wasn't just me; my friends, my sisters, all of us had done this, and it wasn't some innocent game. It was mass killing, and we were guilty of crimes so heinous that my mind could barely comprehend them. Flashes of faces ran through my head, random people whose lives we had taken, all of them dead because of me.

Even though I felt the thought creeping up on me and tried to will it away, I was still shocked by the way I burst out crying once I pictured that tiny little blonde girl on the grass four years earlier, Carolyn's voice echoing in my mind. *"I saved her for you."* I shook my head, trying to make the memory go away. But it wouldn't. Neither would the memories of all the other people I had killed before and since then. Not just me, but all of us. I wondered just what the official body count might be, then screwed my eyes shut, trying to will that thought away as well. It didn't work, but then I was distracted by a voice.

"Now you understand," Tim said, "just as I did."

I looked up, thankful to have something to think about other than the horrible memories that were driving me into uncontrollable despair. Recognizing his voice, I expected to see Tim standing next to me, and I did, but there was something different about him. He looked almost the same as before, the same clothes he had been wearing, the same squinty eyes and curly brown hair, his arms folded in a superior, arrogant manner. But there was one main difference: He was transparent, like a ghost.

I jumped back, trying to make sense of what I was seeing. He looked at me calmly, his gaze following me as I staggered backwards, crawling in an upside-down crab-like motion. "Tim!" I halfway whispered. "Are you… Are you dead?"

He smiled. "No. But I probably will be soon."

Not feeling much reassurance, I said, "But… you're a ghost!"

"Astral projection, actually," he said coolly. "You've heard about that, I'm sure." I had, but it wasn't a particular psychic ability that Dennis or I had, at least as far as I knew. All I could do was nod.

"Believe me, this is about as much of a surprise to me as it is to you," he said, looking around. He seemed remarkably nonchalant. "But it was apparently a side effect of my cribbing off of your powers all along, using them to amplify my own. I think you made this happen."

I sort of understood. Tim's body was still tied up and lying on the couch inside, but now his spirit had somehow traveled out of it and was talking to me. Then I realized something else. "You possessed me. That's why I jumped into the pool."

"If you like," he said, and I was beginning to get annoyed with his aggravatingly calm tone.

"And now I'm probably going to get killed when the others get back!"

"They're still pretty far away. We've got time."

"Time for what?"

"For us to try to fix this."

Back inside, I tried to use my powers to heal Tim's body. That had been his suggestion. But try as I might, the energy I projected at him seemed to do no good. Tim's "ghost," or astral body, had also disappeared. I was alone again with the body of my dying friend.

"I'm sorry, Tim," I said. "I really didn't..." I sighed. There were so many things for me to regret, and I worried about what else there might be to come. "It's all my fault."

"No, it's mine," he said, rematerializing next to me.

"Where did you go?"

"It has to do with me draining off your powers," he said. "It's difficult to explain in terms you would understand."

"But I've been psychic for a long time, Tim. I know how this stuff works."

"That's..." He paused, looking pensive. "That's not exactly what I mean. I see things differently now..." He paused again, this time looking scared, his head darting to one side like he had just heard something.

"What?"

"They've started killing," he said. "They'll be on their way back soon."

"You can see them?" I realized that, like me, he could visualize what our friends were doing far away. I did the same, seeing them at some newly built shopping center somewhere to the south. Susanna and the others were preying on their victims, and for the first time in my life, the image of that horrified me.

"Yes, but only..." Tim began, then disappeared. It was like having a conversation with a flickering light bulb. A few moments later, he reappeared. "We don't have much time. You need to hide my body before they get back."

"Why? They'll probably leave you alone if…"

"No, they won't. Like you did, they're going to get impatient. You need to put me somewhere safe where I can heal. I can feel that the power you put into me earlier helped a little, but it's not nearly enough. I can't just jump back into my body and be conscious again, at least, not yet."

What he was saying sounded somewhat logical, but everything was happening so fast. I just had to trust that he knew what he was talking about. I speculated on where we might be able to hide him, but he already had that figured out, too.

"There's a big storage shed way back in the yard behind the house," he said. "You'll have to drag me in there. It will be quicker if you go through the kitchen and use the back door."

It proved to be quite an effort to get him all the way to where he was indicating, but I managed to. I no longer had the superhuman strength of a vampire, but I found that my powers helped. I wasn't even sure if I was telekinetically making his body lighter or was just increasing my own physical strength, but it didn't matter. The result was the same; I was able to drag him along through the house and the yard. Without my powers, I might not have been able to do it on my own.

For the few minutes that it took me to transport Tim to the storage shed, I was alone with my thoughts. I realized that even though my physical strength had returned to normal now that the vampire potion's effects were gone from me, my psychic powers remained at the same level. I also realized that this was how Tim kept appearing to me as a ghost, figuring out the pattern to his appearances and disappearances. If I used my powers for anything, he couldn't be there; they were what was allowing him to appear in the first place. Whatever level of psychic ability he normally possessed, it was at least for the moment linked to mine. For all I knew, his own powers were all that was still keeping him alive.

As I struggled along with his body, I also had more time to think about everything that had happened, and some of the resentment I had felt before began to crop up. I still felt guilty over having been a vampire, but I was still mad at him for betraying us to Life Force and almost getting us killed. Maybe we were never in any real danger from them, but it was still a really shitty thing for him to do.

Once I had him in the shed, which was more like a small cottage, his ghostly self materialized again as I was taking the ropes off his body. "There isn't time for that," he said. "You need to go."

"Go where?" I asked, panic beginning to set in as I visualized the others returning soon. Tim flickered away again.

I got up from the floor and hurried out of the cottage, closing the door behind me and hoping that no one would think to look for him there once they realized that he was missing. Moreover, I hoped that they wouldn't be able to find me. I pictured a field of invisibility around my body, and I ran back toward the house, realizing that I had cut a swath through the overgrown grass by dragging Tim's body through it earlier. I could only hope that no one would notice, or else it would lead them straight to him.

I reached the pool area again, and a familiar sound caught my ear. It was the Jacuzzi, still bubbling away. Before I had a chance to turn it off, a lone bat flew into view at ground level several yards in front of me. It changed into Carolyn, who gave me a surprised look.

"What are you doing out here?" she asked. There was nothing threatening in her tone; she instead seemed amused. "Aren't you supposed to be inside guarding our little Tim?"

I tried to look natural, not bone-chillingly terrified like I felt. "Oh, yeah," I said. "I just… I just came out here to check on something." I had lied my way out of plenty of jams in the past, but I knew that this was going to be a major test of my acting skills.

"Check on what?" she asked. I hadn't thought that far ahead. Instead, I changed the subject.

"Where's everybody else?" I asked.

"Oh, they're on their way," she said, letting out a small laugh. "Damon and I got into a little fight earlier, so I stormed off acting like I was mad. I'm not really, but I'm letting him think that for a little bit." She smiled throughout the entire conversation. It was hard to look at her, to think that this wasn't really my sister; this was a monster that would probably tear my throat out any second.

"Oh," I said, letting out a nervous laugh. "What were you fighting about?"

She rolled her eyes, but she didn't stop grinning. "He made some dumb joke about Susanna being all 'hot' or something when she was killing this guy. I was a little pissed off for a second, but I know he didn't really mean it. I'm just setting him up for later when we can have… make…" She trailed off, looking at me strangely.

"What?" I asked, but I knew the answer.

"Why are your clothes wet, Ray?" She was looking me up and down, an odd smile replacing her previous, more aloof one.

"They're not! I mean… I was just sweating a lot from… um…"

She shook her head slowly, her eyes locked onto mine. Her fangs were beginning to show, her widening grin only breaking for a moment to allow her to speak. "Oh, this is too good."

I began to back away from her involuntarily. "Carolyn, please. Just… just don't. Let me help change you back, and then you'll understand."

"Oh, Ray," she said condescendingly as she matched my steps. "You of all people should know that's not going to work."

I glanced around as I backed up, wondering if there might be something I could use as a weapon against her. At the same time, I was afraid to look away from her, as if doing so would allow her to pounce on me. Then I realized that it didn't make a difference either way.

"I never really did forgive you, you know," she said, "for trying to kill me like that."

"I didn't…!" I started to say, but I bumped into a metal chair that was behind me, then stumbled past it. We were heading in the wrong direction; if I could get her over to the hot tub, I might be able to lure her in.

"Yes you *di-id!*" she sang. "And now I suppose you think you can beg me to say all is forgiven." She paused, standing still for a moment and looking away. Smirking and narrowing her eyes, she looked back at me. "How about you give that a try, Ray? It'll be fun."

"Hey!" a voice called out, and Carolyn turned around to look. Using the distraction, I raced past her. I could hear her pursuing me, but if my plan worked, that would be perfect. Unfortunately, things didn't go as I'd hoped, and I heard her footsteps behind me suddenly give way to a faint flapping sound.

The rapid thudding of her wings suddenly filled my right ear, and I let out a short shriek, thinking that she was about to bite into my neck. Instead, she whizzed on past my head and beat me to the Jacuzzi, changing back to her person form and using the control panel to turn the water jets off. She then looked back up at me with that same predatory smile.

"Nice try," she said.

"Carolyn!" Tim's voice called out again, this time from a different direction. She looked around but then quickly back at me, not wanting to give me a second chance to get away.

"Is that you, Tim?" she called out, not taking her eyes off of me. "Why don't you come out and stand next to your little friend? The two of you can wait here until the others get back."

I realized that she was right, that it was probably only a matter of minutes before they arrived, if that. Somehow, I needed to gain some kind of advantage. But Carolyn was faster than me; if I ran, she could just catch up to me as a bat.

"Over here!" Tim called out. Once again, his voice came from a completely different direction; this time it sounded like it was coming from the front corner of the house. Carolyn looked around, clearly as confused as I was as to how Tim could be moving around so quickly. Then I realized that because he was more or less a ghost, he could probably appear anywhere, or at least anywhere nearby.

Regaining at least some of my bravery, I reached over to my side and picked up another of the aluminum deck chairs, holding it up defensively. I had hoped that this would be a threatening gesture, but Carolyn just laughed.

"Oh, okay! What are you going to do now, chair me to death?"

"Ray!" Tim's voice rang out again. I could see him this time, barely visible in the darkness behind Carolyn, but she didn't turn around, only peered behind her cautiously without actually looking. "Do it now!" Tim cried.

Carolyn was unable to resist the urge to look, so I ran at her with the chair, knocking her over with it. She struggled against it as she clattered to the ground, and as she did so, I made a break for the Jacuzzi controls. A harsh scraping noise came from behind, and the chair quickly skidded past me and into the larger pool.

"Oh no you don't!" she called out as she clambered up to me, and she managed to grab my wrist just before I reached the controls.

"Ray," Tim's voice whispered in my ear urgently. "You have the power. Use it." I wasn't sure if he was visible or not; I didn't turn my head to look. But finally, I realized what I needed to do. Had I not been so frightened and out of my element, I probably would have come up with the solution earlier.

"Okay, Ray," Carolyn said more harshly, pinning my arm to the pavement and maneuvering herself onto my back. "I think we've played long enough." Her left hand shoved my other shoulder down, and for a moment, I was reminded of the times when we were much younger, back when she was much more of a tomboy. We would sometimes watch professional wrestling on TV, then try our own hand at wrestling in the red den. Usually, it was all in fun, but sometimes, one of us would accidentally hurt the other, causing things to escalate into an actual fight.

"I'm not going to kill you yet," she continued. "We'll wait for everyone else to arrive. Then we can catch both you and that little nerd Tim, and... then... we..."

She lost the ability to speak, then loosened her grip on me and straightened up, sliding off of me and sitting on her knees. I stood up stiffly, my psychic powers working as hard as they could to keep her mind under my control. I turned around and looked at her, and she was grimacing, trying to fight against me.

"Sss... stop it, Ray..." she managed to whisper through clenched teeth. Then, per my direction, she stood up, walked past me, and landed in the small pool.

"I'm sorry," I said, bending down and pressing the *ON* button.

The jets bubbled into life again, and I felt the pain in Carolyn's mind briefly before releasing my hold on her, staggering back as I watched her get changed from a sadistic killer back into my sister, the girl I had grown up with, or at least, the girl she was in between the times we had taken that damned potion and turned ourselves into murderers. She screamed as the transformation took place, and once I was sure she was human again, I helped her out of the tub and onto the wet pavement. She lay there on her side, crying uncontrollably.

I tried to console her by placing a hand on her shoulder, but she punched at me absently, her hand quickly returning to cover her face. She sobbed more and more heavily, then finally managed to say with a voice muffled through tightly pressed palms, "What did you make me *do!?*" Her crying continued for a few more moments, this time taking the form of shallow, almost silent breaths. "Oh, God," she whispered. "Crowley..."

"Carolyn," I said gently. Then, more urgently, I added, "Carolyn."

She stopped crying suddenly, then took her hands away from her face, looking up at me. The look in her eyes was unfamiliar to me, at least on her own face. I had occasionally seen it from time to time when we had killed people, this shocked look they would sometimes get when they realized that they were already dead, that no matter what they did to try to resist, they were experiencing the final moments of their lives. Up until that night, I had barely understood what that look meant.

"Carolyn," I repeated, helping her as she straightened up and started to regain her composure.

"Stop saying my name," she almost whispered. "Just stop." She shook her head quickly, water splattering from her highlighted blonde hair, which looked almost brown while wet.

"We need to get out of here," I said. "We need to hide and get some…"

"Just shut up!" she shrieked, shoving me away. I toppled backwards, surprised at first. But I couldn't really blame her for being so upset. Very quickly, though, she changed her tone, and her breathing went from labored gasps to a more calm rhythm.

"Okay," she said, her eyes darting around but avoiding mine. "Okay. You're right. We need to get the hell out of here." She quickly wiped tears from her eyes as she spoke, then stood up uneasily.

"We should look for some weapons," I said, unsure of how she would respond.

"Yes, I know. See those buckets?" She pointed to the side of the house, and I saw what she was indicating, some large plastic buckets I had seen before but never given much thought. There were several of them, some blue and some grey, each about two or three feet tall and with thin, metal handles. Most of them had labels on them with small writing that I couldn't make out from that far away.

"What can we do with those?" I asked.

"We fill them with water from the pool," she explained. "I'm thinking that in that amount, splashing a vampire with it would count as running water. Make sense?"

"I guess," I said. I could picture what she was describing, and I hoped it would work.

"It's been a while since I had to think on my feet like this," she said, sounding almost amused. I was tempted to make a joke, but I was still feeling a little shaky after her recent lashing out at me, afraid she might do it again. And, truth be told, I wasn't really in a joking mood.

"Wait," I said, realizing again that being under pressure like this was crippling my ability to spot the obvious. "Why not just use the hose? It's right over there." We were somewhat far from the faucet it was connected to, which didn't seem to be a problem at first. But then, I realized it was too late: The rest of the vampires had already returned, their nearly silent bat forms landing nearby and transforming.

"Ssshit!" Carolyn hissed, stepping closer to my side.

"Well, well, well," Dennis said with a smile, fangs punctuating his pudgy face. "Isn't this interesting?" I realized as he spoke that even though I had expected to psychically sense their approach, Dennis had cloaked them before they arrived. He also had obviously figured out that we were human, and I could tell from their expressions that the others knew as well.

"I'll say," Damon said, grinning evilly.

"Looks like we'll get to have some dessert," Nick said, stepping forward slowly along with the others. "I guess Tim wasn't the only traitor after all, huh?" He gave me a pointed look.

"No, it's not like that!" I said in a pleading tone.

"Then what is it like, Ray?" Susanna asked sarcastically. As it had been with Carolyn, it was amazing how different everyone looked to me now that I was human and they were the vampires. I was terrified, and I couldn't see any way out of this. Maybe if Tim helped us with more of his astral tricks, we might have a chance, but even then, we were outnumbered. I couldn't come up with a response to Susanna's rhetorical question, but then Carl chimed in.

"It's 'like' we're going to have a really good time killing these two," he said, then let out his usual goofy laugh. It had never sounded so threatening to me before. "But then, let's see… How do we want to go about this? Both at once? Or maybe we should take turns, do one, then the other."

"I know which one I want," Damon said, eyeing Carolyn menacingly.

"Damon!" Carolyn called out. "No!"

"Oh, yes," he said, nodding his head, his fun-loving expression an evil parody of what it usually was. "Definitely."

"I want some of her, too," Dennis said. "Don't hog it all for yourself."

I wondered if Damon might get mad at Dennis for this, but instead, he just laughed, giving him a sideways glance. "Sure," he said. "We can share." All the while, the group was slowly advancing on us step by step, and Carolyn and I were backing up in sync. At this point, though, Carolyn stopped.

"Damon, it's me!" she pleaded. "You can't!" Her tone was somewhere between screaming and crying, and I could hear the heartbreak in her voice.

I reached out with my mind, hoping that I could subdue them psychically. I wasn't sure if I could control this many people at once, but it was worth a try. The five of them stopped walking, but then Susanna said, "No." Her eyes lit up bright yellow, and then the others did the same. I felt my power bouncing back to me, making me dizzy for a moment.

"Nice try," Dennis said.

"Yeah," Carl said. "Your stupid psychic crap isn't going to save you this time."

"Time to feed, then," Nick said, eyeing me eagerly. He and the other boys began advancing again.

"Wait," Susanna said with authority, holding out her arm. "Everyone stop for a second."

"What?" Carl asked. "Are you fucking kidding me? Let's just kill them already."

"Not yet," she said, her expression unreadable. For a foolish moment, I thought that she might have come to her senses. But when she began smiling again, I knew that things were about to get worse. "Let's let them go. Just for a minute or two. It will be more fun with a chase."

Carl laughed, looking over at her. "You mean, give them a running start?" He looked back at me and Carolyn. "Sure, I can see us doing that."

"No!" Nick said angrily. "Let's just…"

"Shut up, Nick!" Susanna snarled at him. "I'm in charge here, not you."

He clammed up, looking surprised, then more subdued. "Fine. Let's play your little game."

Carl covered his eyes with his hands, his evil grin never fading. "One o'clock," he said, "two o'clock…"

Carolyn grabbed my hand and pulled me away, and we ran as fast as we could towards the woods.

"Where the hell have you been?" I asked Tim's apparition. It had been only a couple of minutes since we had run from the house, and Carolyn and I had found a group of bushes among the dark trees that seemed like a good place to hide for the moment.

"There wouldn't have been any point in me trying to distract them while they were all together," Tim said simply. "Instead, I planted an idea to get them to draw this out."

"Is that why Susanna let us go?" I asked.

"One of the reasons," he said.

"What do you mean?"

"Um, guys?" Carolyn whispered cautiously. "Anyone want to explain to me how Tim here is a ghost?"

I quickly caught her up on the details, explaining astral projection to her and how Tim had somehow been using a combination of his powers and my own to manifest himself like this. I was a little confused about what had happened earlier when I tried to use my powers to control the others, though. "Does that mean that Susanna is psychic, too?" I asked.

"Everyone is psychic," Tim said, "at least a little bit. It only becomes more manifest in those of us who choose to develop it further."

"And they've still got Dennis on their side," I pointed out. "That must have been why I couldn't make it work. Anything I try to do can just be cancelled out by him."

"Correct," Tim said. "You might fare better in individual confrontations, though."

"You sound different," Carolyn said, putting her finger on something that had been bugging me for a while, but I hadn't fully realized it until then. There was something strange about the way he talked, almost like he was older and more mature, or at least less of a kid. He had always been intelligent in an almost annoying way, but even so, somewhere in there was still always the same old mischievous, clever Tim. This ghost-like version of him was somewhat ominous.

"I *am* different," he said. "I can't really explain it now."

"I don't suppose you could explain why you betrayed us to Life Force like that, then," Carolyn said bitterly.

"That was a mistake. I know that now. My thinking at the time was that they might be able to save us, to turn us back to human. We certainly weren't going to do that on our own. Things had gone too far."

"You don't know that!" I said. "If you'd wanted to change back, you should have just said so!"

Carolyn let out a small *"hmph"* sound. "Okay, yeah, I kind of get it now. But even then, those guys would have killed us if they'd gotten the chance." She seemed to have gotten over the idea of Tim as a weird astral figure by this point, as she was no longer staring at him — or through him — and began shuffling around in the nearby dirt, doing something I couldn't see.

"I know," Tim said. "I told them not to bring wooden stakes and the like when they intercepted us, but they wouldn't listen. As I said, it was a mistake on my part. And for that, I'm sorry." For a moment, I understood, and I forgave him, at least internally. "And I'm also sorry for this entire thing."

"What do you..." I started to say, but I was distracted by a sudden movement from Carolyn, who had just jerked her arm violently, causing some debris to hit me. "What are you doing?"

"Improvising," she said simply. "Carry on."

Not knowing what she was up to, I continued talking to Tim. "What do you mean, 'this entire thing?'"

"Whether or not you remember it," he said, "I was the one who came up with the idea of using the vampire potion in the first place." This revelation hit me pretty hard, but once my memory kicked in, I remembered. Way back when Carl had lost that race, we all wanted to do something to comfort him, and Susanna happened to tell me about her vampire potion. I had the dream that we took it, told Tim about it, and then he suggested that we do so for revenge. For the first time in quite a while, the chronology of those events clicked into place in my head.

Before I had a chance to think about this further, we were interrupted by a voice calling out something like *"Yarrrr!"* as someone descended from the tree above us, two glowing yellow eyes zooming straight toward me. I managed to roll out of the way at the last second, and whoever it was hit the ground with a thud. It was dark in the woods, so I couldn't quite make out who it was as they stood up from the ground. A small amount of light from the house filtered this far out, but not much.

"Okay," Nick's voice said. I could see from his silhouette that he had both hands raised in a menacing gesture. "Who's first?"

"Neither," Carolyn said, apparently feeling a lot more calm than I did.

"Nick…" I began.

"Shut it, Ray," he shot back. His eyes lit up again, and I noticed that, like everything else about the vampires, they looked different to me now that I was human. They seemed brighter than I remembered, almost painful to look at in the darkness, like staring into a flashlight. Their glow also faintly illuminated our surroundings, and I noticed that Carolyn was holding her arm out straight. Something was in her hand.

"Pssh…" Nick said, halfway laughing. "What do you think you're going to do with that?"

"This," Carolyn said, jumping forward and right up to Nick. I called out her name, afraid that she was about to get bitten. There was a scream, but it wasn't hers.

I could barely make out Nick's writhing form as he cried out from the ground below. I had seen the transformation from vampire back to human enough times by then to recognize it even in the dark, but I was still confused. "What did you do?" I asked Carolyn, who had backed up and was standing next to me.

"Touched him with a cross," she said, holding up the object she'd been carrying.

"Where did you get a cross from?"

"Made it. Just now." She handed the cross to me, and I felt around it with my fingers. It was made from two thick sticks, pieces of branches maybe, which were tied together with what felt like smooth, thin rope. As my fingers reached an exposed, wet part of it, I realized that the rope was in fact a vine.

"Improvising," I said. "I get it."

Nick, meanwhile, had recovered from being changed back, and he stood up slowly. "Yeah," he said bitterly. "Thanks a fucking lot. Now I can get killed along with the rest of you bastards."

"Nick, calm down," I said.

"No, *you* calm down! I can't believe I let you talk me into all this in the first place!"

"Guys, just stop," Carolyn said. "Nick, what about the others?"

He was quiet for a moment. "They're still at the house. They let me go off on my own first to try and find you two." He filled us in on what they were planning, which wasn't very detailed. The idea had been that Nick was going to chase us out of the woods; they had no idea that we'd actually be able to fight back. But mostly, they were just toying with us, wanting to have as much fun as possible tracking us down and eventually killing us. Nick was understandably surprised at Tim's current status as an astral projection, and we learned that the others hadn't yet been inside the house, so they didn't know that his body had been moved.

"So what do we do?" I asked. "Make ourselves some more weapons out of sticks?"

"That's not a bad idea," Nick said, picking up a long branch from the ground. I heard a snap, then could just barely make out the newly made wooden stake as he held it up.

"Let's try to avoid using something like that if we can," Carolyn said. "We don't want to actually kill any of them."

"Says you," Nick grumbled. He then knelt down and began pulling at another branch.

"What we really need to do is get back to the tunnel," I said. "If we could make it back to the old house, we could get some weapons from there. Maybe some of Life Force's are still in the front yard!"

"We can't just leave Tim's body here," Carolyn said. "Sooner or later, someone is bound to find it. My guess would be Dennis."

She was right. I realized that getting Dennis changed back should be our top priority. The fact that the remaining vampires still had a psychic on their side certainly gave them an advantage. As tempting as it was to just run away and try to escape via the tunnel, what we really needed to do was confront the others.

"I really don't think we stand much of a chance without real weapons," Nick said. "Wait, didn't you say that fire would work against them?"

"Yes," I said, but I wasn't sure where he was going with this.

"Crap," he said. "Never mind. I thought for a second that we might… It doesn't matter. My lighter is still in the house."

"What are you doing with a lighter?" Carolyn asked. "You're too young to smoke."

"I don't smoke! I just… you know…"

"Like to set things on fire sometimes," I said.

"Oh, well that's all right, then," Carolyn said sarcastically.

"That's not important right now!" I said. "We need to figure out what to do."

"The tunnel wouldn't be an option anyway, I just realized," Carolyn said. "We didn't bring any flashlights with us, remember?"

"Crap, you're right," I said. Because of our permanent night vision, there hadn't been any need.

"I brought one," Tim said. "But it's still at the house, too, over near the pool."

"Maybe we could feel our way along in the dark," Nick said. "It's pretty much a straight line, right?"

At first I thought that might work, and I said so, but then I remembered that whenever anyone touched the walls or the roof, they crumbled away. I worried that if one were to do that too much, the entire tunnel might collapse in on them.

"He's right," Tim said. "The mystical force keeping the walls in place and maintaining the wormhole effect would become too compromised."

There was silence for a few seconds, followed by Carolyn saying, "I have absolutely no idea what you just said, but I take it that means 'no.'"

"What do worms have to do with any of this?" Nick asked. "I thought you said it was vampires who made that thing."

"They did," I said, also confused.

"Dennis was close to the proper explanation earlier," Tim said. "He was thinking of that game where one underground passage on-screen was equivalent to…"

"Shh!" I said, finally noticing something different. Because we had been talking, I had been distracted, but I suddenly realized that things had gone quiet over at the house. Earlier, I had just been able to make out the vampires' voices and occasional laughter, but that had died off for at least a minute or two.

"No, keep going!" Dennis's voice said from very close by. "I want to hear all about how I was properly explaining or whatever."

I looked around in the darkness, trying to figure out which direction the voice was coming from. There were slow, deliberate footsteps cracking among the leaves and twigs, but I couldn't figure out just where they were. For just a second, I tried to make my eyes glow to help me see in the dark better, then felt like an idiot once I remembered I could no longer do that. I still had my powers, though.

I tried to find Dennis psychically, but it was like he wasn't there. He must have been cloaking himself. I scanned a broader area, and I was able to sense that Susanna, Carl, and Damon were still waiting near the house. Like they had done with Nick, they must have been letting Dennis try his luck against us on his own. As I let my mind relax and stopped using my powers, I heard Tim whispering in my ear.

"You need to stop doing that. I can't manifest when you do."

"Then what am I supposed to do?" I whispered back angrily.

"Let me help." I looked to my right where his voice had been coming from, but there was nothing there.

A few seconds later, there was the sound of a small crash, and I heard someone stumbling over some bushes nearby. Dennis cried out, more in frustration than from any pain. "What the hell's wrong with my legs?" he said.

It was enough noise for us to determine his position, so we hurried over to where he was. He was sprawled out on the ground next to a tree with a couple of small bushes at its base, pounding on his legs with his fists. By this point, we had been in the dark long enough for me to see better with what little light there was. His legs suddenly came back to life and straightened out, and he began struggling to stand up.

"That was me, I'm afraid," Tim said, materializing next to him.

"Tim? You're awake? No, wait, there's something wrong…"

"Dennis," I said, "just be still." I focused my powers on him, willing him to stand motionless. Not surprisingly, he fought back.

His eyes lit up, and I could feel his mind pushing back against mine. I pushed back more, but he was stronger than I expected. The more I fought against him, the harder it got, and it felt like we were evenly matched. I began to grunt with effort as the struggle continued, focused on nothing but trying to hold him back. I was vaguely aware of some movement to his left, and then a searing pain shot through my arm, sending me toppling backwards.

Dennis cried out, and once I disengaged my mind from his, the pain stopped. Carolyn was standing next to him holding her makeshift cross, and Dennis was clutching at his left arm, then at his head. After a few moments of agony, he was human again.

"Ray…" he said in a broken voice. "Ray, I'm sorry. All of you, really. I can't… Oh, God…"

I knelt down and held out a hand to him, touching his shoulder. "It's okay. You're okay now."

"No! Nothing is okay!"

"Dennis, you need to get it together," Carolyn said. "Tell us what the others are planning."

He sniffled, and I could tell that he was fighting back tears. "They're not… I mean… They're not going to wait anymore. I was a distraction."

"Run!" Tim shouted. "Straight to the house! Now!"

As we bolted out of the woods, I could hear some movement among the trees behind us. Susanna and the others were nearby, and for all I knew, they might descend upon us at any moment. I ran as fast as I could, hoping to reach the pool in time. If we could just get close enough to the Jacuzzi again, there might be a chance to change the others back and get out of this alive. Better still, I might be able to make it to the faucet and use the hose. I also considered jumping into the pool, thinking that might keep me safe from getting bitten. But it wasn't running water, so one of the vampires might just follow me in and kill me underwater. The safest thing I could think of was to get to the hose.

These thoughts were interrupted by the sound of a girl screaming behind me, and for a moment, I hoped that it was Susanna. Maybe someone had managed to catch her and change her back. My body went cold as Susanna's bat form landed in front of me and changed, a malevolent smile on her face. I struggled to stop running and avoid toppling right into her. The scream I had heard was Carolyn's, and I feared the worst.

"Well now," Susanna said, leering at me. "This should be interesting."

I stood there, panting from the exertion, unsure what to do. I was unarmed, and I hadn't even made it to the pavement surrounding the pool. I heard voices nearby, including what sounded like some shouting and a struggle, but I was too preoccupied with my current situation. I really hoped that Carolyn wasn't dead, but I also had to try to keep myself from getting killed.

"Ray!" Nick called out as he caught up to me. "Here!" He shoved a pointed, broken branch into my hand, and I took it without thinking. As far as wooden stakes went, it wasn't elegant, but it would probably do the job. Nick was holding one, too, and he held it up as a sort of demonstration to me, then turned toward Susanna. I just stood there.

"Damn it," Susanna said with an angry sigh. She changed into a bat and flew up into the sky.

I looked around, wondering where everyone else was. I saw Damon running toward me, which scared me until I realized that Carolyn and Dennis were running along with him. He was human again, too.

"Are you all right?" Carolyn asked me. "What happened?"

"Susanna. She tried to…" I didn't want to finish that sentence.

"She got away," Nick said simply, then looked up at Damon. "And that still leaves…"

Without warning, a bat swooped down onto Nick's neck. He screamed and struggled to fight it off, and I leapt forward to help him before I even knew what I was doing. Grabbing the squirming brown figure with both hands, I managed to wrench it away and slam it onto the ground, where it transformed into Carl. He was twisted into a strange position, but he quickly recovered, then looked up at me and Nick with extreme hatred.

Briefly looking around at the others present, he said, "You are so dead. All of you." And with that, he changed back into a bat and flew away.

Having regrouped inside the house, we were a little more confident. The odds were more in our favor. If we could just manage to survive and change Susanna and Carl back to normal, this would all be over and we could go home. But I also kept getting this nagging feeling that something bad was going to happen instead.

Although Tim had discouraged me from using my powers, I was still aware of the presence of the two remaining vampires, who had for a while been perched on the house's chimney and talking quietly. They still wanted to get us, but they were being careful. But Tim preferred to continue to stay incarnate as a transparent version of himself, which couldn't happen whenever I did anything psychic.

This meant that Dennis would have to be the group's designated telepath. He kept quiet while the rest of us talked in the living room, concentrating on Susanna and Carl's movements. From time to time, he let us know when they did something, but it wasn't very useful.

Initially, they had remained on the chimney, but then they seemed to arbitrarily move to different locations along the roof. A little later, they were circling the house separately, not making any attempts to get inside.

"They're biding their time," Tim's ghost said to us, "waiting for the right moment to strike."

"Well, that's helpful," Carolyn said, rolling her eyes. "Got any ideas on how to actually deal with them?"

"That's up to you."

In the meantime, we had gathered up what weapons we could. It turned out that Damon had in fact salvaged a crossbow from Life Force's attack on our house, but I warned him that he should only use it to threaten the vampires, not actually shoot them with it. If it were at all possible, we wanted to change them back, not kill them. And while I didn't say it aloud to anyone, I worried that the latter might end up being a real possibility. I still had the wooden stake Nick had given me tucked halfway into the pocket of my denim shorts, but I really hoped that I wouldn't have to end up using it.

Fortunately, there were less deadly alternatives. As we had hoped, there was some garlic powder on the well-stocked spice rack in the kitchen, and Carolyn was working on finding other things in the kitchen with which to make more crosses. I realized that because both she and Susanna had brought their make-up and hairspray from the old house, there were two more potential weapons upstairs. I asked Carolyn if she would mind if I took the two cans from the bathroom, but she just gave me a confused look, briefly stopping her latest craft project on the tile counter.

"What in the world do you want my hairspray for?" she asked.

"So we can light it on fire," I said. "Like the guys and I did in that field that time. I was thinking that we might be able to set a trap for them, luring them into a patch of it, you know."

"Hmm," Carolyn said simply, then got back to her work. "Sure, fine. Whatever."

"Stay away from my mousse, though," Damon said. That was one thing about him that was odd to me, the fact that he used hair products even though he was a guy. But apparently that was just one of his things, part of his rock star image. In any other situation, I might have made a joke about it, but none of us were in the mood for that.

The fact that things had calmed down for the moment meant that we were all getting a chance to think about things more clearly, which made things very somber. Each and every one of us knew that we had been doing unspeakably horrible things to innocent people all this time, a feeling that started with that initial wave of intense guilt once we became human again. That had never happened before, and once I had enough time to ponder that, I realized that it must have been yet another unexpected side effect of the different potion Susanna had gotten us to take this time.

I made my way out of the kitchen and through the living room, where Dennis was still sitting motionless and looking straight ahead. "Anything?" I asked him.

"Not really. They went over by the pool for a little bit, but I couldn't really see what they were doing. It's difficult, like maybe they know I'm trying to look in on them and are trying to keep their thoughts scattered." He frowned, then added bitterly, "Or maybe I'm just not as great at this as you are."

That hurt a bit. "No, Dennis, you're fine. Your powers have definitely gotten stronger. I could feel that when you were fighting back in the woods."

"Yeah, and it's probably all because of the potion and being vampires, and you know what? I really don't want to talk about it." He never once looked over at me.

All I could think to say in response was, "Okay," and I headed for the stairs. "Just let us know if anything changes."

"Yes, sir."

"It's guilt he's feeling," Tim's ghost said to me. "He needs to work through it."

"I know," I said angrily. "You don't have to tell me that. We're all feeling it."

"Something just occurred to me," Nick said from his place on the couch.

"What's that?" I asked.

"Well, while we're all supposedly safely locked in here, and I'm not even sure about that given that we've only locked the doorknob and can't find the key to the deadbolt..."

"Yeah, I know," I said. "For all I know, Susanna and I accidentally buried it with what was left of those two scientists. We looked around a few times..."

"I know!" he interrupted. "That's not what I'm talking about. It's the fact that we're in here, but Tim's actual body, not the see-through overly smart and annoying version of him here, is still back in that cottage you mentioned. What's to stop Carl and Susanna from finding him in there and slurping up what's left of him?"

"That's a good point," I said, turning back to look at Tim. I expected him to look worried, but as before, he was remarkably calm. "Any chance your body has healed enough to where you could get back into it and be normal again?"

"Not yet," he said, then just looked at me.

"Okay, whatever," I said. "I need to take care of something upstairs."

After gathering the two cans of hairspray from the bathroom, I walked back down the hall, trying to come up with ways to actually use them against Carl or Susanna if I got the chance. I had this idea that I could spray a big patch of the stuff on the ground outside with a trail leading away from it, and then if they were to land there, I could surprise them by using Nick's lighter to ignite the flammable substance and change them back. They might get a little burned, but hopefully not too much. As long as it changed them back to human, I was willing to risk it.

"They're inside!" Dennis's voice blared out from downstairs. "Everyone! They're inside the house!"

I started to rush down the stairs while Dennis continued to shout, but I couldn't make out what he was saying. Then I heard something behind me, a rapid stomping accompanied by heavy breathing. Not looking back, I continued to barrel down the red carpet of the stairwell. I saw Damon appear at the base of the stairs, his newly acquired crossbow held aloft.

"Back it up, Carl!" he shouted, aiming somewhere behind me. I ducked, but then I stumbled, dropping the metal cans and grabbing onto the handrail to try to break my fall. The stomping behind me disappeared, and over my own labored breathing, I could barely make out the sound of flapping wings fading away.

Another noise caught my attention, something metal clanging to the floor. As near as I could make out, it was coming from the kitchen. Carolyn was shouting something, and Damon called out her name as he rushed in her direction, still holding the crossbow.

I picked up the cans of hairspray and hurried after him, forgetting that on their own, they weren't effective weapons. I briefly got the idea that I could just spray the stinky stuff at an attacking vampire and ward them off that way, then realized the ridiculousness of that plan. Still, I followed Damon to the kitchen, only to be almost run over by Carolyn and Nick fleeing in the opposite direction.

"You'd better run!" I heard Susanna shouting after them. I realized that she and Carl had somehow broken into the house on the top floor, and because there were two separate stairwells in the house, Carl had pursued me down one of them while Susanna had made her way down the one that led straight to the kitchen. I wasn't used to houses this big and complicated; our house back in town only had the one small staircase that went up to Susanna's room and the attic. This house had three stories, which was much more square footage to deal with.

We had ended up in the living room, the six of us suddenly cornered. That number suddenly changed to five when Tim's astral self winked out of existence, prompting Dennis to say with a sneer, "Oh, that's convenient!"

"And very interesting!" Susanna said, smiling as she stood in the doorway to the kitchen. "I wonder how that works, exactly." She began to slink towards us with an evil grin, her fangs showing prominently. She looked like one of those supposedly sexy but mostly cheesy actresses from those old vampire movies we'd tried to watch, only much more real and threatening.

"Maybe we should let them live long enough to tell us," Carl said, standing on the opposite side of the room by the base of the stairs. His tone was similar to Susanna's, sort of purring in an overly dramatic way. Had he done that at any other time, I might have laughed at him, but he was a lot more scary than I had ever seen him be.

"Guys!" Damon said forcefully. "Weapons! Use them!" He held up his crossbow, then smacked me on the shoulder, prompting me to lift up one of the cans of hairspray I was holding.

"Here," Nick said. He yanked the can from my hand and then quickly reached into his pocket, whipping out his lighter. In an almost lightning-fast motion, he flicked the switch on the lighter and positioned it in front of the can, igniting the aerosol in a quick burst of flame. This surprised me, but when I looked over at Susanna, I saw that she was even more shocked. She lost her confident stance and stopped moving towards us.

"You like that?" Nick asked arrogantly. "How about this?" He again flicked his lighter and sprayed more flame, this time for several seconds. He then began to advance on Susanna.

"Don't hurt her!" Carolyn called out, holding one of her homemade crosses up. As near as I could tell, it was constructed of two butter knives held together with some kind of tape.

"Hold this," Damon said, handing his crossbow to me. I had no idea how to handle such a contraption, but it didn't matter. What he was doing was trading weapons, taking the other can of hairspray from me and pulling another lighter from his own pocket, preparing to create another impromptu flamethrower.

"I thought you quit," Carolyn said to him, but he shushed her with a dismissive gesture. He began stepping in Carl's direction, flicking his lighter and creating another jet of flame. Unlike Nick, he kept his flame burning steadily. I wondered how long it could last.

Carl's confident expression evaporated. The front door was directly to his left, so he grabbed the knob, flung open the door, and raced outside.

"Get her!" someone called from behind me. There was a whoosh of flame, followed immediately by Susanna's bat form flying directly overhead and out the door.

"After them!" I shouted.

We rushed outside and looked around hoping to spot them. But because we no longer had our special night vision, spotting bats in the dark sky was more or less impossible. The fact that the immense porch was covered in massive floodlights didn't help, either.

I got a strange feeling that something was wrong, and after a few seconds of pointlessly scanning the sky, I looked back at the front of the house. Too late, I saw Susanna and Carl perched above the door frame. Before I could say anything, they flew back inside, and the door slammed behind them. I rushed up to it and pounded furiously, and the others joined me once they realized what had happened. The only response I got from inside came from one of the small windows on either side of the door: Carl was flipping us the bird, and I could hear him laughing.

The situation had been reversed, the challenge having become how to get back into the house to change Carl and Susanna back. Despite this, most of us were definitely feeling more confident that we could succeed. That was probably because we finally had weapons, and we had seen their effectiveness as deterrents.

We gathered on the front lawn and tried to figure out what to do. I wondered if they might not be aware of the back door that I had used earlier to take Tim's body out, but Dennis reminded me of how they had flown around the house several times, probably familiarizing themselves with every aspect of it that they could. Besides, we had already locked that door ourselves.

I still liked my idea of setting a trap with the hairspray, but there were two major flaws in that plan: We would have to lure them outside, and they would somehow have to end up standing in the precise spot necessary to get caught by the flames.

"I could just spray some around the porch," I offered.

"Ray, forget it," Carolyn said. "It's just not going to work. And we shouldn't waste however much we've got left."

"She's right," Dennis said. "The flamethrower thing seems to work best, anyway. They seem genuinely afraid of that."

"We could just leave, you know," Nick said, holding up Tim's flashlight, which he'd recovered from the pool area. "We can make it through the tunnel now. If they want to keep on being big spooky vampires and all, why not just let them?"

"Because we're the first people they're going to want to track down and kill!" Carolyn said, incredulous at his suggestion.

Nick rolled his eyes. "Yeah, well, maybe I should just go off on my own."

"No you won't, dipshit," Damon said. "Anyone who strays from the group is vulnerable. We have to stick together."

"Gee, how incredibly not lame and clichéd," Nick said.

"Quit arguing, everybody," I said. "We need to figure stuff out."

There was a bit more going back and forth, and given that my flammable trap idea was out, I fell back on an earlier strategy that had worked: the hose by the pool. Leading everyone around the house to it, I also figured that making sure the Jacuzzi was on would be an added advantage; we might be able to force either or both of the vampires into it. I mentioned this to everyone, then reintroduced Carolyn's idea of filling up those big plastic buckets with water as well.

"Well, so much for that idea," Dennis said, pointing at the side of the house.

I didn't see it at first, but then I did. The hose had been stretched and torn apart right at the base of the faucet, rendering it useless. Either Carl or Susanna must have realized that it was a potential hazard to them. Not surprisingly, we found that they had similarly disabled the hot tub: The control panel for it had been smashed to pieces.

Still, even without these options, we still had our other weapons, and if we could just somehow get the others to come outside and confront us, we'd have a chance to use them. I wondered what they were planning, if they might be about to sneak up on us at any moment. I psychically scanned the house briefly, finding that they were still in the living room, but I couldn't really make out any specifics when it came to their thoughts. All I sensed was a fierce hatred and determination from them.

When I stopped my scan, Tim's astral self reappeared. "I don't suppose you have any ideas?" I asked him. "You've been pretty quiet for a while."

"There is one thing that might work," he said, "but I'm reluctant to try it, and for purely selfish reasons."

"What are you talking about?" Nick asked.

"You've seen how I can use my own powers to influence people. One thing I could try would be to psychically split Susanna and Carl apart, to make the vampire side of them fight with the human side. Both versions are still within them."

I tried to wrap my head around this, to picture what he was saying. I got this image in my mind of his ghostly self turning into some kind of bolt of energy and then zapping Susanna and Carl, separating each of them into two different incarnations, one vampire, one human.

"No, not like that," Tim said, apparently reading my mind. I found the realization that he could do that so easily disturbing. "I said psychically, not physically."

"Does anyone here have the slightest clue what they're talking about?" Nick asked impatiently.

"Kind of," Dennis said, nodding slowly. "You mean kind of jumbling up their minds? Get them to doubt themselves and maybe turn around to our way of thinking?"

"In a sense," Tim said. He still had that same strange way of speaking, like he was some wise old man trying to get us mere children to understand his complex teachings. "But there is a problem."

"And what's that?" I asked.

"To do so would use up a lot of power on my part. I don't think I would be able to recover physically if I were to do that. You would have to let me die."

Everyone pondered this for a few moments. Carolyn looked sad, while Nick looked indifferent, almost bored. I expected him to pipe up with something sarcastic about how Tim would just have to bite the bullet and tell everyone goodbye.

Before he got the chance, I said, "That's not an option. We all need to come out of this alive, each and every one of us. I don't care what it takes."

"I agree," Carolyn said. "There's got to be another way."

"Here goes nothing," Damon said, holding up the crossbow. Per his instructions, I had sprayed a heavy amount of hairspray onto the tip of its arrow, and then after that, Nick stepped forward and lit it. The result was a flaming arrow not unlike those I had seen in movies set in olden days with primitive warriors trying to set fire to their enemies' stronghold.

"This is foolish," Tim's apparition said, his arms folded. "You really should reconsider."

"Pipe down, Casper," Nick said.

Damon smirked, then pulled the trigger and sent the fiery arrow shooting towards the large living room window, the idea being that it would burst through and start a fire, scaring Carl and Susanna out. Instead, the flame went out mid-air, and the arrow bounced harmlessly off the window pane, landing with a disappointing clatter on the porch beneath it.

"Good plan, Damon," Dennis said. "Any more bright ideas?"

"We could try something more substantial," Nick said. "Like lighting a brick on fire and… Oh. Never mind."

"Yeah, right, Nick," Carolyn said. "Why don't you pick up a big fiery brick and burn your hand off?"

"Well, it's better than Captain Poofy Hair's lame-ass idea here!" he shot back.

"There's got to be a way to lure them out," I said.

"They'll come out," Tim said, "eventually."

"We can't wait around for that. We have to be the ones in control."

"Ray's right," Dennis said. "What we really need to do is just break in, bust down the door somehow and rush in, flames ready and all that." He held up a large stick he'd found, the tip of which had also been soaked in hairspray; he'd wanted to make a torch out of it.

"Break in…" Nick said, sounding inspired. "Wait a minute." He paced around for a few seconds. "Hey, Captain Poof, you got a credit card on you?"

Damon sneered at the insult, but then his face brightened. "I see where you're going." He quickly reached into his back pocket, pulled out a wallet, and thumbed through it. "Here," he said, handing a small plastic card to Nick. "You any good at that? I never really learned how, but I knew other guys who could."

"What are you two talking about?" I asked.

"Oh," Carolyn said knowingly. "Okay. Yeah." She smiled. "I'm not going to ask."

"Ask what?" I almost shouted. "Why are we talking about credit cards?" I only had a vague sense of what those were used for, and I couldn't see what money could possibly have to do with our current situation.

Nick led us up the large concrete steps to the front door, Damon's card in hand. "There's this thing you can do," he said, "that works on some locks and not so much on others, but if it works…" He stopped talking as he got down on his knees, his face going right up to the doorknob. "Yeah, I think so. As long as they haven't managed to lock the deadbolt."

He started carefully shoving the credit card into the crack between the door and its frame, moving it back and forth a few times as he made a some barely audible vocal sounds. After about half a minute, his body went still, and then he grabbed at the doorknob and leaned on the door with his shoulder, pushing on it gently. "There," he said, almost in a whisper. "Easier than I thought. Everyone, get ready."

"Okay," Damon said, setting his empty crossbow down. "Here." He positioned Dennis's arm so that his "torch" was held aloft, then used his lighter to ignite it. Dennis looked eagerly at the flame as it burned blue and orange, obviously proud of his newly vital weapon.

"And you," he said, handing me his lighter. My left hand held one of the cans of hairspray. "Light the lighter first, then hold it to the can as you squeeze the nozzle, then let go of the button on the lighter. It's easy." I nodded. He looked over at Carolyn, who had a determined look on her face as she held her shining cross up. We were ready.

I glanced over at Tim, who was still standing at the base of the porch stairs, arms folded and looking on disapprovingly. I wasn't sure why he was being so resistant all of a sudden; maybe he was somehow angry that we didn't go along with his earlier plan, the one that would wind up with us leaving him to die.

"I'll wait here by the door in case they try to slip out again," Nick whispered, "and I'll be ready for them if they do."

I nodded, first at Nick and then at Damon, suddenly finding myself once again reminded of *Miami Vice* with us playing the part of the cops about to bust inside. It occurred to me that we should have placed someone at the back door as well in order to have the place properly surrounded, but it was too late. The plan was in motion.

Nick slammed the door open, then pressed himself against the wall as the rest of us went running inside, weapons at the ready. I looked around the room quickly, making sure to glance up at the ceiling just in case the vampires were perched up there. Damon, Carolyn, Dennis, and I strode into the room confidently, each of us hoping to spot a target. During this, I caught a glimpse of Nick slipping back out the door, his own weapon ready to catch them if they tried to escape.

"Where are they?" Dennis asked.

"Maybe upstairs?" Carolyn offered.

"Or the kitchen," I added.

"You two are the psychics," Damon said. "You tell me."

"Whoa, wait," Carolyn said, her hand reaching out to Damon's arm.

"What?" I asked. By this point, we had reached the middle of the living room, but there was no one else in sight.

"That smell…" she said, looking around. I hadn't noticed anything; the only unusual odor was the one coming from Dennis's makeshift torch. But then I did notice something, a familiar, bitter sort of smell. And there was something else: a hissing sound somewhere to my right. It was coming from the fireplace.

Carolyn froze, looking every bit as frightened as she had earlier in the night when she and I were confronted by the other vampires. She was gripping Damon's arm tightly, and while he looked annoyed at first, he then got the same expression she had. The penny finally dropped in my head as well, and at the same time, he and I shouted, "Run!"

Everyone but Dennis bolted for the door; he was still looking around and trying to figure out what was happening. Because he had come into the house behind us, this meant that Damon bumped into him, causing him to drop his torch. It continued to burn as it hit the carpet, and when Dennis began to kneel down to pick it up, Carolyn shrieked, "Leave it!"

Damon struggled to pull Dennis away, and Carolyn raced out the doorway, telling Nick to run as she passed him. Dennis seemed angry and confused, but then everything finally clicked for him, something I felt telepathically. I wasn't even sure if I had projected a correct understanding of the situation into his mind or if I had just picked up on his own revelation, but it didn't matter.

As we rushed outside, Damon reached for the knob and slammed the door behind us, and we tumbled down the stone steps to the lawn below. Nick kept asking what was going on, and Carolyn shouted something to him about the gas.

"What gas?" he asked. "Did you find them? Where are they?"

My back was to the house, and I watched as Nick's confused expression became even more bewildered as it was illuminated by the sudden brightness. There was a huge whooshing sound accompanied by glass shattering, and I looked behind me to see part of the house exploding. I felt a wave of heat overtake me, and I squinted as I involuntarily shielded my eyes. The living room had been destroyed, and flames began quickly shooting up the sides of the house, smoke pouring out all over the place.

"What the hell?" Nick exclaimed, but then he suddenly squatted down and picked up the can of hairspray that he'd dropped when the house had burst into flames. "Get down!" he shouted at me, and I did, not knowing what was happening.

I saw a bat flying at Nick, but before it could reach him, he flicked his lighter and created a jet of flame from the canister. The bat ran straight into the stream of fire, then instantly transformed into Carl mid-air. Carl continued to fly in a downward arc to the ground, smoke briefly coming from his body until it tumbled to the ground and rolled for several feet.

Running over to him, I could see in the light from the burning house that he was writhing in pain, and I wasn't sure how much of that was from being burned or from changing back from vampire to human. As I reached him, I found that he appeared to be mostly uninjured, but he was still crying out and clutching at his right arm. He was also openly weeping, which I suspected was from the wave of guilt he must be feeling, the same one each of us had experienced.

"Carl!" I called, kneeling down and reaching out to him. He managed to sit up, but he avoided looking at me. "Carl! Are you okay?" He rocked back and forth as he sat, still cradling his arm, which I realized must have been hurt when he landed.

"Your arm!" I said. "Is it broken?"

"I…" he started to say, but then he just cried some more, shaking his head and screwing his eyes shut. The rest of the group rushed up and gathered around.

"Carl, what happened?" Carolyn asked.

"I… I'm sorry, you guys," he said through tears, trying to regain his composure. "I thought that…" He broke down again, unable to do anything but cry and hold his injured arm.

"Let me see," Carolyn said, kneeling down and trying to get a closer look at him.

He snatched away from her, then winced. "It's okay!" he shouted right in her face, then pulled back, looking apologetic. "I mean, I think it's only sprained. I just…" He paused again, looking at the ground to avoid eye contact. "I can't believe what I tried to do in there."

"What do you mean?" I asked. "What did you do?"

Still staring at the ground, he spoke in quick phrases that were occasionally punctuated by heavy sighs and attempts to avoid breaking down in tears. "I got this idea… once we knew that you were trying to b… break back into the house… that I could turn the gas on. The idea was that it… oh, God… I mean, I thought maybe it could put you guys out, like… you know, knock you out, but maybe me and Susanna wouldn't be affected because we were… because we were vampires… I didn't…" He then shrieked, "Oh *God!*" and broke down sobbing, burying his face in his knees as he pulled them up to his chest.

"Susanna!" Carolyn cried out, looking back at the burning house. "Is she still in there? Did she get away?"

Carl shook his head, his face still hidden. "I don't know. I don't know!"

I stood up quickly, looking desperately at the flames. Could my sister still be in there, changed back to human and burning to death?

"Ray!" Carolyn called out to me as I began running back toward the house. Ignoring her, I ran around the corner and back to the pool, vaguely aware that she and at least some of the others were following me.

Keeping an eye on the progress of the blaze, I reached the side of the house and picked up one of the large plastic buckets, then dipped it into the pool to fill it with water. Pulling it back out, I found that it was almost impossibly heavy, but I was determined to carry it back to the front door and try to fight the fire, hopefully finding Susanna and rescuing her.

"That isn't going to work, Ray!" Carolyn shouted, pulling at my shoulder. I shrugged her off, struggling with the bucket. It dropped to the pavement, half of its contents spilling out before I managed to set it upright again.

"We have to help her!" I screamed back. "You guys! Help me!" I directed this to Dennis and Damon, who were standing nearby. Their expressions were reluctant at first, but then they headed over to the empty buckets, looking determined.

"Just fill it up part of the way," Damon said to Dennis as they walked toward the pool.

I looked Carolyn straight in the eye, willing her to see things my way, but not with my psychic powers. I just needed her to stop trying to talk me out of fighting this fire, to either help me or get out of my way. She relented with a strange expression, one that seemed to say, *I still think you're wrong, but I'm going to let you do this.*

Finally unhindered, I began to carry my half-filled bucket of water around to the back of the house, which I realized was burning just as much as the front side. Apparently, the fire had started in both the living room and the kitchen, the stove being a gas appliance as well. Carl had probably turned on the gas flow in both rooms before we had burst in and accidentally started the fire. I had seen scenarios like this on TV a few times before, so I thought I had an idea of how to handle this.

Everything I'd been planning or hoping for suddenly got sidetracked by a voice that rang out in my right ear, growing in volume as it rushed toward me and began to overtake the sound of the house burning next to me. I didn't hear everything it was saying, but the phrase that stood out before I toppled over was something like, "...destroy everything I've worked so hard to build...!"

Susanna slammed into me, my body smashing to the pavement as the bucket I was carrying fell away to the side. Before I knew what was happening, I was on my back, and there was the monstrous version of my big sister on top of me, pinning my arms as she scowled down at me, her fangs seeming to make up her entire mouth as she continued to rail at me almost incoherently.

"Always trying to take over everything and ruin it!" she shrieked at me, gripping my upper arms so tightly that it felt like they were breaking. "I'm going to make you sorry you ever lived!"

My hand managed to find the wooden stake that had been in the pocket of my shorts all this time; I had almost forgotten about it until it popped out and clattered to the pavement when Susanna tackled me. I gripped it tightly, then managed to maneuver it over my chest, pointing up at hers. I wanted more than anything else in the world for this not to be happening.

"Susanna, please," I said, fighting the pain, both physical and emotional. There might be a way out here, but I really didn't want to take it. "Don't..."

"Pleeeeease…" she said mockingly, still looking down at me with those deadly fangs ready for the kill. She lifted my arms up slightly, then slammed me back onto the pavement, causing my head to hit it. Despite the pain, I managed to hold onto the stake, and I knew that I had to use it.

Susanna screwed her eyes shut, an agonized look breaking out across her face. A second later, a horrible shriek emanated from her, her entire body shaking as her face started to rock back and forth just inches from my own. Before I understood what was happening, I felt the pavement around me becoming wet, water pouring over her body and onto mine.

Because I had been struggling against her this whole time, once she loosened her grip, we were both propelled upward from the ground. She rolled off of me and onto her back, her limbs quivering as she screamed and changed back into her real self. Next to us, I saw Carolyn standing there looking on with pity, an empty plastic bucket in her hand.

Once Susanna stopped screaming, she looked at me with tears in her eyes. "I…" she started to say, looking more vulnerable than I had ever seen. She bit her lower lip for a moment as she blinked heavily, shaking her head slowly. "You have no idea how sorry…" she began, but then another explosion rang out from the house.

Susanna stood up shakily, almost falling over. "We have to get out of here," she said firmly, looking over at the flames as they continued to pour out, the smoke looking almost like rapidly moving storm clouds streaming into the sky.

I stood up and looked around, seeing that everyone had eventually gathered near to Susanna, Carolyn, and me. Carl was holding his arm out slightly in a weird way, and he looked like he was still in pain. We were reunited, minus one person.

"Where's Tim?" Susanna asked.

There wasn't much time left. The main house was continuing to burn, and we feared that it wouldn't be long before the flames spread to the surrounding lawn, possibly engulfing the trees and, most importantly, the cottage. Tim's body was still in there, and we had to get him out.

On the way to it, Susanna and Carl were caught up by the rest of us on the details, how Tim was using his powers to keep himself alive, though he'd warned us that his time was running out.

"I need your help," his ghost said to me as we entered the cottage, where his body was still lying on its back like Sleeping Beauty.

In the flickering light coming from the nearby house, I saw Susanna look down at Tim's body, then at his apparition. "That's too weird," she said gravely.

"What do you mean?" I asked Tim.

"Get me out onto the grass," he said, pointing at his own body. "Hurry."

"What are we doing?" Carl asked as he and I picked the limp form up from the floor by its legs and shoulders.

"Just hurry!" Carolyn said.

We carried Tim outside and laid him back down onto the ground as instructed. Carolyn and Damon worked to get the remaining ropes off of him. I had an idea of what was going on here, but what Tim said next surprised me.

"I need you — all of you — to help bring me back to life."

"What?" Carl asked. "What can we do? You and Ray and Dennis are the ones with the superpowers."

"No," Tim said. "It needs to be everyone. Form a circle around my body, then join hands."

"Oh my God," Nick said. "Seriously?"

"Nick, just do it!" I said angrily. It was hard to make out his expression in the uneven mix of darkness and light, but I was pretty sure he was giving me a dirty look.

"Fine," he said. "If he says we have to start singing, I'm out of here." He grabbed my right hand, then reached out to Carl, who was on the other side of him.

"That won't be necessary," Tim said. "But I do need the energy of everyone here in order to make the transfer. Ray, you and Dennis should stand at opposite sides."

We did as he said, the seven of us completing the circle around Tim, our hands joined. It reminded me of some of the games we had played in P.E. at school when I was younger, but I knew that this was much more important. In fact, it was more like some bizarre religious ceremony.

"Concentrate your power," Tim said to me, his ghostly form stepping into the middle of the circle. His transparent self passed right through my arm as he did so, and a strange tingle went through that part of my body. He then stood where his body was lying flat, the bottom part of his astral legs disappearing into it. The apparition closed its eyes, arms held outright in a Christ-like manner.

Without being told, I suddenly knew what to do. I closed my eyes, then imagined my psychic power building up within me. I envisioned it as a luminous greenish electricity that grew from the center of my body and flared up, then began traveling around the ring of people like a big circuit. It flowed clockwise through our arms, flaring again for a split second as it reached each person: Susanna, Carolyn, Damon, Dennis, Carl, Nick, me, and then around again. Each loop of energy took several seconds at first, but it got faster each time. I could hear a sound effect of it in my head, a pulsing rhythm, and it got faster and stronger with every loop.

The rapidly increasing circuit continued to pulse through us, and what started out as a slow *whoomp, whoomp, whoomp* grew into a faster *whoompwhoomp whoompwhoomp* the longer it went on. Everyone's life energy was connected. A new sound began to appear, a higher pitched *whsshew, whsshew* that overlaid everything and fit with the original rhythm. I opened my eyes, and I was shocked to find that the green lightning I'd been picturing in my mind was in fact real, its powerful glow whipping around the chain of us just as I had pictured it. In the center of the circle, Tim's ghost was glowing with the same color, and the spot where his astral self connected to his physical body was marked by an ever brightening green aura. Whatever we were doing, it seemed to be working.

Yet another sound was added to the mix, something that sounded like police car sirens, but it wasn't quite in sync with the energy we were creating. Once I was aware of it, the pulse circling through us slowed down, but I could still tell that it was doing its intended work.

The ghostly version of Tim opened its eyes and smiled, and then it began descending into Tim's body. At almost the same time, the electricity that had been looping around the rest of us suddenly shot inwards, a huge blaze of light seeming to wipe out everything in my field of vision. I simultaneously felt something rushing out of me and something else pushing me backwards, and I lost my grip on Nick's and Susanna's hands, toppling back onto the grass. The weird sights and sounds stopped suddenly, and there I was, my legs splayed on the ground as I quickly propped myself up with my arms.

Tim was doing the same thing, and he looked around at us, surprised. "You're all okay!" Then he looked behind me. "Whoa. That house is on fire." He said it so matter-of-factly that I almost laughed.

"I don't think anyone saw us," Carolyn said, closing the trapdoor behind her.

Both the fire department and the police had shown up at the house just after we had finished bringing Tim back to life. Apparently, someone had seen the fire and reported it. We couldn't risk being caught and having to explain ourselves, so we had to sneak through the woods in order to get to the tunnel's entrance. Fortunately, the law enforcement officials and rescue workers were fully occupied with trying to put out the fire, which by then had spread to the entire house.

There probably wouldn't be much of it left, but we couldn't stick around long enough to find out for fear of being spotted.

"Even if they didn't," Susanna said, "there's still a chance that they might find this tunnel."

"Yeah, or maybe someone else later on," Dennis said.

"Right. We can't risk that. We need to collapse this thing." As she said this, she pointed at the roof of the tunnel, and Nick shone his flashlight upward.

"Can we do that?" Carolyn asked.

"If enough of us touch it and make it crumble, I think so." She reached over and quickly rubbed her hand in a deliberate arc along the far wall, and a huge amount of dirt spilled out from it and onto the floor of the tunnel. It was more than I had ever seen come out when this effect happened; in the past, we had always touched the walls lightly, producing a relatively tiny amount of freed soil.

"Was this what you were talking about before, Tim?" I asked.

"Hmm? When?"

"Earlier. Something about a mystical force… a worm, or wormhole… something. I don't know."

"I really don't know what you're talking about," he said.

"In the woods! Back when…"

"Oh!" he said. "You mean when I was passed out. I'm sorry; I don't remember anything that this supposed ghost-me said or did. I really don't."

"Seriously?" Carolyn asked. "Not one thing?"

"Nope. As far as I'm concerned, I was about to get bitten by all of you, and it felt like I was having a heart attack, and then I woke up in the grass with all of you sitting around me. It felt kind of like time traveling once I realized how long I'd been out."

"Well, that's weird," Carl said.

"That's enough, everyone," Susanna said impatiently. "We have to take care of this. Help me. Nick, you stand back over there and hold the light so we can see."

"Yes, ma'am," he said sarcastically, but he did as he was told.

Following Susanna's lead, Damon, Carolyn, and Carl (though he only used one arm) reached up and touched the roof around the trapdoor, then quickly moved out of the way as mounds of dry dirt came toppling down. The rest of us repeated the process on the walls, which began to tumble inwards. It was a strange thing to see, plus I was a little bit afraid that too much might flow out and end up burying us. But we were fine as long as we got out of the way in time. When we were done, the entire end of the passageway was filled in, and there was no longer any access to the door.

As we made our way back to the house, we stopped several times to collapse more sections of the tunnel, just to be safe. Between those efforts, we talked some about what had happened. Once Tim understood how far apart the two houses were, he began going off on some scientific babble about the tunnel having some kind of space warping properties or something, but nobody was all that interested. We were just too exhausted.

The previous two summers, once everyone was turned back to normal, we were mostly in a good mood, apologizing for turning on each other but otherwise thinking that what we had gone through was pretty cool. We had survived and gotten away with everything without getting caught, and that was the fun of it. But there was none of that excitement or goodwill this time around. We were ashamed of what we had done, even embarrassed.

As a result, our conversation on the way home was limited. Whenever we did talk, it was usually brief, and one of us would apologize for trying to hurt the others or express some kind of regret. That would result in awkward silence, everyone feeling uncomfortable.

"I don't even think we were really ourselves by the end there," Carl said. "We just got so, I don't know, vicious. Like, more than we ever had been. Do you think it was because of the newer potion?" No one said anything. "Susanna?"

"Maybe," was all she said. I wanted her to say something else, to give some kind of explanation for why things got as bad as they did, but she kept quiet. I tried to reach out and give her a sort of telepathic prod, but then I noticed something. That familiar tingle I got in my head when I'd use my psychic powers wasn't there. I tried again to feel it, but it just wouldn't happen.

"Dennis," I said to him quietly, "are your powers working?"

"Nope," he said rather calmly, almost like he didn't care. "All gone. Yours too?"

"Yes! It's like they're... I don't know! Just gone!"

"Thought so. Tim?"

"Yeah, me too," he said. "I think we used them up when you guys were doing that... whatever it was that brought me back. Like I said, I don't remember any of it, so who knows."

This disappointed me a great deal. I'd always liked my powers; being psychic and able to do cool things like that had been fun. But then again, I had always thought the same thing about being a vampire, which I had definitely soured on by this point. Turning myself into a monster that went around killing innocent people wasn't something that was fun and exciting. It was unbelievably horrible, and I regretted every second of it, which was made worse by the fact that I could actually recall all of the details this time, not just of this summer, but all the ones before.

"Maybe it's just as well," Tim said. "Maybe we weren't meant to have such powerful... I don't know... abilities like that."

"Yeah," Nick said, "look how good of a job you did handling them."

"Nick..." I said with an aggravated tone.

"What?" he shot back.

I was ready to say something angry back to him, but I decided against it. "Nothing."

By the time we got back to the basement, all attempts at friendly conversation had died out. Even Carolyn and Damon were barely talking, though they did stick close to each other, occasionally whispering things I couldn't hear. We stuck to practicalities, accomplishing what we needed to in order to put this mess behind us. Tim still blamed himself for starting the entire thing by suggesting that we take the potion back in 1983, but really, there was plenty of blame and guilt to go around.

"So I guess this is the last one," I said, gesturing to the tunnel entrance. "Collapse this one like we did the one at the other house?"

"Definitely," Susanna said. "But before we do, let me just say one thing. This ends here. We're burying this part of our past and never, ever coming back to it. Not one of you is to say anything about it to a single soul for the rest of our lives. I know we all feel terrible about what we did, and that's a good thing, really, but it won't do any of us any good to get all confessional some point further down the road. If anyone talks," she paused, looking at Tim, "or goes to the police or anything stupid like that, we're all screwed. We could go to jail, or worse. Just saying 'I'm sorry' isn't going to cut it."

She looked around at the rest of us, reminding me of some of the teachers I'd had when they would lecture the entire class after we had been misbehaving. The difference here was that she was just as guilty as we were, just as capable of being implicated if word ever got out that we had been responsible for all of the vampire-related carnage that Augusta had endured all these years.

"Do I have everybody's word that you'll keep quiet about this?" She was so authoritative and forceful that there was no room for dissent, but honestly, I agreed with everything she'd said and was pretty sure that the others felt the same way. Everyone nodded solemnly.

"All right," she said. "So let's finish this."

We had been standing in the basement while this lecture had been going on, but then we stepped back into the entrance to the tunnel, repeating our method of using our hands to deactivate whatever the magical substance or spell was that kept the walls, roof, and floor in place. The dirt flowed inwards and filled the space up, and soon enough, what had once been a dark and mysterious opening leading out of our basement was just a grey, sandy, rectangular hole in the wall. We moved the shelves we had previously used to cover up this hole back into place, and with that, we were finished.

There was still a little more cleaning up to be done around the house, which we'd start on the next morning when we got up. After that, my friends would all go home. We hoped that things would be okay, that we could eventually put this guilt behind us and move on, and that we were done with this vampire business once and for all.

We were wrong.

PART FOUR

"Come on," my father said, lightly kicking my foot with his. "He's got to have a name."

"I know," I said impatiently, turning to look at the tiny beagle puppy wobbling on my bedspread, sniffing around and getting to know his new environment. "I just... I don't know." The little black, white, and brown animal didn't look how I expected a beagle to look; I thought that they were white with black ears. My first notion upon being told that he was a beagle was to call him Snoopy, but that seemed stupid given that he looked nothing like the cartoon character. And it seemed too obvious. I also didn't care.

I hadn't asked for this dog, and quite frankly, I didn't feel like I deserved to have it. My father had taken it upon himself to surprise me with him on my birthday, and while I couldn't deny that he was cute and all that, any enthusiasm I expressed over his arrival was mostly faked. Being presented with him just made me feel worse, but I couldn't admit that to my parents, not without telling them the truth. That was completely out of the question.

When they had arrived home after their three-week trip to San Francisco on Saturday, they were surprised to find me and Carolyn in such gloomy moods. The real reason for that was much deeper and darker than anything we could ever tell them, so the only explanation we could give was the lie we told about what had happened to Crowley. The story was that he had gotten run over by a car, and we were both just really upset about it. In truth, we were, but there were a lot more deaths on our consciences than just that one.

I was used to lying to my parents and hiding things from them. It was something that came naturally to me; I'd done it all my life. Aside from making things up to get out of trouble for various little things through the years, there was also the vampire secret. Each time my parents returned from their trips after my friends, sisters, and I had just finished committing horrible atrocities around the city, we acted like nothing had gone on during their absence, and they bought it every single time. The loss of Crowley this time around meant that we had to at least own up to that, but of course we cloaked it in yet another lie.

"How about Ajax?" my father offered.

"What? Dad, that's a floor cleaner, isn't it?"

He laughed and rolled his eyes, then looked down at me with amusement. "No. I mean, yes, maybe it is, but Ajax was also a hero of the Trojan War. Have you read about that in school yet?"

"That was the thing with the horse, right?" I vaguely recalled the story. "This is a dog, not a horse." I winced inside, feeling guilty for briefly finding myself in a joking mood. It passed quickly.

"I know, Ray," he said, nudging me playfully. "But you're right. Maybe that one's a bit too pretentious." I just looked down at my feet, not wanting to make eye contact.

Being such a literary man, my father had started off saying that I should name the puppy after a famous author, first suggesting Byron, who was apparently some big poet from a couple hundred years ago. I'd never heard of him. I put a stop to this line of reasoning immediately after my father's next offering, Bram. There was no way I was going to name this new pet after the guy who wrote *Dracula*, not after what we had been through this summer. I overreacted slightly to this suggestion, then had to try to cover that up. Apparently taking the hint, my father changed tactics and began coming up with names of characters from literature.

There was Old Dan from *Where the Red Fern Grows*, which I remembered having to read in fourth grade. But it seemed stupid to name such a young dog "Old" anything. I had a similar aversion to the name Old Yeller, especially because the only thing I could remember about that book, or more specifically the movie adaptation we watched in school, was how it ended. The last thing I wanted to think about was animals that wound up getting killed.

"There's Argos, too," my dad offered. "You like that one?"

"Hmm," I said as the toy-sized animal moved up behind me on the bed and began sniffing at my back. I turned around to face him, drawing one leg up underneath me and reaching out to pet him. He flinched, then began licking my fingers. That was cute, but I wasn't in the mood for it. "Maybe."

"Argos belonged to Odysseus," my father began, then regaled me with the story of *The Odyssey* and how this man left his faithful dog behind to take this big journey around the world, then came home after many years to find the dog still waiting for him. The dog was old and decrepit by then, and it died soon after. Again, I wasn't thrilled with the idea of dead pets, but I did kind of like the sound of the name.

Still, my foul mood permeated things and kept me feeling cynical. I couldn't help but notice that this conversation was one of the longest I could remember having with my father in ages, and the past couple of days had been the most time we had spent together in years. He and I just weren't that close. He wasn't mean to me or anything, and I didn't hate him; there just never seemed to be any close father-son connection, the kind I thought my friends had with their fathers or the type I would see in family sitcoms. He went to work, paid for things, made small talk at dinner, occasionally had a boring story to tell, and all that. But I never really felt that I could relate to him, to talk to him about anything that was truly important to me. That may have been partly my fault, as I spent so much of my life trying to fake him and my mother out, to slip things past them. But the older I got, the more I resented our lack of closeness, and his sudden interest in me and this new dog struck a nerve in a way I didn't entirely understand.

As these thoughts ran through my head, I vetoed the name Argos with a small amount of smug satisfaction, feeling a bit like I was the one who was always being left behind and neglected, not the fictional dog from the story he was telling.

My father sighed, then thought for a moment. "Pip?"

"What?"

"Pip. He's the main character in *Great Expectations.* Have you read that yet?" I hadn't, though I would the following year at my new school.

"No way. Sounds way too… yippy. Like the dog is going to be yapping and barking all the time."

My father paused. "There's another character called Pocket," he said, lifting the little dog up to his face. The puppy looked over at me with uncertainty, an irritatingly adorable expression that seemed to say, *Get me away from this goofy guy.* I fought back a laugh. "Pocket's a good name!" Dad said in a high pitched voice directed at the dog, pulling him closer. "He's so small! He can fit right in your pocket!" As he said this, he shoved the squirming furry figure at me, first at my face and then down towards my hip. The dog struggled further until he was released, then bounded off the side of the bed and onto the floor.

For a moment, I feared that such a long drop might have been too much for him, and I instinctively knelt down and reached for him, hoping he wasn't hurt. He was fine, and he again approached my outstretched hand and began sniffing and licking at it.

The conversation was beginning to get old. Here was my father trying to act all cute and funny with this loveable little bundle of responsibility he had thrust upon me, and deep down, all I felt was a profound sense of sadness, guilt over everything I had done the past few years. I'd had a pet, and I'd gotten him killed because my friends and sisters and I had grown arrogant enough to put him in harm's way. But I couldn't say a word about any of that; I had to play along.

Many years earlier, my father and I had gone through a similar process, one I had enjoyed at the time. We had combed through my dinosaur books to try to find a name for the lizard I had recently acquired, a small, green anole that I had managed to catch and keep in a jar. My first real passion as a kindergartner had been dinosaurs, and I liked lizards because I knew that they were related to dinosaurs, only smaller. So my dad came up with the idea of compiling a list of names based on the names of actual dinosaurs, like Ally (based on Allosaurus) or Teri (based on Pterodactyl). Eventually, we settled on Rex. The lizard died after a few days, and I was as heartbroken as a six-year-old could be.

"Well, he won't always be," I said.

"Won't always be what?"

"Pocket. Pocket-sized, I mean. How big's he gonna get?"

"Mmm, about the size of a large..." he broke off for some reason. "Well, about this high." He held his hand about ten inches above the surface of the bed.

I stood up and walked over to where the still unnamed puppy had settled into the corner of my bedroom next to the closed door. He was looking up at me with a sheepish expression, and I was annoyed at how endearing I found that. I was ready for this drawn out naming process to be over, and I had half a mind to just declare that his name was Spot and be done with it. Maybe I would grow to like him in time, but for the moment, I just couldn't bring it upon myself to give a damn.

"How about Scout?" my father said, and I looked back at him as he sat there looking eager. His expression wavered as he added, "Technically, that was a female character, but..." He trailed off, looking disappointed, and I heard a strange, rapid ticking sound behind me. I looked back and saw that the puppy was squatting down, a puddle of clear liquid spilling out from behind it onto the hardwood floor, knowing who was going to have to clean it up.

"'Scout' it is, then," I said angrily.

So this was my life. I had spent four years of it having one episodic adventure after another as this stealthy, secretive vampire along with my similarly wicked sisters and delinquent friends, only to be reduced to a guilt-ridden, reticent 13-year-old cleaning up dog piss in the corner of my bedroom. Over the course of the next year or so, I did eventually warm up to Scout and enjoy his company, but it was a slow process. For one thing, I was too caught up in everything else I was feeling, most of it negative.

All teenagers feel misunderstood and alone, but none — or at least almost none — of the ones I knew had a burden like mine. Aside from my guilty conscience over all the wrong I had done, there was also this underlying fear of being found out. What if one of the other former vampires broke down and decided to tell the police, their parents, or someone else? We had all sworn to each other that we wouldn't, but did that really mean anything? The best I could do was to just try to get over things and move on, to trust that the others would keep their promise and not rat us out. I certainly wasn't going to speak up and confess anything, so I hoped that everyone else had the good sense not to as well.

Whenever I felt confident that our secret was safe — it had been for years, after all — I was left with another feeling, one I found hard to understand at the time. Things just felt more empty, sort of lifeless. In the past, each time we had gone back to normal after being vampires, there was still that notion in the back of my mind that we might do it again in a year or two. Whatever had happened, good and bad, and most of which I wouldn't clearly recall until the next time the potion was in my system, we could try again and do things better. We would have more fun and get away with more bad stuff. But that idea was right out from this point on. There was no way we were ever going to allow ourselves to become that evil and depraved again. And although it shouldn't have, that made me a little sad.

In lieu of the excitement the potion had once given us, I was left to pursue a normal, ordinary life, and I tried to be optimistic about that, but it didn't really work. When my popularity had waned in seventh grade, I began to look forward to eighth grade, knowing that I would be going to a brand new school with entirely different people. I wasn't sure why none of my classmates would be attending Bethlehem Baptist

School, why their parents chose to send them elsewhere instead, but I actually liked that. It meant that I could start over, and I vowed that I would find out just who the "in crowd" was and hook up with them as quickly as possible.

My resentment of my classmates at St. Joseph's abated as our time there wound down, and that summer was meant to be the biggest and greatest vampire session ever. In a sense, it was, but only to the extent that things got so out of control that we kind of imploded on ourselves, wrecking any chance or wish to take that damn potion ever again.

There had been a little bit of damage to our house when Life Force had attempted their assault, but Susanna, Carolyn, and Damon were able to pay for quick repairs before our parents came back. My friends did what they could to help, but they were also pretty mad that a lot of their belongings had been lost in the fire at the other house. I had lucked out in that I hadn't gotten around to moving much of my stuff there before everything fell apart, but I quickly shut up about being relieved about that once I realized how disappointed my friends were. Fortunately for them, some of their clothes had been left in the laundry room at my house, so at least they didn't have to go home empty-handed. As for what they might have to tell their parents about what happened to the rest of their things, I left that up to them. I had enough lies and excuses to come up with to cover my own ass.

The city of Augusta went more or less back to normal as far as I knew. Our attacks had stopped, so there was no longer an immediate threat. Still, this had been our most drawn-out killing spree so far, which meant that the body count was higher than ever. There was some mention on the news of the police continuing to investigate for a short time, but that quickly tapered off, and I immediately lost interest in the news.

My birthday was the Sunday following my parents' return, and it was a pretty terrible time. Usually, my sisters and friends would be there for the party and I would get lots of cool presents, but I could barely stand to go through the motions this time. Susanna didn't even stay in town; she ducked out before Mom and Dad got back. I told my friends that I didn't feel like celebrating, which they were fine with. My parents, though, insisted on at least having a low-key party, and they gave me the various things they had planned to, most of them trinkets they had picked up on their trip.

I did my best to be grateful and tried to be happy, but my overall melancholy was hard to hide. In a way, Crowley's death was sort of convenient in that it served as an excuse to hide the bigger reason for my gloom. This led my father to take an extra day off work to get me Scout, which bothered me more than it comforted me.

"I know it's hard," he said to me, "but you have to learn to move on and take on new challenges. A new pet will give you something to focus on, to take your mind off how bad you feel about the last one." Maybe it did. But it didn't make up for all of the other terrible things I'd done.

It didn't take very long for my new school to disappoint me. Going into a new place not knowing anyone had sounded exciting to me at first. The fact that it was a small school didn't bother me, either, even though some of my former classmates had commented on this, like that somehow made it bad. I was looking forward to something different. But while the teachers at Bethlehem were all smiles and friendliness when I first applied to the school and then later when I attended my first day, I got a cold reception from most of the students, many of whom had known each other for years.

My plan to zero in on the popular kids and hook up with them was sabotaged on that first day. After the formalities of first period — which included me being introduced to the class — had wound down, this guy named Aaron bounded over to me and decided that he wanted to be friends. I didn't like the look of him; he seemed like a major geek. Talking to him only confirmed this.

By the time lunch came around, I had figured out that Aaron and his small group of friends were not the people to be hanging around if I wanted to be thought of as cool. I had learned the basics of this at my previous school, picking up not only on people's traits but also the way others looked at and acted towards them. Willing to risk hurting the geeky group's feelings, I ditched them to sit with another group of guys who seemed more laid back and interesting. They weren't exactly jocks, but they seemed more confident and fun, so I adopted my best cool swagger and asked if I could sit with them.

"Sure, man!" one guy said, but I wasn't sure if his friendliness was genuine. There was something sarcastic in his tone, but I tried to ignore it, maybe out of wishful thinking. As I settled into an orange plastic chair and pulled myself up to the table, the boy looked around at his friends, who had uncertain looks on their faces.

"Looks like there's going to be a major Transformer meeting after school again," he said to one of the other boys. No one did any formal introductions, but I would eventually learn that his name was Kirby. Our names would come out in conversation as everyone talked to each other, and there was no need for me to tell them mine, as they already knew it.

"A what?" I asked.

Another boy, Chris, let out a goofy laugh. "Aaron and Jay and them," he said, gesturing to the table where my former acquaintance was sitting with his friends. "Gonna have a major Transformer meetin'."

I wondered briefly if this meant that Transformers were for some reason considered cool among the people at this school, but I quickly realized as the conversation progressed that instead, Aaron and his friends were considered the bottom of the food chain because they were complete nerds, and their being interested in Transformers was one aspect of that. Apparently, one of them had said something at school the previous year along the lines of them having a "Transformers meeting" so they could get together and play with their toys. It was something this group of cooler guys had made fun of them for ever since.

"You're not into all that shit, right?" Kirby asked me.

"Me? Oh, no, definitely not." I turned to glance briefly at the other boys' table. "What a bunch of dorks."

Chris laughed heartily. "'Dorks!' Haven't heard anyone use that word in a long time!"

I felt my face get hot, then looked down at my sandwich, eagerly taking a bite out of it to try to avoid the moment. After swallowing, I looked back up and hoped that things would take a turn for the better.

"So," Kirby said, an odd look on his face. He was smiling at me, but there was something mildly predatory in there as well. "What kinda cars do you like?"

I knew almost nothing about cars aside from the fact that you got into them and they went places. My father had bought cars for both Susanna and Carolyn when they'd turned sixteen, and at the time, I had been excited along with them. Susanna loved her Toyota Celica Supra, and I knew the name of that car well because she repeated it so many times when she'd first gotten it.

"I don't know," I said, trying to sound nonchalant but still interested. "Toyotas are kinda cool."

The table erupted in laughter, and I felt like I had suddenly become several inches smaller. I looked down at my stupid baloney and cheese sandwich and suddenly found the way the mustard was seeping out between the layers of meat and cheese to be the most detailed and important thing in the world. "I mean…" I managed to whisper, but I couldn't think of what to follow it up with.

"Naw, naw, it's okay!" Kirby said, reaching out like he was going to put his hand on my shoulder, but then resting it on the edge of the table, his laughter subsiding. "Japanese cars are *cool!*"

The other boys, all four of them, laughed again, this time a little less heartily. I hated being laughed at, but I tried to salvage the situation.

"Yeah, I know," I said, still trying to sound cool. "That's what my sisters drive. My dad's just kind of into that. He's all proud of his station wagon."

"Station wagon?" Chris asked with a smirk. "Doesn't anyone in your family drive a Mustang or something cool?"

"Well, no," I said, but I tried to keep my tone disdainful like theirs. "My father's kinda… I don't know…" I tried desperately to dig myself out. "He's like… 'This here's the Pontiac Grand Safari!'" I held my hand out, gesturing to an imaginary vehicle like someone on a game show. As I continued to speak, I did so with an exaggerated southern accent, the kind my father would only get whenever he was mad or excited. "Biggest and best model they ever made!"

The guys laughed, and it finally seemed like they were laughing with me, not at me.

Over the course of my first few days there, I got a handle on the different cliques. There was Aaron's, whom I avoided as much as possible, and Kirby's, whom I tried to get in with, but that never really went anywhere. The girls in the class had their own corresponding groups of misfits and popular people, most of the latter being junior varsity cheerleaders. And then there was another group, the smarter, well behaved Christian kids. The religious aspect of this school was something I had known about going in, but it would be a while before I would realize how much more prominent it was compared to my old school.

It had occurred to me when I knew I would be going there that maybe I could find myself a girlfriend among all these new and interesting people. I'd certainly had my fill of being rejected by the girls at St. Joseph's, so I hoped that things would be better at Bethlehem. They weren't.

For one thing, I found a lot of these girls intimidating. They all seemed so much more grown up than what I was used to, but that may have been because even though the girls in seventh grade had begun to mature, become more stylish, and develop more teenager-like attitudes, I still knew who they had been when they were younger. The girls in eighth grade were strangers and were even more done up, all make-up and heavily sprayed permed hair, looking a lot more like high schoolers to me. I knew that mathematically we were the same age, but it didn't feel like it. I therefore had no idea how to approach them, which left me feeling disappointed and lonely.

There was one girl in particular who caught my eye, a tremendously coiffed blonde named Elizabeth Morgan. I wasn't even sure if I actually liked her or not at first, if she was truly attractive or just oddly fascinating. While most of the popular girls had that advanced sense of style that made me nervous, they were still young enough to be slightly awkward with it. One of the cheerleaders, Annie, went through a period where she wore this bizarre looking silver eye shadow that didn't suit her at all, and I also noticed that one of the Christian girls, Tammy, wore this slimy looking pink lipstick that looked almost exactly like she had Pepto Bismol on her lips. These girls would eventually learn what worked and what didn't work for them, but they were still relatively new to it all.

What made Elizabeth so bizarre was how she had absolutely none of that awkwardness, at least not physically. Her hair and make-up were so perfectly flawless that she looked like she'd just stepped off the set of a soap opera or had a hobby of winning beauty contests in her spare time. She looked out of place, maybe like she was trying too hard to be pretty, but she genuinely was. She had a broad smile and deep, captivating blue eyes, but she was also very quiet. One would think that a girl who was so gorgeous would be part of the popular crowd, but she wasn't. She was part of a trio of girls who were sort of between the cheerleaders and the uptight Christians, a corollary to — or maybe the antithesis of — Aaron's dorky group.

Elizabeth's two friends, Helen and Melinda, were the more outspoken ones of the trio. Sometimes I was able to joke around with them, but I found myself more nervous and tongue-tied around

Elizabeth. I got this weird feeling about her, but I wasn't sure why. She kind of looked like someone I might have seen on TV, maybe one of those hokey newscasters Carolyn and I used to make fun of. I couldn't be certain. She was both fascinating and strange.

My crush on her officially began about a month into the school year when I needed to borrow a pen for a test; I had somehow lost mine on my way to class. After unsuccessfully asking several students if I could borrow one, I found my way to Elizabeth's desk, where she was already holding up a blue pen and looking at me with a slight smile.

As I thanked her and took the pen, she said slyly, "You'd better not lose it."

My mind raced for something funny to say, but the best I could come up with was: "What if I do?"

She looked away and back toward the paper on her desk, raising her eyebrows as she said nonchalantly, "Then I guess you won't do very well on the test."

I burned inside from the comeback, but I admitted to myself later that it was a pretty good one. After class, I tried to return the pen to her, but she said I could keep it. I then tried to make some small talk about the test and how I didn't think I did very well on it, but this was interrupted by Melinda.

"Come on, Elizabeth," she said impatiently, holding her stack of books to her chest. "Quit wasting time talking to that loser." That stung, but then she laughed and said to me as she leaned forward, "I'm just kidding!" It was one of the most fake tones I had ever heard a girl speak in. I had in fact also found Melinda attractive when I'd first met her, but all of that evaporated in that moment. Even so, despite the embarrassment surrounding these encounters, I was hooked. I wanted Elizabeth to be my girlfriend, but I had absolutely no idea how to make that happen.

It didn't even occur to me to ask my father for advice. I had long since learned that whenever I did ask him about something, he would just refer me to a book. I never got the "birds and the bees" talk from him; I got the *World Book Encyclopedia* article titled "Sex." My father just wasn't very good when it came to talking, which was one more reason to resent him.

My mother wasn't much help, either, as whenever I would ask her about something, she'd just tell me to ask my father. What I didn't realize at the time was that I probably seemed just as closed off to them, particularly the older and more private I became. I was used to keeping secrets, both those of a supernatural kind and the more mundane aspects of adolescent life. The fact that my days were becoming much more filled with the latter bothered me, but there was nothing I could do about it.

"Why don't you just talk to her?" Tim asked me over the phone.

"I do!" I said. "I mean, I try to. But she's got these two bitchy friends who kind of try to keep her away from me."

"Well, maybe things will work out for you," Tim said. "You've just got to keep hoping." That wasn't much help. After a pause, he said more gently, "You doing okay otherwise? Like, with the whole, you know…"

"I'm fine," I blurted out impatiently. Surprised, I tried to recover. "I mean, yeah, I guess. I try not to think about that whole thing if I can help it."

"Yeah, me too," he said, sounding sad. Tim hadn't been my first choice of friends to talk to, but when I had tried to call both Dennis and Nick earlier, I was told that they weren't home. Carl and I had only spoken once since the end of our vampire session that summer, and while he wasn't unfriendly to me, he didn't strike me as the right person to talk to about this deeply personal stuff. Of all my friends, Tim was the most accessible, and it occurred to me later on that he was the only one who ever actually called me without my calling him first.

"Sort of," he continued. "I guess I do think about it, but in a repentant way."

"A what?"

"Well, part of moving on from something is asking for forgiveness, and it's not like we can really do that, you know, from the people who died. But sometimes I think of their souls and hope that they're out there somewhere, and maybe if I keep telling them and God that I'm sorry, it will somehow make up for it."

His tone was somewhat wistful and was probably meant to be inspiring, but what he was saying actually scared the hell out of me. The idea of the ghosts of all of our past victims looking down on us from heaven was the farthest thing from comforting that I could imagine, to say nothing of what God himself might think of us and what we'd done.

"Yeah, he's gotten a little weird like that," Dennis said to me. It had been a couple of months since we had last talked on the phone, so we had a lot to catch up on. I had in fact spoken to Tim two more times before this conversation, and I told Dennis how Tim's newfound surge in Christian-centered thought was rather off-putting. I didn't necessarily disagree with what he had to say most of the time, but it did seem strange.

"You've talked to him, too?" I asked.

"Not much. A couple of times. For some reason, he seems to want to keep calling, like he wants to check up on me and see if I'm okay."

I laughed, having experienced some of that myself. But while Dennis sounded annoyed or at the very least nonchalant about this, I empathized with Tim on that point. I too wanted to know that my friends were all right after everything that had happened. I wasn't as pushy about it, but it still mattered to me.

"I guess he feels more guilty than the rest of us," I offered. "Like he said, he was the one who came up with the idea for using the potion in the first place."

"And he was the one who took us all down in the end," he added. "That betrayal and all. He probably feels guilty about that, too."

"I don't know. That one's a little harder to figure out."

"How do you mean?"

I tried to think of the right words. "It's just… I get the feeling that he thinks he saved us from ourselves by doing that. Like, 'Gee, thanks Tim for almost getting us all killed!'" I laughed at my own joke, but Dennis only halfway did.

"Now that I think about it, though…" He broke off, not finishing his thought.

"What?"

"Well, it's just that once we brought him back to life, it was like he didn't remember everything. All that stuff he did as a ghost, you know?"

"So?"

"I… I don't know. I'm not sure where I was going with that." He paused. "I mean, I remember everything we did. All of it. All the grim and gory details, and it freaks me out if I think about it too hard."

"Yeah, me too," I admitted.

"So maybe he's got a point. Maybe we do need forgiving."

"Don't tell me you're getting all Jesus-y on me too, Dennis!" I said with a laugh.

"Oh, shut up. You know what I mean."

"I guess." This wasn't something I liked to think about. I had always been brought up to believe in God, but it wasn't something that was very prominent in my life. To me, God was this sort of vague thing that existed, someone big and up there in the clouds watching over everything. I was used to sneaking around and trying to get away with things as far as parents, teachers, and other authority figures were concerned, but I knew deep down that the big invisible overseer of the universe knew everything. Still, no lightning bolts had struck me yet, so I liked to think that either God was too busy to pay close enough attention to me, or else maybe he really was as forgiving as I'd heard people say. Overall, if I thought about this too closely, it bothered me, so I did my best to avoid the concept. But given where I grew up, that was sometimes difficult.

"Speaking of that, how are you liking Bethlehem Baptist?" he asked me.

I sighed. "It's... It's okay. Just not what I expected." Dennis laughed, but I wasn't sure why. "What?"

"Oh, I was just wondering how much fun it might be there with all those uptight Baptists."

"They're not uptight!" I said defensively. "They're just... I don't know, different, I guess." My voice lowered as I lost my conviction. "Yeah, okay, so they are a little weird sometimes, at least compared to the stuff we had at St. Joseph's."

Dennis maintained his light tone as I explained to him how things were at Bethlehem. Every week at St. Joseph's, the entire school had attended chapel services at an adjacent church for an hour. There were hymns, prayers, recitations of scripture — the same passages every time, in fact — and a sermon from the priest which was often generic but was occasionally tied to the time of the year, like a Thanksgiving-themed story or something to do with Christmas. Some students wore robes and carried candles, and it all seemed very theatrical and a bit hokey to me, but I didn't necessarily dislike it. It never really felt all that repressive or anything; it was just something we had to go through, no different from sitting through English class or trying to get through the rigorous physical trials of P.E.

My family usually only attended church on Sundays twice a year at Easter and Christmas, and when we did that, it was at a huge Baptist church in town that dwarfed St. Joseph's Parish. The place was enormous and recently built, yet to me, their ceremonies seemed a lot less formal and more relaxed. No one wore fancy robes or carried big candles around, nor were there padded benches one had to kneel on during the prayers. Everyone just wore nice suits or dresses and behaved themselves by being quiet and respectful of this thing we called God. None of it really mattered to me all that much; I just went through the motions and did what I was supposed to do, usually daydreaming throughout the more boring parts of the service.

So my impression of what Baptists were versus what Episcopalians were was pretty basic. To me, Baptists were more cool and normal while Episcopalians were all ceremonial and a bit strange. Once I knew I was headed to Bethlehem for eighth grade, I was looking forward to things being less official and structured, a misconception I would eventually look back on and laugh about.

I told Dennis that, and he just chuckled again. "And so...?" he asked with a leading tone, a smile in his voice.

"They're really into it here," I said with an exasperated sigh. "I'm mostly okay with it, but... well... Yeah, we still have Chapel every week like back then. But there's no church, so we just have it in the lunchroom, the entire school sitting in there while this guy stands up in front and gives his talk or whatever. That part's not so bad."

"Doesn't sound all that different," Dennis said. "Maybe just a little more dinky."

"Yeah. But then, before almost every class, they do a devotional."

"A what?" He still sounded amused, and I found myself feeling embarrassed and irritated at the same time.

"This thing they do," I tried to explain, "where the teacher reads this story to the class that has something to do with Jesus or some guy who went through a hardship or whatever, and then there's a prayer. It doesn't matter what class it is: History, Biology, whatever. And everyone's supposed to bow their heads and pray along to whatever the teacher is saying. Some of the kids are really into it and close their eyes and everything, and some of us just don't care and look around at each other, thinking it's kind of stupid."

I hadn't actually realized just how much all of this annoyed me until I spelled it out, and I became more angry as I talked. I began to understand that while things at St. Joseph's were religious from time to time, Bethlehem was downright saturated with the whole Christian thing, and I wasn't even sure why that bothered me so much.

Dennis, meanwhile, found all of this hilarious. He went on for a bit about how his public school was so much cooler, that there was none of that religious stuff permeating his experience there. "It's a nice change," he said. "I got enough of that stuff growing up with my dad and all."

"Oh, right!" I said. "He used to be a priest too, right?"

"Used to be," he said pointedly, but then he changed the subject. "So, made any friends there?"

"Not really," I said, my resentment shifting slightly. "I can't really find anyone to fit in with. I don't like the nerds, and the cooler guys don't seem to like me that much. I get along with them okay, but I get the feeling that they look down on me."

Dennis didn't respond for a few seconds. "Still don't have any powers?"

"What? Oh, you mean the psychic stuff. Nope. All gone. I guess we really did use them up bringing Tim back." I missed my powers, and the absence of them was one more reminder that I was just an ordinary kid, that the supernatural era of my life was over. It was a very empty feeling.

"Yeah, same here. Look, I've got to go." He ended the conversation immediately after that, somewhat rudely, I thought. It would be a few more months before we spoke again.

I had meant to tell him more about Bethlehem and its restrictions, like their seemingly arbitrary rules forbidding various things. Some of them were related to their particular interpretation of Christianity, like how boys couldn't have their hair long enough to touch their shirt collars, and girls couldn't wear skirts that were above the knee. Also, while T-shirts were allowed, no one was permitted to wear any that portrayed rock music groups. The powers that be also had some weird aversion to dancing, which was why the upper grades weren't allowed to have a prom like other high schools did.

Along the same lines, certain topics of discussion weren't allowed, though they were occasionally whispered about among the more rebellious students. Sex and anything related to it was strictly out, the idea seeming to be that as long as no one was allowed to talk about it, none of the kids would be tempted to give in to such carnal desires.

I found it interesting that any talk of vampires was similarly curtailed, as it started to come up one day in Biology class. The teacher was talking about how human beings were at the top of the food chain and didn't have any natural predators, which prompted Aaron's nerdy friend Jay to blurt out, "Oh yeah? What about vampires?"

I almost jumped out of my skin at the sound of the word; I completely hadn't been expecting it. That wasn't the first time that had happened, either. Whenever the word would come up out of the blue, it would make me at the very least flinch. On this occasion, I felt myself get hot and was probably blushing, but no one noticed as everyone was too focused on Jay and at the teacher's vehement reaction.

Mrs. Manning, a slightly overweight middle-aged woman with short hair and obnoxiously large glasses, suddenly scowled, giving Jay a look that made everyone in the room glad that she wasn't looking at them. "We do *not* use that word in this school, Jay," she said through clenched teeth. "That kind of thing is satanic and inappropriate."

"Sorry," he managed to squeak out.

I soon learned after talking to Jay after class that this moratorium on talking about vampires was a standing rule that had been established before I started attending the school. Although I didn't particularly like either Aaron or Jay — who was tall and skinny with big ears and very thick glasses, looking like something straight out of the movie *Revenge of the Nerds* — I still talked to them from time to time. The entire eighth grade only had about twenty kids in it, so even though there were cliques, it was impossible for everyone to avoid each other. Some of the other grades were even smaller; the eleventh grade class that year only had nine people in it.

According to Ken, the third and least annoying of this nerd trio, there were a few people in the school who had either friends or relatives who had died during the vampire attacks on the city, so it was a very upsetting subject. The faculty decided that it was best not to talk about it, essentially sweeping things under the rug and trying to make things go away by not talking about them, just as they did with other topics.

And that was fine with me. Talking in secret to Ken and the others about this while I feigned disbelief and aloofness was difficult enough, so the less it was brought up, the better. I didn't want to wind up in a situation where someone might confide in me that their father or best friend had been killed, all the while wondering just which one of my friends or sisters had committed the murder, or if I had done it myself.

While I tried to play it cool by asking the guys if they really believed that vampires were involved — putting forth the explanation that it was some kind of rabid animals like the news media suggested — I was surprised to find that they fully believed it. They even seemed genuinely scared by the idea, Aaron whispering that we had better stop talking about them, or else they might come back. I wanted to say that there was no way that could ever happen, but I didn't dare tip my hand and let on that I knew any more than they did.

But that was the truth as far as I was concerned. I hated the idea of vampires and never wanted to take that stupid potion ever again, and the remorse I felt over the lives we had taken was crippling if I allowed myself to dwell on it. I just wanted to put it all behind me, and if Tim wanted to take the blame for everything and pray on his knees for forgiveness from God, more power to him.

"Oh, sure," Carolyn said with a typical rolling of her eyes. "Like he was the only one who kept that entire thing going. You were just as bad about it."

"No I wasn't!" was the only retort I could think of.

She looked at me sideways and made a sound like *"pfft,"* blowing out of her lips. She was in the middle of folding her laundry, which she brought over to our house once or twice a week since her own apartment didn't have a washer and dryer. "Right. Like you weren't the one going around every couple of years going, 'Come on! Let's be vampires again! It'll be *fuuuun!'"*

"It wasn't like that!" I said, but I hated the fact that she was right.

"What you're doing is called projection," she said. "You're trying to pretend that what you felt back then was what someone else was feeling instead." Since starting college, she had occasionally brought back these little nuggets of wisdom from her Psychology class. Sometimes I found them interesting, but this one was particularly disturbing. I didn't want to believe it.

"Look, Tim said that we'll all be okay as long as we ask for forgiveness from God." I caught myself, realizing as the words came out that I sounded not only like Tim but like the corny people at Bethlehem.

"Yeah, right," Carolyn said, not looking at me and hefting her basket of laundry off of the kitchen table. "I'm sure some invisible guy in the clouds will make it all better."

"Carolyn!" I stopped short of accusing her of blasphemy, again realizing just how much my new school had been influencing me. "You shouldn't... You shouldn't say stuff like that."

She turned and looked at me again after she sat her clothes basket down in the wicker chair in the yellow den. For a moment, she looked sympathetic, but then her expression hardened again. "What you really need to hope is that none of your stupid little friends opens his big mouth and tells anyone what we did. You want to feel bad about it? Fine. You should. We all should. It was a really, really shitty time for all of us." She paused, looking around for her car keys, which she then picked up from the coffee table. Then she turned on me again, her expression even more harsh. "But I tell you what: It was a lot shittier for all those people who died, to say nothing of their families."

I cried myself to sleep that night, the conversation running over and over in my head, which was made worse by picturing other people crying, the ones we had hurt.

Feelings like that came and went. The only thing that kept me going was focusing on everyday, normal life, not dwelling on the past. The problem was that everyday life also sucked sometimes. I was a full-blown emotional teenager by then, caught up in the rigors of schoolwork and social awkwardness.

What friendships I was able to make at school seemed tentative and fluctuating, and I never really felt like I fit in with anyone. Part of me was okay with that, though, as I didn't particularly like most of the people around me. I could get along with them, but in time, I found myself thinking that it was okay to be something of an outcast. These people, students and teachers alike, didn't really understand me. No one did.

My crush on Elizabeth also fluctuated, ranging from my being head over heels for her to deciding that she didn't really matter and that I was better off not being accepted by her and her snobby friends. She could be nice sometimes, but it seemed that if I showed too much interest in her, she'd withdraw and become more resistant to me. When she showed up at school after the Christmas holidays with a much shorter, cropped haircut, I decided that I officially wasn't interested in her anymore because I didn't like how she looked. Nearly all of the girls at school had that same hairstyle: ear-length, permed, sprayed to death, and with this poofy dome-shaped sculpture made out of the bangs in front. It was fashionable at the time, but when I was feeling particularly rejected and cynical, this monotony and conformity was just one more thing to have contempt for.

The repressive nature of Bethlehem itself began to wear on me by the school year's end, so much that I was getting sick of all of the rules, regulations, and Christian insistence on morality. When Easter came around, I decided not to go with my family to church that Sunday, telling my parents that I already got enough of that "churchy" stuff at school. They understood, and not much was said about it afterwards, including when I later opted out of going with them at Christmas and to other services from that point on.

Another family tradition was broken that summer when my parents didn't go to the ALA conference. My father said that it was for financial reasons, that he and my mother would rather save the money than make the trip. He hoped that they would be able to afford to go to the next one the following year, but he said so with a resigned tone. I didn't know the ins and outs of how all of their financial stuff worked, but I assumed that he knew what he was talking about.

It felt weird for them to be home the entire summer. I didn't resent their presence or anything, but I was just used to the rhythm of things, how the school year would end, I would have a lot of spare time at home, they would go off on their trip, and then they'd come back and I'd experience whatever the rest of the summer turned out to be. Sometimes their absence coincided with everyone getting together as vampires and going on our usual murderous sprees, but that was a thing of the past. We would never do that again. So why did I keep thinking about it so much?

Although Susanna hadn't come to Augusta for her birthday the previous year, she did this time, and it was an odd experience for me. I thought I would be glad to see her, but things felt different this time. We had seen each other at Christmas and gotten along more or less okay, but we had only talked on the phone a couple of times over the course of the year, and then only briefly. During this visit, she seemed more distant than ever. She wasn't rude exactly, just unavailable.

I never got a chance to talk to her alone, but I had some questions for her, things that had been bugging me for a while. These had come up during conversations with Dennis and Tim, whom I never actually hung out with in person, incidentally. But as we had been talking occasionally on the phone over the past few months, there were some things that had begun to bother us about the mechanics of everything that happened during our times as vampires, things that didn't quite make sense. I ended up calling her one Saturday afternoon when I had the house to myself, not wanting to risk being overheard by my parents.

"How's the new place?" I asked her.

"It's fine. A little smaller than what I had in Charleston, but I'll make it work." She was in the middle of moving to Columbia to start graduate school in the fall at the University of South Carolina. She was still majoring in English, and from what I could gather, all that she could really do with that degree was wind up being a college professor. That just sounded like going to school forever, which was pretty unappealing to me.

"Oh." I tried to think of a way to segue into what I really wanted to talk about. "Still doing the cheerleading thing?" That wasn't it.

"No, I gave that up a long time ago," she said, sounding bored. "It just didn't hold my interest anymore."

"Yeah, the cheerleaders at my school aren't all that interesting, either."

She laughed. "I can imagine!"

"So..." I tried to figure out what to say. Talking to her suddenly felt as difficult as trying to talk to Elizabeth or any of the other pretty girls at school. "There's something I need to ask you about."

"What?"

"It's..."

"It better not be what I think it's about."

"But...! Susanna, really. I just need to know this one thing." There were in fact several things I wanted to ask her, but I hoped that starting off with one question would get my foot in the door. "It's about AIDS. The disease." AIDS was still relatively new at the time, having gone from something that people thought only gay men could contract to a serious threat to the health and lives of everyone.

"What about it."

"Well, they say you can get it through blood transfusions, so…? Given everything that we did, you know…"

"Yeah, I *know…*" she said with a sneer in her voice. "And don't worry. We're immune to it."

"Really? You mean, because of the potion?"

She sighed. "Yes. Because of that."

"But that's… I mean, according to…" I stopped myself from mentioning Tim's name, realizing that she would become even more angry if I let on that I had been talking about this with other people from the group. "According to what I've heard, it's a deadly disease, and no one's been able to come up with a cure for it!"

"Ray, I gave you your answer. I've already told you that we're not supposed to be discussing this, and we definitely shouldn't be talking about it over the phone. Someone might be listening in."

"Like who?"

"You're too young to understand."

My temper flared. "Why do you always have to pull that crap on me? Whether or not we're immune to AIDS has nothing to do with how old I am!"

Click. The phone sputtered at me, then was nearly silent apart from a quiet hum. A few seconds later, the dial tone sounded in my ear.

I swore, angry both at her and at myself for handling things so poorly. If had been more tactful, I might have been able to put forth some of the other questions I had for her, like how it was possible that we could change into bats and then back to people and still have all of our clothes on. Tim had mentioned that in the book *Dracula,* it was stated that a vampire couldn't enter someone's home unless they were invited first, so how was it that we were able to get into the house in

Evans where the "Vampire Killers" lived? And how had she known precisely how the newer potion was going to affect us in all of its different and unusual ways?

As I fumed, I suddenly had an uncharacteristic moment of empathy. Maybe the reason Susanna was so reluctant to talk about our experiences as vampires wasn't because she was trying to be controlling, but because she was more traumatized by everything than I'd previously known. Maybe she had more reason to feel guilty than any of us. This made me sad, and I began spiraling down into even gloomier thoughts. Had I, or Tim for making the suggestion in the first place, ruined her life by getting her to make the potion for us?

She was right about one thing, but I didn't realize it at the time. I was too young to understand, but not in the way she'd meant. Had I been more mature, experienced, and with a broader vision, it might have occurred to me that if my own sister had somehow built something into a potion that happened to include a vaccine against the most life-threatening disease since cancer, then maybe that was something she should be sharing with the scientific community. Perhaps she should have been majoring in Chemistry rather than wasting her time with this English stuff.

All of this would eventually occur to me and raise more questions in my mind later on down the road, but unfortunately, I would never get an answer to them.

"So, are you looking forward to seeing all of your friends again?" my mother asked me the night before ninth grade began. Her back was to me; she was standing at the kitchen sink and sorting through the dishes from that night's dinner, putting some in the dishwasher and leaving others to soak beforehand.

"Not really," I said. "I mean, maybe. Just not really excited about going back. Summer was way too short."

"That's what happens as you get older," she said. "Time just goes by faster and faster. Just wait until you're an adult! It gets even worse." Sometimes, my mother and I could have decent conversations that actually meant something, but other times it felt like she was just spouting off random clichés in order to have something to say. We had our occasional conflicts and resolutions from time to time, but as it was with my father, I never felt much of a deep connection to her.

Suddenly, she let out a small exclamation as one of the small plates she'd picked up slipped out of her hands and fell into a large pot filled with soapy water. Water splashed upward, some of it onto my mother's shirt, the rest of it onto the counter and the window behind the sink. I found this amusing, but I held back from laughing outright.

After my mother halfway dried herself off, she began wiping up the water from the counter, then moved to the window. She leaned over the sink as she did so, stretching to reach where the drops had landed and were streaking down the glass and along the frame.

"That's strange," she said softly, having looked upward to a portion of the window. "What is that?" She reached toward the upper right corner, but I could tell that she wasn't able to reach what she was looking at.

"What?" I asked her. "Is something wrong?"

She didn't speak, instead stepping back and kneeling down to open the cabinet beneath the sink. She pulled out a small plastic stool, closed the cabinet, then positioned the stool so she could step up on it to get to whatever had piqued her interest. I was curious, too, so I walked over to join her.

"There's…" she began, but she didn't finish her sentence. Instead, she reached out and peeled off a small white piece of masking tape from the wooden frame. "Tape," she said simply, looking at it as it stuck to her thumb. "How did that get there?"

My heart raced as I quickly realized what she had found. This was one of the windows that we had blocked off with garbage bags to keep the sunlight out during our stints as vampires. Apparently, whoever had taken the bags down had missed a piece of tape, and it had gone unnoticed since it was normally hidden behind the small drapes that covered the upper part of the window. Mom called out to my father, who was in the red den watching TV. Presumably, she was thinking that the tape was there because of something he had done, but I didn't want to involve him in this conversation. A lie, some of it partly true, quickly sprang up in my mind.

"Oh, that!" I said, trying to sound nonchalant. "That was from years ago! One of those times when you and Dad were gone to ALA."

Stepping down from the stool, my mother gave me a confused look. "What?"

"When Susanna and Carolyn were here," I said, smiling and trying to play everything off as a joke. "We got this idea to see what the house would look like during the day if we shut out all the light and covered up the windows with trash bags." Mom continued to look baffled. "I know, I know. It was a stupid idea. Not all the windows, I mean!" I laughed again nervously. "Just in here." I was gesturing at the kitchen window with my arm, then turned around and noticed the adjoining yellow den, realizing that if this story were to make any sense, the windows in there would need to have been blocked out, too. "And in there, too," I added. "One big room of darkness in the middle of the day."

Mom laughed, shaking her head. "You kids," she said, smiling. "Always coming up with strange ideas. I can't keep up with you."

As she turned away from me and struggled to get the tape off of her thumb and into the trash can underneath the sink, I thought to myself, *No. You really can't. And you have no idea.*

As had happened before, I realized in that moment exactly why my mother and I weren't all that close: I'd spent my entire life lying to her and getting away with it.

Ninth grade began without a lot of fanfare, though supposedly I was officially considered a high schooler then. But it didn't really feel all that different from being in eighth grade. The biggest difference was that, because I had been at the school for a year, I no longer felt like the new kid, but I still wasn't terribly popular. Most of the time, I could get along okay with everybody, but I never actually felt liked or as if anyone really wanted me around. And because I kind of hated the school anyway, I told myself that it didn't really matter.

Even though I had said to my mother the night before that I wasn't looking forward to seeing anyone, that wasn't entirely true. I was of course eager to see Elizabeth, who turned out to be just as beautiful as ever. Her hair had grown back to almost the length it was when I first met her, and so my crush on her came back full blast. In retrospect, I know that I was probably being unfair to her, judging her mostly on her physical appearance more than anything else. But at that age, my feelings were ruled by my hormones, and I wasn't really capable of anything much deeper than that. It wasn't that my feelings weren't real; they were just rather simple compared to the things adults feel, more straightforward and less convoluted. If she looked good to me and happened to be nice to me, then that was reason enough to declare my love for her, at least in secret.

As before, those feelings had their peaks and valleys throughout the school year depending on how things went between us. Sometimes she was nice; often she was indifferent. Rarely was she ever actually mean, but Melinda and Helen usually took care of that side of things. Even then, sometimes I was able to get along with them as well, but everything was just so back and forth. It was frustrating. I kept thinking that if I could somehow get through whatever barrier was keeping us apart, I could be a good boyfriend to Elizabeth, and my life would suck a lot less. I ached for her sometimes in the way that only a young adolescent boy can, but I was terrified of letting her know for fear that, like previous girls I had tried to pursue, she might turn on me and truly be hateful. I wouldn't have been able to bear that. So I kept quiet.

I still missed my psychic powers, wishing I could somehow get them back. While I didn't like thinking about my time as a vampire, it occurred to me that if I had those powers again, maybe I could use them to make Elizabeth come around. When I thought about that in any detail, though, I remembered the cruel ways I had used my mind to control my victims. That creeped me out, so I stopped thinking along those lines. Every now and then, the thought would resurface, but it disturbed me.

Elizabeth wasn't the only girl I found attractive, either, but she was definitely the prettiest. By this point, the girls my age had lost some of their awkwardness and were better able to do themselves up and look good, plenty of them having natural beauty that shone through better when they weren't trying so hard to overdo it. There was also the fact that there was more cross-pollinating of the grades than at my previous school. My eighth grade Pre-Algebra class, for example, had students from the seventh grade in it, plus one or two from the ninth grade. There was a somewhat cute seventh-grader named Karyn who seemed to genuinely like me for a while, but at the time, I only had eyes for Elizabeth. Once I was in ninth grade, I took a French class that had a student from the tenth grade in it, a funny girl named Sandra whom I liked. She was nice to me, but because she was older and cooler than the girls my age, I considered her out of my league. Had I not been so caught up in my own shyness and reluctance to let on to anyone about my feelings, I might have had a chance with these girls, but I was just too guarded for my own good.

Hormones, particularly testosterone, played another significant role in our lives at that time, though not in a strictly sexual way. All of us boys had it building up inside us, our bodies and minds struggling to adapt to and understand all of the changes happening within and without. There was all of this pent up energy that needed an outlet, and we weren't sure how to handle it. One way this manifest physically was an increase in violent behavior. It was mostly in fun, but it wasn't unusual to see two boys playfully fighting, randomly hitting each other for a few seconds at a time. Most of the time, these boys were friends. Sometimes these exchanges would develop into actual fights, but that was rare, and if anyone were caught doing that by the teachers, they would get detention.

Because the school was as strict as it was, one of the things the more rebellious of us found ourselves doing was trying to see just how far we could stretch the rules before breaking them. Particularly among the boys, this was something that we found common ground in, the lines between the social groups blurring as long as we were having fun being bad. Sometimes it was something over the top, like the time Chris brought an entire duffle bag filled with wadded up balls of paper to Algebra class. Whenever the teacher had her back turned, he would toss one or two of them across the room at some of the other students. The paper balls would then be lobbed back when it was safe. In time, the number of balls being tossed — and sometimes accurately aimed and targeted — increased, and by the time Mrs. Sherwood caught on, the entire room was littered with trash.

Other times, we were more subtle. One day in World History class, someone started emitting a steady hum, which another student picked up on and repeated, then another, then another. This was something we had done at my previous school, and coincidentally enough, I had been thinking about that just a couple of days before. This humming had the expected result of angering the teacher once he noticed it, but he had no way of knowing just who was doing it. But Elizabeth knew, and she gave me a wicked smile, looking up at me from her desk nearby with a smirk that made me melt. She had this way of looking amused where she would keep her chin turned downward toward her chest, almost like she was looking at you out of the top of her head. A simple gesture like that from her was all it would take for whatever waning feelings I might be having for her to shoot back up immediately, leaving me to pine for her and fantasize over and over how wonderful it would be to somehow get together. But I was always too scared to do anything more than think about it.

The fact that she seemed so unattainable to me was only one of the aspects of her that made her so intriguing. As I mentioned, she was rather soft spoken and tended to keep to herself, but occasionally I could get her to talk or joke around — especially when Melinda and Helen weren't there — even if I usually felt awkward after each encounter. I couldn't say why exactly, but I just kept getting this feeling that there was more to her, that she wasn't just another pretty face, as the cliché goes.

One day in Physical Science, Mrs. Manning was talking about various chemicals and elements, how each had different properties and related to each other in different ways. Acids and bases were discussed, and from time to time, she would ask a leading question in hopes of getting someone from the class to come up with the right answer. She explained what solvents were, then went on to tell us that the human body had its own solvents, like saliva or the hydrochloric acid present in our stomachs.

"Some solutes are more resistant to solvents than others," she went on. I was bored senseless by all of this, but I continued to take notes in case this ended up on an upcoming test. Kirby happened to look over at me from the desk in the row next to mine, and I mimed an exaggerated yawn at him. He nodded in agreement and gave me a slight smile, then looked back down at his notes.

"But there could never be a universal solvent," Mrs. Manning said, "a chemical that can dissolve everything. That's why you have to know the properties of different solutes in order to know which solvent to use on them."

My mind started to drift back to Susanna's Chemistry notebook, the one I had found that night with the vampire potion in it. She and that guy Robert had somehow developed the potion based on their knowledge and skills, but had they really learned all of that from this boring crap?

Mrs. Manning put forth another question, and I could tell from her tone that she was getting more excited in that way that teachers who care about their subjects often do. Unfortunately, that enthusiasm is usually wasted on bored, apathetic high schoolers. "So can anyone tell me why there can't be a universal solvent?" She raised her eyebrows high, her mouth hanging open in a vague, expectant smile.

Silence filled the room as she looked around. I thought about her question but couldn't come up with an answer, thinking that she was probably just wrong anyway. I felt that the science classes in this school were sometimes a joke, having learned that the school got its textbooks from a publisher that specialized in Christian-based teaching. All of the history and science books had this weird bent to them that insisted on certain things in order to keep in line with a specific way of thinking. Our Biology book from the previous year had an entire chapter devoted to disproving evolution and natural selection, and our World History book from this year insisted that the single most important invention in the history of mankind was the printing press because it made the Bible available on a large scale. My cynical response to that was that the wheel — or maybe the discovery of fire — was probably a bit more significant, but if I answered "the wheel" instead of "the printing press" on the test that week, my answer would be marked wrong and I would get a bad grade.

But Mrs. Manning wasn't trying to put forth any kind of religious agenda this time. She was asking a legitimate question, but because I couldn't come up with an answer, I just got annoyed. No one else had anything to offer, either. She repeated her question, this time with a hint of exasperation.

A quiet, almost musical voice came from the center of the room, saying almost in a whisper, "What would you put it in?" I turned and saw Elizabeth looking down at her notebook, her finger holding a pencil to it by the eraser, rotating it slowly on its point.

"What?" Mrs. Manning asked eagerly. "Who said that?" All heads turned toward Elizabeth, who still stared down at her now stationary pencil, the point threatening to slip out from under it. "Elizabeth? Was that you? Say that again!"

She looked up at the teacher, gripping the pencil before it fell. She shrugged her shoulders and smiled nervously. "I just meant… If there's something that can dissolve everything else in the world, well, then you couldn't really put it inside of anything, could you?"

Mrs. Manning applauded lightly, laughing. "Exactly," she said.

Elizabeth smiled again, looking a little embarrassed. She then went back to examining what was on her desk while the teacher continued with her lecture. I was floored by how obvious her answer to the question was, how no one else in the class had been able to come up with it, myself included.

While that particular episode had gone well for her, a later one did not. She spoke up in a similar fashion during a chapel service in the lunchroom later that year, again seeming more like she was talking to herself rather than actually wanting to be heard, but the person in charge picked up on what she was saying. And again, I was surprised by the brilliance of what she had to say.

Usually, the man who led these chapel services — which were more like lectures with occasional singing and praying, not nearly as formal as the services at St. Joseph's — was a goofy but occasionally funny guy named Don Lowden. He was Bethlehem Baptist's youth minister, and I probably liked him the best out of all the faculty. That may have just been because I usually only saw him once a week as opposed to the teachers I had to deal with every day, who got on my nerves more and more as time went on.

Sometimes, I would agree with things Don (who insisted that we call him by his first name and not "Mr. Lowden") had to say, but when it came down to it, he was just another authority figure for me to rebel against. They all had this agenda that was somewhat confusing, always pushing the idea that God and Jesus were loving and forgiving, but at the same time, if any of us said or did or even thought anything that was outside the lines of what they considered right, we were horrible sinners who were going to hell. Their methods varied, some more heavy-handed than others, and Don was one of those whose approach was to try to be as clever as possible, almost like he could trick us into adopting his point of view.

My favorite example of this was when he ended one lecture — or sermon — with one of his typical stories from his past, something that he thought would drive a point home and make us think. "When I was in high school," he said, "there was a song that was popular, and it's still popular to this day. I'm sure you've heard it. It's by the Rolling Stones, and it's called 'I Can't Get No Satisfaction.' You know that song?" He began miming playing a guitar as he tunelessly sang the first few words of the song, then looked around the room as some of the kids laughed at his intentionally silly performance. "Mick Jagger's been singing 'I can't get no satisfaction' for over twenty years now," he continued. "And you know why I think that is? It's because he hasn't found Jesus Christ."

My jaw dropped open. Unable to contain myself, I leaned over to Bradley, one of Kirby's friends who happened to be sitting next to me. "Yeah," I whispered, "or maybe it's because he's been making millions of dollars off of it this whole time."

Bradley chuckled, but I got a dirty look from Tammy, who turned around to glare at me from her seat in front of us. She was a particular fan of Don's, plus she was part of that more pious group of students that I didn't associate with very much if I could help it.

This other afternoon, we had a special guest speaker from some place or another that was probably considered important, but as usual, most of us didn't care. He had his things to say, and we either listened or drifted off in our own thoughts as usual. At one point, I happened to be paying attention when he decided to, like Don, relate a personal story that he felt was worth sharing.

"I had this friend who, one day, found a caterpillar in a cocoon," he began.

"Sure you did," Elizabeth murmured, her arms folded and eyes aimed at the floor near the man's feet. She was obviously in a bad mood, which I had picked up on earlier that morning when I tried to say hi to her in the hall, but she just looked past me and kept walking, apparently angry about something. At the time, it pissed me off.

"Excuse me, young lady?" the man said to her.

She looked up at him, her expression a combination of boredom and contempt. She then huffed, saying, "You had a friend who found a cocoon, just like every other guy who probably got this story from a devotional book."

I was shocked at her brashness, but I knew what she meant. Teachers and preachers would often regale their listeners with some story that was supposedly poignant and true, even more so if it had happened to them. Wherever this guy was going with this caterpillar story, it was no doubt going to wind up being something inspirational and with a deep lesson, and Elizabeth had apparently made up her mind that it was fake.

"No, it happened to a friend of mine," the speaker insisted with a stern tone.

Elizabeth seemed unfazed, her eyes fixing on his more fiercely. "What was his name?"

The man faltered. "His… His name was David. Now, please, let me finish." He continued with his story, and Elizabeth went back to looking down and scowling, arms still folded defiantly.

I hoped to find a chance to talk to Elizabeth in the halls afterwards, but I didn't want to do so in the presence of Helen or Melinda. Fortunately, they were nowhere to be seen, so I walked up to Elizabeth while she was getting some books from her locker.

"Hey," I said.

She looked at me, confused and still looking angry, but then she softened. "Hey," she said.

Fighting the urge to clam up, I managed to get the words out: "That was pretty cool the way you told that guy off, I thought."

She turned back to her locker, taking out another book and adding it to the small pile she was holding. "Thanks, I guess."

"He seemed pretty caught out and embarrassed. I thought it was cool as shit!"

She laughed slightly, then gave me a sideways glance that quickly went from sly and gorgeous to horrified as she looked slightly to my left. Half a second later, I felt a hand clamp down on my shoulder from behind, a hand belonging to the principal, Dr. Phillips. He was carrying a yellow-colored piece of paper, which he then gave to Elizabeth. She took it, knowing as well as I did what it was: a detention slip. Her eyebrows moved slightly together as she examined it, and her lips went outward in a small pout.

"You can join us after school next Wednesday, Miss Morgan," Dr. Phillips said, towering over us both. She looked up at him with what I expected to be more defiance, but her expression was unreadable. It was mostly just empty, like she wasn't going to give him the satisfaction of an emotional response.

"And as for you, Mr. Young," he said, turning me slightly towards him by my shoulder, then releasing it, "you too can expect one of those shortly. You know we don't use language like that in this school. Jesus doesn't like that kind of thing." He strode off proudly, his tall, intimidating form disappearing around the hallway corner.

I turned back to Elizabeth, hoping to talk to her more. But she had already slammed her locker door and walked away.

One thing about her that I picked up on after a while was that she seemed to have even more of a problem with the prevalence of Christianity in our school than I did. In my case, I didn't mind Christianity itself as much as I did Bethlehem's particular take on it, this close-minded approach that opposed not only non-Christian faiths but also any of the various denominations outside of the Baptists themselves. Whereas the faculty at St. Joseph's taught us about other belief systems in the manner of *this is what we believe, this is what they believe, and here's how it's different,* Bethlehem's methodology was more like *this is what we believe, we're the ones who are right, and this is why everyone else is wrong.* That bothered me, and once I realized it, it made me have a lot less respect for the teachers, and I became more resistant to anything they had to say.

Coming off of the whole vampire thing, my first few weeks at Bethlehem had me thinking that maybe all of the talk of sinning and forgiveness might be good for me. Initially, I just saw it as quaint, something different from what I was used to. Talking to Tim increased that feeling at first, but then I began to wonder if he had a point. Maybe what we needed the most was redemption. Unfortunately, the increasingly intolerant environment I found myself in had the opposite effect on me, and I pushed back even more.

This made even their best efforts seem laughable to me at times. One afternoon, the class had to gather in the library, the only room in the entire school that had a TV and VCR. We were then subjected to an hour of watching some lunatic televangelist rant about how evil and satanic popular culture was. The speaker, who sometimes talked to his miniscule studio audience and other times directly to the camera, had a beef with just about everything. Any group, practice, or religion that he didn't like was secretly supporting Satan, he insisted, and he could "prove" this with astounding leaps of logic that made no sense whatsoever.

He even went so far as to say that the Smurfs were satanic because their cartoon on TV depicted them using magic. Michael Jackson was also evil because his moonwalk dance resembled walking backwards, which was analogous to regressing into one's past life, which was related to the Hindu belief in reincarnation, and Hinduism was satanic because it wasn't Christianity. He also had wild theories about how various rock groups had made pacts with the devil in order to become famous, the proof of this being various symbols (such as astrological signs) or pictures of magical creatures (such as unicorns) on their album covers.

Some of the students laughed at this ridiculousness, but that would be greeted by a stern look from Mrs. Nesbit, the librarian. She sat with a stack of detention slips on her lap, anticipating our disapproval and possible misbehavior. The more gullible students, meanwhile, swallowed this garbage, and I could tell from their conversations after class that they really did feel that they'd been given this secret insight into just how dangerous the world was.

Not Elizabeth. Her only vocal reaction to watching this videotape, aside from stifling laughs and turning to whisper to her friends from time to time, was to let a single word slip out in a harsh whisper while she slowly shook her head: "Unbelievable!" That had been the exact word going through my mind at the time.

On the way out of class, I ended up behind her and Melinda, who were talking quietly about how stupid the entire thing was. Behind me, I overheard Tammy talking to her friend Jolene.

"I'm so disappointed!" she said. "I really had no idea they were that bad. When I get home, I'm going to throw all my Duran Duran albums in the trash!"

Elizabeth stopped abruptly, and I almost ran into her. The smell of her hair was amazing. She turned around and said vaguely in Tammy's direction, "Ooh! I want them!"

Melinda gave her a sharp jab with her elbow and said, "Shh!" They laughed, as did I, and Melinda didn't seem to mind that I was in on the joke. She then ushered Elizabeth away, trying to keep her out of trouble.

I had heard a rumor that Elizabeth didn't believe in God at all, but this was just hearsay. Had it been an actual fact, she could have been kicked out of school. I had already been told about a P.E. teacher who had been fired for not being Christian the year before I started at Bethlehem, and whether or not that was even legal, I didn't know or care enough to find out. These people were serious about not wanting any bad influences in their presence. If Elizabeth was an atheist, she'd have to keep it to herself.

Being a naturally secretive person myself, I wondered if maybe this was the reason why she was usually so quiet. Or maybe it was just something that the Christian girls made up about her because they were jealous of how pretty she was. I didn't really care either way, but if she didn't believe in God, I wasn't going to turn her in or try to get her burned at the stake for it.

As for me, I didn't know whether to fear God and what punishment he might have in store for me or to doubt his existence due to the fact that we had been allowed to get away with the horrible things we'd done as vampires. Fear certainly seemed to be a big thing with these people, and I realized over time that they all seemed terrified of anything and everything that wasn't exactly like them. Moreover, they seemed to have a compulsive need to try to make everyone else be just like they were. If anyone questioned God, the Bible, or whatever the teacher happened to be saying at that particular moment, they were shouted down — literally, sometimes — and told that questioning was a sin. I wasn't particularly interested in questioning theology, though. I mostly wanted to avoid it, but that was impossible. I at least wanted to keep from thinking about it to the point where it made me feel even more guilty.

The incident at chapel happened a little while after we had watched that videotape of the crazy televangelist, and while I resented having to go to detention, I at least looked forward to getting to see Elizabeth. I hoped to talk to her again and tell her how cool I thought it was that she told that guest speaker off, but really, I just wanted to take advantage of any excuse to have a conversation with her. I lied to my mother about why I had to stay after school on Wednesday, saying that I was working on a project with some other students. As usual, she believed me.

But Elizabeth and I didn't get to talk much, nor did she seem to be in a particularly talkative mood. Everyone had to be quiet during detention anyway, which consisted of an hour of everyone silently copying down words from a long list. It was just busywork made into a punishment.

Occasionally, I would look up from my paper to steal a glance at Elizabeth, a technique I had perfected in terms of doing so stealthily. At least, I thought I had. She caught me doing it more than once this hour, and each time, I would quickly look back down at my paper, pretending she hadn't seen me. But I knew she had. I had been planning to try to talk to her once detention was over, but because I felt embarrassed over getting caught looking at her, I didn't.

As was often the case, I had gone through conversations in my head leading up to this day, thinking of various things I could say to her and imagining what she would say in response, which I would then respond to with something witty and charming. But when the real situation came about, I either skipped out on talking to her altogether or just managed to get a sentence or two out before things derailed and went nothing like I'd planned. Never would I dare let on how I really felt, but she probably knew anyway. But as long as I didn't admit it, that felt safer, the tentative almost-friendship being preferable to the possibility that she would shun me altogether if I were honest about my feelings.

This wasn't just the case with Elizabeth; it applied to all of the "lesser" crushes I had. I lacked the confidence to ever move beyond my fears, and so I remained alone. My shyness became one more thing to hate about myself, and it seemed to get worse the older I got. I used to be the class clown and make the girls laugh. I used to be confident, even arrogant. I used to be in charge of my friends and lead them into battle. I used to be more. I may not have missed being a vampire, but I definitely missed how powerful I had once been.

I also missed my old friends, whom contact with was more sporadic as time went on, and it was always over the phone, not in person. Even when we did talk, it was clear that things had changed. I had only spoken to Carl a couple of times since our last get-together in 1987, and during our most recent conversation, I was surprised when he mentioned that he had started smoking and drinking occasionally. I knew that a few of the guys in my class did that, and while I wasn't the type to try to get them in trouble for it, it wasn't something that interested me. Carl kind of bragged about it, though, I guess because it made him feel more grown up and cool.

"It's not a big deal," he said to me, his voice noticeably deeper than the last time I had talked to him over the phone. "Don't be a dork-head."

I laughed; something about hearing that old insult felt more comforting than demeaning. "Does it... I don't know... Does it interfere with your sports stuff?" I asked.

"What sports stuff?"

"You know, like running and all that track stuff you used to do."

"Oh, I quit doing all that. Grew out of it, I guess."

I couldn't really think of anything to say. "Yeah, I guess." After another uncomfortable silence, I asked him if he ever talked to any of the other guys from the old group.

"Well, Tim kept calling me for a while there, but eventually I had to tell him to fuck off."

I laughed, slightly shocked. "Really?"

"Well, not in those exact words. But I just got tired of him pestering me."

"Oh. What about Dennis? Or Nick?"

"Nick I haven't seen in ages. I ran into Dennis at the mall not too long ago, and he looked completely different. All weird clothes and stuff, plus he lost a lot of weight."

"   R   e   a   l   l   y   ?   "

"Yeah!" He laughed his characteristic gurgling laugh, though it sounded deeper, like he was trying to keep it under control. "Guess we can't call him the fat kid anymore."

"I guess," was all I could think to say.

"Do you…" he began, then paused. "Do you ever miss it? The vampire thing?"

"Carl," I said with a reproachful tone. "Of course not. I mean, I remember it, but I wouldn't say that I miss it. That was some really horrible shit we did, you know."

He sighed. "Yeah, I know. I didn't mean I missed that. Just the other stuff. The fun parts. There were some, right?"

"I suppose. But we shouldn't really think about…"

"Aw, crap," he said suddenly. "My dad just got home. I'd better go." He fumbled to hang up quickly, and that was that.

I sat there holding the phone, annoyed that he'd ended the call so abruptly. As I replaced the receiver, I thought about calling one of my other old friends. The one I hadn't spoken to since we'd been vampires, Nick, sprang to mind, but I wasn't sure if it was worth it to try calling him. The handful of times I'd tried over the past year and a half, he'd always been unavailable for one reason or another. Every single time, his parents said he was either not home or busy doing something, so much that I began to wonder if he was just telling them to tell me that. But I decided to give it a shot anyway, feeling somehow that if I called him right then, I'd catch him.

He picked up on the first ring. "Nick?" I asked, surprised. "It's Ray!"

"Wow, that was weird," he said. Like Carl, his voice sounded more mature than I remembered it, and he also sounded like he'd been caught off guard. "I was just on the phone with my grandmother, and a few seconds after I hung up, it rang again. I thought you were her calling me back."

"Nope. It's me. It's been a long time."

"Yeah, it has."

"So what have you been up to?" I asked him. I was eager to catch up, plus I had been dying to know how he had adjusted to everything after his brief involvement with the vampires.

"Just stuff. You know. School, life, the usual." He didn't sound very happy to hear from me.

"Yeah, school is pretty crappy for me," I said, hoping to get him talking. "There's all these uptight Christians who won't let you do anything or else you'll get in trouble."

"Hmm," he said simply.

"Oh!" I said eagerly. "Here's something I should tell you about. There was this videotape they made us watch of this really stupid guy. He was all, 'Rock music is all satanic! You're goin' to hell if you listen to this stuff!'"

He let out a small laugh. "Yeah, I'm not surprised."

"He even mentioned that group you used to listen to! The Dead Milkmen!" This was a lie, but I thought it might keep the conversation going. "He's all like, 'The Dead Milkmen. Now isn't that just a *nice* name for a band.'" The man hadn't mentioned that group in particular, but he had spoken in similar ways about more mainstream artists.

"Yeah, well, the whole point of them isn't for them to be nice. Guy sounds like an idiot."

"Oh yeah, he was." Silence. "It was kind of funny, though." More silence. "Are you okay? You're not saying much."

"I'm fine, Ray. Just don't have a whole lot to say. Look, if you're worried that I'm going to tell anyone about your stupid little vampire thing, then don't. You know me; I'm not a narc."

"I know!" I said, feeling hurt. "It's not that! I just… I wanted to know how you'd been doing."

"Fine, I said."

"Okay."

"And if you ever decide to get all your little friends together and do that shit again, leave me out of it."

"I'm not! I mean… No, really, Nick, that's never going to happen. I'm sorry that things got as crappy as they did. It usually wasn't that bad. Things just, you know, got out of hand."

"Yeah, they did."

The conversation ended shortly after that.

By the time 1989 began, I pretty much hated everything about my life. The people I went to school with ranged from being okay to despicable, and the teachers were intolerant and in some cases incompetent. Some of them had no business being in front of a classroom, I felt. The girls I liked seemed completely unapproachable, and the few that I was friends with or who might even like me didn't seem like they were worth my time. I found the pious kids boring, the cool guys stupid and rednecky, and the nerdy guys overbearing and always trying to get up in my face.

Some of the boys and girls dated each other, even across grades. I remember being amused at how Annie, the popular cheerleader, seemed to have a different — and always older — boyfriend every other month. I wasn't happy to find out that Kirby had apparently dated (or "gone with") Elizabeth for a brief time the year before I had started attending Bethlehem, which made me jealous of him in a sort of past tense way. When I asked him why they had broken up, and all he could tell me was, "I don't know, man. You'd have to ask her. She was just too weird."

I didn't ask her; God forbid that I let on that I had any interest whatsoever in her dating history. She never went with anyone else, though, as far as I knew. It was like she didn't want to bother getting caught up in all of the drama that the other kids created for themselves. Or maybe Kirby was right, and she just was too weird. She had grown more cold to me lately, which was frustrating.

Overall, I went through the angst that any young teenager suffering from unrequited love would. The slightest positive reaction from Elizabeth would have me feeling over the moon and hopeful that somehow we might get together, while any bad encounter with her would send me into the depths of depression. Every little thing seemed to matter so much.

Life at home wasn't much better. I only dealt with my parents as much as necessary, and while I sensed that they knew I was unhappy, I wasn't sure how much they cared. They probably did, but I had gotten so sullen and morose by then that I wasn't very approachable, even if they had offered to help. They couldn't have helped, anyway. When I wasn't stewing in anger over my complete lack of a social life and my contempt for everyone around me, I was wallowing in guilt and self-pity over my past sins.

Carolyn was similarly inaccessible, even more so since she and Damon had recently broken up. Curious, I had asked her why they had split, but she wouldn't tell me anything other than "Because he's a jerk." I wasn't even sure which of them had been the one to break things off, but maybe it didn't matter. I had my own failed romantic interests to be concerned with.

I was also curious as to how Damon had handled things in terms of having been a vampire and then dealing with the fallout, but I never got the chance to ask him. Because Carolyn had her own apartment, what time they did spend together was usually over there, and the few times he had come over to the house with her, we didn't talk much. We were cordial and friendly to each other, but there was something distant about him. My guess was that he was secretly freaked out about everything and, like the rest of us, just wanted to put it behind him.

Sometime in late spring, an incident happened in Physical Science class that disturbed me. Bradley had this dubious talent of being able to project his saliva in little spurts from his mouth, which he showed off to some of the boys before class began. It wasn't like regular spitting; he didn't even use his lips. He could somehow do something weird to the muscles under his tongue and have these little drops of saliva shoot forward several inches, sometimes even a couple of feet. I had occasionally done this accidentally while eating, opening my mouth a certain way and being surprised by the little drops that flew out. It reminded me of a snake spraying venom, so when I was younger, I thought it was kind of cool.

What wasn't cool was that Bradley, who sat in the desk behind me, took it upon himself to start spitting like this onto the back of my head after class started. Kirby and a couple of the other guys who saw what he was doing found this funny, but I sure as hell didn't. I could just barely feel it, but it was gross, and it pissed me off. No matter how many times I told him to quit, he kept doing it. Any adult would have said that the right thing to do would be to tell Mrs. Manning, but I wasn't going to be a tattletale.

It didn't help that I was already in a bad mood that day. Like other boys my age, my voice had started to deepen during ninth grade, but it didn't happen all at once. The characteristic high-pitched squeaking that happens to some boys during this time is what forces them to speak in a lower register. This sometimes results in teenage boys developing forced, almost comically deep-sounding voices, but they do that because they're terrified of letting out a squeak and getting embarrassed.

I had done a pretty good job of finding my new voice, but this particular morning, I was caught off guard when Helen asked me something while I happened to be facing the other direction. I was sitting in my desk in History class and talking to Aaron about something when she called out to me.

Turning to face her and being surprised that she was talking to me at all, I squeaked out, "What?" It sounded like a bird chirping. Immediately, I realized what I'd done and felt myself blushing.

Things weren't helped by the way Helen's face lit up and she burst out laughing, managing to cough out that she wanted to ask me if she could borrow a pencil. Even though I was angry, I handed her one from my backpack, just wanting the conversation to be over.

That might have been the end of it, but then I was aware that she was whispering with Elizabeth and Melinda in the next row over. I even heard her do a quiet impression of my high-pitched "what?," which resulted in hushed giggles. After class, Helen returned my pencil, saying in an exaggeratedly distorted voice, "Tha-anks, Ra-ay!" This led to peals of laughter from her two friends, and it hurt so much to see Elizabeth enjoying watching me squirm.

So later on in the day when Bradley was taunting me with his amazing and disgusting talent, I was already close to boiling point. He was even leaning forward in his desk sometimes to project the saliva as far as possible, a couple of times making it shoot over my shoulder. A few times, I turned around and gave him a threatening look, but this just egged him on as much as his friends' laughter did. Mrs. Manning, meanwhile, continued on with her boring lecture, completely oblivious to what was happening or what was about to take place.

For a couple of minutes, it looked like Bradley had tired of his little prank and that I would be left in peace. But all that time, I was tense, something inside of me just waiting for him to do it again. And then, right when I had started to relax, a few clear beads shot past me and onto my notebook. A switch flipped.

With lightning-like quickness, I shot up from my desk and circled around, grabbing both side's of Bradley's head and yanking him from his desk with a strength I didn't know I had. He was a good deal taller than me, but he was also lanky and apparently not very strong, as I had him pinned to the floor in a matter of seconds. I was shouting at him, barely aware of what I was saying; it was something along the lines of having had enough and how he had no idea who he was dealing with. The words didn't necessarily make sense, but they conveyed the rage I was feeling.

I was only vaguely aware of the reactions of everyone around us as I continued to punch at the side of his head and shout at him, and he made little to no move to defend himself. His expression was a combination of surprise and fear, and once he started to recover and seemed to be making a move to push himself up from the floor, I forced his head down by the neck by using my forearm to pin him. He began to look more afraid, and I might have crushed his windpipe had not someone begun pulling me off of him from behind.

The switch flipped again, and I stopped my assault, surprised to find that the person who had manhandled me off of Bradley was in fact Mrs. Manning. She held my arms firmly for a few seconds, stopping her incessant cry of, "Boys! Boys!" I relaxed, surprised at what I'd done and apologizing breathlessly to both her and the boy I had felt like killing just a few moments before. Bradley looked up at me from the floor in terror. There were tears in his eyes, and for a brief moment, I relished that.

I had to attend detention weekly for the rest of the school year, as did Bradley, and I was fully aware of the fact that we were both lucky not to have gotten suspended or even expelled. Part of me wished I had been kicked out of that crappy school, but more than that, it shocked me how violent I had become in that brief moment.

Just a few days earlier, I had watched a TV movie based on the old series *The Incredible Hulk,* which I had liked watching as a child. The main character, David Banner, often talked about how he had this beast within him that he would try to keep from letting escape. Inevitably, he would fail, something setting off his anger to the point where he would transform into the Hulk, tearing things up and terrifying everyone around him. While I had occasionally liked to pretend that I was that green, muscular monster as a little kid, this incident with Bradley felt like the first time I truly understood what that feeling was like in real life, to get so angry that I could lose control and lash out at someone like that. For however many seconds it had gone on — thirty, maybe less — I had genuinely wanted to kill him.

This was the first time I had gotten into trouble at school on this scale, and I wasn't able to lie to my parents about it, either. I explained it to them as best as I could, self-justifications and all, and they seemed more or less sympathetic. It was wrong of Bradley to keep spitting at me like that, but that didn't excuse my overreaction. I was genuinely sorry for how out of hand I had gotten, and they seemed to pick up on that, seeing my acceptance of my school-based punishment as enough. Bradley and I had been forced by Dr. Phillips and the school counselor to apologize to each other and shake hands, but there was something weird about him from that point on that I couldn't quite place.

I had wanted to talk to Dennis about this incident shortly after it happened, but I wasn't able to reach him, so I called Tim instead.

"Oh, so you haven't heard?" he asked me.

"Heard what?"

"Dennis got sent to Danson."

"He did what?" I asked with a laugh. I had thought he'd said "dancing," which prompted a rather funny image in my head of Dennis.

"Danson," Tim repeated firmly, "the mental hospital."

Finally, it clicked. Danson Medical was, as near as I understood it, a juvenile detention center for children with mental and emotional problems. I had heard it spoken of from time to time over the years, usually in hushed tones about how some kid or another had been so bad that they had to be sent there.

"Oh my God," I said. "What happened?"

"Apparently he got into drugs and all that," Tim said sadly. "I don't know what kinds exactly; I've never been into that."

I never had been, either. For people like me and Tim, "drugs" was a blanket term that could span all kinds of illegal substances, and we knew very little about them aside from the somewhat hyperbolical warnings we had grown up with along the lines of "Just Say No" and "drugs are bad for you." That gave them a weird sort of mystique, but the image that had been drilled into our heads was that anyone who succumbed to their power wound up becoming a strung-out junkie, someone dangerous to be around. The idea of Dennis becoming like that bothered me, and I wondered just what had happened.

"His dad wouldn't tell me all the details," Tim said.

"You talked to him?"

"Yeah. He sounded pretty sad about it, but also like it was the right thing to do, something that was for his own good."

I tried to digest this. Was my old friend locked in a jail cell somewhere and confined in a straitjacket? Was he blitzed out on some kind of weird drugs, screaming his head off like a crazy person?

"I think he's mostly okay," Tim continued. "I don't think he's in some padded room in a straitjacket or anything. His dad mentioned that he once had to send Joanna there for a little while, too, and she came out of it okay and much better. Apparently, he'd been doing some bad stuff at school, like vandalism. He even smashed a light bulb in one of the locker rooms, leaving broken glass everywhere so the soccer team couldn't take their showers after their game. Ray?"

I realized that I had gone quiet for a few moments, as I'd been distracted by something he'd said a few sentences earlier. I ended our conversation shortly afterwards, lying and saying I needed to go do some homework.

The summer of 1989 felt weird, particularly because of the pattern of things. Since 1983, we had been on this repeating two-year cycle of becoming vampires while my parents were out of town, then gone back to normal as if nothing had happened. Each time, there was the anticipation over the next time we would do it, and while we hadn't deliberately taken the potion precisely every two years, that was how it turned out and what I got used to. Even in 1987 when we first got back together, I found myself thinking ahead, wondering if we would reunite again in another couple of years and have even more fun.

Of course, all that was out of the question. Still, it felt strange when my parents did leave for Dallas in June, leaving me mostly on my own with nothing to do. Carolyn was still in town and had to stay at the house while they were gone in case I needed to be driven anywhere, but we didn't interact much, at least not beyond a superficial level.

There were a few times when I considered asking her what she thought, if things felt as weird for her as they did for me, but I was pretty sure I knew the answer. She didn't even stay at the house the whole time like she was supposed to, telling me instead that I could call her at her apartment if I needed her. I was fine with that, and I knew I'd see her whenever she needed to come by and do her laundry.

I thought of inviting one or two of my old friends over, but that just reminded me of the vampire summers, so I avoided that. And it wasn't like I was close enough to anybody from Bethlehem to want them to come around. Overall, things felt lonely. I played video games on my own, then felt guilty one time when Carolyn came over during that, thinking that the Atari 5200 Damon had given me might be a sad reminder for her, so I turned it off.

"Do you ever talk to him anymore?" I asked her.

"Not if I can help it," she said, putting her latest load of dirty clothes into the washing machine. "But sometimes I run into him. That's the thing that sucks about Augusta."

"What?"

"There's this... I don't know... interconnectedness of people, I guess you could say." She did a gesture with her hands to indicate things being mixed together. "You try to get away from somebody, then find that they know someone who knows someone else... who knows the same person... It's weird."

It seemed for a moment that we might actually have a deep conversation, but she cut me off before I could say more than a few words. She then headed to the kitchen and picked up the phone, calling up one of her friends and asking her if she wanted to hang out that night. Feeling rejected, I skulked off to my room.

The rest of the week, I busied myself with the task of rearranging my bedroom. I decided to change the position of everything in there, the bed, the dresser, the shelves, the desk. There wasn't much point to doing it; I just felt like a change would be good.

Some of the smaller stuff I was able to move on my own, but I needed Carolyn's help for the bigger things. She may have grown from a tomboy to a more elegant young woman, but when necessary, she could still do some heavy lifting. A small part of me hoped that we might bond over this and start having real conversations again, but that never happened. In fact, she failed to show up one morning when she had said she would, leaving me to sleep in a disorganized, half-arranged bedroom that night. When I tried to call her on that the next day, she didn't bother to apologize, nor did she try to berate me for being ungrateful for what help she had given me so far. She just didn't seem to care.

Being left alone with my thoughts for most of that summer proved to be difficult. Sometimes I could distract myself with projects, but other times, I just brooded. And I didn't like where my thoughts sometimes led me. I didn't actually miss the vampire situation, as I knew that it was horrible and something we should never do again. But that didn't stop the dreams.

Since 1987, I'd occasionally had vivid, often disturbing dreams about vampires. One recurring one that I had involved flying around as a bat, but I couldn't control where I was going or how fast. Sometimes I would go so high that I couldn't see the ground below, and other times, I would need to land but then forget how to, afraid that I would crash.

Another early dream also had me as a vampire, and there were other vampires involved, but they weren't my friends or family. Still, in that strange dream logic that fills in gaps in the narrative, I knew I had done something wrong, and the other vampires were after me because of it. I tried my best to run and hide, never actually seeing them but knowing that they were nearby. I ended up standing in the street outside my house, at which point a wooden arrow shot out of nowhere and nailed me right in the heart, and I fell down dead.

I had heard that if someone died in their dream, they would also die in real life, but apparently this wasn't true. I asked Carolyn about it, telling her I'd had a dream in which I'd died but not that it was a vampire dream.

"Ray, think about it," she said. "Think real hard about the logic of that." I tried, but I couldn't see what she was getting at. She shook her head, and her slight smirk told me that she was enjoying imparting this wisdom on me. "Do you know what other people are dreaming? Do you ever know that unless they tell you?"

"No…?" I said uncertainly.

"Well, say somebody has a dream where they die. So then they're dead. It's not like they can then get up and tell someone, 'Hey, I had a dream where I died!'"

That almost made sense. "But then why do they say that people who die in their dreams die in real life?"

"'They' who?" Carolyn asked, still cocky. "It's just something people say, something they hear from someone else, so they think it's true. Or they hear that it actually happened to someone else, like a friend of a friend or someone's relative. But it's never really true. People just think it is. That's how misconceptions get spread around."

Armed with this new knowledge, I felt better. Not only had I learned something, but I also felt like I knew more than the average person, the kind who would go around spreading urban legends like the one I had believed in just a few moments earlier.

After that conversation, I didn't have any more dreams in which I got killed, but I still had dreams about being a vampire. Things were tense and scary, and I always woke up feeling ashamed, both of the dream and of the reality of my past. I hated dreaming about vampires, and it's possible that the fear of doing that just fueled them, turning them into recurring nightmares.

The one that became the most common was that I would be at school and that some vampire trait would suddenly become active in me, and I would have to try to hide it from everyone. Sometimes I would spontaneously grow fangs and try to avoid speaking so no one could see my teeth, but the most common problem was that my eyes would start glowing and I would have to try to hide those. I would screw my eyes shut, but then I couldn't walk anywhere without bumping into things, so I would try to get by as best as I could by briefly squinting.

The dream recurred several times over the years, getting to the point where I knew that it was coming. Certain events would repeat in sequence, and as I realized that they were happening and leading up to the scarier part where the vampire trait would emerge, I would become more and more frightened. Sometimes, this would shock me awake, but usually I was trapped and had to go through everything.

One night, events progressed further than usual, and I came up with the solution of hiding my glowing eyes from everyone with sunglasses if I could get my hands on some. I made my way out of the school building to the parking lot, the idea being that I could search in one of the upperclassmen's cars. But the sunlight was so intense that I was practically blind, and I again had to keep my eyes shut from the pain, only allowing brief glimpses in order to navigate.

Eventually, I found an unlocked car with some sunglasses in it, but once I was back inside, people were laughing at me. They thought I was being pretentious and trying to look cool, and nothing I said or did could convince them otherwise.

Elizabeth, who looked a little different than she did in real life, gave me a sly grin and pointed at me, saying, "I see you!" She laughed haughtily, and Melinda and Helen did the same, the three of them turning and walking away from me. I tried to follow, but for some reason, my legs wouldn't work properly. It was like I had forgotten how to walk, and I kept falling onto the floor, trying unsuccessfully to get up and follow them, to offer some kind of explanation.

Suddenly, someone behind me grabbed me painfully by the shoulder and spun me around. Towering over me was Dr. Phillips, his eyes glowing red and his mouth covered in blood. He smiled at me menacingly, his arm still outstretched toward me. He started to speak in some demonic voice that sounded like it was being played backwards, and I was jolted awake in fear.

I didn't get any more sleep that night. I was terrified that if I did fall asleep, I would just go back into the same nightmare. Fortunately, there was only about an hour left before my alarm was set to go off, so I lay in bed for a while, then decided to get up early. It was my first day back at school.

As usual, I was dreading going back, wondering what new bullshit I would have to put up with this year. The only bright spot was getting to see Elizabeth again, but that wasn't entirely a comfort, either. My on and off crush on her was so frustrating because I couldn't seem to make it go anywhere, but I also couldn't let it go. She was just too beautiful and captivating, and I was a 15-year-old boy enslaved to his passions. I figured that tenth grade would be filled with more of the same unrequited love and feelings of shyness and loneliness.

I also wasn't looking forward to seeing Bradley again, but then I found out that he hadn't come back that year.

"Yeah, he was too afraid of you, Ray," Kirby said sarcastically. "He had to go to another school so you wouldn't beat him up."

I laughed nervously, unsure how to take this particular joke. I knew Kirby was kidding, but there was something else in there. After that big fight the previous school year, people's reactions had varied. Bradley had seemed terrified of me at the time of the fight, and afterwards, he was just really quiet and avoided me. His friends, including Kirby, had made fun of him for the way he had cried and how I had "beat the ever-living crap out of him," as Chris put it.

The well-behaved Christian kids — who were, perhaps not coincidentally, the ones who were the most studious and got the best grades — avoided me, which I was fine with. And while Aaron and his geeky group thought what I had done was really cool because I stood up for myself, I didn't feel the same way. I was embarrassed about it, and when they tried to cheer me on and congratulate me, I told them off.

Elizabeth's trio of friends was just indifferent. It was like they didn't want to acknowledge that anything had happened at all. Maybe that was because I had gotten so much attention, and their way of taking me down a peg was to ignore me. I worried that Elizabeth might be afraid of me for some reason, thinking that I was this really dangerous person that she needed to avoid. But mostly, she didn't say anything to me at all, which also hurt.

Now that tenth grade was beginning, I hoped for a fresh start. With Bradley gone, maybe there wouldn't be anything to set me off again. But I wondered if some new problems might crop up, and I might end up getting violent again. I didn't want that to happen, but there was something at the edge of my psyche that seemed to be warning me that it would.

Since Bethlehem was a very small school, it was underfunded and understaffed, which was one more reason to dislike the place and think of it as a joke. I had been simultaneously amused and apprehensive to find out that Dr. Phillips, normally just the principal of the school, would be doubling as our homeroom teacher that year. This ended up having something of a diminishing effect over time, turning him from this distant, overlord-like authority figure to just another boring teacher trying to shove Christian morals down our throats.

The most interesting new development on my first day, though, was Elizabeth's new appearance. She was still impossibly beautiful and flawlessly made up, but her hair had changed. Instead of the precise curls meticulously sprayed into place that I had gotten so used to seeing, her hair was now straight and slightly shorter, reaching about halfway to her shoulders. It still looked somewhat fried and overly styled, and she still had that same dome-like sculpture of bangs above her forehead, but she looked good. Her friends and even some of the more popular girls complimented her on her new look, and I couldn't keep my eyes off of her as I tried to take it all in.

"It suits you more!" Helen said to her, gently touching Elizabeth's hair with the back of her hand. Her hair wasn't platinum blonde, but more like it had some brown mixed in with it. Back at St. Joseph's, Valerie's friend Andrea had hair that was almost the same color, and I'd heard her describe this as "dishwater blonde." Helen continued, "It frames your face really well. Maybe I should try that, too."

"I don't think it would work for me," Melinda said, sitting on the other side, her desk pulled up next to Elizabeth's. "I never liked my hair straight."

This made me laugh inside; I was reminded of a time in ninth grade when Melinda had come to school with her hair in a ponytail, but because it was so overly permed and curly, the ponytail had taken on this weird round shape that was exactly the same size as her head. It was like she had two heads at once, one following the other around. I thought it looked incredibly stupid, and she never repeated the style again, probably because one of her friends must have told her afterwards that it wasn't a good look for her.

"But it does look good on you," Melinda added.

"Thanks," Elizabeth said with a slight shrug of her shoulders and a cute grin.

"I know someone else who likes it," Helen said with a smile, and my blood froze as she pointed at me with a mischievous look. The other two girls quickly turned and smiled similarly.

"Yeah, Ray," Elizabeth said. "You can put your eyes back in your head anytime now."

"What?" I almost shouted. "No! I mean..." I faltered, trying to salvage the situation. Aaron, who had unfortunately been assigned to sit in front of me, let out a goofy chortle. I gave him a dirty look, but he just kept on smiling, enjoying my awkward moment as much as the girls were. "I mean, it's just different. That's all. Takes some getting used to. I guess it's cool and all... I don't know."

Elizabeth shook her head, but there was something forgiving in the way that she smiled. I tried to focus on that more than the triumphant, disdainful looks that Melinda and Helen were giving me. "Well, let me know when you're sure," she said.

Thankfully, the bell rang at that moment, and everyone had to get themselves and their desks in order so class could begin. I burned inside from the embarrassment over having been caught staring at Elizabeth so much, but there was something else on my mind.

Sure, it was disconcerting that the girl I had tirelessly admired for two years looked different. And it was humiliating that she and her friends had laughed at me after calling me out on looking at her so intently without any sense of stealth. But the most disturbing thing was that even though this was the first time I had been in Elizabeth's presence for nearly three months, her change in appearance was less of a surprise to me than it should have been. I had seen this new haircut of hers the night before: That was how she had looked in my dream.

If I'd had any doubts up until that point that my psychic powers had returned, they all went out the window at that moment. I had grudgingly accepted that my powers had left me after the incident with bringing Tim back to life, and while I missed having them, there was another part of me that was glad to see them gone. I associated them with being a vampire, especially given how strong and powerful they had gotten during that last summer. A few coincidences had occurred here and there that made me wonder if my powers might be returning, but whenever they did, I tried to write them off. But those occurrences had become too frequent and specific to ignore, culminating in this premonition about Elizabeth.

"You too, huh?" Dennis asked me over the phone. He had been released from Danson near the end of summer and was back home, and I wanted to find out how he was doing, if he was okay. Moreover, I wanted to find out if his powers had returned as well.

"Yeah," I said. "What do you think it means?"

"I don't know," he said airily. He also sounded like he didn't care.

"I wonder if Tim's gotten his back, too," I suddenly realized.

"Maybe you should ask him. I'm sure he'd be eager to talk just like always." His attitude annoyed me, but I was still concerned about him, wondering what he had been through in the hospital. Changing the subject, I asked him about that, but he maintained his distant manner.

"It was fine," he assured me. "Wasn't that bad."

"Did they… I don't know… do stuff to you?"

He laughed a little. "No, it wasn't anything like that. Mostly just a lot of talking and therapy and shit like that. 'How do you feel about…?' blah blah blah. After a while you just learned how to tell them what they wanted to hear, to convince them that you weren't all crazy-ass anymore. One time, they made me write out this big list of all the bad things I'd done, this thing to get me to come to terms with my behavior or something. Of course, I had to leave off one big one in particular, you know."

I understood and said so. "I'm guessing you didn't tell them about the whole psychic thing, either."

He let out an exclamation that sounded like *"pssshhht."* "Are you kidding?" he asked with a laugh. "They'd never have let me out then! But yeah, like you said, it's not as strong as it was before. At least, not by the end. More like when we were first starting out."

I thought about this for a bit. "I wonder if they'll keep getting more powerful."

"Maybe," he said, lapsing back into his previous tone. "Why make such a big deal about it?"

I started to explain how I associated our powers with us being vampires, but as I spoke, I realized that doing so didn't entirely make sense. Our powers had developed as something separate, though the potion did seem to increase them. As we talked things out — which was difficult because Dennis kept being so resistant and apathetic — we concluded that being psychic was just something that naturally occurred in us, and while the powers may have gotten used up or burned out a while ago, they were healing and coming back. That wasn't necessarily a bad thing.

Tim felt differently, though. As he and I talked, I found that he'd developed a similar correlation in his head between the powers and our experiences as vampires, and it disturbed him a great deal that "things seem to be backsliding," as he put it.

"It's not just the psychic thing, Ray," he said worriedly. "It's… well… other stuff. Have you felt it, too?"

"Felt what?"

"I've just been so… I don't know… angry lately. At everything. Like I want to punch my fist through a wall or somebody's…" He broke off, letting out an exasperated sigh. "I don't like it. It really, really bugs me."

"Tim, that could just be you being you," I said, realizing as the words came out that they sounded kind of stupid. "I mean, maybe it's just an adolescence thing. You know, hormones and all that? The teachers at my school are always blaming our bad behavior on stuff like that."

"They're wrong," Tim said firmly, his voice deeper than usual. "I've been praying and praying that this will all just go away, and it isn't working. I hate it."

I wasn't sure what to say. He seemed to need comfort, but I didn't know how to give it. I fumbled around my thoughts trying to come up with something. "Well, maybe praying isn't the way to deal with it."

"Then what the fuck am I supposed to do?" he shouted back. His next sentence revealed that he was just as shocked as I was to hear him talk like that. "I'm sorry, Ray. I'm really, really sorry. That wasn't me. I mean it wasn't like me."

"Maybe you're just having a bad day," I said, again feeling like what I was saying was stupid and ineffectual. "Why don't you try giving me a call in a few days and see if you feel any better."

"Yeah, okay. I will." He sounded genuinely shaken up. "Sorry. I've got to go."

After we got off the phone, I felt bad for him. He certainly wasn't acting normal. But there was something else in the back of my mind that made me feel ashamed when I began to realize what it was. It was the fact that Tim, so often the goody two-shoes who was so smart and in control, seemed to be losing it, and somewhere deep down, I found that amusing. Maybe he wasn't so smart after all.

A couple of nights later, I had another vampire dream, but this one was different. Not much actually happened in it, but it was another one of those where the historical details were filled in by my mind so I could understand what was going on.

The story was that the entire world had changed, and there was a big war between vampires and humans. I was, not surprisingly, one of the vampires, part of a small team of three who had a mission to complete. It had something to do with defending one of the farms, which was what we called these places where human beings were kept in cages until we needed them. It only made sense in the dream, some of these people actually being born and raised in these farms, so isolated from humanity that they never even learned how to speak. They were essentially animals, our food.

There was also a huge dome built over the city, at least, it was called a dome at one point but was more like a huge flat surface supported by rectangular pillars. It was like Augusta had been transformed into one huge parking garage, the sun permanently blotted out so that we vampires could be active any time day or night. The city once famous for its golf courses and gardens had become dead, a place where vampires thrived and ruled.

The only real action that occurred in the dream was a lot of talking among my team of vampires followed by an attack by a team of three humans. Even though they were armed with stakes and crossbows, we easily overpowered them, my teammates claiming their victims as I zeroed in on mine.

I paused when I realized that I recognized her. She had gorgeous, wide brown eyes and very long, straight brown hair that was so dark it was almost black. She was beautiful overall, but there was also something tough about her, a strength in the way she carried herself that made her even more attractive. She also had, oddly enough, a dimple on only one of her cheeks, which made her look distinctive and even kind of cute, despite the fact that she was my enemy.

The reason I recognized her was that in real life, her image often ran through my mind and made me feel wracked with guilt. This was the very last girl I had killed back in 1987, my last victim before being changed back to human that final time. I had no idea who she was or what her name was, but I could clearly remember how she felt as she struggled against me, the softness of her pale neck as I bit into it, and the taste of her hot, salty blood as it rushed into my mouth. She had let out a tiny, pitiful moan as I'd begun to drink from her which, had I been a little older, I might have found arousing. But at the time, it was just one more detail of the experience, something I had tried to forget over the years but never could, just as I could never forget everything else about her.

Realizing who she was and that it didn't make sense for me to be encountering her broke the narrative, making me realize that I was dreaming. This happened to me sometimes in other dreams, the result always being the same: I woke up. As I lay awake in bed for a while, I was as usual shaken up by the memory of my last kill, but I was also disappointed that the dream had to end. Vampire dreams usually disturbed me, but this one had actually been kind of cool, or at least the concept behind it was. It was such a complex, vivid story, and I kept thinking about it, for once hoping that I might drift back into the dream, but that didn't happen.

I did, though, wonder if I might be able to write a book based on the dream's backstory. It certainly had some potential as a dark, post-apocalyptic science fiction tale. I had never been all that keen on writing — or reading, for that matter — but the idea intrigued me. But then I worried that if I were to write this big vampire story, get it published, and become all famous, that could end up being incriminating if anyone were to ever somehow tie me to the real-life events of the past. Besides, my sisters — and probably my friends as well — would probably be pissed off at me for doing it.

That day after school, I found that old copy of *Dracula* that Susanna and I had stolen from Sheling's hotel room. It had been hidden in my closet for a couple of years; I hadn't wanted to just throw it away, but I didn't know what else to do with it. Given how I'd felt about all other vampire-related things since then, I hadn't wanted to read it, either, but the previous night's dream and the brief toying with the idea of writing a vampire novel changed my mind.

After pretending to go to bed that night, I locked my door and settled down into bed with the book and a flashlight, eager to finally read this classic tale. I knew that I shouldn't be doing it or have so much interest in what the book had to say, but that was part of the fun. It was literally a guilty pleasure.

Unfortunately, I couldn't get very far into the book. I quickly remembered the handful of times I had tried to read passages from it before, how the almost hundred-year-old language had come across to me as overly complicated and plodding. It was English, but not quite the same as what I was used to. I knew that language developed and evolved over time, how different and hard to understand things written in Shakespeare's time could be. The text of *Dracula* wasn't quite that old or as hard to understand, but it was off-putting enough that I didn't want to continue reading after that first night. I'd almost fallen asleep during this single attempt.

About a month later, I did what any lazy tenth grader would do in this situation: I read the Cliff's Notes instead. These concise summaries of the great works of literature were often used by teenagers to circumvent having to read the full-length novels assigned to them in school, and often, they were a good substitute. Some teachers, though, were smart enough to get one over on their students by intentionally quizzing them on things that were in the actual book but not in the Cliff's Notes, as I found out that month when I tried this same trick to get out of reading *Wuthering Heights.* While I had gotten used to thinking of the teachers at Bethlehem as stupid and ineffectual, my English teacher that year, Mrs. Cartwright, was actually pretty savvy, at least on this front. I ended up failing a quiz as a result.

But for the purposes of gleaning what knowledge I wanted to from *Dracula,* the Cliff's Notes were more than adequate. I told my mother that I needed to read the book for school, which would have been impossible in reality since vampires were a forbidden topic there, but she didn't know that. As with *Wuthering Heights,* I'd told her that I was still going to read the actual book itself and just use the Cliff's Notes as a guide.

I made it through the entire book in one night, intrigued by what I read but occasionally feeling weird whenever it reminded me of real-life events that I had been trying so hard to forget. What was the most interesting to me were the different abilities that Dracula and the other vampires had and how they either matched up to or were different from the ones we'd had.

At first, I would view anything that differed from us as incorrect and an inconsistency, like how it was said that a vampire couldn't enter someone's home unless invited inside first. Tim had mentioned this to me before, having read the entire book himself like the good little studious nerd he was. Reading that detail myself struck me as odd and even a little bit stupid. How could any of the vampire stories I'd known about growing up ever take place with that kind of a restriction? Since 1987, I had mostly avoided anything vampire-related that I happened to run across on TV, but prior to that, I had seen plenty. Vampires came into people's homes and preyed on them all the time, invitation or not. It was one of the things that made them so scary and powerful. And why would anyone invite a vampire in unless they wanted to be bitten? Had Bram Stoker just gotten that part wrong?

There were other things that were unfamiliar to me, like how one of the vampires was able to get in and out of her tomb by doing this weird thing where her body somehow became flat enough to slip through the cracks, but then she was like a normal person again. We'd never had that ability, but then again, did we maybe have it all along, but we didn't know? That reminded me of the fact that I had never heard of running water being a deterrent to vampires before Susanna mentioned it to us, yet there it was in this book, regardless of my ignorance.

As I read, I became more uncertain of my knowledge, the things I thought I knew about vampires. I was surprised to read that Dracula could turn himself into a wolf, which I didn't like reading because it reminded me of the time I had been involuntarily changed into one, brief though that episode was. Similarly, the physical descriptions and mannerisms of both Dracula and Van Helsing were eerily accurate and disturbing, bringing back to me in vivid detail my confrontations with them in real life. But the most surprising thing of all was finding out that Dracula could walk around in broad daylight. That seemed to go against one of the core things I had always understood about vampires.

After finishing the Cliff's Notes and lying down, I found it hard to get to sleep. So many things were running through my head, though they became muddled the more tired I became. Why were there so many things wrong in the book? Or was my knowledge just too limited? If, as I'd speculated before, Bram Stoker was actually Van Helsing's pen name, then maybe he had intentionally gotten some details wrong in order to throw people off. I wasn't entirely sure if that made sense, but it seemed to at the time.

I also wondered if my other idea was true, that maybe we'd always had these other abilities but just hadn't realized it. Maybe sunlight wasn't actually harmful to us. *Dracula* was, as far as I knew, the oldest vampire story, predating us by almost a hundred years, so who was to say that we were right and it was wrong?

My thoughts began to blur as I approached sleep, but then something else would get me riled up and I'd be awake again. The biggest and most exciting of these was wanting to test my idea by taking the potion again. I couldn't think how I could possibly get Susanna to agree to make it, but maybe I could try to make it myself by somehow getting my hands on a copy of the formula. It would just be a small test, something I could try out briefly and then go back to normal afterwards.

The next morning, I woke up having briefly forgotten about my idea from the night before. While taking a shower, it suddenly popped back into my head, and I was horrified with myself. How could I have possibly thought of taking that potion again? Being vampires wasn't some fun game we had played; it was deadly serious, something terrible we had done that should never be repeated. I had known this for years, so how could I have been so stupid as to forget that, even if just for one night?

I knew that even if I were to somehow be able to manipulate Susanna into giving me the potion or find a way to sneakily do it on my own, I wouldn't just stop being a vampire voluntarily. We had never been able to do that, at least, not the last couple of times. Being that powerful and dangerous was too intoxicating to give up, and hundreds of people had died as a result. I couldn't believe that I'd toyed with the notion at all, and I felt very ashamed.

My thoughts drifted back to this several more times over the next few days, and I continued to berate myself for how stupid that was. I wondered if I might actually have the strength to control myself if I did become a vampire again, but I knew the answer to that. I just might be able to change myself back to human after a day or two, but probably not before some more people got killed. And if I did that, what was to stop any of the former vampires from telling on me? I could end up getting into trouble with the authorities, probably detained somewhere a lot more serious than Danson like Dennis had been. What's more, we could all be implicated, which would be even worse.

My renewed guilt didn't help when it came to the dreams I kept having. Sometimes there would just be brief flashes of vampire-related things, like one I had where Dracula was chasing me around my house. He was being very slow and methodical about it, not running after me but just walking around as I tried to hide, like he knew that he was going to catch me. Because of the way things change in dreams, this vampire then wasn't actually Dracula but some other ancient vampire, a very cocky and confident dark-haired man who boasted about how he knew me and that I couldn't get away from him. He looked familiar, and when I realized that he looked the way my father did in pictures I'd seen of him when he was younger, he laughed at me, sounding just like Dad. That was too much for me to handle, and I woke up.

The recurring nightmare where my eyes would glow while I was at school kept happening, though the variations on it became more complex. In one version, the glowing of my eyes was accompanied by the same musical cue from *The Incredible Hulk* that would occur whenever David Banner's eyes glowed and he transformed into the Hulk. Rather than only lasting a few seconds like on the show, the creepy violin sound was constantly playing, and I was afraid that other people could hear it.

In another dream, I looked in the mirror and saw my eyes ablaze, their glow just like that of a firefly, but steady and constant. This was in fact how our eyes had looked during our final summer as vampires, but I had never actually seen myself like this because I hadn't had a reflection at the time. I held my fists to each side of my head, willing the phenomenon to stop, then feared that I might crush my own skull in the effort. I was reminded of something my sisters and I had done one evening at my aunt and uncle's house when I was little, how we were catching fireflies in the yard and accidentally discovered that if we smashed them into the ground and killed them, they would leave a trail of glowing yellow goo across the grass. I began to wonder if the same thing might happen to me if my head were smashed, if there would be phosphorescent mush everywhere. As I turned to leave the bathroom, a huge hammer swung at me from the open doorway and slammed into my face, and I was jolted awake once again.

Tenth grade was turning out to be just as crappy as my previous two years at Bethlehem, and things showed no signs of improving. One particular morning, I hadn't had a lot of sleep the night before because of yet another vampire nightmare. Kirby and Chris came up to me at my locker after third period, standing on either side of me.

"You want something?" I asked.

"What's that you've got there?" Kirby asked me, looking down at the books I had just taken out of my locker.

"Just my…" I began, but I was interrupted by a nudge to the backs of both of my knees from behind. While Chris did that, Kirby slammed his hands down onto my books, sending them tumbling out of my arms and onto the floor. He then backed away slightly, laughing and sneering at me. He stood there with his arms outstretched, a look of fake surprise on his face like the whole thing had been an accident.

Without thinking, I lunged at him, my right hand reaching for his throat. It made contact, and he let out a slight gurgle as I pressed down. This only lasted for a second or two before Chris grabbed my arms from behind and pulled me backwards, throwing me to one side and onto the floor. A few of the other boys stood nearby and reacted vocally, and I looked up at them angrily, then over at Kirby. I wanted to kill him.

"Careful, man!" he said with an ugly grin. "Don't want to get detention again, do ya?"

With that, he turned and walked away, and the situation dissipated. I lay there on the floor propping myself up and breathing heavily, fighting every urge to jump up and tear his stupid ass to pieces.

Kirby ended up getting detention less than an hour after that for talking back to Mrs. Cartwright, which gave me a little satisfaction. Apparently, the part of my psychic powers that made bad things happen to people who made me angry had come back as well. Still, it wasn't enough. If I'd had my way, my powers would have been even stronger than they'd gotten near the end of that last vampire summer, and his entire body would have burst into flames. I pictured this a few times, hoping it might actually happen. Of course, it didn't.

Back home, I ran the short fight over and over in my head, thinking of how it might have gone differently. I even imagined myself as a vampire again, leaping onto him and ripping his throat to shreds while I lapped up the blood and he begged for mercy. I wouldn't have given any.

A night or two later, I had that same recurring nightmare, but this was another weird variation on it. At first, it seemed like it would be the same dream, the repeated sequences of innocuous events leading up to the scary bit. I walked down the hall past Mrs. Manning's classroom door. I saw a few nondescript children as they fussed about with what looked like hay on the floor of the hallway, and an unseen adult male said to them, "Just play in the little grass." I started to feel anxious as I held my books, looking down at one of them to see the title in big white numbers on a black background: *83*. King, the St. Bernard we used to have when I was little, bounded around the corner in slow motion like something I might see on TV. Usually at this point in the dream, my eyes would start glowing against my will, and things would get progressively scarier.

But this time, nothing about my vision changed; there was no yellow or green hue to what I saw. That creepy musical violin cue kicked in, and that unnerved me, but there was no indication that I had become a vampire and needed to hide it from everyone. Instead, I came upon a crowd of people who were my age, though how I knew this while their backs were to me probably only made sense in dream logic. They turned around to face me simultaneously, the violin music increasing in intensity. Their eyes were all glowing, and they smiled at me, their mouths full of fangs. As usual, I woke up from the shock, too terrified to go back to sleep.

"I was afraid you were going to say that," Susanna said over the phone. "The same thing's been happening to me."

"Really?" I asked. I was surprised that she was speaking to me at all, particularly since I'd brought up the topic of vampires. But after talking to some of the other former vampires and finding out that they were also having nightmares and violent urges, I had to find out if she had been, too.

"Yeah," she said with a sigh. "Just the other night, I was in a bar, and these two dumb drunk guys got into a fight. And I just sat on my stool and watched, barely reacting at all. Everyone else was backing up and trying to get out of the way, but I was just sitting there with my screwdriver, sipping away like I was watching a boxing match on TV."

"You had a screwdriver?"

"It's the name of a drink, Ray."

"Oh."

"Well, anyway, a few people then tried to break up the fight, which just made things worse. Then this one girl got knocked backwards and into me, spilling her drink on me. I went ballistic. I shoved her away, then spun her around and punched her right in the face. *Punched* her! I've never done anything like that."

"What did she do?"

"That was the…" She paused. "She didn't really do anything. I think she was too stunned. She just stood there looking at me stupidly, one hand held to her face and her mouth wide open. Then I jumped on her and knocked her to the floor, and then…" She paused again.

"What?"

"Well, at first I just started slapping her. Really hard. And then I got this idea in my head to hurt her more, to swipe at her face with my nails, like a bobcat or something. Just… *shwwwp!* I wanted to draw blood. If… whoever that guy was hadn't pulled me off of her and dragged me outside, I don't know what else I would have done. After I got kicked out, I just sat on the sidewalk next to the wall and vibrated for a few minutes. It was scary."

"I'll bet," I said, feeling genuinely sympathetic. I had learned that whenever Susanna was scared, things were really serious. "So what do you think is happening?"

There was another pause. "What do *you* think is happening, Ray?"

"I don't know! I mean, I've got… I don't know… a theory or two…"

"Like what. You tell me what you think and then I'll tell you what I think might be going on."

"Well, Carl, who I hadn't talked to in forever until a couple of days ago, said he thought it might be some kind of withdrawal thing. Like alcoholics get when they quit drinking. Delirious… something…"

"Delirium tremens," she told me.

"Yeah. He said that they get all crazy and shake a lot, feeling all tense and nervous. So maybe we're experiencing something similar involving the potion."

"Possibly," she said. "Maybe."

"And Tim seemed to think something else, kind of the opposite, I guess. Remember the potion that those two scientist guys injected us with? The one that turned us into werewolves?"

"Yes," she said gravely.

"Well, that one was more or less based on the older one, the one that you and that guy Robert made. They were working from his notes, right?"

"That's how I remember it."

"So Tim was thinking that maybe since they gave us that one, it was like a double dose of the potion. We'd already taken your formula, and then with that one on top of it, it just kind of built up. Like it never really got out of our systems."

"It's still in there," Susanna said slowly. "That's along the lines of what I was thinking, too."

"So what does that mean?" I asked, my voice almost cracking, but I caught it just in time. Switching to a whisper, I asked, "Are we… I don't know, still vampires or something?"

"Not exactly," she said. "At least, I don't think so. Have you ever heard of LSD?" I had, and I said so. "And flashbacks?"

I'd heard of that as well, how people who weren't using the drug at the time felt its effects come back on their own without warning. The notion of something similar happening with the vampire potion scared the hell out of me, but it also fit with what I'd experienced recently.

After relaying some of these thoughts to Susanna, she asked me, "What about your other friend? The one who came in near the end along with… oh, what's his name… Damon? The one with the stupid haircut."

I snorted briefly. "You mean Nick? I don't know. I haven't talked to him in a long time. He was pretty pissed off about everything last time I did."

"You should talk to him," she said.

"Why?"

"To test the theory about the second dose of the potion. Nick and Damon weren't exposed to that. They joined up afterwards, remember?"

"Oh! You're right."

"I'd really like to know if those two are having the same symptoms we are. What about Carolyn?"

"What about her? Oh, you mean, has she been doing the same. I haven't asked her; I wanted to talk to you about it first. She doesn't like to talk about the whole thing." That wasn't the main reason I hadn't asked her, though. The deeper truth was that I didn't like to talk to her about it because of the brutally honest things she said to me, making me feel bad for perpetuating things and stringing them along until they got as bad as they did.

"Find out from her, just to be sure," she said. "And... Hmm, that part might be a little difficult."

"What part?"

"I don't suppose you have Damon's phone number, do you?"

I didn't; there was no reason for me to. "But Carolyn did tell me that she runs into him sometimes. Oh, I see what you mean. She's probably not going to want to talk to him, but you want to find out if he's been having the symptoms. But even if he is or isn't, what do we do then?"

"Find out what you can and call me back," she said authoritatively. "Once we have more information to go on, we can figure things out from there."

After we hung up, I realized that it felt weird to be making these plans with my oldest sister. In a way, it was like when we would be building up to each of the vampire summers, scheming and preparing. When the entire group was together as vampires, we would do a lot of the same. I'd missed her being this cooperative, the past couple of years being nothing but coldness and distance from her.

I found myself smiling at these thoughts, then angry. This wasn't something I should be enjoying. For all I knew, these flashbacks were a sign of something much worse, and if we didn't get them taken care of soon, terrible things could happen. I wasn't sure just what that might be, and if I thought too hard about it, I'd become too frightened to act.

Nick was, not surprisingly, less than pleased to see me. I was going to call him, but I was afraid that he might hang up on me before I had a chance to explain things. So I just showed up at his house. He was a little taller, and his hair had grown out a lot. The top part was still cropped and sort of purposefully unkempt, but the back hung down in long, black ringlets that went past his shoulders. His expression, meanwhile, was the same disdainful one I had always known, only more hostile.

"Look," I said, "I'm sorry to barge in on you like this, but..."

"No you're not," he snapped back, but his tone was nonchalant. "I'm sure you planned the whole thing out."

"Not exactly," I said, annoyed that he was right. "Is anyone else here?" I looked over his shoulder into the rest of the house while he leaned against the side of the open front door.

"No. Any reason why I shouldn't kick your ass right now?"

I'd expected this. "Probably not," I said, "but that's kind of what I wanted to talk to you about."

"Me kicking your ass? In that case, come on in!" He surprised me by laughing at his own joke and gesturing that I follow him inside. I did so, wary of what might happen. After he shut the door behind us, I turned to him, suddenly realizing that I didn't want to take my eyes off of him. If he had been having the same violent tendencies that the rest of us had, I might be in danger.

"So what's this about? I told you I didn't want to have anything to do with all that vampire shit again, so it better not be that."

"Not exactly," I repeated. "Just..." I tried to remember the speeches I'd rehearsed on my way over. "Have you been having... I don't know... problems lately?"

He gave me a curious look. "What are you talking about?"

"Like, urges and stuff. Violent stuff. Wanting to kick people's asses. Besides me, I mean."

He began to look worried. "How did you know…" He broke off, then shook his head quickly. "Ray, whatever it is you're selling, I don't want any part of it. I told you that before."

"Nightmares?" I asked, feeling triumphant when his expression went from defiant to scared. "Been having dreams about vampires, by any chance? Like ones where you are one?"

His face then hardened. "Okay, you need to leave. Now."

"No!" I shouted, surprising myself. "Nick, it's not just you. We've all been having them. Bad dreams. Violent thoughts. Even urges to be vampires again. And we don't want it. It just seems to be happening, and we're trying to figure out why."

"I thought it was just me," he said quietly, looking down at the floor, his hand still resting on the doorknob. He then looked up at me. "Goddamn it, Ray, what did you assholes do to me?"

Susanna ended up calling Carolyn before I had a chance to talk to her, confirming that she too had been having the same weird feelings as everyone else. That was just as well; I hadn't been looking forward to approaching her about all of this. She'd also convinced Carolyn to get in touch with Damon, which wasn't an easy task.

"Still, now that you've told me that Nick has been having the same cravings, I think it's safe to assume that Damon has as well," she said.

"So what does that mean?" I still had no idea what we were supposed to do with all of this data, but I hoped that Susanna had some kind of plan.

"Well, first of all, it means that the theory about that extra potion some of us were given is incorrect. That is, it's not the reason we're all feeling like this."

"Okay, got it. So what is the reason?"

"I think I'd rather wait to say until we can all get together as a group. I think I know the solution, but…"

"But what? Damn it, Susanna, don't start getting all secretive and withholding things again. I sometimes think that that's the whole reason we're in this mess."

"What?" She sounded genuinely offended by this.

"You pulled that crap back in '87. Not telling us ahead of time all of those weird side effects the potion was going to have. That wound up with all of us getting captured and almost… I don't know… enslaved by those stupid mad scientists or whatever they were. If you'd just told us what we needed to know…"

"All right, all right!" she said exasperatedly. After a sigh, she added, "Maybe you're right. I… Well, back then, I was trying to keep things a surprise. I thought it would be more fun that way."

"And we all know how that turned out," I said bitterly.

"Fine." She sighed again. "I think," she began with a pause, "that the flashback theory is the most likely one. And the reason we're experiencing that is because we never took the antidote."

"What? The cure?"

"Sure, if you want to call it that. If you remember, aside from when we tried giving it to Carolyn the first time around, every other time, we were 'cured' by what your friend Carl called the 'vampire killers.' I thought that was enough."

Very quickly, I saw where she was going. "So… So by not taking the cure — the antidote, whatever — we just let the potion stay within us to…"

"To lie dormant," she said. "But it's still been in there all along. I think that if we all drink the antidote, it will cancel things out and we'll be okay again."

"Really back to normal," I said, relieved at the thought. If something could finally end this nightmare, I was all for it. "So, what, do we need to get together again and do that?"

"That would be safest, I think." I could tell from her tone that she was thinking through things as she talked, still working them out in her head. I was doing the same, but then a snag in the plan came up.

"I really don't think Carolyn's going to be too keen on another reunion if Damon's going to be there," I said. "As far as I can tell, she totally hates him now."

"Yes, she does."

"Do you know why? I mean, I know they broke up and all, but…" I trailed off, unsure how to finish that sentence. I had seen some of the people at my school get together and later break up, and sometimes they were able to be friendly to each other afterwards, sometimes not. But Carolyn seemed pretty vehement when it came to the topic of Damon, so I wasn't sure how she would feel about this idea. Then I was distracted by another thought. "And Nick. He's talked like he never wants to see the rest of us, either."

"Well, he's just going to have to get over that. It has to be the entire group together, everyone at once." She sounded adamant.

"Yeah, I suppose you're right. And who knows, maybe it would be nice to get to see everyone again."

"This isn't some big happy reunion, Ray. It's just… necessary."

"I know, I know. So when are we going to do it?"

"Let me see," she said, then went quiet.

"The sooner the better, I'd say. Carl told me about this thing that happened with him last week at his school, where this girl pissed him off and he threw a book at her, just barely missing her head. He said that he meant to hit her with it, and had it actually made impact, well…"

"Hmm," Susanna said simply, like she hadn't been listening. "Sorry. I'm checking my calendar. I've got a break in my classes on the 19th and 20th, so maybe we can do it then."

"But that's two weeks from now! Can't we do it sooner?"

"Best I can do, I'm afraid."

"I'm just worried that if we wait too long, things could get worse."

"We'll just have to hope not," she said. "Keep control. It'll be over soon."

"It better be," I said. "I just want this stuff out of me once and for all."

The next two weeks were difficult to get through, not least because the same weird feelings and urges kept occurring. I had to fight hard to keep my anger in check, which wasn't easy at school. There were times when I would be walking down the halls between classes and picture myself tearing up everything in sight, ripping the lockers from the walls and crushing them, punching holes in the walls, or jumping up and breaking the fluorescent light fixtures overhead. I wasn't sure if all of this violent imagery was helping me or making things worse, but the idea was that if I could just imagine destroying property instead of killing the people around me, that was better.

Things weren't helped by the fact that Kirby and his friends still seemed intent on trying to get me into trouble. Apparently, they thought that provoking me was funny. They even tried to manipulate things so that I would get into a fight with Aaron, and while I didn't entirely dislike the idea of pounding his pointy little head into the ground, I knew better than to give in to any belligerent urges.

"Kirby said you were talking shit about me to him the other day," I said to Aaron. "Is that true?"

"Huh? No!" He looked shocked, maybe even scared, and I believed him. The story as Kirby told it to me earlier didn't really make sense. Why would Aaron go up to him and say stuff about me when he barely talked to him at all in the first place?

I told him this, and he agreed. "He probably just wants to get us in trouble."

"More than that, I think it's just some big joke to all of them."

"Hey! Maybe we could stage something! Like, make them think we're going to fight and then don't."

I considered this briefly, then decided against it. "Nah, I don't see much point in that." Truthfully, I was afraid of losing control, even in a staged confrontation. I wished that I could just hide out from the rest of the world until Susanna came into town with the antidote, but that wasn't possible.

Also, because I was so aware of what I hoped was an upcoming ending to all of this inner turmoil, that seemed to make me more conscious of it. Knowing precisely what it was heightened that feeling. Before, I had just been confused and not sure what was happening to me, but now that I knew, it was harder to try to ignore it or think it might go away. I wasn't just in a bad mood or being a typical difficult teenager; something biochemical was raging inside of me, and I wondered how much longer I could keep it at bay.

Sometimes I was okay, but other times, I was so angry that it frightened me. My feelings toward Elizabeth and other girls fluctuated as well. One minute, I would like them and have genuine affection for them, and then the slightest little thing would set me off and make me hate them. I looked forward to a time when I could finally get back to normal, not alternating between thinking that Elizabeth was this wonderfully intriguing person with TV star good looks and hidden depths of intellect, only to later think that she was just some Barbie doll snob who needed to loosen the hell up, just like her stupid snooty friends.

The nightmares continued; usually I had the recurring one about vampire traits emerging while I was at school. Sometimes, the other people in the dream were my present-day classmates and teachers, but there were also times when there were people I hadn't thought of in years, some reaching as far back as kindergarten. It all made sense in the context of the story, but once I was awake, I would realize how odd it was that Kirby was in the same class as Antonio, for example.

Just a few nights before everyone was scheduled to gather and take the antidote, I had another one of these mixed-cast versions of the nightmare, but it was also one where the sequence of events deviated from the norm. This time, I tried the sunglasses method to hide my glowing eyes, but the glasses broke somehow, and I couldn't keep them on. Aaron happened to catch my eye while I looked around hoping that no one had noticed, and instead of freaking out like he should have, he just kind of nodded, then looked away.

Elizabeth got my attention from the other direction, asking me if she could borrow a pen. Like Aaron, she either didn't notice my eyes or didn't care that they were glowing. Then it was her handing me the pen, not the other way around, which again seemed to make sense because of the weird dream logic.

This went on for a while, people reacting to me strangely, as if my being a vampire was perfectly acceptable. I got this feeling of resentment from somewhere, like maybe people had a problem with it but weren't saying so, but the overall impression I got was that it wasn't a big deal. Or it wasn't a secret. Either way, it weirded me out.

When my alarm went off, I realized that somehow, the usually terrifying recurring nightmare had somehow found its way to another place. It wasn't a happy ending, but it had somehow shifted. It was just less unsettling than usual; for once, I didn't wake up with my heart pounding. But it still disturbed me.

Finally, the night of October 20th arrived, and everyone met in secret in a hotel room at the Westchester Suites. Leading up to this, I found myself feeling more and more anxious, hoping that things would go well. Susanna was right, though: This wasn't some happy occasion in which everyone would be glad to see each other. In the past, I had happily anticipated these gatherings, but hindsight made me realize that every time we had done that, the long term result was always that lots of people ended up dying. I would later wonder if calling off this meeting would have somehow prevented the same thing from happening.

But things played out as they did, everyone arriving and eager to get through this as quickly and painlessly as possible. There was some conversation, but it wasn't like before. Everyone was guarded and suspicious, and there was clearly some resentment floating around over everything that had happened.

Not everyone arrived at once. It wasn't like everybody could just tell their parents that they were meeting up at a hotel to take an antidote to a vampire potion, so things had to be done surreptitiously. Carolyn had picked me up from my house with the pretense that she was taking me around to help me practice driving, as I had my learner's permit by then.

On the way to the hotel, we had picked up Carl and Tim from their houses, and it was weird seeing them again after so long. Like Nick, they looked somewhat the same, just older and different, more developed. Carl was lankier than ever, while Tim seemed to have lost a lot of his youthful perkiness and exuberance. All of my former friends had settled into our deeper, more mature voices, and while I had heard these over the phone, it was unnerving to experience in person those tones emanating from older versions of the faces I had grown up with.

Susanna had paid for the hotel room herself, something she mentioned more than once because she clearly resented having to do so. Her initial idea had been for everyone to gather at Carolyn's apartment, but Carolyn vetoed that idea because of Damon. She didn't want him to know where she lived. I had no idea precisely why that was, but because she was so insistent about it, I didn't push it and had to tell Susanna that we would have to meet somewhere else. Grudgingly, she'd settled on a hotel instead.

We arrived to find Susanna and Damon already there, and it was also weird seeing him again. He was friendly to everyone as we walked in, which was a welcome change from the way he had acted toward me the last few times I'd seen him. He looked pretty much the same as I'd remembered, though I noticed that one side of his face seemed red and slightly bruised.

"What happened to you?" I asked.

"Oh, that," he said, touching a hand to his face and wincing. "Got into a fight earlier. Nothing really worth talking about. Things happen, you know?" He flashed a smile, his eyebrows raised in a comical manner.

"Typical of what's been happening to the rest of us, huh?" I offered, and he nodded.

He greeted Tim and Carl as they came into the room behind me. I liked his attitude; it was a sharp contrast to the tension I felt, worrying that old resentments might resurface this night. Dennis hadn't arrived yet, but I wondered if maybe he and Carl might set each other off like in the past. The last thing I wanted was for our violent urges to bubble up during this meeting and get out of control.

The biggest potential for that came with Carolyn's entrance to the room. I had no idea how recently she and Damon had seen each other or just what the nature of their animosity was, but I hoped that they would be able to keep things civil. Seeing Damon be so friendly and charming briefly put me at ease, and it reminded me of why I had always liked him so much. He was just such a cool person, the kind of guy I always wanted to be like. If I could just be as suave and sociable as he was, I thought, maybe I'd be better at approaching the girls I liked at school.

"Carolyn," he said as she entered, more formally than he had greeted the rest of us and nodding politely. She huffed and looked away, trying to find anything else in the room to look at. "Look, I know this is uncomfortable, but…"

"Ya think?" she practically spat at him, her forehead creased in anger.

"Carolyn, please!" he said, reaching out to her. I felt a little sorry for him, knowing from a lifetime's worth of experience what it was like to be on the wrong end of Carolyn's wrath. "I'm just hoping we can smooth things over, to make up for the past." She continued to stare up at him coldly, her arms folded. "I just want to do the right thing."

"The right thing," she said quietly but firmly, "would have been not to cheat on me in the first place and fuck all of your little groupies."

"Okay, okay," Susanna said loudly, stepping in and taking Carolyn's arm. She pulled her away from the door and past the rest of us, leading her into another section of the hotel room. This room was bigger than the one Sheling had a couple of years ago; it had a separate bedroom, almost like a small apartment. As Susanna led Carolyn into this other room, she continued speaking in a simultaneously soothing and condescending manner. "This is exactly the kind of stuff we need to avoid. We're all on edge here, so let's just calm down and…" I lost track of her words as she went out of earshot.

It was an uncomfortable situation for all of us, and Damon looked embarrassed. My own feelings of resentment were beginning to well up inside, but they were interrupted by a knock at the door. Carl, the nearest to it, turned the handle and let Dennis in.

"Everyone here?" he asked nonchalantly as he stepped inside, looking around the room and up at the ceiling.

"Not yet, dork-head," Carl said playfully. Dennis smiled weakly, but like the rest of us, he didn't seem to be in a particularly great mood.

I hadn't seen him for ages, and as Carl had mentioned to me before, he looked completely different. He was much taller, and while he had always been a pudgy kid, it was kind of like his overall weight had remained the same but he had just been stretched to become taller and thinner. He still had the same round face and squinty eyes, but his hair was much longer, one length all around and almost to his shoulders, like a girl's. He wore weird clothes that were reminiscent of the hippies of the 1960s, though with a modern bent.

"We're still waiting for Nick," I said.

"Well, that should be exciting," he said sarcastically. "Who's...?" he began, then gestured to the partition that led to the other room, where Susanna and Carolyn were whispering fiercely.

"My sisters," I said a little theatrically. "You remember them."

"Oh yeah," he said, and I didn't like the hint of innuendo in his voice. Something on my face must have indicated this. "Oh, calm down," he added, rolling his eyes and then plopping down on the bed. "So once our favorite skater jerk gets here, can we get this shit over with and take the cure?"

"That's what I'm hoping," Tim said, sitting down on the bed as well. "I'm ready to get this stuff gone for good."

There was an uncomfortable silence, each of us looking around and trying to think of something to say. I settled down into a chair next to a small round table, avoiding looking at Damon. He was the one who broke the silence, asking Dennis how he had gotten to the hotel.

He started to mention something about a cab, but this was interrupted by yet another knock at the door, the final one we had been waiting for.

"About time," Carl said, walking over from the table I'd been sitting at and jerking open the door. "Come on in!" he said exaggeratedly. "We've been waiting!"

Nick just gave him an apathetic look as he came in, pushing past him rudely as he took in his surroundings.

"Hey, Nick!" Damon said with a friendly grin and a wave. "Nice hair, by the way. Very punk rock."

"Fuck off," Nick said coldly, his eyes narrowing more than usual. Damon's face fell, which was just as well considering that if he had kept up that same stupid grin for a second longer, I might not have been able to resist the growing urge I had to leap up from my chair and knock his teeth down his throat.

This was a guy I had always admired, and I had been sad when he and Carolyn had broken up because he'd always seemed so cool. Just a few moments ago, I had learned that he had cheated on my sister, which made him the lowest form of life in my book. That was the kind of shit the guys I knew at school did, the jerks like Kirby and those asshole upperclassmen who hurt the girls that I wished I could be with. I always told myself that I would never do anything like that to them if I ever got a chance to be their boyfriend, and anyone who would was a worthless scum who didn't deserve to live. Worse still, not only was Damon just as bad, but he had cheated on my own sister, whom I suddenly felt very protective of.

Remembering what was more important at the moment, I fought these feelings down, afraid that I might lose it. Like Susanna had said to Carolyn earlier, we needed to focus on what needed to be done and not let things get out of control. Then I realized that I hadn't actually heard her say that, but maybe it was just my psychic powers playing up again.

Before I could muse on this further, my sisters came in from the other room, Carolyn still angry and not looking at Damon, and Susanna carrying a large clear beaker full of liquid. As she set it down on the table by the window, I suddenly realized that I was quite thirsty, but then I began to wonder if the formula might taste weird. After taking a moment to check the drapes to make sure no one could see inside, Susanna turned to address the group.

"Okay," she said purposefully, "we just need to do this and get it over with. I know that we've all been experiencing strange things, which I think is because we never actually took the antidote, so the vampire potion never really got eliminated. It's like when Carolyn did take the cure back in '83, but it took too long to work, leaving time for the vampire inside of her to rage against it and struggle to survive..."

"Holy shit, really?" Carolyn interrupted. "More speeches? Just shut the hell up and let's do this already!"

"Amen to that," Nick muttered from behind me, which made me want to turn around and punch him.

"Fine!" Susanna almost shouted, scowling and pushing her hair back over her right ear. She lifted the beaker from the table and began pouring the clear liquid into small glasses. They were each about two inches high, a complex crystal pattern at their bases. Then I noticed something strange: There were only four of them.

"Susanna," I said, suddenly feeling more apprehensive, "that's not enough glasses."

"I know," she said, not looking up as she continued to distribute the antidote among them. "That's all the glasses for this room that the hotel provided. Four glasses, eight people. We'll have to share. It'll be enough."

"You sure?" Carl asked.

"Trust me," she said. Finishing up, she looked at the beaker curiously, noticing that there was still a little bit of the antidote left in it, yet all four of the glasses were full. "One of these days," she said quietly and with a frown, "I'm going to get that right."

"Never mind that," I said, stepping forward and picking up one of the glasses. The liquid sloshed around, and I was careful not to spill it. "So we're sharing, so…?"

Susanna quickly pointed around at each of us. "Ray, you drink half of this one. I'll drink the other half. Carolyn, you and… Okay, no… You and Dennis drink from that one, half a glass each." She portioned out the other glasses to the rest of the group. "If any of you feel icky about drinking after someone else," she added sarcastically, "get over it."

I smiled at this, nervous but eager to finally take this cure and fix everything that had been going so wrong. I was tense, but this finally felt like the moment when things would be put right. I pulled the glass to my lips and prepared to sip, but then something else happened.

My hand began shaking. I had no idea why, but there it was, my hand rapidly jerking back and forth in front of my face, letting drops of the precious antidote spill out over the edges of the glass even as I tried to will them not to. I fought to counter this, thinking that it was some nervous thing that I could conquer if I just concentrated enough. But it wasn't working.

"Screw this," I heard myself say, but I hadn't meant to. Before I even knew that I'd done it, I reached back and slung the glass away from me, some of the antidote spewing out as it sailed across the room. I thought the glass might shatter as it hit the wall, but instead it just clunked against it, the clear liquid temporarily coloring the white wall with a dull grey pattern.

Surprisingly, Susanna didn't say anything, nor did anyone else. The room had grown unnaturally quiet all of a sudden. I looked around at the others and saw that Tim, Dennis, and Nick had followed my lead, their empty hands still outstretched after having thrown their glasses away to other parts of the room, the cure discarded and having spilled out uselessly onto the floor. I looked at them and the others, feeling confused but also sure of my convictions, thinking simultaneously that I had done the right thing and that I'd made the worst mistake of my life.

Tim's face caught my eye, and I looked at him, uncertain of what I was feeling. My heart was pounding, and my breathing began to get heavier. I could tell that he was doing the same thing, his expression a mixture of curiosity and horror. A quick glance around the room revealed that the same thing was happening to everyone, and as my fingers started to tingle and go numb, I realized what was about to take place. At least, I thought I did.

This was almost the same experience as before, what happened to us when we took the vampire potion. We hadn't, but the transformation seemed to be happening anyway. I couldn't accept that, and I was terrified, at least partly. That is, half of me felt that way. There was another part of me that was sensing the inevitability of it and even wanting to just give in and let it happen. Maybe I was even glad. These thoughts raced through my head, and I was so confused that I wasn't sure just what I was thinking or if it even mattered.

As the physical sensations increased and the familiar sound of rushing blood began to fill my ears, I managed to glance over at Dennis, who had been propping himself up against the dresser, his head facing downward. When I looked at him, his head rose, and I was shocked to see that his eyes were glowing. This wasn't something that normally happened during our transformation, and even more unusually, our eyes had never glowed pure white.

Everyone was mostly standing still, struggling against some unknown, inner force, which was how things usually were when we changed. But something else was happening here. I looked around and saw that everyone else had the same bright white eyes, some of them squinting hard and grabbing their heads as if that might somehow make this stop.

A new, weird sound began, like if someone were holding down the far right key on a synthesizer keyboard and turning up the volume steadily. Then, I saw a white orb start to form on Susanna's chest, but it wasn't like it was coming from her skin and shining through her clothes. It was just there, flat against her body, growing quickly and spreading over her torso. The room began to get brighter, but this made it harder for me to see clearly, not easier. Afraid to, but unable to resist, I looked down in horror to find that the same thing was happening to my chest.

This phenomenon then started to stretch outward from me, the white glow elongating itself and pulling away from my upper body. I screwed my eyes shut, panicking and trying to will all of this to stop, whatever it was. It felt like something was being torn out of my very being, not just my body. A few moments later, the whiteness — which I could see even when my eyes were closed — abruptly ceased along with that piercing sound effect, which had reached a painful crescendo. All of the other strange sensations stopped, and I felt relief for a moment, that is, until I opened my eyes.

What I saw was impossible. It took me a few seconds to process the information, and even then, I still couldn't believe it. Standing just a few inches in front of me was an exact copy of myself. My very first thought was that someone had placed a full-length mirror in front of me, but it only took a moment for me to realize that this wasn't true. This figure looked wrong to me precisely because it wasn't a mirror image, what I was used to seeing. He had my face, my body, my clothes, everything, but the part in his dark brown hair was on the opposite side of where I expected to see it, as was the small curved scar on his left cheek. The very first thing I noticed, though, was how the clothes were similarly distorted. I was wearing my blue denim jacket that night, which I decorated with a handful of buttons and badges that I thought looked cool, one of my attempts at being fashionable. Normally, I'd see those in the mirror with their designs and words reversed, but there they were on this new version of me, on the opposite side I usually saw them and facing the right way around.

I almost went into shock when I finally figured out who this duplicate of me was, which happened when he smiled at me. He gave me an evil, triumphant grin, which was punctuated with two sharp fangs on either side.

Before I could react, he quickly reached back with both arms bent at the elbows and his palms held up, then shot them forward and pushed me backward. I tumbled into someone behind me, then was knocked to the left and into the side of the bed, my vision obscured for a few moments as a room full of people scrambled around me. It was complete chaos, and there was lots of shouting. Some of the voices expressed complete bewilderment while others were full of rage. I heard a latch opening and someone shouting, "Go, go, go!" urgently, a voice I didn't immediately recognize until I realized that it was my own, or rather, my copy's.

Righting myself on the floor, I saw the other versions of ourselves racing out of the hotel room door, then got up and staggered after them. Out in the parking lot, I could see the eight figures running, and I was unnerved when Carl's duplicate turned back and looked at me briefly and gave me a sly grin. Then, one by one, the vampires quickly dissolved into small puffs of colored smoke, flying away into the night sky as bats.

I stood in the doorway and held onto the frame, feeling like I might collapse. Susanna was to my right, and I could feel the others behind me, everyone gasping as they recovered.

"Susanna," Carolyn said, her whispering voice quickly rising to a shout, "what the *hell* was all *that?*"

"I don't know!" she said, her voice quivering. "I really don't know."

The rest of our time in the hotel room that night was spent trying to understand just what had happened. Everyone was upset, myself included, but the best way I could think to cope was to try to figure things out. We needed to know what we were dealing with.

Carolyn had started openly weeping, and Carl, looking somewhat awkward, found himself holding her as she sat next to him on the bed and cried into his chest. Damon offered to get everyone drinks from the soda machine down the hall, and Nick went with him to help carry them back. Tim and I were both pacing, trying to talk things out and come up with the right questions, while Dennis just sat on the floor with his back against the foot of the bed, saying nothing. Susanna was sitting at the table staring away from everyone and nervously smoking a cigarette. I'd never seen her do that or even knew that it was something she did, but when Dennis had offered one to her, she didn't refuse.

Once the initial shock had worn off, we were able to assess the situation, at least as far as we understood it. Our vampire selves had somehow manifested as separate beings, and they were on the loose.

"We should go after them!" I said.

"And do what?" Dennis asked. "Get ourselves killed?"

"What I want to know is why they didn't just kill us to begin with," Tim said. "You'd think they could have."

"Just be glad they didn't," Carl said sternly. Then, a little more quietly, he added, "I really hope they don't come back."

"Why would they?" Dennis asked gloomily. "They got what they wanted. They escaped. Escaped from inside of us."

I thought this over, trying to see the logic in it. I then looked over at Carolyn, who had stopped crying and pulled away from Carl, sniffling. "Sorry," she said to him gently.

"It's okay," he said as he wiped at the dampness on his shirt.

Damon knocked on the door and shouted, "It's us!" I walked clumsily over Dennis's spot on the floor and reached for the handle, but Carolyn whispered at me anxiously.

"Wait! It could be them!"

"Of course it's…" I began, but then I realized what she meant. Peering through the peephole, I saw the distorted image of Damon and Nick, each of them carrying cans of soda. "No, it's okay," I said, turning back to Carolyn and seeing that she still looked worried.

I opened the door and let them in, and they entered and distributed the drinks. Carolyn just sat hers next to her on the bed, leaving it unopened. Susanna barely acknowledged the can Damon placed on the table. Opening mine and drinking from it quickly, I looked out of the open doorway, wondering if I might see any approaching bats. There was nothing.

Closing the door behind me, I sat down at the table across from Susanna. The smoke from her cigarette barely bothered me, though it was strange to see her indulging in the habit. My father had smoked up until I was about five or six years old before giving it up, so there was actually something familiar and comforting about the smell. Really, I was grasping at straws, trying to find anything soothing in the middle of this hellish situation.

"So, Susanna," Carolyn began, the tears wiped clean from her face and an angry edge to her voice, "did you know?"

Susanna's expression remained vacant. "Did I know what?"

"What would happen."

Vacancy shifted to sadness. "No. I didn't know." She dabbed her cigarette on the edge of the ashtray, a small bit of orange ember falling from it and immediately turning to grey.

"This wasn't another one of your big surprises, then?" Dennis called out from the foot of the bed. "Like all of those hilarious side effects you didn't tell us about a couple of years ago?"

"No! How can you even…" She broke off, jamming the almost finished cigarette into the ashtray to put it out. "No, I know. I can understand how you might think that. But I swear, I've never seen anything like this before."

"How about you come up with a way to fix it?" he shot back, still facing away from us and toward the dresser.

"Come on, Dennis," Tim said. "Lay off. It's not her fault."

"It's not?"

"Look," I said, "this isn't the way to deal with this."

"Okay, then what is?" Dennis went on, finally getting up from the floor and turning to face us. As he straightened up, I noticed how much more intimidating he looked now that he was taller. "Why don't you tell us what we should do, fearless leader."

I looked down at the table. "I… I don't know. I just feel like we should do something."

"He's right," Tim said. "Those vampires are out there right now, and I think we can all guess what they're doing. I bet if we watch the news tonight, it will be just like before. Killings all around town and no good explanation for it."

"But it's not like before," I said. "That's the problem. Back then, it was us. We did it, outmaneuvered the police, all that. But now we have no control over things. Those others can go around and do whatever they want."

"And for all we know, we could be implicated," Damon said. That was an unpleasant thought.

"Fucking great," Nick said. "Thanks so much, you guys. We've all pretty much screwed ourselves entirely."

"Shut up, Nick," I said wearily. "You're not helping."

"And you are?" he shot back. "How about you and your genius sister there figure out a way out of this mess?" I glanced up at Susanna, wondering if she might turn on him. She just sat there, staring at the ashtray.

"Shouldn't we try to go after them like Ray said?" Tim offered. "Seems like it's kind of our responsibility to do so."

"But how?" I asked. "We don't even know where they are."

"And what's to stop them from killing us?" Carl asked worriedly. "If they really are exact copies of us, or, you know, who we were when we were vampires, they're pretty damn powerful."

There was an uncomfortable silence. It made sense that we should try to track the vampires down and kill them, but would we stand a chance against them? The rest of the city never did, and we were just regular people now, too.

"I think Carl's right," Susanna said finally, putting her hands down onto the table and then pushing her chair back as she stood up. "We need to get out of here." She sounded more determined, but there was still something fragile in her voice. I had never seen her this withdrawn before. She didn't seem like herself.

"If those vampires out there really are just like us," Tim said, "they could come to the same conclusions we just did and see us as a threat. You're right, Susanna, we should go."

"And then what?" I asked.

"I don't know," Susanna said, still looking broken and defeated.

What followed over the next few days and nights was hard to take in. I had hoped that Susanna would recover from the shock and help me and the others form some kind of plan, but instead, she just returned to Columbia. All she could say was that she didn't know what to do and would try to come up with something, but she was so nonchalant about it. Resentfully, I got the impression that all she wanted to do was run and hide.

Dennis was similarly withdrawn, and Nick made it profanely clear as everyone was leaving the hotel that night that he never wanted to see or hear from any of us again. Tim, Carl, and I all seemed to think that we should stay in touch and try to do something, but we had no idea what. Damon had also expressed an interest in pursuing this initiative, but after Carolyn cursed him out and told him to stay away from her and her family, he left angrily, saying that he would handle things his own way. Carolyn also avoided coming over to the house for a while and ignored my phone calls.

As expected, the news broadcasts over the weekend began to report mysterious killings that were similar to the ones in the past, the authorities trying to blame them on dangerous animals while the more astute public started worrying about vampires again. I intentionally hadn't watched the news for more than two years by this point; whenever I saw it, it was just another reminder of the horrible things we had done. Back then, we leered at everyone's clueless speculation, relishing it like the clever and destructive monsters that we were. But it was no longer fun. For the first time, I began to see what it must have been like for everyone else all those years, to wonder what might happen next and if people I cared about were in danger.

The vampires, our "clones," as Tim took to calling them, appeared to be concentrating their attacks in South Augusta, though there were other reports indicating a few kills closer to the inner city. So far, it looked like they weren't interested in coming after us, which was a small comfort. As I watched the taped news reports, I speculated about the upcoming body count, knowing that if we didn't do something to stop the vampires, that would continue to escalate.

Returning to school on Monday was a bizarre experience. There were hushed mentions of the supposed return of vampires to Augusta, but no one could talk about it openly or else some uptight teacher would swoop in and serve them with a detention slip for talking about something so "satanic." Everything looked and felt so different to me, these idiots huddling around with their preoccupations with piety, popularity, and their wishes to be thought of as attractive and interesting, while I knew that something more important was going on. I knew what it was, and they didn't. In a perverse way, that made me feel more confident.

When Kirby and his friends tried to talk down to me or lure me into something that would lead to a fight, I ignored them. They didn't matter. My crushes on Elizabeth and the handful of other girls I liked also took a back seat. Aside from the fact that I had something else to concentrate on and worry about, I had the added benefit of no longer having that demon inside of me, the vampire that had been haunting me from within and making me act so moody and strange. Perhaps for the first time in years, I was truly myself. I wasn't happy about the bigger picture and how dangerous the situation had become, but at least I finally felt capable of dealing with things rationally.

Tim had suggested that the few of us who were willing should arm ourselves similarly to the way Life Force had done, garlic and crosses and wooden stakes and all. Carl wondered if we might be able to get in touch with those people again, but we had no way to do so, nor had there been any mention of them in the news. For all we knew, their arrest back in 1987 had been the end of them, plus it wasn't like they would have had a reason to stick around after we as vampires were cured and back to normal shortly after. Damon had seemed interested in pursuing this new threat, but I still didn't have his phone number, and I still wasn't sure if I could forgive him for cheating on Carolyn and put my resentment towards him aside. For the moment, we seemed to be on our own.

The idea was that the three of us might be able to track the vampire clones down and kill them, but we still didn't know just how to do that. We were all still teenagers, ordinary kids despite our extraordinary past. It was exciting and maybe even romantic to think that we could be the heroes of this tragedy and put things right, but the practicality of actually making that happen eluded us.

As the week went on, I continued to tape the news to see if I could track the vampires' movements, similar to the way we had documented our own attacks on a map two years before. By this point, I had my own TV and VCR in my room, which made keeping this work from my parents easier.

It took me a couple of nights to notice it, but there was something unfamiliar in the pattern that emerged, if one could even call it a pattern. All this time, I had been trying to imagine just what our vampire clones might be doing, picturing them gathering in secret somewhere and carefully plotting things out. I envisioned the other Ray and the other Susanna in charge of the group, making plans and telling everyone where they should kill. At first, it seemed like the bodies that were turning up were well spread out, which was to be expected. But then the following night and the one after that, the locations tended to be very near to their previous ones. That is, the attacks were still widespread geographically on any given night, but there didn't seem to be much variation as the nights went on. Perhaps this was some new strategy of Susanna's, I figured.

"Yeah, I noticed that, too," Tim said. He, Carl, and I were sitting in Carl's sister's car in the Regency Mall parking lot, hoping to spot some activity. Karen was off at college at the University of Georgia, and she had left her car at home, using the campus's public transportation and friends to get around town instead. Technically, we were breaking the law by having Carl borrow the car and bring us here since we were too young to drive, but it's not like we ever let something like that stop us. Plus, Carl and Karen's parents were out of town.

"I didn't," Carl said simply, looking up out of the windshield toward the sky.

"Well, it's what seems to be happening," Tim said from the back seat. "If the current rate of migration continues, at least one or two of them may end up attacking here tonight."

"Let's hope so," I said determinedly, though part of me was nervous. We had armed ourselves with as much anti-vampire weaponry as we could, including some wooden stakes I had gathered that were in fact pointed sticks used to put small signs in the ground. I had stolen the signs from various yards around my neighborhood over the past couple of nights.

"Hard to believe it's already been a week since all that shit went down," Carl said, meaning our meeting in the hotel room.

"I know," I said. It was unfortunate that we'd had to wait a week for the three of us to get together, but doing so on school nights just wasn't practical. That meant that every night, eight more people died. I mentioned this to the others.

"Yeah, that sucks," Carl said.

"At least it gave us time to gather some data," Tim offered.

"I'm sure all the…" Carl began, but then he stopped. I could tell from his sarcastic tone what he was about to say. "Never mind."

"No, you're right," I said. "You were going to say that that's not a lot of comfort to all the people who've already died."

"Still reading people's minds?" Carl said, giving me a snide look.

"Not really, I mean, kind of. That was just logic."

"Can you still do all that, though? I can't believe I just now thought of that. Why don't you just use your psychic woo-woo shit to find out where these vampires are so we can kill them?"

"It's not like it was," I said, both with sadness and defensiveness. "It's more subtle these days. Like vague impressions of stuff…"

"Or premonitions after the fact," Tim added.

"Huh?"

I smiled, realizing that even though he and I had never talked about this, Tim must have grown up with the same phenomenon I had where I wouldn't realize I'd had a premonition about something until it happened. A simple event would occur, something very specific and obscure, and then I'd remember that I'd foreseen it a day or two before. We explained this to Carl.

"Yeah, but wasn't there that other thing you guys could do? You and Dennis did it once, I remember. Where you like… I don't know… merged your powers or something, and that made them stronger." He made a gesture of his hands coming together and the tips of his fingers becoming entwined.

"That's a thought," I said, turning to look at Tim.

He shrugged his shoulders, but I could tell that he was similarly inspired. "Couldn't hurt," he said.

"Okay," I said, "concentrate." I closed my eyes, and I reached out with my mind to Tim. Although I couldn't actually see it, I imagined that Carl was looking back and forth between us expectantly. There was silence for a few seconds apart from the sound of everyone breathing.

"Anything?" Carl asked.

"A little," Tim said. "I can feel something, but it's not very…" He didn't finish his sentence.

I could feel something, too, but it was nothing more than a vague tingle. I reached out farther, trying to scan the surrounding area. I got the impression that Tim was doing the same. But nothing came of this. Our powers just weren't what they used to be.

It took some convincing to get Dennis to join us the following night. He didn't seem to think it would do any good, but I managed to convince him that with three psychics combining our powers, we just might be able to get a strong enough connection to make something really happen. Once again, Carl had borrowed Karen's car, and he began to worry that the smell of garlic might linger in it.

"She probably won't notice it over the smell of pot," Dennis said snidely.

"Oh, shut up," Carl said. "Karen's not into all that. You're thinking of your own sister."

"Suck it," Dennis said, making a rude gesture towards his crotch.

"That's enough, you two," I said.

"Yeah, come on!" Tim said. "Let's just see if this works. According to the news, the vampire activity last night didn't reach this far north, but it was close. So I'm willing to bet that at least one vampire comes here tonight."

Dennis let out a sound like *"nyih-nyih-nyinyinyih,"* making fun of the nerdy way Tim had been speaking. It was a shame that we weren't getting along better. The night before, Carl, Tim, and I had gotten along fairly well, so much that it made me nostalgic for the old days. I had to check that feeling; it wasn't like I missed us being vampires and going around killing people. But once or twice, it almost felt like we were all in third grade again, the old crew having fun together.

Saturday night was different. Dennis hadn't even wanted Carl to pick him up from his house and insisted on taking a cab to meet us at the mall instead. And once all four of us were in the car together, things weren't as pleasant as I had hoped.

"Oh, quit being a douchebag," I said to Dennis, turning around and facing him and Tim in the back seat. "Let's try it. Concentrate; try to join our minds. You remember how."

"Yeah, I do," he said with a slight smile. "In fact, last time I remember doing this, we were looking for you." He gave Tim a pointed look.

Tim laughed nervously. "I remember that. That night was so scary. I was convinced you guys were going to kill me."

"We almost did," Dennis said simply. There was much less regret in his voice than I would have liked.

Animosities temporarily set aside, we joined our minds together and tried to scan for any vampires in the area. Aside from a slightly more pronounced tingling sensation along the sides of my head, nothing really happened.

"Well, so much for that," Dennis said.

"Let's not give up just yet," I said. "Maybe they just haven't arrived."

"Maybe," Dennis said, seeming more engaged and thoughtful. "And even if they do, do you really think we can take them?"

"Sure," Carl said. "According to Ray and Tim, they seem to be attacking solo, so that will mean it's four against one."

"Yeah, but four *people* against one vampire," Dennis said. "Even with those odds…"

We sat in silence, Dennis's last few words echoing in our heads. Eventually, the conversation resumed, and I pointed out something that had been disturbing me over the past several days.

"The thing that's really bad this time is that these copies of us, the clones, well, they're not going on a limited timetable like we did. We'd be vampires for a week or two, then stop. I mean, yeah, a lot of people died, and that's really horrible. I'm sure the rest of you feel as guilty about that as I do." I expected some kind of affirmation, but everyone just kept quiet. "But what's bad here is that these clones don't have any reason to stop. They can just keep on going."

"Which is why we have to stop them," Tim added.

"Do you think they're immortal?" Carl asked. "You know, like real vampires?"

"I hadn't thought of that," I said. "Maybe. Probably."

"The way I figure it," Tim said, "they're just like we were when we were vampires. Presumably, they have all of the same abilities we had. And all of the limitations."

"Like how their victims don't come back to life," Carl said, the idea seeming to have just occurred to him. "Not like those other vampires we met that time. That creepy-ass guy and his slutty looking girlfriend who went around resurrecting the bodies."

"Or Dracula," Tim said.

"Don't remind me of that shit," Dennis said.

"Yeah, I guess that was pretty…" He froze, interrupting himself. "Whoa. Did you feel that?"

I had. There was something, a sort of psychic ping. "Yes," I said nervously.

"Me too," Dennis said, looking through the back seat window.

"What?" Carl asked. "Something psychic?"

"Yeah, just a twinge," I said, also looking around to see if I could spot anything.

"Here, I'll roll down the windows," Carl said. "Might give you guys better reception."

That may or may not have made a difference, but I felt it again, this vague notion that there was another presence nearby, a vampire. As the four windows of the car hummed down, I said to Tim and Dennis, "Quick! Concentrate!"

We did, and the vision became more clear. There was a bat somewhere nearby, which I could see flapping through the night sky. The trouble was that I had no idea where it was; it was like watching a documentary on TV, a close-up shot of a bat flying but no sense of context.

"Where is it?" Carl asked frantically.

"I can't tell," Tim said, sounding frustrated. "Somewhere."

"Maybe if we get out of the car..." Carl said, opening his door and grabbing his dad's crossbow, which had been waiting in the floorboard next to his feet. He hadn't brought it the night before, but this night, he was more well armed and ready for action.

The rest of us got out, grabbing various weapons. If there was a vampire here, we wanted to get it. Unfortunately, this brief amount of physical activity broke our concentration, and the psychic link was lost.

"Where is it?" Carl asked, crossbow raised.

I exhaled sharply, frustrated. "I can't tell!"

"Should we join..." Tim began, but he was interrupted by a scream from nearby.

"This way!" Carl called, and we hurried after him across the parking lot. We had parked far away from most of the cars there, and from what I could tell, the person we were hoping to save had done the same thing for whatever reason.

We arrived at the scene too late, spotting the other version of Dennis as he stood up over the prone body of a woman. She lay there dead, face down with her long, straight blonde hair spread out after having been pushed to one side while she had been fed upon. The vampire Dennis turned and looked back at us halfway through wiping his mouth with the sleeve of his shirt.

He was an exact copy of my old friend, or at least, the more grown-up and hippie-looking version of him. Dennis's change in style and attitude had been unsettling enough, but I had begun to get used to it despite our difficulty in getting along as teenagers. But the sight of the thing that stood over that woman's body and leered at us was even harder to take in. It was Dennis, but not Dennis. Its mouth was covered with blood, and I could just barely make out the fangs from this far away.

"Get him!" I shouted to the others as we approached, my wooden stake held high. The vampire glared at us angrily, and it seemed for a moment that we might have a fight on our hands.

But then his expression changed as his gaze panned across us: He went from looking defiant to less certain. Maybe he realized that he was outnumbered. Before we could reach him, the bloody-faced figure morphed into a bat in an orange-colored puff of smoke, and we were left looking up at it as it flew away. Coming to a halt, we found ourselves next to the body of a dead woman.

I had seen lots of dead bodies in my time. The others and I had caused so many deaths, and at the time, we had been smug about it, proud of what we'd done. But this was entirely different. At our feet was a corpse, the remnants of a life ended. It was the most disgusting thing I had ever seen, the way it looked like a life-sized marionette that had been discarded and twisted unnaturally. I found myself staggering back from it, fighting the urge to vomit. Carl started to reach down as he said something about feeling for a pulse, but Dennis shouted, "Don't touch it!"

We managed to get out of there before anyone else arrived. Shaken, we had run back to the car and sped out of there, rationalizing that someone else would find the body and report it to the police. Dennis had at first insisted on taking another cab back home, but then he agreed that getting as far away from there as quickly as possible was the best course of action.

Everyone was shocked and breathing heavily, but we slowly came back to ourselves. I warned Carl to stop speeding; the last thing we needed was for us to get pulled over by a cop. He agreed and did his best to control his driving. After a while, he turned on the radio, tuning it until I told him to concentrate on driving while I tried to find something for us to listen to.

As I turned the dial, the static hissing between the stations, I thought about how the vampire version of Dennis had unnerved me, but I wasn't sure exactly why. After all, I had seen him as a vampire plenty of times back in the day. But there was something about seeing him that way while I was just a regular human being that frightened me. Maybe it was because I felt more vulnerable, but then, we had been the ones with the weapons.

I started to settle on a station that was playing Queen's song "Another One Bites the Dust," but Dennis blurted out, "Turn that shit off." I wasn't sure if he meant the radio or just that particular song, but I assumed the former and turned the volume knob to the *OFF* position.

For a brief second, I considered telling the guys the story of when I killed the jogger who was listening to that song on his Walkman, then immediately thought better of it. Then I remembered that crazy televangelist we'd been forced to watch at school. One of his claims was that if you played the song "Another One Bites the Dust" backwards, there was a hidden message that said, "It's fun to smoke marijuana." The idea of subliminal messages in songs influencing people and making them do bad things was mildly intriguing to me, but I was pretty sure it was full of crap.

Instead, I kept quiet. I could tell from everyone's mood that this was not the time for funny anecdotes. Dennis sat with his arms folded tightly and was looking out the window the whole time, probably even more shaken up by seeing his vampire self than the rest of us were.

"You okay?" Tim asked him gently.

"No," he said bitterly. "You try seeing yourself brutally murdering someone and see how you feel."

"But it wasn't you," Tim insisted. "That was the vampire. The monster you used to be, that all of us used to be. That part's been expunged, exorcised from you."

"You think that's true?" Carl asked.

"I know it is! Think about how much more normal you've felt since the clones emerged. All of that hate and rage that was stewing inside… Now it's all been put somewhere else. It was the potion that did it to us. That's why we did all of that bad stuff, or rather, why *they* did it. Now's our chance to make things right, to get rid of them once and for all and bury this."

This made sense to me. Over the past two years, I had struggled with so much guilt and hated myself for everything I had done as a vampire. But if what Tim was saying was true, none of that had really been my fault. There was another version of me — of all of us — who was truly to blame. To track these monsters down and destroy them was our chance for redemption.

"That's a wonderful little speech, Tim," Dennis said snidely. "I wonder how many times you practiced it."

"No!" Tim said. "I mean… I don't…" He slumped back in his seat. "I'm just trying to help," he added quietly.

Not long afterwards, we arrived at Dennis's house, which was a weird feeling for me. I hadn't been there in years, but seeing it brought back all sorts of memories. For a moment, I hoped that Dennis might invite the rest of us inside so we could discuss things, but he just slammed the car door and quickly walked away, not even saying goodbye. It was the last time that the four of us would ever be together.

As I continued to monitor the TV news to try to keep track of the vampires, I noticed a disturbing trend. Their attacks were getting closer, edging away from South Augusta and moving towards downtown. This still put them way out of range of my house or my friends' homes, but it still worried me. Were they getting bolder? Had they been avoiding the main part of the city because they feared that the others and I might kill them? Surely Dennis's clone had told the rest about our abortive attack on him at the mall.

I worried that things might escalate, that eventually, they would start striking closer to home. I started keeping a cross and a small wooden stake in the drawer of the night table by my bed, hoping that my mother wouldn't find them if she happened to get nosy. My parents had in fact noticed and commented on the mentions of vampire activity in the news, but they were dismissive about it, thinking that there must be a more rational explanation. I of course couldn't tell them what I knew.

But overall, the city seemed to be accepting the fact that there were vampires on the loose. The news reporters would still talk about "alleged vampire activity" in their fake and professional manner, but after all these years, it was hard even for them to deny that when bodies kept piling up drained of blood, that was what was really going on.

An interesting development along these lines caught my notice one afternoon when I happened upon a program called *Augusta Events.* I had seen it from time to time but never thought much of it; it was this low-budget show produced by the local cable company that was boring and not worth watching unless I wanted to see bland people try to act like they were professional news reporters. The only reason I had ever seen it was that it happened to air on channel 3, which was what my TV had to be tuned to in order for me to use the VCR.

On the rare occasions when Carolyn and I were able to get along during her visits to the house, we would sometimes watch a few minutes of this or other cable access shows on channel 3 and laugh at them together. *Augusta Events* was hilarious in particular because it tried its best to be interesting, but it was just so dull and ineffectual. This one afternoon, though, my attention was caught by the topic being discussed: vampires.

I was intrigued by the fact that this pathetic show was making an attempt to cover this serious topic, and I wondered what their take on it might be. Almost instinctively, I shoved my VHS tape back into the machine and hit the "record" and "play" buttons, knowing that I might be taping over some of the news from the night before. But something told me that this would be important to capture.

The host sat in an oversized brown chair that looked like a very short couch, a soft pink background behind her. Cheesy synthesizer music played over the intro and faded out as she began talking, a just barely outdated-looking computerized caption overlaid on her face bearing the words *VAMPIRES IN AUGUSTA*.

"Hello, and welcome to *Augusta Events*," the woman said, enunciating her words in a cloying, precise way. "I'm your host, Eden Garris. Today on *Augusta Events*, we discuss a somewhat controversial topic, that of alleged vampires infiltrating the Garden City." Her expression changed slightly, her brow becoming creased, but it looked very forced. "Many deaths have occurred recently in our city, which seem to echo the spates of killings that occurred just a few years ago. Are there really supernatural creatures attacking your loved ones? Or is there some other explanation?"

"Lady, you have no idea," I said to the TV screen, simultaneously amused and in wonderment. My attitude completely changed when the camera angle switched to a wide shot, revealing the show's guests.

"My guests today include some experts in the field as well as some local eyewitnesses who claim to have seen real life vampire activity," the host continued. There were four men seated in two pairs of chairs on either side of her, and they looked mostly boring and uninteresting to me as well, apart from one. To my surprise, there was Damon on my TV screen.

Seeing someone I knew on TV was a rare thing. For a moment, I felt excited to see my sister's ex-boyfriend on a show, but then I remembered that he was a cheating bastard whom I despised. Even so, I couldn't help but notice how cool and at ease he looked as the host introduced him and the other guests, each of them getting their own close-up and caption. His read *DAMON CAMPBELL, Eyewitness to Assault.* He smiled in a warm and friendly manner at the host, as did the others.

Once the initial shock had worn off, I began to worry. Was this jerk going on TV — even if it were only this crappy local program — to rat us out? I had always feared that something like this might happen, that one of us might crack under the guilt and try to save his own ass or turn us in, or possibly both.

"Dr. Shepard," the host said, beginning with the man to Damon's right, "as an expert in animal care and behavior, are you in line with the thinking that these killings... and not just these most recent ones, but the ones over the years... could be caused by some kind of animal?"

"Well," the man said with a slight laugh, "I would hardly call myself an expert on all animals, but generally speaking, I would say so." He was a friendly looking man with short grey hair and a matching beard, a veterinarian according to his introductory caption. He continued to smile as he spoke, almost unnervingly given the grim topic being discussed. "For a start, the cases seemed at least at first to be seasonal, occurring for short times during the summer months, then ceasing without explanation. This would suggest some sort of migratory behavior, though I am unaware of similar cases elsewhere at the same time of year. This most recent turn of events, however, has occurred in the fall, not the summer, which I can't explain.

"Another notion that has been put forth is that of rabies, which could be possible. The rabid animals, perhaps bats as some people have claimed, could in theory make their attacks, then die shortly afterwards. As for what would cause such a rabid... er... *rapid* and widespread outbreak, I can't say."

"So you don't believe that vampires are involved in any way," the host said.

Dr. Shepard's face fell for a second, but then he resumed his smiling demeanor. "Well, now, I wouldn't say that. I'm... I'm not one to dismiss any explanation entirely, as unbelievable as it might be. It could be that we are dealing with some as yet unknown strain of vampire bat, though, as I've said before when consulted about this, vampire bats, while they do exist, aren't like what you see in the movies. They are just one of the hundreds of species of bat known throughout the world, and they generally don't feed on humans. Furthermore, they are confined to South America, not this continent. But that..."

"So you..." the host began, but the vet had one more point to make. "I'm sorry, go ahead."

"I was just going to say that it could be possible that some new strain of vampire bat may have made its way to North America, and we're only just now finding out about it. That's the joy of science: There's always something new to learn."

This man's cheerful manner was getting on my nerves, mostly because I was dying to find out what Damon was going to say. The other two guests, a college professor and some kind of religious man, would soon get their turns to give their own bullshit takes, but what Damon ended up saying blew my mind.

"Mr. Campbell..."

"Damon is fine, thanks," he said with a cheeky grin.

"Damon, then," the host said with a sheepish laugh. Damon continued to smile at her as he raised his eyebrows, being as charming as ever. I realized that he was being flirty, which surprised me a little because the woman was black. I wasn't opposed to interracial relationships, but my limited experience and mostly white-bread upbringing still led me to consider such things out of the ordinary.

"As I was going to say, you probably have a very different take on things than Dr. Shepard here. You claim to have been attacked by an actual vampire and survived. Isn't that right?"

"Yes, that certainly is right!" he said, still grinning widely, but his tone had a hint of sadness to it. Knowing him as well as I did, though, I could tell that he was faking it. What was he up to? "It happened just a few nights ago, when I was leaving Noble, that new club downtown. Have you been there?" He raised his eyebrows again and cocked his head slightly as he asked her this.

"No, no, I haven't," she said quickly. "Please, go on."

"Well, like I said, I was leaving the club, and then out of nowhere, this man came at me and tried to bite me. Given everything I'd seen on the news, I realized that this was a vampire, like the ones I'd been hearing about. I hadn't even believed in vampires until that very moment, but you can bet I started to real quick! It was a really, really terrifying thing." With this last sentence, his tone went from increasingly excited to more somber. He was still lying, I could tell. After all, I had grown up being a liar myself, so I knew how to spot one.

"Go on," the host said, clearly intrigued.

"Well, there was no one else around to help, so I had to fight the monster off all on my own. I held him back the best I could, kind of holding his face like this…" He held out his hand in a cupping motion, and as he did, his face twisted. "You know, like this? Right. But then, something strange happened. The vampire's face began to change, sort of to… I don't know, *morph* is the best way I can put it. At first, he looked like someone I didn't recognize, and then, for whatever reason, his face twisted and shifted until it looked exactly like mine." He rocked his head back and forth to illustrate his story. There was a hushed reaction from the host and one or two of the other guests, and Damon let his words sink in.

"I know! It was the weirdest thing. And it wasn't just the face, either, I mean, this guy all of a sudden looked *just* like me. Same face, same hair, same everything." As he said this, he reached back and lightly touched his carefully coiffed hair, that same poofy style that looked fine on someone like him, but it wasn't something I would ever think of attempting for myself.

"Anyway, after I recovered from that, I managed to shove him off of me. I'd seen this tree beside me just before that, so before he could get up, I snapped off a branch, just a little thing, like this, you see…" He indicated a span of about ten inches between his two index fingers. "And then, when the vampire came at me again, I used the branch like a wooden stake and got him right through the heart." He mimed doing this as he spoke, then sat back in his chair, looking pleased with himself but also faking apprehension. "I was lucky to get away."

"And so the vampire died?" the host asked, her eyes rapt.

"Yeah. I have to say that it was really weird seeing someone who looked just like me lying there dead. I'm not proud of it, but all I could think to do was run."

"I understand. Or at least, I can as much as someone who's never been in that situation. So why do you think it suddenly changed and looked like you?"

"I have no idea. Maybe it was, I don't know… Maybe they make themselves look like other people as a disguise?"

"If I may," a voice from off-camera spoke. It was one of the other guests. The picture cut to a wide shot showing everyone, and it became clear that the man to Eden Garris's left had spoken. "Sorry to interrupt, but I just wanted to say that what this young man is describing is not outside the realm of traditional vampire folklore."

"Dr. Prescott, professor of English," Garris said hurriedly as the camera zoomed in on the man. He had thick, curly grey hair and large, amber tinted glasses that were out of style, the kind one would expect to see on someone in the late 1970s. "You were saying?"

"The ability of vampires to shape-shift is a common theme in vampire literature. Most people these days only know what they see in the old Christopher Lee movies, but actually, vampires have traditionally been known to take all sorts of forms, not only bats, but wolves, dogs, cats… Virtually anything they want to, depending on the story. *Dracula* is just the most famous story, but there are many others, some of them much older and from all parts of the world."

"Really," the host said. "I didn't realize that."

"Yes. Sorry to interrupt. I just wanted to say that even though Mr. Campbell's story here sounds out of the ordinary, in the larger context, a vampire in human form could very well take on the appearance of another person for its own ends. Please, go on," he concluded, holding out a hand in Damon's direction.

The camera cut to him, and he looked pleased. "So you're saying that he copied my face, my entire appearance, for some evil purpose?" He said this eagerly, like he needed Prescott's approval, but I had picked up on where he was going with all of this. He was still acting, weaving his lie. Although it pained me to do so, I found myself admiring him again. "I wonder how he did that. Like, maybe he was reading my thoughts, or something."

"I'm sorry; I don't follow," Prescott said off-camera.

Damon looked pensive. "It's just that… That same night, a little later, I saw another vampire, and this time, I was too scared to fight. I just ran again, barely making it to my car in time to get away." There was suddenly something different about his tone; he was more quiet, looking down at his lap more, only glancing up a few times to look at Garris and the college professor. "This one was a girl, and she looked just like my ex-girlfriend's sister. Scared the hell out of me."

"I would offer, then," Prescott said, "that these vampires can not only mimic forms but read thoughts. Had you encountered your former girlfriend's sister recently? Or thought of her?"

"Actually, yeah," Damon said, looking up. "I saw her a couple of weeks ago. Wasn't a good time." He wasn't lying anymore.

"I see. Vampires being able to read minds is also a well documented trait. It's how they get inside of us, finding ways to make us do what they want."

"Dr. Prescott," the host said, turning her body toward him, "when you say all of this, do you say it from the perspective of a believer in the supernatural, or are you merely someone who knows all of the old stories and can just pull stuff out at random?" The camera was tight on her, so Prescott's off-screen reaction wasn't visible. "I'm sorry, what I mean is: Do you just think of these as stories and are knowledgeable about their history, or do you truly think that vampires are real and alive in the city?"

"A bit of both, I suppose."

The program continued on for its full half hour, during which the fourth guest threw out his own ideas. His was a more spiritual view, and he had some crackpot idea that because Halloween was approaching, that might have something to do with everything that was going on, either real vampires or some kind of hoax. He also put forth an idea that involved the Grim Reaper or the Angel of Death, saying that in some belief systems, this specter takes on a person's form when it appears to them to take their life. That might be related to Damon's story, he suggested.

Most of what was said on this show was completely false as far as I knew, but I felt an odd satisfaction from that. People were seriously discussing the topic of vampires, but they had it all wrong. The truth was that my friends, sisters, and I were at the core of this, but if everyone was willing to believe other things, that was fine with me. In a way, it got us off the hook.

I hadn't thought much about the danger of there being vampires identical to us running around the city, at least not in the sense of us being identified by eyewitnesses. Up until that point, the clones had been killing far enough away that the chances of anyone who knew us seeing them was fairly slim. But if somebody had, for example, seen my clone killing someone and also happened to know the real me, that could put me in some serious danger. I hadn't considered this, but Damon obviously had.

On the phone, Susanna sounded impressed, though reluctant at the same time. "I have to admit," she said, "that's pretty damn brilliant. I wish I'd thought of that."

"He was pretty convincing," I said. "I probably would have believed him if I hadn't known how full of shit he was. But like I said, the show's probably going to repeat a lot of times for at least a couple of weeks. That's how they do it on that channel, just showing the same crappy local shows over and over until they make new ones."

"Good," she said. "I guess that helps a little."

"What about the rest of it?"

"Hmm?"

"Have you thought about, I don't know, some other way to get rid of… you know, them?"

She sighed. "Not really. In fact, what you just told me pretty much blew my only idea out of the water."

"What do you mean? About Damon's story?"

"The part of it that was true," she said meaningfully. "You're sure that the bit about my double attacking him was real?"

"Yeah, definitely. Almost the entire time, he was all, 'Look at me! I'm a cool guy!' You know, with that big *'ehhhh'* smile of his. But just for that one part, when he was talking about you… I mean the other you, he started to clam up. I think he genuinely did almost get killed and was freaked out by it."

"Which means," she said, "that taking the antidote after the fact didn't work. I had hoped that maybe if I did that, it would eliminate my clone, make her disappear. Apparently, it didn't."

This was something that had crossed my mind, too, the idea of getting her to make another batch of the antidote so we could try again. Prior to this night, I hadn't been able to get in touch with her in order to suggest it. I said so, adding, "But I guess that idea is out."

"Yeah," she said bitterly.

"Any other ideas?"

"No."

I wasn't sure whether or not I should tell Carolyn about Damon's TV appearance, but Susanna told me that I should make sure that everyone else knew about the program and took the time to watch it. That way, they could at least know what the cover story was in case any of them ever encountered a situation where they had to explain to someone that if they saw one of their clones, it wasn't really them. It was a convoluted lie, but it served its purpose.

I expected Carolyn to lash out at me when I mentioned Damon to her, which she did initially. But then she sat and listened to the story, going from impatient to attentive. She echoed Susanna's sentiment that Damon's ploy had been a good one.

"Always such a good liar," she said, unfolding her arms and leaning back on them as she sat on the corner of my bed. I was sitting facing away from my desk, occasionally rolling my chair over a small, familiar ripple in the hardwood floor, one that had been caused by water damage several years earlier. "Asshole or not, he's good at what he does. And you're right; I guess it does kind of help, at least for covering our tracks. Still doesn't make things right, though."

"I know," I said. "You wanna see the tape?"

She shook her head quickly and let out a *"pssht"* sound. "Hell no. As far as I'm concerned, I never want to see that prick again."

"I know," I repeated. "He was totally hitting on the host, by the way. This black woman named Eden Garrison or something like that."

"Oh, he'll hit on anyone. Black, white, Chinese, whatever. He doesn't care. Anyone with a pulse, really."

"Yeah, I know some guys like that at school. And the girls just flock to them like they don't have a clue."

"They do," she said pointedly, then looked over toward the window for a moment. "Did you ever notice how Damon would pull that shit with Mom, too?"

"With Mom? No!"

"Oh, he totally would. Especially when we were first dating. Like he'd do this…" She imitated the tilting head gesture I'd seen him do on the show. "Or this…" She squinted her right eye slightly while doing an accurate impression of Damon's trademark grin.

"Yeah, I think I saw him do that, too."

"Yeah. It was all some big thing of his, trying to flatter people by being like, 'You're going to like me because I'm deigning to act flirty with you.'"

"And he did that to Mom? Isn't that… I don't know… kind of…"

"Fucked up? Pretty much, yeah. He just did it to win her over. She and Dad weren't too thrilled with him at first, you know."

I remembered that, some objections centering around his being older than Carolyn. By this point in my life, I'd learned to recognize the signs of a jerk playing a girl's heartstrings, knowing full well that he would turn around just a few weeks later and treat her like crap. But back during the era Carolyn was describing, I was just too young to pick up on any of that.

This brief period of civil conversation between me and Carolyn, comforting though it might have been, didn't do anything to solve the overall problem. The vampires were still out there, and the killings were still going on. On a more personal front, my social life at school wasn't doing all that great, either. Part of me didn't care, being preoccupied with the ongoing menace threatening our city. But another part of me still did; I couldn't ignore the fact that I still had to live the life of a normal 15-year-old boy.

I continued to study the news in an attempt to figure out the vampires' strategy, but it was frustrating. They had seemed to be edging toward downtown, but then more killings would occur farther south again, most of them individual and spread out but occasionally clustered or in pairs. Also, sometimes there were more than eight victims per night, other times less. That could just be because the police weren't finding the bodies immediately, or maybe not at all. I just didn't know.

Still, one thing I did find was that Damon's story had indeed been catching on. On the news, a few eyewitnesses claimed to have seen vampires that looked either like themselves or people they knew. None of this could have been true, so my only guess was that people were lying or mistaken. I hadn't realized how much the power of suggestion — and repetition, considering how many times that *Augusta Events* episode aired — could convince people that false things were true. Then again, I'd already seen a videotape of a crazy televangelist convince a classmate of mine to throw away her record albums just because he claimed they were satanic.

As far as trying to get the guys together again to go out and hunt down the vampires — something I hoped would become a regular thing — that wasn't working. With his parents back in town, Carl couldn't steal his sister's car anymore to drive us around, and Dennis stopped returning my calls. I realized that his sixteenth birthday was coming up on the 11th, at which point he'd be able to drive, and maybe that's precisely why he began avoiding me.

Carolyn could have helped on that front, but she refused to. She was far too scared of the idea of trying to confront her clone or any of the others, thinking that none of us would stand a chance against them. I was afraid she might be right. After all, when we were the vampires, we were pretty much unstoppable. It was only our own failings that did us in, our group falling apart and winding up being changed back to regular people. That wasn't going to happen this time. And if we couldn't go out and stop them, who would?

I spent several days struggling with my inability to solve this crisis, wondering what would happen if we couldn't fix things. Would the vampires just keep going? Could somebody else, maybe another group like Life Force, spring up and save the day? I was surprised one day in early November when hope came from an unexpected source.

"Somebody named Nick called you," my mother told me, and I must have betrayed myself by showing too much surprise. "What? Isn't he a friend of yours? He said he was."

Recovering, I said, "Used to be, I guess. We don't talk much anymore."

"Well, he said he wanted you to call him. Something about a game you used to play when you were younger. Is something wrong?" She looked more amused than concerned.

"No, no," I said. "Just surprised to hear from him. He was kind of a jerk, someone I knew back at St. Joseph's."

"Well then maybe this is a chance for you two to make up for lost time, to mend some fences."

I involuntarily rolled my eyes at this, but I checked myself. "Yeah, maybe," I said.

It took a while for me to find a good time to call Nick; I didn't want my parents to overhear. After dinner, while they were safely in the other end of the house watching *Jeopardy!* in the red den, I called from the phone in their room.

"A game, huh?" I said to him.

"Oh, shut it, Ray," he said. "Your mom asked what I was calling about, so I had to make something up. I figured you'd be able to figure it out from that." His tone was anything but friendly, so I abandoned my attempts to joke around.

"So what's up?" I asked as toughly as I could.

"I managed to kill the… the other me last night. I thought you should know."

Hearing this gave me an unexpected chill. "What? Really? How?"

"Don't get me wrong, Ray," he said, his voice deep and quiet. "I'm not telling you this because I want to say all is forgiven or any shit like that. I'm just sharing information, stuff you can tell the others that might help."

I understood, and I said so. "What happened?"

"I tracked him down, stalked him even. I knew he needed to go down, so I made it happen."

"Yeah, but how?"

"I guess the best way to explain it is to say that I tried to think of what I would do if I were him. He was me, after all, just a vampire. So I wondered where I'd go, or he would go, who he'd want to kill…" He went quiet for a moment.

Trying to fill the gap, I offered, "I kind of tried to do that, too, watching the news and seeing where the clones were killing. But I couldn't figure out how to make that work, I mean, to do anything with it."

"Yeah well, whatever. There was…" He stopped again. "You know, I was going to leave this part of the story out, but what the hell. There was this girl I went out with a few months ago. Alex. Well, Alexandra, but she went by Alex."

"Yeah?" I wasn't sure what his dating history had to do with anything.

"My clone killed her. Just last week."

I felt another chill, only having just recovered from the previous one. This time, my hair stood up. "Oh shit, Nick. I'm sorry. That really sucks."

"Yeah, it does. We'd broken up, but… She was really cool. Shaved head, lots of piercings in her ears, stuff like that. Cool chick. She really was."

"Damn, Nick." The vision I got in my head wasn't of the kind of girl I would find attractive; instead I thought of the video I had seen a year or so earlier for a song by The Dead Milkmen called "Punk Rock Girl." But for Nick, this Alex girl was probably his ideal, and for her to have gotten killed by his clone must have been devastating.

I started to mention this, but instead I asked a more obvious question: "Why did he do that?"

"Because… well… Probably a lot of reasons. I was pretty pissed at her when we broke up. And I even… Oh, what the hell. I told her about us."

"About who?"

"Us. The vampires."

I felt yet another chill, but this one was tinged with anger. "You did *what.*" I realized as the words came out that I had adopted Susanna's technique of saying a question as if it were a statement when she got mad.

"Don't worry about it; she's dead," Nick said bitterly.

"I know, I just… Damn it, Nick, do you realize how much trouble we could get into if…"

"You're damn right I do!" he interrupted. "But no, my clone killed her. Maybe for that same reason."

I seethed for a moment, then took in what he was saying. "To keep her quiet. Shit. Yeah, I get it now." We sat in silence for a few more seconds, listening to each other's breathing. "Why did you tell her?"

"I don't know," he said, sounding more vulnerable, a bit like his younger self. "She didn't believe me, anyway. I was trying to tell her that all that bad stuff that happened a couple of years ago was because of us, and she just laughed, telling me I was full of it." There was a sigh, and then he spoke again, his voice abruptly changing and becoming more stern. "Anyway, that's not what I wanted to tell you about. It's about what happened when I killed my clone."

"How did you manage to do it, anyway? When some of the guys and I tried to go after one of them, it just changed into a bat and flew away before we could get to him."

"Yeah, well, I saw that coming. For mine, I mean. But here's what surprised me: He was afraid of me."

"Really?"

"Yeah. I mean, not all terrified, but I could just tell. There was a look he got the first time I confronted him that I recognized, one I'd get if I was… well…"

"Afraid?"

"In trouble," he said.

My memory drifted back to a story he'd told me in seventh grade, this time that he flipped off a cop and gotten chased by him. The man was on foot, and Nick was on his skateboard, so he managed to get up enough speed to get away. However, he was so distracted by what had happened that he'd wound up falling and scraping himself up, injuries he later cleaned up in the bathroom once he was home.

I could still hear the younger, more high-pitched voice of Nick in my head: "Then I kept thinking, 'What if he comes and finds me? What if he knows where I live?' In the mirror, I had this weird look on my face, like…" He'd recreated the expression for me, darting his eyes around and doing something weird with his lips, pursing them. It looked almost like he might be about to throw up, but not quite that severe.

Back then, Nick could admit to feeling that vulnerable. But in the present, he was too concerned with being tough and aloof. "That's the best way I can describe it," he said, continuing the story about his clone. "He got away that time, but the next night, I found him at Basement Records downtown. You've been there, right? Near that new coffee shop?"

I hadn't actually been in there, but I knew where he was talking about. It was rumored at school to be a place where lots of punks, weirdos, and dangerous people hung out, that is, Nick's kind of people.

"Well anyway, I remembered this one time when Alex and I were at the store, where this fat dick-head behind the counter yelled at us because he thought she was trying to steal something. I told her after we left that I'd go back and fuck him up, but she warned me not to. But that's… Yeah, I guess I should explain that, too. I'd been checking the news and seeing where some of the killing was happening, and even before she… before she died, I noticed that some of them were places she and I used to go. At first I thought it was just coincidence. But when one of my friends who works at Be Caffeinated told me that Alex got killed just outside there, I figured it out."

"That it was your clone."

"Yeah. So I went after him. He even admitted killing her, bragging about it, just before he got away that first time. But he never tried to attack me. Then finally, I managed to catch him at Basement, probably there about to kill that guy. I dusted him with garlic powder, and that got him all disabled and screaming and shit, long enough for me to knock him on his ass and stake him."

I pictured all of this as he told his story. "You got him through the heart? And that killed him?"

"More than that," he said, a hint of surprise in his voice. "He completely disappeared. Like a ghost. Well, first he screamed a lot and coughed up blood, which I've gotta say is not something you want to see an exact copy of yourself doing."

"But he just vanished?"

"Yep, like he never even existed."

There was a pause as I processed this. "At least you got your revenge," I said, thinking that it sounded kind of lame.

"I guess," he said resignedly. "There were a few other people around when it happened, too, and they all clapped and cheered after I stood up from the sidewalk, but that just got on my nerves. I didn't feel like celebrating. But they were all, 'He killed the vampire! Did you see that?' All this crap. I didn't want to stick around, so I left. And that was pretty much it."

"Man…" was all I could think to say. Things were quiet for several seconds, but then Nick had something else to add.

"Oh, that was the other thing. When the clone died, or disappeared, whatever it did, I felt this weird… well, feeling. It was like a thread detached from my chest. Kind of like this invisible umbilical cord, something connecting me to the vampire. It was almost… I don't know… spiritual, or maybe psychic. You know more about that kind of stuff than I do.”

“I’ve never heard of anything like that, though,” I admitted.

“Well, it was definitely there, something real. My guess would be that if you were to kill your own clone, you’d feel it, too.”

“Did it hurt?”

“No, no, nothing like that. Just a weird sort of *snip,* and this image in my head of this long thread or cord floating away from my chest and into nothing. Kind of like a vision, now that I think about it, but not an actual hallucination.”

“An impression, maybe,” I offered.

“That’s as good a word as any, I guess.” There was a pause, then a sigh. “And that’s really all I can tell you. You should probably let all the others know, too, and maybe it’ll help. But from this point on, Ray, I’m done. Completely. Don’t ever call me again about this shit. Or anything. You and your stupid friends dragged me into this years ago, and I’m tired of my life getting all fucked up by it. I hope you manage to get rid of the other vampires and all that, but as far as I’m concerned, you’re on your own.”

“Okay,” I said, angry at myself for feeling so hurt by his words. I should have been tough and shot something back at him, but I knew he was right. “Sorry,” I managed to say.

“Yeah.”

Eager to pass on this new information, I set about getting in touch with the rest of the former vampires, starting with Susanna.

“So, that’s what that was,” she said thoughtfully.

“What what was?” I asked.

“That thread detaching thing he described. I felt that a few days ago, but I had no idea what it was at the time.”

“You mean…”

“The vampire copy of me is dead,” she said meaningfully. “Someone must have killed it.”

I pondered this for a moment. "But it wasn't you?"

"No. How could I? I've just been sitting here in Columbia, hiding out and hoping for the best." She sounded ashamed, which wasn't something I was used to hearing from her.

"Hmm. So that means…" I tried to find the right words. "The city is fighting back. I'd been wondering maybe if some group like Life Force might pop up again."

"Probably not on that scale," she said. "Or at least, not as public. The police might just round them up again." She paused again. "I guess we kind of screwed ourselves in that regard."

"But it sounds like at least some people are doing something!" I said hopefully. Then a more gloomy thought hit me. "Then again, that might just mean that more people are going to get killed if they get in over their heads."

"Probably." After another pause, she added, "I'm just glad I didn't have to face her myself. The thought of that scared the crap out of me. I was so sure that any night now, this evil, identical version of me would show up at my apartment and try to kill me."

"You think she would have flown all the way to Columbia?"

"Well, I hoped not, but I guess it doesn't matter now." She sounded relieved, but still cautious. "But what was the other thing your friend said? About his duplicate being afraid?"

"What? Afraid? I'm not sure. He was a little vague. Something like the clone thought he'd get in trouble or something. Didn't make a lot of sense to me."

"It might…" she said, her voice trailing off.

"How?"

"Give me a minute." There was a long silence, and I wasn't sure what she was doing. After ten or fifteen seconds, she said, "Okay. Just had to think through something there."

"About what?"

"So Nick's clone was afraid of him for some reason, and you also said before that when you and the others went after Dennis's clone, it just flew away without a fight."

"Well, sure. There were four of us and only one of him."

"Ray," she said, a hint of condescension in her voice. "Dennis was there, wasn't he?" I answered her. "Come on," she said with a leading tone. "Put it together."

Finally, it clicked. I slapped my hand to my forehead, amazed that I hadn't seen it before. My mind immediately flashed back to a comic book I'd gotten when I was six years old, an issue of *The Incredible Hulk*. For some reason, that character kept popping up in my life. I had loved the TV show as a little kid, but I had only owned a couple of issues of the comic book it was based on. That was because my mother was opposed to comics, saying that they weren't "real books" and that I should read other things instead. My father was more lax about that, being of the opinion that anything that encouraged young children to read was good.

Because I only had these two issues of the comic, I reread them constantly. The more intriguing of them was the one called "If I Kill You... I Die!" While the normal storyline involved David Banner — or Bruce Banner as he was known in the comics — transforming into the Hulk against his will, this story was interesting in that Banner and the Hulk somehow got separated into two different people, existing side by side. The Hulk hated Banner and wanted to get rid of him, saying that he felt like a prisoner inside the other's body. But Banner protested, insisting that if the Hulk killed him, the source from which he'd come, he would die as well.

It was a pretty deep concept for a six-year-old to take in, but I understood it pretty well at the time. That is, I did once Susanna explained it to me. Back then, we were still young enough to get along and comfortably spend time together. That was just before the gap in our ages began to force us apart, her hurtling into adolescence and leaving me behind. Carolyn and I remained close for a few more years, the two of us having more in common than our snobby older sister.

"If I kill you, I die," I said to Susanna meaningfully, and I could picture her nodding her head. "I haven't thought about that in years."

"Me neither. But it makes sense, doesn't it? God, I wish I'd thought of that before. It explains why those vampire versions didn't just kill us in the hotel room that night when they first emerged. They couldn't."

I realized that the same thing had been bugging me all along. Finally, I understood why those clones had rushed out of the room, and it explained why both Dennis's and Nick's clones hadn't tried to attack them. In a larger sense, it meant that if any of us were to confront our clones one on one, we actually had the advantage.

Inspired by this new knowledge, I felt confident for the first time in weeks. I passed the new information on to everyone else, and while I hoped that Carolyn might regain some confidence and be willing to drive me and maybe Tim or Carl around to hunt down the vampires, she still refused, too scared to act.

When I went to bed on Sunday night, I thought about this and was sympathetic, but I still knew that things had to be done. Our clones were out there killing innocent people, and even if a few others might be taking up arms and doing the dirty work for us, when it all came down to it, we still had a responsibility to get rid of the vampires. They existed because of us, and they needed to be eliminated. If we could just manage to do that, this whole nightmare could be put to an end. Now that I knew that I had nothing to fear from my clone, I felt a renewed sense of purpose.

But could I really do it? Nick's description of what it was like killing his clone unnerved me. When I was a vampire, I had killed lots of people, enjoying it as I did it. But things were different now. I wasn't a murderer anymore. When I tried to picture myself successfully conquering my double and plunging a wooden stake through his heart, the idea made me squirm. That whole "coughing up blood" comment of Nick's made me picture the other version of me doing the same thing, and it was a difficult thing to envision. I'd seen it happen in cheesy vampire movies before, but could I really stomach seeing that happen, to drive the stake through the monster's heart?

I got my answer the following day, but not in a way I could have expected.

"I'm afraid I have some bad news," Dr. Phillips said, standing in front of our homeroom class with his hands pressed together like someone saying a prayer. When I first saw him do this, my sarcastic nature kicked in, and I wondered what kind of crap this middle-aged balding jerk might have to say.

"Our friend and classmate," he continued, "Elizabeth Morgan, whom we all loved and cherished, passed away at her home this weekend."

My entire body went numb. It felt like something rushed through me, an invisible force plowing its way through my entire being. I let out a gasp, as did some of the other students. Almost without thinking, I looked over at Elizabeth's empty desk, thinking somehow that Dr. Phillips must have been wrong, that Elizabeth would be sitting right there, only then remembering that I had noticed just a few minutes before that she wasn't in class. I then realized that not only was her desk vacant, but Helen's and Melinda's were as well. Everyone in the class was murmuring anxiously.

"I know," Dr. Phillips continued, holding up his hand. "It's a difficult thing to take in. We're all upset about it."

"What happened?" Tammy asked, which prompted an even more pained look from our teacher.

"That's... The details have... yet to be determined," he said, and I could tell that he was lying. I knew exactly what had happened to Elizabeth, and I fought back tears as the implications of it sunk in. As my classmate's whispers began to mix with the sounds of some of the girls' muffled crying, that became more and more difficult.

Dr. Phillips tried to maintain control. "You may have noticed that two more of our friends, Melinda Maxwell and Helen Richards, are also absent." A small shriek rang out from the rear of the classroom, and I turned back to see Annie, who was usually so confident and pretty, grasping at her mouth, her eyes squinting tightly and wet with tears.

"I'm sorry," Dr. Phillips said hastily, holding up a hand. "I'm sorry. Helen and Melinda are fine. I should have worded that better." A collective sigh rushed through the room. "Because the two of them were so close to Elizabeth, the school decided to let them stay home today. We were informed of the news early this morning."

The numbness of the initial shock having passed, my body began to feel like it was on fire. I wanted to burst out crying, even screaming, but another part of me still cared about what everyone else would think. I didn't want to display that kind of emotion. The guys in the class would probably think I was a baby if I did. I dared to glance over at Aaron and his friends, then felt a small sense of relief to see that they too seemed to be struggling to keep it together.

"I can see that the rest of you are..." he continued, then faltered, lowering his head for a moment. Unexpectedly, I found myself feeling bad for him. I hated this guy, but for the first time, I sympathized with him. Conveying this to the class couldn't have been easy.

He cleared his throat, facing everyone again. "Because of the impact of this, that is, I can see how deeply affected we all are... If anyone here feels the need to go home today, please raise your hand. You won't be penalized for missing class."

Hands shot up immediately from the right side of the room where the well-behaved, pious do-gooders were barely holding back from breaking down. It struck me as odd that these kids — the ones who had almost nothing in common with the rebellious girl I loved — were so upset. But it was genuine. That much I knew. Following their lead, I slowly put my own hand up as well.

Had the bad kids, myself included, immediately opted for a free holiday from school, it might have been seen as a cop-out, just an excuse for some time off. But one by one, everybody in the class raised their hands, and I found that touching. We were all mourning the loss of someone we cared about, even if we hadn't known just how much until we'd been told that she was gone.

"I see," Dr. Phillips said, nodding his head slowly. There was something in his expression that I had never seen before, a slight smile that seemed warm and almost proud. "I'll make arrangements with Debbie… uh… Ms. Carlton, to call everyone's parents to come pick them up. Excuse me." With that, he rushed out of the room.

Left on our own, everyone was free to talk without adult supervision. While some of the students took this as an opportunity to let their tears out and comfort each other, the people on my side of the classroom wanted to speculate.

"Do you think it was vampires who got her?" Aaron blurted out.

"I bet it was!" Jay said. "They're still going around killing people!" I didn't want to hear this. Apparently, neither did Kirby.

"You shut up with that shit right now," he said angrily.

"We were just wondering!" Aaron said defensively.

"Well, you just keep on wondering and shut the fuck up," Kirby said firmly.

"But we just thought…" Jay began, then broke off, uncertain. "What do you think, Ray?" This whole time, I had been staring down at my desk, holding my knuckles to my temples and trying my best not to break down and cry. Most of the conversation had been heard by me, not seen, apart from what happened to be in my peripheral vision.

Fighting to control my voice, I said sternly: "I think Kirby is right." I flinched inwardly, realizing how weird it was for me to be saying those words.

"It's these new feet." That was the last thing I had said to Elizabeth before she died. The previous Friday, I had been walking near her and her friends down a small flight of three or four stairs outside one of our classrooms, and I tripped. I didn't stumble enough to fall down, but it was a noticeable mistake and therefore embarrassing. Elizabeth and the other girls saw, and as I recovered, I joked, "It's these new feet." It was a joke, a variation on one I'd used with other people once or twice before when I jumbled up my words and stammered, saying, "It's this new tongue. I'm still getting used to it." I couldn't even remember where I'd picked the joke up from; I'd probably seen a funny actor or a stand-up comic say it on TV. And it usually got a positive reaction for me, a smile or even a laugh.

This time around, Elizabeth had gotten the joke, probably because she'd been around for one of my "new tongue" references before. Helen and Melinda just looked at me with a combination of confusion and contempt, sighing and shaking their heads as they walked on. Elizabeth, meanwhile, gave me one of those smiles she was so good at, the kind that looked like she was trying to fight it, but not really. That wasn't the last time I saw her that day, but it was the final bit of interaction we'd had. I hated the fact that the last thing I'd said to her had been so trivial and stupid.

On the way home, I'd thought about this and countless other things, sitting silently in the passenger seat and looking out the window, barely aware of the cars and houses we passed as my mother drove. She'd asked me early on if I wanted to talk about things, then quickly backtracked once she realized how upset I was. "It's okay," she'd said. "We can talk about it later if you want to." I didn't.

Instead, I holed up in my room with the door locked, lying in bed and crying as quietly as possible into my pillow. The girl I loved was dead, and it was my fault. I may not have been the one who actually killed her, but I knew who had, and if it weren't for me, he wouldn't exist. If it weren't for me, Elizabeth would still be alive.

I ran things over and over in my head, wishing that they weren't true but knowing that they were. I wondered what I should have done differently, if I could have somehow warned her that my clone might go after her, but honestly, that hadn't even occurred to me. I had been more concerned with the other people he and the vampires had been killing, but even then, most of those were far away and out of scope. That is, I knew that people were dying, and I felt bad about that, but they weren't people that I actually knew. They were generic, abstract victims. For the first time, I knew what it must have been like for the friends and relatives of all those people. The beautiful girl I had lost wasn't merely a statistic; she was someone I loved, and when I thought about how cowardly I had been while she was alive, too afraid to just tell her how I felt, I hated myself even more.

But I was also confused. Why had my clone killed her? I liked Elizabeth, and she wasn't a threat to us, either the former vampires or the rogue duplicates. She didn't know anything about that. I could understand why Nick's clone had killed his ex-girlfriend for fear of her exposing us, but was that really the reason?

As for how I knew that my clone had done it, that was just something that clicked in my head the moment Dr. Phillips announced her death. My conversation with Nick had immediately coalesced with some recent and not-so-recent memories of my own, a scheme I'd come up with a couple of years before to try to get Elizabeth's phone number.

Back when I was at St. Joseph's, a student directory was published each year that listed everyone's name, address, and telephone number. Presumably this was to facilitate communication among parents, teachers, and students, but there were occasional downsides to having that much information so readily available. Sure, I could use the directory to get in touch with my friends, but I could also use it to prank call Dennis's house in fourth grade, which I did. Other students did similar things.

In sixth grade, I called Valerie to ask about the homework I'd missed one day when I'd been out sick, though it would have made more sense to call Dennis or one of my closer friends instead. I just used that as an excuse to talk to her since I liked her, hoping that we might talk about other things as well. She and I still got along at that point, so we did talk, but the conversation soon became awkward and meaningless, and my crush on her never went anywhere. Also, because the directory listed her address, I took note of it. One day in seventh grade, I was riding with Carolyn in her car, and when we happened by Dresden Way, the street Valerie lived on, I got her to drive down it so I could see her house. It was a pointless exercise, but it meant something to me to see the actual place where the object of my affection lived.

But at Bethlehem, there was no such directory. Either the school didn't have the resources to print such a thing, or for all I knew, there was some biblical reason along the lines of *thou shalt not stalk thine classmates.* I didn't think of all of this as stalking, nor did I know the term at the time. I'd just gotten used to the idea of knowing where the people I went to school with lived. In the summer of 1987, when the others and I had studied the map of Augusta, I would occasionally spot street names and find myself saying things like, "Oh, so that's where Bryan lives!" It just made things seem more coherent and real in terms of knowing and picturing where everyone was.

So when I got to know Elizabeth and became obsessed with her, it bugged me that I didn't know where she lived, what her phone number was, nothing. The same was true for most of my other classmates, but of course, she was the one I wondered about the most. I cooked up this elaborate scheme to find out her number, thinking that if I could just call her and talk to her, maybe we could get to know each other, get together, and live happily ever after. It was a dumb idea, but not to a lonely and smitten 13-year-old.

The plan was that I would first ask her what street she lived on. She would tell me something like "Whatever Street." Presumably, she'd want to know why I'd asked, and I would tell her that there was a family in my neighborhood with the same last name as hers, and

I had been wondering if she in fact lived nearby. I knew she didn't, but armed with the knowledge of her last name and her street name, I could then go through the phone book and find out which Morgans lived on Whatever Street, and then I'd know her number.

This idea was abandoned not long after I came up with it. Helen happened to mention at school one day that Elizabeth lived near Lake Olmstead, which wasn't too far from our school. I knew where that was, but the mention of it unnerved me. We had killed there back in 1983, and I didn't like being reminded of our time as vampires. Furthermore, I realized that even if I were able to stealthily find out Elizabeth's phone number, I would never be able to work up the nerve to just call her out of the blue and strike up a conversation with her. It was hard enough to talk to her in person, so why did I think that I could call her after being so sneaky? Back at my old school, that kind of behavior was understandable and acceptable because it was so easy to find the information. But at this new point in my life, it would have just seemed creepy and way too obvious in terms of how much I liked her, not suave and clever like I first thought it might be.

When I got a little older and was approaching the age to drive, the idea resurfaced. I'd heard some of the upperclassmen at Bethlehem talk about how they would go around town on Friday and Saturday nights and stop by friends' houses, plus I remembered how some of Carolyn's friends had occasionally done the same thing. A group of them would just show up at our home when she was in high school, and an impromptu session of hanging out and joking around would commence. A couple of times, a single friend of hers would show up, bored and looking for something to do, and they'd go off somewhere together.

I vaguely knew the area where Elizabeth lived, but if I knew the exact address, then maybe I could be one of those cool teenaged friends who just showed up at a classmate's house and said, "Hey, you wanna hang out?" We'd drive off into the sunset and have great times, or something like that. It would have to wait until I was sixteen, which wouldn't happen until the following year.

This was just something that went through my mind a month before the emergence of the clones happened, one of the more normal ideas that had to do with everyday life and my crush on the most gorgeous girl in school, or so I thought. Looking back on it, I realized that a lot of these thoughts were somewhat psycho and disturbing, and I wondered if they had anything to do with the latent vampire traits that had resurfaced up until the time of the emergence.

That tied in with how I knew what my clone had done. He had probably stalked her, hanging around her neighborhood until he figured out which house was hers, then attacked and killed her. He may have done it for the same reason Nick's clone killed his ex, or maybe not. It didn't really matter. What did matter was that I was certain of one thing: I was going to track down that disgusting piece of trash and drive a stake right through his heart.

The anger and determination helped to push aside the overwhelming sadness I felt, but only briefly. Avenging Elizabeth's death seemed like the right thing to do, but how could I go about it? When I watched the news that night, the sporadic vampire activity in the report still did nothing to clue me in as to how to track any of the monsters down, let alone the main one I was after. I tried to use my psychic powers to sense him, but they just weren't strong enough for that. For all I knew, his powers were just as strong as mine had gotten a couple of years before, and he was able to cloak himself and possibly the others as well.

Getting to sleep that night was difficult. I was sad, angry, and frustrated. The fact that I couldn't figure out a way to find my clone and kill him made me feel useless. Trying to focus on the logistics of that was really just a distraction anyway, something to keep myself from spiraling down into another fit of crying over the loss of Elizabeth. She had been so beautiful, so smart, and such a cool girl, and I had wasted all that time hiding behind my shyness and trying to conceal how I really felt about her. And for what? So I could avoid being rejected? To keep from being ridiculed by my friends or hers? If I could just go back in time somehow and do things differently…

I took the flashlight out of my night table, then reached down to the small shelf underneath it. That was where I kept all of my school annuals, and it wasn't uncommon for me to take them out occasionally and thumb through them, usually to look at pictures of the girls I liked. It only took me a few seconds to find the page with Elizabeth's ninth grade class photo; I'd turned to that page probably a hundred times. She looked different back then, her hair still all poofed up and curly, not straight like it had been in tenth grade. But she was still impossibly gorgeous. There she was in black and white, a slight misinterpretation of her true beauty: that wicked smile, her wide, expressive eyes having a slight squint to them, her looking at the camera in a way that seemed to say, *I know something you don't.*

Getting out the annual had been a mistake. I slammed the book shut and shoved it back onto the shelf, my body beginning to quake with emotion as I fought back the latest wave of tears. Turning the flashlight off and replacing it in the drawer, I slammed my body back onto the bed and lay there, looking up at the ceiling in the dark. I heaved as quietly as possible, not wanting my parents to hear me. I felt a cold prick in my right ear as one of my tears made its way along my temple and into the earhole, something that would happen if I cried while lying on my back. Annoyed, I sat up and wiped at my ear, then punched the mattress in frustration.

I'd killed her. I had killed the girl that I loved more than anyone else in the world. And even if I could kill my clone, that wouldn't bring her back. She was gone, just like all of the other people we had killed over the years. This death felt more personal, more real. It even felt more real than the kill I had actually made myself a few years ago, the one when Carolyn got me to drain the life of that helpless little blonde girl. *I saved her for you.* Those words would always cut through my heart whenever I'd remember them. I had thought of it as a mercy killing at the time, but what had happened next? Who had found her body and the bodies of the other people in the yard that night? How much did her family mourn for her? How much did they hate whoever had done it, even if they didn't know who was to blame?

More tears streamed down my face, some of them making their way into my open mouth, which was hurting from all of the grimacing. Their saltiness reminded me of the taste of blood, though sharper and not as warm. The fact that I knew the difference between the two flavors disgusted me.

I didn't dream about Elizabeth that night, which was simultaneously disappointing and a relief. Part of me wanted to see her in my dreams because I missed her, but if I had, the dream might have turned scary like those recurring nightmares. Mostly I dreamed about random stuff, but every now and then, I would get this eerie feeling, like something was just around the corner. It was like the signs that usually led to a nightmare were almost there, but not quite. Whenever I would start to feel even a twinge of that, I would wake up, then quickly fall back to sleep and dream of something else.

By the time I finally did dream about her, it was a few nights later, and I wound up telling Carolyn about it the following evening. She had been both sympathetic and berating of me as I told her about Elizabeth's death and the guilt I felt, telling me that I should feel guilty given all that had happened, but also holding back some and being more gentle. Despite our differences, she still seemed saddened by seeing her little brother in so much pain.

"She wouldn't talk to me," I explained. "We were at school, and I wanted to talk to her. In the dream, I didn't even remember that she'd died. It was like that never happened. But I just wanted so bad to tell her something, something like… Yeah, that was it. I was sorry. I don't remember what about, just… I'd tried to tell her something earlier, and she hadn't understood, and I didn't want to tell her while her friends were there."

"How come?"

"I don't like them. Or they don't like me. These two girls she always hung out with, real *bit*... I mean... just... I don't know. It was something private."

"Like how much you liked her?" I thought she might be making fun of me, but the lack of her usual sneer told me that she was asking a genuine question.

"No, it wasn't that. Something more simple. I'm not sure. It's hard to remember dreams, you know."

"I know. But dreams are important. Did she say anything at all?"

"No. She'd just look at me, sort of... I don't know, uninterested, maybe? Is that a word?" Carolyn nodded. "And she just kept walking away, and I couldn't keep up. That was pretty much the whole dream. It only went on for a couple of minutes, but I kept thinking about it all day today."

"What were things like for you at her funeral?" she asked.

I looked down at the kitchen table. "I didn't go. I just couldn't."

"What? Ray, you really should have gone."

"Why?" I shot back, feeling defensive. "So I could see her dead body lying there in a coffin? So I could cry my eyes out and not be able to tell any of the people there just how much I knew about how..." I broke off, realizing that I'd raised my voice. Our parents were in the red den, just two rooms away, and I didn't want them to hear what we were talking about. Carolyn picked up on this, and she made a gesture with her hand and led me into the yellow den. We started to sit down on the couch in front of the window, but then I remembered that if Scout saw us from the backyard, he would start barking. He always did that whenever he saw someone in the house. Instead, I just let Carolyn sit in the wicker chair while I leaned up against the doorway to the kitchen.

"You really should have gone, you know," she said to me. "Funerals are meant to give people a sense of closure."

"I know," I said. "Mom said the same thing. But it just wasn't something I was comfortable with. Just too upsetting."

"You were too young to remember Granny, right?"

"Yeah. I think I was two when she died, maybe three."

"Well, I was older, old enough to know her. In fact, the last real memory I have of her was me yelling at her and telling her I hated her."

"What?" I'd never heard this story.

"It was a few months before she went into the hospital after her… Was it a stroke or an aneurysm? I can't remember. But anyway, the last time I really talked to her, we were out at her house, and I did something wrong. I think I talked back to her or said something bad… something like that. So she made me go out into the yard, you know, that big yard over by the garden, and get a branch off of a tree."

"What for?"

"She called it a 'switch.' Some old tradition, I think. A kid is bad, and they have to go out and pick their own 'switch' so the parent or whoever can spank them with it. Really thin, like this." She indicated a space of about a quarter of an inch with her fingers. "Hurts like hell, apparently."

This was all new to me. I'd always heard that Granny was a nice woman, a typical, sweet old lady. I could just barely remember her, tall and thin with curly white hair. To think that she would punish my sister in such a cruel way was unsettling, and I said so.

"Oh, she was usually really nice. But whatever it was I said to her that time really set her off. I wish I could remember what it was. But anyway, I'd heard about this kind of punishment before. A friend of mine from school told me about when it happened to her, when her father beat her with a switch until her legs bled." She shuddered, then got a more wistful look. "Can't remember her name, either. Elise, maybe? Anyway, it doesn't matter. The point is that I walked out of that house and never went back inside. I pretended at first like I was looking for a switch, but then thought, screw it, I'll just stay out here until Mom gets back. No way was I going back in there and let her do that to me."

"Did she come out and look for you?"

"No, which surprised me. And then a little later, when Mom picked me and Susanna up, I didn't say a word. But Granny made sure to tell her about it, that I should be 'whipped,' as she put it, when we got home. Thankfully, that never happened. The whole thing was forgotten."

"Hmm," I said simply.

"But what I didn't forget," she said meaningfully, "was the very last thing I said to her when she chased me out of the house. I turned around and said as loud as I could, 'I *hate* you!' Just like that." She squinted, clenched her fists, and shook as she whispered the scream to me, and I could picture her as a little girl doing it. "That was the last thing I ever said to her, and then two or three months later, she died. I always regretted that."

I understood what she was saying. It was a sad story, but I wasn't sure how relevant it was to how I felt about Elizabeth and her death. I'd never hated her, though I had occasionally gotten snippy with her at times when I was feeling irritated over her not returning my affection.

"That's sad," I said. "I never knew about all that."

"Yeah, well, I never told you. But the reason I bring it up is because I did at least get some kind of sense of peace at Granny's funeral, or at least, at the viewing."

"The what?"

"There's this thing they do, where… Well, aside from just the funeral, they have this thing before called the viewing. It's at the funeral home, not the actual graveyard. At the funeral, the coffin is closed. They call it a 'viewing' because that's when the coffin is open, and you see the actual body in it. It's kind of creepy."

I tried not to picture Elizabeth lying dead in a coffin. It didn't work. I looked down and shuddered, prompting Carolyn to say, "Yeah, I know. But the point is that you see the body, so there's no denying that the person is gone, and it's your last chance to say goodbye to them. And that's what I did with Granny. I remember standing by the coffin next to Dad and Susanna, and then I reached up and touched the edge of it. I whispered to her, 'Sorry,' hoping that she could hear me."

She'd choked up a little with this last sentence. I imagined myself doing the same thing at Elizabeth's viewing. "So…" I searched for the right words. "Did it do any good?"

"I think so," she said.

After thinking over this for a few moments, I decided to tell her what I knew about Elizabeth's funeral, things I'd heard people at school say about it. Even though I'd skipped out on going, at least I'd gotten some secondhand experience.

"Like what?" Carolyn asked me.

"Well, I don't know. Just little things. Like hearing how upset her mother was, crying and all that. I don't think I could have handled seeing that, knowing what I know." She gave me a quizzical look. "About how she died." Then she nodded quickly.

"Oh, and there was another thing," I added. "One of her friends, one of the ones I mentioned earlier, told me how some woman there sang this church song, 'His Eye Is on the Sparrow.' According to the preacher, it was Elizabeth's favorite song. That struck me as a little bit strange."

"How come?"

"Elizabeth wasn't really a religious person. She was always getting in trouble at school for questioning all that." Carolyn smiled slightly. "What?"

"Oh, nothing. Doesn't matter. So… what, do you think her friend was lying to you?"

"No, no, nothing like that. But I did feel kind of pissed that Helen and Melinda were suddenly being all nice to me given how they seemed to do everything they could to keep Elizabeth away from me when she was alive. No, I was just thinking that maybe the preacher guy didn't know what he was talking about." I paused, then surprised myself by letting out a little laugh.

Carolyn's smile grew more warm. "And you wish you could tell her about that, don't you?"

I went back to being sad. "Yeah. I guess so."

"Look," she said, standing up from the chair, her car keys in hand. "I get that you didn't want to be around all those people being so upset. That's understandable. But I do think you should at least go see her grave and get that sense of closure I mentioned."

I pondered this. Could I bear it? Given everything that Carolyn was saying, it made sense to give it a try. "Yeah," I said with a sigh. "Maybe you're right. Maybe it would help, even if only a little bit."

"Do you know where it is? Do you want me to take you by there tomorrow?" As I thought about this and was about to say yes, she then looked pained. "Ohhh, crap. Hang on. Sorry. I already have plans with Catherine to go to Athens this weekend."

"Who?"

"Friend of mine. She knows all these cool stores and stuff downtown… Says it's a really neat place. I've never been, though… Anyway, sorry. Maybe when I get back on Sunday?"

I agreed. "But…" I began to say, then broke off.

"What?"

"Can I just…? I don't know. When we go, could you, like, wait in the car or something? If I'm going to be standing by her grave and talking and being all emotional and stuff, I'd rather do it on my own." I'd seen people do such things on TV and in movies, and as our plan formed, I pictured myself doing the same thing. It just needed to be something I did on my own, not with someone else standing there and making me feel self-conscious.

"Sure," she said, heading for the back door.

"Thanks, by the way," I said, and she paused and turned back. "I think going by there and giving her one last goodbye will help. Maybe her ghost will hear me or something. It's not as sad as the thing with you and Granny, but I hate thinking that her last memory of me was me cracking some dumb joke about my feet."

She had been smiling up until that last sentence, but then her face fell. "Wait, what?" she asked, looking confused.

I wasn't sure what had been unclear. "That thing I told you about. The last thing I said to her."

She looked down at the floor, then back up at me with a sad expression. "I thought you understood," she said softly.

"What are you talking about?"

She started to speak, then stopped, avoiding eye contact. "Look, we'll talk about it when I get back. See you later." With that, she went out the back door, and I stood there, perplexed for almost a full minute. During that, I heard her starting up her car and backing out of the driveway.

Finally, it clicked. When I realized what she'd meant, I broke down again, running through the den and to the bathroom to throw up what little dinner I'd managed to eat that night into the sink. When I recovered from that, I looked up at the mirror. Seeing myself through bleary, bloodshot eyes, I hated the person I saw.

How could I have been so self-centered? All this time, I'd been thinking about Elizabeth's death from my own narrow point of view, and I'd thought for a brief time during my conversation with Carolyn that I'd been given some insight into the bigger picture, how I should have been looking at things. But one thing had completely slipped my mind: Elizabeth's last memory of me, of Ray Young, was not that stupid incident at school. It was of my clone attacking and killing her.

I lay on my bed, tortured by the notion that Elizabeth must have believed that I had been the one who killed her. That was probably her last memory altogether. She didn't know anything about the clones. Maybe she had seen that TV show that Damon was on and bought into the lie that vampires could look like anyone they wanted, but still, the last thing she'd probably experienced was the terror of being murdered by someone identical to me. I couldn't live with that thought, but I couldn't make it go away.

This had to stop. I wasn't sure which was more painful: the grief or the guilt. And it wasn't like Elizabeth's death was the only one on my conscience. I'd dealt with that for years, the knowledge that I'd been both directly and indirectly responsible for countless people dying. For a short time, I'd bought into one of Tim's ideas, a Christian belief called predestination. If everyone's fate was already decided by God, then the people we killed were going to die anyway, and we were just part of that bigger plan. When I'd tried running this by Carolyn at one point, she had balked at the idea and called it a cop-out. And she was right.

Even though I had settled on the notion that the vampires out there were separate beings from us, and I liked Tim's other belief that killing them was our chance at redemption, that still didn't make things right. We couldn't let those monsters continue to fly around the city and kill whoever they wanted. Whether they were killing total strangers or people we knew wasn't relevant. It was just that once someone I knew and cared about died, that was what it took to shake me awake and into action.

As the hours crawled by, I tried to come up with a solution. When I finally did, I was struck by the simplicity of it. It was drastic, and I wasn't sure if I could go through with it. In fact, I wound up trying to talk myself out of it more than once throughout the rest of the night. This led to my coming up with a plan B, but I doubted if that one would even work. I was pretty sure that my original idea was the only way out. But first, there was something else I needed to do.

It took forever for my parents to go to bed that night, and to be safe, I waited for almost a full hour afterwards. I turned the knob on my bedroom door as slowly as possible, making sure that there were no audible clicks as it unlocked. It had been a long time since I had tried to sneak through my own house, and I silently swore each time a section of the floor creaked. I moved quietly and carefully, making my way around to the front door, through the living room, and then to the kitchen. Opening the refrigerator door without making a sound was almost impossible, but I hoped that it was still muffled enough that my parents wouldn't hear it.

Once I had what I needed, I crept through the kitchen, stopping by the sink to pick up a large steak knife I had noticed earlier in the night just before Carolyn and I had talked. As I put it into my backpack, I glanced over at the table, picturing for a moment some of the times my sisters, my friends, and I had gathered there. It made me sad, but it also made me more determined.

Everything had to be in slow motion. If anything I did made the slightest sound and my mother or father got up and found me, I'd be screwed. It wasn't like I could tell them what I was doing, and I realized just before reaching the back door that I probably should have come up with a cover story just in case I did get caught. Pausing for a moment after gently picking up Mom's car keys from a small shelf, I ran through a couple of ideas. Settling on one I figured they would swallow, I continued with my plan.

I made it outside just fine and carefully locked the door behind me. As expected, I heard Scout beginning to move around in the backyard, and in sharp contrast to my earlier actions, I raced around the carport and over to the corner of the fence near his doghouse, slinging my backpack onto the ground and reaching into the outermost pocket.

"It's okay!" I whispered to him as he joined me at the fence and began jumping around, letting out little whimpers. "It's me! It's just me, Scout. Shh. Shh shh shh. Here. I've got something for you if you'll be quiet." I unwrapped the slice of cheese I'd gotten from the refrigerator. It seemed like the cellophane made more noise than anything else had so far. I pushed the slice through the chain-link fence, and he gobbled it up eagerly. Cheese was always a good way to get him to do what I wanted. What I wanted most from him now was for him not to bark.

Satisfied that Scout would keep quiet for at least a few minutes, I quickly made my way into the car, hurrying to close the door so that the interior light wouldn't be visible if Mom or Dad happened to have heard anything and might be looking out the window. I wasn't even sure if the carport was visible from their bedroom, but I wasn't taking any chances. I shifted the car into neutral, then quietly got back out of the car and began pushing it from the front. It was difficult at first, but once I got it going, the car moved more easily than I expected. Once I had it about three quarters of the way down the driveway, I got in and started it up, hoping that the sound of the engine was far enough away from the house.

Leaving the lights off, I sped backwards out of the driveway, just barely missing the mailbox. Once on the road, I headed for the corner and turned the lights on. I circled around the block and drove by the house once more, checking for any signs that someone had gotten up. As far as I could tell, I'd gotten away safely.

I was nervous as I drove, but I couldn't help but feel a thrill of satisfaction over how successful I'd been so far. I knew what I was doing was risky, but then, what in my life hadn't been? With a laugh, I realized that this was actually one of the most conventionally criminal things I had ever done. Besides, if Carl could "borrow" his sister's car, why couldn't I pull this off?

"I've gone through a lot of trouble to come see you tonight," I whispered, looking down at the grave. I said it with a smile, but I grew sad again when I looked back at the tombstone. Beneath the words *ELIZABETH P. MORGAN* were the dates of her birth and death: *SEPTEMBER 19, 1973 — NOVEMBER 12, 1989.* It reminded me of something several people had mentioned at school, how it was such a shame that she had died so young.

"I… I've thought a lot about what I wanted to say to you," I continued, "and I'm not sure if it's going to do any good, if you can hear me or anything. But I'd like to think that you can. Otherwise, there's not much point. But I need to get this out, to let you know that it wasn't me who killed you. It was someone else. Someone who looks exactly like me. I know it doesn't make sense, but it's the truth." I paused, taking a moment to look around the cemetery, which was lit intermittently by various streetlights along the concrete paths. My mother's car was parked quite a long way away out by the road, and I hoped that its presence wouldn't attract the attention of the police or anyone else. I knew that I wasn't supposed to be here, but I had to be.

"Hopefully no one will show up and ask me what I'm doing at some girl's grave at two o'clock in the morning," I said, my words echoing my thoughts. "My sister Carolyn was supposed to bring me by here in a couple of days, but I couldn't let another night go by letting that… well, first of all, with the thought that you went to your grave thinking that it was me that murdered you. And maybe…" I breathed in deeply without meaning to, the tears welling up in me. Forcing out a breath, I continued: "Maybe it was. Kind of. The Ray that you saw, the one who… you know… He wasn't actually me. He was a vampire version of me, a separate person that I'm going to make damn sure doesn't kill anyone else." I began shaking as I said this, adrenaline building up as I fought all kinds of emotions sweeping through me.

Trying to regain my composure, I sighed and said, "I'm sorry. I don't really know what I'm doing here. Just kind of winging it. But this seems like something important that I need to do. So I'm just going to tell you about it."

I'd been standing by the tombstone this whole time, my voice rising from a whisper to more of a hushed murmur as I became more relaxed. I squatted down and gently rested my left hand on the granite, a strange tingle passing through my fingers as I felt the coldness of the rock. It was like doing so made Elizabeth's death all the more real, and I suddenly felt incredibly weak.

I found myself sitting, almost as if my legs had given way beneath me, but it wasn't quite that dramatic. I just felt the need to sit down. I had been so tense for such an extended period of time, not realizing just how much until I allowed myself to sit on the grass and just pour my feelings out.

"Let me just tell you how it happened," I said, "and maybe it will make some kind of sense." And so I told her everything, going all the way back to Carl's failure at the qualifying race at the YMCA. I told her about the potion, how we had taken it almost as a prank to begin with, how things quickly got out of control, our turning on each other and becoming human again, and how that cycle repeated itself two more times before things finally imploded and couldn't continue anymore. Sometimes I glossed over things, and other times, I went into more detail than necessary, like the way our bat forms looked different in 1987 as opposed to the previous two summers. I would then catch myself and realize that I didn't need to explain every single thing.

When that happened, I'd laugh and berate myself. "Sorry, I'm doing it again," I said at one point. "Hell, I've probably been rambling for close to an hour by now." I let out another small laugh, but it was tinged with sadness. "I just realized that this is the longest I've ever talked to you. I was always too scared to when you were alive. Kinda pathetic, huh?" In that moment, I remembered the way she sometimes laughed, this gentle, almost forced chuckle. It was like she wasn't so much laughing at whatever stupid joke I cracked, but more like she was laughing at how bad I was at hiding how head over heels I was for her. She had probably known the entire time. "Yeah, you probably did know," I said, again shifting between thinking internally and speaking aloud. "Just wish I'd had the guts to tell you at the time."

I could feel tears starting to well up, so I buckled down and tried to keep telling the story. It took me through my time at Bethlehem and the weird things that led to the clones coming about, and I emphasized once again that the Ray who had killed her wasn't really me, but him.

I started to go into detail about mine and some of the other former vampires' ideas about just how they came to be and what they were, but then I stopped short, realizing that I was stalling. I stood up, not bothering to brush the loose grass and dirt from my jeans.

"And that's why I came here tonight," I said firmly, trying to convince myself to be tough. I also realized that I was speaking in almost a normal voice, though still more quiet than usual. I'd been at the grave undisturbed long enough to believe that no one was there to overhear me. "I've figured out how to get rid of the other Ray and make sure he doesn't do any more damage. I'm just sorry that I didn't do it in time to save you, Elizabeth. I really, really am. I just needed to come here and tell you all this, and I hope that wherever you are, you can hear me. I love you. I really do. And I'm sorry that I never had the courage to say so."

I took another deep breath. Was I done? There was more I could say, but it would be more like thinking aloud, trying to work things out. I considered telling her my plan, or actually plans, since there were a few variations running through my head.

"Should I tell you…?" I whispered. "Okay, sure, why not. Well, I started off trying to think of a way to find my clone, which has been hard so far because of the psychic stuff I told you about. I think he's shielding himself from me. But what I'm hoping is that he can still sense me. And if that's true, I'm going to send him a sort of psychic message, or just an impression maybe, that will get him to go to a certain place. I've always had this thing where I'll think things and someone else will say them, so the idea here is to do that deliberately, hopefully with the one person most receptive to my own thoughts, another *me.* "

I was pacing back and forth as I talked this plan out. I then turned back to the grave with a smile and said, "Are you getting all this so far?" It surprised me how much I joked around throughout all of this; I fully expected as I drove out here that I would be falling apart and bawling my eyes out the whole time. I wasn't sure if I was acting this way out of nervousness or fear, or maybe it really was comforting to me to feel like I could talk to Elizabeth, to anyone, about this. If I had told anybody else the rest of my plan, they would have tried to stop me, and here was someone who couldn't.

"I don't even know if it's going to work. But there is another solution, the one that was my original plan, actually. See, if I die, then so does he. That's why he won't attack me. I've got this knife back in the car, this big, sharp thing about this long." I indicated with my fingers the length of the blade, about six inches. "Should do the trick." I paused again, shuddering at the idea of taking my own life, plunging the blade into my stomach like some noble Japanese warrior committing ritual suicide.

"I thought about trying to bring him here," I continued, sounding more calm than I felt. "But then I thought that that would be disrespectful to you, or something. So instead I'm going to bring it back to where he... where I made my first kill. Ending this at the YMCA seems appropriate, I think.

"And yeah, there's a flaw in the plan, I know. He may not come. And if he doesn't come by sunrise, then I'm doing it anyway. I'm ending it. I've done so many horrible things, and I don't deserve to live. Neither does he. I can't let that piece of shit keep running around free and killing more people. Again, I'm sorry that I didn't think of this before he got to you."

I lowered my head and closed my eyes, thinking some more. Could I really do what I was saying? Was this the only way? The variations on my plan began to resurface, ones I had discarded earlier. Maybe I could just lure him to me and then kill him. But he'd probably just fly away as soon as he saw me. A new idea began to form as I pictured myself with the knife to my belly, warning him that if he left, I'd kill myself and therefore him as well. But then, *I'll kill you if you don't stay here and let me kill you* didn't really work. The only way I could come out of this alive would be to somehow convince him to stick around long enough. But how?

Something occurred to me. What if, instead of destroying him, I could manipulate him? The suicide thing could be a weapon, so to speak. Maybe I could force him to betray the other vampires, to lead me and possibly the others to them so we could finish them off once and for all. After all, Tim had tried to do something similar to us with Life Force, so maybe I could adapt that idea. If the evil Ray really were an almost exact copy of me, this might even appeal to him. We were both control freaks, after all.

Before I could continue this line of reasoning, I heard something. I'd heard a few noises throughout my time at the grave that made me stop talking and listen carefully, wondering if someone might be around. But it always turned out to be nothing; because it was autumn, things kept falling off the trees and scaring me. I got used to it after a while and learned to ignore it. But this was different. It was slow, steady, and repetitive, though not in an exact pattern. I heard leaves crunching along with the occasional twig here and there.

I looked around, trying to determine where the sound was coming from. I also hoped that it would stop like the earlier noises had, that it would turn out to be nothing. But it didn't. Someone was here.

Finally, I saw it. A figure was approaching, making its way among the graves in more or less a straight line, though it had to zigzag occasionally to make it through their vaguely grid-like arrangement. I crouched down, hoping to hide, but I knew that it was probably too late. Whoever it was must have seen me, as they were heading in my direction. I thought at first that it might be a policeman or a security guard, but as the person got closer, I realized that the clothes weren't right. They were lightly colored, possibly even white, but looking bluish due to the dim electrical light.

I began to wonder: Had my clone already picked up on my thoughts? Had he beaten me at my own game, coming here for our final confrontation? No, it couldn't be. My clone didn't have long, straight, blonde hair. And he wouldn't be wearing a white turtleneck sweater with pale, acid-washed blue jeans. As Elizabeth came into view, my heart started pounding wildly. My neck seemed to be pounding along with it.

I stood up, clutching at my chest with one hand and trying to steady myself on her gravestone with the other. "Elizabeth?" I almost hissed, my entire head feeling numb. "How can you be...? You can't!" My voice raised to full volume. "You *can't!*"

For half a second, I'd been delighted to see her, thinking that somehow, this whole mess about her having died was just a mistake. Everyone had been wrong the entire time, and here she was, still alive. But it only took me another moment or two to realize just what had happened. And it was impossible.

She was just a few feet from me now, and I continued to see her more clearly the closer she got. She looked different in a way I couldn't put my finger on, but it was definitely her, and the difference in her appearance that I was immediately sure of scared the hell out of me. She strode toward me confidently, doing that same thing I'd always loved where she'd tilt her chin downward and appear to be looking up at me as she smiled. Sometimes, she'd accentuate this look by biting her lower lip, which was what she was doing now. That was what made her fangs show so prominently.

"You can't..." I repeated, going back to a whisper. "Our victims don't come back," I choked out, tears beginning to well up. She shook her head, her vicious smile never fading. She looked so smart, so powerful. It was terrifying.

I realized that I'd been holding my hands out toward her, like that would somehow protect me. I started to look behind me, wondering if I could make a run for it but knowing that it wouldn't do any good. By the time I turned back to look at her, her face was right in front of mine, a wild look in her wide, blue eyes. Before I could say anything else, she shoved at me with superhuman strength, and I tumbled backwards onto the ground. The agony in my chest from where she had pushed me was coupled with the pain I felt in my back from sliding across the grass and dirt. I might have hit my head, too, but I was too scared to care. Within seconds, she was on top of me, her lower body draped over my torso as she quickly grabbed both of my wrists and pinned them to the ground.

"Stop!" I shrieked, trying to force myself up, but it was pointless. "Don't!" She just kept on grinning at me, and even in the dim light, I could still see those fangs. As her head leaned out of my field of vision and moved towards the left side of my neck, I knew what was coming next.

Everything I'd done, every lie I'd told, every life I'd taken, had led to this moment. Despite all of the confusion and terror I was feeling, I was certain of one thing: I was going to die. After all, I deserved it.

TO BE CONTINUED

ABOUT THE AUTHOR

T. Marshall Bunn grew up in Augusta, Georgia, and has lived several places up and down the east coast since. He currently lives in Rockville, Maryland and works as an audiovisual preservation librarian.

9 798986 101613